I0640787

THE MYSTERY OF EDWIN DROOD

Sir David Madden was a member of HM Diplomatic Service for 34 years, and retired after serving as British High Commissioner in Cyprus and subsequently British Ambassador in Greece. He was then Political Advisor to the EU Peace-Keeping Force in Bosnia and Herzegovina, before returning home to Oxford. He is a Senior Member of St Antony's College, Oxford, and chairs the Development Committee of South East European Studies at Oxford (SEESOX). He takes a close interest in animal welfare: he is a Trustee both of The Brooke Hospital for Animals and of Compassion in World Farming, a patron of the Voice for Ethical Research in Oxford, and promotes the development of the Universal Declaration on Animal Welfare. He is working on two new books.

THE
MYSTERY
OF
EDWIN DROOD

BY
CHARLES DICKENS

COMPLETED BY
DAVID MADDEN

UNTHANK
BOOKS

First published by
Unthank Books of London and Norwich 2011

Second edition 2015

Printed and bound in Great Britain
by Lightning Source, Milton Keynes

All Rights Reserved
Part II © David Madden 2011

The right of David Madden to be identified as
author of Part II of this work has been
asserted in accordance with Section 77 of
the Copyright, Designs and Patents Act of 1988

A CIP record for this book is available
from the British Library

Any resemblance to persons fictional or real
who are living, dead or undead is purely coincidental

ISBN 978-0-9564223-3-0

Cover Design & Typesetting by
Green Door Design for Publishing

Cover Image © Gracie Carver

Contents

The Mystery of Edwin Drood – Part 2

INTRODUCTION
- David Madden -

CHARLES DICKENS' FINAL masterpiece was left unfinished, and none of the second half was written.

The book was due to appear in twelve monthly instalments beginning in April 1870. Dickens wrote six of these, and prepared the first three for publication in April-June. The remaining three appeared after his death, in July-September. For Dickens died suddenly, on 9th June, the day after writing his famous description of sunlight: "A brilliant morning shines on the old city…Changes of glorious light…penetrate into the Cathedral, subdue its earthy odour, and preach the Resurrection and the Life…flecks of brightness dart into the sternest marble corners of the building, fluttering there like wings." This helps end the first half of the book on a note of exultation.

What Dickens has left us is a marvellous example of the work of his late period. After a striking opening, he builds his novel and characters with his accustomed vigour and imagination, demonstrating that he remained at the height of his powers when he died. It is a tragedy that he left it unfinished: but also a challenge. What follows is an attempt to complete what Dickens started, to do so in a way which is true to what can be divined of his intentions, to set the new alongside the old, and thus to offer readers a version which is at least completed, albeit by a surrogate. Dickens was born in 1812; and my hope is to encourage people to return to this memorable novel in his anniversary year.

The approach which I have followed flows from this underlying aim. The first and most obvious aspect is the structure. Publication by instalment imposes its own logic: the separate parts have to be rounded off, and the new ones launched, as is done in the first half, most obviously between Chapters 16 and 17 (the ends of instalments are clearly delineated in the text). It also requires a certain degree of repetition to keep salient traits and other details in the reader's mind over the course of a year. Secondly, Dickens sets his tale in both past and present, depending on chapter, content and characters (scenes involving one of the protagonists invariably use the present tense, others attract the past): though certain passages of the novel reveal that Dickens is looking back at events which are meant to have happened in the fictional town of Cloisterham (Rochester) some years previously. Thirdly, there are his borrowings and references. To take just one of many influences on the first half, there is a quotation from Macbeth in a title and echoes of the play in the text. The second half needs to reflect the format and rhythm and fabric of the first.

More complicated is the question of Dickens' intentions: how did he mean to continue and finish his story? The materials for answering this question lie in the evidence from himself and also from those who knew him and his work, from the text he has left, the characters he has created, and the interplay between them, from the clues contained in the first half, and from the loose ends which are left untied at the half-way point (though some may have knowingly been left obscure).

An important caveat is that Dickens played his cards close to his chest, and may not have revealed to others his precise or final ideas, and may indeed have changed his mind; so the testimony of his family and associates cannot be totally relied on, especially on the details: though they appear to provide noteworthy pointers to what was in Dickens' mind as he planned his work.

It would, I suppose, be possible to complete *Edwin Drood* in the modern vernacular, or set in the present day, or during the Second World War – an approach much beloved by those staging Shakespeare and opera. This is not the path I have followed.

Dickens' number plans for the book are extant, and give a fascinating glimpse into the workings of the novelist's mind (was the Blustrous Philanthropist to be Mr Honeythunder or Mr Honeyblast? we follow the progression of the eponymous central character from James Wakefield to Edwyn Brood to Edwin Brude to Edwyn Drood to Edwin Drude and then finally and conclusively to Edwin Drood: there are already references to scenes and phrases which play a vital part in the work, especially those involving Drood's uncle Jasper); but the notes become progressively thinner in content, there are none for the sixth instalment, and total silence on the second part. The word murder is used twice, however, once apparently with reference to uncle and nephew; and there are other dark hints about the uncle ("quarrel, (fomented by Jasper)", "Jasper lays his ground", "Jasper's artful turn" etc).

Contemporary testimony is thin but consistent. There is a recorded exchange between Dickens and his son Charles Dickens, Junior. To the son's comment, "Of course, Edwin Drood was murdered?" Dickens' reply was "Of course; what else do you suppose?" John Forster, Dickens' literary executor and first biographer, wrote of the novel, that "The story…was to be that of a murder of a nephew by his uncle." According to Charles Allston Collins, Dickens' son-in-law and first designer of the front cover, "Edwin Drood was never to reappear, he having been murdered by Jasper".

The weight of this accumulated evidence seems to leave little doubt that Drood was murdered by his uncle Jasper; and since this is so unambiguously hinted at in what Dickens actually wrote in his six instalments, a further conclusion is that "The Mystery of Edwin Drood" is not an early whodunit, competing with the writing of Dickens' colleague Wilkie Collins, but a novel about the disappearance and death of Drood, presumably to include how Jasper managed to carry it out, how he was discovered and punished, and how these circumstances affected both him and the other dramatis personae. As Dickens' daughter Katey reminds us, her father "was quite as deeply fascinated and absorbed in the study of the criminal Jasper, as in the dark and sinister crime that has given the book its title".

Forster provides other indicators of elements to feature in the second half of the novel. He describes Dickens' intention to include "the review of the murderer's career by himself at the close", and to set the final chapters in the condemned cell. The illustrator for the book, Luke Fildes, confirms a plan to visit Maidstone Gaol for an illustration: never undertaken, because Dickens was dead and Drood left unfinished.

Fildes also offers another detail. He records Dickens as telling him for a picture of Jasper: "I must have the double necktie! It is necessary, for Jasper strangles Edwin Drood with it." And indeed it appears in Dickens' text. In chapter 14, Jasper is wearing, on the evening of Drood's disappearance, "a large black scarf of strong close-woven silk." This would seem to establish Jasper's intention to strangle Drood: but later Jasper, drugged by opium, mutters "No struggle, no consciousness of peril, no entreaty". Might Dickens have had a further trick up his sleeve? My earlier caution about the evidence of the collaborators is particularly relevant on this kind of point.

Next are the clues left by Dickens in his text. There is one big one. When Edwin decides not to show the engagement ring to Rosa after they have ended their betrothal by mutual consent, but to keep it secure in his inside pocket, Dickens writes: "...there was one chain forged in the moment of that small conclusion, riveted to the foundations of heaven and earth, and gifted with invincible force to hold and drag." I think that we can safely assume that this is an important moment, and that the ring is destined to play a further part in the story; and indeed that the circumstances of its reappearance will be directly related to the disappearance of Drood. And, again, testimony from Forster seems to confirm this: "discovery of the murderer was to be baffled till towards the close, when, by means of a gold ring which had resisted the corrosive effects of the lime into which he had thrown the body," the persons of murderer and murdered were to be identified.

Another unexplained detail seems significant. The stonemason Durdles walking among the gravestones, "surrounded by his works, like a popular Author", points out to Jasper the sarcophagus of "your own brother-in-law". There is no reference to Jasper's sister, though we know that she also is dead; just to the brother-in-law.

There are other words or phrases which may give an inkling of what Dickens had in store. The repeated references in the opening lines to the tower and the spike appear telling. The various keys in the possession of Durdles receive special attention, especially when Jasper is present. The tower in particular remains a regular theme, for example in the case of Jasper's night excursion with Durdles (in Dickens' words, "an unaccountable sort of expedition"). Then, on the night of the great storm and of Drood's disappearance ("No such power of wind has blown for many a winter-night. Chimneys topple in the streets...the violent rushes abate not..."), the tower is still at the centre of events: "some stones have been displaced upon the summit of the great tower." The scene seems to be set for some cataclysmic event or events involving the tower.

Intimations of mesmerism are scattered about the text: Jasper's "look of intentness and intensity" in looking at Drood, his "strange power of suddenly including the sketch [of Rosa] over the chimneypiece" in their dialogue, Rosa's "old horrible feeling of being compelled by him". It is hard to avoid the conclusion that these powers may have played a role in the killing of Drood by Jasper: or at least that Dickens was giving himself the opportunity to use this theme when the moment came to describe the murder.

Some "clues" are more questionable. Forster wrote of Neville

Landless "who was himself, I think, to have perished in assisting… finally to unmask and seize the murderer". Some have seen a hint of an untimely end in Dickens' text: Crisparkle says to Neville "I wish your eyes were not quite so large and not quite so bright". But large and bright eyes are hardly a signal that someone is to perish in unmasking and seizing a murderer; while they are quite consistent with a lengthy period of enforced isolation and study away from the world, and accompanying mental turmoil as a result of being unjustly suspected of Drood's murder. Dickens describes Neville as having a prisonous look.

I see from the notes to my Penguin version of Drood that a reference to Neville's sister Helena running away from home in Ceylon when young "dressed as a boy" has on occasion been used to suggest that the proto-detective Datchery is really Helena in disguise; but the timing does not fit, for after Datchery takes up residence in Cloisterham, Helena departs from the city to attend her brother's fortunes in Holborn, where Rosa duly finds her when she flees to London shortly afterwards. It is obvious that Datchery wears a white wig, presumably to make himself look older; but there is not much else in the way of hiding identity, and he invariably wears a "tightish blue surtout". Another note in my same guide comments that this was a frockcoat worn tightly buttoned to show off the figure: hardly ideal concealment for Helena, whose appearance would seem pretty unmistakeable both in Dickens' text and in Fildes' illustrations.

Then there is the dog. About a year before the 'unaccountable sort of expedition" up the Tower, the previous Christmas Eve, Durdles had been woken from drunken sleep by "the ghost of one terrific shriek, which shriek was followed by the ghost of the howl of a dog: a long dismal woeful howl, such as a dog gives when a person's dead." Being told this, Jasper is abrupt, fierce, scornful and impatient. Clearly this episode suggests some kind of premonition, since Drood disappeared the following Christmas Eve. But is it a clue, or a loose end, or a device to help build the atmosphere, or simply an illustrative detail designed to tell us more about Jasper?

There is also the "Sapsea Fragment". The relationship of these few manuscript pages (about an incident related by Sapsea in the first person) to the book remains uncertain; but since there are parallels between Sapsea's account of his conversation with a character named Poker, and the first meeting in the fifth instalment between Sapsea and Datchery (of whom Poker may have been an early version), it seems reasonably clear that it was not intended in this form for the second part, and it does not therefore feature in my version.

Finally, the characters. Dickens has assembled and presented his usual rich gallery: they are also clues, indeed they are the chief ones, for it is their personalities, and the interaction between them, which will continue to carry the story forward, and tell us how it is likely to end, if we read them aright.

The characters have to act and speak and think (and develop) in the second part; and they have to do so in a way which is consistent with the style of the first part. This is the final element of the challenge of completing Drood: to reflect something of the voice of Dickens without sounding like a parody or a pastiche or even a rejected script for a Monty Python sketch. One possible advantage I had was my experience as a diplomat. Diplomats are protean figures who have to learn to ventriloquise, to assume the aura and authority of their governments, but also to understand other countries, to sound different notes as necessary in arguing a case, to play a variety of roles and see situations from a variety of viewpoints, to listen to others, to develop access and familiarity while remaining objective observers, and above all to narrate a complicated story involving many characters. So I attempted to make use of this experience in this work of reconstruction (a term I use, because it is a reasonable assumption that on 8/9 June 1870 Dickens had a fairly clear view of how he would end the book, even if he did not commit it to paper).

Out of this jigsaw, I have tried to create and present a credible conclusion to the novel. I am by no means an expert on Dickens or the bibliography on Drood; but I hope that it will interest those who are, and give pleasure to others. I intend it as a tribute to Charles Dickens, and to his unmatched and undimmed ability to involve, excite and entertain.

David Madden
Oxford
2011

My special thanks are due to: Robin Jones, who has doubled as agent and publisher; to Margaret-Alice, who made the connection between us; to my sister-in-law Claire, who first gave me the idea of completing Drood; to my wife Anthea, who tolerated many hours when my mind was in the nineteenth rather than the twenty-first century; and above all to Charles Dickens, who has given all of us and the world so much.

PART I
- Charles Dickens -

CHAPTER I
The Dawn

An ancient English Cathedral Tower? How can the ancient English Cathedral tower be here! The well-known massive grey square tower of its old Cathedral? How can that be here! There is no spike of rusty iron in the air, between the eye and it, from any point of the real prospect. What is the spike that intervenes, and who has set it up? Maybe it is set up by the Sultan's orders for the impaling of a horde of Turkish robbers, one by one. It is so, for cymbals clash, and the Sultan goes by to his palace in long procession. Ten thousand scimitars flash in the sunlight, and thrice ten thousand dancing-girls strew flowers. Then, follow white elephants caparisoned in countless gorgeous colours, and infinite in number and attendants. Still the Cathedral Tower rises in the background, where it cannot be, and still no writhing figure is on the grim spike. Stay! Is the spike so low a thing as the rusty spike on the top of a post of an old bedstead that has tumbled all awry? Some vague period of drowsy laughter must be devoted to the consideration of this possibility.

Shaking from head to foot, the man whose scattered consciousness has thus fantastically pieced itself together, at length rises, supports his trembling frame upon his arms, and looks around. He is in the meanest and closest of small rooms. Through the ragged window-curtain, the light of early day steals in from a miserable court. He lies, dressed, across a large unseemly bed, upon a bedstead that has indeed given way under the weight upon it. Lying, also dressed and also across the bed, not longwise, are a Chinaman, a Lascar, and a haggard woman. The two first are in a sleep or stupor; the last is blowing at a kind of pipe, to kindle it. And as she blows, and shading it with her lean hand, concentrates its red spark of light, it serves in the dim morning as a lamp to show him what he sees of her.

'Another?' says this woman, in a querulous, rattling whisper. 'Have another?'

He looks about him, with his hand to his forehead.

'Ye've smoked as many as five since ye come in at midnight,' the woman goes on, as she chronically complains. 'Poor me, poor me, my head is so bad. Them two come in after ye. Ah, poor me, the business is slack, is slack! Few Chinamen about the Docks, and fewer Lascars, and no ships coming in, these say! Here's another ready for ye, deary. Ye'll remember like a good soul, won't ye, that the market price is dreffle high just now? More nor three shillings and sixpence for a thimbleful! And ye'll remember that nobody but me (and Jack Chinaman t'other side the court; but he can't do it as well as me) has the true secret of mixing it? Ye'll pay up accordingly, deary, won't ye?'

She blows at the pipe as she speaks, and, occasionally bubbling at it, inhales much of its contents.

'O me, O me, my lungs is weak, my lungs is bad! It's nearly ready for ye, deary. Ah, poor me, poor me, my poor hand shakes like to drop off! I see ye coming-to, and I ses to my poor self, "I'll have another ready for him, and he'll bear in mind the market price of opium, and pay according." O my poor head! I makes my pipes of old penny ink-bottles, ye see, deary – this is one – and I fits-in a mouthpiece, this way, and I takes my mixter out of this thimble with this little horn spoon; and so I fills, deary. Ah, my poor nerves! I got Heavens-hard drunk for sixteen year afore I took to this; but this don't hurt me, not to speak of. And it takes away the hunger as well as wittles, deary.'

She hands him the nearly-emptied pipe, and sinks back, turning over on her face.

He rises unsteadily from the bed, lays the pipe upon the hearth-stone, draws back the ragged curtain, and looks with repugnance at his three companions. He notices that the woman has opium-smoked herself into a strange likeness of the Chinaman. His form of cheek, eye, and temple, and his colour, are repeated in her. Said Chinaman convulsively wrestles with one of his many Gods or Devils, perhaps, and snarls horribly. The Lascar laughs and dribbles at the mouth. The hostess is still.

'What visions can *she* have?' the waking man muses, as he turns her face towards him, and stands looking down at it. 'Visions of many butchers' shops, and public-houses, and much credit? Of an increase of hideous customers, and this horrible bedstead set upright again, and this horrible court swept clean? What can she rise to, under any quantity of opium, higher than that! – Eh?'

He bends down his ear, to listen to her mutterings.

'Unintelligible!'

As he watches the spasmodic shoots and darts that break out of her

4

face and limbs, like fitful lightning out of a dark sky, some contagion in them seizes upon him: insomuch that he has to withdraw himself to a lean arm-chair by the hearth – placed there, perhaps, for such emergencies – and to sit in it, holding tight, until he has got the better of this unclean spirit of imitation.

Then he comes back, pounces on the Chinaman, and seizing him with both hands by the throat, turns him violently on the bed. The Chinaman clutches the aggressive hands, resists, gasps, and protests.

'What do you say?'

A watchful pause.

'Unintelligible!'

Slowly loosening his grasp as he listens to the incoherent jargon with an attentive frown, he turns to the Lascar and fairly drags him forth upon the floor. As he falls, the Lascar starts into a half-risen attitude, glares with his eyes, lashes about him fiercely with his arms, and draws a phantom knife. It then becomes apparent that the woman has taken possession of this knife, for safety's sake; for, she too starting up, and restraining and expostulating with him, the knife is visible in her dress, not in his, when they drowsily drop back, side by side.

There has been chattering and clattering enough between them, but to no purpose. When any distinct word has been flung into the air, it has had no sense or sequence. Wherefore 'unintelligible!' is again the comment of the watcher, made with some reassured nodding of his head, and a gloomy smile. He then lays certain silver money on the table, finds his hat, gropes his way down the broken stairs, gives a good morning to some rat-ridden doorkeeper, in bed in a black hutch beneath the stairs, and passes out.

That same afternoon, the massive grey square tower of an old Cathedral rises before the sight of a jaded traveller. The bells are going for daily vesper service, and he must needs attend it, one would say, from his haste to reach the open Cathedral door. The choir are getting on their sullied white robes, in a hurry, when he arrives among them, gets on his own robe, and falls into the procession filing in to service. Then, the Sacristan locks the iron-barred gates that divide the sanctuary from the chancel, and all of the procession having scuttled into their places, hide their faces; and then the intoned words, 'WHEN THE WICKED MAN – ' rise among groins of arches and beams of roof, awakening muttered thunder.

CHAPTER II
A Dean, and a Chapter Also

WHOSOEVER HAS OBSERVED that sedate and clerical bird, the rook, may perhaps have noticed that when he wings his way homeward towards nightfall, in a sedate and clerical company, two rooks will suddenly detach themselves from the rest, will retrace their flight for some distance, and will there poise and linger; conveying to mere men the fancy that it is of some occult importance to the body politic, that this artful couple should pretend to have renounced connection with it.

Similarly, service being over in the old Cathedral with the square tower, and the choir scuffling out again, and divers venerable persons of rook-like aspect dispersing, two of these latter retrace their steps, and walk together in the echoing Close.

Not only is the day waning, but the year. The low sun is fiery and yet cold behind the monastery ruin, and the Virginia creeper on the Cathedral wall has showered half its deep-red leaves down on the pavement. There has been rain this afternoon, and a wintry shudder goes among the little pools on the cracked, uneven flag-stones, and through the giant elm-trees as they shed a gust of tears. Their fallen leaves lie strewn thickly about. Some of these leaves, in a timid rush, seek sanctuary within the low arched Cathedral door; but two men coming out resist them, and cast them forth again with their feet; this done, one of the two locks the door with a goodly key, and the other flits away with a folio music-book.

'Mr. Jasper was that, Tope?'

'Yes, Mr. Dean.'

'He has stayed late.'

'Yes, Mr. Dean. I have stayed for him, your Reverence. He has been took a little poorly.'

'Say "taken," Tope – to the Dean,' the younger rook interposes in a low tone with this touch of correction, as who should say: 'You may offer bad grammar to the laity, or the humbler clergy, not to the Dean.'

Mr. Tope, Chief Verger and Showman, and accustomed to be high with excursion parties, declines with a silent loftiness to perceive that any

6

suggestion has been tendered to him.

'And when and how has Mr. Jasper been taken – for, as Mr. Crisparkle has remarked, it is better to say taken – taken – ' repeats the Dean; 'when and how has Mr. Jasper been Taken – '

'Taken, sir,' Tope deferentially murmurs.

' – Poorly, Tope?'

'Why, sir, Mr. Jasper was that breathed – '

'I wouldn't say "That breathed," Tope,' Mr. Crisparkle interposes with the same touch as before. 'Not English – to the Dean.'

'Breathed to that extent,' the Dean (not unflattered by this indirect homage) condescendingly remarks, 'would be preferable.'

'Mr. Jasper's breathing was so remarkably short' – thus discreetly does Mr. Tope work his way round the sunken rock – 'when he came in, that it distressed him mightily to get his notes out: which was perhaps the cause of his having a kind of fit on him after a little. His memory grew DAZED.' Mr. Tope, with his eyes on the Reverend Mr. Crisparkle, shoots this word out, as defying him to improve upon it: 'and a dimness and giddiness crept over him as strange as ever I saw: though he didn't seem to mind it particularly, himself. However, a little time and a little water brought him out of his DAZE.' Mr. Tope repeats the word and its emphasis, with the air of saying: 'As I *have* made a success, I'll make it again.'

'And Mr. Jasper has gone home quite himself, has he?' asked the Dean.

'Your Reverence, he has gone home quite himself. And I'm glad to see he's having his fire kindled up, for it's chilly after the wet, and the Cathedral had both a damp feel and a damp touch this afternoon, and he was very shivery.'

They all three look towards an old stone gatehouse crossing the Close, with an arched thoroughfare passing beneath it. Through its latticed window, a fire shines out upon the fast-darkening scene, involving in shadow the pendent masses of ivy and creeper covering the building's front. As the deep Cathedral-bell strikes the hour, a ripple of wind goes through these at their distance, like a ripple of the solemn sound that hums through tomb and tower, broken niche and defaced statue, in the pile close at hand.

'Is Mr. Jasper's nephew with him?' the Dean asks.

'No, sir,' replied the Verger, 'but expected. There's his own solitary shadow betwixt his two windows – the one looking this way, and the one looking down into the High Street – drawing his own curtains now.'

'Well, well,' says the Dean, with a sprightly air of breaking up the little conference, 'I hope Mr. Jasper's heart may not be too much set upon his nephew. Our affections, however laudable, in this transitory world, should never master us; we should guide them, guide them. I find I am not disagreeably reminded of my dinner, by hearing my dinner-bell. Perhaps, Mr. Crisparkle, you will, before going home, look in on Jasper?'

'Certainly, Mr. Dean. And tell him that you had the kindness to desire to know how he was?'

'Ay; do so, do so. Certainly. Wished to know how he was. By all means. Wished to know how he was.'

With a pleasant air of patronage, the Dean as nearly cocks his quaint hat as a Dean in good spirits may, and directs his comely gaiters towards the ruddy dining-room of the snug old red-brick house where he is at present, 'in residence' with Mrs. Dean and Miss Dean.

Mr. Crisparkle, Minor Canon, fair and rosy, and perpetually pitching himself head-foremost into all the deep running water in the surrounding country; Mr. Crisparkle, Minor Canon, early riser, musical, classical, cheerful, kind, good-natured, social, contented, and boy-like; Mr. Crisparkle, Minor Canon and good man, lately 'Coach' upon the chief Pagan high roads, but since promoted by a patron (grateful for a well-taught son) to his present Christian beat; betakes himself to the gatehouse, on his way home to his early tea.

'Sorry to hear from Tope that you have not been well, Jasper.'

'O, it was nothing, nothing!'

'You look a little worn.'

'Do I? O, I don't think so. What is better, I don't feel so. Tope has made too much of it, I suspect. It's his trade to make the most of everything appertaining to the Cathedral, you know.'

'I may tell the Dean – I call expressly from the Dean – that you are all right again?'

The reply, with a slight smile, is: 'Certainly; with my respects and thanks to the Dean.'

'I'm glad to hear that you expect young Drood.'

'I expect the dear fellow every moment.'

'Ah! He will do you more good than a doctor, Jasper.'

'More good than a dozen doctors. For I love him dearly, and I don't love doctors, or doctors' stuff.'

Mr. Jasper is a dark man of some six-and-twenty, with thick, lustrous, well-arranged black hair and whiskers. He looks older than he is, as dark men often do. His voice is deep and good, his face and figure are good, his manner is a little sombre. His room is a little sombre, and may have had its influence in forming his manner. It is mostly in shadow. Even when the sun shines brilliantly, it seldom touches the grand piano in the recess, or the folio music-books on the stand, or the book-shelves on the wall, or the unfinished picture of a blooming schoolgirl hanging over the chimneypiece; her flowing brown hair tied with a blue riband, and her beauty remarkable for a quite childish, almost babyish, touch of saucy discontent, comically conscious of itself. (There is not the least artistic merit in this picture, which is a mere daub; but it is clear that the painter has made it humorously – one might almost say, revengefully – like the original.)

'We shall miss you, Jasper, at the "Alternate Musical Wednesdays" to-night; but no doubt you are best at home. Good-night. God bless you! "Tell me, shep-herds, te-e-ell me; tell me-e-e, have you seen (have you seen, have you seen, have you seen) my-y-y Flo-o-ora-a pass this way!"' Melodiously good Minor Canon the Reverend Septimus Crisparkle thus delivers himself, in musical rhythm, as he withdraws his amiable face from the doorway and conveys it down-stairs.

Sounds of recognition and greeting pass between the Reverend Septimus and somebody else, at the stair-foot. Mr. Jasper listens, starts from his chair, and catches a young fellow in his arms, exclaiming:

'My dear Edwin!'

'My dear Jack! So glad to see you!'

'Get off your greatcoat, bright boy, and sit down here in your own corner. Your feet are not wet? Pull your boots off. Do pull your boots off.'

'My dear Jack, I am as dry as a bone. Don't moddley-coddley, there's a good fellow. I like anything better than being moddley-coddleyed.'

With the check upon him of being unsympathetically restrained in a genial outburst of enthusiasm, Mr. Jasper stands still, and looks on intently at the young fellow, divesting himself of his outward coat, hat, gloves, and so forth. Once for all, a look of intentness and intensity – a look of hungry, exacting, watchful, and yet devoted affection – is always, now and ever afterwards, on the Jasper face whenever the Jasper face is addressed in this direction. And whenever it is so addressed, it is never, on this occasion or on any other, dividedly addressed; it is always concentrated.

'Now I am right, and now I'll take my corner, Jack. Any dinner, Jack?'

Mr. Jasper opens a door at the upper end of the room, and discloses a small inner room pleasantly lighted and prepared, wherein a comely dame is in the act of setting dishes on table.

'What a jolly old Jack it is!' cries the young fellow, with a clap of his hands. 'Look here, Jack; tell me; whose birthday is it?'

'Not yours, I know,' Mr. Jasper answers, pausing to consider.

'Not mine, you know? No; not mine, *I* know! Pussy's!'

Fixed as the look the young fellow meets, is, there is yet in it some strange power of suddenly including the sketch over the chimneypiece.

'Pussy's, Jack! We must drink Many happy returns to her. Come, uncle; take your dutiful and sharp-set nephew in to dinner.'

As the boy (for he is little more) lays a hand on Jasper's shoulder, Jasper cordially and gaily lays a hand on *his* shoulder, and so Marseillaise-wise they go in to dinner.

'And, Lord! here's Mrs. Tope!' cries the boy. 'Lovelier than ever!'

'Never you mind me, Master Edwin,' retorts the Verger's wife; 'I can take care of myself.'

'You can't. You're much too handsome. Give me a kiss because it's Pussy's birthday.'

'I'd Pussy you, young man, if I was Pussy, as you call her,' Mrs. Tope blushingly retorts, after being saluted. 'Your uncle's too much wrapt up in you, that's where it is. He makes so much of you, that it's my opinion you think you've only to call your Pussys by the dozen, to make 'em come.'

'You forget, Mrs. Tope,' Mr. Jasper interposes, taking his place at the table with a genial smile, 'and so do you, Ned, that Uncle and Nephew are words prohibited here by common consent and express agreement. For what we are going to receive His holy name be praised!'

'Done like the Dean! Witness, Edwin Drood! Please to carve, Jack, for I can't.'

This sally ushers in the dinner. Little to the present purpose, or to any purpose, is said, while it is in course of being disposed of. At length the cloth is drawn, and a dish of walnuts and a decanter of rich-coloured sherry are placed upon the table.

'I say! Tell me, Jack,' the young fellow then flows on: 'do you really and truly feel as if the mention of our relationship divided us at all? *I* don't.'

'Uncles as a rule, Ned, are so much older than their nephews,' is the reply, 'that I have that feeling instinctively.'

'As a rule! Ah, may-be! But what is a difference in age of half-a-dozen years or so? And some uncles, in large families, are even younger than their nephews. By George, I wish it was the case with us!'

'Why?'

'Because if it was, I'd take the lead with you, Jack, and be as wise as Begone, dull Care! that turned a young man grey, and Begone, dull Care! that turned an old man to clay. – Halloa, Jack! Don't drink.'

'Why not?'

'Asks why not, on Pussy's birthday, and no Happy returns proposed! Pussy, Jack, and many of 'em! Happy returns, I mean.'

Laying an affectionate and laughing touch on the boy's extended hand, as if it were at once his giddy head and his light heart, Mr. Jasper drinks the toast in silence.

'Hip, hip, hip, and nine times nine, and one to finish with, and all that, understood. Hooray, hooray, hooray! – And now, Jack, let's have a little talk about Pussy. Two pairs of nut-crackers? Pass me one, and take the other.' Crack. 'How's Pussy getting on Jack?'

'With her music? Fairly.'

'What a dreadfully conscientious fellow you are, Jack! But *I* know, Lord bless you! Inattentive, isn't she?'

'She can learn anything, if she will.'

'*If* she will! Egad, that's it. But if she won't?'

Crack! – on Mr. Jasper's part.

'How's she looking, Jack?'

Mr. Jasper's concentrated face again includes the portrait as he returns: 'Very like your sketch indeed.'

'I *am* a little proud of it,' says the young fellow, glancing up at the sketch with complacency, and then shutting one eye, and taking a corrected prospect of it over a level bridge of nut-crackers in the air: 'Not badly hit off from memory. But I ought to have caught that expression pretty well, for I have seen it often enough.'

Crack! – on Edwin Drood's part.

Crack! – on Mr. Jasper's part.

'In point of fact,' the former resumes, after some silent dipping among his fragments of walnut with an air of pique, 'I see it whenever I go to see Pussy. If I don't find it on her face, I leave it there. – You know I do, Miss Scornful Pert. Booh!' With a twirl of the nut-crackers at the portrait.

Crack! crack! crack. Slowly, on Mr. Jasper's part.

Crack. Sharply on the part of Edwin Drood.

Silence on both sides.

'Have you lost your tongue, Jack?'

'Have you found yours, Ned?'

'No, but really; – isn't it, you know, after all – '

Mr. Jasper lifts his dark eyebrows inquiringly.

'Isn't it unsatisfactory to be cut off from choice in such a matter? There, Jack! I tell you! If I could choose, I would choose Pussy from all the pretty girls in the world.'

'But you have not got to choose.'

'That's what I complain of. My dead and gone father and Pussy's dead and gone father must needs marry us together by anticipation. Why the – Devil, I was going to say, if it had been respectful to their memory – couldn't they leave us alone?'

'Tut, tut, dear boy,' Mr. Jasper remonstrates, in a tone of gentle deprecation.

'Tut, tut? Yes, Jack, it's all very well for *you*. *You* can take it easily. *Your* life is not laid down to scale, and lined and dotted out for you, like a surveyor's plan. *You* have no uncomfortable suspicion that you are forced upon anybody, nor has anybody an uncomfortable suspicion that she is forced upon you, or that you are forced upon her. *You* can choose for yourself. Life, for *you*, is a plum with the natural bloom on; it hasn't been over-carefully wiped off for *you* – '

'Don't stop, dear fellow. Go on.'

'Can I anyhow have hurt your feelings, Jack?'

'How can you have hurt my feelings?'

'Good Heaven, Jack, you look frightfully ill! There's a strange film come over your eyes.'

Mr. Jasper, with a forced smile, stretches out his right hand, as if at once to disarm apprehension and gain time to get better. After a while he says faintly:

'I have been taking opium for a pain – an agony – that sometimes overcomes me. The effects of the medicine steal over me like a blight or a cloud, and pass. You see them in the act of passing; they will be gone directly. Look away from me. They will go all the sooner.'

With a scared face the younger man complies by casting his eyes downward at the ashes on the hearth. Not relaxing his own gaze on the fire, but rather strengthening it with a fierce, firm grip upon his elbow-chair, the elder sits for a few moments rigid, and then, with thick drops standing on his forehead, and a sharp catch of his breath, becomes as he was before. On his so subsiding in his chair, his nephew gently and assiduously tends him while he quite recovers. When Jasper is restored, he lays a tender hand upon his nephew's shoulder, and, in a tone of voice less troubled than the purport of his words – indeed with something of raillery or banter in it – thus addresses him:

'There is said to be a hidden skeleton in every house; but you thought there was none in mine, dear Ned.'

'Upon my life, Jack, I did think so. However, when I come to consider that even in Pussy's house – if she had one – and in mine – if I had one – '

'You were going to say (but that I interrupted you in spite of myself) what a quiet life mine is. No whirl and uproar around me, no distracting commerce or calculation, no risk, no change of place, myself devoted to the art I pursue, my business my pleasure.'

'I really was going to say something of the kind, Jack; but you see, you, speaking of yourself, almost necessarily leave out much that I should have put in. For instance: I should have put in the foreground your being so much respected as Lay Precentor, or Lay Clerk, or whatever you call it, of this Cathedral; your enjoying the reputation of having done such wonders with the choir; your choosing your society, and holding such an independent position in this queer old place; your gift of teaching (why, even Pussy, who don't like being taught, says there never was such a Master as you are!), and your connexion.'

'Yes; I saw what you were tending to. I hate it.'

'Hate it, Jack?' (Much bewildered.)

'I hate it. The cramped monotony of my existence grinds me away by the grain. How does our service sound to you?'

'Beautiful! Quite celestial!'

'It often sounds to me quite devilish. I am so weary of it. The echoes of my own voice among the arches seem to mock me with my daily drudging round. No wretched monk who droned his life away in that gloomy place, before me, can have been more tired of it than I am. He

13

could take for relief (and did take) to carving demons out of the stalls and seats and desks. What shall I do? Must I take to carving them out of my heart?'

'I thought you had so exactly found your niche in life, Jack,' Edwin Drood returns, astonished, bending forward in his chair to lay a sympathetic hand on Jasper's knee, and looking at him with an anxious face.

'I know you thought so. They all think so.'

'Well, I suppose they do,' says Edwin, meditating aloud. 'Pussy thinks so.'

'When did she tell you that?'

'The last time I was here. You remember when. Three months ago.'

'How did she phrase it?'

'O, she only said that she had become your pupil, and that you were made for your vocation.'

The younger man glances at the portrait. The elder sees it in him.

'Anyhow, my dear Ned,' Jasper resumes, as he shakes his head with a grave cheerfulness, 'I must subdue myself to my vocation: which is much the same thing outwardly. It's too late to find another now. This is a confidence between us.'

'It shall be sacredly preserved, Jack.'

'I have reposed it in you, because – '

'I feel it, I assure you. Because we are fast friends, and because you love and trust me, as I love and trust you. Both hands, Jack.'

As each stands looking into the other's eyes, and as the uncle holds the nephew's hands, the uncle thus proceeds:

'You know now, don't you, that even a poor monotonous chorister and grinder of music – in his niche – may be troubled with some stray sort of ambition, aspiration, restlessness, dissatisfaction, what shall we call it?'

'Yes, dear Jack.'

'And you will remember?'

'My dear Jack, I only ask you, am I likely to forget what you have said with so much feeling?'

'Take it as a warning, then.'

In the act of having his hands released, and of moving a step back, Edwin pauses for an instant to consider the application of these last words. The instant over, he says, sensibly touched:

'I am afraid I am but a shallow, surface kind of fellow, Jack, and that my headpiece is none of the best. But I needn't say I am young; and perhaps I shall not grow worse as I grow older. At all events, I hope I have something impressible within me, which feels – deeply feels – the disinterestedness of your painfully laying your inner self bare, as a warning to me.'

Mr. Jasper's steadiness of face and figure becomes so marvellous that his breathing seems to have stopped.

'I couldn't fail to notice, Jack, that it cost you a great effort, and that you were very much moved, and very unlike your usual self. Of course I knew that you were extremely fond of me, but I really was not prepared for your, as I may say, sacrificing yourself to me in that way.'

Mr. Jasper, becoming a breathing man again without the smallest stage of transition between the two extreme states, lifts his shoulders, laughs, and waves his right arm.

'No; don't put the sentiment away, Jack; please don't; for I am very much in earnest. I have no doubt that that unhealthy state of mind which you have so powerfully described is attended with some real suffering, and is hard to bear. But let me reassure you, Jack, as to the chances of its overcoming me. I don't think I am in the way of it. In some few months less than another year, you know, I shall carry Pussy off from school as Mrs. Edwin Drood. I shall then go engineering into the East, and Pussy with me. And although we have our little tiffs now, arising out of a certain unavoidable flatness that attends our love-making, owing to its end being all settled beforehand, still I have no doubt of our getting on capitally then, when it's done and can't be helped. In short, Jack, to go back to the old song I was freely quoting at dinner (and who knows old songs better than you?), my wife shall dance, and I will sing, so merrily pass the day. Of Pussy's being beautiful there cannot be a doubt; – and when you are good besides, Little Miss Impudence,' once more apostrophising the portrait, 'I'll burn your comic likeness, and paint your music-master another.'

Mr. Jasper, with his hand to his chin, and with an expression of musing benevolence on his face, has attentively watched every animated look and gesture attending the delivery of these words. He remains in that attitude after they are spoken, as if in a kind of fascination attendant on his strong interest in the youthful spirit that he loves so well. Then he says with a quiet smile:

'You won't be warned, then?'

'No, Jack.'

'You can't be warned, then?'

'No, Jack, not by you. Besides that I don't really consider myself in danger, I don't like your putting yourself in that position.'

'Shall we go and walk in the churchyard?'

'By all means. You won't mind my slipping out of it for half a moment to the Nuns' House, and leaving a parcel there? Only gloves for Pussy; as many pairs of gloves as she is years old to-day. Rather poetical, Jack?'

Mr. Jasper, still in the same attitude, murmurs: ' "Nothing half so sweet in life," Ned!'

'Here's the parcel in my greatcoat-pocket. They must be presented to-night, or the poetry is gone. It's against regulations for me to call at night, but not to leave a packet. I am ready, Jack!'

Mr. Jasper dissolves his attitude, and they go out together.

CHAPTER III
The Nuns' House

FOR SUFFICIENT REASONS, which this narrative will itself unfold as it advances, a fictitious name must be bestowed upon the old Cathedral town. Let it stand in these pages as Cloisterham. It was once possibly known to the Druids by another name, and certainly to the Romans by another, and to the Saxons by another, and to the Normans by another; and a name more or less in the course of many centuries can be of little moment to its dusty chronicles.

An ancient city, Cloisterham, and no meet dwelling-place for any one with hankerings after the noisy world. A monotonous, silent city, deriving an earthy flavour throughout from its Cathedral crypt, and so abounding in vestiges of monastic graves, that the Cloisterham children grow small salad in the dust of abbots and abbesses, and make dirt-pies of nuns and friars; while every ploughman in its outlying fields renders to once puissant Lord Treasurers, Archbishops, Bishops, and such-like, the attention which the Ogre in the story-book desired to render to his unbidden visitor, and grinds their bones to make his bread.

A drowsy city, Cloisterham, whose inhabitants seem to suppose, with an inconsistency more strange than rare, that all its changes lie behind it, and that there are no more to come. A queer moral to derive from antiquity, yet older than any traceable antiquity. So silent are the streets of Cloisterham (though prone to echo on the smallest provocation), that of a summer-day the sunblinds of its shops scarce dare to flap in the south wind; while the sun-browned tramps, who pass along and stare, quicken their limp a little, that they may the sooner get beyond the confines of its oppressive respectability. This is a feat not difficult of achievement, seeing that the streets of Cloisterham city are little more than one narrow street by which you get into it and get out of it: the rest being mostly disappointing yards with pumps in them and no thoroughfare – exception made of the Cathedral-close, and a paved Quaker settlement, in colour and general confirmation very like a Quakeress's bonnet, up in a shady corner.

In a word, a city of another and a bygone time is Cloisterham, with its hoarse Cathedral-bell, its hoarse rooks hovering about the Cathedral tower, its hoarser and less distinct rooks in the stalls far beneath. Fragments of old wall, saint's chapel, chapter-house, convent and monastery, have got incongruously or obstructively built into many of its houses and gardens, much as kindred jumbled notions have become incorporated into many of its citizens' minds. All things in it are of the past. Even its single pawnbroker takes in no pledges, nor has he for a long time, but offers vainly an unredeemed stock for sale, of which the costlier articles are dim and pale old watches apparently in a slow perspiration, tarnished sugar-tongs with ineffectual legs, and odd volumes of dismal books. The most abundant and the most agreeable evidences of progressing life in Cloisterham are the evidences of vegetable life in many gardens; even its drooping and despondent little theatre has its poor strip of garden, receiving the foul fiend, when he ducks from its stage into the infernal regions, among scarlet-beans or oyster-shells, according to the season of the year.

In the midst of Cloisterham stands the Nuns' House: a venerable brick edifice, whose present appellation is doubtless derived from the legend of its conventual uses. On the trim gate enclosing its old courtyard is a resplendent brass plate flashing forth the legend: 'Seminary for Young Ladies. Miss Twinkleton.' The house-front is so old and worn, and the brass plate is so shining and staring, that the general result has reminded imaginative strangers of a battered old beau with a large modern eye-glass stuck in his blind eye.

Whether the nuns of yore, being of a submissive rather than a stiff-necked generation, habitually bent their contemplative heads to avoid collision with the beams in the low ceilings of the many chambers of their House; whether they sat in its long low windows telling their beads for their mortification, instead of making necklaces of them for their adornment; whether they were ever walled up alive in odd angles and jutting gables of the building for having some ineradicable leaven of busy mother Nature in them which has kept the fermenting world alive ever since; these may be matters of interest to its haunting ghosts (if any), but constitute no item in Miss Twinkleton's half-yearly accounts. They are neither of Miss Twinkleton's inclusive regulars, nor of her extras. The lady who undertakes the poetical department of the establishment at so much (or so little) a quarter has no pieces in her list of recitals bearing on such unprofitable questions.

As, in some cases of drunkenness, and in others of animal

magnetism, there are two states of consciousness which never clash, but each of which pursues its separate course as though it were continuous instead of broken (thus, if I hide my watch when I am drunk, I must be drunk again before I can remember where), so Miss Twinkleton has two distinct and separate phases of being. Every night, the moment the young ladies have retired to rest, does Miss Twinkleton smarten up her curls a little, brighten up her eyes a little, and become a sprightlier Miss Twinkleton than the young ladies have ever seen. Every night, at the same hour, does Miss Twinkleton resume the topics of the previous night, comprehending the tenderer scandal of Cloisterham, of which she has no knowledge whatever by day, and references to a certain season at Tunbridge Wells (airily called by Miss Twinkleton in this state of her existence 'The Wells'), notably the season wherein a certain finished gentleman (compassionately called by Miss Twinkleton, in this stage of her existence, 'Foolish Mr. Porters') revealed a homage of the heart, whereof Miss Twinkleton, in her scholastic state of existence, is as ignorant as a granite pillar. Miss Twinkleton's companion in both states of existence, and equally adaptable to either, is one Mrs. Tisher: a deferential widow with a weak back, a chronic sigh, and a suppressed voice, who looks after the young ladies' wardrobes, and leads them to infer that she has seen better days. Perhaps this is the reason why it is an article of faith with the servants, handed down from race to race, that the departed Tisher was a hairdresser.

The pet pupil of the Nuns' House is Miss Rosa Bud, of course called Rosebud; wonderfully pretty, wonderfully childish, wonderfully whimsical. An awkward interest (awkward because romantic) attaches to Miss Bud in the minds of the young ladies, on account of its being known to them that a husband has been chosen for her by will and bequest, and that her guardian is bound down to bestow her on that husband when he comes of age. Miss Twinkleton, in her seminarial state of existence, has combated the romantic aspect of this destiny by affecting to shake her head over it behind Miss Bud's dimpled shoulders, and to brood on the unhappy lot of that doomed little victim. But with no better effect – possibly some unfelt touch of foolish Mr. Porters has undermined the endeavour – than to evoke from the young ladies an unanimous bedchamber cry of 'O, what a pretending old thing Miss Twinkleton is, my dear!'

The Nuns' House is never in such a state of flutter as when this allotted husband calls to see little Rosebud. (It is unanimously understood by the young ladies that he is lawfully entitled to this privilege, and that if Miss

Twinkleton disputed it, she would be instantly taken up and transported.) When his ring at the gate-bell is expected, or takes place, every young lady who can, under any pretence, look out of window, looks out of window; while every young lady who is 'practising,' practises out of time; and the French class becomes so demoralised that the mark goes round as briskly as the bottle at a convivial party in the last century.

On the afternoon of the day next after the dinner of two at the gatehouse, the bell is rung with the usual fluttering results.

'Mr. Edwin Drood to see Miss Rosa.'

This is the announcement of the parlour-maid in chief. Miss Twinkleton, with an exemplary air of melancholy on her, turns to the sacrifice, and says, 'You may go down, my dear.' Miss Bud goes down, followed by all eyes.

Mr. Edwin Drood is waiting in Miss Twinkleton's own parlour: a dainty room, with nothing more directly scholastic in it than a terrestrial and a celestial globe. These expressive machines imply (to parents and guardians) that even when Miss Twinkleton retires into the bosom of privacy, duty may at any moment compel her to become a sort of Wandering Jewess, scouring the earth and soaring through the skies in search of knowledge for her pupils.

The last new maid, who has never seen the young gentleman Miss Rosa is engaged to, and who is making his acquaintance between the hinges of the open door, left open for the purpose, stumbles guiltily down the kitchen stairs, as a charming little apparition, with its face concealed by a little silk apron thrown over its head, glides into the parlour.

'O! *it is* so ridiculous!' says the apparition, stopping and shrinking. 'Don't, Eddy!'

'Don't what, Rosa?'

'Don't come any nearer, please. It *is* so absurd.'

'What is absurd, Rosa?'

'The whole thing is. It *is* so absurd to be an engaged orphan and it *is* so absurd to have the girls and the servants scuttling about after one, like mice in the wainscot; and it *is* so absurd to be called upon!'

The apparition appears to have a thumb in the corner of its mouth while making this complaint.

'You give me an affectionate reception, Pussy, I must say.'

'Well, I will in a minute, Eddy, but I can't just yet. How are you?' (very shortly.)

'I am unable to reply that I am much the better for seeing you, Pussy, inasmuch as I see nothing of you.'

This second remonstrance brings a dark, bright, pouting eye out from a corner of the apron; but it swiftly becomes invisible again, as the apparition exclaims: 'O good gracious! you have had half your hair cut off!'

'I should have done better to have had my head cut off, I think,' says Edwin, rumpling the hair in question, with a fierce glance at the looking-glass, and giving an impatient stamp. 'Shall I go?'

'No; you needn't go just yet, Eddy. The girls would all be asking questions why you went.'

'Once for all, Rosa, will you uncover that ridiculous little head of yours and give me a welcome?'

The apron is pulled off the childish head, as its wearer replies: 'You're very welcome, Eddy. There! I'm sure that's nice. Shake hands. No, I can't kiss you, because I've got an acidulated drop in my mouth.'

'Are you at all glad to see me, Pussy?'

'O, yes, I'm dreadfully glad. – Go and sit down. – Miss Twinkleton.'

It is the custom of that excellent lady when these visits occur, to appear every three minutes, either in her own person or in that of Mrs. Tisher, and lay an offering on the shrine of Propriety by affecting to look for some desiderated article. On the present occasion Miss Twinkleton, gracefully gliding in and out, says in passing: 'How do you do, Mr. Drood? Very glad indeed to have the pleasure. Pray excuse me. Tweezers. Thank you!'

'I got the gloves last evening, Eddy, and I like them very much. They are beauties.'

'Well, that's something,' the affianced replies, half grumbling. 'The smallest encouragement thankfully received. And how did you pass your birthday, Pussy?'

'Delightfully! Everybody gave me a present. And we had a feast. And we had a ball at night.'

'A feast and a ball, eh? These occasions seem to go off tolerably well without me, Pussy.'

'De-lightfully!' cries Rosa, in a quite spontaneous manner, and without the least pretence of reserve.

'Hah! And what was the feast?'

'Tarts, oranges, jellies, and shrimps.'

'Any partners at the ball?'

'We danced with one another, of course, sir. But some of the girls made game to be their brothers. It *was* so droll!'

'Did anybody make game to be – '

'To be you? O dear yes!' cries Rosa, laughing with great enjoyment. 'That was the first thing done.'

'I hope she did it pretty well,' says Edwin rather doubtfully.

'O, it was excellent! – I wouldn't dance with you, you know.'

Edwin scarcely seems to see the force of this; begs to know if he may take the liberty to ask why?

'Because I was so tired of you,' returns Rosa. But she quickly adds, and pleadingly too, seeing displeasure in his face: 'Dear Eddy, you were just as tired of me, you know.'

'Did I say so, Rosa?'

'Say so! Do you ever say so? No, you only showed it. O, she did it so well!' cries Rosa, in a sudden ecstasy with her counterfeit betrothed.

'It strikes me that she must be a devilish impudent girl,' says Edwin Drood. 'And so, Pussy, you have passed your last birthday in this old house.'

'Ah, yes!' Rosa clasps her hands, looks down with a sigh, and shakes her head.

'You seem to be sorry, Rosa.'

'I am sorry for the poor old place. Somehow, I feel as if it would miss me, when I am gone so far away, so young.'

'Perhaps we had better stop short, Rosa?'

She looks up at him with a swift bright look; next moment shakes her head, sighs, and looks down again.

'That is to say, is it, Pussy, that we are both resigned?'

She nods her head again, and after a short silence, quaintly bursts out with: 'You know we must be married, and married from here, Eddy, or the poor girls will be so dreadfully disappointed!'

For the moment there is more of compassion, both for her and for himself, in her affianced husband's face, than there is of love. He checks the look, and asks: 'Shall I take you out for a walk, Rosa dear?'

Rosa dear does not seem at all clear on this point, until her face, which has been comically reflective, brightens. 'O, yes, Eddy; let us go for a walk! And I tell you what we'll do. You shall pretend that you are engaged to somebody else, and I'll pretend that I am not engaged to anybody, and then we shan't quarrel.'

'Do you think that will prevent our falling out, Rosa?'

'I know it will. Hush! Pretend to look out of window – Mrs. Tisher!'

Through a fortuitous concourse of accidents, the matronly Tisher heaves in sight, says, in rustling through the room like the legendary ghost of a dowager in silken skirts: 'I hope I see Mr. Drood well; though I needn't ask, if I may judge from his complexion. I trust I disturb no one; but there *was* a paper-knife – O, thank you, I am sure!' and disappears with her prize.

'One other thing you must do, Eddy, to oblige me,' says Rosebud. 'The moment we get into the street, you must put me outside, and keep close to the house yourself – squeeze and graze yourself against it.'

'By all means, Rosa, if you wish it. Might I ask why?'

'O! because I don't want the girls to see you.'

'It's a fine day; but would you like me to carry an umbrella up?'

'Don't be foolish, sir. You haven't got polished leather boots on,' pouting, with one shoulder raised.

'Perhaps that might escape the notice of the girls, even if they did see me,' remarks Edwin, looking down at his boots with a sudden distaste for them.

'Nothing escapes their notice, sir. And then I know what would happen. Some of them would begin reflecting on me by saying (for *they* are free) that they never will on any account engage themselves to lovers without polished leather boots. Hark! Miss Twinkleton. I'll ask for leave.'

That discreet lady being indeed heard without, inquiring of nobody in a blandly conversational tone as she advances: 'Eh? Indeed! Are you quite sure you saw my mother-of-pearl button-holder on the work-table in my room?' is at once solicited for walking leave, and graciously accords it. And soon the young couple go out of the Nuns' House, taking all precautions against the discovery of the so vitally defective boots of Mr. Edwin Drood: precautions, let us hope, effective for the peace of Mrs. Edwin Drood that is to be.

'Which way shall we take, Rosa?'

Rosa replies: 'I want to go to the Lumps-of-Delight shop.'

'To the – ?'

'A Turkish sweetmeat, sir. My gracious me, don't you understand anything? Call yourself an Engineer, and not know *that*?'

'Why, how should I know it, Rosa?'

'Because I am very fond of them. But O! I forgot what we are to pretend. No, you needn't know anything about them; never mind.'

So he is gloomily borne off to the Lumps-of-Delight shop, where Rosa makes her purchase, and, after offering some to him (which he rather indignantly declines), begins to partake of it with great zest: previously taking off and rolling up a pair of little pink gloves, like rose-leaves, and occasionally putting her little pink fingers to her rosy lips, to cleanse them from the Dust of Delight that comes off the Lumps.

'Now, be a good-tempered Eddy, and pretend. And so you are engaged?'

'And so I am engaged.'

'Is she nice?'

'Charming.'

'Tall?'

'Immensely tall!' Rosa being short.

'Must be gawky, I should think,' is Rosa's quiet commentary.

'I beg your pardon; not at all,' contradiction rising in him.

'What is termed a fine woman; a splendid woman.'

'Big nose, no doubt,' is the quiet commentary again.

'Not a little one, certainly,' is the quick reply, (Rosa's being a little one.)

'Long pale nose, with a red knob in the middle. I know the sort of nose,' says Rosa, with a satisfied nod, and tranquilly enjoying the Lumps.

'You *don't* know the sort of nose, Rosa,' with some warmth; 'because it's nothing of the kind.'

'Not a pale nose, Eddy?'

'No.' Determined not to assent.

'A red nose? O! I don't like red noses. However; to be sure she can always powder it.'

'She would scorn to powder it,' says Edwin, becoming heated.

'Would she? What a stupid thing she must be! Is she stupid in everything?'

'No; in nothing.'

After a pause, in which the whimsically wicked face has not been unobservant of him, Rosa says:

'And this most sensible of creatures likes the idea of being carried off to Egypt; does she, Eddy?'

'Yes. She takes a sensible interest in triumphs of engineering skill: especially when they are to change the whole condition of an undeveloped country.'

'Lor!' says Rosa, shrugging her shoulders, with a little laugh of wonder.

'Do you object,' Edwin inquires, with a majestic turn of his eyes downward upon the fairy figure: 'do you object, Rosa, to her feeling that interest?'

'Object? my dear Eddy! But really, doesn't she hate boilers and things?'

'I can answer for her not being so idiotic as to hate Boilers,' he returns with angry emphasis; 'though I cannot answer for her views about Things; really not understanding what Things are meant.'

'But don't she hate Arabs, and Turks, and Fellahs, and people?'

'Certainly not.' Very firmly.

'At least she *must* hate the Pyramids? Come, Eddy?'

'Why should she be such a little – tall, I mean – goose, as to hate the Pyramids, Rosa?'

'Ah! you should hear Miss Twinkleton,' often nodding her head, and much enjoying the Lumps, 'bore about them, and then you wouldn't ask. Tiresome old burying-grounds! Isises, and Ibises, and Cheopses, and Pharaohses; who cares about them? And then there was Belzoni, or somebody, dragged out by the legs, half-choked with bats and dust. All the girls say: Serve him right, and hope it hurt him, and wish he had been quite choked.'

The two youthful figures, side by side, but not now arm-in-arm, wander discontentedly about the old Close; and each sometimes stops and slowly imprints a deeper footstep in the fallen leaves.

'Well!' says Edwin, after a lengthy silence. 'According to custom. We can't get on, Rosa.'

Rosa tosses her head, and says she don't want to get on.

'That's a pretty sentiment, Rosa, considering.'

'Considering what?'

'If I say what, you'll go wrong again.'

'*You'll* go wrong, you mean, Eddy. Don't be ungenerous.'

'Ungenerous! I like that!'

'Then I *don't* like that, and so I tell you plainly,' Rosa pouts.

'Now, Rosa, I put it to you. Who disparaged my profession, my destination – '

'You are not going to be buried in the Pyramids, I hope?' she interrupts, arching her delicate eyebrows. 'You never said you were. If you are, why haven't you mentioned it to me? I can't find out your plans by instinct.'

'Now, Rosa, you know very well what I mean, my dear.'

'Well then, why did you begin with your detestable red-nosed giantesses? And she would, she would, she would, she would, she WOULD powder it!' cries Rosa, in a little burst of comical contradictory spleen.

'Somehow or other, I never can come right in these discussions,' says Edwin, sighing and becoming resigned.

'How is it possible, sir, that you ever can come right when you're always wrong? And as to Belzoni, I suppose he's dead; – I'm sure I hope he is – and how can his legs or his chokes concern you?'

'It is nearly time for your return, Rosa. We have not had a very happy walk, have we?'

'A happy walk? A detestably unhappy walk, sir. If I go up-stairs the moment I get in and cry till I can't take my dancing lesson, you are responsible, mind!'

'Let us be friends, Rosa.'

'Ah!' cries Rosa, shaking her head and bursting into real tears, 'I wish we *could* be friends! It's because we can't be friends, that we try one another so. I am a young little thing, Eddy, to have an old heartache; but I really, really have, sometimes. Don't be angry. I know you have one yourself too often. We should both of us have done better, if What is to be had been left What might have been. I am quite a little serious thing now, and not teasing you. Let each of us forbear, this one time, on our own account, and on the other's!'

Disarmed by this glimpse of a woman's nature in the spoilt child, though for an instant disposed to resent it as seeming to involve the enforced infliction of himself upon her, Edwin Drood stands watching her as she childishly cries and sobs, with both hands to the handkerchief at her eyes, and then – she becoming more composed, and indeed beginning in her young inconstancy to laugh at herself for having been so moved – leads her to a seat hard by, under the elm-trees.

'One clear word of understanding, Pussy dear. I am not clever out of my own line – now I come to think of it, I don't know that I am particularly clever in it – but I want to do right. There is not – there may be – I really don't see my way to what I want to say, but I must say it before we part – there is not any other young – '

'O no, Eddy! It's generous of you to ask me; but no, no, no!'

They have come very near to the Cathedral windows, and at this moment the organ and the choir sound out sublimely. As they sit listening to the solemn swell, the confidence of last night rises in young Edwin Drood's mind, and he thinks how unlike this music is to that discordance.

'I fancy I can distinguish Jack's voice,' is his remark in a low tone in connection with the train of thought.

'Take me back at once, please,' urges his Affianced, quickly laying her light hand upon his wrist. 'They will all be coming out directly; let us get away. O, what a resounding chord! But don't let us stop to listen to it; let us get away!'

Her hurry is over as soon as they have passed out of the Close. They go arm-in-arm now, gravely and deliberately enough, along the old High-street, to the Nuns' House. At the gate, the street being within sight empty, Edwin bends down his face to Rosebud's.

She remonstrates, laughing, and is a childish schoolgirl again.

'Eddy, no! I'm too sticky to be kissed. But give me your hand, and I'll blow a kiss into that.'

He does so. She breathes a light breath into it and asks, retaining it and looking into it: –

'Now say, what do you see?'

'See, Rosa?'

'Why, I thought you Egyptian boys could look into a hand and see all sorts of phantoms. Can't you see a happy Future?'

For certain, neither of them sees a happy Present, as the gate opens and closes, and one goes in, and the other goes away.

CHAPTER IV
Mr. Sapsea

ACCEPTING THE JACKASS as the type of self-sufficient stupidity and conceit – a custom, perhaps, like some few other customs, more conventional than fair – then the purest jackass in Cloisterham is Mr. Thomas Sapsea, Auctioneer.

Mr. Sapsea 'dresses at' the Dean; has been bowed to for the Dean, in mistake; has even been spoken to in the street as My Lord, under the impression that he was the Bishop come down unexpectedly, without his chaplain. Mr. Sapsea is very proud of this, and of his voice, and of his style. He has even (in selling landed property) tried the experiment of slightly intoning in his pulpit, to make himself more like what he takes to be the genuine ecclesiastical article. So, in ending a Sale by Public Auction, Mr. Sapsea finishes off with an air of bestowing a benediction on the assembled brokers, which leaves the real Dean – a modest and worthy gentleman – far behind.

Mr. Sapsea has many admirers; indeed, the proposition is carried by a large local majority, even including non-believers in his wisdom, that he is a credit to Cloisterham. He possesses the great qualities of being portentous and dull, and of having a roll in his speech, and another roll in his gait; not to mention a certain gravely flowing action with his hands, as if he were presently going to Confirm the individual with whom he holds discourse. Much nearer sixty years of age than fifty, with a flowing outline of stomach, and horizontal creases in his waistcoat; reputed to be rich; voting at elections in the strictly respectable interest; morally satisfied that nothing but he himself has grown since he was a baby; how can dunder-headed Mr. Sapsea be otherwise than a credit to Cloisterham, and society?

Mr. Sapsea's premises are in the High-street, over against the Nuns' House. They are of about the period of the Nuns' House, irregularly modernised here and there, as steadily deteriorating generations found, more and more, that they preferred air and light to Fever and the Plague. Over the doorway is a wooden effigy, about half life-size, representing

Mr. Sapsea's father, in a curly wig and toga, in the act of selling. The chastity of the idea, and the natural appearance of the little finger, hammer, and pulpit, have been much admired.

Mr. Sapsea sits in his dull ground-floor sitting-room, giving first on his paved back yard; and then on his railed-off garden. Mr. Sapsea has a bottle of port wine on a table before the fire – the fire is an early luxury, but pleasant on the cool, chilly autumn evening – and is characteristically attended by his portrait, his eight-day clock, and his weather-glass. Characteristically, because he would uphold himself against mankind, his weather-glass against weather, and his clock against time.

By Mr. Sapsea's side on the table are a writing-desk and writing materials. Glancing at a scrap of manuscript, Mr. Sapsea reads it to himself with a lofty air, and then, slowly pacing the room with his thumbs in the arm-holes of his waistcoat, repeats it from memory: so internally, though with much dignity, that the word 'Ethelinda' is alone audible.

There are three clean wineglasses in a tray on the table. His serving-maid entering, and announcing 'Mr. Jasper is come, sir,' Mr. Sapsea waves 'Admit him,' and draws two wineglasses from the rank, as being claimed.

'Glad to see you, sir. I congratulate myself on having the honour of receiving you here for the first time.' Mr. Sapsea does the honours of his house in this wise.

'You are very good. The honour is mine and the self-congratulation is mine.'

'You are pleased to say so, sir. But I do assure you that it is a satisfaction to me to receive you in my humble home. And that is what I would not say to everybody.' Ineffable loftiness on Mr. Sapsea's part accompanies these words, as leaving the sentence to be understood: 'You will not easily believe that your society can be a satisfaction to a man like myself; nevertheless, it is.'

'I have for some time desired to know you, Mr. Sapsea.'

'And I, sir, have long known you by reputation as a man of taste. Let me fill your glass. I will give you, sir,' says Mr. Sapsea, filling his own:

> 'When the French come over,
> May we meet them at Dover!'

This was a patriotic toast in Mr. Sapsea's infancy, and he is therefore fully convinced of its being appropriate to any subsequent era.

'You can scarcely be ignorant, Mr. Sapsea,' observes Jasper, watching the auctioneer with a smile as the latter stretches out his legs before the fire, 'that you know the world.'

'Well, sir,' is the chuckling reply, 'I think I know something of it; something of it.'

'Your reputation for that knowledge has always interested and surprised me, and made me wish to know you. For Cloisterham is a little place. Cooped up in it myself, I know nothing beyond it, and feel it to be a very little place.'

'If I have not gone to foreign countries, young man,' Mr. Sapsea begins, and then stops: – 'You will excuse me calling you young man, Mr. Jasper? You are much my junior.'

'By all means.'

'If I have not gone to foreign countries, young man, foreign countries have come to me. They have come to me in the way of business, and I have improved upon my opportunities. Put it that I take an inventory, or make a catalogue. I see a French clock. I never saw him before, in my life, but I instantly lay my finger on him and say "Paris!" I see some cups and saucers of Chinese make, equally strangers to me personally: I put my finger on them, then and there, and I say "Pekin, Nankin, and Canton." It is the same with Japan, with Egypt, and with bamboo and sandalwood from the East Indies; I put my finger on them all. I have put my finger on the North Pole before now, and said "Spear of Esquimaux make, for half a pint of pale sherry!"'

'Really? A very remarkable way, Mr. Sapsea, of acquiring a knowledge of men and things.'

'I mention it, sir,' Mr. Sapsea rejoins, with unspeakable complacency, 'because, as I say, it don't do to boast of what you are; but show how you came to be it, and then you prove it.'

'Most interesting. We were to speak of the late Mrs. Sapsea.'

'We were, sir.' Mr. Sapsea fills both glasses, and takes the decanter into safe keeping again. 'Before I consult your opinion as a man of taste on this little trifle' – holding it up – 'which is *but* a trifle, and still has required some thought, sir, some little fever of the brow, I ought perhaps to describe the character of the late Mrs. Sapsea, now dead three quarters of a year.'

Mr. Jasper, in the act of yawning behind his wineglass, puts down that screen and calls up a look of interest. It is a little impaired in its expressiveness by his having a shut-up gape still to dispose of, with watering eyes.

'Half a dozen years ago, or so,' Mr. Sapsea proceeds, 'when I had enlarged my mind up to – I will not say to what it now is, for that might seem to aim at too much, but up to the pitch of wanting another mind to be absorbed in it – I cast my eye about me for a nuptial partner. Because, as I say, it is not good for man to be alone.'

Mr. Jasper appears to commit this original idea to memory.

'Miss Brobity at that time kept, I will not call it the rival establishment to the establishment at the Nuns' House opposite, but I will call it the other parallel establishment down town. The world did have it that she showed a passion for attending my sales, when they took place on half holidays, or in vacation time. The world did put it about, that she admired my style. The world did notice that as time flowed by, my style became traceable in the dictation-exercises of Miss Brobity's pupils. Young man, a whisper even sprang up in obscure malignity, that one ignorant and besotted Churl (a parent) so committed himself as to object to it by name. But I do not believe this. For is it likely that any human creature in his right senses would so lay himself open to be pointed at, by what I call the finger of scorn?'

Mr. Jasper shakes his head. Not in the least likely. Mr. Sapsea, in a grandiloquent state of absence of mind, seems to refill his visitor's glass, which is full already; and does really refill his own, which is empty.

'Miss Brobity's Being, young man, was deeply imbued with homage to Mind. She revered Mind, when launched, or, as I say, precipitated, on an extensive knowledge of the world. When I made my proposal, she did me the honour to be so overshadowed with a species of Awe, as to be able to articulate only the two words, "O Thou!" meaning myself. Her limpid blue eyes were fixed upon me, her semi-transparent hands were clasped together, pallor overspread her aquiline features, and, though encouraged to proceed, she never did proceed a word further. I disposed of the parallel establishment by private contract, and we became as nearly one as could be expected under the circumstances. But she never could, and she never did, find a phrase satisfactory to her perhaps-too-favourable estimate of my intellect. To the very last (feeble action of liver), she addressed me in the same unfinished terms.'

Mr. Jasper has closed his eyes as the auctioneer has deepened his voice. He now abruptly opens them, and says, in unison with the deepened voice 'Ah!' – rather as if stopping himself on the extreme verge of adding – 'men!'

'I have been since,' says Mr. Sapsea, with his legs stretched out, and solemnly enjoying himself with the wine and the fire, 'what you behold me; I have been since a solitary mourner; I have been since, as I say, wasting my evening conversation on the desert air. I will not say that I have reproached myself; but there have been times when I have asked myself the question: What if her husband had been nearer on a level with her? If she had not had to look up quite so high, what might the stimulating action have been upon the liver?'

Mr. Jasper says, with an appearance of having fallen into dreadfully low spirits, that he 'supposes it was to be.'

'We can only suppose so, sir,' Mr. Sapsea coincides. 'As I say, Man proposes, Heaven disposes. It may or may not be putting the same thought in another form; but that is the way I put it.'

Mr. Jasper murmurs assent.

'And now, Mr. Jasper,' resumes the auctioneer, producing his scrap of manuscript, 'Mrs. Sapsea's monument having had full time to settle and dry, let me take your opinion, as a man of taste, on the inscription I have (as I before remarked, not without some little fever of the brow) drawn out for it. Take it in your own hand. The setting out of the lines requires to be followed with the eye, as well as the contents with the mind.'

Mr. Jasper complying, sees and reads as follows:

ETHELINDA,

Reverential Wife of

MR. THOMAS SAPSEA,

AUCTIONEER, VALUER, ESTATE AGENT, &c.,

OF THIS CITY.

Whose Knowledge of the World,

Though somewhat extensive,

Never brought him acquainted with

A SPIRIT

More capable of

LOOKING UP TO HIM.

STRANGER PAUSE

And ask thyself the Question,

CANST THOU DO LIKEWISE?

If Not,

WITH A BLUSH RETIRE.

Mr. Sapsea having risen and stationed himself with his back to the fire, for the purpose of observing the effect of these lines on the countenance of a man of taste, consequently has his face towards the door, when his serving-maid, again appearing, announces, 'Durdles is come, sir!' He promptly draws forth and fills the third wineglass, as being now claimed, and replies, 'Show Durdles in.'

'Admirable!' quoth Mr. Jasper, handing back the paper.

'You approve, sir?'

'Impossible not to approve. Striking, characteristic, and complete.'

The auctioneer inclines his head, as one accepting his due and giving a receipt; and invites the entering Durdles to take off that glass of wine (handing the same), for it will warm him.

Durdles is a stonemason; chiefly in the gravestone, tomb, and monument way, and wholly of their colour from head to foot. No man is better known in Cloisterham. He is the chartered libertine of the place. Fame trumpets him a wonderful workman – which, for aught that anybody knows, he may be (as he never works); and a wonderful sot – which everybody knows he is. With the Cathedral crypt he is better acquainted than any living authority; it may even be than any dead one. It is said that the intimacy of this acquaintance began in his habitually resorting to that secret place, to lock-out the Cloisterham boy-populace, and sleep off fumes of liquor: he having ready access to the Cathedral, as contractor for rough repairs. Be this as it may, he does know much about it, and, in the demolition of impedimental fragments of wall, buttress, and pavement, has seen strange sights. He often speaks of himself in the third person; perhaps, being a little misty as to his own identity, when he narrates; perhaps impartially adopting the Cloisterham nomenclature in reference to a character of acknowledged distinction. Thus he will say, touching his strange sights: 'Durdles come upon the old chap,' in reference to a buried magnate of ancient time and high degree, 'by striking right into the coffin with his pick. The old chap gave Durdles a look with his open eyes, as much as to say, "Is your name Durdles? Why, my man, I've been waiting for you a devil of a time!" And then he turned to powder.' With a two-foot rule always in his pocket, and a mason's hammer all but always in his hand, Durdles goes continually sounding and tapping all about and about the Cathedral; and whenever he says to Tope: 'Tope, here's another old 'un in here!' Tope announces it to the Dean as an established discovery.

In a suit of coarse flannel with horn buttons, a yellow neckerchief with draggled ends, an old hat more russet-coloured than black, and laced boots of the hue of his stony calling, Durdles leads a hazy, gipsy sort of life, carrying his dinner about with him in a small bundle, and sitting on all manner of tombstones to dine. This dinner of Durdles's has become quite a Cloisterham institution: not only because of his never appearing in public without it, but because of its having been, on certain renowned occasions, taken into custody along with Durdles (as drunk and incapable), and exhibited before the Bench of justices at the townhall. These occasions, however, have been few and far apart: Durdles being as seldom drunk as sober. For the rest, he is an old bachelor, and he lives in a little antiquated hole of a house that was never finished: supposed to be built, so far, of stones stolen from the city wall. To this abode there is an approach, ankle-deep in stone chips, resembling a petrified grove of tombstones, urns, draperies, and broken columns, in all stages of sculpture. Herein two journeymen incessantly chip, while other two journeymen, who face each other, incessantly saw stone; dipping as regularly in and out of their sheltering sentry-boxes, as if they were mechanical figures emblematical of Time and Death.

To Durdles, when he had consumed his glass of port, Mr. Sapsea intrusts that precious effort of his Muse. Durdles unfeelingly takes out his two-foot rule, and measures the lines calmly, alloying them with stone-grit.

'This is for the monument, is it, Mr. Sapsea?'

'The Inscription. Yes.' Mr. Sapsea waits for its effect on a common mind.

'It'll come in to a eighth of a inch,' says Durdles. 'Your servant, Mr. Jasper. Hope I see you well.'

'How are you Durdles?'

'I've got a touch of the Tombatism on me, Mr. Jasper, but that I must expect.'

'You mean the Rheumatism,' says Sapsea, in a sharp tone. (He is nettled by having his composition so mechanically received.)

'No, I don't. I mean, Mr. Sapsea, the Tombatism. It's another sort from Rheumatism. Mr. Jasper knows what Durdles means. You get among them Tombs afore it's well light on a winter morning, and keep on, as the Catechism says, a-walking in the same all the days of your life, and *you'll* know what Durdles means.'

'It is a bitter cold place,' Mr. Jasper assents, with an antipathetic shiver.

'And if it's bitter cold for you, up in the chancel, with a lot of live breath smoking out about you, what the bitterness is to Durdles, down in the crypt among the earthy damps there, and the dead breath of the old 'uns,' returns that individual, 'Durdles leaves you to judge. – Is this to be put in hand at once, Mr. Sapsea?'

Mr. Sapsea, with an Author's anxiety to rush into publication, replies that it cannot be out of hand too soon.

'You had better let me have the key then,' says Durdles.

'Why, man, it is not to be put inside the monument!'

'Durdles knows where it's to be put, Mr. Sapsea; no man better. Ask 'ere a man in Cloisterham whether Durdles knows his work.'

Mr. Sapsea rises, takes a key from a drawer, unlocks an iron safe let into the wall, and takes from it another key.

'When Durdles puts a touch or a finish upon his work, no matter where, inside or outside, Durdles likes to look at his work all round, and see that his work is a-doing him credit,' Durdles explains, doggedly.

The key proffered him by the bereaved widower being a large one, he slips his two-foot rule into a side-pocket of his flannel trousers made for it, and deliberately opens his flannel coat, and opens the mouth of a large breast-pocket within it before taking the key to place it in that repository.

'Why, Durdles!' exclaims Jasper, looking on amused, 'you are undermined with pockets!'

'And I carries weight in 'em too, Mr. Jasper. Feel those!' producing two other large keys.

'Hand me Mr. Sapsea's likewise. Surely this is the heaviest of the three.'

'You'll find 'em much of a muchness, I expect,' says Durdles. 'They all belong to monuments. They all open Durdles's work. Durdles keeps the keys of his work mostly. Not that they're much used.'

'By the bye,' it comes into Jasper's mind to say, as he idly examines the keys, 'I have been going to ask you, many a day, and have always forgotten. You know they sometimes call you Stony Durdles, don't you?'

'Cloisterham knows me as Durdles, Mr. Jasper.'

'I am aware of that, of course. But the boys sometimes – '

'O! if you mind them young imps of boys – ' Durdles gruffly interrupts.

'I don't mind them any more than you do. But there was a discussion the other day among the Choir, whether Stony stood for Tony;' clinking one key against another.

('Take care of the wards, Mr. Jasper.')

'Or whether Stony stood for Stephen;' clinking with a change of keys.

('You can't make a pitch pipe of 'em, Mr. Jasper.')

'Or whether the name comes from your trade. How stands the fact?'

Mr. Jasper weighs the three keys in his hand, lifts his head from his idly stooping attitude over the fire, and delivers the keys to Durdles with an ingenuous and friendly face.

But the stony one is a gruff one likewise, and that hazy state of his is always an uncertain state, highly conscious of its dignity, and prone to take offence. He drops his two keys back into his pocket one by one, and buttons them up; he takes his dinner-bundle from the chair-back on which he hung it when he came in; he distributes the weight he carries, by tying the third key up in it, as though he were an Ostrich, and liked to dine off cold iron; and he gets out of the room, deigning no word of answer.

Mr. Sapsea then proposes a hit at backgammon, which, seasoned with his own improving conversation, and terminating in a supper of cold roast beef and salad, beguiles the golden evening until pretty late. Mr. Sapsea's wisdom being, in its delivery to mortals, rather of the diffuse than the epigrammatic order, is by no means expended even then; but his visitor intimates that he will come back for more of the precious commodity on future occasions, and Mr. Sapsea lets him off for the present, to ponder on the instalment he carries away.

* D *

CHAPTER V

Mr. Durdles and Friend

JOHN JASPER, ON his way home through the Close, is brought to a stand-still by the spectacle of Stony Durdles, dinner-bundle and all, leaning his back against the iron railing of the burial-ground enclosing it from the old cloister-arches; and a hideous small boy in rags flinging stones at him as a well-defined mark in the moonlight. Sometimes the stones hit him, and sometimes they miss him, but Durdles seems indifferent to either fortune. The hideous small boy, on the contrary, whenever he hits Durdles, blows a whistle of triumph through a jagged gap, convenient for the purpose, in the front of his mouth, where half his teeth are wanting; and whenever he misses him, yelps out 'Mulled agin!' and tries to atone for the failure by taking a more correct and vicious aim.

'What are you doing to the man?' demands Jasper, stepping out into the moonlight from the shade.

'Making a cock-shy of him,' replies the hideous small boy.

'Give me those stones in your hand.'

'Yes, I'll give 'em you down your throat, if you come a-ketching hold of me,' says the small boy, shaking himself loose, and backing. 'I'll smash your eye, if you don't look out!'

'Baby-Devil that you are, what has the man done to you?'

'He won't go home.'

'What is that to you?'

'He gives me a 'apenny to pelt him home if I ketches him out too late,' says the boy. And then chants, like a little savage, half stumbling and half dancing among the rags and laces of his dilapidated boots: –

> 'Widdy widdy wen!
> I – ket – ches – Im – out – ar – ter – ten,
> Widdy widdy wy!
> Then – E – don't – go – then – I – shy –
> Widdy Widdy Wake-cock warning!'

– with a comprehensive sweep on the last word, and one more delivery at Durdles.

This would seem to be a poetical note of preparation, agreed upon, as a caution to Durdles to stand clear if he can, or to betake himself homeward.

John Jasper invites the boy with a beck of his head to follow him (feeling it hopeless to drag him, or coax him), and crosses to the iron railing where the Stony (and stoned) One is profoundly meditating.

'Do you know this thing, this child?' asks Jasper, at a loss for a word that will define this thing.

'Deputy,' says Durdles, with a nod.

'Is that its – his – name?'

'Deputy,' assents Durdles.

'I'm man-servant up at the Travellers' Twopenny in Gas Works Garding,' this thing explains. 'All us man-servants at Travellers' Lodgings is named Deputy. When we're chock full and the Travellers is all a-bed I come out for my 'elth.' Then withdrawing into the road, and taking aim, he resumes:

> 'Widdy widdy wen!
> I – ket – ches – Im – out – ar – ter —'

'Hold your hand,' cries Jasper, 'and don't throw while I stand so near him, or I'll kill you! Come, Durdles; let me walk home with you to-night. Shall I carry your bundle?'

'Not on any account,' replies Durdles, adjusting it. 'Durdles was making his reflections here when you come up, sir, surrounded by his works, like a poplar Author. – Your own brother-in-law;' introducing a sarcophagus within the railing, white and cold in the moonlight. 'Mrs. Sapsea;' introducing the monument of that devoted wife. 'Late Incumbent;' introducing the Reverend Gentleman's broken column. 'Departed Assessed Taxes;' introducing a vase and towel, standing on what might represent the cake of soap. 'Former pastrycook and Muffin-maker, much respected;' introducing gravestone. 'All safe and sound here, sir, and all Durdles's work. Of the common folk, that is merely bundled up in turf and brambles, the less said the better. A poor lot, soon forgot.'

'This creature, Deputy, is behind us,' says Jasper, looking back. 'Is he to follow us?'

The relations between Durdles and Deputy are of a capricious kind; for, on Durdles's turning himself about with the slow gravity of beery suddenness, Deputy makes a pretty wide circuit into the road and stands on the defensive.

'You never cried Widdy Warning before you begun to-night,' says Durdles, unexpectedly reminded of, or imagining, an injury.

'Yer lie, I did,' says Deputy, in his only form of polite contradiction.

'Own brother, sir,' observes Durdles, turning himself about again, and as unexpectedly forgetting his offence as he had recalled or conceived it; 'own brother to Peter the Wild Boy! But I gave him an object in life.'

'At which he takes aim?' Mr. Jasper suggests.

'That's it, sir,' returns Durdles, quite satisfied; 'at which he takes aim. I took him in hand and gave him an object. What was he before? A destroyer. What work did he do? Nothing but destruction. What did he earn by it? Short terms in Cloisterham jail. Not a person, not a piece of property, not a winder, not a horse, nor a dog, nor a cat, nor a bird, nor a fowl, nor a pig, but what he stoned, for want of an enlightened object. I put that enlightened object before him, and now he can turn his honest halfpenny by the three penn'orth a week.'

'I wonder he has no competitors.'

'He has plenty, Mr. Jasper, but he stones 'em all away. Now, I don't know what this scheme of mine comes to,' pursues Durdles, considering about it with the same sodden gravity; 'I don't know what you may precisely call it. It ain't a sort of a – scheme of a – National Education?'

'I should say not,' replies Jasper.

'*I* should say not,' assents Durdles; 'then we won't try to give it a name.'

'He still keeps behind us,' repeats Jasper, looking over his shoulder; 'is he to follow us?'

'We can't help going round by the Travellers' Twopenny, if we go the short way, which is the back way,' Durdles answers, 'and we'll drop him there.'

So they go on; Deputy, as a rear rank one, taking open order, and invading the silence of the hour and place by stoning every wall, post, pillar, and other inanimate object, by the deserted way.

'Is there anything new down in the crypt, Durdles?' asks John Jasper.

'Anything old, I think you mean,' growls Durdles. 'It ain't a spot for novelty.'

'Any new discovery on your part, I meant.'

'There's a old 'un under the seventh pillar on the left as you go down the broken steps of the little underground chapel as formerly was; I make him out (so fur as I've made him out yet) to be one of them old 'uns with a crook. To judge from the size of the passages in the walls, and of the steps and doors, by which they come and went, them crooks must have been a good deal in the way of the old 'uns! Two on 'em meeting promiscuous must have hitched one another by the mitre pretty often, I should say.'

Without any endeavour to correct the literality of this opinion, Jasper surveys his companion – covered from head to foot with old mortar, lime, and stone grit – as though he, Jasper, were getting imbued with a romantic interest in his weird life.

'Yours is a curious existence.'

Without furnishing the least clue to the question, whether he receives this as a compliment or as quite the reverse, Durdles gruffly answers: 'Yours is another.'

'Well! inasmuch as my lot is cast in the same old earthy, chilly, never-changing place, Yes. But there is much more mystery and interest in your connection with the Cathedral than in mine. Indeed, I am beginning to have some idea of asking you to take me on as a sort of student, or free 'prentice, under you, and to let me go about with you sometimes, and see some of these odd nooks in which you pass your days.'

The Stony One replies, in a general way, 'All right. Everybody knows where to find Durdles, when he's wanted.' Which, if not strictly true, is approximately so, if taken to express that Durdles may always be found in a state of vagabondage somewhere.

'What I dwell upon most,' says Jasper, pursuing his subject of romantic interest, 'is the remarkable accuracy with which you would seem to find out where people are buried. – What is the matter? That bundle is in your way; let me hold it.'

Durdles has stopped and backed a little (Deputy, attentive to all his movements, immediately skirmishing into the road), and was looking about for some ledge or corner to place his bundle on, when thus relieved of it.

'Just you give me my hammer out of that,' says Durdles, 'and I'll show you.'

Clink, clink. And his hammer is handed him.

'Now, lookee here. You pitch your note, don't you, Mr. Jasper?'

'Yes.'

'So I sound for mine. I take my hammer, and I tap.' (Here he strikes the pavement, and the attentive Deputy skirmishes at a rather wider range, as supposing that his head may be in requisition.) 'I tap, tap, tap. Solid! I go on tapping. Solid still! Tap again. Holloa! Hollow! Tap again, persevering. Solid in hollow! Tap, tap, tap, to try it better. Solid in hollow; and inside solid, hollow again! There you are! Old 'un crumbled away in stone coffin, in vault!'

'Astonishing!'

'I have even done this,' says Durdles, drawing out his two-foot rule (Deputy meanwhile skirmishing nearer, as suspecting that Treasure may be about to be discovered, which may somehow lead to his own enrichment, and the delicious treat of the discoverers being hanged by the neck, on his evidence, until they are dead). 'Say that hammer of mine's a wall – my work. Two; four; and two is six,' measuring on the pavement. 'Six foot inside that wall is Mrs. Sapsea.'

'Not really Mrs. Sapsea?'

'Say Mrs. Sapsea. Her wall's thicker, but say Mrs. Sapsea. Durdles taps, that wall represented by that hammer, and says, after good sounding: "Something betwixt us!" Sure enough, some rubbish has been left in that same six-foot space by Durdles's men!'

Jasper opines that such accuracy 'is a gift.'

'I wouldn't have it at a gift,' returns Durdles, by no means receiving the observation in good part. 'I worked it out for myself. Durdles comes by *his* knowledge through grubbing deep for it, and having it up by the roots when it don't want to come. – Holloa you Deputy!'

'Widdy!' is Deputy's shrill response, standing off again.

'Catch that ha'penny. And don't let me see any more of you to-night, after we come to the Travellers' Twopenny.'

'Warning!' returns Deputy, having caught the halfpenny, and appearing by this mystic word to express his assent to the arrangement.

They have but to cross what was once the vineyard, belonging to what was once the Monastery, to come into the narrow back lane wherein stands the crazy wooden house of two low stories currently known as the Travellers' Twopenny: – a house all warped and distorted, like the morals of the travellers, with scant remains of a lattice-work porch over the door, and also of a rustic fence before its stamped-out garden; by reason of the travellers being so bound to the premises by a tender sentiment (or so fond of having a fire by the roadside in the course of the day), that they can never be persuaded or threatened into departure, without violently possessing themselves of some wooden forget-me-not, and bearing it off.

The semblance of an inn is attempted to be given to this wretched place by fragments of conventional red curtaining in the windows, which rags are made muddily transparent in the night-season by feeble lights of rush or cotton dip burning dully in the close air of the inside. As Durdles and Jasper come near, they are addressed by an inscribed paper lantern over the door, setting forth the purport of the house. They are also addressed by some half-dozen other hideous small boys – whether twopenny lodgers or followers or hangers-on of such, who knows! – who, as if attracted by some carrion-scent of Deputy in the air, start into the moonlight, as vultures might gather in the desert, and instantly fall to stoning him and one another.

'Stop, you young brutes,' cries Jasper angrily, 'and let us go by!'

This remonstrance being received with yells and flying stones, according to a custom of late years comfortably established among the police regulations of our English communities, where Christians are stoned on all sides, as if the days of Saint Stephen were revived, Durdles remarks of the young savages, with some point, that 'they haven't got an object,' and leads the way down the lane.

At the corner of the lane, Jasper, hotly enraged, checks his companion and looks back. All is silent. Next moment, a stone coming rattling at his hat, and a distant yell of 'Wake-Cock! Warning!' followed by a crow, as from some infernally-hatched Chanticleer, apprising him under whose victorious fire he stands, he turns the corner into safety, and takes Durdles home: Durdles stumbling among the litter of his stony yard as if he were going to turn head foremost into one of the unfinished tombs.

John Jasper returns by another way to his gatehouse, and entering softly with his key, finds his fire still burning. He takes from a locked press a peculiar-looking pipe, which he fills – but not with tobacco – and, having adjusted the contents of the bowl, very carefully, with a little instrument, ascends an inner staircase of only a few steps, leading to two rooms. One of these is his own sleeping chamber: the other is his nephew's. There is a light in each.

His nephew lies asleep, calm and untroubled. John Jasper stands looking down upon him, his unlighted pipe in his hand, for some time, with a fixed and deep attention. Then, hushing his footsteps, he passes to his own room, lights his pipe, and delivers himself to the Spectres it invokes at midnight.

CHAPTER VI

Philanthropy in Minor Canon Corner

THE REVEREND SEPTIMUS Crisparkle (Septimus, because six little brother Crisparkles before him went out, one by one, as they were born, like six weak little rushlights, as they were lighted), having broken the thin morning ice near Cloisterham Weir with his amiable head, much to the invigoration of his frame, was now assisting his circulation by boxing at a looking-glass with great science and prowess. A fresh and healthy portrait the looking-glass presented of the Reverend Septimus, feinting and dodging with the utmost artfulness, and hitting out from the shoulder with the utmost straightness, while his radiant features teemed with innocence, and soft-hearted benevolence beamed from his boxing-gloves.

It was scarcely breakfast-time yet, for Mrs. Crisparkle – mother, not wife of the Reverend Septimus – was only just down, and waiting for the urn. Indeed, the Reverend Septimus left off at this very moment to take the pretty old lady's entering face between his boxing-gloves and kiss it. Having done so with tenderness, the Reverend Septimus turned to again, countering with his left, and putting in his right, in a tremendous manner.

'I say, every morning of my life, that you'll do it at last, Sept,' remarked the old lady, looking on; 'and so you will.'

'Do what, Ma dear?'

'Break the pier-glass, or burst a blood-vessel.'

'Neither, please God, Ma dear. Here's wind, Ma. Look at this!' In a concluding round of great severity, the Reverend Septimus administered and escaped all sorts of punishment, and wound up by getting the old lady's cap into Chancery – such is the technical term used in scientific circles by the learned in the Noble Art – with a lightness of touch that hardly stirred the lightest lavender or cherry riband on it. Magnanimously releasing the defeated, just in time to get his gloves into a drawer and feign to be looking out of window in a contemplative state of mind when a servant entered, the Reverend Septimus then gave place to the urn and other preparations for breakfast. These completed, and the two alone again, it was pleasant to see (or would have been, if there had been any one to see it, which there never was), the old lady standing to say the Lord's Prayer aloud, and her son, Minor Canon nevertheless, standing with bent head to hear it, he being within five years of forty: much as he had stood to hear the same words from the same lips when he was within five months of four.

What is prettier than an old lady – except a young lady – when her eyes are bright, when her figure is trim and compact, when her face is cheerful and calm, when her dress is as the dress of a china shepherdess: so dainty in its colours, so individually assorted to herself, so neatly moulded on her? Nothing is prettier, thought the good Minor Canon frequently, when taking his seat at table opposite his long-widowed mother. Her thought at such times may be condensed into the two words that oftenest did duty together in all her conversations: 'My Sept!'

They were a good pair to sit breakfasting together in Minor Canon Corner, Cloisterham. For Minor Canon Corner was a quiet place in the shadow of the Cathedral, which the cawing of the rooks, the echoing footsteps of rare passers, the sound of the Cathedral bell, or the roll of the Cathedral organ, seemed to render more quiet than absolute silence. Swaggering fighting men had had their centuries of ramping and raving about Minor Canon Corner, and beaten serfs had had their centuries of drudging and dying there, and powerful monks had had their centuries of being sometimes useful and sometimes harmful there, and behold they were all gone out of Minor Canon Corner, and so much the better. Perhaps one of the highest uses of their ever having been there, was, that there might be left behind, that blessed air of tranquillity which pervaded Minor Canon Corner, and that serenely romantic state of the mind – productive for the most part of pity and forbearance – which is engendered by a sorrowful story that is all told, or a pathetic play that is played out.

Red-brick walls harmoniously toned down in colour by time, strong-rooted ivy, latticed windows, panelled rooms, big oaken beams in little places, and stone-walled gardens where annual fruit yet ripened upon monkish trees, were the principal surroundings of pretty old Mrs. Crisparkle and the Reverend Septimus as they sat at breakfast.

'And what, Ma dear,' inquired the Minor Canon, giving proof of a wholesome and vigorous appetite, 'does the letter say?'

The pretty old lady, after reading it, had just laid it down upon the breakfast-cloth. She handed it over to her son.

Now, the old lady was exceedingly proud of her bright eyes being so clear that she could read writing without spectacles. Her son was also so proud of the circumstance, and so dutifully bent on her deriving the utmost possible gratification from it, that he had invented the pretence that he himself could *not* read writing without spectacles. Therefore he now assumed a pair, of grave and prodigious proportions, which not only seriously inconvenienced his nose and his breakfast, but seriously impeded his perusal of the letter. For, he had the eyes of a microscope and a telescope combined, when they were unassisted.

'It's from Mr. Honeythunder, of course,' said the old lady, folding her arms.

'Of course,' assented her son. He then lamely read on:

‘ “Haven of Philanthropy,
‘ “Chief Offices, London, Wednesday.

‘ “DEAR MADAM,

‘ “I write in the – ;” In the what's this? What does he write in?'

'In the chair,' said the old lady.

The Reverend Septimus took off his spectacles, that he might see her face, as he exclaimed:

'Why, what should he write in?'

'Bless me, bless me, Sept,' returned the old lady, 'you don't see the context! Give it back to me, my dear.'

Glad to get his spectacles off (for they always made his eyes water), her son obeyed: murmuring that his sight for reading manuscript got worse and worse daily.

‘ “I write,” ’ his mother went on, reading very perspicuously and precisely, ‘ “from the chair, to which I shall probably be confined for some hours.” ’

Septimus looked at the row of chairs against the wall, with a half-protesting and half-appealing countenance.

‘ “We have,” ’ the old lady read on with a little extra emphasis, ‘ “a meeting of our Convened Chief Composite Committee of Central and District Philanthropists, at our Head Haven as above; and it is their unanimous pleasure that I take the chair.” ’

Septimus breathed more freely, and muttered: 'O! if he comes to *that*, let him.'

‘ “Not to lose a day's post, I take the opportunity of a long report being read, denouncing a public miscreant – ” ’

'It is a most extraordinary thing,' interposed the gentle Minor Canon, laying down his knife and fork to rub his ear in a vexed manner, 'that these Philanthropists are always denouncing somebody. And it is another most extraordinary thing that they are always so violently flush of miscreants!'

' "Denouncing a public miscreant – " ' – the old lady resumed, ' "to get our little affair of business off my mind. I have spoken with my two wards, Neville and Helena Landless, on the subject of their defective education, and they give in to the plan proposed; as I should have taken good care they did, whether they liked it or not." '

'And it is another most extraordinary thing,' remarked the Minor Canon in the same tone as before, 'that these philanthropists are so given to seizing their fellow-creatures by the scruff of the neck, and (as one may say) bumping them into the paths of peace. – I beg your pardon, Ma dear, for interrupting.'

' "Therefore, dear Madam, you will please prepare your son, the Rev. Mr. Septimus, to expect Neville as an inmate to be read with, on Monday next. On the same day Helena will accompany him to Cloisterham, to take up her quarters at the Nuns' House, the establishment recommended by yourself and son jointly. Please likewise to prepare for her reception and tuition there. The terms in both cases are understood to be exactly as stated to me in writing by yourself, when I opened a correspondence with you on this subject, after the honour of being introduced to you at your sister's house in town here. With compliments to the Rev. Mr. Septimus, I am, Dear Madam, Your affectionate brother (In Philanthropy), LUKE HONEYTHUNDER." '

'Well, Ma,' said Septimus, after a little more rubbing of his ear, 'we must try it. There can be no doubt that we have room for an inmate, and that I have time to bestow upon him, and inclination too. I must confess to feeling rather glad that he is not Mr. Honeythunder himself. Though that seems wretchedly prejudiced – does it not? – for I never saw him. Is he a large man, Ma?'

'I should call him a large man, my dear,' the old lady replied after some hesitation, 'but that his voice is so much larger.'

'Than himself?'

'Than anybody.'

'Hah!' said Septimus. And finished his breakfast as if the flavour of the Superior Family Souchong, and also of the ham and toast and eggs, were a little on the wane.

Mrs. Crisparkle's sister, another piece of Dresden china, and matching her so neatly that they would have made a delightful pair of ornaments for the two ends of any capacious old-fashioned chimneypiece, and by right should never have been seen apart, was the childless wife of a clergyman holding Corporation preferment in London City. Mr. Honeythunder in his public character of Professor of Philanthropy had come to know Mrs. Crisparkle during the last re-matching of the china ornaments (in other words during her last annual visit to her sister), after a public occasion of a philanthropic nature, when certain devoted orphans of tender years had been glutted with plum buns, and plump bumptiousness. These were all the antecedents known in Minor Canon Corner of the coming pupils.

'I am sure you will agree with me, Ma,' said Mr. Crisparkle, after thinking the matter over, 'that the first thing to be done, is, to put these young people as much at their ease as possible. There is nothing disinterested in the notion, because we cannot be at our ease with them unless they are at their ease with us. Now, Jasper's nephew is down here at present; and like takes to like, and youth takes to youth. He is a cordial young fellow, and we will have him to meet the brother and sister at dinner. That's three. We can't think of asking him, without asking Jasper. That's four. Add Miss Twinkleton and the fairy bride that is to be, and that's six. Add our two selves, and that's eight. Would eight at a friendly dinner at all put you out, Ma?'

'Nine would, Sept,' returned the old lady, visibly nervous.

'My dear Ma, I particularise eight.'

'The exact size of the table and the room, my dear.'

So it was settled that way: and when Mr. Crisparkle called with his mother upon Miss Twinkleton, to arrange for the reception of Miss Helena Landless at the Nuns' House, the two other invitations having reference to that establishment were proffered and accepted. Miss Twinkleton did, indeed, glance at the globes, as regretting that they were not formed to be taken out into society; but became reconciled to leaving them behind. Instructions were then despatched to the Philanthropist for the departure and arrival, in good time for dinner, of Mr. Neville and Miss Helena; and stock for soup became fragrant in the air of Minor Canon Corner.

In those days there was no railway to Cloisterham, and Mr. Sapsea said there never would be. Mr. Sapsea said more; he said there never should be. And yet, marvellous to consider, it has come to pass, in these days, that Express Trains don't think Cloisterham worth stopping at, but yell and whirl through it on their larger errands, casting the dust off their wheels as a testimony against its insignificance. Some remote fragment of Main Line to somewhere else, there was, which was going to ruin the Money Market if it failed, and Church and State if it succeeded, and (of course), the Constitution, whether or no; but even that had already so unsettled Cloisterham traffic, that the traffic, deserting the high road, came sneaking in from an unprecedented part of the country by a back stable-way, for many years labelled at the corner: 'Beware of the Dog.'

To this ignominious avenue of approach, Mr. Crisparkle repaired, awaiting the arrival of a short, squat omnibus, with a disproportionate heap of luggage on the roof – like a little Elephant with infinitely too much Castle – which was then the daily service between Cloisterham and external mankind. As this vehicle lumbered up, Mr. Crisparkle could hardly see anything else of it for a large outside passenger seated on the box, with his elbows squared, and his hands on his knees, compressing the driver into a most uncomfortably small compass, and glowering about him with a strongly-marked face.

'Is this Cloisterham?' demanded the passenger, in a tremendous voice.

'It is,' replied the driver, rubbing himself as if he ached, after throwing the reins to the ostler. 'And I never was so glad to see it.'

'Tell your master to make his box-seat wider, then,' returned the passenger. 'Your master is morally bound – and ought to be legally, under ruinous penalties – to provide for the comfort of his fellow-man.'

The driver instituted, with the palms of his hands, a superficial perquisition into the state of his skeleton; which seemed to make him anxious.

'Have I sat upon you?' asked the passenger.

'You have,' said the driver, as if he didn't like it at all.

'Take that card, my friend.'

'I think I won't deprive you on it,' returned the driver, casting his eyes over it with no great favour, without taking it. 'What's the good of it to me?'

'Be a Member of that Society,' said the passenger.

'What shall I get by it?' asked the driver.

'Brotherhood,' returned the passenger, in a ferocious voice.

'Thankee,' said the driver, very deliberately, as he got down; 'my mother was contented with myself, and so am I. I don't want no brothers.'

'But you must have them,' replied the passenger, also descending, 'whether you like it or not. I am your brother.'

'I say!' expostulated the driver, becoming more chafed in temper, 'not too fur! The worm *will*, when – '

But here, Mr. Crisparkle interposed, remonstrating aside, in a friendly voice: 'Joe, Joe, Joe! don't forget yourself, Joe, my good fellow!' and then, when Joe peaceably touched his hat, accosting the passenger with: 'Mr. Honeythunder?'

'That is my name, sir.'

'My name is Crisparkle.'

'Reverend Mr. Septimus? Glad to see you, sir. Neville and Helena are inside. Having a little succumbed of late, under the pressure of my public labours, I thought I would take a mouthful of fresh air, and come down with them, and return at night. So you are the Reverend Mr. Septimus, are you?' surveying him on the whole with disappointment, and twisting a double eyeglass by its ribbon, as if he were roasting it, but not otherwise using it. 'Hah! I expected to see you older, sir.'

'I hope you will,' was the good-humoured reply.

'Eh?' demanded Mr. Honeythunder.

'Only a poor little joke. Not worth repeating.'

'Joke? Ay; I never see a joke,' Mr. Honeythunder frowningly retorted. 'A joke is wasted upon me, sir. Where are they? Helena and Neville, come here! Mr. Crisparkle has come down to meet you.'

An unusually handsome lithe young fellow, and an unusually handsome lithe girl; much alike; both very dark, and very rich in colour; she of almost the gipsy type; something untamed about them both; a certain air upon them of hunter and huntress; yet withal a certain air of being the objects of the chase, rather than the followers. Slender, supple, quick of eye and limb; half shy, half defiant; fierce of look; an indefinable kind of pause coming and going on their whole expression, both of face and form, which might be equally likened to the pause before a crouch or a bound. The rough mental notes made in the first five minutes by Mr. Crisparkle would have read thus, *verbatim*.

He invited Mr. Honeythunder to dinner, with a troubled mind (for the discomfiture of the dear old china shepherdess lay heavy on it), and gave his arm to Helena Landless. Both she and her brother, as they walked all together through the ancient streets, took great delight in what he pointed out of the Cathedral and the Monastery ruin, and wondered – so his notes ran on – much as if they were beautiful barbaric captives brought from some wild tropical dominion. Mr. Honeythunder walked in the middle of the road, shouldering the natives out of his way, and loudly developing a scheme he had, for making a raid on all the unemployed persons in the United Kingdom, laying them every one by the heels in jail, and forcing them, on pain of prompt extermination, to become philanthropists.

Mrs. Crisparkle had need of her own share of philanthropy when she beheld this very large and very loud excrescence on the little party. Always something in the nature of a Boil upon the face of society, Mr. Honeythunder expanded into an inflammatory Wen in Minor Canon Corner. Though it was not literally true, as was facetiously charged against him by public unbelievers, that he called aloud to his fellow-creatures: 'Curse your souls and bodies, come here and be blessed!' still his philanthropy was of that gunpowderous sort that the difference between it and animosity was hard to determine. You were to abolish military force, but you were first to bring all commanding officers who had done their duty, to trial by court-martial for that offence, and shoot them. You were to abolish war, but were to make converts by making war upon them, and charging them with loving war as the apple of their eye. You were to have no capital punishment, but were first to sweep off the face of the earth all legislators, jurists, and judges, who were of the contrary opinion. You were to have universal concord, and were to get it by eliminating all the people who wouldn't, or conscientiously couldn't, be concordant. You were to love your brother as yourself, but after an indefinite interval of maligning him (very much as if you hated him), and calling him all manner of names. Above all things, you were to do nothing in private, or on your own account. You were to go to the offices of the Haven of Philanthropy, and put your name down as a Member and a Professing Philanthropist. Then, you were to pay up your subscription, get your card of membership and your riband and medal, and were evermore to live upon a platform, and evermore to say what Mr. Honeythunder said, and what the Treasurer said, and what the sub-Treasurer said, and what the Committee said, and what the sub-Committee said, and what the Secretary said, and what the Vice-Secretary said. And this was usually said in the unanimously-carried resolution under hand and seal, to the effect: 'That this assembled Body of Professing Philanthropists views, with indignant scorn and contempt, not unmixed with utter detestation and loathing abhorrence' – in short, the baseness of all those who do not belong to it, and pledges itself to make as many obnoxious statements as possible about them, without being at all particular as to facts.

The dinner was a most doleful breakdown. The philanthropist

deranged the symmetry of the table, sat himself in the way of the waiting, blocked up the thoroughfare, and drove Mr. Tope (who assisted the parlour-maid) to the verge of distraction by passing plates and dishes on, over his own head. Nobody could talk to anybody, because he held forth to everybody at once, as if the company had no individual existence, but were a Meeting. He impounded the Reverend Mr. Septimus, as an official personage to be addressed, or kind of human peg to hang his oratorical hat on, and fell into the exasperating habit, common among such orators, of impersonating him as a wicked and weak opponent. Thus, he would ask: 'And will you, sir, now stultify yourself by telling me' – and so forth, when the innocent man had not opened his lips, nor meant to open them. Or he would say: 'Now see, sir, to what a position you are reduced. I will leave you no escape. After exhausting all the resources of fraud and falsehood, during years upon years; after exhibiting a combination of dastardly meanness with ensanguined daring, such as the world has not often witnessed; you have now the hypocrisy to bend the knee before the most degraded of mankind, and to sue and whine and howl for mercy!' Whereat the unfortunate Minor Canon would look, in part indignant and in part perplexed; while his worthy mother sat bridling, with tears in her eyes, and the remainder of the party lapsed into a sort of gelatinous state, in which there was no flavour or solidity, and very little resistance.

But the gush of philanthropy that burst forth when the departure of Mr. Honeythunder began to impend, must have been highly gratifying to the feelings of that distinguished man. His coffee was produced, by the special activity of Mr. Tope, a full hour before he wanted it. Mr. Crisparkle sat with his watch in his hand for about the same period, lest he should overstay his time. The four young people were unanimous in believing that the Cathedral clock struck three-quarters, when it actually struck but one. Miss Twinkleton estimated the distance to the omnibus at five-and-twenty minutes' walk, when it was really five. The affectionate kindness of the whole circle hustled him into his greatcoat, and shoved him out into the moonlight, as if he were a fugitive traitor with whom they sympathised, and a troop of horse were at the back door. Mr. Crisparkle and his new charge, who took him to the omnibus, were so fervent in their apprehensions of his catching cold, that they shut him up in it instantly and left him, with still half-an-hour to spare.

CHAPTER VII
More Confidences than One

'I KNOW VERY little of that gentleman, sir,' said Neville to the Minor Canon as they turned back.

'You know very little of your guardian?' the Minor Canon repeated.

'Almost nothing!'

'How came he – '

'To *be* my guardian? I'll tell you, sir. I suppose you know that we come (my sister and I) from Ceylon?'

'Indeed, no.'

'I wonder at that. We lived with a stepfather there. Our mother died there, when we were little children. We have had a wretched existence. She made him our guardian, and he was a miserly wretch who grudged us food to eat, and clothes to wear. At his death, he passed us over to this man; for no better reason that I know of, than his being a friend or connexion of his, whose name was always in print and catching his attention.'

'That was lately, I suppose?'

'Quite lately, sir. This stepfather of ours was a cruel brute as well as a grinding one. It is well he died when he did, or I might have killed him.'

Mr. Crisparkle stopped short in the moonlight and looked at his hopeful pupil in consternation.

'I surprise you, sir?' he said, with a quick change to a submissive manner.

'You shock me; unspeakably shock me.'

The pupil hung his head for a little while, as they walked on, and then said: 'You never saw him beat your sister. I have seen him beat mine, more than once or twice, and I never forgot it.'

'Nothing,' said Mr. Crisparkle, 'not even a beloved and beautiful sister's tears under dastardly ill-usage;' he became less severe, in spite of himself, as his indignation rose; 'could justify those horrible expressions that you used.'

'I am sorry I used them, and especially to you, sir. I beg to recall them. But permit me to set you right on one point. You spoke of my sister's tears. My sister would have let him tear her to pieces, before she would have let him believe that he could make her shed a tear.'

Mr. Crisparkle reviewed those mental notes of his, and was neither at all surprised to hear it, nor at all disposed to question it.

'Perhaps you will think it strange, sir,' – this was said in a hesitating voice – 'that I should so soon ask you to allow me to confide in you, and to have the kindness to hear a word or two from me in my defence?'

'Defence?' Mr. Crisparkle repeated. 'You are not on your defence, Mr. Neville.'

'I think I am, sir. At least I know I should be, if you were better acquainted with my character.'

'Well, Mr. Neville,' was the rejoinder. 'What if you leave me to find it out?'

'Since it is your pleasure, sir,' answered the young man, with a quick change in his manner to sullen disappointment: 'since it is your pleasure to check me in my impulse, I must submit.'

There was that in the tone of this short speech which made the conscientious man to whom it was addressed uneasy. It hinted to him that he might, without meaning it, turn aside a trustfulness beneficial to a mis-shapen young mind and perhaps to his own power of directing and improving it. They were within sight of the lights in his windows, and he stopped.

'Let us turn back and take a turn or two up and down, Mr. Neville, or you may not have time to finish what you wish to say to me. You are hasty in thinking that I mean to check you. Quite the contrary. I invite your confidence.'

'You have invited it, sir, without knowing it, ever since I came here. I say "ever since," as if I had been here a week. The truth is, we came here (my sister and I) to quarrel with you, and affront you, and break away again.'

'Really?' said Mr. Crisparkle, at a dead loss for anything else to say.

'You see, we could not know what you were beforehand, sir; could we?'

'Clearly not,' said Mr. Crisparkle.

'And having liked no one else with whom we have ever been brought into contact, we had made up our minds not to like you.'

'Really?' said Mr. Crisparkle again.

'But we do like you, sir, and we see an unmistakable difference between your house and your reception of us, and anything else we have ever known. This – and my happening to be alone with you – and everything around us seeming so quiet and peaceful after Mr. Honeythunder's departure – and Cloisterham being so old and grave and beautiful, with the moon shining on it – these things inclined me to open my heart.'

'I quite understand, Mr. Neville. And it is salutary to listen to such influences.'

'In describing my own imperfections, sir, I must ask you not to suppose that I am describing my sister's. She has come out of the disadvantages of our miserable life, as much better than I am, as that Cathedral tower is higher than those chimneys.'

Mr. Crisparkle in his own breast was not so sure of this.

'I have had, sir, from my earliest remembrance, to suppress a deadly and bitter hatred. This has made me secret and revengeful. I have been always tyrannically held down by the strong hand. This has driven me, in my weakness, to the resource of being false and mean. I have been stinted of education, liberty, money, dress, the very necessaries of life, the commonest pleasures of childhood, the commonest possessions of youth. This has caused me to be utterly wanting in I don't know what emotions, or remembrances, or good instincts – I have not even a name for the thing, you see! – that you have had to work upon in other young men to whom you have been accustomed.'

'This is evidently true. But this is not encouraging,' thought Mr. Crisparkle as they turned again.

'And to finish with, sir: I have been brought up among abject and servile dependents, of an inferior race, and I may easily have contracted some affinity with them. Sometimes, I don't know but that it may be a drop of what is tigerish in their blood.'

'As in the case of that remark just now,' thought Mr. Crisparkle.

'In a last word of reference to my sister, sir (we are twin children), you ought to know, to her honour, that nothing in our misery ever subdued her, though it often cowed me. When we ran away from it (we ran away four times in six years, to be soon brought back and cruelly punished), the flight was always of her planning and leading. Each time she dressed as a boy, and showed the daring of a man. I take it we were seven years old when we first decamped; but I remember, when I lost the pocket-knife with which she was to have cut her hair short, how desperately she tried to tear it out, or bite it off. I have nothing further to say, sir, except that I hope you will bear with me and make allowance for me.'

'Of that, Mr. Neville, you may be sure,' returned the Minor Canon. 'I don't preach more than I can help, and I will not repay your confidence with a sermon. But I entreat you to bear in mind, very seriously and steadily, that if I am to do you any good, it can only be with your own assistance; and that you can only render that, efficiently, by seeking aid from Heaven.'

'I will try to do my part, sir.'

'And, Mr. Neville, I will try to do mine. Here is my hand on it. May God bless our endeavours!'

They were now standing at his house-door, and a cheerful sound of voices and laughter was heard within.

'We will take one more turn before going in,' said Mr. Crisparkle, 'for I want to ask you a question. When you said you were in a changed mind concerning me, you spoke, not only for yourself, but for your sister too?'

'Undoubtedly I did, sir.'

'Excuse me, Mr. Neville, but I think you have had no opportunity of communicating with your sister, since I met you. Mr. Honeythunder was very eloquent; but perhaps I may venture to say, without ill-nature, that he rather monopolised the occasion. May you not have answered for your sister without sufficient warrant?'

Neville shook his head with a proud smile.

'You don't know, sir, yet, what a complete understanding can exist between my sister and me, though no spoken word – perhaps hardly as much as a look – may have passed between us. She not only feels as I have described, but she very well knows that I am taking this opportunity of speaking to you, both for her and for myself.'

Mr. Crisparkle looked in his face, with some incredulity; but his face expressed such absolute and firm conviction of the truth of what he said, that Mr. Crisparkle looked at the pavement, and mused, until they came to his door again.

'I will ask for one more turn, sir, this time,' said the young man, with a rather heightened colour rising in his face. 'But for Mr. Honeythunder's – I think you called it eloquence, sir?' (somewhat slyly.)

'I – yes, I called it eloquence,' said Mr. Crisparkle.

'But for Mr. Honeythunder's eloquence, I might have had no need to ask you what I am going to ask you. This Mr. Edwin Drood, sir: I think that's the name?'

'Quite correct,' said Mr. Crisparkle. 'D-r-double o-d.'

'Does he – or did he – read with you, sir?'

'Never, Mr. Neville. He comes here visiting his relation, Mr. Jasper.'

'Is Miss Bud his relation too, sir?'

('Now, why should he ask that, with sudden superciliousness?' thought Mr. Crisparkle.) Then he explained, aloud, what he knew of the little story of their betrothal.

'O! *that's* it, is it?' said the young man. 'I understand his air of proprietorship now!'

This was said so evidently to himself, or to anybody rather than Mr. Crisparkle, that the latter instinctively felt as if to notice it would be almost tantamount to noticing a passage in a letter which he had read by chance over the writer's shoulder. A moment afterwards they re-entered the house.

Mr. Jasper was seated at the piano as they came into his drawing-room, and was accompanying Miss Rosebud while she sang. It was a consequence of his playing the accompaniment without notes, and of her being a heedless little creature, very apt to go wrong, that he followed her lips most attentively, with his eyes as well as hands; carefully and softly hinting the key-note from time to time. Standing with an arm drawn round her, but with a face far more intent on Mr. Jasper than on her singing, stood Helena, between whom and her brother an instantaneous recognition passed, in which Mr. Crisparkle saw, or thought he saw, the understanding that had been spoken of, flash out. Mr. Neville then took his admiring station, leaning against the piano, opposite the singer; Mr. Crisparkle sat down by the china shepherdess; Edwin Drood gallantly furled and unfurled Miss Twinkleton's fan; and that lady passively claimed that sort of exhibitor's proprietorship in the accomplishment on view, which Mr. Tope, the Verger, daily claimed in the Cathedral service.

The song went on. It was a sorrowful strain of parting, and the fresh young voice was very plaintive and tender. As Jasper watched the pretty lips, and ever and again hinted the one note, as though it were a low whisper from himself, the voice became less steady, until all at once the singer broke into a burst of tears, and shrieked out, with her hands over her eyes: 'I can't bear this! I am frightened! Take me away!'

With one swift turn of her lithe figure Helena laid the little beauty on a sofa, as if she had never caught her up. Then, on one knee beside her, and with one hand upon her rosy mouth, while with the other she appealed to all the rest, Helena said to them: 'It's nothing; it's all over; don't speak to her for one minute, and she is well!'

Jasper's hands had, in the same instant, lifted themselves from the keys, and were now poised above them, as though he waited to resume. In that attitude he yet sat quiet: not even looking round, when all the rest had changed their places and were reassuring one another.

'Pussy's not used to an audience; that's the fact,' said Edwin Drood. 'She got nervous, and couldn't hold out. Besides, Jack, you are such a conscientious master, and require so much, that I believe you make her afraid of you. No wonder.'

'No wonder,' repeated Helena.

'There, Jack, you hear! You would be afraid of him, under similar circumstances, wouldn't you, Miss Landless?'

'Not under any circumstances,' returned Helena.

Jasper brought down his hands, looked over his shoulder, and begged to thank Miss Landless for her vindication of his character. Then he fell to dumbly playing, without striking the notes, while his little pupil was taken to an open window for air, and was otherwise petted and restored. When she was brought back, his place was empty. 'Jack's gone, Pussy,' Edwin told her. 'I am more than half afraid he didn't like to be charged with being the Monster who had frightened you.' But she answered never a word, and shivered, as if they had made her a little too cold.

Miss Twinkleton now opining that indeed these were late hours, Mrs. Crisparkle, for finding ourselves outside the walls of the Nuns' House, and that we who undertook the formation of the future wives and mothers of England (the last words in a lower voice, as requiring to be communicated in confidence) were really bound (voice coming up again) to set a better example than one of rakish habits, wrappers were put in requisition, and the two young cavaliers volunteered to see the ladies home. It was soon done, and the gate of the Nuns' House closed upon them.

The boarders had retired, and only Mrs. Tisher in solitary vigil awaited the new pupil. Her bedroom being within Rosa's, very little introduction or explanation was necessary, before she was placed in charge of her new friend, and left for the night.

'This is a blessed relief, my dear,' said Helena. 'I have been dreading all day, that I should be brought to bay at this time.'

'There are not many of us,' returned Rosa, 'and we are good-natured girls; at least the others are; I can answer for them.'

'I can answer for you,' laughed Helena, searching the lovely little face with her dark, fiery eyes, and tenderly caressing the small figure. 'You will be a friend to me, won't you?'

'I hope so. But the idea of my being a friend to you seems too absurd, though.'

'Why?'

'O, I am such a mite of a thing, and you are so womanly and handsome. You seem to have resolution and power enough to crush me. I shrink into nothing by the side of your presence even.'

'I am a neglected creature, my dear, unacquainted with all accomplishments, sensitively conscious that I have everything to learn, and deeply ashamed to own my ignorance.'

'And yet you acknowledge everything to me!' said Rosa.

'My pretty one, can I help it? There is a fascination in you.'

'O! is there though?' pouted Rosa, half in jest and half in earnest. 'What a pity Master Eddy doesn't feel it more!'

Of course her relations towards that young gentleman had been already imparted in Minor Canon Corner.

'Why, surely he must love you with all his heart!' cried Helena, with an earnestness that threatened to blaze into ferocity if he didn't.

'Eh? O, well, I suppose he does,' said Rosa, pouting again; 'I am sure I have no right to say he doesn't. Perhaps it's my fault. Perhaps I am not as nice to him as I ought to be. I don't think I am. But it *is* so ridiculous!'

Helena's eyes demanded what was.

'*We* are,' said Rosa, answering as if she had spoken. 'We are such a ridiculous couple. And we are always quarrelling.'

'Why?'

'Because we both know we are ridiculous, my dear!' Rosa gave that answer as if it were the most conclusive answer in the world.

Helena's masterful look was intent upon her face for a few moments, and then she impulsively put out both her hands and said:

'You will be my friend and help me?'

'Indeed, my dear, I will,' replied Rosa, in a tone of affectionate childishness that went straight and true to her heart; 'I will be as good a friend as such a mite of a thing can be to such a noble creature as you.

And be a friend to me, please; I don't understand myself: and I want a friend who can understand me, very much indeed.'

Helena Landless kissed her, and retaining both her hands said:

'Who is Mr. Jasper?'

Rosa turned aside her head in answering: 'Eddy's uncle, and my music-master.'

'You do not love him?'

'Ugh!' She put her hands up to her face, and shook with fear or horror.

'You know that he loves you?'

'O, don't, don't, don't!' cried Rosa, dropping on her knees, and clinging to her new resource. 'Don't tell me of it! He terrifies me. He haunts my thoughts, like a dreadful ghost. I feel that I am never safe from him. I feel as if he could pass in through the wall when he is spoken of.' She actually did look round, as if she dreaded to see him standing in the shadow behind her.

'Try to tell me more about it, darling.'

'Yes, I will, I will. Because you are so strong. But hold me the while, and stay with me afterwards.'

'My child! You speak as if he had threatened you in some dark way.'

'He has never spoken to me about – that. Never.'

'What has he done?'

'He has made a slave of me with his looks. He has forced me to understand him, without his saying a word; and he has forced me to keep silence, without his uttering a threat. When I play, he never moves his eyes from my hands. When I sing, he never moves his eyes from my lips. When he corrects me, and strikes a note, or a chord, or plays a passage, he himself is in the sounds, whispering that he pursues me as a lover, and commanding me to keep his secret. I avoid his eyes, but he forces me to see them without looking at them. Even when a glaze comes over them (which is sometimes the case), and he seems to wander away into a frightful sort of dream in which he threatens most, he obliges me to know it, and to know that he is sitting close at my side, more terrible to me than ever.'

'What is this imagined threatening, pretty one? What is threatened?'

'I don't know. I have never even dared to think or wonder what it is.'

'And was this all, to-night?'

'This was all; except that to-night when he watched my lips so closely as I was singing, besides feeling terrified I felt ashamed and passionately hurt. It was as if he kissed me, and I couldn't bear it, but cried out. You must never breathe this to any one. Eddy is devoted to him. But you said to-night that you would not be afraid of him, under any circumstances, and that gives me – who am so much afraid of him – courage to tell only you. Hold me! Stay with me! I am too frightened to be left by myself.'

The lustrous gipsy-face drooped over the clinging arms and bosom, and the wild black hair fell down protectingly over the childish form. There was a slumbering gleam of fire in the intense dark eyes, though they were then softened with compassion and admiration. Let whomsoever it most concerned look well to it!

CHAPTER VIII
Daggers Drawn

THE TWO YOUNG men, having seen the damsels, their charges, enter the courtyard of the Nuns' House, and finding themselves coldly stared at by the brazen door-plate, as if the battered old beau with the glass in his eye were insolent, look at one another, look along the perspective of the moonlit street, and slowly walk away together.

'Do you stay here long, Mr. Drood?' says Neville.

'Not this time,' is the careless answer. 'I leave for London again, to-morrow. But I shall be here, off and on, until next Midsummer; then I shall take my leave of Cloisterham, and England too; for many a long day, I expect.'

'Are you going abroad?'

'Going to wake up Egypt a little,' is the condescending answer.

'Are you reading?'

'Reading?' repeats Edwin Drood, with a touch of contempt. 'No. Doing, working, engineering. My small patrimony was left a part of the capital of the Firm I am with, by my father, a former partner; and I am a charge upon the Firm until I come of age; and then I step into my modest share in the concern. Jack – you met him at dinner – is, until then, my guardian and trustee.'

'I heard from Mr. Crisparkle of your other good fortune.'

'What do you mean by my other good fortune?'

Neville has made his remark in a watchfully advancing, and yet furtive and shy manner, very expressive of that peculiar air already noticed, of being at once hunter and hunted. Edwin has made his retort with an abruptness not at all polite. They stop and interchange a rather heated look.

'I hope,' says Neville, 'there is no offence, Mr. Drood, in my innocently referring to your betrothal?'

'By George!' cries Edwin, leading on again at a somewhat quicker pace; 'everybody in this chattering old Cloisterham refers to it. I wonder no public-house has been set up, with my portrait for the sign of The Betrothed's Head. Or Pussy's portrait. One or the other.'

'I am not accountable for Mr. Crisparkle's mentioning the matter to me, quite openly,' Neville begins.

'No; that's true; you are not,' Edwin Drood assents.

'But,' resumes Neville, 'I am accountable for mentioning it to you. And I did so, on the supposition that you could not fail to be highly proud of it.'

Now, there are these two curious touches of human nature working the secret springs of this dialogue. Neville Landless is already enough impressed by Little Rosebud, to feel indignant that Edwin Drood (far below her) should hold his prize so lightly. Edwin Drood is already enough impressed by Helena, to feel indignant that Helena's brother (far below her) should dispose of him so coolly, and put him out of the way so entirely.

However, the last remark had better be answered. So, says Edwin:

'I don't know, Mr. Neville' (adopting that mode of address from Mr. Crisparkle), 'that what people are proudest of, they usually talk most about; I don't know either, that what they are proudest of, they most like other people to talk about. But I live a busy life, and I speak under correction by you readers, who ought to know everything, and I daresay do.'

By this time they had both become savage; Mr. Neville out in the open; Edwin Drood under the transparent cover of a popular tune, and a stop now and then to pretend to admire picturesque effects in the moonlight before him.

'It does not seem to me very civil in you,' remarks Neville, at length, 'to reflect upon a stranger who comes here, not having had your advantages, to try to make up for lost time. But, to be sure, I was not brought up in "busy life," and my ideas of civility were formed among Heathens.'

'Perhaps, the best civility, whatever kind of people we are brought up among,' retorts Edwin Drood, 'is to mind our own business. If you will set me that example, I promise to follow it.'

'Do you know that you take a great deal too much upon yourself?' is the angry rejoinder, 'and that in the part of the world I come from, you would be called to account for it?'

'By whom, for instance?' asks Edwin Drood, coming to a halt, and surveying the other with a look of disdain.

But, here a startling right hand is laid on Edwin's shoulder, and Jasper stands between them. For, it would seem that he, too, has strolled round by the Nuns' House, and has come up behind them on the shadowy side of the road.

'Ned, Ned, Ned!' he says; 'we must have no more of this. I don't like this. I have overheard high words between you two. Remember, my dear boy, you are almost in the position of host to-night. You belong, as it were, to the place, and in a manner represent it towards a stranger. Mr. Neville is a stranger, and you should respect the obligations of hospitality. And, Mr. Neville,' laying his left hand on the inner shoulder of that young gentleman, and thus walking on between them, hand to shoulder on either side: 'you will pardon me; but I appeal to you to govern your temper too. Now, what is amiss? But why ask! Let there be nothing amiss, and the question is superfluous. We are all three on a good understanding, are we not?'

After a silent struggle between the two young men who shall speak last, Edwin Drood strikes in with: 'So far as I am concerned, Jack, there is no anger in me.'

'Nor in me,' says Neville Landless, though not so freely; or perhaps so carelessly. 'But if Mr. Drood knew all that lies behind me, far away from here, he might know better how it is that sharp-edged words have sharp edges to wound me.'

'Perhaps,' says Jasper, in a soothing manner, 'we had better not qualify our good understanding. We had better not say anything having the appearance of a remonstrance or condition; it might not seem generous. Frankly and freely, you see there is no anger in Ned. Frankly and freely, there is no anger in you, Mr. Neville?'

'None at all, Mr. Jasper.' Still, not quite so frankly or so freely; or, be it said once again, not quite so carelessly perhaps.

'All over then! Now, my bachelor gatehouse is a few yards from here, and the heater is on the fire, and the wine and glasses are on the table, and it is not a stone's throw from Minor Canon Corner. Ned, you are up and away to-morrow. We will carry Mr. Neville in with us, to take a stirrup-cup.'

'With all my heart, Jack.'

'And with all mine, Mr. Jasper.' Neville feels it impossible to say less, but would rather not go. He has an impression upon him that he has lost hold of his temper; feels that Edwin Drood's coolness, so far from being infectious, makes him red-hot.

Mr. Jasper, still walking in the centre, hand to shoulder on either side, beautifully turns the Refrain of a drinking song, and they all go up to his rooms. There, the first object visible, when he adds the light of a lamp to that of the fire, is the portrait over the chimneypicce. It is not an object calculated to improve the understanding between the two young men, as rather awkwardly reviving the subject of their difference. Accordingly, they both glance at it consciously, but say nothing. Jasper, however (who would appear from his conduct to have gained but an imperfect clue to the cause of their late high words), directly calls attention to it.

'You recognise that picture, Mr. Neville?' shading the lamp to throw the light upon it.

'I recognise it, but it is far from flattering the original.'

'O, you are hard upon it! It was done by Ned, who made me a present of it.'

'I am sorry for that, Mr. Drood.' Neville apologises, with a real intention to apologise; 'if I had known I was in the artist's presence – '

'O, a joke, sir, a mere joke,' Edwin cuts in, with a provoking yawn. 'A little humouring of Pussy's points! I'm going to paint her gravely, one of these days, if she's good.'

The air of leisurely patronage and indifference with which this is said, as the speaker throws himself back in a chair and clasps his hands at the back of his head, as a rest for it, is very exasperating to the excitable and excited Neville. Jasper looks observantly from the one to the other, slightly smiles, and turns his back to mix a jug of mulled wine at the fire. It seems to require much mixing and compounding.

'I suppose, Mr. Neville,' says Edwin, quick to resent the indignant protest against himself in the face of young Landless, which is fully as visible as the portrait, or the fire, or the lamp: 'I suppose that if you painted the picture of your lady love – '

'I can't paint,' is the hasty interruption.

'That's your misfortune, and not your fault. You would if you could. But if you could, I suppose you would make her (no matter what she was in reality), Juno, Minerva, Diana, and Venus, all in one. Eh?'

'I have no lady love, and I can't say.'

'If I were to try my hand,' says Edwin, with a boyish boastfulness getting up in him, 'on a portrait of Miss Landless – in earnest, mind you; in earnest – you should see what I could do!'

'My sister's consent to sit for it being first got, I suppose? As it never will be got, I am afraid I shall never see what you can do. I must bear the loss.'

Jasper turns round from the fire, fills a large goblet glass for Neville, fills a large goblet glass for Edwin, and hands each his own; then fills for himself, saying:

'Come, Mr. Neville, we are to drink to my nephew, Ned. As it is his foot that is in the stirrup – metaphorically – our stirrup-cup is to be devoted to him. Ned, my dearest fellow, my love!'

Jasper sets the example of nearly emptying his glass, and Neville follows it. Edwin Drood says, 'Thank you both very much,' and follows the double example.

'Look at him,' cries Jasper, stretching out his hand admiringly and tenderly, though rallyingly too. 'See where he lounges so easily, Mr. Neville! The world is all before him where to choose. A life of stirring work and interest, a life of change and excitement, a life of domestic ease and love! Look at him!'

Edwin Drood's face has become quickly and remarkably flushed with the wine; so has the face of Neville Landless. Edwin still sits thrown back in his chair, making that rest of clasped hands for his head.

'See how little he heeds it all!' Jasper proceeds in a bantering vein. 'It is hardly worth his while to pluck the golden fruit that hangs ripe on the tree for him. And yet consider the contrast, Mr. Neville. You and I have no prospect of stirring work and interest, or of change and excitement, or of domestic ease and love. You and I have no prospect (unless you are more fortunate than I am, which may easily be), but the tedious unchanging round of this dull place.'

'Upon my soul, Jack,' says Edwin, complacently, 'I feel quite apologetic for having my way smoothed as you describe. But you know what I know, Jack, and it may not be so very easy as it seems, after all. May it, Pussy?' To the portrait, with a snap of his thumb and finger. 'We have got to hit it off yet; haven't we, Pussy? You know what I mean, Jack.'

His speech has become thick and indistinct. Jasper, quiet and self-possessed, looks to Neville, as expecting his answer or comment. When Neville speaks, *his* speech is also thick and indistinct.

'It might have been better for Mr. Drood to have known some hardships,' he says, defiantly.

'Pray,' retorts Edwin, turning merely his eyes in that direction, 'pray why might it have been better for Mr. Drood to have known some hardships?'

'Ay,' Jasper assents, with an air of interest; 'let us know why?'

'Because they might have made him more sensible,' says Neville, 'of good fortune that is not by any means necessarily the result of his own merits.'

Mr. Jasper quickly looks to his nephew for his rejoinder.

'Have *you* known hardships, may I ask?' says Edwin Drood, sitting upright.

Mr. Jasper quickly looks to the other for his retort.

'I have.'

'And what have they made you sensible of?'

Mr. Jasper's play of eyes between the two holds good throughout the dialogue, to the end.

'I have told you once before to-night.'

'You have done nothing of the sort.'

'I tell you I have. That you take a great deal too much upon yourself.'

'You added something else to that, if I remember?'

'Yes, I did say something else.'

'Say it again.'

'I said that in the part of the world I come from, you would be called to account for it.'

'Only there?' cries Edwin Drood, with a contemptuous laugh. 'A long way off, I believe? Yes; I see! That part of the world is at a safe distance.'

'Say here, then,' rejoins the other, rising in a fury. 'Say anywhere! Your vanity is intolerable, your conceit is beyond endurance; you talk as if you were some rare and precious prize, instead of a common boaster. You are a common fellow, and a common boaster.'

'Pooh, pooh,' says Edwin Drood, equally furious, but more collected; 'how should you know? You may know a black common fellow, or a black common boaster, when you see him (and no doubt you have a large acquaintance that way); but you are no judge of white men.'

This insulting allusion to his dark skin infuriates Neville to that violent degree, that he flings the dregs of his wine at Edwin Drood, and is in the act of flinging the goblet after it, when his arm is caught in the nick of time by Jasper.

'Ned, my dear fellow!' he cries in a loud voice; 'I entreat you, I command you, to be still!' There has been a rush of all the three, and a clattering of glasses and overturning of chairs. 'Mr. Neville, for shame!

66

Give this glass to me. Open your hand, sir. I WILL have it!'

But Neville throws him off, and pauses for an instant, in a raging passion, with the goblet yet in his uplifted hand. Then, he dashes it down under the grate, with such force that the broken splinters fly out again in a shower; and he leaves the house.

When he first emerges into the night air, nothing around him is still or steady; nothing around him shows like what it is; he only knows that he stands with a bare head in the midst of a blood-red whirl, waiting to be struggled with, and to struggle to the death.

But, nothing happening, and the moon looking down upon him as if he were dead after a fit of wrath, he holds his steam-hammer beating head and heart, and staggers away. Then, he becomes half-conscious of having heard himself bolted and barred out, like a dangerous animal; and thinks what shall he do?

Some wildly passionate ideas of the river dissolve under the spell of the moonlight on the Cathedral and the graves, and the remembrance of his sister, and the thought of what he owes to the good man who has but that very day won his confidence and given him his pledge. He repairs to Minor Canon Corner, and knocks softly at the door.

It is Mr. Crisparkle's custom to sit up last of the early household, very softly touching his piano and practising his favourite parts in concerted vocal music. The south wind that goes where it lists, by way of Minor Canon Corner on a still night, is not more subdued than Mr. Crisparkle at such times, regardful of the slumbers of the china shepherdess.

His knock is immediately answered by Mr. Crisparkle himself. When he opens the door, candle in hand, his cheerful face falls, and disappointed amazement is in it.

'Mr. Neville! In this disorder! Where have you been?'

'I have been to Mr. Jasper's, sir. With his nephew.'

'Come in.'

The Minor Canon props him by the elbow with a strong hand (in a strictly scientific manner, worthy of his morning trainings), and turns him into his own little book-room, and shuts the door.'

'I have begun ill, sir. I have begun dreadfully ill.'

'Too true. You are not sober, Mr. Neville.'

'I am afraid I am not, sir, though I can satisfy you at another time that I have had a very little indeed to drink, and that it overcame me in the strangest and most sudden manner.'

'Mr. Neville, Mr. Neville,' says the Minor Canon, shaking his head with a sorrowful smile; 'I have heard that said before.'

'I think – my mind is much confused, but I think – it is equally true of Mr. Jasper's nephew, sir.'

'Very likely,' is the dry rejoinder.

'We quarrelled, sir. He insulted me most grossly. He had heated that tigerish blood I told you of to-day, before then.'

'Mr. Neville,' rejoins the Minor Canon, mildly, but firmly: 'I request you not to speak to me with that clenched right hand. Unclench it, if you please.'

'He goaded me, sir,' pursues the young man, instantly obeying, 'beyond my power of endurance. I cannot say whether or no he meant it at first, but he did it. He certainly meant it at last. In short, sir,' with an irrepressible outburst, 'in the passion into which he lashed me, I would have cut him down if I could, and I tried to do it.'

'You have clenched that hand again,' is Mr. Crisparkle's quiet commentary.

'I beg your pardon, sir.'

'You know your room, for I showed it you before dinner; but I will accompany you to it once more. Your arm, if you please. Softly, for the house is all a-bed.'

Scooping his hand into the same scientific elbow-rest as before, and backing it up with the inert strength of his arm, as skilfully as a Police Expert, and with an apparent repose quite unattainable by novices, Mr. Crisparkle conducts his pupil to the pleasant and orderly old room prepared for him. Arrived there, the young man throws himself into a chair, and, flinging his arms upon his reading-table, rests his head upon them with an air of wretched self-reproach.

The gentle Minor Canon has had it in his thoughts to leave the room, without a word. But looking round at the door, and seeing this dejected figure, he turns back to it, touches it with a mild hand, says 'Good night!' A sob is his only acknowledgment. He might have had many a worse; perhaps, could have had few better.

Another soft knock at the outer door attracts his attention as he goes down-stairs. He opens it to Mr. Jasper, holding in his hand the pupil's hat.

'We have had an awful scene with him,' says Jasper, in a low voice.

'Has it been so bad as that?'

'Murderous!'

Mr. Crisparkle remonstrates: 'No, no, no. Do not use such strong words.'

'He might have laid my dear boy dead at my feet. It is no fault of his, that he did not. But that I was, through the mercy of God, swift and strong with him, he would have cut him down on my hearth.'

The phrase smites home. 'Ah!' thinks Mr. Crisparkle, 'his own words!'

'Seeing what I have seen to-night, and hearing what I have heard,' adds Jasper, with great earnestness, 'I shall never know peace of mind when there is danger of those two coming together, with no one else to interfere. It was horrible. There is something of the tiger in his dark blood.'

'Ah!' thinks Mr. Crisparkle, 'so he said!'

'You, my dear sir,' pursues Jasper, taking his hand, 'even you, have accepted a dangerous charge.'

'You need have no fear for me, Jasper,' returns Mr. Crisparkle, with a quiet smile. 'I have none for myself.'

'I have none for myself,' returns Jasper, with an emphasis on the last pronoun, 'because I am not, nor am I in the way of being, the object of his hostility. But you may be, and my dear boy has been. Good night!'

Mr. Crisparkle goes in, with the hat that has so easily, so almost imperceptibly, acquired the right to be hung up in his hall; hangs it up; and goes thoughtfully to bed.

CHAPTER IX
Birds in the Bush

ROSA, HAVING NO relation that she knew of in the world, had, from the seventh year of her age, known no home but the Nuns' House, and no mother but Miss Twinkleton. Her remembrance of her own mother was of a pretty little creature like herself (not much older than herself it seemed to her), who had been brought home in her father's arms, drowned. The fatal accident had happened at a party of pleasure. Every fold and colour in the pretty summer dress, and even the long wet hair, with scattered petals of ruined flowers still clinging to it, as the dead young figure, in its sad, sad beauty lay upon the bed, were fixed indelibly in Rosa's recollection. So were the wild despair and the subsequent bowed-down grief of her poor young father, who died broken-hearted on the first anniversary of that hard day.

The betrothal of Rosa grew out of the soothing of his year of mental distress by his fast friend and old college companion, Drood: who likewise had been left a widower in his youth. But he, too, went the silent road into which all earthly pilgrimages merge, some sooner, and some later; and thus the young couple had come to be as they were.

The atmosphere of pity surrounding the little orphan girl when she first came to Cloisterham, had never cleared away. It had taken brighter hues as she grew older, happier, prettier; now it had been golden, now roseate, and now azure; but it had always adorned her with some soft light of its own. The general desire to console and caress her, had caused her to be treated in the beginning as a child much younger than her years; the same desire had caused her to be still petted when she was a child no longer. Who should be her favourite, who should anticipate this or that small present, or do her this or that small service; who should take her home for the holidays; who should write to her the oftenest when they were separated, and whom she would most rejoice to see again when they were reunited; even these gentle rivalries were not without their slight dashes of bitterness in the Nuns' House. Well for the poor Nuns in their day, if they hid no harder strife under their veils and rosaries!

Thus Rosa had grown to be an amiable, giddy, wilful, winning little creature; spoilt, in the sense of counting upon kindness from all around her; but not in the sense of repaying it with indifference. Possessing an exhaustless well of affection in her nature, its sparkling waters had freshened and brightened the Nuns' House for years, and yet its depths had never yet been moved: what might betide when that came to pass; what developing changes might fall upon the heedless head, and light heart, then; remained to be seen.

By what means the news that there had been a quarrel between the two young men overnight, involving even some kind of onslaught by Mr. Neville upon Edwin Drood, got into Miss Twinkleton's establishment before breakfast, it is impossible to say. Whether it was brought in by the birds of the air, or came blowing in with the very air itself, when the casement windows were set open; whether the baker brought it kneaded into the bread, or the milkman delivered it as part of the adulteration of his milk; or the housemaids, beating the dust out of their mats against the gateposts, received it in exchange deposited on the mats by the town atmosphere; certain it is that the news permeated every gable of the old building before Miss Twinkleton was down, and that Miss Twinkleton herself received it through Mrs. Tisher, while yet in the act of dressing; or (as she might have expressed the phrase to a parent or guardian of a mythological turn) of sacrificing to the Graces.

Miss Landless's brother had thrown a bottle at Mr. Edwin Drood.

Miss Landless's brother had thrown a knife at Mr. Edwin Drood.

A knife became suggestive of a fork; and Miss Landless's brother had thrown a fork at Mr. Edwin Drood.

As in the governing precedence of Peter Piper, alleged to have picked the peck of pickled pepper, it was held physically desirable to have evidence of the existence of the peck of pickled pepper which Peter Piper was alleged to have picked; so, in this case, it was held psychologically important to know why Miss Landless's brother threw a bottle, knife, or fork-or bottle, knife, *and* fork – for the cook had been given to understand it was all three – at Mr. Edwin Drood?

Well, then. Miss Landless's brother had said he admired Miss Bud. Mr. Edwin Drood had said to Miss Landless's brother that he had no business to admire Miss Bud. Miss Landless's brother had then 'up'd' (this was the cook's exact information) with the bottle, knife, fork, and decanter (the decanter now coolly flying at everybody's head, without the least introduction), and thrown them all at Mr. Edwin Drood.

Poor little Rosa put a forefinger into each of her ears when these rumours began to circulate, and retired into a corner, beseeching not to be told any more; but Miss Landless, begging permission of Miss Twinkleton to go and speak with her brother, and pretty plainly showing that she would take it if it were not given, struck out the more definite course of going to Mr. Crisparkle's for accurate intelligence.

When she came back (being first closeted with Miss Twinkleton, in order that anything objectionable in her tidings might be retained by that discreet filter), she imparted to Rosa only, what had taken place; dwelling with a flushed cheek on the provocation her brother had received, but almost limiting it to that last gross affront as crowning 'some other words between them,' and, out of consideration for her new friend, passing lightly over the fact that the other words had originated in her lover's taking things in general so very easily. To Rosa direct, she brought a petition from her brother that she would forgive him; and, having delivered it with sisterly earnestness, made an end of the subject.

It was reserved for Miss Twinkleton to tone down the public mind of the Nuns' House. That lady, therefore, entering in a stately manner what plebeians might have called the school-room, but what, in the patrician language of the head of the Nuns' House, was euphuistically, not to say round-aboutedly, denominated 'the apartment allotted to study,' and saying with a forensic air, 'Ladies!' all rose. Mrs. Tisher at the same time grouped herself behind her chief, as representing Queen Elizabeth's first historical female friend at Tilbury fort. Miss Twinkleton then proceeded to remark that Rumour, Ladies, had been represented by the bard of Avon – needless were it to mention the immortal SHAKESPEARE, also called the Swan of his native river, not improbably with some reference to the ancient superstition that that bird of graceful plumage (Miss Jennings will please stand upright) sang sweetly on the approach of death, for which we have no ornithological authority, – Rumour, Ladies, had been represented by that bard – hem! –

> 'who drew
> The celebrated Jew,'

as painted full of tongues. Rumour in Cloisterham (Miss Ferdinand will honour me with her attention) was no exception to the great limner's portrait of Rumour elsewhere. A slight *fracas* between two young gentlemen occurring last night within a hundred miles of these peaceful walls (Miss Ferdinand, being apparently incorrigible, will have the kindness to write out this evening, in the original language, the first four fables of our vivacious neighbour, Monsieur La Fontaine) had been very grossly exaggerated by Rumour's voice. In the first alarm and anxiety arising from our sympathy with a sweet young friend, not wholly to be dissociated from one of the gladiators in the bloodless arena in question (the impropriety of Miss Reynolds's appearing to stab herself in the hand with a pin, is far too obvious, and too glaringly unladylike, to be pointed out), we descended from our maiden elevation to discuss this uncongenial and this unfit theme. Responsible inquiries having assured us that it was but one of those 'airy nothings' pointed at by the Poet (whose name and date of birth Miss Giggles will supply within half an hour), we would now discard the subject, and concentrate our minds upon the grateful labours of the day.

But the subject so survived all day, nevertheless, that Miss Ferdinand got into new trouble by surreptitiously clapping on a paper moustache at dinner-time, and going through the motions of aiming a water-bottle at Miss Giggles, who drew a table-spoon in defence.

Now, Rosa thought of this unlucky quarrel a great deal, and thought of it with an uncomfortable feeling that she was involved in it, as cause, or consequence, or what not, through being in a false position altogether as to her marriage engagement. Never free from such uneasiness when she was with her affianced husband, it was not likely that she would be free from it when they were apart. To-day, too, she was cast in upon herself, and deprived of the relief of talking freely with her new friend, because the quarrel had been with Helena's brother, and Helena undisguisedly avoided the subject as a delicate and difficult one to herself. At this critical time, of all times, Rosa's guardian was announced as having come to see her.

Mr. Grewgious had been well selected for his trust, as a man of incorruptible integrity, but certainly for no other appropriate quality discernible on the surface. He was an arid, sandy man, who, if he had been put into a grinding-mill, looked as if he would have ground immediately into high-dried snuff. He had a scanty flat crop of hair, in colour and consistency like some very mangy yellow fur tippet; it was so unlike hair, that it must have been a wig, but for the stupendous improbability of anybody's voluntarily sporting such a head. The little play of feature that his face presented, was cut deep into it, in a few hard curves that made it more like work; and he had certain notches in his forehead, which looked as though Nature had been about to touch them into sensibility or refinement, when she had impatiently thrown away the chisel, and said: 'I really cannot be worried to finish off this man; let him go as he is.'

With too great length of throat at his upper end, and too much ankle-bone and heel at his lower; with an awkward and hesitating manner; with a shambling walk; and with what is called a near sight – which perhaps prevented his observing how much white cotton stocking he displayed to the public eye, in contrast with his black suit – Mr. Grewgious still had some strange capacity in him of making on the whole an agreeable impression.

Mr. Grewgious was discovered by his ward, much discomfited by being in Miss Twinkleton's company in Miss Twinkleton's own sacred room. Dim forebodings of being examined in something, and not coming well out of it, seemed to oppress the poor gentleman when found in these circumstances.

'My dear, how do you do? I am glad to see you. My dear, how much improved you are. Permit me to hand you a chair, my dear.'

Miss Twinkleton rose at her little writing-table, saying, with general sweetness, as to the polite Universe: 'Will you permit me to retire?'

'By no means, madam, on my account. I beg that you will not move.'

'I must entreat permission to *move*,' returned Miss Twinkleton, repeating the word with a charming grace; 'but I will not withdraw, since you are so obliging. If I wheel my desk to this corner window, shall I be in the way?'

'Madam! In the way!'

'You are very kind. – Rosa, my dear, you will be under no restraint, I am sure.'

Here Mr. Grewgious, left by the fire with Rosa, said again: 'My dear, how do you do? I am glad to see you, my dear.' And having waited for her to sit down, sat down himself.

'My visits,' said Mr. Grewgious, 'are, like those of the angels – not that I compare myself to an angel.'

'No, sir,' said Rosa.

'Not by any means,' assented Mr. Grewgious. 'I merely refer to my visits, which are few and far between. The angels are, we know very well, up-stairs.'

Miss Twinkleton looked round with a kind of stiff stare.

'I refer, my dear,' said Mr. Grewgious, laying his hand on Rosa's, as the possibility thrilled through his frame of his otherwise seeming to take the awful liberty of calling Miss Twinkleton my dear; 'I refer to the other young ladies.'

Miss Twinkleton resumed her writing.

Mr. Grewgious, with a sense of not having managed his opening point quite as neatly as he might have desired, smoothed his head from back to front as if he had just dived, and were pressing the water out – this smoothing action, however superfluous, was habitual with him – and took a pocket-book from his coat-pocket, and a stump of black-lead pencil from his waistcoat-pocket.

'I made,' he said, turning the leaves: 'I made a guiding memorandum or so – as I usually do, for I have no conversational powers whatever – to which I will, with your permission, my dear, refer. "Well and happy." Truly. You are well and happy, my dear? You look so.'

'Yes, indeed, sir,' answered Rosa.

'For which,' said Mr. Grewgious, with a bend of his head towards the corner window, 'our warmest acknowledgments are due, and I am sure are rendered, to the maternal kindness and the constant care and consideration of the lady whom I have now the honour to see before me.'

This point, again, made but a lame departure from Mr. Grewgious, and never got to its destination; for, Miss Twinkleton, feeling that the courtesies required her to be by this time quite outside the conversation, was biting the end of her pen, and looking upward, as waiting for the descent of an idea from any member of the Celestial Nine who might have one to spare.

Mr. Grewgious smoothed his smooth head again, and then made another reference to his pocket-book; lining out 'well and happy,' as disposed of.

' "Pounds, shillings, and pence," is my next note. A dry subject for a young lady, but an important subject too. Life is pounds, shillings, and pence. Death is – ' A sudden recollection of the death of her two parents seemed to stop him, and he said in a softer tone, and evidently inserting the negative as an after-thought: 'Death is *not* pounds, shillings, and pence.'

His voice was as hard and dry as himself, and Fancy might have ground it straight, like himself, into high-dried snuff. And yet, through the very limited means of expression that he possessed, he seemed to express kindness. If Nature had but finished him off, kindness might have been recognisable in his face at this moment. But if the notches in his forehead wouldn't fuse together, and if his face would work and couldn't play, what could he do, poor man!

' "Pounds, shillings, and pence." You find your allowance always sufficient for your wants, my dear?'

Rosa wanted for nothing, and therefore it was ample.

'And you are not in debt?'

Rosa laughed at the idea of being in debt. It seemed, to her inexperience, a comical vagary of the imagination. Mr. Grewgious stretched his near sight to be sure that this was her view of the case. 'Ah!' he said, as comment, with a furtive glance towards Miss Twinkleton, and lining out pounds, shillings, and pence: 'I spoke of having got among the angels! So I did!'

Rosa felt what his next memorandum would prove to be, and was blushing and folding a crease in her dress with one embarrassed hand, long before he found it.

' "Marriage." Hem!' Mr. Grewgious carried his smoothing hand down over his eyes and nose, and even chin, before drawing his chair a little nearer, and speaking a little more confidentially: 'I now touch, my dear, upon the point that is the direct cause of my troubling you with the present visit. Othenwise, being a particularly Angular man, I should not have intruded here. I am the last man to intrude into a sphere for which I am so entirely unfitted. I feel, on these premises, as if I was a bear – with the cramp – in a youthful Cotillon.'

His ungainliness gave him enough of the air of his simile to set Rosa off laughing heartily.

'It strikes you in the same light,' said Mr. Grewgious, with perfect calmness. 'Just so. To return to my memorandum. Mr. Edwin has been to and fro here, as was arranged. You have mentioned that, in your quarterly letters to me. And you like him, and he likes you.'

'I *like* him very much, sir,' rejoined Rosa.

'So I said, my dear,' returned her guardian, for whose ear the timid emphasis was much too fine. 'Good. And you correspond.'

'We write to one another,' said Rosa, pouting, as she recalled their epistolary differences.

'Such is the meaning that I attach to the word "correspond" in this application, my dear,' said Mr. Grewgious. 'Good. All goes well, time works on, and at this next Christmas-time it will become necessary, as a matter of form, to give the exemplary lady in the corner window, to whom we are so much indebted, business notice of your departure in the ensuing half-year. Your relations with her are far more than business relations, no doubt; but a residue of business remains in them, and business is business ever. I am a particularly Angular man,' proceeded Mr. Grewgious, as if it suddenly occurred to him to mention it, 'and I am not used to give anything away. If, for these two reasons, some competent Proxy would give *you* away, I should take it very kindly.'

Rosa intimated, with her eyes on the ground, that she thought a substitute might be found, if required.

'Surely, surely,' said Mr. Grewgious. 'For instance, the gentleman who teaches Dancing here – he would know how to do it with graceful propriety. He would advance and retire in a manner satisfactory to the feelings of the officiating clergyman, and of yourself, and the bridegroom, and all parties concerned. I am – I am a particularly Angular man,' said Mr. Grewgious, as if he had made up his mind to screw it out at last: 'and should only blunder.'

Rosa sat still and silent. Perhaps her mind had not got quite so far as the ceremony yet, but was lagging on the way there.

'Memorandum, "Will." Now, my dear,' said Mr. Grewgious, referring to his notes, disposing of 'Marriage' with his pencil, and taking a paper from his pocket; 'although. I have before possessed you with the contents of your father's will, I think it right at this time to leave a certified copy of it in your hands. And although Mr. Edwin is also aware of its contents, I think it right at this time likewise to place a certified copy of it in Mr. Jasper's hand – '

'Not in his own!' asked Rosa, looking up quickly. 'Cannot the copy go to Eddy himself?'

'Why, yes, my dear, if you particularly wish it; but I spoke of Mr. Jasper as being his trustee.'

'I do particularly wish it, if you please,' said Rosa, hurriedly and earnestly; 'I don't like Mr. Jasper to come between us, in any way.'

'It is natural, I suppose,' said Mr. Grewgious, 'that your young husband should be all in all. Yes. You observe that I say, I suppose. The fact is, I am a particularly Unnatural man, and I don't know from my own knowledge.'

Rosa looked at him with some wonder.

'I mean,' he explained, 'that young ways were never my ways. I was the only offspring of parents far advanced in life, and I half believe I was born advanced in life myself. No personality is intended towards the name you will so soon change, when I remark that while the general growth of people seem to have come into existence, buds, I seem to have come into existence a chip. I was a chip – and a very dry one – when I first became aware of myself. Respecting the other certified copy, your wish shall be complied with. Respecting your inheritance, I think you know all. It is an annuity of two hundred and fifty pounds. The savings upon that annuity, and some other items to your credit, all duly carried to account, with vouchers, will place you in possession of a lump-sum of money, rather exceeding Seventeen Hundred Pounds. I am empowered to advance the cost of your preparations for your marriage out of that fund. All is told.'

'Will you please tell me,' said Rosa, taking the paper with a prettily knitted brow, but not opening it: 'whether I am right in what I am going to say? I can understand what you tell me, so very much better than what I read in law-writings. My poor papa and Eddy's father made their agreement together, as very dear and firm and fast friends, in order that we, too, might be very dear and firm and fast friends after them?'

'Just so.'

'For the lasting good of both of us, and the lasting happiness of both of us?'

'Just so.'

'That we might be to one another even much more than they had been to one another?'

'Just so.'

'It was not bound upon Eddy, and it was not bound upon me, by any forfeit, in case – '

'Don't be agitated, my dear. In the case that it brings tears into your affectionate eyes even to picture to yourself – in the case of your not marrying one another – no, no forfeiture on either side. You would then have been my ward until you were of age. No worse would have befallen you. Bad enough perhaps!'

'And Eddy?'

'He would have come into his partnership derived from his father, and into its arrears to his credit (if any), on attaining his majority, just as now.'

Rosa, with her perplexed face and knitted brow, bit the corner of her attested copy, as she sat with her head on one side, looking abstractedly on the floor, and smoothing it with her foot.

'In short,' said Mr. Grewgious, 'this betrothal is a wish, a sentiment, a friendly project, tenderly expressed on both sides. That it was strongly felt, and that there was a lively hope that it would prosper, there can be no doubt. When you were both children, you began to be accustomed to it, and it *has* prospered. But circumstances alter cases; and I made this visit to-day, partly, indeed principally, to discharge myself of the duty of telling you, my dear, that two young people can only be betrothed in marriage (except as a matter of convenience, and therefore mockery and misery) of their own free will, their own attachment, and their own assurance (it may or it may not prove a mistaken one, but we must take our chance of that), that they are suited to each other, and will make each other happy. Is it to be supposed, for example, that if either of your fathers were living now, and had any mistrust on that subject, his mind would not be changed by the change of circumstances involved in the change of your years? Untenable, unreasonable, inconclusive, and preposterous!'

Mr. Grewgious said all this, as if he were reading it aloud; or, still more, as if he were repeating a lesson. So expressionless of any approach to spontaneity were his face and manner.

'I have now, my dear,' he added, blurring out 'Will' with his pencil, 'discharged myself of what is doubtless a formal duty in this case, but still a duty in such a case. Memorandum, "Wishes." My dear, is there any wish of yours that I can further?'

Rosa shook her head, with an almost plaintive air of hesitation in want of help.

'Is there any instruction that I can take from you with reference to your affairs?'

'I – I should like to settle them with Eddy first, if you please,' said Rosa, plaiting the crease in her dress.

'Surely, surely,' returned Mr. Grewgious. 'You two should be of one mind in all things. Is the young gentleman expected shortly?'

'He has gone away only this morning. He will be back at Christmas.'

'Nothing could happen better. You will, on his return at Christmas, arrange all matters of detail with him; you will then communicate with me; and I will discharge myself (as a mere business acquaintance) of my business responsibilities towards the accomplished lady in the corner window. They will accrue at that season.' Blurring pencil once again. 'Memorandum, "Leave." Yes. I will now, my dear, take my leave.'

'Could I,' said Rosa, rising, as he jerked out of his chair in his ungainly way: 'could I ask you, most kindly to come to me at Christmas, if I had anything particular to say to you?'

'Why, certainly, certainly,' he rejoined; apparently – if such a word can be used of one who had no apparent lights or shadows about him – complimented by the question. 'As a particularly Angular man, I do not fit smoothly into the social circle, and consequently I have no other engagement at Christmas-time than to partake, on the twenty-fifth, of a boiled turkey and celery sauce with a – with a particularly Angular clerk I have the good fortune to possess, whose father, being a Norfolk farmer, sends him up (the turkey up), as a present to me, from the neighbourhood of Norwich. I should be quite proud of your wishing to see me, my dear. As a professional Receiver of rents, so very few people *do* wish to see me, that the novelty would be bracing.'

For his ready acquiescence, the grateful Rosa put her hands upon his shoulders, stood on tiptoe, and instantly kissed him.

'Lord bless me!' cried Mr. Grewgious. 'Thank you, my dear! The honour is almost equal to the pleasure. Miss Twinkleton, madam, I have had a most satisfactory conversation with my ward, and I will now release you from the incumbrance of my presence.'

'Nay, sir,' rejoined Miss Twinkleton, rising with a gracious condescension: 'say not incumbrance. Not so, by any means. I cannot permit you to say so.'

'Thank you, madam. I have read in the newspapers,' said Mr. Grewgious, stammering a little, 'that when a distinguished visitor (not that I am one: far from it) goes to a school (not that this is one: far from it), he asks for a holiday, or some sort of grace. It being now the afternoon in the – College – of which you are the eminent head, the young ladies might gain nothing, except in name, by having the rest of the day allowed them. But if there is any young lady at all under a cloud, might I solicit – '

'Ah, Mr. Grewgious, Mr. Grewgious!' cried Miss Twinkleton, with a chastely-rallying forefinger. 'O you gentlemen, you gentlemen! Fie for shame, that you are so hard upon us poor maligned disciplinarians of our sex, for your sakes! But as Miss Ferdinand is at present weighed down by an incubus' – Miss Twinkleton might have said a pen-and-ink-ubus of writing out Monsieur La Fontaine – 'go to her, Rosa my dear, and tell her the penalty is remitted, in deference to the intercession of your guardian, Mr. Grewgious.'

Miss Twinkleton here achieved a curtsey, suggestive of marvels happening to her respected legs, and which she came out of nobly, three yards behind her starting-point.

As he held it incumbent upon him to call on Mr. Jasper before leaving Cloisterham, Mr. Grewgious went to the gatehouse, and climbed its postern stair. But Mr. Jasper's door being closed, and presenting on a slip of paper the word 'Cathedral,' the fact of its being service-time was borne into the mind of Mr. Grewgious. So he descended the stair again, and, crossing the Close, paused at the great western folding-door of the Cathedral, which stood open on the fine and bright, though short-lived, afternoon, for the airing of the place.

'Dear me,' said Mr. Grewgious, peeping in, 'it's like looking down the throat of Old Time.'

Old Time heaved a mouldy sigh from tomb and arch and vault; and gloomy shadows began to deepen in corners; and damps began to rise from green patches of stone; and jewels, cast upon the pavement of the nave from stained glass by the declining sun, began to perish. Within the grill-gate of the chancel, up the steps surmounted loomingly by the fast-darkening organ, white robes could be dimly seen, and one feeble voice, rising and falling in a cracked, monotonous mutter, could at intervals be faintly heard. In the free outer air, the river, the green pastures, and the brown arable lands, the teeming hills and dales, were reddened by the sunset: while the distant little windows in windmills and farm homesteads, shone, patches of bright beaten gold. In the Cathedral, all became grey, murky, and sepulchral, and the cracked monotonous mutter went on like a dying voice, until the organ and the choir burst forth, and drowned it in a sea of music. Then, the sea fell, and the dying voice made another feeble effort, and then the sea rose high, and beat its life out, and lashed the roof, and surged among the arches, and pierced the heights of the great tower; and then the sea was dry, and all was still.

Mr. Grewgious had by that time walked to the chancel-steps, where he met the living waters coming out.

'Nothing is the matter?' Thus Jasper accosted him, rather quickly. 'You have not been sent for?'

'Not at all, not at all. I came down of my own accord. I have been to my pretty ward's, and am now homeward bound again.'

'You found her thriving?'

'Blooming indeed. Most blooming. I merely came to tell her, seriously, what a betrothal by deceased parents is.'

'And what is it – according to your judgment?'

Mr. Grewgious noticed the whiteness of the lips that asked the question, and put it down to the chilling account of the Cathedral.

'I merely came to tell her that it could not be considered binding, against any such reason for its dissolution as a want of affection, or want of disposition to carry it into effect, on the side of either party.'

'May I ask, had you any especial reason for telling her that?'

Mr. Grewgious answered somewhat sharply: 'The especial reason of doing my duty, sir. Simply that.' Then he added: 'Come, Mr. Jasper; I know your affection for your nephew, and that you are quick to feel on his behalf. I assure you that this implies not the least doubt of, or disrespect to, your nephew.'

'You could not,' returned Jasper, with a friendly pressure of his arm, as they walked on side by side, 'speak more handsomely.'

Mr. Grewgious pulled off his hat to smooth his head, and, having smoothed it, nodded it contentedly, and put his hat on again.

'I will wager,' said Jasper, smiling – his lips were still so white that he was conscious of it, and bit and moistened them while speaking: 'I will wager that she hinted no wish to be released from Ned.'

'And you will win your wager, if you do,' retorted Mr. Grewgious. 'We should allow some margin for little maidenly delicacies in a young motherless creature, under such circumstances, I suppose; it is not in my line; what do you think?'

'There can be no doubt of it.'

'I am glad you say so. Because,' proceeded Mr. Grewgious, who had all this time very knowingly felt his way round to action on his remembrance of what she had said of Jasper himself: 'because she seems to have some little delicate instinct that all preliminary arrangements had best be made between Mr. Edwin Drood and herself, don't you see? She don't want us, don't you know?'

Jasper touched himself on the breast, and said, somewhat indistinctly: 'You mean me.'

Mr. Grewgious touched himself on the breast, and said: 'I mean us. Therefore, let them have their little discussions and councils together, when Mr. Edwin Drood comes back here at Christmas; and then you and I will step in, and put the final touches to the business.'

'So, you settled with her that you would come back at Christmas?' observed Jasper. 'I see! Mr. Grewgious, as you quite fairly said just now, there is such an exceptional attachment between my nephew and me, that I am more sensitive for the dear, fortunate, happy, happy fellow than for myself. But it is only right that the young lady should be considered, as you have pointed out, and that I should accept my cue from you. I accept it. I understand that at Christmas they will complete their preparations for May, and that their marriage will be put in final train by themselves, and that nothing will remain for us but to put ourselves in train also, and have everything ready for our formal release from our trusts, on Edwin's birthday.'

'That is my understanding,' assented Mr. Grewgious, as they shook hands to part. 'God bless them both!'

'God save them both!' cried Jasper.

'I said, bless them,' remarked the former, looking back over his shoulder.

'I said, save them,' returned the latter. 'Is there any difference?'

* D *

CHAPTER X
Smoothing the Way

IT HAS BEEN often enough remarked that women have a curious power of divining the characters of men, which would seem to be innate and instinctive; seeing that it is arrived at through no patient process of reasoning, that it can give no satisfactory or sufficient account of itself, and that it pronounces in the most confident manner even against accumulated observation on the part of the other sex. But it has not been quite so often remarked that this power (fallible, like every other human attribute) is for the most part absolutely incapable of self-revision; and that when it has delivered an adverse opinion which by all human lights is subsequently proved to have failed, it is undistinguishable from prejudice, in respect of its determination not to be corrected. Nay, the very possibility of contradiction or disproof, however remote, communicates to this feminine judgment from the first, in nine cases out of ten, the weakness attendant on the testimony of an interested witness; so personally and strongly does the fair diviner connect herself with her divination.

'Now, don't you think, Ma dear,' said the Minor Canon to his mother one day as she sat at her knitting in his little book-room, 'that you are rather hard on Mr. Neville?'

'No, I do *not*, Sept,' returned the old lady.

'Let us discuss it, Ma.'

'I have no objection to discuss it, Sept. I trust, my dear, I am always open to discussion.' There was a vibration in the old lady's cap, as though she internally added: 'and I should like to see the discussion that would change *my* mind!'

'Very good, Ma,' said her conciliatory son. 'There is nothing like being open to discussion.'

'I hope not, my dear,' returned the old lady, evidently shut to it.

'Well! Mr. Neville, on that unfortunate occasion, commits himself under provocation.'

'And under mulled wine,' added the old lady.

84

'I must admit the wine. Though I believe the two young men were much alike in that regard.'

'I don't,' said the old lady.

'Why not, Ma?'

'Because I *don't*,' said the old lady. 'Still, I am quite open to discussion.'

'But, my dear Ma, I cannot see how we are to discuss, if you take that line.'

'Blame Mr. Neville for it, Sept, and not me,' said the old lady, with stately severity.

'My dear Ma! why Mr. Neville?'

'Because,' said Mrs. Crisparkle, retiring on first principles, 'he came home intoxicated, and did great discredit to this house, and showed great disrespect to this family.'

'That is not to be denied, Ma. He was then, and he is now, very sorry for it.'

'But for Mr. Jasper's well-bred consideration in coming up to me, next day, after service, in the Nave itself, with his gown still on, and expressing his hope that I had not been greatly alarmed or had my rest violently broken, I believe I might never have heard of that disgraceful transaction,' said the old lady.

'To be candid, Ma, I think I should have kept it from you if I could: though I had not decidedly made up my mind. I was following Jasper out, to confer with him on the subject, and to consider the expediency of his and my jointly hushing the thing up on all accounts, when I found him speaking to you. Then it was too late.'

'Too late, indeed, Sept. He was still as pale as gentlemanly ashes at what had taken place in his rooms overnight.'

'If I *had* kept it from you, Ma, you may be sure it would have been for your peace and quiet, and for the good of the young men, and in my best discharge of my duty according to my lights.'

The old lady immediately walked across the room and kissed him: saying, 'Of course, my dear Sept, I am sure of that.'

'However, it became the town-talk,' said Mr. Crisparkle, rubbing his ear, as his mother resumed her seat, and her knitting, 'and passed out of my power.'

'And I said then, Sept,' returned the old lady, 'that I thought ill of Mr. Neville. And I say now, that I think ill of Mr. Neville. And I said then, and I say now, that I hope Mr. Neville may come to good, but I don't believe he will.' Here the cap vibrated again considerably.

'I am sorry to hear you say so, Ma – '

'I am sorry to say so, my dear,' interposed the old lady, knitting on firmly, 'but I can't help it.'

' – For,' pursued the Minor Canon, 'it is undeniable that Mr. Neville is exceedingly industrious and attentive, and that he improves apace, and that he has – I hope I may say – an attachment to me.'

'There is no merit in the last article, my dear,' said the old lady, quickly; 'and if he says there is, I think the worse of him for the boast.'

'But, my dear Ma, he never said there was.'

'Perhaps not,' returned the old lady; 'still, I don't see that it greatly signifies.'

There was no impatience in the pleasant look with which Mr. Crisparkle contemplated the pretty old piece of china as it knitted; but there was, certainly, a humorous sense of its not being a piece of china to argue with very closely.

'Besides, Sept, ask yourself what he would be without his sister. You know what an influence she has over him; you know what a capacity she has; you know that whatever he reads with you, he reads with her. Give her her fair share of your praise, and how much do you leave for him?'

At these words Mr. Crisparkle fell into a little reverie, in which he thought of several things. He thought of the times he had seen the brother and sister together in deep converse over one of his own old college books; now, in the rimy mornings, when he made those sharpening pilgrimages to Cloisterham Weir; now, in the sombre evenings, when he faced the wind at sunset, having climbed his favourite outlook, a beetling fragment of monastery ruin; and the two studious figures passed below him along the margin of the river, in which the town fires and lights already shone, making the landscape bleaker. He thought how the consciousness had stolen upon him that in teaching one, he was teaching two; and how he had almost insensibly adapted his explanations to both minds – that with which his own was daily in contact, and that which he only approached through it. He thought of the gossip that had reached him from the Nuns' House, to the effect that Helena, whom he had mistrusted as so proud and fierce, submitted herself to the fairy-bride (as he called her), and learnt from her what she knew. He thought of the picturesque alliance between those two, externally so very different. He thought – perhaps most of all – could it be that these things were yet but so many weeks old, and had become an integral part of his life?

As, whenever the Reverend Septimus fell a-musing, his good mother took it to be an infallible sign that he 'wanted support,' the blooming old lady made all haste to the dining-room closet, to produce from it the support embodied in a glass of Constantia and a home-made biscuit. It was a most wonderful closet, worthy of Cloisterham and of Minor Canon Corner. Above it, a portrait of Handel in a flowing wig beamed down at the spectator, with a knowing air of being up to the contents of the closet, and a musical air of intending to combine all its harmonies in one delicious fugue. No common closet with a vulgar door on hinges, openable all at once, and leaving nothing to be disclosed by degrees, this rare closet had a lock in mid-air, where two perpendicular slides met; the one falling down, and the other pushing up. The upper slide, on being pulled down (leaving the lower a double mystery), revealed deep shelves of pickle-jars, jam-pots, tin canisters, spice-boxes, and agreeably outlandish vessels of blue and white, the luscious lodgings of preserved tamarinds and ginger. Every benevolent inhabitant of this retreat had his name inscribed upon his stomach. The pickles, in a uniform of rich brown double-breasted buttoned coat, and yellow or sombre drab continuations, announced their portly forms, in printed capitals, as Walnut, Gherkin, Onion, Cabbage, Cauliflower, Mixed, and other members of that noble family. The jams, as being of a less masculine temperament, and as wearing curlpapers, announced themselves in feminine caligraphy, like a soft whisper, to be Raspberry, Gooseberry, Apricot, Plum, Damson, Apple, and Peach. The scene closing on these charmers, and the lower slide ascending, oranges were revealed, attended by a mighty japanned sugar-box, to temper their acerbity if unripe. Home-made biscuits waited at the Court of these Powers, accompanied by a goodly fragment of plum-cake, and various slender ladies' fingers, to be dipped into sweet wine and kissed. Lowest of all, a compact leaden-vault enshrined the sweet wine and a stock of cordials: whence issued whispers of Seville Orange, Lemon, Almond, and Caraway-seed. There was a crowning air upon this closet of closets, of having been for ages hummed through by the Cathedral bell and organ, until those venerable bees had made sublimated honey of everything in store; and it was always observed that every dipper among the shelves (deep, as has been noticed, and swallowing up head, shoulders, and elbows) came forth again mellow-faced, and seeming to have undergone a saccharine transfiguration.

The Reverend Septimus yielded himself up quite as willing a victim to a nauseous medicinal herb-closet, also presided over by the china shepherdess, as to this glorious cupboard. To what amazing infusions of gentian, peppermint, gilliflower, sage, parsley, thyme, rue, rosemary, and dandelion, did his courageous stomach submit itself! In what wonderful wrappers, enclosing layers of dried leaves, would he swathe his rosy and contented face, if his mother suspected him of a toothache! What botanical blotches would he cheerfully stick upon his cheek, or forehead, if the dear old lady convicted him of an imperceptible pimple there! Into this herbaceous penitentiary, situated on an upper staircase-landing: a low and narrow whitewashed cell, where bunches of dried leaves hung from rusty hooks in the ceiling, and were spread out upon shelves, in company with portentous bottles: would the Reverend Septimus submissively be led, like the highly popular lamb who has so long and unresistingly been led to the slaughter, and there would he, unlike that lamb, bore nobody but himself. Not even doing that much, so that the old lady were busy and pleased, he would quietly swallow what was given him, merely taking a corrective dip of hands and face into the great bowl of dried rose-leaves, and into the other great bowl of dried lavender, and then would go out, as confident in the sweetening powers of Cloisterham Weir and a wholesome mind, as Lady Macbeth was hopeless of those of all the seas that roll.

In the present instance the good Minor Canon took his glass of Constantia with an excellent grace, and, so supported to his mother's satisfaction, applied himself to the remaining duties of the day. In their orderly and punctual progress they brought round Vesper Service and twilight. The Cathedral being very cold, he set off for a brisk trot after service; the trot to end in a charge at his favourite fragment of ruin, which was to be carried by storm, without a pause for breath.

He carried it in a masterly manner, and, not breathed even then, stood looking down upon the river. The river at Cloisterham is sufficiently near the sea to throw up oftentimes a quantity of seaweed. An unusual quantity had come in with the last tide, and this, and the confusion of the water, and the restless dipping and flapping of the noisy gulls, and an angry light out seaward beyond the brown-sailed barges that were turning black, foreshadowed a stormy night. In his mind he was contrasting the wild and noisy sea with the quiet harbour of Minor Canon Corner, when Helena and Neville Landless passed below him. He had had the two together in his thoughts all day, and at once climbed down to speak to them together. The footing was rough in an uncertain light for any tread save that of a good climber; but the Minor Canon was as good a climber as most men, and stood beside them before many good climbers would have been half-way down.

'A wild evening, Miss Landless! Do you not find your usual walk with your brother too exposed and cold for the time of year? Or at all events, when the sun is down, and the weather is driving in from the sea?'

Helena thought not. It was their favourite walk. It was very retired.

'It is very retired,' assented Mr. Crisparkle, laying hold of his opportunity straightway, and walking on with them. 'It is a place of all others where one can speak without interruption, as I wish to do. Mr. Neville, I believe you tell your sister everything that passes between us?'

'Everything, sir.'

'Consequently,' said Mr. Crisparkle, 'your sister is aware that I have repeatedly urged you to make some kind of apology for that unfortunate occurrence which befell on the night of your arrival here.' In saying it he looked to her, and not to him; therefore it was she, and not he, who replied:

'Yes.'

'I call it unfortunate, Miss Helena,' resumed Mr. Crisparkle, 'forasmuch as it certainly has engendered a prejudice against Neville. There is a notion about, that he is a dangerously passionate fellow, of an uncontrollable and furious temper: he is really avoided as such.'

'I have no doubt he is, poor fellow,' said Helena, with a look of proud compassion at her brother, expressing a deep sense of his being ungenerously treated. 'I should be quite sure of it, from your saying so; but what you tell me is confirmed by suppressed hints and references that I meet with every day.'

'Now,' Mr. Crisparkle again resumed, in a tone of mild though firm persuasion, 'is not this to be regretted, and ought it not to be amended? These are early days of Neville's in Cloisterham, and I have no fear of his outliving such a prejudice, and proving himself to have been misunderstood. But how much wiser to take action at once, than to trust to uncertain time! Besides, apart from its being politic, it is right. For there can be no question that Neville was wrong.'

'He was provoked,' Helena submitted.

'He was the assailant,' Mr. Crisparkle submitted.

They walked on in silence, until Helena raised her eyes to the Minor Canon's face, and said, almost reproachfully: 'O Mr. Crisparkle, would you have Neville throw himself at young Drood's feet, or at Mr. Jasper's, who maligns him every day? In your heart you cannot mean it. From your heart you could not do it, if his case were yours.'

'I have represented to Mr. Crisparkle, Helena,' said Neville, with a glance of deference towards his tutor, 'that if I could do it from my heart, I would. But I cannot, and I revolt from the pretence. You forget however, that to put the case to Mr. Crisparkle as his own, is to suppose to have done what I did.'

'I ask his pardon,' said Helena.

'You see,' remarked Mr. Crisparkle, again laying hold of his opportunity, though with a moderate and delicate touch, 'you both instinctively acknowledge that Neville did wrong. Then why stop short, and not otherwise acknowledge it?'

'Is there no difference,' asked Helena, with a little faltering in her manner; 'between submission to a generous spirit, and submission to a base or trivial one?'

Before the worthy Minor Canon was quite ready with his argument in reference to this nice distinction, Neville struck in:

'Help me to clear myself with Mr. Crisparkle, Helena. Help me to convince him that I cannot be the first to make concessions without mockery and falsehood. My nature must be changed before I can do so, and it is not changed. I am sensible of inexpressible affront, and deliberate aggravation of inexpressible affront, and I am angry. The plain truth is, I am still as angry when I recall that night as I was that night.'

'Neville,' hinted the Minor Canon, with a steady countenance, 'you have repeated that former action of your hands, which I so much dislike.'

'I am sorry for it, sir, but it was involuntary. I confessed that I was still as angry.'

'And I confess,' said Mr. Crisparkle, 'that I hoped for better things.'

'I am sorry to disappoint you, sir, but it would be far worse to deceive you, and I should deceive you grossly if I pretended that you had softened me in this respect. The time may come when your powerful influence will do even that with the difficult pupil whose antecedents you know; but it has not come yet. Is this so, and in spite of my struggles against myself, Helena?'

She, whose dark eyes were watching the effect of what he said on Mr. Crisparkle's face, replied – to Mr. Crisparkle, not to him: 'It is so.' After a short pause, she answered the slightest look of inquiry conceivable, in her brother's eyes, with as slight an affirmative bend of her own head; and he went on:

'I have never yet had the courage to say to you, sir, what in full openness I ought to have said when you first talked with me on this subject. It is not easy to say, and I have been withheld by a fear of its seeming ridiculous, which is very strong upon me down to this last moment, and might, but for my sister, prevent my being quite open with you even now. – I admire Miss Bud, sir, so very much, that I cannot bear her being treated with conceit or indifference; and even if I did not feel that I had an injury against young Drood on my own account, I should feel that I had an injury against him on hers.'

Mr. Crisparkle, in utter amazement, looked at Helena for corroboration, and met in her expressive face full corroboration, and a plea for advice.

'The young lady of whom you speak is, as you know, Mr. Neville, shortly to be married,' said Mr. Crisparkle, gravely; 'therefore your admiration, if it be of that special nature which you seem to indicate, is outrageously misplaced. Moreover, it is monstrous that you should take upon yourself to be the young lady's champion against her chosen husband. Besides, you have seen them only once. The young lady has become your sister's friend; and I wonder that your sister, even on her behalf, has not checked you in this irrational and culpable fancy.'

'She has tried, sir, but uselessly. Husband or no husband, that fellow is incapable of the feeling with which I am inspired towards the beautiful young creature whom he treats like a doll. I say he is as incapable of it, as he is unworthy of her. I say she is sacrificed in being bestowed upon him. I say that I love her, and despise and hate him!' This with a face so flushed, and a gesture so violent, that his sister crossed to his side, and caught his arm, remonstrating, 'Neville, Neville!'

Thus recalled to himself, he quickly became sensible of having lost the guard he had set upon his passionate tendency, and covered his face with his hand, as one repentant and wretched.

Mr. Crisparkle, watching him attentively, and at the same time meditating how to proceed, walked on for some paces in silence. Then he spoke:

'Mr. Neville, Mr. Neville, I am sorely grieved to see in you more traces of a character as sullen, angry, and wild, as the night now closing in. They are of too serious an aspect to leave me the resource of treating the infatuation you have disclosed, as undeserving serious consideration. I give it very serious consideration, and I speak to you accordingly. This feud between you and young Drood must not go on. I cannot permit it to go on any longer, knowing what I now know from you, and you living under my roof. Whatever prejudiced and unauthorised constructions your blind and envious wrath may put upon his character, it is a frank, good-natured character. I know I can trust to it for that. Now, pray observe what I am about to say. On reflection, and on your sister's representation, I am willing to admit that, in making peace with young Drood, you have a right to be met half-way. I will engage that you shall be, and even that young Drood shall make the first advance. This condition fulfilled, you will pledge me the honour of a Christian gentleman that the quarrel is for ever at an end on your side. What may be in your heart when you give him your hand, can only be known to the Searcher of all hearts; but it will never go well with you, if there be any treachery there. So far, as to that; next as to what I must again speak of as your infatuation. I understand it to have been confided to me, and to be known to no other person save your sister and yourself. Do I understand aright?'

Helena answered in a low voice: 'It is only known to us three who are here together.'

'It is not at all known to the young lady, your friend?'

'On my soul, no!'

'I require you, then, to give me your similar and solemn pledge, Mr. Neville, that it shall remain the secret it is, and that you will take no other action whatsoever upon it than endeavouring (and that most earnestly) to erase it from your mind. I will not tell you that it will soon pass; I will not tell you that it is the fancy of the moment; I will not tell you that such caprices have their rise and fall among the young and ardent every hour; I will leave you undisturbed in the belief that it has few parallels or none, that it will abide with you a long time, and that it will be very difficult to conquer. So much the more weight shall I attach to the pledge I require from you, when it is unreservedly given.'

The young man twice or thrice essayed to speak, but failed.

'Let me leave you with your sister, whom it is time you took home,' said Mr. Crisparkle. 'You will find me alone in my room by-and-by.'

'Pray do not leave us yet,' Helena implored him. 'Another minute.'

'I should not,' said Neville, pressing his hand upon his face, 'have needed so much as another minute, if you had been less patient with me, Mr. Crisparkle, less considerate of me, and less unpretendingly good and true. O, if in my childhood I had known such a guide!'

'Follow your guide now, Neville,' murmured Helena, 'and follow him to Heaven!'

There was that in her tone which broke the good Minor Canon's voice, or it would have repudiated her exaltation of him. As it was, he laid a finger on his lips, and looked towards her brother.

'To say that I give both pledges, Mr. Crisparkle, out of my innermost heart, and to say that there is no treachery in it, is to say nothing!' Thus Neville, greatly moved. 'I beg your forgiveness for my miserable lapse into a burst of passion.'

'Not mine, Neville, not mine. You know with whom forgiveness lies, as the highest attribute conceivable. Miss Helena, you and your brother are twin children. You came into this world with the same dispositions, and you passed your younger days together surrounded by the same adverse circumstances. What you have overcome in yourself, can you not overcome in him? You see the rock that lies in his course. Who but you can keep him clear of it?'

'Who but you, sir?' replied Helena. 'What is my influence, or my weak wisdom, compared with yours!'

'You have the wisdom of Love,' returned the Minor Canon, 'and it was the highest wisdom ever known upon this earth, remember. As to mine – but the less said of that commonplace commodity the better. Good night!'

She took the hand he offered her, and gratefully and almost reverently raised it to her lips.

'Tut!' said the Minor Canon softly, 'I am much overpaid!' and turned away.

Retracing his steps towards the Cathedral Close, he tried, as he went along in the dark, to think out the best means of bringing to pass what he had promised to effect, and what must somehow be done. 'I shall probably be asked to marry them,' he reflected, 'and I would they were married and gone! But this presses first.'

He debated principally whether he should write to young Drood, or whether he should speak to Jasper. The consciousness of being popular with the whole Cathedral establishment inclined him to the latter course, and the well-timed sight of the lighted gatehouse decided him to take it. 'I will strike while the iron is hot,' he said, 'and see him now.'

Jasper was lying asleep on a couch before the fire, when, having ascended the postern-stair, and received no answer to his knock at the door, Mr. Crisparkle gently turned the handle and looked in. Long afterwards he had cause to remember how Jasper sprang from the couch in a delirious state between sleeping and waking, and crying out: 'What is the matter? Who did it?'

'It is only I, Jasper. I am sorry to have disturbed you.'

93

The glare of his eyes settled down into a look of recognition, and he moved a chair or two, to make a way to the fireside.

'I was dreaming at a great rate, and am glad to be disturbed from an indigestive after-dinner sleep. Not to mention that you are always welcome.'

'Thank you. I am not confident,' returned Mr. Crisparkle, as he sat himself down in the easy-chair placed for him, 'that my subject will at first sight be quite as welcome as myself; but I am a minister of peace, and I pursue my subject in the interests of peace. In a word, Jasper, I want to establish peace between these two young fellows.'

A very perplexed expression took hold of Mr. Jasper's face; a very perplexing expression too, for Mr. Crisparkle could make nothing of it.

'How?' was Jasper's inquiry, in a low and slow voice, after a silence.

'For the "How" I come to you. I want to ask you to do me the great favour and service of interposing with your nephew (I have already interposed with Mr. Neville), and getting him to write you a short note, in his lively way, saying that he is willing to shake hands. I know what a good-natured fellow he is, and what influence you have with him. And without in the least defending Mr. Neville, we must all admit that he was bitterly stung.'

Jasper turned that perplexed face towards the fire. Mr. Crisparkle continuing to observe it, found it even more perplexing than before, inasmuch as it seemed to denote (which could hardly be) some close internal calculation.

'I know that you are not prepossessed in Mr. Neville's favour,' the Minor Canon was going on, when Jasper stopped him:

'You have cause to say so. I am not, indeed.'

'Undoubtedly; and I admit his lamentable violence of temper, though I hope he and I will get the better of it between us. But I have exacted a very solemn promise from him as to his future demeanour towards your nephew, if you do kindly interpose; and I am sure he will keep it.'

'You are always responsible and trustworthy, Mr. Crisparkle. Do you really feel sure that you can answer for him so confidently?'

'I do.'

The perplexed and perplexing look vanished.

'Then you relieve my mind of a great dread, and a heavy weight,' said Jasper; 'I will do it.'

Mr. Crisparkle, delighted by the swiftness and completeness of his success, acknowledged it in the handsomest terms.

'I will do it,' repeated Jasper, 'for the comfort of having your guarantee against my vague and unfounded fears. You will laugh – but do you keep a Diary?'

'A line for a day; not more.'

'A line for a day would be quite as much as my uneventful life would need, Heaven knows,' said Jasper, taking a book from a desk, 'but that my Diary is, in fact, a Diary of Ned's life too. You will laugh at this entry; you will guess when it was made:

'Past midnight. – After what I have just now seen, I have a morbid dread upon me of some horrible consequences resulting to my dear boy, that I cannot reason with or in any way contend against. All my efforts are vain. The demoniacal passion of this Neville Landless, his strength in his fury, and his savage rage for the destruction of its object, appal me. So profound is the impression, that twice since I have gone into my dear boy's room, to assure myself of his sleeping safely, and not lying dead in his blood.

'Here is another entry next morning:

'Ned up and away. Light-hearted and unsuspicious as ever. He laughed when I cautioned him, and said he was as good a man as Neville Landless any day. I told him that might be, but he was not as bad a man. He continued to make light of it, but I travelled with him as far as I could, and left him most unwillingly. I am unable to shake off these dark intangible presentiments of evil – if feelings founded upon staring facts are to be so called.

'Again and again,' said Jasper, in conclusion, twirling the leaves of the book before putting it by, 'I have relapsed into these moods, as other entries show. But I have now your assurance at my back, and shall put it in my book, and make it an antidote to my black humours.'

'Such an antidote, I hope,' returned Mr. Crisparkle, 'as will induce you before long to consign the black humours to the flames. I ought to be the last to find any fault with you this evening, when you have met my wishes so freely; but I must say, Jasper, that your devotion to your nephew has made you exaggerative here.'

'You are my witness,' said Jasper, shrugging his shoulders, 'what my state of mind honestly was, that night, before I sat down to write, and in what words I expressed it. You remember objecting to a word I used, as being too strong? It was a stronger word than any in my Diary.'

'Well, well. Try the antidote,' rejoined Mr. Crisparkle; 'and may it give you a brighter and better view of the case! We will discuss it no more now. I have to thank you for myself, thank you sincerely.'

'You shall find,' said Jasper, as they shook hands, 'that I will not do the thing you wish me to do, by halves. I will take care that Ned, giving way at all, shall give way thoroughly.'

On the third day after this conversation, he called on Mr. Crisparkle with the following letter:

MY DEAR JACK,

'I am touched by your account of your interview with Mr. Crisparkle, whom I much respect and esteem. At once I openly say that I forgot myself on that occasion quite as much as Mr. Landless did, and that I wish that bygone to be a bygone, and all to be right again.

'Look here, dear old boy. Ask Mr. Landless to dinner on Christmas Eve (the better the day the better the deed), and let there be only we three, and let us shake hands all round there and then, and say no more about it.

My Dear Jack,

Ever your most affectionate,

"EDWIN DROOD.

P.S. Love to Miss Pussy at the next music lesson.

'You expect Mr. Neville, then?' said Mr. Crisparkle.

'I count upon his coming,' said Mr. Jasper.

Chapter XI
A Picture and a Ring

BEHIND THE MOST ancient part of Holborn, London, where certain gabled houses some centuries of age still stand looking on the public way, as if disconsolately looking for the Old Bourne that has long run dry, is a little nook composed of two irregular quadrangles, called Staple Inn. It is one of those nooks, the turning into which out of the clashing street, imparts to the relieved pedestrian the sensation of having put cotton in his ears, and velvet soles on his boots. It is one of those nooks where a few smoky sparrows twitter in smoky trees, as though they called to one another, 'Let us play at country,' and where a few feet of garden-mould and a few yards of gravel enable them to do that refreshing violence to their tiny understandings. Moreover, it is one of those nooks which are legal nooks; and it contains a little Hall, with a little lantern in its roof: to what obstructive purposes devoted, and at whose expense, this history knoweth not.

In the days when Cloisterham took offence at the existence of a railroad afar off, as menacing that sensitive constitution, the property of us Britons: the odd fortune of which sacred institution it is to be in exactly equal degrees croaked about, trembled for, and boasted of, whatever happens to anything, anywhere in the world: in those days no neighbouring architecture of lofty proportions had arisen to overshadow Staple Inn. The westering sun bestowed bright glances on it, and the south-west wind blew into it unimpeded.

Neither wind nor sun, however, favoured Staple Inn one December afternoon towards six o'clock, when it was filled with fog, and candles shed murky and blurred rays through the windows of all its then-occupied sets of chambers; notably from a set of chambers in a corner house in the little inner quadrangle, presenting in black and white over its ugly portal the mysterious inscription:

P

J   T

1747

In which set of chambers, never having troubled his head about the inscription, unless to bethink himself at odd times on glancing up at it, that haply it might mean Perhaps John Thomas, or Perhaps Joe Tyler, sat Mr. Grewgious writing by his fire.

Who could have told, by looking at Mr. Grewgious, whether he had ever known ambition or disappointment? He had been bred to the Bar, and had laid himself out for chamber practice; to draw deeds; 'convey the wise it call,' as Pistol says. But Conveyancing and he had made such a very indifferent marriage of it that they had separated by consent – if there can be said to be separation where there has never been coming together.

No. Coy Conveyancing would not come to Mr. Grewgious. She was wooed, not won, and they went their several ways. But an Arbitration being blown towards him by some unaccountable wind, and he gaining great credit in it as one indefatigable in seeking out right and doing right, a pretty fat Receivership was next blown into his pocket by a wind more traceable to its source. So, by chance, he had found his niche. Receiver and Agent now, to two rich estates, and deputing their legal business, in an amount worth having, to a firm of solicitors on the floor below, he had snuffed out his ambition (supposing him to have ever lighted it), and had settled down with his snuffers for the rest of his life under the dry vine and fig-tree of P. J. T., who planted in seventeen-forty-seven.

Many accounts and account-books, many files of correspondence, and several strong boxes, garnished Mr. Grewgious's room. They can scarcely be represented as having lumbered it, so conscientious and precise was their orderly arrangement. The apprehension of dying suddenly, and leaving one fact or one figure with any incompleteness or obscurity attaching to it, would have stretched Mr. Grewgious stone-dead any day. The largest fidelity to a trust was the life-blood of the man. There are sorts of life-blood that course more quickly, more gaily, more attractively; but there is no better sort in circulation.

There was no luxury in his room. Even its comforts were limited to its being dry and warm, and having a snug though faded fireside. What may be called its private life was confined to the hearth, and an easy-chair, and an old-fashioned occasional round table that was brought out upon the rug after business hours, from a corner where it elsewise remained turned up like a shining mahogany shield. Behind it, when standing thus on the defensive, was a closet, usually containing something good to drink. An outer room was the clerk's room; Mr. Grewgious's sleeping-room was across the common stair; and he held some not empty cellarage at the bottom of the common stair. Three hundred days in the year, at least, he crossed over to the hotel in Furnival's Inn for his dinner, and after dinner crossed back again, to make the most of these simplicities until it should become broad business day once more, with P. J. T., date seventeen-forty-seven.

As Mr. Grewgious sat and wrote by his fire that afternoon, so did the clerk of Mr. Grewgious sit and write by *his* fire. A pale, puffy-faced, dark-haired person of thirty, with big dark eyes that wholly wanted lustre, and a dissatisfied doughy complexion, that seemed to ask to be sent to the baker's, this attendant was a mysterious being, possessed of some strange power over Mr. Grewgious. As though he had been called into existence, like a fabulous Familiar, by a magic spell which had failed when required to dismiss him, he stuck tight to Mr. Grewgious's stool, although Mr. Grewgious's comfort and convenience would manifestly have been advanced by dispossessing him. A gloomy person with tangled locks, and a general air of having been reared under the shadow of that baleful tree of Java which has given shelter to more lies than the whole botanical kingdom, Mr. Grewgious, nevertheless, treated him with unaccountable consideration.

'Now, Bazzard,' said Mr. Grewgious, on the entrance of his clerk: looking up from his papers as he arranged them for the night: 'what is in the wind besides fog?'

'Mr. Drood,' said Bazzard.

'What of him?'

'Has called,' said Bazzard.

'You might have shown him in.'

'I am doing it,' said Bazzard.

The visitor came in accordingly.

'Dear me!' said Mr. Grewgious, looking round his pair of office candles. 'I thought you had called and merely left your name and gone. How do you do, Mr. Edwin? Dear me, you're choking!'

'It's this fog,' returned Edwin; 'and it makes my eyes smart, like Cayenne pepper.'

'Is it really so bad as that? Pray undo your wrappers. It's fortunate I have so good a fire; but Mr. Bazzard has taken care of me.'

'No I haven't,' said Mr. Bazzard at the door.

'Ah! then it follows that I must have taken care of myself without observing it,' said Mr. Grewgious. 'Pray be seated in my chair. No. I beg! Coming out of such an atmosphere, in *my* chair.'

Edwin took the easy-chair in the corner; and the fog he had brought in with him, and the fog he took off with his greatcoat and neck-shawl, was speedily licked up by the eager fire.

'I look,' said Edwin, smiling, 'as if I had come to stop.'

' – By the by,' cried Mr. Grewgious; 'excuse my interrupting you; do stop. The fog may clear in an hour or two. We can have dinner in from just across Holborn. You had better take your Cayenne pepper here than outside; pray stop and dine.'

'You are very kind,' said Edwin, glancing about him as though attracted by the notion of a new and relishing sort of gipsy-party.

'Not at all,' said Mr. Grewgious; '*you* are very kind to join issue with a bachelor in chambers, and take pot-luck. And I'll ask,' said Mr. Grewgious, dropping his voice, and speaking with a twinkling eye, as if inspired with a bright thought: 'I'll ask Bazzard. He mightn't like it else. – Bazzard!'

Bazzard reappeared.

'Dine presently with Mr. Drood and me.'

'If I am ordered to dine, of course I will, sir,' was the gloomy answer.

'Save the man!' cried Mr. Grewgious. 'You're not ordered; you're invited.'

'Thank you, sir,' said Bazzard; 'in that case I don't care if I do.'

'That's arranged. And perhaps you wouldn't mind,' said Mr. Grewgious, 'stepping over to the hotel in Furnival's, and asking them to send in materials for laying the cloth. For dinner we'll have a tureen of the hottest and strongest soup available, and we'll have the best made-dish that can be recommended, and we'll have a joint (such as a haunch of mutton), and we'll have a goose, or a turkey, or any little stuffed thing of that sort that may happen to be in the bill of fare – in short, we'll have whatever there is on hand.'

These liberal directions Mr. Grewgious issued with his usual air of reading an inventory, or repeating a lesson, or doing anything else by rote. Bazzard, after drawing out the round table, withdrew to execute them.

'I was a little delicate, you see,' said Mr. Grewgious, in a lower tone, after his clerk's departure, 'about employing him in the foraging or commissariat department. Because he mightn't like it.'

'He seems to have his own way, sir,' remarked Edwin.

'His own way?' returned Mr. Grewgious. 'O dear no! Poor fellow, you quite mistake him. If he had his own way, he wouldn't be here.'

'I wonder where he would be!' Edwin thought. But he only thought it, because Mr. Grewgious came and stood himself with his back to the other corner of the fire, and his shoulder-blades against the chimneypiece, and collected his skirts for easy conversation.

'I take it, without having the gift of prophecy, that you have done me the favour of looking in to mention that you are going down yonder – where I can tell you, you are expected – and to offer to execute any little commission from me to my charming ward, and perhaps to sharpen me up a bit in any proceedings? Eh, Mr. Edwin?'

'I called, sir, before going down, as an act of attention.'

'Of attention!' said Mr. Grewgious. 'Ah! of course, not of impatience?'

'Impatience, sir?'

Mr. Grewgious had meant to be arch – not that he in the remotest degree expressed that meaning – and had brought himself into scarcely supportable proximity with the fire, as if to burn the fullest effect of his archness into himself, as other subtle impressions are burnt into hard metals. But his archness suddenly flying before the composed face and manner of his visitor, and only the fire remaining, he started and rubbed himself.

'I have lately been down yonder,' said Mr. Grewgious, rearranging his skirts; 'and that was what I referred to, when I said I could tell you you are expected.'

'Indeed, sir! Yes; I knew that Pussy was looking out for me.'

'Do you keep a cat down there?' asked Mr. Grewgious.

Edwin coloured a little as he explained: 'I call Rosa Pussy.'

'O, really,' said Mr. Grewgious, smoothing down his head; 'that's very affable.'

Edwin glanced at his face, uncertain whether or no he seriously objected to the appellation. But Edwin might as well have glanced at the face of a clock.

'A pet name, sir,' he explained again.

'Umps,' said Mr. Grewgious, with a nod. But with such an extraordinary compromise between an unqualified assent and a qualified dissent, that his visitor was much disconcerted.

'Did PRosa – ' Edwin began by way of recovering himself.

'PRosa?' repeated Mr. Grewgious.

'I was going to say Pussy, and changed my mind; – did she tell you anything about the Landlesses?'

'No,' said Mr. Grewgious. 'What is the Landlesses? An estate? A villa? A farm?'

'A brother and sister. The sister is at the Nuns' House, and has become a great friend of P – '

'PRosa's,' Mr. Grewgious struck in, with a fixed face.

'She is a strikingly handsome girl, sir, and I thought she might have been described to you, or presented to you perhaps?'

'Neither,' said Mr. Grewgious. 'But here is Bazzard.'

Bazzard returned, accompanied by two waiters – an immovable waiter, and a flying waiter; and the three brought in with them as much fog as gave a new roar to the fire. The flying waiter, who had brought everything on his shoulders, laid the cloth with amazing rapidity and dexterity; while the immovable waiter, who had brought nothing, found fault with him. The flying waiter then highly polished all the glasses he had brought, and the immovable waiter looked through them. The flying waiter then flew across Holborn for the soup, and flew back again, and then took another flight for the made-dish, and flew back again, and then took another flight for the joint and poultry, and flew back again, and between whiles took supplementary flights for a great variety of articles, as it was discovered from time to time that the immovable waiter had forgotten them all. But let the flying waiter cleave the air as he might, he was always reproached on his return by the immovable waiter for bringing fog with him, and being out of breath. At the conclusion of the repast, by which time the flying waiter was severely blown, the immovable waiter gathered up the tablecloth under his arm with a grand air, and having sternly (not to say with indignation) looked on at the flying waiter while he set the clean glasses round, directed a valedictory glance towards Mr. Grewgious, conveying: 'Let it be clearly understood between us that the reward is mine, and that Nil is the claim of this slave,' and pushed the flying waiter before him out of the room.

It was like a highly-finished miniature painting representing My Lords of the Circumlocution Department, Commandership-in-Chief of any sort, Government. It was quite an edifying little picture to be hung on the line in the National Gallery.

As the fog had been the proximate cause of this sumptuous repast, so the fog served for its general sauce. To hear the out-door clerks sneezing, wheezing, and beating their feet on the gravel was a zest far surpassing

Doctor Kitchener's. To bid, with a shiver, the unfortunate flying waiter shut the door before he had opened it, was a condiment of a profounder flavour than Harvey. And here let it be noticed, parenthetically, that the leg of this young man, in its application to the door, evinced the finest sense of touch: always preceding himself and tray (with something of an angling air about it), by some seconds: and always lingering after he and the tray had disappeared, like Macbeth's leg when accompanying him off the stage with reluctance to the assassination of Duncan.

The host had gone below to the cellar, and had brought up bottles of ruby, straw-coloured, and golden drinks, which had ripened long ago in lands where no fogs are, and had since lain slumbering in the shade. Sparkling and tingling after so long a nap, they pushed at their corks to help the corkscrew (like prisoners helping rioters to force their gates), and danced out gaily. If P. J. T. in seventeen-forty-seven, or in any other year of his period, drank such wines – then, for a certainty, P. J. T. was Pretty Jolly Too.

Externally, Mr. Grewgious showed no signs of being mellowed by these glowing vintages. Instead of his drinking them, they might have been poured over him in his high-dried snuff form, and run to waste, for any lights and shades they caused to flicker over his face. Neither was his manner influenced. But, in his wooden way, he had observant eyes for Edwin; and when at the end of dinner, he motioned Edwin back to his own easy-chair in the fireside corner, and Edwin sank luxuriously into it after very brief remonstrance, Mr. Grewgious, as he turned his seat round towards the fire too, and smoothed his head and face, might have been seen looking at his visitor between his smoothing fingers.

'Bazzard!' said Mr. Grewgious, suddenly turning to him.

'I follow you, sir,' returned Bazzard; who had done his work of consuming meat and drink in a workmanlike manner, though mostly in speechlessness.

'I drink to you, Bazzard; Mr. Edwin, success to Mr. Bazzard!'

'Success to Mr. Bazzard!' echoed Edwin, with a totally unfounded appearance of enthusiasm, and with the unspoken addition: 'What in, I wonder!'

'And May!' pursued Mr. Grewgious – 'I am not at liberty to be definite – May! – my conversational powers are so very limited that I know I shall not come well out of this – May! – it ought to be put imaginatively, but I have no imagination – May! – the thorn of anxiety is as nearly the mark as I am likely to get – May it come out at last!'

Mr. Bazzard, with a frowning smile at the fire, put a hand into his tangled locks, as if the thorn of anxiety were there; then into his waistcoat, as if it were there; then into his pockets, as if it were there. In all these movements he was closely followed by the eyes of Edwin, as if that young gentleman expected to see the thorn in action. It was not produced, however, and Mr. Bazzard merely said: 'I follow you, sir, and I thank you.'

'I am going,' said Mr. Grewgious, jingling his glass on the table with one hand, and bending aside under cover of the other, to whisper to Edwin, 'to drink to my ward. But I put Bazzard first. He mightn't like it else.'

This was said with a mysterious wink; or what would have been a wink, if, in Mr. Grewgious's hands, it could have been quick enough. So Edwin winked responsively, without the least idea what he meant by doing so.

'And now,' said Mr. Grewgious, 'I devote a bumper to the fair and fascinating Miss Rosa. Bazzard, the fair and fascinating Miss Rosa!'

'I follow you, sir,' said Bazzard, 'and I pledge you!'

'And so do I!' said Edwin.

'Lord bless me,' cried Mr. Grewgious, breaking the blank silence which of course ensued: though why these pauses *should* come upon us when we have performed any small social rite, not directly inducive of self-examination or mental despondency, who can tell? 'I am a particularly Angular man, and yet I fancy (if I may use the word, not having a morsel of fancy), that I could draw a picture of a true lover's state of mind, to-night.'

'Let us follow you, sir,' said Bazzard, 'and have the picture.'

'Mr. Edwin will correct it where it's wrong,' resumed Mr. Grewgious, 'and will throw in a few touches from the life. I dare say it is wrong in many particulars, and wants many touches from the life, for I was born a Chip, and have neither soft sympathies nor soft experiences. Well! I hazard the guess that the true lover's mind is completely permeated by the beloved object of his affections. I hazard the guess that her dear name is precious to him, cannot be heard or repeated without emotion, and is preserved sacred. If he has any distinguishing appellation of fondness for her, it is reserved for her, and is not for common ears. A name that it would be a privilege to call her by, being alone with her own bright self, it would be a liberty, a coldness, an insensibility, almost a breach of good faith, to flaunt elsewhere.'

It was wonderful to see Mr. Grewgious sitting bolt upright, with his hands on his knees, continuously chopping this discourse out of himself: much as a charity boy with a very good memory might get his catechism said: and evincing no correspondent emotion whatever, unless in a certain occasional little tingling perceptible at the end of his nose.

'My picture,' Mr. Grewgious proceeded, 'goes on to represent (under correction from you, Mr. Edwin), the true lover as ever impatient to be in the presence or vicinity of the beloved object of his affections; as caring very little for his case in any other society; and as constantly seeking that. If I was to say seeking that, as a bird seeks its nest, I should make an ass of myself, because that would trench upon what I understand to be poetry; and I am so far from trenching upon poetry at any time, that I never, to my knowledge, got within ten thousand miles of it. And I am besides totally unacquainted with the habits of birds, except the birds of Staple Inn, who seek their nests on ledges, and in gutter-pipes and chimneypots, not constructed for them by the beneficent hand of Nature. I beg, therefore, to be understood as foregoing the bird's-nest. But my picture does represent the true lover as having no existence separable from that of the beloved object of his affections, and as living at once a doubled life and a halved life. And if I do not clearly express what I mean by that, it is either for the reason that having no conversational powers, I cannot express what I mean, or that having no meaning, I do not mean what I fail to express. Which, to the best of my belief, is not the case.'

Edwin had turned red and turned white, as certain points of this picture came into the light. He now sat looking at the fire, and bit his lip.

'The speculations of an Angular man,' resumed Mr. Grewgious, still sitting and speaking exactly as before, 'are probably erroneous on so globular a topic. But I figure to myself (subject, as before, to Mr. Edwin's correction), that there can be no coolness, no lassitude, no doubt, no indifference, no half fire and half smoke state of mind, in a real lover. Pray am I at all near the mark in my picture?'

As abrupt in his conclusion as in his commencement and progress, he jerked this inquiry at Edwin, and stopped when one might have supposed him in the middle of his oration.

'I should say, sir,' stammered Edwin, 'as you refer the question to me – '

'Yes,' said Mr. Grewgious, 'I refer it to you, as an authority.'

'I should say, then, sir,' Edwin went on, embarrassed, 'that the picture you have drawn is generally correct; but I submit that perhaps you may be rather hard upon the unlucky lover.'

'Likely so,' assented Mr. Grewgious, 'likely so. I am a hard man in the grain.'

'He may not show,' said Edwin, 'all he feels; or he may not – '

There he stopped so long, to find the rest of his sentence, that Mr. Grewgious rendered his difficulty a thousand times the greater by unexpectedly striking in with:

'No to be sure; he *may* not!'

After that, they all sat silent; the silence of Mr. Bazzard being occasioned by slumber.

'His responsibility is very great, though,' said Mr. Grewgious at length, with his eyes on the fire.

Edwin nodded assent, with *his* eyes on the fire.

'And let him be sure that he trifles with no one,' said Mr. Grewgious; 'neither with himself, nor with any other.'

Edwin bit his lip again, and still sat looking at the fire.

'He must not make a plaything of a treasure. Woe betide him if he does! Let him take that well to heart,' said Mr. Grewgious.

Though he said these things in short sentences, much as the supposititious charity boy just now referred to might have repeated a verse or two from the Book of Proverbs, there was something dreamy (for so literal a man) in the way in which he now shook his right forefinger at the live coals in the grate, and again fell silent.

But not for long. As he sat upright and stiff in his chair, he suddenly rapped his knees, like the carved image of some queer Joss or other coming out of its reverie, and said: 'We must finish this bottle, Mr. Edwin. Let me help you. I'll help Bazzard too, though he *is* asleep. He mightn't like it else.'

He helped them both, and helped himself, and drained his glass, and stood it bottom upward on the table, as though he had just caught a bluebottle in it.

'And now, Mr. Edwin,' he proceeded, wiping his mouth and hands upon his handkerchief: 'to a little piece of business. You received from me, the other day, a certified copy of Miss Rosa's father's will. You knew its contents before, but you received it from me as a matter of business. I should have sent it to Mr. Jasper, but for Miss Rosa's wishing it to come straight to you, in preference. You received it?'

'Quite safely, sir.'

'You should have acknowledged its receipt,' said Mr. Grewgious; 'business being business all the world over. However, you did not.'

'I meant to have acknowledged it when I first came in this evening, sir.'

'Not a business-like acknowledgment,' returned Mr. Grewgious; 'however, let that pass. Now, in that document you have observed a few words of kindly allusion to its being left to me to discharge a little trust, confided to me in conversation, at such time as I in my discretion may think best.'

'Yes, sir.'

'Mr. Edwin, it came into my mind just now, when I was looking at the fire, that I could, in my discretion, acquit myself of that trust at no better time than the present. Favour me with your attention, half a minute.'

He took a bunch of keys from his pocket, singled out by the candle-light the key he wanted, and then, with a candle in his hand, went to a bureau or escritoire, unlocked it, touched the spring of a little secret drawer, and took from it an ordinary ring-case made for a single ring. With this in his hand, he returned to his chair. As he held it up for the young man to see, his hand trembled.

'Mr. Edwin, this rose of diamonds and rubies delicately set in gold, was a ring belonging to Miss Rosa's mother. It was removed from her dead hand, in my presence, with such distracted grief as I hope it may never be my lot to contemplate again. Hard man as I am, I am not hard enough for that. See how bright these stones shine!' opening the case. 'And yet the eyes that were so much brighter, and that so often looked upon them with a light and a proud heart, have been ashes among ashes, and dust among dust, some years! If I had any imagination (which it is needless to say I have not), I might imagine that the lasting beauty of these stones was almost cruel.'

He closed the case again as he spoke.

'This ring was given to the young lady who was drowned so early in her beautiful and happy career, by her husband, when they first plighted their faith to one another. It was he who removed it from her unconscious hand, and it was he who, when his death drew very near, placed it in mine. The trust in which I received it, was, that, you and Miss Rosa growing to manhood and womanhood, and your betrothal prospering and coming to maturity, I should give it to you to place upon her finger. Failing those desired results, it was to remain in my possession.'

Some trouble was in the young man's face, and some indecision was in the action of his hand, as Mr. Grewgious, looking steadfastly at him, gave him the ring.

'Your placing it on her finger,' said Mr. Grewgious, 'will be the solemn seal upon your strict fidelity to the living and the dead. You are going to her, to make the last irrevocable preparations for your marriage. Take it with you.'

The young man took the little case, and placed it in his breast.

'If anything should be amiss, if anything should be even slightly wrong, between you; if you should have any secret consciousness that you are committing yourself to this step for no higher reason than because you have long been accustomed to look forward to it; then,' said Mr. Grewgious, 'I charge you once more, by the living and by the dead, to bring that ring back to me!'

Here Bazzard awoke himself by his own snoring; and, as is usual in such cases, sat apoplectically staring at vacancy, as defying vacancy to accuse him of having been asleep.

'Bazzard!' said Mr. Grewgious, harder than ever.

'I follow you, sir,' said Bazzard, 'and I have been following you.'

'In discharge of a trust, I have handed Mr. Edwin Drood a ring of diamonds and rubies. You see?'

Edwin reproduced the little case, and opened it; and Bazzard looked into it.

'I follow you both, sir,' returned Bazzard, 'and I witness the transaction.'

Evidently anxious to get away and be alone, Edwin Drood now resumed his outer clothing, muttering something about time and appointments. The fog was reported no clearer (by the flying waiter, who alighted from a speculative flight in the coffee interest), but he went out into it; and Bazzard, after his manner, 'followed' him.

Mr. Grewgious, left alone, walked softly and slowly to and fro, for an hour and more. He was restless to-night, and seemed dispirited.

'I hope I have done right,' he said. 'The appeal to him seemed necessary. It was hard to lose the ring, and yet it must have gone from me very soon.'

He closed the empty little drawer with a sigh, and shut and locked the escritoire, and came back to the solitary fireside.

'Her ring,' he went on. 'Will it come back to me? My mind hangs about her ring very uneasily to-night. But that is explainable. I have had it so long, and I have prized it so much! I wonder – '

He was in a wondering mood as well as a restless; for, though he checked himself at that point, and took another walk, he resumed his wondering when he sat down again.

'I wonder (for the ten-thousandth time, and what a weak fool I, for what can it signify now!) whether he confided the charge of their orphan child to me, because he knew – Good God, how like her mother she has become!'

'I wonder whether he ever so much as suspected that some one doted on her, at a hopeless, speechless distance, when he struck in and won her. I wonder whether it ever crept into his mind who that unfortunate some one was!'

'I wonder whether I shall sleep to-night! At all events, I will shut out the world with the bedclothes, and try.'

Mr. Grewgious crossed the staircase to his raw and foggy bedroom, and was soon ready for bed. Dimly catching sight of his face in the misty looking-glass, he held his candle to it for a moment.

'A likely some one, *you*, to come into anybody's thoughts in such an aspect!' he exclaimed. 'There! there! there! Get to bed, poor man, and cease to jabber!'

With that, he extinguished his light, pulled up the bedclothes around him, and with another sigh shut out the world. And yet there are such unexplored romantic nooks in the unlikeliest men, that even old tinderous and touchwoody P. J. T. Possibly Jabbered Thus, at some odd times, in or about seventeen-forty-seven.

CHAPTER XII
A Night with Durdles

WHEN MR. SAPSEA has nothing better to do, towards evening, and finds the contemplation of his own profundity becoming a little monotonous in spite of the vastness of the subject, he often takes an airing in the Cathedral Close and thereabout. He likes to pass the churchyard with a swelling air of proprietorship, and to encourage in his breast a sort of benignant-landlord feeling, in that he has been bountiful towards that meritorious tenant, Mrs. Sapsea, and has publicly given her a prize. He likes to see a stray face or two looking in through the railings, and perhaps reading his inscription. Should he meet a stranger coming from the churchyard with a quick step, he is morally convinced that the stranger is 'with a blush retiring,' as monumentally directed.

Mr. Sapsea's importance has received enhancement, for he has become Mayor of Cloisterham. Without mayors, and many of them, it cannot be disputed that the whole framework of society – Mr. Sapsea is confident that he invented that forcible figure – would fall to pieces. Mayors have been knighted for 'going up' with addresses: explosive machines intrepidly discharging shot and shell into the English Grammar. Mr. Sapsea may 'go up' with an address. Rise, Sir Thomas Sapsea! Of such is the salt of the earth.

Mr. Sapsea has improved the acquaintance of Mr. Jasper, since their first meeting to partake of port, epitaph, backgammon, beef, and salad. Mr. Sapsea has been received at the gatehouse with kindred hospitality; and on that occasion Mr. Jasper seated himself at the piano, and sang to him, tickling his ears – figuratively – long enough to present a considerable area for tickling. What Mr. Sapsea likes in that young man is, that he is always ready to profit by the wisdom of his elders, and that he is sound, sir, at the core. In proof of which, he sang to Mr. Sapsea that evening, no kickshaw ditties, favourites with national enemies, but gave him the genuine George the Third home-brewed; exhorting him (as 'my brave boys') to reduce to a smashed condition all other islands but this island, and all continents, peninsulas, isthmuses, promontories, and other geographical forms of land soever, besides sweeping the seas in all

110

directions. In short, he rendered it pretty clear that Providence made a distinct mistake in originating so small a nation of hearts of oak, and so many other verminous peoples.

Mr. Sapsea, walking slowly this moist evening near the churchyard with his hands behind him, on the look-out for a blushing and retiring stranger, turns a corner, and comes instead into the goodly presence of the Dean, conversing with the Verger and Mr. Jasper. Mr. Sapsea makes his obeisance, and is instantly stricken far more ecclesiastical than any Archbishop of York or Canterbury.

'You are evidently going to write a book about us, Mr. Jasper,' quoth the Dean; 'to write a book about us. Well! We are very ancient, and we ought to make a good book. We are not so richly endowed in possessions as in age; but perhaps you will put *that* in your book, among other things, and call attention to our wrongs.'

Mr. Tope, as in duty bound, is greatly entertained by this.

'I really have no intention at all, sir,' replies Jasper, 'of turning author or archæologist. It is but a whim of mine. And even for my whim, Mr. Sapsea here is more accountable than I am.'

'How so, Mr. Mayor?' says the Dean, with a nod of good-natured recognition of his Fetch. 'How is that, Mr. Mayor?'

'I am not aware,' Mr. Sapsea remarks, looking about him for information, 'to what the Very Reverend the Dean does me the honour of referring.' And then falls to studying his original in minute points of detail.

'Durdles,' Mr. Tope hints.

'Ay!' the Dean echoes; 'Durdles, Durdles!'

'The truth is, sir,' explains Jasper, 'that my curiosity in the man was first really stimulated by Mr. Sapsea. Mr. Sapsea's knowledge of mankind and power of drawing out whatever is recluse or odd around him, first led to my bestowing a second thought upon the man: though of course I had met him constantly about. You would not be surprised by this, Mr. Dean, if you had seen Mr. Sapsea deal with him in his own parlour, as I did.'

'O!' cries Sapsea, picking up the ball thrown to him with ineffable complacency and pomposity; 'yes, yes. The Very Reverend the Dean refers to that? Yes. I happened to bring Durdles and Mr. Jasper together. I regard Durdles as a Character.'

'A character, Mr. Sapsea, that with a few skilful touches you turn inside out,' says Jasper.

'Nay, not quite that,' returns the lumbering auctioneer. 'I may have a little influence over him, perhaps; and a little insight into his character, perhaps. The Very Reverend the Dean will please to bear in mind that I have seen the world.' Here Mr. Sapsea gets a little behind the Dean, to inspect his coat-buttons.

'Well!' says the Dean, looking about him to see what has become of his copyist: 'I hope, Mr. Mayor, you will use your study and knowledge of Durdles to the good purpose of exhorting him not to break our worthy and respected Choir-Master's neck; we cannot afford it; his head and voice are much too valuable to us.'

Mr. Tope is again highly entertained, and, having fallen into respectful convulsions of laughter, subsides into a deferential murmur, importing that surely any gentleman would deem it a pleasure and an honour to have his neck broken, in return for such a compliment from such a source.

'I will take it upon myself, sir,' observes Sapsea loftily, 'to answer for Mr. Jasper's neck. I will tell Durdles to be careful of it. He will mind what *I* say. How is it at present endangered?' he inquires, looking about him with magnificent patronage.

'Only by my making a moonlight expedition with Durdles among the tombs, vaults, towers, and ruins,' returns Jasper. 'You remember suggesting, when you brought us together, that, as a lover of the picturesque, it might be worth my while?'

'I remember!' replies the auctioneer. And the solemn idiot really believes that he does remember.

'Profiting by your hint,' pursues Jasper, 'I have had some day-rambles with the extraordinary old fellow, and we are to make a moonlight hole-and-corner exploration to-night.'

'And here he is,' says the Dean.

Durdles with his dinner-bundle in his hand, is indeed beheld slouching towards them. Slouching nearer, and perceiving the Dean, he pulls off his hat, and is slouching away with it under his arm, when Mr. Sapsea stops him.

'Mind you take care of my friend,' is the injunction Mr. Sapsea lays upon him.

'What friend o' yourn is dead?' asks Durdles. 'No orders has come in for any friend o' yourn.'

'I mean my live friend there.'

'O! him?' says Durdles. 'He can take care of himself, can Mister Jarsper.'

'But do you take care of him too,' says Sapsea.

Whom Durdles (there being command in his tone) surlily surveys from head to foot.

'With submission to his Reverence the Dean, if you'll mind what concerns you, Mr. Sapsea, Durdles he'll mind what concerns him.'

'You're out of temper,' says Mr. Sapsea, winking to the company to observe how smoothly he will manage him. 'My friend concerns me, and Mr. Jasper is my friend. And you are my friend.'

'Don't you get into a bad habit of boasting,' retorts Durdles, with a grave cautionary nod. 'It'll grow upon you.'

'You are out of temper,' says Sapsea again; reddening, but again winking to the company.

'I own to it,' returns Durdles; 'I don't like liberties.'

Mr. Sapsea winks a third wink to the company, as who should say: 'I think you will agree with me that I have settled *his* business;' and stalks out of the controversy.

Durdles then gives the Dean a good evening, and adding, as he puts his hat on, 'You'll find me at home, Mister Jarsper, as agreed, when you want me; I'm a-going home to clean myself,' soon slouches out of sight. This going home to clean himself is one of the man's incomprehensible compromises with inexorable facts; he, and his hat, and his boots, and his clothes, never showing any trace of cleaning, but being uniformly in one condition of dust and grit.

The lamplighter now dotting the quiet Close with specks of light, and running at a great rate up and down his little ladder with that object – his little ladder under the sacred shadow of whose inconvenience generations had grown up, and which all Cloisterham would have stood aghast at the idea of abolishing – the Dean withdraws to his dinner, Mr. Tope to his tea, and Mr. Jasper to his piano. There, with no light but that of the fire, he sits chanting choir-music in a low and beautiful voice, for two or three hours; in short, until it has been for some time dark, and the moon is about to rise.

Then he closes his piano softly, softly changes his coat for a pea-jacket, with a goodly wicker-cased bottle in its largest pocket, and putting on a low-crowned, flap-brimmed hat, goes softly out. Why does he move so softly to-night? No outward reason is apparent for it. Can there be any sympathetic reason crouching darkly within him?

Repairing to Durdles's unfinished house, or hole in the city wall, and seeing a light within it, he softly picks his course among the gravestones, monuments, and stony lumber of the yard, already touched here and there, sidewise, by the rising moon. The two journeymen have left their two great saws sticking in their blocks of stone; and two skeleton journeymen out of the Dance of Death might be grinning in the shadow of their sheltering sentry-boxes, about to slash away at cutting out the gravestones of the next two people destined to die in Cloisterham. Likely enough, the two think little of that now, being alive, and perhaps merry. Curious, to make a guess at the two; – or say one of the two!

'Ho! Durdles!'

The light moves, and he appears with it at the door. He would seem to have been 'cleaning himself' with the aid of a bottle, jug, and tumbler; for no other cleansing instruments are visible in the bare brick room with rafters overhead and no plastered ceiling, into which he shows his visitor.

'Are you ready?'

'I am ready, Mister Jarsper. Let the old 'uns come out if they dare, when we go among their tombs. My spirit is ready for 'em.'

'Do you mean animal spirits, or ardent?'

'The one's the t'other,' answers Durdles, 'and I mean 'em both.'

He takes a lantern from a hook, puts a match or two in his pocket wherewith to light it, should there be need; and they go out together, dinner-bundle and all.

Surely an unaccountable sort of expedition! That Durdles himself, who is always prowling among old graves, and ruins, like a Ghoul – that he should be stealing forth to climb, and dive, and wander without an object, is nothing extraordinary; but that the Choir-Master or any one else should hold it worth his while to be with him, and to study moonlight effects in such company is another affair. Surely an unaccountable sort of expedition, therefore!

''Ware that there mound by the yard-gate, Mister Jarsper.'

'I see it. What is it?'

'Lime.'

Mr. Jasper stops, and waits for him to come up, for he lags behind. 'What you call quick-lime?'

'Ay!' says Durdles; 'quick enough to eat your boots. With a little handy stirring, quick enough to eat your bones.'

They go on, presently passing the red windows of the Travellers' Twopenny, and emerging into the clear moonlight of the Monks' Vineyard. This crossed, they come to Minor Canon Corner: of which the greater part lies in shadow until the moon shall rise higher in the sky.

The sound of a closing house-door strikes their ears, and two men come out. These are Mr. Crisparkle and Neville. Jasper, with a strange and sudden smile upon his face, lays the palm of his hand upon the breast of Durdles, stopping him where he stands.

At that end of Minor Canon Corner the shadow is profound in the existing state of the light: at that end, too, there is a piece of old dwarf wall, breast high, the only remaining boundary of what was once a garden, but is now the thoroughfare. Jasper and Durdles would have turned this wall in another instant; but, stopping so short, stand behind it.

'Those two are only sauntering,' Jasper whispers; 'they will go out into the moonlight soon. Let us keep quiet here, or they will detain us, or want to join us, or what not.'

Durdles nods assent, and falls to munching some fragments from his bundle. Jasper folds his arms upon the top of the wall, and, with his chin resting on them, watches. He takes no note whatever of the Minor Canon, but watches Neville, as though his eye were at the trigger of a loaded rifle, and he had covered him, and were going to fire. A sense of destructive power is so expressed in his face, that even Durdles pauses in his munching, and looks at him, with an unmunched something in his cheek.

Meanwhile Mr. Crisparkle and Neville walk to and fro, quietly talking together. What they say, cannot be heard consecutively; but Mr. Jasper has already distinguished his own name more than once.

'This is the first day of the week,' Mr. Crisparkle can be distinctly heard to observe, as they turn back; 'and the last day of the week is Christmas Eve.'

'You may be certain of me, sir.'

The echoes were favourable at those points, but as the two approach, the sound of their talking becomes confused again. The word 'confidence,' shattered by the echoes, but still capable of being pieced together, is uttered by Mr. Crisparkle. As they draw still nearer, this fragment of a reply is heard: 'Not deserved yet, but shall be, sir.' As they turn away again, Jasper again hears his own name, in connection with the words from Mr. Crisparkle: 'Remember that I said I answered for you confidently.' Then the sound of their talk becomes confused again; they halting for a little while, and some earnest action on the part of Neville succeeding. When they move once more, Mr. Crisparkle is seen to look up at the sky, and to point before him. They then slowly disappear; passing out into the moonlight at the opposite end of the Corner.

It is not until they are gone, that Mr. Jasper moves. But then he turns to Durdles, and bursts into a fit of laughter. Durdles, who still has that suspended something in his cheek, and who sees nothing to laugh at, stares at him until Mr. Jasper lays his face down on his arms to have his laugh out. Then Durdles bolts the something, as if desperately resigning himself to indigestion.

Among those secluded nooks there is very little stir or movement after dark. There is little enough in the high tide of the day, but there is next to none at night. Besides that the cheerfully frequented High Street lies nearly parallel to the spot (the old Cathedral rising between the two), and is the natural channel in which the Cloisterham traffic flows, a certain awful hush pervades the ancient pile, the cloisters, and the churchyard, after dark, which not many people care to encounter. Ask the first hundred citizens of Cloisterham, met at random in the streets at noon, if they believed in Ghosts, they would tell you no; but put them to choose at night between these eerie Precincts and the thoroughfare of shops, and you would find that ninety-nine declared for the longer round and the more frequented way. The cause of this is not to be found in any local superstition that attaches to the Precincts – albeit a mysterious lady, with a child in her arms and a rope dangling from her neck, has been seen flitting about there by sundry witnesses as intangible as herself – but it is to be sought in the innate shrinking of dust with the breath of life in it from dust out of which the breath of life has passed; also, in the widely diffused, and almost as widely unacknowledged, reflection: 'If the dead do, under any circumstances, become visible to the living, these are such likely surroundings for the purpose that I, the living, will get out of them as soon as I can.' Hence, when Mr. Jasper and Durdles pause to glance around them, before descending into the crypt by a small side door, of which the latter has a key, the whole expanse of moonlight in their view is utterly deserted. One might fancy that the tide of life was stemmed by Mr. Jasper's own gatehouse. The murmur of the tide is heard beyond; but no wave passes the archway, over which his lamp burns red behind his curtain, as if the building were a Lighthouse.

They enter, locking themselves in, descend the rugged steps, and are down in the Crypt. The lantern is not wanted, for the moonlight strikes in at the groined windows, bare of glass, the broken frames for which cast patterns on the ground. The heavy pillars which support the roof engender masses of black shade, but between them there are lanes of light. Up and down these lanes they walk, Durdles discoursing of the 'old uns' he yet counts on disinterring, and slapping a wall, in which he considers 'a whole family on 'em' to be stoned and earthed up, just as if he were a familiar friend of the family. The taciturnity of Durdles is for the time overcome by Mr. Jasper's wicker bottle, which circulates freely; – in the sense, that is to say, that its contents enter freely into Mr. Durdles's circulation, while Mr. Jasper only rinses his mouth once, and casts forth the rinsing.

They are to ascend the great Tower. On the steps by which they rise to the Cathedral, Durdles pauses for new store of breath. The steps are very dark, but out of the darkness they can see the lanes of light they have traversed. Durdles seats himself upon a step. Mr. Jasper seats himself upon another. The odour from the wicker bottle (which has somehow passed into Durdles's keeping) soon intimates that the cork has been taken out; but this is not ascertainable through the sense of sight, since neither can descry the other. And yet, in talking, they turn to one another, as though their faces could commune together.

'This is good stuff, Mister Jarsper!'

'It is very good stuff, I hope. – I bought it on purpose.'

'They don't show, you see, the old uns don't, Mister Jarsper!'

'It would be a more confused world than it is, if they could.'

'Well, it *would* lead towards a mixing of things,' Durdles acquiesces: pausing on the remark, as if the idea of ghosts had not previously presented itself to him in a merely inconvenient light, domestically or chronologically. 'But do you think there may be Ghosts of other things, though not of men and women?'

'What things? Flower-beds and watering-pots? horses and harness?'

'No. Sounds.'

'What sounds?'

'Cries.'

'What cries do you mean? Chairs to mend?'

'No. I mean screeches. Now I'll tell you, Mr. Jarsper. Wait a bit till I put the bottle right.' Here the cork is evidently taken out again, and replaced again. 'There! *Now* it's right! This time last year, only a few days later, I happened to have been doing what was correct by the season, in the way of giving it the welcome it had a right to expect, when them town-boys set on me at their worst. At length I gave 'em the slip, and turned in here. And here I fell asleep. And what woke me? The ghost of a cry. The ghost of one terrific shriek, which shriek was followed by the ghost of the howl of a dog: a long, dismal, woeful howl, such as a dog gives when a person's dead. That was *my* last Christmas Eve.'

'What do you mean?' is the very abrupt, and, one might say, fierce retort.

'I mean that I made inquiries everywhere about, and, that no living ears but mine heard either that cry or that howl. So I say they was both ghosts; though why they came to me, I've never made out.'

'I thought you were another kind of man,' says Jasper, scornfully.

'So I thought myself,' answers Durdles with his usual composure; 'and yet I was picked out for it.'

Jasper had risen suddenly, when he asked him what he meant, and he now says, 'Come; we shall freeze here; lead the way.'

Durdles complies, not over-steadily; opens the door at the top of the steps with the key he has already used; and so emerges on the Cathedral level, in a passage at the side of the chancel. Here, the moonlight is so very bright again that the colours of the nearest stained-glass window are thrown upon their faces. The appearance of the unconscious Durdles, holding the door open for his companion to follow, as if from the grave, is ghastly enough, with a purple hand across his face, and a yellow splash upon his brow; but he bears the close scrutiny of his companion in an insensible way, although it is prolonged while the latter fumbles among his pockets for a key confided to him that will open an iron gate, so to enable them to pass to the staircase of the great tower.

'That and the bottle are enough for you to carry,' he says, giving it to Durdles; 'hand your bundle to me; I am younger and longer-winded than you.' Durdles hesitates for a moment between bundle and bottle; but gives the preference to the bottle as being by far the better company, and consigns the dry weight to his fellow-explorer.

Then they go up the winding staircase of the great tower, toilsomely, turning and turning, and lowering their heads to avoid the stairs above, or the rough stone pivot around which they twist. Durdles has lighted his lantern, by drawing from the cold, hard wall a spark of that mysterious fire which lurks in everything, and, guided by this speck, they clamber up among the cobwebs and the dust. Their way lies through strange places. Twice or thrice they emerge into level, low-arched galleries, whence they can look down into the moon-lit nave; and where Durdles, waving his lantern, waves the dim angels' heads upon the corbels of the roof, seeming to watch their progress. Anon they turn into narrower and steeper staircases, and the night-air begins to blow upon them, and the chirp of some startled jackdaw or frightened rook precedes the heavy beating of wings in a confined space, and the beating down of dust and straws upon their heads. At last, leaving their light behind a stair – for it blows fresh up here – they look down on Cloisterham, fair to see in the moonlight: its ruined habitations and sanctuaries of the dead, at the tower's base: its moss-softened red-tiled roofs and red-brick houses of the living, clustered beyond: its river winding down from the mist on the horizon, as though that were its source, and already heaving with a restless knowledge of its approach towards the sea.

Once again, an unaccountable expedition this! Jasper (always moving softly with no visible reason) contemplates the scene, and especially that stillest part of it which the Cathedral overshadows. But he contemplates Durdles quite as curiously, and Durdles is by times conscious of his watchful eyes.

Only by times, because Durdles is growing drowsy. As aëronauts lighten the load they carry, when they wish to rise, similarly Durdles has lightened the wicker bottle in coming up. Snatches of sleep surprise him on his legs, and stop him in his talk. A mild fit of calenture seizes him, in which he deems that the ground so far below, is on a level with the tower, and would as lief walk off the tower into the air as not. Such is his state when they begin to come down. And as aëronauts make themselves heavier when they wish to descend, similarly Durdles charges himself with more liquid from the wicker bottle, that he may come down the better.

The iron gate attained and locked – but not before Durdles has tumbled twice, and cut an eyebrow open once – they descend into the crypt again, with the intent of issuing forth as they entered. But, while returning among those lanes of light, Durdles becomes so very uncertain, both of foot and speech, that he half drops, half throws himself down, by one of the heavy pillars, scarcely less heavy than itself, and indistinctly appeals to his companion for forty winks of a second each.

'If you will have it so, or must have it so,' replies Jasper, 'I'll not leave you here. Take them, while I walk to and fro.'

Durdles is asleep at once; and in his sleep he dreams a dream.

It is not much of a dream, considering the vast extent of the domains of dreamland, and their wonderful productions; it is only remarkable for being unusually restless and unusually real. He dreams of lying there, asleep, and yet counting his companion's footsteps as he walks to and fro. He dreams that the footsteps die away into distance of time and of space, and that something touches him, and that something falls from his hand. Then something clinks and gropes about, and he dreams that he is alone for so long a time, that the lanes of light take new directions as the moon advances in her course. From succeeding unconsciousness he passes into a dream of slow uneasiness from cold; and painfully awakes to a perception of the lanes of light – really changed, much as he had dreamed – and Jasper walking among them, beating his hands and feet.

'Holloa!' Durdles cries out, unmeaningly alarmed.

'Awake at last?' says Jasper, coming up to him. 'Do you know that your forties have stretched into thousands?'

'No.'

'They have though.'

'What's the time?'

'Hark! The bells are going in the Tower!'

They strike four quarters, and then the great bell strikes.

'Two!' cries Durdles, scrambling up; 'why didn't you try to wake me, Mister Jarsper?'

'I did. I might as well have tried to wake the dead – your own family of dead, up in the corner there.'

'Did you touch me?'

'Touch you! Yes. Shook you.'

As Durdles recalls that touching something in his dream, he looks down on the pavement, and sees the key of the crypt door lying close to where he himself lay.

'I dropped you, did I?' he says, picking it up, and recalling that part of his dream. As he gathers himself up again into an upright position, or into a position as nearly upright as he ever maintains, he is again conscious of being watched by his companion.

'Well?' says Jasper, smiling, 'are you quite ready? Pray don't hurry.'

'Let me get my bundle right, Mister Jarsper, and I'm with you.' As he ties it afresh, he is once more conscious that he is very narrowly observed.

'What do you suspect me of, Mister Jarsper?' he asks, with drunken displeasure. 'Let them as has any suspicions of Durdles name 'em.'

'I've no suspicions of you, my good Mr. Durdles; but I have

suspicions that my bottle was filled with something stiffer than either of us supposed. And I also have suspicions,' Jasper adds, taking it from the pavement and turning it bottom upwards, 'that it's empty.'

Durdles condescends to laugh at this. Continuing to chuckle when his laugh is over, as though remonstrant with himself on his drinking powers, he rolls to the door and unlocks it. They both pass out, and Durdles relocks it, and pockets his key.

'A thousand thanks for a curious and interesting night,' says Jasper, giving him his hand; 'you can make your own way home?'

'I should think so!' answers Durdles. 'If you was to offer Durdles the affront to show him his way home, he wouldn't go home.

> 'Durdles wouldn't go home till morning;
> And then Durdles wouldn't go home,

Durdles wouldn't.' This with the utmost defiance.

'Good-night, then.'

'Good-night, Mister Jarsper.'

Each is turning his own way, when a sharp whistle rends the silence, and the jargon is yelped out:

> 'Widdy widdy wen!
> I – ket – ches – Im – out – ar – ter – ten.
> Widdy widdy wy!
> Then – E – don't – go – then – I – shy –
> Widdy Widdy Wake-cock warning!'

Instantly afterwards, a rapid fire of stones rattles at the Cathedral wall, and the hideous small boy is beheld opposite, dancing in the moonlight.

'What! Is that baby-devil on the watch there!' cries Jasper in a fury: so quickly roused, and so violent, that he seems an older devil himself. 'I shall shed the blood of that impish wretch! I know I shall do it!' Regardless of the fire, though it hits him more than once, he rushes at Deputy, collars him, and tries to bring him across. But Deputy is not to be so easily brought across. With a diabolical insight into the strongest part of his position, he is no sooner taken by the throat than he curls up his legs, forces his assailant to hang him, as it were, and gurgles in his throat, and screws his body, and twists, as already undergoing the first agonies of strangulation. There is nothing for it but to drop him. He instantly gets himself together, backs over to Durdles, and cries to his assailant, gnashing the great gap in front of his mouth with rage and malice:

'I'll blind yer, s'elp me! I'll stone yer eyes out, s'elp me! If I don't have yer eyesight, bellows me!' At the same time dodging behind Durdles, and snarling at Jasper, now from this side of him, and now from that: prepared, if pounced upon, to dart away in all manner of curvilinear directions, and, if run down after all, to grovel in the dust, and cry: 'Now, hit me when I'm down! Do it!'

'Don't hurt the boy, Mister Jarsper,' urges Durdles, shielding him. 'Recollect yourself.'

'He followed us to-night, when we first came here!'

'Yer lie, I didn't!' replies Deputy, in his one form of polite contradiction.

'He has been prowling near us ever since!'

'Yer lie, I haven't,' returns Deputy. 'I'd only jist come out for my 'elth when I see you two a-coming out of the Kinfreederel. If –

'I – ket – ches – Im – out – ar – ter – ten!'

(with the usual rhythm and dance, though dodging behind Durdles), 'it ain't *any* fault, is it?'

'Take him home, then,' retorts Jasper, ferociously, though with a strong check upon himself, 'and let my eyes be rid of the sight of you!'

Deputy, with another sharp whistle, at once expressing his relief, and his commencement of a milder stoning of Mr. Durdles, begins stoning that respectable gentleman home, as if he were a reluctant ox. Mr. Jasper goes to his gatehouse, brooding. And thus, as everything comes to an end, the unaccountable expedition comes to an end – for the time.

* D *

CHAPTER XIII
Both at their Best

MISS TWINKLETON'S ESTABLISHMENT was about to undergo a serene hush. The Christmas recess was at hand. What had once, and at no remote period, been called, even by the erudite Miss Twinkleton herself, 'the half;' but what was now called, as being more elegant, and more strictly collegiate, 'the term,' would expire to-morrow. A noticeable relaxation of discipline had for some few days pervaded the Nuns' House. Club suppers had occurred in the bedrooms, and a dressed tongue had been carved with a pair of scissors, and handed round with the curling tongs. Portions of marmalade had likewise been distributed on a service of plates constructed of curlpaper; and cowslip wine had been quaffed from the small squat measuring glass in which little Rickitts (a junior of weakly constitution) took her steel drops daily. The housemaids had been bribed with various fragments of riband, and sundry pairs of shoes more or less down at heel, to make no mention of crumbs in the beds; the airiest costumes had been worn on these festive occasions; and the daring Miss Ferdinand had even surprised the company with a sprightly solo on the comb-and-curlpaper, until suffocated in her own pillow by two flowing-haired executioners.

Nor were these the only tokens of dispersal. Boxes appeared in the bedrooms (where they were capital at other times), and a surprising amount of packing took place, out of all proportion to the amount packed. Largess, in the form of odds and ends of cold cream and pomatum, and also of hairpins, was freely distributed among the attendants. On charges of inviolable secrecy, confidences were interchanged respecting golden youth of England expected to call, 'at home,' on the first opportunity. Miss Giggles (deficient in sentiment) did indeed profess that she, for her part, acknowledged such homage by making faces at the golden youth; but this young lady was outvoted by an immense majority.

On the last night before a recess, it was always expressly made a point of honour that nobody should go to sleep, and that Ghosts should be encouraged by all possible means. This compact invariably broke down, and all the young ladies went to sleep very soon, and got up very early.

The concluding ceremony came off at twelve o'clock on the day of departure; when Miss Twinkleton, supported by Mrs. Tisher, held a drawing-room in her own apartment (the globes already covered with brown Holland), where glasses of white-wine and plates of cut pound-cake were discovered on the table. Miss Twinkleton then said: Ladies, another revolving year had brought us round to that festive period at which the first feelings of our nature bounded in our – Miss Twinkleton was annually going to add 'bosoms,' but annually stopped on the brink of that expression, and substituted 'hearts.' Hearts; our hearts. Hem! Again a revolving year, ladies, had brought us to a pause in our studies – let us hope our greatly advanced studies – and, like the mariner in his bark, the warrior in his tent, the captive in his dungeon, and the traveller in his various conveyances, we yearned for home. Did we say, on such an occasion, in the opening words of Mr. Addison's impressive tragedy:

> 'The dawn is overcast, the morning lowers,
> And heavily in clouds brings on the day,
> The great, th' important day – ?'

Not so. From horizon to zenith all was *couleur de rose*, for all was redolent of our relations and friends. Might *we* find *them* prospering as *we* expected; might *they* find *us* prospering as *they* expected! Ladies, we would now, with our love to one another, wish one another good-bye, and happiness, until we met again. And when the time should come for our resumption of those pursuits which (here a general depression set in all round), pursuits which, pursuits which; – then let us ever remember what was said by the Spartan General, in words too trite for repetition, at the battle it were superfluous to specify.

The handmaidens of the establishment, in their best caps, then handed the trays, and the young ladies sipped and crumbled, and the bespoken coaches began to choke the street. Then leave-taking was not long about; and Miss Twinkleton, in saluting each young lady's cheek, confided to her an exceedingly neat letter, addressed to her next friend at law, 'with Miss Twinkleton's best compliments' in the corner. This missive she handed with an air as if it had not the least connexion with the bill, but were something in the nature of a delicate and joyful surprise.

So many times had Rosa seen such dispersals, and so very little did she know of any other Home, that she was contented to remain where she was, and was even better contented than ever before, having her latest friend with her. And yet her latest friendship had a blank place in it of which she could not fail to be sensible. Helena Landless, having been a party to her brother's revelation about Rosa, and having entered into that compact of silence with Mr. Crisparkle, shrank from any allusion to Edwin Drood's name. Why she so avoided it, was mysterious to Rosa, but she perfectly perceived the fact. But for the fact, she might have relieved her own little perplexed heart of some of its doubts and hesitations, by taking Helena into her confidence. As it was, she had no such vent: she could only ponder on her own difficulties, and wonder more and more why this avoidance of Edwin's name should last, now that she knew – for so much Helena had told her – that a good understanding was to be reëstablished between the two young men, when Edwin came down.

It would have made a pretty picture, so many pretty girls kissing Rosa in the cold porch of the Nuns' House, and that sunny little creature peeping out of it (unconscious of sly faces carved on spout and gable peeping at her), and waving farewells to the departing coaches, as if she represented the spirit of rosy youth abiding in the place to keep it bright and warm in its desertion. The hoarse High Street became musical with the cry, in various silvery voices, 'Good-bye, Rosebud darling!' and the effigy of Mr. Sapsea's father over the opposite doorway seemed to say to mankind: 'Gentlemen, favour me with your attention to this charming little last lot left behind, and bid with a spirit worthy of the occasion!' Then the staid street, so unwontedly sparkling, youthful, and fresh for a few rippling moments, ran dry, and Cloisterham was itself again.

If Rosebud in her bower now waited Edwin Drood's coming with an uneasy heart, Edwin for his part was uneasy too. With far less force of purpose in his composition than the childish beauty, crowned by acclamation fairy queen of Miss Twinkleton's establishment, he had a conscience, and Mr. Grewgious had pricked it. That gentleman's steady convictions of what was right and what was wrong in such a case as his, were neither to be frowned aside nor laughed aside. They would not be moved. But for the dinner in Staple Inn, and but for the ring he carried in the breast pocket of his coat, he would have drifted into their wedding-day without another pause for real thought, loosely trusting that all would go well, left alone. But that serious putting him on his truth to the living and the dead had brought him to a check. He must either give the ring to Rosa, or he must take it back. Once put into this narrowed way of action, it was curious that he began to consider Rosa's claims upon him more unselfishly than he had ever considered them before, and began to be less sure of himself than he had ever been in all his easy-going days.

'I will be guided by what she says, and by how we get on,' was his decision, walking from the gatehouse to the Nuns' House. 'Whatever comes of it, I will bear his words in mind, and try to be true to the living and the dead.'

Rosa was dressed for walking. She expected him. It was a bright, frosty day, and Miss Twinkleton had already graciously sanctioned fresh air. Thus they got out together before it became necessary for either Miss Twinkleton, or the deputy high-priest Mrs. Tisher, to lay even so much as one of those usual offerings on the shrine of Propriety.

'My dear Eddy,' said Rosa, when they had turned out of the High Street, and had got among the quiet walks in the neighbourhood of the Cathedral and the river: 'I want to say something very serious to you. I have been thinking about it for a long, long time.'

'I want to be serious with you too, Rosa dear. I mean to be serious and earnest.'

'Thank you, Eddy. And you will not think me unkind because I begin, will you? You will not think I speak for myself only, because I speak first? That would not be generous, would it? And I know you are generous!'

He said, 'I hope I am not ungenerous to you, Rosa.' He called her Pussy no more. Never again.

'And there is no fear,' pursued Rosa, 'of our quarrelling, is there? Because, Eddy,' clasping her hand on his arm, 'we have so much reason to be very lenient to each other!'

'We will be, Rosa.'

'That's a dear good boy! Eddy, let us be courageous. Let us change to brother and sister from this day forth.'

'Never be husband and wife?'

'Never!'

Neither spoke again for a little while. But after that pause he said, with some effort:

'Of course I know that this has been in both our minds, Rosa, and of course I am in honour bound to confess freely that it does not originate with you.'

'No, nor with you, dear,' she returned, with pathetic earnestness. 'That sprung up between us. You are not truly happy in our engagement; I am not truly happy in it. O, I am so sorry, so sorry!' And there she broke into tears.

'I am deeply sorry too, Rosa. Deeply sorry for you.'

'And I for you, poor boy! And I for you!'

This pure young feeling, this gentle and forbearing feeling of each towards the other, brought with it its reward in a softening light that seemed to shine on their position. The relations between them did not look wilful, or capricious, or a failure, in such a light; they became elevated into something more self-denying, honourable, affectionate, and true.

'If we knew yesterday,' said Rosa, as she dried her eyes, 'and we did know yesterday, and on many, many yesterdays, that we were far from right together in those relations which were not of our own choosing, what better could we do to-day than change them? It is natural that we should be sorry, and you see how sorry we both are; but how much better to be sorry now than then!'

'When, Rosa?'

'When it would be too late. And then we should be angry, besides.'

Another silence fell upon them.

'And you know,' said Rosa innocently, 'you couldn't like me then; and you can always like me now, for I shall not be a drag upon you, or a worry to you. And I can always like you now, and your sister will not tease or trifle with you. I often did when I was not your sister, and I beg your pardon for it.'

'Don't let us come to that, Rosa; or I shall want more pardoning than I like to think of.'

'No, indeed, Eddy; you are too hard, my generous boy, upon yourself. Let us sit down, brother, on these ruins, and let me tell you how it was with us. I think I know, for I have considered about it very much since you were here last time. You liked me, didn't you? You thought I was a nice little thing?'

'Everybody thinks that, Rosa.'

'Do they?' She knitted her brow musingly for a moment, and then flashed out with the bright little induction: 'Well, but say they do. Surely it was not enough that you should think of me only as other people did; now, was it?'

The point was not to be got over. It was not enough.

'And that is just what I mean; that is just how it was with us,' said Rosa. 'You liked me very well, and you had grown used to me, and had grown used to the idea of our being married. You accepted the situation as an inevitable kind of thing, didn't you? It was to be, you thought, and why discuss or dispute it?'

It was new and strange to him to have himself presented to himself so clearly, in a glass of her holding up. He had always patronised her, in his superiority to her share of woman's wit. Was that but another instance of something radically amiss in the terms on which they had been gliding towards a life-long bondage?

'All this that I say of you is true of me as well, Eddy. Unless it was, I might not be bold enough to say it. Only, the difference between us was, that by little and little there crept into my mind a habit of thinking about it, instead of dismissing it. My life is not so busy as yours, you see, and I have not so many things to think of. So I thought about it very much, and I cried about it very much too (though that was not your fault, poor boy); when all at once my guardian came down, to prepare for my leaving the Nuns' House. I tried to hint to him that I was not quite settled in my mind, but I hesitated and failed, and he didn't understand me. But he is a good, good man. And he put before me so kindly, and yet so strongly, how seriously we ought to consider, in our circumstances, that I resolved to speak to you the next moment we were alone and grave. And if I seemed to come to it easily just now, because I came to it all at once, don't think it was so really, Eddy, for O, it was very, very hard, and O, I am very, very sorry!'

Her full heart broke into tears again. He put his arm about her waist, and they walked by the river-side together.

'Your guardian has spoken to me too, Rosa dear. I saw him before I left London.' His right hand was in his breast, seeking the ring; but he checked it, as he thought: 'If I am to take it back, why should I tell her of it?'

'And that made you more serious about it, didn't it, Eddy? And if I had not spoken to you, as I have, you would have spoken to me? I hope you can tell me so? I don't like it to be *all* my doing, though it *is* so much better for us.'

'Yes, I should have spoken; I should have put everything before you; I came intending to do it. But I never could have spoken to you as you have spoken to me, Rosa.'

'Don't say you mean so coldly or unkindly, Eddy, please, if you can help it.'

'I mean so sensibly and delicately, so wisely and affectionately.'

'That's my dear brother!' She kissed his hand in a little rapture. 'The dear girls will be dreadfully disappointed,' added Rosa, laughing, with the dewdrops glistening in her bright eyes. 'They have looked forward to it so, poor pets!'

'Ah! but I fear it will be a worse disappointment to Jack,' said Edwin

Drood, with a start. 'I never thought of Jack!'

Her swift and intent look at him as he said the words could no more be recalled than a flash of lightning can. But it appeared as though she would have instantly recalled it, if she could; for she looked down, confused, and breathed quickly.

'You don't doubt its being a blow to Jack, Rosa?'

She merely replied, and that evasively and hurriedly: Why should she? She had not thought about it. He seemed, to her, to have so little to do with it.

'My dear child! can you suppose that any one so wrapped up in another – Mrs. Tope's expression: not mine – as Jack is in me, could fail to be struck all of a heap by such a sudden and complete change in my life? I say sudden, because it will be sudden to *him*, you know.'

She nodded twice or thrice, and her lips parted as if she would have assented. But she uttered no sound, and her breathing was no slower.

'How shall I tell Jack?' said Edwin, ruminating. If he had been less occupied with the thought, he must have seen her singular emotion. 'I never thought of Jack. It must be broken to him, before the town-crier knows it. I dine with the dear fellow to-morrow and next day – Christmas Eve and Christmas Day – but it would never do to spoil his feast-days. He always worries about me, and moddley-coddleys in the merest trifles. The news is sure to overset him. How on earth shall this be broken to Jack?'

'He must be told, I suppose?' said Rosa.

'My dear Rosa! who ought to be in our confidence, if not Jack?'

'My guardian promised to come down, if I should write and ask him. I am going to do so. Would you like to leave it to him?'

'A bright idea!' cried Edwin. 'The other trustee. Nothing more natural. He comes down, he goes to Jack, he relates what we have agreed upon, and he states our case better than we could. He has already spoken feelingly to you, he has already spoken feelingly to me, and he'll put the whole thing feelingly to Jack. That's it! I am not a coward, Rosa, but to tell you a secret, I am a little afraid of Jack.'

'No, no! you are not afraid of him!' cried Rosa, turning white, and clasping her hands.

'Why, sister Rosa, sister Rosa, what do you see from the turret?' said Edwin, rallying her. 'My dear girl!'

'You frightened me.'

129

'Most unintentionally, but I am as sorry as if I had meant to do it. Could you possibly suppose for a moment, from any loose way of speaking of mine, that I was literally afraid of the dear fond fellow? What I mean is, that he is subject to a kind of paroxysm, or fit – I saw him in it once – and I don't know but that so great a surprise, coming upon him direct from me whom he is so wrapped up in, might bring it on perhaps. Which – and this is the secret I was going to tell you – is another reason for your guardian's making the communication. He is so steady, precise, and exact, that he will talk Jack's thoughts into shape, in no time: whereas with me Jack is always impulsive and hurried, and, I may say, almost womanish.'

Rosa seemed convinced. Perhaps from her own very different point of view of 'Jack,' she felt comforted and protected by the interposition of Mr. Grewgious between herself and him.

And now, Edwin Drood's right hand closed again upon the ring in its little case, and again was checked by the consideration: 'It is certain, now, that I am to give it back to him; then why should I tell her of it?' That pretty sympathetic nature which could be so sorry for him in the blight of their childish hopes of happiness together, and could so quietly find itself alone in a new world to weave fresh wreaths of such flowers as it might prove to bear, the old world's flowers being withered, would be grieved by those sorrowful jewels; and to what purpose? Why should it be? They were but a sign of broken joys and baseless projects; in their very beauty they were (as the unlikeliest of men had said) almost a cruel satire on the loves, hopes, plans, of humanity, which are able to forecast nothing, and are so much brittle dust. Let them be. He would restore them to her guardian when he came down; he in his turn would restore them to the cabinet from which he had unwillingly taken them; and there, like old letters or old vows, or other records of old aspirations come to nothing, they would be disregarded, until, being valuable, they were sold into circulation again, to repeat their former round.

Let them be. Let them lie unspoken of, in his breast. However distinctly or indistinctly he entertained these thoughts, he arrived at the conclusion, Let them be. Among the mighty store of wonderful chains that are for ever forging, day and night, in the vast iron-works of time and circumstance, there was one chain forged in the moment of that small conclusion, riveted to the foundations of heaven and earth, and gifted with invincible force to hold and drag.

They walked on by the river. They began to speak of their separate plans. He would quicken his departure from England, and she would remain where she was, at least as long as Helena remained. The poor dear girls should have their disappointment broken to them gently, and, as the first preliminary, Miss Twinkleton should be confided in by Rosa, even in advance of the reappearance of Mr. Grewgious. It should be made clear in all quarters that she and Edwin were the best of friends. There had never been so serene an understanding between them since they were first affianced. And yet there was one reservation on each side; on hers, that she intended through her guardian to withdraw herself immediately from the tuition of her music-master; on his, that he did already entertain some wandering speculations whether it might ever come to pass that he would know more of Miss Landless.

The bright, frosty day declined as they walked and spoke together. The sun dipped in the river far behind them, and the old city lay red before them, as their walk drew to a close. The moaning water cast its seaweed duskily at their feet, when they turned to leave its margin; and the rooks hovered above them with hoarse cries, darker splashes in the darkening air.

'I will prepare Jack for my flitting soon,' said Edwin, in a low voice, 'and I will but see your guardian when he comes, and then go before they speak together. It will be better done without my being by. Don't you think so?'

'Yes.'

'We know we have done right, Rosa?'

'Yes.'

'We know we are better so, even now?'

'And shall be far, far better so by-and-by.'

Still there was that lingering tenderness in their hearts towards the old positions they were relinquishing, that they prolonged their parting. When they came among the elm-trees by the Cathedral, where they had last sat together, they stopped as by consent, and Rosa raised her face to his, as she had never raised it in the old days; – for they were old already.

'God bless you, dear! Good-bye!'

'God bless you, dear! Good-bye!'

They kissed each other fervently.

'Now, please take me home, Eddy, and let me be by myself.'

'Don't look round, Rosa,' he cautioned her, as he drew her arm through his, and led her away. 'Didn't you see Jack?'

'No! Where?'

'Under the trees. He saw us, as we took leave of each other. Poor fellow! he little thinks we have parted. This will be a blow to him, I am much afraid!'

She hurried on, without resting, and hurried on until they had passed under the gatehouse into the street; once there, she asked:

'Has he followed us? You can look without seeming to. Is he behind?'

'No. Yes, he is! He has just passed out under the gateway. The dear, sympathetic old fellow likes to keep us in sight. I am afraid he will be bitterly disappointed!'

She pulled hurriedly at the handle of the hoarse old bell, and the gate soon opened. Before going in, she gave him one last, wide, wondering look, as if she would have asked him with imploring emphasis: 'O! don't you understand?' And out of that look he vanished from her view.

CHAPTER XIV
When Shall These Three Meet Again?

CHRISTMAS EVE IN Cloisterham. A few strange faces in the streets; a few other faces, half strange and half familiar, once the faces of Cloisterham children, now the faces of men and women who come back from the outer world at long intervals to find the city wonderfully shrunken in size, as if it had not washed by any means well in the meanwhile. To these, the striking of the Cathedral clock, and the cawing of the rooks from the Cathedral tower, are like voices of their nursery time. To such as these, it has happened in their dying hours afar off, that they have imagined their chamber-floor to be strewn with the autumnal leaves fallen from the elm-trees in the Close: so have the rustling sounds and fresh scents of their earliest impressions revived when the circle of their lives was very nearly traced, and the beginning and the end were drawing close together.

Seasonable tokens are about. Red berries shine here and there in the lattices of Minor Canon Corner; Mr. and Mrs. Tope are daintily sticking sprigs of holly into the carvings and sconces of the Cathedral stalls, as if they were sticking them into the coat-button-holes of the Dean and Chapter. Lavish profusion is in the shops: particularly in the articles of currants, raisins, spices, candied peel, and moist sugar. An unusual air of gallantry and dissipation is abroad; evinced in an immense bunch of mistletoe hanging in the greengrocer's shop doorway, and a poor little Twelfth Cake, culminating in the figure of a Harlequin – such a very poor little Twelfth Cake, that one would rather called it a Twenty-fourth Cake or a Forty-eighth Cake – to be raffled for at the pastrycook's, terms one shilling per member. Public amusements are not wanting. The Wax-Work which made so deep an impression on the reflective mind of the Emperor of China is to be seen by particular desire during Christmas Week only, on the premises of the bankrupt livery-stable-keeper up the lane; and a new grand comic Christmas pantomime is to be produced at the Theatre: the latter heralded by the portrait of Signor Jacksonini the clown, saying 'How do you do to-morrow?' quite as large as life, and almost as miserably. In short, Cloisterham is up and doing: though from this description the High School and Miss Twinkleton's are to be excluded. From the former establishment the scholars have gone home, every one of them in love with one of Miss Twinkleton's young ladies (who knows nothing about it); and only the handmaidens flutter occasionally in the windows of the latter. It is noticed, by the bye, that these damsels become, within the limits of decorum, more skittish when thus intrusted with the concrete representation of their sex, than when dividing the representation with Miss Twinkleton's young ladies.

Three are to meet at the gatehouse to-night. How does each one of the three get through the day?

Neville Landless, though absolved from his books for the time by Mr. Crisparkle – whose fresh nature is by no means insensible to the charms of a holiday – reads and writes in his quiet room, with a concentrated air, until it is two hours past noon. He then sets himself to clearing his table, to arranging his books, and to tearing up and burning his stray papers. He makes a clean sweep of all untidy accumulations, puts all his drawers in order, and leaves no note or scrap of paper undestroyed, save such memoranda as bear directly on his studies. This done, he turns to his wardrobe, selects a few articles of ordinary wear – among them, change of stout shoes and socks for walking – and packs these in a knapsack. This knapsack is new, and he bought it in the High Street yesterday. He also purchased, at the same time and at the same place, a heavy walking-stick; strong in the handle for the grip of the hand, and iron-shod. He tries this, swings it, poises it, and lays it by, with the knapsack, on a window-seat. By this time his arrangements are complete.

He dresses for going out, and is in the act of going – indeed has left his room, and has met the Minor Canon on the staircase, coming out of his bedroom upon the same story – when he turns back again for his walking-stick, thinking he will carry it now. Mr. Crisparkle, who has paused on the staircase, sees it in his hand on his immediately reappearing, takes it from him, and asks him with a smile how he chooses a stick?

'Really I don't know that I understand the subject,' he answers. 'I chose it for its weight.'

'Much too heavy, Neville; *much* too heavy.'

'To rest upon in a long walk, sir?'

'Rest upon?' repeats Mr. Crisparkle, throwing himself into pedestrian form. 'You don't rest upon it; you merely balance with it.'

'I shall know better, with practice, sir. I have not lived in a walking country, you know.'

'True,' says Mr. Crisparkle. 'Get into a little training, and we will have a few score miles together. I should leave you nowhere now. Do you come back before dinner?'

'I think not, as we dine early.'

Mr. Crisparkle gives him a bright nod and a cheerful good-bye; expressing (not without intention) absolute confidence and ease.

Neville repairs to the Nuns' House, and requests that Miss Landless may be informed that her brother is there, by appointment. He waits at the gate, not even crossing the threshold; for he is on his parole not to put himself in Rosa's way.

His sister is at least as mindful of the obligation they have taken on themselves as he can be, and loses not a moment in joining him. They meet affectionately, avoid lingering there, and walk towards the upper inland country.

'I am not going to tread upon forbidden ground, Helena,' says Neville, when they have walked some distance and are turning; 'you will understand in another moment that I cannot help referring to – what shall I say? – my infatuation.'

'Had you not better avoid it, Neville? You know that I can hear nothing.'

'You can hear, my dear, what Mr. Crisparkle has heard, and heard with approval.'

'Yes; I can hear so much.'

'Well, it is this. I am not only unsettled and unhappy myself, but I am conscious of unsettling and interfering with other people. How do I know that, but for my unfortunate presence, you, and – and – the rest of that former party, our engaging guardian excepted, might be dining cheerfully in Minor Canon Corner to-morrow? Indeed it probably would be so. I can see too well that I am not high in the old lady's opinion, and it is easy to understand what an irksome clog I must be upon the hospitalities of her orderly house – especially at this time of year – when I must be kept asunder from this person, and there is such a reason for my not being brought into contact with that person, and an unfavourable reputation has preceded me with such another person; and so on. I have put this very gently to Mr. Crisparkle, for you know his self-denying ways; but still I have put it. What I have laid much greater stress upon at the same time is, that I am engaged in a miserable struggle with myself, and that a little change and absence may enable me to come through it the better. So, the weather being bright and hard, I am going on a walking expedition, and intend taking myself out of everybody's way (my own included, I hope) to-morrow morning.'

'When to come back?'

'In a fortnight.'

'And going quite alone?'

'I am much better without company, even if there were any one but you to bear me company, my dear Helena.'

'Mr. Crisparkle entirely agrees, you say?'

'Entirely. I am not sure but that at first he was inclined to think it rather a moody scheme, and one that might do a brooding mind harm. But we took a moonlight walk last Monday night, to talk it over at leisure, and I represented the case to him as it really is. I showed him that I do want to conquer myself, and that, this evening well got over, it is surely better that I should be away from here just now, than here. I could hardly help meeting certain people walking together here, and that could do no good, and is certainly not the way to forget. A fortnight hence, that chance will probably be over, for the time; and when it again arises for the last time, why, I can again go away. Farther, I really do feel hopeful of bracing exercise and wholesome fatigue. You know that Mr. Crisparkle allows such things their full weight in the preservation of his own sound mind in his own sound body, and that his just spirit is not likely to maintain one set of natural laws for himself and another for me. He yielded to my view of the matter, when convinced that I was honestly in earnest; and so, with his full consent, I start to-morrow morning. Early enough to be not only out of the streets, but out of hearing of the bells, when the good people go to church.'

Helena thinks it over, and thinks well of it. Mr. Crisparkle doing so, she would do so; but she does originally, out of her own mind, think well of it, as a healthy project, denoting a sincere endeavour and an active attempt at self-correction. She is inclined to pity him, poor fellow, for going away solitary on the great Christmas festival; but she feels it much more to the purpose to encourage him. And she does encourage him.

He will write to her?

He will write to her every alternate day, and tell her all his adventures.

Does he send clothes on in advance of him?

'My dear Helena, no. Travel like a pilgrim, with wallet and staff. My wallet – or my knapsack – is packed, and ready for strapping on; and here is my staff!'

He hands it to her; she makes the same remark as Mr. Crisparkle, that it is very heavy; and gives it back to him, asking what wood it is? Ironwood.

Up to this point he has been extremely cheerful. Perhaps, the having to carry his case with her, and therefore to present it in its brightest aspect, has roused his spirits. Perhaps, the having done so with success, is followed by a revulsion. As the day closes in, and the city-lights begin to spring up before them, he grows depressed.

'I wish I were not going to this dinner, Helena.'

'Dear Neville, is it worth while to care much about it? Think how soon it will be over.'

'How soon it will be over!' he repeats gloomily. 'Yes. But I don't like it.'

There may be a moment's awkwardness, she cheeringly represents to him, but it can only last a moment. He is quite sure of himself.

'I wish I felt as sure of everything else, as I feel of myself,' he answers her.

'How strangely you speak, dear! What do you mean?'

'Helena, I don't know. I only know that I don't like it. What a strange dead weight there is in the air!'

She calls his attention to those copperous clouds beyond the river, and says that the wind is rising. He scarcely speaks again, until he takes leave of her, at the gate of the Nuns' House. She does not immediately enter, when they have parted, but remains looking after him along the street. Twice he passes the gatehouse, reluctant to enter. At length, the Cathedral clock chiming one quarter, with a rapid turn he hurries in.

And so *he* goes up the postern stair.

Edwin Drood passes a solitary day. Something of deeper moment than he had thought, has gone out of his life; and in the silence of his own chamber he wept for it last night. Though the image of Miss Landless still hovers in the background of his mind, the pretty little affectionate creature, so much firmer and wiser than he had supposed, occupies its stronghold. It is with some misgiving of his own unworthiness that he thinks of her, and of what they might have been to one another, if he had been more in earnest some time ago; if he had set a higher value on her; if, instead of accepting his lot in life as an inheritance of course, he had studied the right way to its appreciation and enhancement. And still, for all this, and though there is a sharp heartache in all this, the vanity and caprice of youth sustain that handsome figure of Miss Landless in the background of his mind.

That was a curious look of Rosa's when they parted at the gate. Did it mean that she saw below the surface of his thoughts, and down into their twilight depths? Scarcely that, for it was a look of astonished and keen inquiry. He decides that he cannot understand it, though it was remarkably expressive.

As he only waits for Mr. Grewgious now, and will depart immediately after having seen him, he takes a sauntering leave of the ancient city and its neighbourhood. He recalls the time when Rosa and he walked here or there, mere children, full of the dignity of being engaged. Poor children! he thinks, with a pitying sadness.

Finding that his watch has stopped, he turns into the jeweller's shop, to have it wound and set. The jeweller is knowing on the subject of a bracelet, which he begs leave to submit, in a general and quite aimless way. It would suit (he considers) a young bride, to perfection; especially if of a rather diminutive style of beauty. Finding the bracelet but coldly looked at, the jeweller invites attention to a tray of rings for gentlemen; here is a style of ring, now, he remarks – a very chaste signet – which gentlemen are much given to purchasing, when changing their condition. A ring of a very responsible appearance. With the date of their wedding-day engraved inside, several gentlemen have preferred it to any other kind of memento.

The rings are as coldly viewed as the bracelet. Edwin tells the tempter that he wears no jewellery but his watch and chain, which were his father's; and his shirt-pin.

'That I was aware of,' is the jeweller's reply, 'for Mr. Jasper dropped in for a watch-glass the other day, and, in fact, I showed these articles to him, remarking that if he *should* wish to make a present to a gentleman relative, on any particular occasion – But he said with a smile that he had an inventory in his mind of all the jewellery his gentleman relative ever wore; namely, his watch and chain, and his shirt-pin.' Still (the jeweller considers) that might not apply to all times, though applying to the present time. 'Twenty minutes past two, Mr. Drood, I set your watch at. Let me recommend you not to let it run down, sir.'

Edwin takes his watch, puts it on, and goes out, thinking: 'Dear old Jack! If I were to make an extra crease in my neckcloth, he would think it worth noticing!'

He strolls about and about, to pass the time until the dinner-hour. It somehow happens that Cloisterham seems reproachful to him to-day; has fault to find with him, as if he had not used it well; but is far more pensive with him than angry. His wonted carelessness is replaced by a wistful looking at, and dwelling upon, all the old landmarks. He will soon be far away, and may never see them again, he thinks. Poor youth! Poor youth!

As dusk draws on, he paces the Monks' Vineyard. He has walked to and fro, full half an hour by the Cathedral chimes, and it has closed in dark, before he becomes quite aware of a woman crouching on the ground near a wicket gate in a corner. The gate commands a cross bye-path, little used in the gloaming; and the figure must have been there all the time, though he has but gradually and lately made it out.

He strikes into that path, and walks up to the wicket. By the light of a lamp near it, he sees that the woman is of a haggard appearance, and that her weazen chin is resting on her hands, and that her eyes are staring – with an unwinking, blind sort of steadfastness – before her.

Always kindly, but moved to be unusually kind this evening, and having bestowed kind words on most of the children and aged people he has met, he at once bends down, and speaks to this woman.

'Are you ill?'

'No, deary,' she answers, without looking at him, and with no departure from her strange blind stare.

'Are you blind?'

'No, deary.'

'Are you lost, homeless, faint? What is the matter, that you stay here in the cold so long, without moving?'

By slow and stiff efforts, she appears to contract her vision until it can rest upon him; and then a curious film passes over her, and she begins to shake.

He straightens himself, recoils a step, and looks down at her in a dread amazement; for he seems to know her.

'Good Heaven!' he thinks, next moment. 'Like Jack that night!'

As he looks down at her, she looks up at him, and whimpers: 'My lungs is weakly; my lungs is dreffle bad. Poor me, poor me, my cough is rattling dry!' and coughs in confirmation horribly.

'Where do you come from?'

'Come from London, deary.' (Her cough still rending her.)

'Where are you going to?'

'Back to London, deary. I came here, looking for a needle in a haystack, and I ain't found it. Look'ee, deary; give me three-and-sixpence, and don't you be afeard for me. I'll get back to London then, and trouble no one. I'm in a business. – Ah, me! It's slack, it's slack, and times is very bad! – but I can make a shift to live by it.'

'Do you eat opium?'

'Smokes it,' she replies with difficulty, still racked by her cough. 'Give me three-and-sixpence, and I'll lay it out well, and get back. If you don't give me three-and-sixpence, don't give me a brass farden. And if you do give me three-and-sixpence, deary, I'll tell you something.'

He counts the money from his pocket, and puts it in her hand. She instantly clutches it tight, and rises to her feet with a croaking laugh of satisfaction.

'Bless ye! Hark'ee, dear genl'mn. What's your Chris'en name?'

'Edwin.'

'Edwin, Edwin, Edwin,' she repeats, trailing off into a drowsy repetition of the word; and then asks suddenly: 'Is the short of that name Eddy?'

'It is sometimes called so,' he replies, with the colour starting to his face.

'Don't sweethearts call it so?' she asks, pondering.

'How should I know?'

'Haven't you a sweetheart, upon your soul?'

'None.'

She is moving away, with another 'Bless ye, and thank'ee, deary!' when he adds: 'You were to tell me something; you may as well do so.'

'So I was, so I was. Well, then. Whisper. You be thankful that your name ain't Ned.'

He looks at her quite steadily, as he asks: 'Why?'

'Because it's a bad name to have just now.'

'How a bad name?'

'A threatened name. A dangerous name.'

'The proverb says that threatened men live long,' he tells her, lightly.

'Then Ned – so threatened is he, wherever he may be while I am a-talking to you, deary – should live to all eternity!' replies the woman.

She has leaned forward to say it in his ear, with her forefinger shaking before his eyes, and now huddles herself together, and with another 'Bless ye, and thank'ee!' goes away in the direction of the Travellers' Lodging House.

This is not an inspiriting close to a dull day. Alone, in a sequestered place, surrounded by vestiges of old time and decay, it rather has a tendency to call a shudder into being. He makes for the better-lighted streets, and resolves as he walks on to say nothing of this to-night, but to mention it to Jack (who alone calls him Ned), as an odd coincidence, to-morrow; of course only as a coincidence, and not as anything better worth remembering.

Still, it holds to him, as many things much better worth remembering never did. He has another mile or so, to linger out before the dinner-hour; and, when he walks over the bridge and by the river, the woman's words are in the rising wind, in the angry sky, in the troubled water, in the flickering lights. There is some solemn echo of them even in the Cathedral chime, which strikes a sudden surprise to his heart as he turns in under the archway of the gatehouse.

And so *he* goes up the postern stair.

John Jasper passes a more agreeable and cheerful day than either of his guests. Having no music-lessons to give in the holiday season, his time is his own, but for the Cathedral services. He is early among the shopkeepers, ordering little table luxuries that his nephew likes. His nephew will not be with him long, he tells his provision-dealers, and so must be petted and made much of. While out on his hospitable preparations, he looks in on Mr. Sapsea; and mentions that dear Ned, and that inflammable young spark of Mr. Crisparkle's, are to dine at the gatehouse to-day, and make up their difference. Mr. Sapsea is by no means friendly towards the inflammable young spark. He says that his complexion is 'Un-English.' And when Mr. Sapsea has once declared anything to be Un-English, he considers that thing everlastingly sunk in the bottomless pit.

John Jasper is truly sorry to hear Mr. Sapsea speak thus, for he knows right well that Mr. Sapsea never speaks without a meaning, and that he has a subtle trick of being right. Mr. Sapsea (by a very remarkable coincidence) is of exactly that opinion.

Mr. Jasper is in beautiful voice this day. In the pathetic supplication to have his heart inclined to keep this law, he quite astonishes his fellows by his melodious power. He has never sung difficult music with such skill and harmony, as in this day's Anthem. His nervous temperament is occasionally prone to take difficult music a little too quickly; to-day, his time is perfect.

These results are probably attained through a grand composure of the spirits. The mere mechanism of his throat is a little tender, for he wears, both with his singing-robe and with his ordinary dress, a large black scarf of strong close-woven silk, slung loosely round his neck. But his composure is so noticeable, that Mr. Crisparkle speaks of it as they come out from Vespers.

'I must thank you, Jasper, for the pleasure with which I have heard you to-day. Beautiful! Delightful! You could not have so outdone yourself, I hope, without being wonderfully well.'

'I *am* wonderfully well.'

'Nothing unequal,' says the Minor Canon, with a smooth motion of his hand: 'nothing unsteady, nothing forced, nothing avoided; all thoroughly done in a masterly manner, with perfect self-command.'

'Thank you. I hope so, if it is not too much to say.'

'One would think, Jasper, you had been trying a new medicine for that occasional indisposition of yours.'

'No, really? That's well observed; for I have.'

'Then stick to it, my good fellow,' says Mr. Crisparkle, clapping him on the shoulder with friendly encouragement, 'stick to it.'

'I will.'

'I congratulate you,' Mr. Crisparkle pursues, as they come out of the Cathedral, 'on all accounts.'

'Thank you again. I will walk round to the Corner with you, if you don't object; I have plenty of time before my company come; and I want to say a word to you, which I think you will not be displeased to hear.'

'What is it?'

'Well. We were speaking, the other evening, of my black humours.'

Mr. Crisparkle's face falls, and he shakes his head deploringly.

'I said, you know, that I should make you an antidote to those black humours; and you said you hoped I would consign them to the flames.'

'And I still hope so, Jasper.'

'With the best reason in the world! I mean to burn this year's Diary at the year's end.'

'Because you – ?' Mr. Crisparkle brightens greatly as he thus begins.

'You anticipate me. Because I feel that I have been out of sorts, gloomy, bilious, brain-oppressed, whatever it may be. You said I had been exaggerative. So I have.'

Mr. Crisparkle's brightened face brightens still more.

'I couldn't see it then, because I *was* out of sorts; but I am in a healthier state now, and I acknowledge it with genuine pleasure. I made a great deal of a very little; that's the fact.'

'It does me good,' cries Mr. Crisparkle, 'to hear you say it!'

'A man leading a monotonous life,' Jasper proceeds, 'and getting his nerves, or his stomach, out of order, dwells upon an idea until it loses its proportions. That was my case with the idea in question. So I shall burn the evidence of my case, when the book is full, and begin the next volume with a clearer vision.'

'This is better,' says Mr. Crisparkle, stopping at the steps of his own door to shake hands, 'than I could have hoped.'

'Why, naturally,' returns Jasper. 'You had but little reason to hope that I should become more like yourself. You are always training yourself to be, mind and body, as clear as crystal, and you always are, and never change; whereas I am a muddy, solitary, moping weed. However, I have got over that mope. Shall I wait, while you ask if Mr. Neville has left for my place? If not, he and I may walk round together.'

'I think,' says Mr. Crisparkle, opening the entrance-door with his key, 'that he left some time ago; at least I know he left, and I think he has not come back. But I'll inquire. You won't come in?'

'My company wait,' said Jasper, with a smile.

The Minor Canon disappears, and in a few moments returns. As he thought, Mr. Neville has not come back; indeed, as he remembers now, Mr. Neville said he would probably go straight to the gatehouse.

'Bad manners in a host!' says Jasper. 'My company will be there before me! What will you bet that I don't find my company embracing?'

'I will bet – or I would, if ever I did bet,' returns Mr. Crisparkle, 'that your company will have a gay entertainer this evening.'

Jasper nods, and laughs good-night!

He retraces his steps to the Cathedral door, and turns down past it to the gatehouse. He sings, in a low voice and with delicate expression, as he walks along. It still seems as if a false note were not within his power to-night, and as if nothing could hurry or retard him. Arriving thus under the arched entrance of his dwelling, he pauses for an instant in the shelter to pull off that great black scarf, and hang it in a loop upon his arm. For that brief time, his face is knitted and stern. But it immediately clears, as he resumes his singing, and his way.

And so *he* goes up the postern stair.

The red light burns steadily all the evening in the lighthouse on the margin of the tide of busy life. Softened sounds and hum of traffic pass it and flow on irregularly into the lonely Precincts; but very little else goes by, save violent rushes of wind. It comes on to blow a boisterous gale.

The Precincts are never particularly well lighted; but the strong blasts of wind blowing out many of the lamps (in some instances shattering the frames too, and bringing the glass rattling to the ground), they are unusually dark to-night. The darkness is augmented and confused, by flying dust from the earth, dry twigs from the trees, and great ragged fragments from the rooks' nests up in the tower. The trees themselves so toss and creak, as this tangible part of the darkness madly whirls about, that they seem in peril of being torn out of the earth: while ever and again a crack, and a rushing fall, denote that some large branch has yielded to the storm.

Not such power of wind has blown for many a winter night. Chimneys topple in the streets, and people hold to posts and corners, and to one another, to keep themselves upon their feet. The violent rushes abate not, but increase in frequency and fury until at midnight, when the streets are empty, the storm goes thundering along them, rattling at all the latches, and tearing at all the shutters, as if warning the people to get up and fly with it, rather than have the roofs brought down upon their brains.

Still, the red light burns steadily. Nothing is steady but the red light.

All through the night the wind blows, and abates not. But early in the morning, when there is barely enough light in the east to dim the stars, it begins to lull. From that time, with occasional wild charges, like a wounded monster dying, it drops and sinks; and at full daylight it is dead.

It is then seen that the hands of the Cathedral clock are torn off; that lead from the roof has been stripped away, rolled up, and blown into the Close; and that some stones have been displaced upon the summit of the great tower. Christmas morning though it be, it is necessary to send up workmen, to ascertain the extent of the damage done. These, led by Durdles, go aloft; while Mr. Tope and a crowd of early idlers gather down in Minor Canon Corner, shading their eyes and watching for their appearance up there.

This cluster is suddenly broken and put aside by the hands of Mr.

Jasper; all the gazing eyes are brought down to the earth by his loudly inquiring of Mr. Crisparkle, at an open window:

'Where is my nephew?'

'He has not been here. Is he not with you?'

'No. He went down to the river last night, with Mr. Neville, to look at the storm, and has not been back. Call Mr. Neville!'

'He left this morning, early.'

'Left this morning early? Let me in! let me in!'

There is no more looking up at the tower, now. All the assembled eyes are turned on Mr. Jasper, white, half-dressed, panting, and clinging to the rail before the Minor Canon's house.

CHAPTER XV
Impeached

NEVILLE LANDLESS HAD started so early and walked at so good a pace, that when the church-bells began to ring in Cloisterham for morning service, he was eight miles away. As he wanted his breakfast by that time, having set forth on a crust of bread, he stopped at the next roadside tavern to refresh.

Visitors in want of breakfast – unless they were horses or cattle, for which class of guests there was preparation enough in the way of water-trough and hay – were so unusual at the sign of The Tilted Wagon, that it took a long time to get the wagon into the track of tea and toast and bacon. Neville in the interval, sitting in a sanded parlour, wondering in how long a time after he had gone, the sneezy fire of damp fagots would begin to make somebody else warm.

Indeed, The Tilted Wagon, as a cool establishment on the top of a hill, where the ground before the door was puddled with damp hoofs and trodden straw; where a scolding landlady slapped a moist baby (with one red sock on and one wanting), in the bar; where the cheese was cast aground upon a shelf, in company with a mouldy tablecloth and a green-handled knife, in a sort of cast-iron canoe; where the pale-faced bread shed tears of crumb over its shipwreck in another canoe; where the family linen, half washed and half dried, led a public life of lying about; where everything to drink was drunk out of mugs, and everything else was suggestive of a rhyme to mugs; The Tilted Wagon, all these things considered, hardly kept its painted promise of providing good entertainment for Man and Beast. However, Man, in the present case, was not critical, but took what entertainment he could get, and went on again after a longer rest than he needed.

He stopped at some quarter of a mile from the house, hesitating whether to pursue the road, or to follow a cart track between two high hedgerows, which led across the slope of a breezy heath, and evidently struck into the road again by-and-by. He decided in favour of this latter track, and pursued it with some toil; the rise being steep, and the way

146

worn into deep ruts.

He was labouring along, when he became aware of some other pedestrians behind him. As they were coming up at a faster pace than his, he stood aside, against one of the high banks, to let them pass. But their manner was very curious. Only four of them passed. Other four slackened speed, and loitered as intending to follow him when he should go on. The remainder of the party (half-a-dozen perhaps) turned, and went back at a great rate.

He looked at the four behind him, and he looked at the four before him. They all returned his look. He resumed his way. The four in advance went on, constantly looking back; the four in the rear came closing up.

When they all ranged out from the narrow track upon the open slope of the heath, and this order was maintained, let him diverge as he would to either side, there was no longer room to doubt that he was beset by these fellows. He stopped, as a last test; and they all stopped.

'Why do you attend upon me in this way?' he asked the whole body. 'Are you a pack of thieves?'

'Don't answer him,' said one of the number; he did not see which. 'Better be quiet.'

'Better be quiet?' repeated Neville. 'Who said so?'

Nobody replied.

'It's good advice, whichever of you skulkers gave it,' he went on angrily. 'I will not submit to be penned in between four men there, and four men there. I wish to pass, and I mean to pass, those four in front.'

They were all standing still; himself included.

'If eight men, or four men, or two men, set upon one,' he proceeded, growing more enraged, 'the one has no chance but to set his mark upon some of them. And, by the Lord, I'll do it, if I am interrupted any farther!'

Shouldering his heavy stick, and quickening his pace, he shot on to pass the four ahead. The largest and strongest man of the number changed swiftly to the side on which he came up, and dexterously closed with him and went down with him; but not before the heavy stick had descended smartly.

'Let him be!' said this man in a suppressed voice, as they struggled together on the grass. 'Fair play! His is the build of a girl to mine, and he's got a weight strapped to his back besides. Let him alone. I'll manage him.'

After a little rolling about, in a close scuffle which caused the faces of both to be besmeared with blood, the man took his knee from Neville's chest, and rose, saying: 'There! Now take him arm-in-arm, any two of you!'

It was immediately done.

'As to our being a pack of thieves, Mr. Landless,' said the man, as he spat out some blood, and wiped more from his face; 'you know better than that at midday. We wouldn't have touched you if you hadn't forced us. We're going to take you round to the high road, anyhow, and you'll find help enough against thieves there, if you want it. – Wipe his face, somebody; see how it's a-trickling down him!'

When his face was cleansed, Neville recognised in the speaker, Joe, driver of the Cloisterham omnibus, whom he had seen but once, and that on the day of his arrival.

'And what I recommend you for the present, is, don't talk, Mr. Landless. You'll find a friend waiting for you, at the high road – gone ahead by the other way when we split into two parties – and you had much better say nothing till you come up with him. Bring that stick along, somebody else, and let's be moving!'

Utterly bewildered, Neville stared around him and said not a word. Walking between his two conductors, who held his arms in theirs, he went on, as in a dream, until they came again into the high road, and into the midst of a little group of people. The men who had turned back were among the group; and its central figures were Mr. Jasper and Mr. Crisparkle. Neville's conductors took him up to the Minor Canon, and there released him, as an act of deference to that gentleman.

'What is all this, sir? What is the matter? I feel as if I had lost my senses!' cried Neville, the group closing in around him.

'Where is my nephew?' asked Mr. Jasper, wildly.

'Where is your nephew?' repeated Neville, 'Why do you ask me?'

'I ask you,' retorted Jasper, 'because you were the last person in his company, and he is not to be found.'

'Not to be found!' cried Neville, aghast.

'Stay, stay,' said Mr. Crisparkle. 'Permit me, Jasper. Mr. Neville, you are confounded; collect your thoughts; it is of great importance that you should collect your thoughts; attend to me.'

'I will try, sir, but I seem mad.'

'You left Mr. Jasper last night with Edwin Drood?'

'Yes.'

'At what hour?'

'Was it at twelve o'clock?' asked Neville, with his hand to his confused head, and appealing to Jasper.

'Quite right,' said Mr. Crisparkle; 'the hour Mr. Jasper has already named to me. You went down to the river together?'

'Undoubtedly. To see the action of the wind there.'

'What followed? How long did you stay there?'

'About ten minutes; I should say not more. We then walked together to your house, and he took leave of me at the door.'

'Did he say that he was going down to the river again?'

'No. He said that he was going straight back.'

The bystanders looked at one another, and at Mr. Crisparkle. To whom Mr. Jasper, who had been intensely watching Neville, said, in a low, distinct, suspicious voice: 'What are those stains upon his dress?'

All eyes were turned towards the blood upon his clothes.

'And here are the same stains upon this stick!' said Jasper, taking it from the hand of the man who held it. 'I know the stick to be his, and he carried it last night. What does this mean?'

'In the name of God, say what it means, Neville!' urged Mr. Crisparkle.

'That man and I,' said Neville, pointing out his late adversary, 'had a struggle for the stick just now, and you may see the same marks on him, sir. What was I to suppose, when I found myself molested by eight people? Could I dream of the true reason when they would give me none at all?'

They admitted that they had thought it discreet to be silent, and that the struggle had taken place. And yet the very men who had seen it looked darkly at the smears which the bright cold air had already dried.

'We must return, Neville,' said Mr. Crisparkle; 'of course you will be glad to come back to clear yourself?'

'Of course, sir.'

'Mr. Landless will walk at my side,' the Minor Canon continued, looking around him. 'Come, Neville!'

They set forth on the walk back; and the others, with one exception, straggled after them at various distances. Jasper walked on the other side of Neville, and never quitted that position. He was silent, while Mr. Crisparkle more than once repeated his former questions, and while Neville repeated his former answers; also, while they both hazarded some explanatory conjectures. He was obstinately silent, because Mr. Crisparkle's manner directly appealed to him to take some part in the discussion, and no appeal would move his fixed face. When they drew near to the city, and it was suggested by the Minor Canon that they might do well in calling on the Mayor at once, he assented with a stern nod; but he spake no word until they stood in Mr. Sapsea's parlour.

Mr. Sapsea being informed by Mr. Crisparkle of the circumstances under which they desired to make a voluntary statement before him, Mr. Jasper broke silence by declaring that he placed his whole reliance, humanly speaking, on Mr. Sapsea's penetration. There was no conceivable reason why his nephew should have suddenly absconded, unless Mr. Sapsea could suggest one, and then he would defer. There was no intelligible likelihood of his having returned to the river, and been accidentally drowned in the dark, unless it should appear likely to Mr. Sapsea, and then again he would defer. He washed his hands as clean as he could of all horrible suspicions, unless it should appear to Mr. Sapsea that some such were inseparable from his last companion before his disappearance (not on good terms with previously), and then, once more, he would defer. His own state of mind, he being distracted with doubts, and labouring under dismal apprehensions, was not to be safely trusted; but Mr. Sapsea's was.

Mr. Sapsea expressed his opinion that the case had a dark look; in short (and here his eyes rested full on Neville's countenance), an Un-English complexion. Having made this grand point, he wandered into a denser haze and maze of nonsense than even a mayor might have been expected to disport himself in, and came out of it with the brilliant discovery that to take the life of a fellow-creature was to take something that didn't belong to you. He wavered whether or no he should at once issue his warrant for the committal of Neville Landless to jail, under circumstances of grave suspicion; and he might have gone so far as to do it but for the indignant protest of the Minor Canon: who undertook for the young man's remaining in his own house, and being produced by his own hands, whenever demanded. Mr. Jasper then understood Mr. Sapsea to suggest that the river should be dragged, that its banks should be rigidly examined, that particulars of the disappearance should be sent to all outlying places and to London, and that placards and advertisements should be widely circulated imploring Edwin Drood, if for any unknown reason he had withdrawn himself from his uncle's home and society, to take pity on that loving kinsman's sore bereavement and distress, and somehow inform him that he was yet alive. Mr. Sapsea was perfectly understood, for this was exactly his meaning (though he had said nothing about it); and measures were taken towards all these ends immediately.

It would be difficult to determine which was the more oppressed with horror and amazement: Neville Landless, or John Jasper. But that Jasper's position forced him to be active, while Neville's forced him to be passive, there would have been nothing to choose between them. Each was bowed down and broken.

With the earliest light of the next morning, men were at work upon the river, and other men – most of whom volunteered for the service – were examining the banks. All the livelong day the search went on; upon the river, with barge and pole, and drag and net; upon the muddy and rushy shore, with jack-boots, hatchet, spade, rope, dogs, and all imaginable appliances. Even at night, the river was specked with lanterns, and lurid with fires; far-off creeks, into which the tide washed as it changed, had their knots of watchers, listening to the lapping of the stream, and looking out for any burden it might bear; remote shingly causeways near the sea, and lonely points off which there was a race of water, had their unwonted flaring cressets and rough-coated figures when the next day dawned; but no trace of Edwin Drood revisited the light of the sun.

All that day, again, the search went on. Now, in barge and boat; and now ashore among the osiers, or tramping amidst mud and stakes and jagged stones in low-lying places, where solitary watermarks and signals of strange shapes showed like spectres, John Jasper worked and toiled. But to no purpose; for still no trace of Edwin Drood revisited the light of the sun.

Setting his watches for that night again, so that vigilant eyes should be kept on every change of tide, he went home exhausted. Unkempt and disordered, bedaubed with mud that had dried upon him, and with much of his clothing torn to rags, he had but just dropped into his easy-chair, when Mr. Grewgious stood before him.

'This is strange news,' said Mr. Grewgious.

'Strange and fearful news.'

Jasper had merely lifted up his heavy eyes to say it, and now dropped them again as he drooped, worn out, over one side of his easy-chair.

Mr. Grewgious smoothed his head and face, and stood looking at the fire.

'How is your ward?' asked Jasper, after a time, in a faint, fatigued voice.

'Poor little thing! You may imagine her condition.'

'Have you seen his sister?' inquired Jasper, as before.

'Whose?'

The curtness of the counter-question, and the cool, slow manner in which, as he put it, Mr. Grewgious moved his eyes from the fire to his companion's face, might at any other time have been exasperating. In his depression and exhaustion, Jasper merely opened his eyes to say: 'The suspected young man's.'

'Do you suspect him?' asked Mr. Grewgious.

'I don't know what to think. I cannot make up my mind.'

'Nor I,' said Mr. Grewgious. 'But as you spoke of him as the suspected young man, I thought you *had* made up your mind. – I have just left Miss Landless.'

'What is her state?'

'Defiance of all suspicion, and unbounded faith in her brother.'

'Poor thing!'

'However,' pursued Mr. Grewgious, 'it is not of her that I came to speak. It is of my ward. I have a communication to make that will surprise you. At least, it has surprised me.'

Jasper, with a groaning sigh, turned wearily in his chair.

'Shall I put it off till to-morrow?' said Mr. Grewgious. 'Mind, I warn you, that I think it will surprise you!'

More attention and concentration came into John Jasper's eyes as they caught sight of Mr. Grewgious smoothing his head again, and again looking at the fire; but now, with a compressed and determined mouth.

'What is it?' demanded Jasper, becoming upright in his chair.

'To be sure,' said Mr. Grewgious, provokingly slowly and internally, as he kept his eyes on the fire: 'I might have known it sooner; she gave me the opening; but I am such an exceedingly Angular man, that it never occurred to me; I took all for granted.'

'What is it?' demanded Jasper once more.

Mr. Grewgious, alternately opening and shutting the palms of his hands as he warmed them at the fire, and looking fixedly at him sideways, and never changing either his action or his look in all that followed, went on to reply.

'This young couple, the lost youth and Miss Rosa, my ward, though so long betrothed, and so long recognising their betrothal, and so near being married – '

Mr. Grewgious saw a staring white face, and two quivering white lips, in the easy-chair, and saw two muddy hands gripping its sides. But for the hands, he might have thought he had never seen the face.

' – This young couple came gradually to the discovery (made on both sides pretty equally, I think), that they would be happier and better, both in their present and their future lives, as affectionate friends, or say rather as brother and sister, than as husband and wife.'

Mr. Grewgious saw a lead-coloured face in the easy-chair, and on its surface dreadful starting drops or bubbles, as if of steel.

'This young couple formed at length the healthy resolution of interchanging their discoveries, openly, sensibly, and tenderly. They met for that purpose. After some innocent and generous talk, they agreed to dissolve their existing, and their intended, relations, for ever and ever.'

Mr. Grewgious saw a ghastly figure rise, open-mouthed, from the easy-chair, and lift its outspread hands towards its head.

'One of this young couple, and that one your nephew, fearful, however, that in the tenderness of your affection for him you would be bitterly disappointed by so wide a departure from his projected life, forbore to tell you the secret, for a few days, and left it to be disclosed by me, when I should come down to speak to you, and he would be gone. I speak to you, and he is gone.'

Mr. Grewgious saw the ghastly figure throw back its head, clutch its hair with its hands, and turn with a writhing action from him.

'I have now said all I have to say: except that this young couple parted, firmly, though not without tears and sorrow, on the evening when you last saw them together.'

Mr. Grewgious heard a terrible shriek, and saw no ghastly figure, sitting or standing; saw nothing but a heap of torn and miry clothes upon the floor.

Not changing his action even then, he opened and shut the palms of his hands as he warmed them, and looked down at it.

CHAPTER XVI
Devoted

WHEN JOHN JASPER recovered from his fit or swoon, he found himself being tended by Mr. and Mrs. Tope, whom his visitor had summoned for the purpose. His visitor, wooden of aspect, sat stiffly in a chair, with his hands upon his knees, watching his recovery.

'There! You've come to nicely now, sir,' said the tearful Mrs. Tope; 'you were thoroughly worn out, and no wonder!'

'A man,' said Mr. Grewgious, with his usual air of repeating a lesson, 'cannot have his rest broken, and his mind cruelly tormented, and his body overtaxed by fatigue, without being thoroughly worn out.'

'I fear I have alarmed you?' Jasper apologised faintly, when he was helped into his easy-chair.

'Not at all, I thank you,' answered Mr. Grewgious.

'You are too considerate.'

'Not at all, I thank you,' answered Mr. Grewgious again.

'You must take some wine, sir,' said Mrs. Tope, 'and the jelly that I had ready for you, and that you wouldn't put your lips to at noon, though I warned you what would come of it, you know, and you not breakfasted; and you must have a wing of the roast fowl that has been put back twenty times if it's been put back once. It shall all be on table in five minutes, and this good gentleman belike will stop and see you take it.'

This good gentleman replied with a snort, which might mean yes, or no, or anything or nothing, and which Mrs. Tope would have found highly mystifying, but that her attention was divided by the service of the table.

'You will take something with me?' said Jasper, as the cloth was laid.

'I couldn't get a morsel down my throat, I thank you,' answered Mr. Grewgious.

Jasper both ate and drank almost voraciously. Combined with the hurry in his mode of doing it, was an evident indifference to the taste of what he took, suggesting that he ate and drank to fortify himself against any other failure of the spirits, far more than to gratify his palate. Mr. Grewgious in the meantime sat upright, with no expression in his face, and a hard kind of imperturbably polite protest all over him: as though he would have said, in reply to some invitation to discourse; 'I couldn't originate the faintest approach to an observation on any subject whatever, I thank you.'

'Do you know,' said Jasper, when he had pushed away his plate and glass, and had sat meditating for a few minutes: 'do you know that I find some crumbs of comfort in the communication with which you have so much amazed me?'

'*Do* you?' returned Mr. Grewgious, pretty plainly adding the unspoken clause: 'I don't, I thank you!'

'After recovering from the shock of a piece of news of my dear boy, so entirely unexpected, and so destructive of all the castles I had built for him; and after having had time to think of it; yes.'

'I shall be glad to pick up your crumbs,' said Mr. Grewgious, dryly.

'Is there not, or is there – if I deceive myself, tell me so, and shorten my pain – is there not, or is there, hope that, finding himself in this new position, and becoming sensitively alive to the awkward burden of explanation, in this quarter, and that, and the other, with which it would load him, he avoided the awkwardness, and took to flight?'

'Such a thing might be,' said Mr. Grewgious, pondering.

'Such a thing has been. I have read of cases in which people, rather than face a seven days' wonder, and have to account for themselves to the idle and impertinent, have taken themselves away, and been long unheard of.'

'I believe such things have happened,' said Mr. Grewgious, pondering still.

'When I had, and could have, no suspicion,' pursued Jasper, eagerly following the new track, 'that the dear lost boy had withheld anything from me – most of all, such a leading matter as this – what gleam of light was there for me in the whole black sky? When I supposed that his intended wife was here, and his marriage close at hand, how could I entertain the possibility of his voluntarily leaving this place, in a manner that would be so unaccountable, capricious, and cruel? But now that I know what you have told me, is there no little chink through which day pierces? Supposing him to have disappeared of his own act, is not his disappearance more accountable and less cruel? The fact of his having just parted from your ward, is in itself a sort of reason for his going away.

It does not make his mysterious departure the less cruel to me, it is true; but it relieves it of cruelty to her.'

Mr. Grewgious could not but assent to this.

'And even as to me,' continued Jasper, still pursuing the new track, with ardour, and, as he did so, brightening with hope: 'he knew that you were coming to me; he knew that you were intrusted to tell me what you have told me; if your doing so has awakened a new train of thought in my perplexed mind, it reasonably follows that, from the same premises, he might have foreseen the inferences that I should draw. Grant that he did foresee them; and even the cruelty to me – and who am I! – John Jasper, Music Master, vanishes!' –

Once more, Mr. Grewgious could not but assent to this.

'I have had my distrusts, and terrible distrusts they have been,' said Jasper; 'but your disclosure, overpowering as it was at first – showing me that my own dear boy had had a great disappointing reservation from me, who so fondly loved him, kindles hope within me. You do not extinguish it when I state it, but admit it to be a reasonable hope. I begin to believe it possible:' here he clasped his hands: 'that he may have disappeared from among us of his own accord, and that he may yet be alive and well.'

Mr. Crisparkle came in at the moment. To whom Mr. Jasper repeated:

'I begin to believe it possible that he may have disappeared of his own accord, and may yet be alive and well.'

Mr. Crisparkle taking a seat, and inquiring: 'Why so?' Mr. Jasper repeated the arguments he had just set forth. If they had been less plausible than they were, the good Minor Canon's mind would have been in a state of preparation to receive them, as exculpatory of his unfortunate pupil. But he, too, did really attach great importance to the lost young man's having been, so immediately before his disappearance, placed in a new and embarrassing relation towards every one acquainted with his projects and affairs; and the fact seemed to him to present the question in a new light.

'I stated to Mr. Sapsea, when we waited on him,' said Jasper: as he really had done: 'that there was no quarrel or difference between the two young men at their last meeting. We all know that their first meeting was unfortunately very far from amicable; but all went smoothly and quietly when they were last together at my house. My dear boy was not in his usual spirits; he was depressed – I noticed that – and I am bound henceforth to dwell upon the circumstance the more, now that I know there was a special reason for his being depressed: a reason, moreover, which may possibly have induced him to absent himself.'

'I pray to Heaven it may turn out so!' exclaimed Mr. Crisparkle.

'*I* pray to Heaven it may turn out so!' repeated Jasper. 'You know – and Mr. Grewgious should now know likewise – that I took a great prepossession against Mr. Neville Landless, arising out of his furious conduct on that first occasion. You know that I came to you, extremely apprehensive, on my dear boy's behalf, of his mad violence. You know that I even entered in my Diary, and showed the entry to you, that I had dark forebodings against him. Mr. Grewgious ought to be possessed of the whole case. He shall not, through any suppression of mine, be informed of a part of it, and kept in ignorance of another part of it. I wish him to be good enough to understand that the communication he has made to me has hopefully influenced my mind, in spite of its having been, before this mysterious occurrence took place, profoundly impressed against young Landless.'

This fairness troubled the Minor Canon much. He felt that he was not as open in his own dealing. He charged against himself reproachfully that he had suppressed, so far, the two points of a second strong outbreak of temper against Edwin Drood on the part of Neville, and of the passion of jealousy having, to his own certain knowledge, flamed up in Neville's breast against him. He was convinced of Neville's innocence of any part in the ugly disappearance; and yet so many little circumstances combined so wofully against him, that he dreaded to add two more to their cumulative weight. He was among the truest of men; but he had been balancing in his mind, much to its distress, whether his volunteering to tell these two fragments of truth, at this time, would not be tantamount to a piecing together of falsehood in the place of truth.

However, here was a model before him. He hesitated no longer. Addressing Mr. Grewgious, as one placed in authority by the revelation he had brought to bear on the mystery (and surpassingly Angular Mr. Grewgious became when he found himself in that unexpected position), Mr. Crisparkle bore his testimony to Mr. Jasper's strict sense of justice, and, expressing his absolute confidence in the complete clearance of his pupil from the least taint of suspicion, sooner or later, avowed that his confidence in that young gentleman had been formed, in spite of his confidential knowledge that his temper was of the hottest and fiercest, and that it was directly incensed against Mr. Jasper's nephew, by the circumstance of his romantically supposing himself to be enamoured of the same young lady. The sanguine reaction manifest in Mr. Jasper was proof even against this unlooked-for declaration. It turned him paler; but he repeated that he would cling to the hope he had derived from Mr. Grewgious; and that if no trace of his dear boy were found, leading to the dreadful inference that he had been made away with, he would cherish unto the last stretch of possibility the idea, that he might have absconded of his own wild will.

Now, it fell out that Mr. Crisparkle, going away from this conference still very uneasy in his mind, and very much troubled on behalf of the young man whom he held as a kind of prisoner in his own house, took a memorable night walk.

He walked to Cloisterham Weir.

He often did so, and consequently there was nothing remarkable in his footsteps tending that way. But the preoccupation of his mind so hindered him from planning any walk, or taking heed of the objects he passed, that his first consciousness of being near the Weir, was derived from the sound of the falling water close at hand.

'How did I come here!' was his first thought, as he stopped.

'Why did I come here!' was his second.

Then, he stood intently listening to the water. A familiar passage in his reading, about airy tongues that syllable men's names, rose so unbidden to his ear, that he put it from him with his hand, as if it were tangible.

It was starlight. The Weir was full two miles above the spot to which the young men had repaired to watch the storm. No search had been made up here, for the tide had been running strongly down, at that time of the night of Christmas Eve, and the likeliest places for the discovery of a body, if a fatal accident had happened under such circumstances, all lay – both when the tide ebbed, and when it flowed again – between that spot and the sea. The water came over the Weir, with its usual sound on a cold starlight night, and little could be seen of it; yet Mr. Crisparkle had a strange idea that something unusual hung about the place.

He reasoned with himself: What was it? Where was it? Put it to the proof. Which sense did it address?

No sense reported anything unusual there. He listened again, and his sense of hearing again checked the water coming over the Weir, with its usual sound on a cold starlight night.

Knowing very well that the mystery with which his mind was occupied, might of itself give the place this haunted air, he strained those hawk's eyes of his for the correction of his sight. He got closer to the Weir, and peered at its well-known posts and timbers. Nothing in the least unusual was remotely shadowed forth. But he resolved that he would come back early in the morning.

The Weir ran through his broken sleep, all night, and he was back again at sunrise. It was a bright frosty morning. The whole composition before him, when he stood where he had stood last night, was clearly discernible in its minutest details. He had surveyed it closely for some minutes, and was about to withdraw his eyes, when they were attracted keenly to one spot.

He turned his back upon the Weir, and looked far away at the sky, and at the earth, and then looked again at that one spot. It caught his sight again immediately, and he concentrated his vision upon it. He could not lose it now, though it was but such a speck in the landscape. It fascinated his sight. His hands began plucking off his coat. For it struck him that at that spot – a corner of the Weir – something glistened, which did not move and come over with the glistening water-drops, but remained stationary.

He assured himself of this, he threw off his clothes, he plunged into the icy water, and swam for the spot. Climbing the timbers, he took from them, caught among their interstices by its chain, a gold watch, bearing engraved upon its back E. D.

He brought the watch to the bank, swam to the Weir again, climbed it, and dived off. He knew every hole and corner of all the depths, and dived and dived and dived, until he could bear the cold no more. His notion was, that he would find the body; he only found a shirt-pin sticking in some mud and ooze.

With these discoveries he returned to Cloisterham, and, taking Neville Landless with him, went straight to the Mayor. Mr. Jasper was sent for, the watch and shirt-pin were identified, Neville was detained, and the wildest frenzy and fatuity of evil report rose against him. He was of that vindictive and violent nature, that but for his poor sister, who alone had influence over him, and out of whose sight he was never to be trusted, he would be in the daily commission of murder. Before coming to England he had caused to be whipped to death sundry 'Natives' – nomadic persons, encamping now in Asia, now in Africa, now in the West Indies, and now at the North Pole – vaguely supposed in Cloisterham to be always black, always of great virtue, always calling themselves Me, and everybody else Massa or Missie (according to sex), and always reading tracts of the obscurest meaning, in broken English, but always accurately understanding them in the purest mother tongue. He had nearly brought

Mrs. Crisparkle's grey hairs with sorrow to the grave. (Those original expressions were Mr. Sapsea's.) He had repeatedly said he would have Mr. Crisparkle's life. He had repeatedly said he would have everybody's life, and become in effect the last man. He had been brought down to Cloisterham, from London, by an eminent Philanthropist, and why? Because that Philanthropist had expressly declared: 'I owe it to my fellow-creatures that he should be, in the words of BENTHAM, where he is the cause of the greatest danger to the smallest number.'

These dropping shots from the blunderbusses of blunderheadedness might not have hit him in a vital place. But he had to stand against a trained and well-directed fire of arms of precision too. He had notoriously threatened the lost young man, and had, according to the showing of his own faithful friend and tutor who strove so hard for him, a cause of bitter animosity (created by himself, and stated by himself), against that ill-starred fellow. He had armed himself with an offensive weapon for the fatal night, and he had gone off early in the morning, after making preparations for departure. He had been found with traces of blood on him; truly, they might have been wholly caused as he represented, but they might not, also. On a search-warrant being issued for the examination of his room, clothes, and so forth, it was discovered that he had destroyed all his papers, and rearranged all his possessions, on the very afternoon of the disappearance. The watch found at the Weir was challenged by the jeweller as one he had wound and set for Edwin Drood, at twenty minutes past two on that same afternoon; and it had run down, before being cast into the water; and it was the jeweller's positive opinion that it had never been re-wound. This would justify the hypothesis that the watch was taken from him not long after he left Mr. Jasper's house at midnight, in company with the last person seen with him, and that it had been thrown away after being retained some hours. Why thrown away? If he had been murdered, and so artfully disfigured, or concealed, or both, as that the murderer hoped identification to be impossible, except from something that he wore, assuredly the murderer would seek to remove from the body the most lasting, the best known, and the most easily recognisable, things upon it. Those things would be the watch and shirt-pin. As to his opportunities of casting them into the river; if he were the object of these suspicions, they were easy. For, he had been seen by many persons, wandering about on that side of the city – indeed on all sides of it – in a miserable and seemingly half-distracted manner. As to the choice of the spot, obviously such criminating evidence had better take its chance of being found anywhere, rather than upon himself, or in his possession. Concerning the reconciliatory nature of the appointed meeting between the two young men, very little could be made of that in young Landless's favour; for it distinctly appeared that the meeting originated, not with him, but with Mr. Crisparkle, and that it had been urged on by Mr. Crisparkle; and who could say how unwillingly, or in what ill-conditioned mood, his enforced pupil had gone to it? The more his case was looked into, the weaker it became in every point. Even the broad suggestion that the lost young man had absconded, was rendered additionally improbable on the showing of the young lady from whom he had so lately parted; for; what did she say, with great earnestness and sorrow, when interrogated? That he had, expressly and enthusiastically, planned with her, that he would await the arrival of her guardian, Mr. Grewgious. And yet, be it observed, he disappeared before that gentleman appeared.

On the suspicions thus urged and supported, Neville was detained, and re-detained, and the search was pressed on every hand, and Jasper laboured night and day. But nothing more was found. No discovery being made, which proved the lost man to be dead, it at length became necessary to release the person suspected of having made away with him. Neville was set at large. Then, a consequence ensued which Mr. Crisparkle had too well foreseen. Neville must leave the place, for the place shunned him and cast him out. Even had it not been so, the dear old china shepherdess would have worried herself to death with fears for her son, and with general trepidation occasioned by their having such an inmate. Even had that not been so, the authority to which the Minor Canon deferred officially, would have settled the point.

'Mr. Crisparkle,' quoth the Dean, 'human justice may err, but it must act according to its lights. The days of taking sanctuary are past. This young man must not take sanctuary with us.'

'You mean that he must leave my house, sir?'

'Mr. Crisparkle,' returned the prudent Dean, 'I claim no authority in your house. I merely confer with you, on the painful necessity you find yourself under, of depriving this young man of the great advantages of your counsel and instruction.'

'It is very lamentable, sir,' Mr. Crisparkle represented.

'Very much so,' the Dean assented.

'And if it be a necessity – ' Mr. Crisparkle faltered.

'As you unfortunately find it to be,' returned the Dean.

Mr. Crisparkle bowed submissively: 'It is hard to prejudge his case, sir, but I am sensible that – '

'Just so. Perfectly. As you say, Mr. Crisparkle,' interposed the Dean, nodding his head smoothly, 'there is nothing else to be done. No doubt, no doubt. There is no alternative, as your good sense has discovered.'

'I am entirely satisfied of his perfect innocence, sir, nevertheless.'

'We-e-ell!' said the Dean, in a more confidential tone, and slightly glancing around him, 'I would not say so, generally. Not generally. Enough of suspicion attaches to him to – no, I think I would not say so, generally.'

Mr. Crisparkle bowed again.

'It does not become us, perhaps,' pursued the Dean, 'to be partisans. Not partisans. We clergy keep our hearts warm and our heads cool, and we hold a judicious middle course.'

'I hope you do not object, sir, to my having stated in public, emphatically, that he will reappear here, whenever any new suspicion may be awakened, or any new circumstance may come to light in this extraordinary matter?'

'Not at all,' returned the Dean. 'And yet, do you know, I don't think,' with a very nice and neat emphasis on those two words: 'I *don't think* I would state it emphatically. State it? Ye-e-es! But emphatically? No-o-o. I *think* not. In point of fact, Mr. Crisparkle, keeping our hearts warm and our heads cool, we clergy need do nothing emphatically.'

So Minor Canon Row knew Neville Landless no more; and he went whithersoever he would, or could, with a blight upon his name and fame.

It was not until then that John Jasper silently resumed his place in the choir. Haggard and red-eyed, his hopes plainly had deserted him, his sanguine mood was gone, and all his worst misgivings had come back. A day or two afterwards, while unrobing, he took his Diary from a pocket of his coat, turned the leaves, and with an impressive look, and without one spoken word, handed this entry to Mr. Crisparkle to read:

'My dear boy is murdered. The discovery of the watch and shirt-pin convinces me that he was murdered that night, and that his jewellery was taken from him to prevent identification by its means. All the delusive hopes I had founded on his separation from his betrothed wife, I give to the winds. They perish before this fatal discovery. I now swear, and record the oath on this page, That I nevermore will discuss this mystery with any human creature until I hold the clue to it in my hand. That I never will relax in my secrecy or in my search. That I will fasten the crime of the murder of my dear dead boy upon the murderer. And, That I devote myself to his destruction.'

* D *

CHAPTER XVII
Philanthropy, Professional and Unprofessional

FULL HALF A year had come and gone, and Mr. Crisparkle sat in a waiting-room in the London chief offices of the Haven of Philanthropy, until he could have audience of Mr. Honeythunder.

In his college days of athletic exercises, Mr. Crisparkle had known professors of the Noble Art of fisticuffs, and had attended two or three of their gloved gatherings. He had now an opportunity of observing that as to the phrenological formation of the backs of their heads, the Professing Philanthropists were uncommonly like the Pugilists. In the development of all those organs which constitute, or attend, a propensity to 'pitch into' your fellow-creatures, the Philanthropists were remarkably favoured. There were several Professors passing in and out, with exactly the aggressive air upon them of being ready for a turn-up with any Novice who might happen to be on hand, that Mr. Crisparkle well remembered in the circles of the Fancy. Preparations were in progress for a moral little Mill somewhere on the rural circuit, and other Professors were backing this or that Heavy-Weight as good for such or such speech-making hits, so very much after the manner of the sporting publicans, that the intended Resolutions might have been Rounds. In an official manager of these displays much celebrated for his platform tactics, Mr. Crisparkle recognised (in a suit of black) the counterpart of a deceased benefactor of his species, an eminent public character, once known to fame as Frosty-faced Fogo, who in days of yore superintended the formation of the magic circle with the ropes and stakes. There were only three conditions of resemblance wanting between these Professors and those. Firstly, the Philanthropists were in very bad training: much too fleshy, and presenting, both in face and figure, a superabundance of what is known to Pugilistic Experts as Suet Pudding. Secondly, the Philanthropists had not the good temper of the Pugilists, and used worse language. Thirdly, their fighting code stood in great need of revision, as empowering them not only to bore their man to the ropes, but to bore him to the confines of distraction; also to hit him when he was down, hit him anywhere and anyhow, kick him, stamp upon him, gouge him, and maul him behind his back without mercy. In these last particulars the Professors of the Noble Art were much nobler than the Professors of Philanthropy.

Mr. Crisparkle was so completely lost in musing on these similarities and dissimilarities, at the same time watching the crowd which came and went by, always, as it seemed, on errands of antagonistically snatching something from somebody, and never giving anything to anybody, that his name was called before he heard it. On his at length responding, he was shown by a miserably shabby and underpaid stipendiary Philanthropist (who could hardly have done worse if he had taken service with a declared enemy of the human race) to Mr. Honeythunder's room.

'Sir,' said Mr. Honeythunder, in his tremendous voice, like a schoolmaster issuing orders to a boy of whom he had a bad opinion, 'sit down.'

Mr. Crisparkle seated himself.

Mr. Honeythunder having signed the remaining few score of a few thousand circulars, calling upon a corresponding number of families without means to come forward, stump up instantly, and be Philanthropists, or go to the Devil, another shabby stipendiary Philanthropist (highly disinterested, if in earnest) gathered these into a basket and walked off with them.

'Now, Mr. Crisparkle,' said Mr. Honeythunder, turning his chair half round towards him when they were alone, and squaring his arms with his hands on his knees, and his brows knitted, as if he added, I am going to make short work of *you*: 'Now, Mr. Crisparkle, we entertain different views, you and I, sir, of the sanctity of human life.'

'Do we?' returned the Minor Canon.

'We do, sir?'

'Might I ask you,' said the Minor Canon: 'what are your views on that subject?'

'That human life is a thing to be held sacred, sir.'

'Might I ask you,' pursued the Minor Canon as before: 'what you suppose to be my views on that subject?'

'By George, sir!' returned the Philanthropist, squaring his arms still more, as he frowned on Mr. Crisparkle: 'they are best known to yourself.'

'Readily admitted. But you began by saying that we took different views, you know. Therefore (or you could not say so) you must have set up some views as mine. Pray, what views *have* you set up as mine?'

'Here is a man – and a young man,' said Mr. Honeythunder, as if that made the matter infinitely worse, and he could have easily borne the loss of an old one, 'swept off the face of the earth by a deed of violence. What do you call that?'

'Murder,' said the Minor Canon.

'What do you call the doer of that deed, sir?'

'A murderer,' said the Minor Canon.

'I am glad to hear you admit so much, sir,' retorted Mr. Honeythunder, in his most offensive manner; 'and I candidly tell you that I didn't expect it.' Here he lowered heavily at Mr. Crisparkle again.

'Be so good as to explain what you mean by those very unjustifiable expressions.'

'I don't sit here, sir,' returned the Philanthropist, raising his voice to a roar, 'to be browbeaten.'

'As the only other person present, no one can possibly know that better than I do,' returned the Minor Canon very quietly. 'But I interrupt your explanation.'

'Murder!' proceeded Mr. Honeythunder, in a kind of boisterous reverie, with his platform folding of his arms, and his platform nod of abhorrent reflection after each short sentiment of a word. 'Bloodshed! Abel! Cain! I hold no terms with Cain. I repudiate with a shudder the red hand when it is offered me.'

Instead of instantly leaping into his chair and cheering himself hoarse, as the Brotherhood in public meeting assembled would infallibly have done on this cue, Mr. Crisparkle merely reversed the quiet crossing of his legs, and said mildly: 'Don't let me interrupt your explanation – when you begin it.'

'The Commandments say, no murder. NO murder, sir!' proceeded Mr. Honeythunder, platformally pausing as if he took Mr. Crisparkle to task for having distinctly asserted that they said: You may do a little murder, and then leave off.

'And they also say, you shall bear no false witness,' observed Mr. Crisparkle.

'Enough!' bellowed Mr. Honeythunder, with a solemnity and severity that would have brought the house down at a meeting, 'E-e-nough! My late wards being now of age, and I being released from a trust which I cannot contemplate without a thrill of horror, there are the accounts which you have undertaken to accept on their behalf, and there is a statement of the balance which you have undertaken to receive, and which you cannot receive too soon. And let me tell you, sir, I wish that, as a man and a Minor Canon, you were better employed,' with a nod. 'Better employed,' with another nod. 'Bet-ter em-ployed!' with another and the three nods added up.

Mr. Crisparkle rose; a little heated in the face, but with perfect command of himself.

'Mr. Honeythunder,' he said, taking up the papers referred to: 'my being better or worse employed than I am at present is a matter of taste and opinion. You might think me better employed in enrolling myself a member of your Society.'

'Ay, indeed, sir!' retorted Mr. Honeythunder, shaking his head in a threatening manner. 'It would have been better for you if you had done that long ago!'

'I think otherwise.'

'Or,' said Mr. Honeythunder, shaking his head again, 'I might think one of your profession better employed in devoting himself to the discovery and punishment of guilt than in leaving that duty to be undertaken by a layman.'

'I may regard my profession from a point of view which teaches me that its first duty is towards those who are in necessity and tribulation, who are desolate and oppressed,' said Mr. Crisparkle. 'However, as I have quite clearly satisfied myself that it is no part of my profession to make professions, I say no more of that. But I owe it to Mr. Neville, and to Mr. Neville's sister (and in a much lower degree to myself), to say to you that I *know* I was in the full possession and understanding of Mr. Neville's mind and heart at the time of this occurrence; and that, without in the least colouring or concealing what was to be deplored in him and required to be corrected, I feel certain that his tale is true. Feeling that certainty, I befriend him. As long as that certainty shall last, I will befriend him. And if any consideration could shake me in this resolve, I should be so ashamed of myself for my meanness, that no man's good opinion – no, nor no woman's – so gained, could compensate me for the loss of my own.'

Good fellow! manly fellow! And he was so modest, too. There was no more self-assertion in the Minor Canon than in the schoolboy who had stood in the breezy playing-fields keeping a wicket. He was simply and staunchly true to his duty alike in the large case and in the small. So all true souls ever are. So every true soul ever was, ever is, and ever will be.

There is nothing little to the really great in spirit.

'Then who do you make out did the deed?' asked Mr. Honeythunder, turning on him abruptly.

'Heaven forbid,' said Mr. Crisparkle, 'that in my desire to clear one man I should lightly criminate another! I accuse no one.'

'Tcha!' ejaculated Mr. Honeythunder with great disgust; for this was by no means the principle on which the Philanthropic Brotherhood usually proceeded. 'And, sir, you are not a disinterested witness, we must bear in mind.'

'How am I an interested one?' inquired Mr. Crisparkle, smiling innocently, at a loss to imagine.

'There was a certain stipend, sir, paid to you for your pupil, which may have warped your judgment a bit,' said Mr. Honeythunder, coarsely.

'Perhaps I expect to retain it still?' Mr. Crisparkle returned, enlightened; 'do you mean that too?'

'Well, sir,' returned the professional Philanthropist, getting up and thrusting his hands down into his trousers-pockets, 'I don't go about measuring people for caps. If people find I have any about me that fit 'em, they can put 'em on and wear 'em, if they like. That's their look out: not mine.'

Mr. Crisparkle eyed him with a just indignation, and took him to task thus:

'Mr. Honeythunder, I hoped when I came in here that I might be under no necessity of commenting on the introduction of platform manners or platform manœuvres among the decent forbearances of private life. But you have given me such a specimen of both, that I should be a fit subject for both if I remained silent respecting them. They are detestable.'

'They don't suit *you*, I dare say, sir.'

'They are,' repeated Mr. Crisparkle, without noticing the interruption, 'detestable. They violate equally the justice that should belong to Christians, and the restraints that should belong to gentlemen. You assume a great crime to have been committed by one whom I, acquainted with the attendant circumstances, and having numerous reasons on my side, devoutly believe to be innocent of it. Because I differ from you on that vital point, what is your platform resource? Instantly to turn upon me, charging that I have no sense of the enormity of the crime itself, but am its aider and abettor! So, another time – taking me as representing your opponent in other cases – you set up a platform credulity; a moved and seconded and carried-unanimously profession of faith in some ridiculous delusion or mischievous imposition. I decline to believe it, and you fall back upon your platform resource of proclaiming that I believe nothing; that because I will not bow down to a false God of your making, I deny the true God! Another time you make the platform discovery that War is a calamity, and you propose to abolish it by a string of twisted resolutions tossed into the air like the tail of a kite. I do not admit the discovery to be yours in the least, and I have not a grain of faith in your remedy. Again, your platform resource of representing me as revelling in the horrors of a battle-field like a fiend incarnate! Another time, in another of your undiscriminating platform rushes, you would punish the sober for the drunken. I claim consideration for the comfort, convenience, and refreshment of the sober; and you presently make platform proclamation that I have a depraved desire to turn Heaven's creatures into swine and wild beasts! In all such cases your movers, and your seconders, and your supporters – your regular Professors of all degrees, run amuck like so many mad Malays; habitually attributing the lowest and basest motives with the utmost recklessness (let me call your attention to a recent instance in yourself for which you should blush), and quoting figures which you know to be as wilfully onesided as a statement of any complicated account that should be all Creditor side and no Debtor, or all Debtor side and no Creditor. Therefore it is, Mr. Honeythunder, that I consider the platform a sufficiently bad example and a sufficiently bad school, even in public life; but hold that, carried into private life, it becomes an unendurable nuisance.'

'These are strong words, sir!' exclaimed the Philanthropist.

'I hope so,' said Mr. Crisparkle. 'Good morning.'

He walked out of the Haven at a great rate, but soon fell into his regular brisk pace, and soon had a smile upon his face as he went along, wondering what the china shepherdess would have said if she had seen him pounding Mr. Honeythunder in the late little lively affair. For Mr. Crisparkle had just enough of harmless vanity to hope that he had hit hard, and to glow with the belief that he had trimmed the Philanthropic Jacket pretty handsomely.

He took himself to Staple Inn, but not to P. J. T. and Mr. Grewgious. Full many a creaking stair he climbed before he reached some attic rooms in a corner, turned the latch of their unbolted door, and stood beside the table of Neville Landless.

An air of retreat and solitude hung about the rooms and about their inhabitant. He was much worn, and so were they. Their sloping ceilings, cumbrous rusty locks and grates, and heavy wooden bins and beams, slowly mouldering withal, had a prisonous look, and he had the haggard face of a prisoner. Yet the sunlight shone in at the ugly garret-window, which had a penthouse to itself thrust out among the tiles; and on the cracked and smoke-blackened parapet beyond, some of the deluded sparrows of the place rheumatically hopped, like little feathered cripples who had left their crutches in their nests; and there was a play of living leaves at hand that changed the air, and made an imperfect sort of music in it that would have been melody in the country.

The rooms were sparely furnished, but with good store of books. Everything expressed the abode of a poor student. That Mr. Crisparkle had been either chooser, lender, or donor of the books, or that he combined the three characters, might have been easily seen in the friendly beam of his eyes upon them as he entered.

'How goes it, Neville?'

'I am in good heart, Mr. Crisparkle, and working away.'

'I wish your eyes were not quite so large and not quite so bright,' said the Minor Canon, slowly releasing the hand he had taken in his.

'They brighten at the sight of you,' returned Neville. 'If you were to fall away from me, they would soon be dull enough.'

'Rally, rally!' urged the other, in a stimulating tone. 'Fight for it, Neville!'

'If I were dying, I feel as if a word from you would rally me; if my pulse had stopped, I feel as if your touch would make it beat again,' said Neville. 'But I *have* rallied, and am doing famously.'

Mr. Crisparkle turned him with his face a little more towards the light.

'I want to see a ruddier touch here, Neville,' he said, indicating his own healthy cheek by way of pattern. 'I want more sun to shine upon you.'

Neville drooped suddenly, as he replied in a lowered voice: 'I am not hardy enough for that, yet. I may become so, but I cannot bear it yet. If you had gone through those Cloisterham streets as I did; if you had seen, as I did, those averted eyes, and the better sort of people silently giving me too much room to pass, that I might not touch them or come near them, you wouldn't think it quite unreasonable that I cannot go about in the daylight.'

'My poor fellow!' said the Minor Canon, in a tone so purely sympathetic that the young man caught his hand, 'I never said it was unreasonable; never thought so. But I should like you to do it.'

'And that would give me the strongest motive to do it. But I cannot yet. I cannot persuade myself that the eyes of even the stream of strangers I pass in this vast city look at me without suspicion. I feel marked and tainted, even when I go out – as I do only – at night. But the darkness covers me then, and I take courage from it.'

Mr. Crisparkle laid a hand upon his shoulder, and stood looking down at him.

'If I could have changed my name,' said Neville, 'I would have done so. But as you wisely pointed out to me, I can't do that, for it would look like guilt. If I could have gone to some distant place, I might have found relief in that, but the thing is not to be thought of, for the same reason. Hiding and escaping would be the construction in either case. It seems a little hard to be so tied to a stake, and innocent; but I don't complain.'

'And you must expect no miracle to help you, Neville,' said Mr. Crisparkle, compassionately.

'No, sir, I know that. The ordinary fulness of time and circumstances is all I have to trust to.'

'It will right you at last, Neville.'

'So I believe, and I hope I may live to know it.'

But perceiving that the despondent mood into which he was falling cast a shadow on the Minor Canon, and (it may be) feeling that the broad hand upon his shoulder was not then quite as steady as its own natural strength had rendered it when it first touched him just now, he brightened and said:

'Excellent circumstances for study, anyhow! and you know, Mr. Crisparkle, what need I have of study in all ways. Not to mention that you have advised me to study for the difficult profession of the law, specially, and that of course I am guiding myself by the advice of such a friend and helper. Such a good friend and helper!'

He took the fortifying hand from his shoulder, and kissed it. Mr. Crisparkle beamed at the books, but not so brightly as when he had entered.

'I gather from your silence on the subject that my late guardian is adverse, Mr. Crisparkle?'

The Minor Canon answered: 'Your late guardian is a – a most

unreasonable person, and it signifies nothing to any reasonable person whether he is *ad*verse, *per*verse, or the *re*verse.'

'Well for me that I have enough with economy to live upon,' sighed Neville, half wearily and half cheerily, 'while I wait to be learned, and wait to be righted! Else I might have proved the proverb, that while the grass grows, the steed starves!'

He opened some books as he said it, and was soon immersed in their interleaved and annotated passages; while Mr. Crisparkle sat beside him, expounding, correcting, and advising. The Minor Canon's Cathedral duties made these visits of his difficult to accomplish, and only to be compassed at intervals of many weeks. But they were as serviceable as they were precious to Neville Landless.

When they had got through such studies as they had in hand, they stood leaning on the window-sill, and looking down upon the patch of garden. 'Next week,' said Mr. Crisparkle, 'you will cease to be alone, and will have a devoted companion.'

'And yet,' returned Neville, 'this seems an uncongenial place to bring my sister to.'

'I don't think so,' said the Minor Canon. 'There is duty to be done here; and there are womanly feeling, sense, and courage wanted here.'

'I meant,' explained Neville, 'that the surroundings are so dull and unwomanly, and that Helena can have no suitable friend or society here.'

'You have only to remember,' said Mr. Crisparkle, 'that you are here yourself, and that she has to draw you into the sunlight.'

They were silent for a little while, and then Mr. Crisparkle began anew.

'When we first spoke together, Neville, you told me that your sister had risen out of the disadvantages of your past lives as superior to you as the tower of Cloisterham Cathedral is higher than the chimneys of Minor Canon Corner. Do you remember that?'

'Right well!'

'I was inclined to think it at the time an enthusiastic flight. No matter what I think it now. What I would emphasise is, that under the head of Pride your sister is a great and opportune example to you.'

'Under *all* heads that are included in the composition of a fine character, she is.'

'Say so; but take this one. Your sister has learnt how to govern what is proud in her nature. She can dominate it even when it is wounded through her sympathy with you. No doubt she has suffered deeply in those same streets where you suffered deeply. No doubt her life is darkened by the cloud that darkens yours. But bending her pride into a grand composure that is not haughty or aggressive, but is a sustained confidence in you and in the truth, she has won her way through those streets until she passes along them as high in the general respect as any one who treads them. Every day and hour of her life since Edwin Drood's disappearance, she has faced malignity and folly – for you – as only a brave nature well directed can. So it will be with her to the end. Another and weaker kind of pride might sink broken-hearted, but never such a pride as hers: which knows no shrinking, and can get no mastery over her.'

The pale cheek beside him flushed under the comparison, and the hint implied in it.

'I will do all I can to imitate her,' said Neville.

'Do so, and be a truly brave man, as she is a truly brave woman,' answered Mr. Crisparkle stoutly. 'It is growing dark. Will you go my way with me, when it is quite dark? Mind! it is not I who wait for darkness.'

Neville replied, that he would accompany him directly. But Mr. Crisparkle said he had a moment's call to make on Mr. Grewgious as an act of courtesy, and would run across to that gentleman's chambers, and rejoin Neville on his own doorstep, if he would come down there to meet him.

Mr. Grewgious, bolt upright as usual, sat taking his wine in the dusk at his open window; his wineglass and decanter on the round table at his elbow; himself and his legs on the window-seat; only one hinge in his whole body, like a bootjack.

'How do you do, reverend sir?' said Mr. Grewgious, with abundant offers of hospitality, which were as cordially declined as made. 'And how is your charge getting on over the way in the set that I had the pleasure of recommending to you as vacant and eligible?'

Mr. Crisparkle replied suitably.

'I am glad you approve of them,' said Mr. Grewgious, 'because I entertain a sort of fancy for having him under my eye.'

As Mr. Grewgious had to turn his eye up considerably before he could see the chambers, the phrase was to be taken figuratively and not literally.

'And how did you leave Mr. Jasper, reverend sir?' said Mr. Grewgious.

Mr. Crisparkle had left him pretty well.

'And where did you leave Mr. Jasper, reverend sir?' Mr. Crisparkle had left him at Cloisterham.

'And when did you leave Mr. Jasper, reverend sir?' That morning.

'Umps!' said Mr. Grewgious. 'He didn't say he was coming, perhaps?'

'Coming where?'

'Anywhere, for instance?' said Mr. Grewgious.

'No.'

'Because here he is,' said Mr. Grewgious, who had asked all these questions, with his preoccupied glance directed out at window. 'And he don't look agreeable, does he?'

Mr. Crisparkle was craning towards the window, when Mr. Grewgious added:

'If you will kindly step round here behind me, in the gloom of the room, and will cast your eye at the second-floor landing window in yonder house, I think you will hardly fail to see a slinking individual in whom I recognise our local friend.'

'You are right!' cried Mr. Crisparkle.

'Umps!' said Mr. Grewgious. Then he added, turning his face so abruptly that his head nearly came into collision with Mr. Crisparkle's: 'what should you say that our local friend was up to?'

The last passage he had been shown in the Diary returned on Mr. Crisparkle's mind with the force of a strong recoil, and he asked Mr. Grewgious if he thought it possible that Neville was to be harassed by the keeping of a watch upon him?

'A watch?' repeated Mr. Grewgious musingly. 'Ay!'

'Which would not only of itself haunt and torture his life,' said Mr. Crisparkle warmly, 'but would expose him to the torment of a perpetually reviving suspicion, whatever he might do, or wherever he might go.'

'Ay!' said Mr. Grewgious musingly still. 'Do I see him waiting for you?'

'No doubt you do.'

'Then *would* you have the goodness to excuse my getting up to see you out, and to go out to join him, and to go the way that you were going, and to take no notice of our local friend?' said Mr. Grewgious. 'I entertain a sort of fancy for having *him* under my eye to-night, do you know?'

Mr. Crisparkle, with a significant need complied; and rejoining Neville, went away with him. They dined together, and parted at the yet unfinished and undeveloped railway station: Mr. Crisparkle to get home; Neville to walk the streets, cross the bridges, make a wide round of the city in the friendly darkness, and tire himself out.

It was midnight when he returned from his solitary expedition and climbed his staircase. The night was hot, and the windows of the staircase were all wide open. Coming to the top, it gave him a passing chill of surprise (there being no rooms but his up there) to find a stranger sitting on the window-sill, more after the manner of a venturesome glazier than an amateur ordinarily careful of his neck; in fact, so much more outside the window than inside, as to suggest the thought that he must have come up by the water-spout instead of the stairs.

The stranger said nothing until Neville put his key in his door; then, seeming to make sure of his identity from the action, he spoke:

'I beg your pardon,' he said, coming from the window with a frank and smiling air, and a prepossessing address; 'the beans.'

Neville was quite at a loss.

'Runners,' said the visitor. 'Scarlet. Next door at the back.'

'O,' returned Neville. 'And the mignonette and wall-flower?'

'The same,' said the visitor.

'Pray walk in.'

'Thank you.'

Neville lighted his candles, and the visitor sat down. A handsome gentleman, with a young face, but with an older figure in its robustness and its breadth of shoulder; say a man of eight-and-twenty, or at the utmost thirty; so extremely sunburnt that the contrast between his brown visage and the white forehead shaded out of doors by his hat, and the glimpses of white throat below the neckerchief, would have been almost ludicrous but for his broad temples, bright blue eyes, clustering brown hair, and laughing teeth.

'I have noticed,' said he; ' – my name is Tartar.'

Neville inclined his head.

'I have noticed (excuse me) that you shut yourself up a good deal, and that you seem to like my garden aloft here. If you would like a little more of it, I could throw out a few lines and stays between my windows and yours, which the runners would take to directly. And I have some boxes, both of mignonette and wall-flower, that I could shove on along the gutter (with a boathook I have by me) to your windows, and draw back again when they wanted watering or gardening, and shove on again when they were ship-shape; so that they would cause you no trouble. I couldn't take this liberty without asking your permission, so I venture to ask it. Tartar, corresponding set, next door.'

175

'You are very kind.'

'Not at all. I ought to apologise for looking in so late. But having noticed (excuse me) that you generally walk out at night, I thought I should inconvenience you least by awaiting your return. I am always afraid of inconveniencing busy men, being an idle man.'

'I should not have thought so, from your appearance.'

'No? I take it as a compliment. In fact, I was bred in the Royal Navy, and was First Lieutenant when I quitted it. But, an uncle disappointed in the service leaving me his property on condition that I left the Navy, I accepted the fortune, and resigned my commission.'

'Lately, I presume?'

'Well, I had had twelve or fifteen years of knocking about first. I came here some nine months before you; I had had one crop before you came. I chose this place, because, having served last in a little corvette, I knew I should feel more at home where I had a constant opportunity of knocking my head against the ceiling. Besides, it would never do for a man who had been aboard ship from his boyhood to turn luxurious all at once. Besides, again; having been accustomed to a very short allowance of land all my life, I thought I'd feel my way to the command of a landed estate, by beginning in boxes.'

Whimsically as this was said, there was a touch of merry earnestness in it that made it doubly whimsical.

'However,' said the Lieutenant, 'I have talked quite enough about myself. It is not my way, I hope; it has merely been to present myself to you naturally. If you will allow me to take the liberty I have described, it will be a charity, for it will give me something more to do. And you are not to suppose that it will entail any interruption or intrusion on you, for that is far from my intention.'

Neville replied that he was greatly obliged, and that he thankfully accepted the kind proposal.

'I am very glad to take your windows in tow,' said the Lieutenant. 'From what I have seen of you when I have been gardening at mine, and you have been looking on, I have thought you (excuse me) rather too studious and delicate. May I ask, is your health at all affected?'

'I have undergone some mental distress,' said Neville, confused, 'which has stood me in the stead of illness.'

'Pardon me,' said Mr. Tartar.

With the greatest delicacy he shifted his ground to the windows again, and asked if he could look at one of them. On Neville's opening it, he immediately sprang out, as if he were going aloft with a whole watch in an emergency, and were setting a bright example.

'For Heaven's sake,' cried Neville, 'don't do that! Where are you going Mr. Tartar? You'll be dashed to pieces!'

'All well!' said the Lieutenant, coolly looking about him on the housetop. 'All taut and trim here. Those lines and stays shall be rigged before you turn out in the morning. May I take this short cut home, and say good-night?'

'Mr. Tartar!' urged Neville. 'Pray! It makes me giddy to see you!'

But Mr. Tartar, with a wave of his hand and the deftness of a cat, had already dipped through his scuttle of scarlet runners without breaking a leaf, and 'gone below.'

Mr. Grewgious, his bedroom window-blind held aside with his hand, happened at the moment to have Neville's chambers under his eye for the last time that night. Fortunately his eye was on the front of the house and not the back, or this remarkable appearance and disappearance might have broken his rest as a phenomenon. But Mr. Grewgious seeing nothing there, not even a light in the windows, his gaze wandered from the windows to the stars, as if he would have read in them something that was hidden from him. Many of us would, if we could; but none of us so much as know our letters in the stars yet – or seem likely to do it, in this state of existence – and few languages can be read until their alphabets are mastered.

CHAPTER XVIII
A Settler in Cloisterham

AT ABOUT THIS time a stranger appeared in Cloisterham; a white-haired personage, with black eyebrows. Being buttoned up in a tightish blue surtout, with a buff waistcoat and grey trousers, he had something of a military air, but he announced himself at the Crozier (the orthodox hotel, where he put up with a portmanteau) as an idle dog who lived upon his means; and he farther announced that he had a mind to take a lodging in the picturesque old city for a month or two, with a view of settling down there altogether. Both announcements were made in the coffee-room of the Crozier, to all whom it might or might not concern, by the stranger as he stood with his back to the empty fireplace, waiting for his fried sole, veal cutlet, and pint of sherry. And the waiter (business being chronically slack at the Crozier) represented all whom it might or might not concern, and absorbed the whole of the information.

This gentleman's white head was unusually large, and his shock of white hair was unusually thick and ample. 'I suppose, waiter,' he said, shaking his shock of hair, as a Newfoundland dog might shake his before sitting down to dinner, 'that a fair lodging for a single buffer might be found in these parts, eh?'

The waiter had no doubt of it.

'Something old,' said the gentleman. 'Take my hat down for a moment from that peg, will you? No, I don't want it; look into it. What do you see written there?'

The waiter read: 'Datchery.'

'Now you know my name,' said the gentleman; 'Dick Datchery. Hang it up again. I was saying something old is what I should prefer, something odd and out of the way; something venerable, architectural, and inconvenient.'

'We have a good choice of inconvenient lodgings in the town, sir, I think,' replied the waiter, with modest confidence in its resources that way; 'indeed, I have no doubt that we could suit you that far, however particular you might be. But a architectural lodging!' That seemed to trouble the waiter's head, and he shook it.

'Anything Cathedraly, now,' Mr. Datchery suggested.

'Mr. Tope,' said the waiter, brightening, as he rubbed his chin with his hand, 'would be the likeliest party to inform in that line.'

'Who is Mr. Tope?' inquired Dick Datchery.

The waiter explained that he was the Verger, and that Mrs. Tope had indeed once upon a time let lodgings herself or offered to let them; but that as nobody had ever taken them, Mrs. Tope's window-bill, long a Cloisterham Institution, had disappeared; probably had tumbled down one day, and never been put up again.

'I'll call on Mrs. Tope,' said Mr. Datchery, 'after dinner.'

So when he had done his dinner, he was duly directed to the spot, and sallied out for it. But the Crozier being an hotel of a most retiring disposition, and the waiter's directions being fatally precise, he soon became bewildered, and went boggling about and about the Cathedral Tower, whenever he could catch a glimpse of it, with a general impression on his mind that Mrs. Tope's was somewhere very near it, and that, like the children in the game of hot boiled beans and very good butter, he was warm in his search when he saw the Tower, and cold when he didn't see it.

He was getting very cold indeed when he came upon a fragment of burial-ground in which an unhappy sheep was grazing. Unhappy, because a hideous small boy was stoning it through the railings, and had already lamed it in one leg, and was much excited by the benevolent sportsmanlike purpose of breaking its other three legs, and bringing it down.

''It 'im agin!' cried the boy, as the poor creature leaped; 'and made a dint in his wool.'

'Let him be!' said Mr. Datchery. 'Don't you see you have lamed him?'

'Yer lie,' returned the sportsman. ''E went and lamed isself. I see 'im do it, and I giv' 'im a shy as a Widdy-warning to 'im not to go a-bruisin' 'is master's mutton any more.'

'Come here.'

'I won't; I'll come when yer can ketch me.'

'Stay there then, and show me which is Mr. Tope's.'

'Ow can I stay here and show you which is Topeseses, when Topeseses is t'other side the Kinfreederal, and over the crossings, and round ever so many comers? Stoo-pid! Ya-a-ah!'

'Show me where it is, and I'll give you something.'

'Come on, then.'

This brisk dialogue concluded, the boy led the way, and by-and-by stopped at some distance from an arched passage, pointing.

'Lookie yonder. You see that there winder and door?'

'That's Tope's?'

'Yer lie; it ain't. That's Jarsper's.'

'Indeed?' said Mr. Datchery, with a second look of some interest.

'Yes, and I ain't a-goin' no nearer 'IM, I tell yer.'

'Why not?'

''Cos I ain't a-goin' to be lifted off my legs and 'ave my braces bust and be choked; not if I knows it, and not by 'Im. Wait till I set a jolly good flint a-flyin' at the back o' 'is jolly old 'ed some day! Now look t'other side the harch; not the side where Jarsper's door is; t'other side.'

'I see.'

'A little way in, o' that side, there's a low door, down two steps. That's Topeseses with 'is name on a hoval plate.'

'Good. See here,' said Mr. Datchery, producing a shilling. 'You owe me half of this.'

'Yer lie! I don't owe yer nothing; I never seen yer.'

'I tell you you owe me half of this, because I have no sixpence in my pocket. So the next time you meet me you shall do something else for me, to pay me.'

'All right, give us 'old.'

'What is your name, and where do you live?'

'Deputy. Travellers' Twopenny, 'cross the green.'

The boy instantly darted off with the shilling, lest Mr. Datchery should repent, but stopped at a safe distance, on the happy chance of his being uneasy in his mind about it, to goad him with a demon dance expressive of its irrevocability.

Mr. Datchery, taking off his hat to give that shock of white hair of his another shake, seemed quite resigned, and betook himself whither he had been directed.

Mr. Tope's official dwelling, communicating by an upper stair with Mr. Jasper's (hence Mrs. Tope's attendance on that gentleman), was of very modest proportions, and partook of the character of a cool dungeon. Its ancient walls were massive, and its rooms rather seemed to have been dug out of them, than to have been designed beforehand with any reference to them. The main door opened at once on a chamber of no describable shape, with a groined roof, which in its turn opened on another chamber of no describable shape, with another groined roof: their windows small, and in the thickness of the walls. These two chambers, close as to their atmosphere, and swarthy as to their illumination by natural light, were the apartments which Mrs. Tope had so long offered to an unappreciative city. Mr. Datchery, however, was more appreciative. He found that if he sat with the main door open he would enjoy the passing society of all comers to and fro by the gateway, and would have light enough. He found that if Mr. and Mrs. Tope, living overhead, used for their own egress and ingress a little side stair that came plump into the Precincts by a door opening outward, to the surprise and inconvenience of a limited public of pedestrians in a narrow way, he would be alone, as in a separate residence. He found the rent moderate, and everything as quaintly inconvenient as he could desire. He agreed, therefore, to take the lodging then and there, and money down, possession to be had next evening, on condition that reference was permitted him to Mr. Jasper as occupying the gatehouse, of which on the other side of the gateway, the Verger's hole-in-the-wall was an appanage or subsidiary part.

The poor dear gentleman was very solitary and very sad, Mrs. Tope said, but she had no doubt he would 'speak for her.' Perhaps Mr. Datchery had heard something of what had occurred there last winter?

Mr. Datchery had as confused a knowledge of the event in question, on trying to recall it, as he well could have. He begged Mrs. Tope's pardon when she found it incumbent on her to correct him in every detail of his summary of the facts, but pleaded that he was merely a single buffer getting through life upon his means as idly as he could, and that so many people were so constantly making away with so many other people, as to render it difficult for a buffer of an easy temper to preserve the circumstances of the several cases unmixed in his mind.

Mr. Jasper proving willing to speak for Mrs. Tope, Mr. Datchery, who had sent up his card, was invited to ascend the postern staircase. The Mayor was there, Mr. Tope said; but he was not to be regarded in the light of company, as he and Mr. Jasper were great friends.

'I beg pardon,' said Mr. Datchery, making a leg with his hat under his arm, as he addressed himself equally to both gentlemen; 'a selfish precaution on my part, and not personally interesting to anybody but myself. But as a buffer living on his means, and having an idea of doing it in this lovely place in peace and quiet, for remaining span of life, I beg to ask if the Tope family are quite respectable?'

Mr. Jasper could answer for that without the slightest hesitation.

'That is enough, sir,' said Mr. Datchery.

'My friend the Mayor,' added Mr. Jasper, presenting Mr. Datchery with a courtly motion of his hand towards that potentate; 'whose recommendation is actually much more important to a stranger than that of an obscure person like myself, will testify in their behalf, I am sure.'

'The Worshipful the Mayor,' said Mr. Datchery, with a low bow, 'places me under an infinite obligation.'

'Very good people, sir, Mr. and Mrs. Tope,' said Mr. Sapsea, with condescension. 'Very good opinions. Very well behaved. Very respectful. Much approved by the Dean and Chapter.'

'The Worshipful the Mayor gives them a character,' said Mr. Datchery, 'of which they may indeed be proud. I would ask His Honour (if I might be permitted) whether there are not many objects of great interest in the city which is under his beneficent sway?'

'We are, sir,' returned Mr. Sapsea, 'an ancient city, and an ecclesiastical city. We are a constitutional city, as it becomes such a city to be, and we uphold and maintain our glorious privileges.'

'His Honour,' said Mr. Datchery, bowing, 'inspires me with a desire to know more of the city, and confirms me in my inclination to end my days in the city.'

'Retired from the Army, sir?' suggested Mr. Sapsea.

'His Honour the Mayor does me too much credit,' returned Mr. Datchery.

'Navy, sir?' suggested Mr. Sapsea.

'Again,' repeated Mr. Datchery, 'His Honour the Mayor does me too much credit.'

'Diplomacy is a fine profession,' said Mr. Sapsea, as a general remark.

'There, I confess, His Honour the Mayor is too many for me,' said Mr. Datchery, with an ingenious smile and bow; 'even a diplomatic bird must fall to such a gun.'

Now this was very soothing. Here was a gentleman of a great, not to say a grand, address, accustomed to rank and dignity, really setting a fine example how to behave to a Mayor. There was something in that third-person style of being spoken to, that Mr. Sapsea found particularly recognisant of his merits and position.

'But I crave pardon,' said Mr. Datchery. 'His Honour the Mayor will bear with me, if for a moment I have been deluded into occupying his time, and have forgotten the humble claims upon my own, of my hotel, the Crozier.'

'Not at all, sir,' said Mr. Sapsea. 'I am returning home, and if you would like to take the exterior of our Cathedral in your way, I shall be glad to point it out.'

'His Honour the Mayor,' said Mr. Datchery, 'is more than kind and gracious.'

As Mr. Datchery, when he had made his acknowledgments to Mr. Jasper, could not be induced to go out of the room before the Worshipful, the Worshipful led the way down-stairs; Mr. Datchery following with his hat under his arm, and his shock of white hair streaming in the evening breeze.

'Might I ask His Honour,' said Mr. Datchery, 'whether that gentleman we have just left is the gentleman of whom I have heard in the neighbourhood as being much afflicted by the loss of a nephew, and concentrating his life on avenging the loss?'

'That is the gentleman. John Jasper, sir.'

'Would His Honour allow me to inquire whether there are strong suspicions of any one?'

'More than suspicions, sir,' returned Mr. Sapsea; 'all but certainties.'

'Only think now!' cried Mr. Datchery.

'But proof, sir, proof must be built up stone by stone,' said the Mayor. 'As I say, the end crowns the work. It is not enough that justice should be morally certain; she must be immorally certain – legally, that is.'

'His Honour,' said Mr. Datchery, 'reminds me of the nature of the law. Immoral. How true!'

'As I say, sir,' pompously went on the Mayor, 'the arm of the law is a strong arm, and a long arm. That is the may I put it. A strong arm and a long arm.'

'How forcible! – And yet, again, how true!' murmured Mr. Datchery.

'And without betraying, what I call the secrets of the prison-house,' said Mr. Sapsea; 'the secrets of the prison-house is the term I used on the bench.'

'And what other term than His Honour's would express it?' said Mr. Datchery.

'Without, I say, betraying them, I predict to you, knowing the iron will of the gentleman we have just left (I take the bold step of calling it iron, on account of its strength), that in this case the long arm will reach, and the strong arm will strike. – This is our Cathedral, sir. The best judges are pleased to admire it, and the best among our townsmen own to being a little vain of it.'

All this time Mr. Datchery had walked with his hat under his arm, and his white hair streaming. He had an odd momentary appearance upon him of having forgotten his hat, when Mr. Sapsea now touched it; and he clapped his hand up to his head as if with some vague expectation of finding another hat upon it.

'Pray be covered, sir,' entreated Mr. Sapsea; magnificently plying: 'I shall not mind it, I assure you.'

'His Honour is very good, but I do it for coolness,' said Mr. Datchery.

Then Mr. Datchery admired the Cathedral, and Mr. Sapsea pointed it out as if he himself had invented and built it: there were a few details indeed of which he did not approve, but those he glossed over, as if the workmen had made mistakes in his absence. The Cathedral disposed of, he led the way by the churchyard, and stopped to extol the beauty of the evening – by chance – in the immediate vicinity of Mrs. Sapsea's epitaph.

'And by the by,' said Mr. Sapsea, appearing to descend from an elevation to remember it all of a sudden; like Apollo shooting down from Olympus to pick up his forgotten lyre; '*that* is one of our small lions. The partiality of our people has made it so, and strangers have been seen taking a copy of it now and then. I am not a judge of it myself, for it is a little work of my own. But it was troublesome to turn, sir; I may say, difficult to turn with elegance.'

Mr. Datchery became so ecstatic over Mr. Sapsea's composition, that, in spite of his intention to end his days in Cloisterham, and therefore his probably having in reserve many opportunities of copying it, he would have transcribed it into his pocket-book on the spot, but for the slouching towards them of its material producer and perpetuator, Durdles, whom Mr. Sapsea hailed, not sorry to show him a bright example of behaviour to superiors.

'Ah, Durdles! This is the mason, sir; one of our Cloisterham worthies; everybody here knows Durdles. Mr. Datchery, Durdles a gentleman who is going to settle here.'

'I wouldn't do it if I was him,' growled Durdles. 'We're a heavy lot.'

'You surely don't speak for yourself, Mr. Durdles,' returned Mr. Datchery, 'any more than for His Honour.'

'Who's His Honour?' demanded Durdles.

'His Honour the Mayor.'

'I never was brought afore him,' said Durdles, with anything but the look of a loyal subject of the mayoralty, 'and it'll be time enough for me to Honour him when I am. Until which, and when, and where:

'Mister Sapsea is his name,
   England is his nation,
Cloisterham's his dwelling-place,
   Aukshneer's his occupation.'

Here, Deputy (preceded by a flying oyster-shell) appeared upon the scene, and requested to have the sum of threepence instantly 'chucked' to him by Mr. Durdles, whom he had been vainly seeking up and down, as lawful wages overdue. While that gentleman, with his bundle under his arm, slowly found and counted out the money, Mr. Sapsea informed the new settler of Durdles's habits, pursuits, abode, and reputation. 'I suppose a curious stranger might come to see you, and your works, Mr. Durdles, at any odd time?' said Mr. Datchery upon that.

'Any gentleman is welcome to come and see me any evening if he brings liquor for two with him,' returned Durdles, with a penny between his teeth and certain halfpence in his hands; 'or if he likes to make it twice two, he'll be doubly welcome.'

'I shall come. Master Deputy, what do you owe me?'

'A job.'

'Mind you pay me honestly with the job of showing me Mr. Durdles's house when I want to go there.'

Deputy, with a piercing broadside of whistle through the whole gap in his mouth, as a receipt in full for all arrears, vanished.

The Worshipful and the Worshipper then passed on together until they parted, with many ceremonies, at the Worshipful's door; even then the Worshipper carried his hat under his arm, and gave his streaming white hair to the breeze.

Said Mr. Datchery to himself that night, as he looked at his white hair in the gas-lighted looking-glass over the coffee-room chimneypiece at the Crozier, and shook it out: 'For a single buffer, of an easy temper, living idly on his means, I have had a rather busy afternoon!'

CHAPTER XIX
Shadow on the Sun-Dial

AGAIN MISS TWINKLETON has delivered her valedictory address, with the accompaniments of white-wine and pound-cake, and again the young ladies have departed to their several homes. Helena Landless has left the Nuns' House to attend her brother's fortunes, and pretty Rosa is alone.

Cloisterham is so bright and sunny in these summer days, that the Cathedral and the monastery-ruin show as if their strong walls were transparent. A soft glow seems to shine from within them, rather than upon them from without, such is their mellowness as they look forth on the hot corn-fields and the smoking roads that distantly wind among them. The Cloisterham gardens blush with ripening fruit. Time was when travel-stained pilgrims rode in clattering parties through the city's welcome shades; time is when wayfarers, leading a gipsy life between haymaking time and harvest, and looking as if they were just made of the dust of the earth, so very dusty are they, lounge about on cool door-steps, trying to mend their unmendable shoes, or giving them to the city kennels as a hopeless job, and seeking others in the bundles that they carry, along with their yet unused sickles swathed in bands of straw. At all the more public pumps there is much cooling of bare feet, together with much bubbling and gurgling of drinking with hand to spout on the part of these Bedouins; the Cloisterham police meanwhile looking askant from their beats with suspicion, and manifest impatience that the intruders should depart from within the civic bounds, and once more fry themselves on the simmering high-roads.

On the afternoon of such a day, when the last Cathedral service is done, and when that side of the High Street on which the Nuns' House stands is in grateful shade, save where its quaint old garden opens to the west between the boughs of trees, a servant informs Rosa, to her terror, that Mr. Jasper desires to see her.

If he had chosen his time for finding her at a disadvantage, he could have done no better. Perhaps he has chosen it. Helena Landless is gone, Mrs. Tisher is absent on leave, Miss Twinkleton (in her amateur state of existence) has contributed herself and a veal pie to a picnic.

'O why, why, why, did you say I was at home!' cried Rosa, helplessly.

The maid replies, that Mr. Jasper never asked the question.

That he said he knew she was at home, and begged she might be told that he asked to see her.

'What shall I do! what shall I do!' thinks Rosa, clasping her hands.

Possessed by a kind of desperation, she adds in the next breath, that she will come to Mr. Jasper in the garden. She shudders at the thought of being shut up with him in the house; but many of its windows command the garden, and she can be seen as well as heard there, and can shriek in the free air and run away. Such is the wild idea that flutters through her mind.

She has never seen him since the fatal night, except when she was questioned before the Mayor, and then he was present in gloomy watchfulness, as representing his lost nephew and burning to avenge him. She hangs her garden-hat on her arm, and goes out. The moment she sees him from the porch, leaning on the sun-dial, the old horrible feeling of being compelled by him, asserts its hold upon her. She feels that she would even then go back, but that he draws her feet towards him. She cannot resist, and sits down, with her head bent, on the garden-seat beside the sun-dial. She cannot look up at him for abhorrence, but she has perceived that he is dressed in deep mourning. So is she. It was not so at first; but the lost has long been given up, and mourned for, as dead.

He would begin by touching her hand. She feels the intention, and draws her hand back. His eyes are then fixed upon her, she knows, though her own see nothing but the grass.

'I have been waiting,' he begins, 'for some time, to be summoned back to my duty near you.'

After several times forming her lips, which she knows he is closely watching, into the shape of some other hesitating reply, and then into none, she answers: 'Duty, sir?'

'The duty of teaching you, serving you as your faithful music-master.'

'I have left off that study.'

'Not left off, I think. Discontinued. I was told by your guardian that you discontinued it under the shock that we have all felt so acutely. When will you resume?'

'Never, sir.'

'Never? You could have done no more if you had loved my dear boy.'

'I did love him!' cried Rosa, with a flash of anger.

'Yes; but not quite – not quite in the right way, shall I say? Not in the intended and expected way. Much as my dear boy was, unhappily, too self-conscious and self-satisfied (I'll draw no parallel between him and you in that respect) to love as he should have loved, or as any one in his place would have loved – must have loved!'

She sits in the same still attitude, but shrinking a little more.

'Then, to be told that you discontinued your study with me, was to be politely told that you abandoned it altogether?' he suggested.

'Yes,' says Rosa, with sudden spirit, 'The politeness was my guardian's, not mine. I told him that I was resolved to leave off, and that I was determined to stand by my resolution.'

'And you still are?'

'I still am, sir. And I beg not to be questioned any more about it. At all events, I will not answer any more; I have that in my power.'

She is so conscious of his looking at her with a gloating admiration of the touch of anger on her, and the fire and animation it brings with it, that even as her spirit rises, it falls again, and she struggles with a sense of shame, affront, and fear, much as she did that night at the piano.

'I will not question you any more, since you object to it so much; I will confess – '

'I do not wish to hear you, sir,' cries Rosa, rising.

This time he does touch her with his outstretched hand. In shrinking from it, she shrinks into her seat again.

'We must sometimes act in opposition to our wishes,' he tells her in a low voice. 'You must do so now, or do more harm to others than you can ever set right.'

'What harm?'

'Presently, presently. You question *me*, you see, and surely that's not fair when you forbid me to question you. Nevertheless, I will answer the question presently. Dearest Rosa! Charming Rosa!'

She starts up again.

This time he does not touch her. But his face looks so wicked and menacing, as he stands leaning against the sun-dial-setting, as it were, his black mark upon the very face of day – that her flight is arrested by horror as she looks at him.

188

'I do not forget how many windows command a view of us,' he says, glancing towards them. 'I will not touch you again; I will come no nearer to you than I am. Sit down, and there will be no mighty wonder in your music-master's leaning idly against a pedestal and speaking with you, remembering all that has happened, and our shares in it. Sit down, my beloved.'

She would have gone once more – was all but gone – and once more his face, darkly threatening what would follow if she went, has stopped her. Looking at him with the expression of the instant frozen on her face, she sits down on the seat again.

'Rosa, even when my dear boy was affianced to you, I loved you madly; even when I thought his happiness in having you for his wife was certain, I loved you madly; even when I strove to make him more ardently devoted to you, I loved you madly; even when he gave me the picture of your lovely face so carelessly traduced by him, which I feigned to hang always in my sight for his sake, but worshipped in torment for years, I loved you madly; in the distasteful work of the day, in the wakeful misery of the night, girded by sordid realities, or wandering through Paradises and Hells of visions into which I rushed, carrying your image in my arms, I loved you madly.'

If anything could make his words more hideous to her than they are in themselves, it would be the contrast between the violence of his look and delivery, and the composure of his assumed attitude.

'I endured it all in silence. So long as you were his, or so long as I supposed you to be his, I hid my secret loyally. Did I not?'

This lie, so gross, while the mere words in which it is told are so true, is more than Rosa can endure. She answers with kindling indignation: 'You were as false throughout, sir, as you are now. You were false to him, daily and hourly. You know that you made my life unhappy by your pursuit of me. You know that you made me afraid to open his generous eyes, and that you forced me, for his own trusting, good, good sake, to keep the truth from him, that you were a bad, bad man!'

His preservation of his easy attitude rendering his working features and his convulsive hands absolutely diabolical, he returns, with a fierce extreme of admiration:

'How beautiful you are! You are more beautiful in anger than in repose. I don't ask you for your love; give me yourself and your hatred; give me yourself and that pretty rage; give me yourself and that enchanting scorn; it will be enough for me.'

Impatient tears rise to the eyes of the trembling little beauty, and her face flames; but as she again rises to leave him in indignation, and seek protection within the house, he stretches out his hand towards the porch, as though he invited her to enter it.

'I told you, you rare charmer, you sweet witch, that you must stay and hear me, or do more harm than can ever be undone. You asked me what harm. Stay, and I will tell you. Go, and I will do it!'

Again Rosa quails before his threatening face, though innocent of its meaning, and she remains. Her panting breathing comes and goes as if it would choke her; but with a repressive hand upon her bosom, she remains.

'I have made my confession that my love is mad. It is so mad, that had the ties between me and my dear lost boy been one silken thread less strong, I might have swept even him from your side, when you favoured him.'

A film comes over the eyes she raises for an instant, as though he had turned her faint.

'Even him,' he repeats. 'Yes, even him! Rosa, you see me and you hear me. Judge for yourself whether any other admirer shall love you and live, whose life is in my hand.'

'What do you mean, sir?'

'I mean to show you how mad my love is. It was hawked through the late inquiries by Mr. Crisparkle, that young Landless had confessed to him that he was a rival of my lost boy. That is an inexpiable offence in my eyes. The same Mr. Crisparkle knows under my hand that I have devoted myself to the murderer's discovery and destruction, be he whom he might, and that I determined to discuss the mystery with no one until I should hold the clue in which to entangle the murderer as in a net. I have since worked patiently to wind and wind it round him; and it is slowly winding as I speak.'

'Your belief, if you believe in the criminality of Mr. Landless, is not Mr. Crisparkle's belief, and he is a good man,' Rosa retorts.

'My belief is my own; and I reserve it, worshipped of my soul! Circumstances may accumulate so strongly *even against an innocent man*, that directed, sharpened, and pointed, they may slay him. One wanting link discovered by perseverance against a guilty man, proves his guilt, however slight its evidence before, and he dies. Young Landless stands in deadly peril either way.'

'If you really suppose,' Rosa pleads with him, turning paler, 'that I favour Mr. Landless, or that Mr. Landless has ever in any way addressed himself to me, you are wrong.'

He puts that from him with a slighting action of his hand and a curled lip.

'I was going to show you how madly I love you. More madly now than ever, for I am willing to renounce the second object that has arisen in my life to divide it with you; and henceforth to have no object in existence but you only. Miss Landless has become your bosom friend. You care for her peace of mind?'

'I love her dearly.'

'You care for her good name?'

'I have said, sir, I love her dearly.'

'I am unconsciously,' he observes with a smile, as he folds his hands upon the sun-dial and leans his chin upon them, so that his talk would seem from the windows (faces occasionally come and go there) to be of the airiest and playfullest – 'I am unconsciously giving offence by questioning again. I will simply make statements, therefore, and not put questions. You do care for your bosom friend's good name, and you do care for her peace of mind. Then remove the shadow of the gallows from her, dear one!'

'You dare propose to me to – '

'Darling, I dare propose to you. Stop there. If it be bad to idolise you, I am the worst of men; if it be good, I am the best. My love for you is above all other love, and my truth to you is above all other truth. Let me have hope and favour, and I am a forsworn man for your sake.'

Rosa puts her hands to her temples, and, pushing back her hair, looks wildly and abhorrently at him, as though she were trying to piece together what it is his deep purpose to present to her only in fragments.

'Reckon up nothing at this moment, angel, but the sacrifices that I lay at those dear feet, which I could fall down among the vilest ashes and kiss, and put upon my head as a poor savage might. There is my fidelity to my dear boy after death. Tread upon it!'

With an action of his hands, as though he cast down something precious.

'There is the inexpiable offence against my adoration of you. Spurn it!'

With a similar action.

'There are my labours in the cause of a just vengeance for six toiling months. Crush them!'

With another repetition of the action.

'There is my past and my present wasted life. There is the desolation of my heart and my soul. There is my peace; there is my despair. Stamp them into the dust; so that you take me, were it even mortally hating me!'

The frightful vehemence of the man, now reaching its full height, so additionally terrifies her as to break the spell that has held her to the spot. She swiftly moves towards the porch; but in an instant he is at her side, and speaking in her ear.

'Rosa, I am self-repressed again. I am walking calmly beside you to the house. I shall wait for some encouragement and hope. I shall not strike too soon. Give me a sign that you attend to me.'

She slightly and constrainedly moves her hand.

'Not a word of this to any one, or it will bring down the blow, as certainly as night follows day. Another sign that you attend to me.'

She moves her hand once more.

'I love you, love you, love you! If you were to cast me off now – but you will not – you would never be rid of me. No one should come between us. I would pursue you to the death.'

The handmaid coming out to open the gate for him, he quietly pulls off his hat as a parting salute, and goes away with no greater show of agitation than is visible in the effigy of Mr. Sapsea's father opposite. Rosa faints in going up-stairs, and is carefully carried to her room and laid down on her bed. A thunderstorm is coming on, the maids say, and the hot and stifling air has overset the pretty dear: no wonder; they have felt their own knees all of a tremble all day long.

CHAPTER XX
A Flight

Rosa no sooner came to herself than the whole of the late interview was before her. It even seemed as if it had pursued her into her insensibility, and she had not had a moment's unconsciousness of it. What to do, she was at a frightened loss to know: the only one clear thought in her mind was, that she must fly from this terrible man.

But where could she take refuge, and how could she go? She had never breathed her dread of him to any one but Helena. If she went to Helena, and told her what had passed, that very act might bring down the irreparable mischief that he threatened he had the power, and that she knew he had the will, to do. The more fearful he appeared to her excited memory and imagination, the more alarming her responsibility appeared; seeing that a slight mistake on her part, either in action or delay, might let his malevolence loose on Helena's brother.

Rosa's mind throughout the last six months had been stormily confused. A half-formed, wholly unexpressed suspicion tossed in it, now heaving itself up, and now sinking into the deep; now gaining palpability, and now losing it. Jasper's self-absorption in his nephew when he was alive, and his unceasing pursuit of the inquiry how he came by his death, if he were dead, were themes so rife in the place, that no one appeared able to suspect the possibility of foul play at his hands. She had asked herself the question, 'Am I so wicked in my thoughts as to conceive a wickedness that others cannot imagine?' Then she had considered, Did the suspicion come of her previous recoiling from him before the fact? And if so, was not that a proof of its baselessness? Then she had reflected, 'What motive could he have, according to my accusation?' She was ashamed to answer in her mind, 'The motive of gaining *me*!' And covered her face, as if the lightest shadow of the idea of founding murder on such an idle vanity were a crime almost as great.

She ran over in her mind again, all that he had said by the sun-dial in the garden. He had persisted in treating the disappearance as murder, consistently with his whole public course since the finding of the watch

193

and shirt-pin. If he were afraid of the crime being traced out, would he not rather encourage the idea of a voluntary disappearance? He had even declared that if the ties between him and his nephew had been less strong, he might have swept 'even him' away from her side. Was that like his having really done so? He had spoken of laying his six months' labours in the cause of a just vengeance at her feet. Would he have done that, with that violence of passion, if they were a pretence? Would he have ranged them with his desolate heart and soul, his wasted life, his peace and his despair? The very first sacrifice that he represented himself as making for her, was his fidelity to his dear boy after death. Surely these facts were strong against a fancy that scarcely dared to hint itself. And yet he was so terrible a man! In short, the poor girl (for what could she know of the criminal intellect, which its own professed students perpetually misread, because they persist in trying to reconcile it with the average intellect of average men, instead of identifying it as a horrible wonder apart) could get by no road to any other conclusion than that he *was* a terrible man, and must be fled from.

She had been Helena's stay and comfort during the whole time. She had constantly assured her of her full belief in her brother's innocence, and of her sympathy with him in his misery. But she had never seen him since the disappearance, nor had Helena ever spoken one word of his avowal to Mr. Crisparkle in regard of Rosa, though as a part of the interest of the case it was well known far and wide. He was Helena's unfortunate brother, to her, and nothing more. The assurance she had given her odious suitor was strictly true, though it would have been better (she considered now) if she could have restrained herself from so giving it. Afraid of him as the bright and delicate little creature was, her spirit swelled at the thought of his knowing it from her own lips.

But where was she to go? Anywhere beyond his reach, was no reply to the question. Somewhere must be thought of. She determined to go to her guardian, and to go immediately. The feeling she had imparted to Helena on the night of their first confidence, was so strong upon her – the feeling of not being safe from him, and of the solid walls of the old convent being powerless to keep out his ghostly following of her – that no reasoning of her own could calm her terrors. The fascination of repulsion had been upon her so long, and now culminated so darkly, that she felt as if he had power to bind her by a spell. Glancing out at window, even now, as she rose to dress, the sight of the sun-dial on which he had leaned when he declared himself, turned her cold, and made her shrink from it, as though he had invested it with some awful quality from his own nature.

She wrote a hurried note to Miss Twinkleton, saying that she had sudden reason for wishing to see her guardian promptly, and had gone to him; also, entreating the good lady not to be uneasy, for all was well with her. She hurried a few quite useless articles into a very little bag, left the note in a conspicuous place, and went out, softly closing the gate after her.

It was the first time she had ever been even in Cloisterham High Street alone. But knowing all its ways and windings very well, she hurried straight to the corner from which the omnibus departed. It was, at that very moment, going off.

'Stop and take me, if you please, Joe. I am obliged to go to London.'

In less than another minute she was on her road to the railway, under Joe's protection. Joe waited on her when she got there, put her safely into the railway carriage, and handed in the very little bag after her, as though it were some enormous trunk, hundredweights heavy, which she must on no account endeavour to lift.

'Can you go round when you get back, and tell Miss Twinkleton that you saw me safely off, Joe?'

'It shall be done, Miss.'

'With my love, please, Joe.'

'Yes, Miss – and I wouldn't mind having it myself!' But Joe did not articulate the last clause; only thought it.

Now that she was whirling away for London in real earnest, Rosa was at leisure to resume the thoughts which her personal hurry had checked. The indignant thought that his declaration of love soiled her; that she could only be cleansed from the stain of its impurity by appealing to the honest and true; supported her for a time against her fears, and confirmed her in her hasty resolution. But as the evening grew darker and darker, and the great city impended nearer and nearer, the doubts usual in such cases began to arise. Whether this was not a wild proceeding, after all; how Mr. Grewgious might regard it; whether she should find him at the journey's end; how she would act if he were absent; what might become of her, alone, in a place so strange and crowded; how if she had but waited and taken counsel first; whether, if she could now go back, she would not do it thankfully; a multitude of such uneasy speculations disturbed her, more and more as they accumulated. At length the train came into London over the housetops; and down below lay the gritty streets with their yet un-needed lamps a-glow, on a hot, light, summer night.

'Hiram Grewgious, Esquire, Staple Inn, London.' This was all Rosa knew of her destination; but it was enough to send her rattling away again in a cab, through deserts of gritty streets, where many people crowded at the corner of courts and byways to get some air, and where many other people walked with a miserably monotonous noise of shuffling of feet on hot paving-stones, and where all the people and all their surroundings were so gritty and so shabby!

There was music playing here and there, but it did not enliven the case. No barrel-organ mended the matter, and no big drum beat dull care away. Like the chapel bells that were also going here and there, they only seemed to evoke echoes from brick surfaces, and dust from everything. As to the flat wind-instruments, they seemed to have cracked their hearts and souls in pining for the country.

Her jingling conveyance stopped at last at a fast-closed gateway, which appeared to belong to somebody who had gone to bed very early, and was much afraid of housebreakers; Rosa, discharging her conveyance, timidly knocked at this gateway, and was let in, very little bag and all, by a watchman.

'Does Mr. Grewgious live here?'

'Mr. Grewgious lives there, Miss,' said the watchman, pointing further in.

So Rosa went further in, and, when the clocks were striking ten, stood on P. J. T.'s doorsteps, wondering what P. J. T. had done with his street-door.

Guided by the painted name of Mr. Grewgious, she went up-stairs and softly tapped and tapped several times. But no one answering, and Mr. Grewgious's door-handle yielding to her touch, she went in, and saw her guardian sitting on a window-seat at an open window, with a shaded lamp placed far from him on a table in a corner.

Rosa drew nearer to him in the twilight of the room. He saw her, and he said, in an undertone: 'Good Heaven!'

Rosa fell upon his neck, with tears, and then he said, returning her embrace:

'My child, my child! I thought you were your mother! – But what, what, what,' he added, soothingly, 'has happened? My dear, what has brought you here? Who has brought you here?'

'No one. I came alone.'

'Lord bless me!' ejaculated Mr. Grewgious. 'Came alone! Why didn't you write to me to come and fetch you?'

'I had no time. I took a sudden resolution. Poor, poor Eddy!'

'Ah, poor fellow, poor fellow!'

'His uncle has made love to me. I cannot bear it,' said Rosa, at once with a burst of tears, and a stamp of her little foot; 'I shudder with horror of him, and I have come to you to protect me and all of us from him, if you will?'

'I will,' cried Mr. Grewgious, with a sudden rush of amazing energy. 'Damn him!

> 'Confound his politics!
> Frustrate his knavish tricks!
> On Thee his hopes to fix?
> Damn him again!'

After this most extraordinary outburst, Mr. Grewgious, quite beside himself, plunged about the room, to all appearance undecided whether he was in a fit of loyal enthusiasm, or combative denunciation.

He stopped and said, wiping his face: 'I beg your pardon, my dear, but you will be glad to know I feel better. Tell me no more just now, or I might do it again. You must be refreshed and cheered. What did you take last? Was it breakfast, lunch, dinner, tea, or supper? And what will you take next? Shall it be breakfast, lunch, dinner, tea, or supper?'

The respectful tenderness with which, on one knee before her, he helped her to remove her hat, and disentangle her pretty hair from it, was quite a chivalrous sight. Yet who, knowing him only on the surface, would have expected chivalry – and of the true sort, too; not the spurious – from Mr. Grewgious?

'Your rest too must be provided for,' he went on; 'and you shall have the prettiest chamber in Furnival's. Your toilet must be provided for, and you shall have everything that an unlimited head chambermaid – by which expression I mean a head chambermaid not limited as to outlay – can procure. Is that a bag?' he looked hard at it; sooth to say, it required hard looking at to be seen at all in a dimly lighted room: 'and is it your property, my dear?'

'Yes, sir. I brought it with me.'

'It is not an extensive bag,' said Mr. Grewgious, candidly, 'though admirably calculated to contain a day's provision for a canary-bird. Perhaps you brought a canary-bird?'

Rosa smiled and shook her head.

'If you had, he should have been made welcome,' said Mr. Grewgious, 'and I think he would have been pleased to be hung upon a nail outside and pit himself against our Staple sparrows; whose execution must be admitted to be not quite equal to their intention. Which is the case with so many of us! You didn't say what meal, my dear. Have a nice jumble of all meals.'

Rosa thanked him, but said she could only take a cup of tea. Mr. Grewgious, after several times running out, and in again, to mention such supplementary items as marmalade, eggs, watercresses, salted fish, and frizzled ham, ran across to Furnival's without his hat, to give his various directions. And soon afterwards they were realised in practice, and the board was spread.

'Lord bless my soul,' cried Mr. Grewgious, putting the lamp upon it, and taking his seat opposite Rosa; 'what a new sensation for a poor old Angular bachelor, to be sure!'

Rosa's expressive little eyebrows asked him what he meant?

'The sensation of having a sweet young presence in the place, that whitewashes it, paints it, papers it, decorates it with gilding, and makes it Glorious!' said Mr. Grewgious. 'Ah me! Ah me!'

As there was something mournful in his sigh, Rosa, in touching him with her tea-cup, ventured to touch him with her small hand too.

'Thank you, my dear,' said Mr. Grewgious. 'Ahem! Let's talk!'

'Do you always live here, sir?' asked Rosa.

'Yes, my dear.'

'And always alone?'

'Always alone; except that I have daily company in a gentleman by the name of Bazzard, my clerk.'

'*He* doesn't live here?'

'No, he goes his way, after office hours. In fact, he is off duty here, altogether, just at present; and a firm down-stairs, with which I have business relations, lend me a substitute. But it would be extremely difficult to replace Mr. Bazzard.'

'He must be very fond of you,' said Rosa.

'He bears up against it with commendable fortitude if he is,' returned Mr. Grewgious, after considering the matter. 'But I doubt if he is. Not particularly so. You see, he is discontented, poor fellow.'

'Why isn't he contented?' was the natural inquiry.

'Misplaced,' said Mr. Grewgious, with great mystery.

Rosa's eyebrows resumed their inquisitive and perplexed expression.

'So misplaced,' Mr. Grewgious went on, 'that I feel constantly apologetic towards him. And he feels (though he doesn't mention it) that I have reason to be.'

Mr. Grewgious had by this time grown so very mysterious, that Rosa did not know how to go on. While she was thinking about it Mr. Grewgious suddenly jerked out of himself for the second time:

'Let's talk. We were speaking of Mr. Bazzard. It's a secret, and moreover it is Mr. Bazzard's secret; but the sweet presence at my table makes me so unusually expansive, that I feel I must impart it in inviolable confidence. What do you think Mr. Bazzard has done?'

'O dear!' cried Rosa, drawing her chair a little nearer, and her mind reverting to Jasper, 'nothing dreadful, I hope?'

'He has written a play,' said Mr. Grewgious, in a solemn whisper. 'A tragedy.'

Rosa seemed much relieved.

'And nobody,' pursued Mr. Grewgious in the same tone, 'will hear, on any account whatever, of bringing it out.'

Rosa looked reflective, and nodded her head slowly; as who should say, 'Such things are, and why are they!'

'Now, you know,' said Mr. Grewgious, '*I* couldn't write a play.'

'Not a bad one, sir?' said Rosa, innocently, with her eyebrows again in action.

'No. If I was under sentence of decapitation, and was about to be instantly decapitated, and an express arrived with a pardon for the condemned convict Grewgious if he wrote a play, I should be under the necessity of resuming the block, and begging the executioner to proceed to extremities, – meaning,' said Mr. Grewgious, passing his hand under his chin, 'the singular number, and this extremity.'

Rosa appeared to consider what she would do if the awkward supposititious case were hers.

'Consequently,' said Mr. Grewgious, 'Mr. Bazzard would have a sense of my inferiority to himself under any circumstances; but when I am his master, you know, the case is greatly aggravated.'

Mr. Grewgious shook his head seriously, as if he felt the offence to be a little too much, though of his own committing.

'How came you to be his master, sir?' asked Rosa.

'A question that naturally follows,' said Mr. Grewgious. 'Let's talk. Mr. Bazzard's father, being a Norfolk farmer, would have furiously laid about him with a flail, a pitch-fork, and every agricultural implement available for assaulting purposes, on the slightest hint of his son's having written a play. So the son, bringing to me the father's rent (which I receive), imparted his secret, and pointed out that he was determined to pursue his genius, and that it would put him in peril of starvation, and that he was not formed for it.'

'For pursuing his genius, sir?'

'No, my dear,' said Mr. Grewgious, 'for starvation. It was impossible to deny the position, that Mr. Bazzard was not formed to be starved, and Mr. Bazzard then pointed out that it was desirable that I should stand between him and a fate so perfectly unsuited to his formation. In that way Mr. Bazzard became my clerk, and he feels it very much.'

'I am glad he is grateful,' said Rosa.

'I didn't quite mean that, my dear. I mean, that he feels the degradation. There are some other geniuses that Mr. Bazzard has become acquainted with, who have also written tragedies, which likewise nobody will on any account whatever hear of bringing out, and these choice spirits dedicate their plays to one another in a highly panegyrical manner. Mr. Bazzard has been the subject of one of these dedications. Now, you know, I never had a play dedicated to *me*!'

Rosa looked at him as if she would have liked him to be the recipient of a thousand dedications.

'Which again, naturally, rubs against the grain of Mr. Bazzard,' said Mr. Grewgious. 'He is very short with me sometimes, and then I feel that he is meditating, "This blockhead is my master! A fellow who couldn't write a tragedy on pain of death, and who will never have one dedicated to him with the most complimentary congratulations on the high position he has taken in the eyes of posterity!" Very trying, very trying. However, in giving him directions, I reflect beforehand: "Perhaps he may not like this," or "He might take it ill if I asked that;" and so we get on very well. Indeed, better than I could have expected.'

'Is the tragedy named, sir?' asked Rosa.

'Strictly between ourselves,' answered Mr. Grewgious, 'it has a dreadfully appropriate name. It is called The Thorn of Anxiety. But Mr. Bazzard hopes – and I hope – that it will come out at last.'

It was not hard to divine that Mr. Grewgious had related the Bazzard history thus fully, at least quite as much for the recreation of his ward's mind from the subject that had driven her there, as for the gratification of his own tendency to be social and communicative.

'And now, my dear,' he said at this point, 'if you are not too tired to tell me more of what passed to-day – but only if you feel quite able – I should be glad to hear it. I may digest it the better, if I sleep on it to-night.'

Rosa, composed now, gave him a faithful account of the interview. Mr. Grewgious often smoothed his head while it was in progress, and begged to be told a second time those parts which bore on Helena and Neville. When Rosa had finished, he sat grave, silent, and meditative for a while.

'Clearly narrated,' was his only remark at last, 'and, I hope, clearly put away here,' smoothing his head again. 'See, my dear,' taking her to the open window, 'where they live! The dark windows over yonder.'

'I may go to Helena to-morrow?' asked Rosa.

'I should like to sleep on that question to-night,' he answered doubtfully. 'But let me take you to your own rest, for you must need it.'

With that Mr. Grewgious helped her to get her hat on again, and hung upon his arm the very little bag that was of no earthly use, and led her by the hand (with a certain stately awkwardness, as if he were going to walk a minuet) across Holborn, and into Furnival's Inn. At the hotel door, he confided her to the Unlimited head chambermaid, and said that while she went up to see her room, he would remain below, in case she should wish it exchanged for another, or should find that there was anything she wanted.

Rosa's room was airy, clean, comfortable, almost gay. The Unlimited had laid in everything omitted from the very little bag (that is to say, everything she could possibly need), and Rosa tripped down the great many stairs again, to thank her guardian for his thoughtful and affectionate care of her.

'Not at all, my dear,' said Mr. Grewgious, infinitely gratified; 'it is I who thank you for your charming confidence and for your charming company. Your breakfast will be provided for you in a neat, compact, and graceful little sitting-room (appropriate to your figure), and I will come to you at ten o'clock in the morning. I hope you don't feel very strange indeed, in this strange place.'

'O no, I feel so safe!'

'Yes, you may be sure that the stairs are fire-proof,' said Mr. Grewgious, 'and that any outbreak of the devouring element would be perceived and suppressed by the watchmen.'

'I did not mean that,' Rosa replied. 'I mean, I feel so safe from him.'

'There is a stout gate of iron bars to keep him out,' said Mr. Grewgious, smiling; 'and Furnival's is fire-proof, and specially watched and lighted, and *I* live over the way!' In the stoutness of his knight-errantry, he seemed to think the last-named protection all sufficient. In the same spirit he said to the gate-porter as he went out, 'If some one staying in the hotel should wish to send across the road to me in the night, a crown will be ready for the messenger.' In the same spirit, he walked up and down outside the iron gate for the best part of an hour, with some solicitude; occasionally looking in between the bars, as if he had laid a dove in a high roost in a cage of lions, and had it on his mind that she might tumble out.

* D *

CHAPTER XXI
A Recognition

NOTHING OCCURRED IN the night to flutter the tired dove; and the dove arose refreshed. With Mr. Grewgious, when the clock struck ten in the morning, came Mr. Crisparkle, who had come at one plunge out of the river at Cloisterham.

'Miss Twinkleton was so uneasy, Miss Rosa,' he explained to her, 'and came round to Ma and me with your note, in such a state of wonder, that, to quiet her, I volunteered on this service by the very first train to be caught in the morning. I wished at the time that you had come to me; but now I think it best that you did *as* you did, and came to your guardian.'

'I did think of you,' Rosa told him; 'but Minor Canon Corner was so near him – '

'I understand. It was quite natural.'

'I have told Mr. Crisparkle,' said Mr. Grewgious, 'all that you told me last night, my dear. Of course I should have written it to him immediately; but his coming was most opportune. And it was particularly kind of him to come, for he had but just gone.'

'Have you settled,' asked Rosa, appealing to them both, 'what is to be done for Helena and her brother?'

'Why really,' said Mr. Crisparkle, 'I am in great perplexity. If even Mr. Grewgious, whose head is much longer than mine, and who is a whole night's cogitation in advance of me, is undecided, what must I be!'

The Unlimited here put her head in at the door – after having rapped, and been authorised to present herself – announcing that a gentleman wished for a word with another gentleman named Crisparkle, if any such gentleman were there. If no such gentleman were there, he begged pardon for being mistaken.

'Such a gentleman is here,' said Mr. Crisparkle, 'but is engaged just now.'

'Is it a dark gentleman?' interposed Rosa, retreating on her guardian.

'No, Miss, more of a brown gentleman.'

'You are sure not with black hair?' asked Rosa, taking courage.

'Quite sure of that, Miss. Brown hair and blue eyes.'

'Perhaps,' hinted Mr. Grewgious, with habitual caution, 'it might be well to see him, reverend sir, if you don't object. When one is in a difficulty or at a loss, one never knows in what direction a way out may chance to open. It is a business principle of mine, in such a case, not to close up any direction, but to keep an eye on every direction that may present itself. I could relate an anecdote in point, but that it would be premature.'

'If Miss Rosa will allow me, then? Let the gentleman come in,' said Mr. Crisparkle.

The gentleman came in; apologised, with a frank but modest grace, for not finding Mr. Crisparkle alone; turned to Mr. Crisparkle, and smilingly asked the unexpected question: 'Who am I?'

'You are the gentleman I saw smoking under the trees in Staple Inn, a few minutes ago.'

'True. There I saw you. Who else am I?'

Mr. Crisparkle concentrated his attention on a handsome face, much sunburnt; and the ghost of some departed boy seemed to rise, gradually and dimly, in the room.

The gentleman saw a struggling recollection lighten up the Minor Canon's features, and smiling again, said: 'What will you have for breakfast this morning? You are out of jam.'

'Wait a moment!' cried Mr. Crisparkle, raising his right hand. 'Give me another instant! Tartar!'

The two shook hands with the greatest heartiness, and then went the wonderful length – for Englishmen – of laying their hands each on the other's shoulders, and looking joyfully each into the other's face.

'My old fag!' said Mr. Crisparkle.

'My old master!' said Mr. Tartar.

'You saved me from drowning!' said Mr. Crisparkle.

'After which you took to swimming, you know!' said Mr. Tartar.

'God bless my soul!' said Mr. Crisparkle.

'Amen!' said Mr. Tartar.

And then they fell to shaking hands most heartily again.

'Imagine,' exclaimed Mr. Crisparkle, with glistening eyes: 'Miss Rosa Bud and Mr. Grewgious, imagine Mr. Tartar, when he was the smallest of juniors, diving for me, catching me, a big heavy senior, by the hair of the head, and striking out for the shore with me like a water-giant!'

'Imagine my not letting him sink, as I was his fag!' said Mr. Tartar. 'But the truth being that he was my best protector and friend, and did me more good than all the masters put together, an irrational impulse seized me to pick him up, or go down with him.'

'Hem! Permit me, sir, to have the honour,' said Mr. Grewgious, advancing with extended hand, 'for an honour I truly esteem it. I am proud to make your acquaintance. I hope you didn't take cold. I hope you were not inconvenienced by swallowing too much water. How have you been since?'

It was by no means apparent that Mr. Grewgious knew what he said, though it was very apparent that he meant to say something highly friendly and appreciative.

If Heaven, Rosa thought, had but sent such courage and skill to her poor mother's aid! And he to have been so slight and young then!

'I don't wish to be complimented upon it, I thank you; but I think I have an idea,' Mr. Grewgious announced, after taking a jog-trot or two across the room, so unexpected and unaccountable that they all stared at him, doubtful whether he was choking or had the cramp – 'I *think* I have an idea. I believe I have had the pleasure of seeing Mr. Tartar's name as tenant of the top set in the house next the top set in the corner?'

'Yes, sir,' returned Mr. Tartar. 'You are right so far.'

'I am right so far,' said Mr. Grewgious. 'Tick that off;' which he did, with his right thumb on his left. 'Might you happen to know the name of your neighbour in the top set on the other side of the party-wall?' coming very close to Mr. Tartar, to lose nothing of his face, in his shortness of sight.

'Landless.'

'Tick that off,' said Mr. Grewgious, taking another trot, and then coming back. 'No personal knowledge, I suppose, sir?'

'Slight, but some.'

'Tick that off,' said Mr. Grewgious, taking another trot, and again coming back. 'Nature of knowledge, Mr. Tartar?'

'I thought he seemed to be a young fellow in a poor way, and I asked his leave – only within a day or so – to share my flowers up there with him; that is to say, to extend my flower-garden to his windows.'

'Would you have the kindness to take seats?' said Mr. Grewgious. 'I *have* an idea!'

They complied; Mr. Tartar none the less readily, for being all abroad; and Mr. Grewgious, seated in the centre, with his hands upon his knees, thus stated his idea, with his usual manner of having got the statement by heart.

'I cannot as yet make up my mind whether it is prudent to hold open communication under present circumstances, and on the part of the fair member of the present company, with Mr. Neville or Miss Helena. I have reason to know that a local friend of ours (on whom I beg to bestow a passing but a hearty malediction, with the kind permission of my reverend friend) sneaks to and fro, and dodges up and down. When not doing so himself, he may have some informant skulking about, in the person of a watchman, porter, or such-like hanger-on of Staple. On the other hand, Miss Rosa very naturally wishes to see her friend Miss Helena, and it would seem important that at least Miss Helena (if not her brother too, through her) should privately know from Miss Rosa's lips what has occurred, and what has been threatened. Am I agreed with generally in the views I take?'

'I entirely coincide with them,' said Mr. Crisparkle, who had been very attentive.

'As I have no doubt I should,' added Mr. Tartar, smiling, 'if I understood them.'

'Fair and softly, sir,' said Mr. Grewgious; 'we shall fully confide in you directly, if you will favour us with your permission. Now, if our local friend should have any informant on the spot, it is tolerably clear that such informant can only be set to watch the chambers in the occupation of Mr. Neville. He reporting, to our local friend, who comes and goes there, our local friend would supply for himself, from his own previous knowledge, the identity of the parties. Nobody can be set to watch all Staple, or to concern himself with comers and goers to other sets of chambers: unless, indeed, mine.'

'I begin to understand to what you tend,' said Mr. Crisparkle, 'and highly approve of your caution.'

'I needn't repeat that I know nothing yet of the why and wherefore,' said Mr. Tartar; 'but I also understand to what you tend, so let me say at once that my chambers are freely at your disposal.'

'There!' cried Mr. Grewgious, smoothing his head triumphantly, 'now we have all got the idea. You have it, my dear?'

'I think I have,' said Rosa, blushing a little as Mr. Tartar looked quickly towards her.

'You see, you go over to Staple with Mr. Crisparkle and Mr. Tartar,' said Mr. Grewgious; 'I going in and out, and out and in alone, in my usual way; you go up with those gentlemen to Mr. Tartar's rooms; you look into Mr. Tartar's flower-garden; you wait for Miss Helena's appearance there, or you signify to Miss Helena that you are close by; and you communicate with her freely, and no spy can be the wiser.'

'I am very much afraid I shall be – '

'Be what, my dear?' asked Mr. Grewgious, as she hesitated. 'Not frightened?'

'No, not that,' said Rosa, shyly; 'in Mr. Tartar's way. We seem to be appropriating Mr. Tartar's residence so very coolly.'

'I protest to you,' returned that gentleman, 'that I shall think the better of it for evermore, if your voice sounds in it only once.'

Rosa, not quite knowing what to say about that, cast down her eyes, and turning to Mr. Grewgious, dutifully asked if she should put her hat on? Mr. Grewgious being of opinion that she could not do better, she withdrew for the purpose. Mr. Crisparkle took the opportunity of giving Mr. Tartar a summary of the distresses of Neville and his sister; the opportunity was quite long enough, as the hat happened to require a little extra fitting on.

Mr. Tartar gave his arm to Rosa, and Mr. Crisparkle walked, detached, in front.

'Poor, poor Eddy!' thought Rosa, as they went along.

Mr. Tartar waved his right hand as he bent his head down over Rosa, talking in an animated way.

'It was not so powerful or so sun-browned when it saved Mr. Crisparkle,' thought Rosa, glancing at it; 'but it must have been very steady and determined even then.'

Mr. Tartar told her he had been a sailor, roving everywhere for years and years.

'When are you going to sea again?' asked Rosa.

'Never!'

Rosa wondered what the girls would say if they could see her crossing the wide street on the sailor's arm. And she fancied that the passers-by must think her very little and very helpless, contrasted with the strong figure that could have caught her up and carried her out of any danger, miles and miles without resting.

She was thinking further, that his far-seeing blue eyes looked as if they had been used to watch danger afar off, and to watch it without flinching, drawing nearer and nearer: when, happening to raise her own eyes, she found that he seemed to be thinking something about *them*.

This a little confused Rosebud, and may account for her never afterwards quite knowing how she ascended (with his help) to his garden in the air, and seemed to get into a marvellous country that came into sudden bloom like the country on the summit of the magic bean-stalk. May it flourish for ever!

CHAPTER XXII
A Gritty State of Things comes on

MR. TARTAR'S CHAMBERS were the neatest, the cleanest, and the best-ordered chambers ever seen under the sun, moon, and stars. The floors were scrubbed to that extent, that you might have supposed the London blacks emancipated for ever, and gone out of the land for good. Every inch of brass-work in Mr. Tartar's possession was polished and burnished, till it shone like a brazen mirror. No speck, nor spot, nor spatter soiled the purity of any of Mr. Tartar's household gods, large, small, or middle-sized. His sitting-room was like the admiral's cabin, his bath-room was like a dairy, his sleeping-chamber, fitted all about with lockers and drawers, was like a seedsman's shop; and his nicely-balanced cot just stirred in the midst, as if it breathed. Everything belonging to Mr. Tartar had quarters of its own assigned to it: his maps and charts had their quarters; his books had theirs; his brushes had theirs; his boots had theirs; his clothes had theirs; his case-bottles had theirs; his telescopes and other instruments had theirs. Everything was readily accessible. Shelf, bracket, locker, hook, and drawer were equally within reach, and were equally contrived with a view to avoiding waste of room, and providing some snug inches of stowage for something that would have exactly fitted nowhere else. His gleaming little service of plate was so arranged upon his sideboard as that a slack salt-spoon would have instantly betrayed itself; his toilet implements were so arranged upon his dressing-table as that a toothpick of slovenly deportment could have been reported at a glance. So with the curiosities he had brought home from various voyages. Stuffed, dried, repolished, or otherwise preserved, according to their kind; birds, fishes, reptiles, arms, articles of dress, shells, seaweeds, grasses, or memorials of coral reef; each was displayed in its especial place, and each could have been displayed in no better place. Paint and varnish seemed to be kept somewhere out of sight, in constant readiness to obliterate stray finger-marks wherever any might become perceptible in Mr. Tartar's chambers. No man-of-war was ever kept more spick and span from careless touch. On this bright summer day, a neat awning was rigged over Mr. Tartar's flower-garden as only a sailor can rig it, and there was a sea-going air upon the whole effect, so delightfully complete, that the flower-garden might have appertained to stern-windows afloat, and the whole concern might have bowled away gallantly with all on board, if Mr. Tartar had only clapped to his lips the speaking-trumpet that was slung in a corner, and given hoarse orders to heave the anchor up, look alive there, men, and get all sail upon her!

Mr. Tartar doing the honours of this gallant craft was of a piece with the rest. When a man rides an amiable hobby that shies at nothing and kicks nobody, it is only agreeable to find him riding it with a humorous sense of the droll side of the creature. When the man is a cordial and an earnest man by nature, and withal is perfectly fresh and genuine, it may be doubted whether he is ever seen to greater advantage than at such a time. So Rosa would have naturally thought (even if she hadn't been conducted over the ship with all the homage due to the First Lady of the Admiralty, or First Fairy of the Sea), that it was charming to see and hear Mr. Tartar half laughing at, and half rejoicing in, his various contrivances. So Rosa would have naturally thought, anyhow, that the sunburnt sailor showed to great advantage when, the inspection finished, he delicately withdrew out of his admiral's cabin, beseeching her to consider herself its Queen, and waving her free of his flower-garden with the hand that had had Mr. Crisparkle's life in it.

'Helena! Helena Landless! Are you there?'

'Who speaks to me? Not Rosa?' Then a second handsome face appearing.

'Yes, my darling!'

'Why, how did you come here, dearest?'

'I – I don't quite know,' said Rosa with a blush; 'unless I am dreaming!'

Why with a blush? For their two faces were alone with the other flowers. Are blushes among the fruits of the country of the magic bean-stalk?

'I am not dreaming,' said Helena, smiling. 'I should take more for granted if I were. How do we come together – or so near together – so very unexpectedly?'

Unexpectedly indeed, among the dingy gables and chimney-pots of P. J. T.'s connection, and the flowers that had sprung from the salt sea. But Rosa, waking, told in a hurry how they came to be together, and all the why and wherefore of that matter.

'And Mr. Crisparkle is here,' said Rosa, in rapid conclusion; 'and, could you believe it? long ago he saved his life!'

'I could believe any such thing of Mr. Crisparkle,' returned Helena, with a mantling face.

(More blushes in the bean-stalk country!)

'Yes, but it wasn't Crisparkle,' said Rosa, quickly putting in the correction.

'I don't understand, love.'

'It was very nice of Mr. Crisparkle to be saved,' said Rosa, 'and he couldn't have shown his high opinion of Mr. Tartar more expressively. But it was Mr. Tartar who saved him.'

Helena's dark eyes looked very earnestly at the bright face among the leaves, and she asked, in a slower and more thoughtful tone:

'Is Mr. Tartar with you now, dear?'

'No; because he has given up his rooms to me – to us, I mean. It is such a beautiful place!'

'Is it?'

'It is like the inside of the most exquisite ship that ever sailed. It is like – it is like – '

'Like a dream?' suggested Helena.

Rosa answered with a little nod, and smelled the flowers.

Helena resumed, after a short pause of silence, during which she seemed (or it was Rosa's fancy) to compassionate somebody: 'My poor Neville is reading in his own room, the sun being so very bright on this side just now. I think he had better not know that you are so near.'

'O, I think so too!' cried Rosa very readily.

'I suppose,' pursued Helena, doubtfully, 'that he must know by-and-by all you have told me; but I am not sure. Ask Mr. Crisparkle's advice, my darling. Ask him whether I may tell Neville as much or as little of what you have told me as I think best.'

Rosa subsided into her state-cabin, and propounded the question. The Minor Canon was for the free exercise of Helena's judgment.

'I thank him very much,' said Helena, when Rosa emerged again with her report. 'Ask him whether it would be best to wait until any more maligning and pursuing of Neville on the part of this wretch shall disclose itself, or to try to anticipate it: I mean, so far as to find out whether any such goes on darkly about us?'

The Minor Canon found this point so difficult to give a confident opinion on, that, after two or three attempts and failures, he suggested a reference to Mr. Grewgious. Helena acquiescing, he betook himself (with a most unsuccessful assumption of lounging indifference) across the quadrangle to P. J. T.'s, and stated it. Mr. Grewgious held decidedly to the general principle, that if you could steal a march upon a brigand or a wild beast, you had better do it; and he also held decidedly to the special case, that John Jasper was a brigand and a wild beast in combination.

Thus advised, Mr. Crisparkle came back again and reported to Rosa, who in her turn reported to Helena. She now steadily pursuing her train of thought at her window, considered thereupon.

'We may count on Mr. Tartar's readiness to help us, Rosa?' she inquired.

O yes! Rosa shyly thought so. O yes, Rosa shyly believed she could almost answer for it. But should she ask Mr. Crisparkle? 'I think your authority on the point as good as his, my dear,' said Helena, sedately, 'and you needn't disappear again for that.' Odd of Helena!

'You see, Neville,' Helena pursued after more reflection, 'knows no one else here: he has not so much as exchanged a word with any one else here. If Mr. Tartar would call to see him openly and often; if he would spare a minute for the purpose, frequently; if he would even do so, almost daily; something might come of it.'

'Something might come of it, dear?' repeated Rosa, surveying her friend's beauty with a highly perplexed face. 'Something might?'

'If Neville's movements are really watched, and if the purpose really is to isolate him from all friends and acquaintance and wear his daily life out grain by grain (which would seem to be the threat to you), does it not appear likely,' said Helena, 'that his enemy would in some way communicate with Mr. Tartar to warn him off from Neville? In which case, we might not only know the fact, but might know from Mr. Tartar what the terms of the communication were.'

'I see!' cried Rosa. And immediately darted into her state-cabin again.

Presently her pretty face reappeared, with a greatly heightened colour, and she said that she had told Mr. Crisparkle, and that Mr. Crisparkle had fetched in Mr. Tartar, and that Mr. Tartar – 'who is waiting now, in case you want him,' added Rosa, with a half look back, and in not a little confusion between the inside of the state-cabin and out – had declared his readiness to act as she had suggested, and to enter on his task that very day.

'I thank him from my heart,' said Helena. 'Pray tell him so.'

Again not a little confused between the Flower-garden and the Cabin,

Rosa dipped in with her message, and dipped out again with more assurances from Mr. Tartar, and stood wavering in a divided state between Helena and him, which proved that confusion is not always necessarily awkward, but may sometimes present a very pleasant appearance.

'And now, darling,' said Helena, 'we will be mindful of the caution that has restricted us to this interview for the present, and will part. I hear Neville moving too. Are you going back?'

'To Miss Twinkleton's?' asked Rosa.

'Yes.'

'O, I could never go there any more. I couldn't indeed, after that dreadful interview!' said Rosa.

'Then where *are* you going, pretty one?'

'Now I come to think of it, I don't know,' said Rosa. 'I have settled nothing at all yet, but my guardian will take care of me. Don't be uneasy, dear. I shall be sure to be somewhere.'

(It did seem likely.)

'And I shall hear of my Rosebud from Mr. Tartar?' inquired Helena.

'Yes, I suppose so; from – ' Rosa looked back again in a flutter, instead of supplying the name. 'But tell me one thing before we part, dearest Helena. Tell me – that you are sure, sure, sure, I couldn't help it.'

'Help it, love?'

'Help making him malicious and revengeful. I couldn't hold any terms with him, could I?'

'You know how I love you, darling,' answered Helena, with indignation; 'but I would sooner see you dead at his wicked feet.'

'That's a great comfort to me! And you will tell your poor brother so, won't you? And you will give him my remembrance and my sympathy? And you will ask him not to hate me?'

With a mournful shake of the head, as if that would be quite a superfluous entreaty, Helena lovingly kissed her two hands to her friend, and her friend's two hands were kissed to her; and then she saw a third hand (a brown one) appear among the flowers and leaves, and help her friend out of sight.

The refection that Mr. Tartar produced in the Admiral's Cabin by merely touching the spring knob of a locker and the handle of a drawer, was a dazzling enchanted repast. Wonderful macaroons, glittering liqueurs, magically-preserved tropical spices, and jellies of celestial tropical fruits, displayed themselves profusely at an instant's notice.

But Mr. Tartar could not make time stand still; and time, with his hard-hearted fleetness, strode on so fast, that Rosa was obliged to come down from the bean-stalk country to earth and her guardian's chambers.

'And now, my dear,' said Mr. Grewgious, 'what is to be done next? To put the same thought in another form; what is to be done with you?'

Rosa could only look apologetically sensible of being very much in her own way and in everybody else's. Some passing idea of living, fireproof, up a good many stairs in Furnival's Inn for the rest of her life, was the only thing in the nature of a plan that occurred to her.

'It has come into my thoughts,' said Mr. Grewgious, 'that as the respected lady, Miss Twinkleton, occasionally repairs to London in the recess, with the view of extending her connection, and being available for interviews with metropolitan parents, if any – whether, until we have time in which to turn ourselves round, we might invite Miss Twinkleton to come and stay with you for a month?'

'Stay where, sir?'

'Whether,' explained Mr. Grewgious, 'we might take a furnished lodging in town for a month, and invite Miss Twinkleton to assume the charge of you in it for that period?'

'And afterwards?' hinted Rosa.

'And afterwards,' said Mr. Grewgious, 'we should be no worse off than we are now.'

'I think that might smooth the way,' assented Rosa.

'Then let us,' said Mr. Grewgious, rising, 'go and look for a furnished lodging. Nothing could be more acceptable to me than the sweet presence of last evening, for all the remaining evenings of my existence; but these are not fit surroundings for a young lady. Let us set out in quest of adventures, and look for a furnished lodging. In the meantime, Mr. Crisparkle here, about to return home immediately, will no doubt kindly see Miss Twinkleton, and invite that lady to co-operate in our plan.'

Mr. Crisparkle, willingly accepting the commission, took his departure; Mr. Grewgious and his ward set forth on their expedition.

As Mr. Grewgious's idea of looking at a furnished lodging was to get on the opposite side of the street to a house with a suitable bill in the window, and stare at it; and then work his way tortuously to the back of the house, and stare at that; and then not go in, but make similar trials of another house, with the same result; their progress was but slow. At length he bethought himself of a widowed cousin, divers times removed, of Mr. Bazzard's, who had once solicited his influence in the lodger world, and who lived in Southampton Street, Bloomsbury Square. This lady's name, stated in uncompromising capitals of considerable size on a brass door-plate, and yet not lucidly as to sex or condition, was BILLICKIN.

Personal faintness, and an overpowering personal candour, were the distinguishing features of Mrs. Billickin's organisation. She came languishing out of her own exclusive back parlour, with the air of having been expressly brought-to for the purpose, from an accumulation of several swoons.

'I hope I see you well, sir,' said Mrs. Billickin, recognising her visitor with a bend.

'Thank you, quite well. And you, ma'am?' returned Mr. Grewgious.

'I am as well,' said Mrs. Billickin, becoming aspirational with excess of faintness, 'as I hever ham.'

'My ward and an elderly lady,' said Mr. Grewgious, 'wish to find a genteel lodging for a month or so. Have you any apartments available, ma'am?'

'Mr. Grewgious,' returned Mrs. Billickin, 'I will not deceive you; far from it. I *have* apartments available.'

This with the air of adding: 'Convey me to the stake, if you will; but while I live, I will be candid.'

'And now, what apartments, ma'am?' asked Mr. Grewgious, cosily. To tame a certain severity apparent on the part of Mrs. Billickin.

'There is this sitting-room – which, call it what you will, it is the front parlour, Miss,' said Mrs. Billickin, impressing Rosa into the conversation: 'the back parlour being what I cling to and never part with; and there is two bedrooms at the top of the 'ouse with gas laid on. I do not tell you that your bedroom floors is firm, for firm they are not. The gas-fitter himself allowed, that to make a firm job, he must go right under your jistes, and it were not worth the outlay as a yearly tenant so to do. The piping is carried above your jistes, and it is best that it should be made known to you.'

Mr. Grewgious and Rosa exchanged looks of some dismay, though they had not the least idea what latent horrors this carriage of the piping might involve. Mrs. Billickin put her hand to her heart, as having eased it of a load.

'Well! The roof is all right, no doubt,' said Mr. Grewgious, plucking up a little.

'Mr. Grewgious,' returned Mrs. Billickin, 'if I was to tell you, sir, that to have nothink above you is to have a floor above you, I should put a deception upon you which I will not do. No, sir. Your slates WILL rattle loose at that elewation in windy weather, do your utmost, best or worst! I defy you, sir, be you what you may, to keep your slates tight, try how you can.' Here Mrs. Billickin, having been warm with Mr. Grewgious, cooled a little, not to abuse the moral power she held over him. 'Consequent,' proceeded Mrs. Billickin, more mildly, but still firmly in her incorruptible candour: 'consequent it would be worse than of no use for me to trapse and travel up to the top of the 'ouse with you, and for you to say, "Mrs. Billickin, what stain do I notice in the ceiling, for a stain I do consider it?" and for me to answer, "I do not understand you, sir." No, sir, I will not be so underhand. I *do* understand you before you pint it out. It is the wet, sir. It do come in, and it do not come in. You may lay dry there half your lifetime; but the time will come, and it is best that you should know it, when a dripping sop would be no name for you.'

Mr. Grewgious looked much disgraced by being prefigured in this pickle.

'Have you any other apartments, ma'am?' he asked.

'Mr. Grewgious,' returned Mrs. Billickin, with much solemnity, 'I have. You ask me have I, and my open and my honest answer air, I have. The first and second floors is wacant, and sweet rooms.'

'Come, come! There's nothing against *them*,' said Mr. Grewgious, comforting himself.

'Mr. Grewgious,' replied Mrs. Billickin, 'pardon me, there is the stairs. Unless your mind is prepared for the stairs, it will lead to inevitable disappointment. You cannot, Miss,' said Mrs. Billickin, addressing Rosa reproachfully, 'place a first floor, and far less a second, on the level footing 'of a parlour. No, you cannot do it, Miss, it is beyond your power, and wherefore try?'

Mrs. Billickin put it very feelingly, as if Rosa had shown a headstrong determination to hold the untenable position.

'Can we see these rooms, ma'am?' inquired her guardian.

'Mr. Grewgious,' returned Mrs. Billickin, 'you can. I will not disguise it from you, sir; you can.'

Mrs. Billickin then sent into her back parlour for her shawl (it being a state fiction, dating from immemorial antiquity, that she could never go anywhere without being wrapped up), and having been enrolled by her attendant, led the way. She made various genteel pauses on the stairs for breath, and clutched at her heart in the drawing-room as if it had very nearly got loose, and she had caught it in the act of taking wing.

'And the second floor?' said Mr. Grewgious, on finding the first satisfactory.

'Mr. Grewgious,' replied Mrs. Billickin, turning upon him with ceremony, as if the time had now come when a distinct understanding on a difficult point must be arrived at, and a solemn confidence established, 'the second floor is over this.'

'Can we see that too, ma'am?'

'Yes, sir,' returned Mrs. Billickin, 'it is open as the day.'

That also proving satisfactory, Mr. Grewgious retired into a window with Rosa for a few words of consultation, and then asking for pen and ink, sketched out a line or two of agreement. In the meantime Mrs. Billickin took a seat, and delivered a kind of Index to, or Abstract of, the general question.

'Five-and-forty shillings per week by the month certain at the time of year,' said Mrs. Billickin, 'is only reasonable to both parties. It is not Bond Street nor yet St. James's Palace; but it is not pretended that it is. Neither is it attempted to be denied – for why should it? – that the Arching leads to a mews. Mewses must exist. Respecting attendance; two is kep', at liberal wages. Words *has* arisen as to tradesmen, but dirty shoes on fresh hearth-stoning was attributable, and no wish for a commission on your orders. Coals is either *by* the fire, or *per* the scuttle.' She emphasised the prepositions as marking a subtle but immense difference. 'Dogs is not viewed with favour. Besides litter, they gets stole, and sharing suspicions is apt to creep in, and unpleasantness takes place.'

By this time Mr. Grewgious had his agreement-lines, and his earnest-money, ready. 'I have signed it for the ladies, ma'am,' he said, 'and you'll have the goodness to sign it for yourself, Christian and Surname, there, if you please.'

'Mr. Grewgious,' said Mrs. Billickin in a new burst of candour, 'no, sir! You must excuse the Christian name.'

Mr. Grewgious stared at her.

'The door-plate is used as a protection,' said Mrs. Billickin, 'and acts as such, and go from it I will not.'

Mr. Grewgious stared at Rosa.

'No, Mr. Grewgious, you must excuse me. So long as this 'ouse is known indefinite as Billickin's, and so long as it is a doubt with the riffraff where Billickin may be hidin', near the street-door or down the airy, and what his weight and size, so long I feel safe. But commit myself to a solitary female statement, no, Miss! Nor would you for a moment wish,' said Mrs. Billickin, with a strong sense of injury, 'to take that advantage of your sex, if you were not brought to it by inconsiderate example.'

Rosa reddening as if she had made some most disgraceful attempt to overreach the good lady, besought Mr. Grewgious to rest content with any signature. And accordingly, in a baronial way, the sign-manual BILLICKIN got appended to the document.

Details were then settled for taking possession on the next day but one, when Miss Twinkleton might be reasonably expected; and Rosa went back to Furnival's Inn on her guardian's arm.

Behold Mr. Tartar walking up and down Furnival's Inn, checking himself when he saw them coming, and advancing towards them!

'It occurred to me,' hinted Mr. Tartar, 'that we might go up the river, the weather being so delicious and the tide serving. I have a boat of my own at the Temple Stairs.'

'I have not been up the river for this many a day,' said Mr. Grewgious, tempted.

'I was never up the river,' added Rosa.

Within half an hour they were setting this matter right by going up the river. The tide was running with them, the afternoon was charming. Mr. Tartar's boat was perfect. Mr. Tartar and Lobley (Mr. Tartar's man) pulled a pair of oars. Mr. Tartar had a yacht, it seemed, lying somewhere down by Greenhithe; and Mr. Tartar's man had charge of this yacht, and was detached upon his present service. He was a jolly-favoured man, with tawny hair and whiskers, and a big red face. He was the dead image of the sun in old woodcuts, his hair and whiskers answering for rays all around him. Resplendent in the bow of the boat, he was a shining sight, with a man-of-war's man's shirt on – or off, according to opinion – and his arms and breast tattooed all sorts of patterns. Lobley seemed to take it easily, and so did Mr. Tartar; yet their oars bent as they pulled, and the boat bounded under them. Mr. Tartar talked as if he were doing nothing, to Rosa who was really doing nothing, and to Mr. Grewgious who was doing this much that he steered all wrong; but what did that matter, when a turn of Mr. Tartar's skilful wrist, or a mere grin of Mr. Lobley's over the bow, put all to rights! The tide bore them on in the gayest and most sparkling manner, until they stopped to dine in some ever-lastingly-green garden, needing no matter-of-fact identification here; and then the tide obligingly turned – being devoted to that party alone for that day; and as they floated idly among some osier-beds, Rosa tried what she could do in the rowing way, and came off splendidly, being much assisted; and Mr. Grewgious tried what he could do, and came off on his back, doubled up with an oar under his chin, being not assisted at all. Then there was an interval of rest under boughs (such rest!) what time Mr. Lobley mopped, and, arranging cushions, stretchers, and the like, danced the tight-rope the whole length of the boat like a man to whom shoes were a superstition and stockings slavery; and then came the sweet return among delicious odours of limes in bloom, and musical ripplings; and, all too soon, the great black city cast its shadow on the waters, and its dark bridges spanned them as death spans life, and the everlastingly-green garden seemed to be left for everlasting, unregainable and far away.

'Cannot people get through life without gritty stages, I wonder?' Rosa thought next day, when the town was very gritty again, and everything had a strange and an uncomfortable appearance of seeming to wait for something that wouldn't come. No. She began to think, that, now the Cloisterham school-days had glided past and gone, the gritty stages would begin to set in at intervals and make themselves wearily known!

Yet what did Rosa expect? Did she expect Miss Twinkleton? Miss Twinkleton duly came. Forth from her back parlour issued the Billickin to receive Miss Twinkleton, and War was in the Billickin's eye from that fell moment.

Miss Twinkleton brought a quantity of luggage with her, having all Rosa's as well as her own. The Billickin took it ill that Miss Twinkleton's mind, being sorely disturbed by this luggage, failed to take in her personal identity with that clearness of perception which was due to its demands. Stateliness mounted her gloomy throne upon the Billickin's brow in consequence. And when Miss Twinkleton, in agitation taking stock of her trunks and packages, of which she had seventeen, particularly counted in the Billickin herself as number eleven, the B. found it necessary to repudiate.

'Things cannot too soon be put upon the footing,' said she, with a candour so demonstrative as to be almost obtrusive, 'that the person of the 'ouse is not a box nor yet a bundle, nor a carpet-bag. No, I am 'ily obleeged to you, Miss Twinkleton, nor yet a beggar.'

This last disclaimer had reference to Miss Twinkleton's distractedly pressing two-and-sixpence on her, instead of the cabman.

Thus cast off, Miss Twinkleton wildly inquired, 'which gentleman' was to be paid? There being two gentlemen in that position (Miss Twinkleton having arrived with two cabs), each gentleman on being paid held forth his two-and-sixpence on the flat of his open hand, and, with a speechless stare and a dropped jaw, displayed his wrong to heaven and earth. Terrified by this alarming spectacle, Miss Twinkleton placed another shilling in each hand; at the same time appealing to the law in flurried accents, and recounting her luggage this time with the two gentlemen in, who caused the total to come out complicated. Meanwhile the two gentlemen, each looking very hard at the last shilling grumblingly, as if it might become eighteen-pence if he kept his eyes on it, descended the doorsteps, ascended their carriages, and drove away, leaving Miss Twinkleton on a bonnet-box in tears.

The Billickin beheld this manifestation of weakness without sympathy, and gave directions for 'a young man to be got in' to wrestle with the luggage. When that gladiator had disappeared from the arena, peace ensued, and the new lodgers dined.

But the Billickin had somehow come to the knowledge that Miss Twinkleton kept a school. The leap from that knowledge to the inference that Miss Twinkleton set herself to teach *her* something, was easy. 'But you don't do it,' soliloquised the Billickin; 'I am not your pupil, whatever she,' meaning Rosa, 'may be, poor thing!'

Miss Twinkleton, on the other hand, having changed her dress and recovered her spirits, was animated by a bland desire to improve the occasion in all ways, and to be as serene a model as possible. In a happy compromise between her two states of existence, she had already become, with her workbasket before her, the equably vivacious companion with a slight judicious flavouring of information, when the Billickin announced herself.

'I will not hide from you, ladies,' said the B., enveloped in the shawl of state, 'for it is not my character to hide neither my motives nor my actions, that I take the liberty to look in upon you to express a 'ope that your dinner was to your liking. Though not Professed but Plain, still her wages should be a sufficient object to her to stimilate to soar above mere roast and biled.'

'We dined very well indeed,' said Rosa, 'thank you.'

'Accustomed,' said Miss Twinkleton with a gracious air, which to the jealous ears of the Billickin seemed to add 'my good woman' – 'accustomed to a liberal and nutritious, yet plain and salutary diet, we have found no reason to bemoan our absence from the ancient city, and the methodical household, in which the quiet routine of our lot has been hitherto cast.'

'I did think it well to mention to my cook,' observed the Billickin with a gush of candour, 'which I 'ope you will agree with, Miss Twinkleton, was a right precaution, that the young lady being used to what we should consider here but poor diet, had better be brought forward by degrees. For, a rush from scanty feeding to generous feeding, and from what you may call messing to what you may call method, do require a power of constitution which is not often found in youth, particular when undermined by boarding-school!'

It will be seen that the Billickin now openly pitted herself against Miss Twinkleton, as one whom she had fully ascertained to be her natural enemy.

'Your remarks,' returned Miss Twinkleton, from a remote moral eminence, 'are well meant, I have no doubt; but you will permit me to observe that they develop a mistaken view of the subject, which can only be imputed to your extreme want of accurate information.'

'My informiation,' retorted the Billickin, throwing in an extra syllable for the sake of emphasis at once polite and powerful – 'my informiation, Miss Twinkleton, were my own experience, which I believe is usually considered to be good guidance. But whether so or not, I was put in youth to a very genteel boarding-school, the mistress being no less a lady than yourself, of about your own age or it may be some years younger, and a poorness of blood flowed from the table which has run through my life.'

'Very likely,' said Miss Twinkleton, still from her distant eminence; 'and very much to be deplored. – Rosa, my dear, how are you getting on with your work?'

'Miss Twinkleton,' resumed the Billickin, in a courtly manner, 'before retiring on the 'int, as a lady should, I wish to ask of yourself, as a lady, whether I am to consider that my words is doubted?'

'I am not aware on what ground you cherish such a supposition,' began Miss Twinkleton, when the Billickin neatly stopped her.

'Do not, if you please, put suppositions betwixt my lips where none such have been imparted by myself. Your flow of words is great, Miss Twinkleton, and no doubt is expected from you by your pupils, and no doubt is considered worth the money. *No* doubt, I am sure. But not paying for flows of words, and not asking to be favoured with them here, I wish to repeat my question.'

'If you refer to the poverty of your circulation,' began Miss Twinkleton, when again the Billickin neatly stopped her.

'I have used no such expressions.'

'If you refer, then, to the poorness of your blood – '

'Brought upon me,' stipulated the Billickin, expressly, 'at a boarding-school – '

'Then,' resumed Miss Twinkleton, 'all I can say is, that I am bound to believe, on your asseveration, that it is very poor indeed. I cannot forbear adding, that if that unfortunate circumstance influences your conversation, it is much to be lamented, and it is eminently desirable that your blood were richer. – Rosa, my dear, how are you getting on with your work?'

'Hem! Before retiring, Miss,' proclaimed the Billickin to Rosa, loftily cancelling Miss Twinkleton, 'I should wish it to be understood between yourself and me that my transactions in future is with you alone. I know no elderly lady here, Miss, none older than yourself.'

'A highly desirable arrangement, Rosa my dear,' observed Miss Twinkleton.

'It is not, Miss,' said the Billickin, with a sarcastic smile, 'that I possess the Mill I have heard of, in which old single ladies could be ground up young (what a gift it would be to some of us), but that I limit myself to you totally.'

'When I have any desire to communicate a request to the person of the house, Rosa my dear,' observed Miss Twinkleton with majestic cheerfulness, 'I will make it known to you, and you will kindly undertake, I am sure, that it is conveyed to the proper quarter.'

'Good-evening, Miss,' said the Billickin, at once affectionately and distantly. 'Being alone in my eyes, I wish you good-evening with best wishes, and do not find myself drove, I am truly 'appy to say, into expressing my contempt for an indiwidual, unfortunately for yourself, belonging to you.'

The Billickin gracefully withdrew with this parting speech, and from that time Rosa occupied the restless position of shuttlecock between these two battledores. Nothing could be done without a smart match being played out. Thus, on the daily-arising question of dinner, Miss Twinkleton would say, the three being present together:

'Perhaps, my love, you will consult with the person of the house, whether she can procure us a lamb's fry; or, failing that, a roast fowl.'

On which the Billickin would retort (Rosa not having spoken a word), 'If you was better accustomed to butcher's meat, Miss, you would not entertain the idea of a lamb's fry. Firstly, because lambs has long been sheep, and secondly, because there is such things as killing-days, and there is not. As to roast fowls, Miss, why you must be quite surfeited with roast fowls, letting alone your buying, when you market for yourself, the agedest of poultry with the scaliest of legs, quite as if you was accustomed to picking 'em out for cheapness. Try a little inwention, Miss. Use yourself to 'ousekeeping a bit. Come now, think of somethink else.'

To this encouragement, offered with the indulgent toleration of a wise and liberal expert, Miss Twinkleton would rejoin, reddening:

'Or, my dear, you might propose to the person of the house a duck.'

'Well, Miss!' the Billickin would exclaim (still no word being spoken by Rosa), 'you do surprise me when you speak of ducks! Not to mention that they're getting out of season and very dear, it really strikes to my heart to see you have a duck; for the breast, which is the only delicate cuts in a duck, always goes in a direction which I cannot imagine where, and your own plate comes down so miserably skin-and-bony! Try again, Miss. Think more of yourself, and less of others. A dish of sweetbreads now, or a bit of mutton. Something at which you can get your equal chance.'

Occasionally the game would wax very brisk indeed, and would be kept up with a smartness rendering such an encounter as this quite tame. But the Billickin almost invariably made by far the higher score; and would come in with side hits of the most unexpected and extraordinary description, when she seemed without a chance.

All this did not improve the gritty state of things in London, or the air that London had acquired in Rosa's eyes of waiting for something that never came. Tired of working, and conversing with Miss Twinkleton, she suggested working and reading: to which Miss Twinkleton readily assented, as an admirable reader, of tried powers. But Rosa soon made the discovery that Miss Twinkleton didn't read fairly. She cut the love-scenes, interpolated passages in praise of female celibacy, and was guilty of other glaring pious frauds. As an instance in point, take the glowing passage: 'Ever dearest and best adored, – said Edward, clasping the dear head to his breast, and drawing the silken hair through his caressing fingers, from which he suffered it to fall like golden rain, – ever dearest and best adored, let us fly from the unsympathetic world and the sterile coldness of the stony-hearted, to the rich warm Paradise of Trust and Love.' Miss Twinkleton's fraudulent version tamely ran thus: 'Ever engaged to me with the consent of our parents on both sides, and the approbation of the silver-haired rector of the district, – said Edward, respectfully raising to his lips the taper fingers so skilful in embroidery, tambour, crochet, and other truly feminine arts, – let me call on thy papa ere to-morrow's dawn has sunk into the west, and propose a suburban establishment, lowly it may be, but within our means, where he will be always welcome as an evening guest, and where every arrangement shall invest economy, and constant interchange of scholastic acquirements with the attributes of the ministering angel to domestic bliss.'

As the days crept on and nothing happened, the neighbours began to say that the pretty girl at Billickin's, who looked so wistfully and so much out of the gritty windows of the drawing-room, seemed to be losing her spirits. The pretty girl might have lost them but for the accident of lighting on some books of voyages and sea-adventure. As a compensation against their romance, Miss Twinkleton, reading aloud, made the most of all the latitudes and longitudes, bearings, winds, currents, offsets, and other statistics (which she felt to be none the less improving because they expressed nothing whatever to her); while Rosa, listening intently, made the most of what was nearest to her heart. So they both did better than before.

CHAPTER XXIII
The Dawn Again

ALTHOUGH MR. CRISPARKLE and John Jasper met daily under the Cathedral roof, nothing at any time passed between them having reference to Edwin Drood, after the time, more than half a year gone by, when Jasper mutely showed the Minor Canon the conclusion and the resolution entered in his Diary. It is not likely that they ever met, though so often, without the thoughts of each reverting to the subject. It is not likely that they ever met, though so often, without a sensation on the part of each that the other was a perplexing secret to him. Jasper as the denouncer and pursuer of Neville Landless, and Mr. Crisparkle as his consistent advocate and protector, must at least have stood sufficiently in opposition to have speculated with keen interest on the steadiness and next direction of the other's designs. But neither ever broached the theme.

False pretence not being in the Minor Canon's nature, he doubtless displayed openly that he would at any time have revived the subject, and even desired to discuss it. The determined reticence of Jasper, however, was not to be so approached. Impassive, moody, solitary, resolute, so concentrated on one idea, and on its attendant fixed purpose, that he would share it with no fellow-creature, he lived apart from human life. Constantly exercising an Art which brought him into mechanical harmony with others, and which could not have been pursued unless he and they had been in the nicest mechanical relations and unison, it is curious to consider that the spirit of the man was in moral accordance or interchange with nothing around him. This indeed he had confided to his lost nephew, before the occasion for his present inflexibility arose.

That he must know of Rosa's abrupt departure, and that he must divine its cause, was not to be doubted. Did he suppose that he had terrified her into silence? or did he suppose that she had imparted to any one – to Mr. Crisparkle himself, for instance – the particulars of his last interview with her? Mr. Crisparkle could not determine this in his mind. He could not but admit, however, as a just man, that it was not, of itself, a crime to fall in love with Rosa, any more than it was a crime to offer to set love above revenge.

The dreadful suspicion of Jasper, which Rosa was so shocked to have received into her imagination, appeared to have no harbour in Mr. Crisparkle's. If it ever haunted Helena's thoughts or Neville's, neither gave it one spoken word of utterance. Mr. Grewgious took no pains to conceal his implacable dislike of Jasper, yet he never referred it, however distantly, to such a source. But he was a reticent as well as an eccentric man; and he made no mention of a certain evening when he warmed his hands at the gatehouse fire, and looked steadily down upon a certain heap of torn and miry clothes upon the floor.

Drowsy Cloisterham, whenever it awoke to a passing reconsideration of a story above six months old and dismissed by the bench of magistrates, was pretty equally divided in opinion whether John Jasper's beloved nephew had been killed by his treacherously passionate rival, or in an open struggle; or had, for his own purposes, spirited himself away. It then lifted up its head, to notice that the bereaved Jasper was still ever devoted to discovery and revenge; and then dozed off again. This was the condition of matters, all round, at the period to which the present history has now attained.

The Cathedral doors have closed for the night; and the Choir-Master, on a short leave of absence for two or three services, sets his face towards London. He travels thither by the means by which Rosa travelled, and arrives, as Rosa arrived, on a hot, dusty evening.

His travelling baggage is easily carried in his hand, and he repairs with it on foot, to a hybrid hotel in a little square behind Aldersgate Street, near the General Post Office. It is hotel, boarding-house, or lodging-house, at its visitor's option. It announces itself, in the new Railway Advertisers, as a novel enterprise, timidly beginning to spring up. It bashfully, almost apologetically, gives the traveller to understand that it does not expect him, on the good old constitutional hotel plan, to order a pint of sweet blacking for his drinking, and throw it away; but insinuates that he may have his boots blacked instead of his stomach, and maybe also have bed, breakfast, attendance, and a porter up all night, for a certain fixed charge. From these and similar premises, many true Britons in the lowest spirits deduce that the times are levelling times, except in the article of high roads, of which there will shortly be not one in England.

He eats without appetite, and soon goes forth again. Eastward and still eastward through the stale streets he takes his way, until he reaches his destination: a miserable court, specially miserable among many such.

He ascends a broken staircase, opens a door, looks into a dark stifling room, and says: 'Are you alone here?'

'Alone, deary; worse luck for me, and better for you,' replies a croaking voice. 'Come in, come in, whoever you be: I can't see you till I light a match, yet I seem to know the sound of your speaking. I'm acquainted with you, ain't I?'

'Light your match, and try.'

'So I will, deary, so I will; but my hand that shakes, as I can't lay it on a match all in a moment. And I cough so, that, put my matches where I may, I never find 'em there. They jump and start, as I cough and cough, like live things. Are you off a voyage, deary?'

'No.'

'Not seafaring?'

'No.'

'Well, there's land customers, and there's water customers. I'm a mother to both. Different from Jack Chinaman t'other side the court. He ain't a father to neither. It ain't in him. And he ain't got the true secret of mixing, though he charges as much as me that has, and more if he can get it. Here's a match, and now where's the candle? If my cough takes me, I shall cough out twenty matches afore I gets a light.'

But she finds the candle, and lights it, before the cough comes on. It seizes her in the moment of success, and she sits down rocking herself to and fro, and gasping at intervals: 'O, my lungs is awful bad! my lungs is wore away to cabbage-nets!' until the fit is over. During its continuance she has had no power of sight, or any other power not absorbed in the struggle; but as it leaves her, she begins to strain her eyes, and as soon as she is able to articulate, she cries, staring:

'Why, it's you!'

'Are you so surprised to see me?'

'I thought I never should have seen you again, deary. I thought you was dead, and gone to Heaven.'

'Why?'

'I didn't suppose you could have kept away, alive, so long, from the poor old soul with the real receipt for mixing it. And you are in mourning too! Why didn't you come and have a pipe or two of comfort? Did they leave you money, perhaps, and so you didn't want comfort?'

'No.'

'Who was they as died, deary?'

'A relative.'

'Died of what, lovey?'

'Probably, Death.'

'We are short to-night!' cries the woman, with a propitiatory laugh. 'Short and snappish we are! But we're out of sorts for want of a smoke. We've got the all-overs, haven't us, deary? But this is the place to cure 'em in; this is the place where the all-overs is smoked off.'

'You may make ready, then,' replies the visitor, 'as soon as you like.'

He divests himself of his shoes, loosens his cravat, and lies across the foot of the squalid bed, with his head resting on his left hand.

'Now you begin to look like yourself,' says the woman approvingly. 'Now I begin to know my old customer indeed! Been trying to mix for yourself this long time, poppet?'

'I have been taking it now and then in my own way.'

'Never take it your own way. It ain't good for trade, and it ain't good for you. Where's my ink-bottle, and where's my thimble, and where's my little spoon? He's going to take it in a artful form now, my deary dear!'

Entering on her process, and beginning to bubble and blow at the faint spark enclosed in the hollow of her hands, she speaks from time to time, in a tone of snuffling satisfaction, without leaving off. When he speaks, he does so without looking at her, and as if his thoughts were already roaming away by anticipation.

'I've got a pretty many smokes ready for you, first and last, haven't I, chuckey?'

'A good many.'

'When you first come, you was quite new to it; warn't ye?'

'Yes, I was easily disposed of, then.'

'But you got on in the world, and was able by-and-by to take your pipe with the best of 'em, warn't ye?'

'Ah; and the worst.'

'It's just ready for you. What a sweet singer you was when you first come! Used to drop your head, and sing yourself off like a bird! It's ready for you now, deary.'

He takes it from her with great care, and puts the mouthpiece to his lips. She seats herself beside him, ready to refill the pipe.

After inhaling a few whiffs in silence, he doubtingly accosts her with:

'Is it as potent as it used to be?'

'What do you speak of, deary?'

'What should I speak of, but what I have in my mouth?'

'It's just the same. Always the identical same.'

'It doesn't taste so. And it's slower.'

'You've got more used to it, you see.'

'That may be the cause, certainly. Look here.' He stops, becomes dreamy, and seems to forget that he has invited her attention. She bends over him, and speaks in his ear.

'I'm attending to you. Says you just now, Look here. Says I now, I'm attending to ye. We was talking just before of your being used to it.'

'I know all that. I was only thinking. Look here. Suppose you had something in your mind; something you were going to do.'

'Yes, deary; something I was going to do?'

'But had not quite determined to do.'

'Yes, deary.'

'Might or might not do, you understand.'

'Yes.' With the point of a needle she stirs the contents of the bowl.

'Should you do it in your fancy, when you were lying here doing this?'

She nods her head. 'Over and over again.'

'Just like me! I did it over and over again. I have done it hundreds of thousands of times in this room.'

'It's to be hoped it was pleasant to do, deary.'

'It *was* pleasant to do!'

He says this with a savage air, and a spring or start at her. Quite unmoved she retouches and replenishes the contents of the bowl with her little spatula. Seeing her intent upon the occupation, he sinks into his former attitude.

'It was a journey, a difficult and dangerous journey. That was the subject in my mind. A hazardous and perilous journey, over abysses where a slip would be destruction. Look down, look down! You see what lies at the bottom there?'

He has darted forward to say it, and to point at the ground, as though at some imaginary object far beneath. The woman looks at him, as his spasmodic face approaches close to hers, and not at his pointing. She seems to know what the influence of her perfect quietude would be; if so, she has not miscalculated it, for he subsides again.

'Well; I have told you I did it here hundreds of thousands of times. What do I say? I did it millions and billions of times. I did it so often, and through such vast expanses of time, that when it was really done, it seemed not worth the doing, it was done so soon.'

'That's the journey you have been away upon,' she quietly remarks.

He glares at her as he smokes; and then, his eyes becoming filmy, answers: 'That's the journey.'

Silence ensues. His eyes are sometimes closed and sometimes open. The woman sits beside him, very attentive to the pipe, which is all the while at his lips.

'I'll warrant,' she observes, when he has been looking fixedly at her for some consecutive moments, with a singular appearance in his eyes of seeming to see her a long way off, instead of so near him: 'I'll warrant you made the journey in a many ways, when you made it so often?'

'No, always in one way.'

'Always in the same way?'

'Ay.'

'In the way in which it was really made at last?'

'Ay.'

'And always took the same pleasure in harping on it?'

'Ay.'

For the time he appears unequal to any other reply than this lazy monosyllabic assent. Probably to assure herself that it is not the assent of a mere automaton, she reverses the form of her next sentence.

'Did you never get tired of it, deary, and try to call up something else for a change?'

He struggles into a sitting posture, and retorts upon her: 'What do you mean? What did I want? What did I come for?'

She gently lays him back again, and before returning him the instrument he has dropped, revives the fire in it with her own breath; then says to him, coaxingly:

'Sure, sure, sure! Yes, yes, yes! Now I go along with you. You was too quick for me. I see now. You come o' purpose to take the journey. Why, I might have known it, through its standing by you so.'

He answers first with a laugh, and then with a passionate setting of his teeth: 'Yes, I came on purpose. When I could not bear my life, I came to get the relief, and I got it. It WAS one! It WAS one!' This repetition with extraordinary vehemence, and the snarl of a wolf.

She observes him very cautiously, as though mentally feeling her way to her next remark. It is: 'There was a fellow-traveller, deary.'

'Ha, ha, ha!' He breaks into a ringing laugh, or rather yell.

'To think,' he cries, 'how often fellow-traveller, and yet not know it! To think how many times he went the journey, and never saw the road!'

The woman kneels upon the floor, with her arms crossed on the coverlet of the bed, close by him, and her chin upon them. In this crouching attitude she watches him. The pipe is falling from his mouth. She puts it back, and laying her hand upon his chest, moves him slightly from side to side. Upon that he speaks, as if she had spoken.

'Yes! I always made the journey first, before the changes of colours and the great landscapes and glittering processions began. They couldn't begin till it was off my mind. I had no room till then for anything else.'

Once more he lapses into silence. Once more she lays her hand upon his chest, and moves him slightly to and fro, as a cat might stimulate a half-slain mouse. Once more he speaks, as if she had spoken.

'What? I told you so. When it comes to be real at last, it is so short that it seems unreal for the first time. Hark!'

'Yes, deary. I'm listening.'

'Time and place are both at hand.'

He is on his feet, speaking in a whisper, and as if in the dark.

'Time, place, and fellow-traveller,' she suggests, adopting his tone, and holding him softly by the arm.

'How could the time be at hand unless the fellow-traveller was? Hush! The journey's made. It's over.'

'So soon?'

'That's what I said to you. So soon. Wait a little. This is a vision. I shall sleep it off. It has been too short and easy. I must have a better vision than this; this is the poorest of all. No struggle, no consciousness of peril, no entreaty – and yet I never saw *that* before.' With a start.

'Saw what, deary?'

'Look at it! Look what a poor, mean, miserable thing it is! *That* must be real. It's over.'

He has accompanied this incoherence with some wild unmeaning gestures; but they trail off into the progressive inaction of stupor, and he lies a log upon the bed.

The woman, however, is still inquisitive. With a repetition of her cat-like action she slightly stirs his body again, and listens; stirs again, and listens; whispers to it, and listens. Finding it past all rousing for the time, she slowly gets upon her feet, with an air of disappointment, and flicks the face with the back of her hand in turning from it.

But she goes no further away from it than the chair upon the hearth. She sits in it, with an elbow on one of its arms, and her chin upon her hand, intent upon him. 'I heard ye say once,' she croaks under her breath, 'I heard ye say once, when I was lying where you're lying, and you were making your speculations upon me, "Unintelligible!" I heard you say so, of two more than me. But don't ye be too sure always; don't be ye too sure, beauty!'

Unwinking, cat-like, and intent, she presently adds: 'Not so potent as it once was? Ah! Perhaps not at first. You may be more right there. Practice makes perfect. I may have learned the secret how to make ye talk, deary.'

He talks no more, whether or no. Twitching in an ugly way from time to time, both as to his face and limbs, he lies heavy and silent. The wretched candle burns down; the woman takes its expiring end between her fingers, lights another at it, crams the guttering frying morsel deep into the candlestick, and rams it home with the new candle, as if she were loading some ill-savoured and unseemly weapon of witchcraft; the new candle in its turn burns down; and still he lies insensible. At length what remains of the last candle is blown out, and daylight looks into the room.

It has not looked very long, when he sits up, chilled and shaking, slowly recovers consciousness of where he is, and makes himself ready to depart. The woman receives what he pays her with a grateful, 'Bless ye, bless ye, deary!' and seems, tired out, to begin making herself ready for sleep as he leaves the room.

But seeming may be false or true. It is false in this case; for, the moment the stairs have ceased to creak under his tread, she glides after him, muttering emphatically: 'I'll not miss ye twice!'

There is no egress from the court but by its entrance. With a weird peep from the doorway, she watches for his looking back. He does not look back before disappearing, with a wavering step. She follows him, peeps from the court, sees him still faltering on without looking back, and holds him in view.

He repairs to the back of Aldersgate Street, where a door immediately opens to his knocking. She crouches in another doorway, watching that one, and easily comprehending that he puts up temporarily at that house. Her patience is unexhausted by hours. For sustenance she can, and does, buy bread within a hundred yards, and milk as it is carried past her.

He comes forth again at noon, having changed his dress, but carrying nothing in his hand, and having nothing carried for him. He is not going back into the country, therefore, just yet. She follows him a little way, hesitates, instantaneously turns confidently, and goes straight into the house he has quitted.

'Is the gentleman from Cloisterham indoors?

'Just gone out.'

'Unlucky. When does the gentleman return to Cloisterham?'

'At six this evening.'

'Bless ye and thank ye. May the Lord prosper a business where a civil question, even from a poor soul, is so civilly answered!'

'I'll not miss ye twice!' repeats the poor soul in the street, and not so civilly. 'I lost ye last, where that omnibus you got into nigh your journey's end plied betwixt the station and the place. I wasn't so much as certain that you even went right on to the place. Now I know ye did. My gentleman from Cloisterham, I'll be there before ye, and bide your coming. I've swore my oath that I'll not miss ye twice!'

Accordingly, that same evening the poor soul stands in Cloisterham High Street, looking at the many quaint gables of the Nuns' House, and getting through the time as she best can until nine o'clock; at which hour she has reason to suppose that the arriving omnibus passengers may have some interest for her. The friendly darkness, at that hour, renders it easy for her to ascertain whether this be so or not; and it is so, for the passenger not to be missed twice arrives among the rest.

'Now let me see what becomes of you. Go on!'

An observation addressed to the air, and yet it might be addressed to the passenger, so compliantly does he go on along the High Street until he comes to an arched gateway, at which he unexpectedly vanishes. The poor soul quickens her pace; is swift, and close upon him entering under the gateway; but only sees a postern staircase on one side of it, and on the other side an ancient vaulted room, in which a large-headed, grey-haired gentleman is writing, under the odd circumstances of sitting open to the thoroughfare and eyeing all who pass, as if he were toll-taker of the gateway: though the way is free.

'Halloa!' he cries in a low voice, seeing her brought to a stand-still: 'who are you looking for?'

'There was a gentleman passed in here this minute, sir.'

'Of course there was. What do you want with him?'

'Where do he live, deary?'

'Live? Up that staircase.'

'Bless ye! Whisper. What's his name, deary?'

'Surname Jasper, Christian name John. Mr. John Jasper.'

'Has he a calling, good gentleman?'

'Calling? Yes. Sings in the choir.'

'In the spire?'

'Choir.'

'What's that?'

Mr. Datchery rises from his papers, and comes to his doorstep. 'Do you know what a cathedral is?' he asks, jocosely.

The woman nods.

'What is it?'

She looks puzzled, casting about in her mind to find a definition, when it occurs to her that it is easier to point out the substantial object itself, massive against the dark-blue sky and the early stars.

'That's the answer. Go in there at seven to-morrow morning, and you may see Mr. John Jasper, and hear him too.'

'Thank ye! Thank ye!'

The burst of triumph in which she thanks him does not escape the notice of the single buffer of an easy temper living idly on his means. He glances at her; clasps his hands behind him, as the wont of such buffers is; and lounges along the echoing Precincts at her side.

'Or,' he suggests, with a backward hitch of his head, 'you can go up at once to Mr. Jasper's rooms there.'

The woman eyes him with a cunning smile, and shakes her head.

'O! you don't want to speak to him?'

She repeats her dumb reply, and forms with her lips a soundless 'No.'

'You can admire him at a distance three times a day, whenever you like. It's a long way to come for that, though.'

The woman looks up quickly. If Mr. Datchery thinks she is to be so induced to declare where she comes from, he is of a much easier temper than she is. But she acquits him of such an artful thought, as he lounges along, like the chartered bore of the city, with his uncovered grey hair blowing about, and his purposeless hands rattling the loose money in the pockets of his trousers.

The chink of the money has an attraction for her greedy ears. 'Wouldn't you help me to pay for my traveller's lodging, dear gentleman, and to pay my way along? I am a poor soul, I am indeed, and troubled with a grievous cough.'

'You know the travellers' lodging, I perceive, and are making directly for it,' is Mr. Datchery's bland comment, still rattling his loose money. 'Been here often, my good woman?'

'Once in all my life.'

'Ay, ay?'

They have arrived at the entrance to the Monks' Vineyard. An appropriate remembrance, presenting an exemplary model for imitation, is revived in the woman's mind by the sight of the place. She stops at the gate, and says energetically:

'By this token, though you mayn't believe it, That a young gentleman gave me three-and-sixpence as I was coughing my breath away on this very grass. I asked him for three-and-sixpence, and he gave it me.'

'Wasn't it a little cool to name your sum?' hints Mr. Datchery, still rattling. 'Isn't it customary to leave the amount open? Mightn't it have had the appearance, to the young gentleman – only the appearance – that he was rather dictated to?'

'Look'ee here, deary,' she replies, in a confidential and persuasive tone, 'I wanted the money to lay it out on a medicine as does me good, and as I deal in. I told the young gentleman so, and he gave it me, and I laid it out honest to the last brass farden. I want to lay out the same sum in the same way now; and if you'll give it me, I'll lay it out honest to the last brass farden again, upon my soul!'

'What's the medicine?'

'I'll be honest with you beforehand, as well as after. It's opium.'

Mr. Datchery, with a sudden change of countenance, gives her a sudden look.

'It's opium, deary. Neither more nor less. And it's like a human creetur so far, that you always hear what can be said against it, but seldom what can be said in its praise.'

Mr. Datchery begins very slowly to count out the sum demanded of him. Greedily watching his hands, she continues to hold forth on the great example set him.

'It was last Christmas Eve, just arter dark, the once that I was here afore, when the young gentleman gave me the three-and-six.' Mr.

Datchery stops in his counting, finds he has counted wrong, shakes his money together, and begins again.

'And the young gentleman's name,' she adds, 'was Edwin.'

Mr. Datchery drops some money, stoops to pick it up, and reddens with the exertion as he asks:

'How do you know the young gentleman's name?'

'I asked him for it, and he told it me. I only asked him the two questions, what was his Chris'en name, and whether he'd a sweetheart? And he answered, Edwin, and he hadn't.'

Mr. Datchery pauses with the selected coins in his hand, rather as if he were falling into a brown study of their value, and couldn't bear to part with them. The woman looks at him distrustfully, and with her anger brewing for the event of his thinking better of the gift; but he bestows it on her as if he were abstracting his mind from the sacrifice, and with many servile thanks she goes her way.

John Jasper's lamp is kindled, and his lighthouse is shining when Mr. Datchery returns alone towards it. As mariners on a dangerous voyage, approaching an iron-bound coast, may look along the beams of the warning light to the haven lying beyond it that may never be reached, so Mr. Datchery's wistful gaze is directed to this beacon, and beyond.

His object in now revisiting his lodging is merely to put on the hat which seems so superfluous an article in his wardrobe. It is half-past ten by the Cathedral clock when he walks out into the Precincts again; he lingers and looks about him, as though, the enchanted hour when Mr. Durdles may be stoned home having struck, he had some expectation of seeing the Imp who is appointed to the mission of stoning him.

In effect, that Power of Evil is abroad. Having nothing living to stone at the moment, he is discovered by Mr. Datchery in the unholy office of stoning the dead, through the railings of the churchyard. The Imp finds this a relishing and piquing pursuit; firstly, because their resting-place is announced to be sacred; and secondly, because the tall headstones are sufficiently like themselves, on their beat in the dark, to justify the delicious fancy that they are hurt when hit.

Mr. Datchery hails with him: 'Halloa, Winks!'

He acknowledges the hail with: 'Halloa, Dick!' Their acquaintance seemingly having been established on a familiar footing.

'But, I say,' he remonstrates, 'don't yer go a-making my name public. I never means to plead to no name, mind yer. When they says to me in the Lock-up, a-going to put me down in the book, "What's your name?" I says to them, "Find out." Likewise when they says, "What's your religion?" I says, "Find out." '

Which, it may be observed in passing, it would be immensely difficult for the State, however statistical, to do.

'Asides which,' adds the boy, 'there ain't no family of Winkses.'

'I think there must be.'

'Yer lie, there ain't. The travellers give me the name on account of my getting no settled sleep and being knocked up all night; whereby I gets one eye roused open afore I've shut the other. That's what Winks means. Deputy's the nighest name to indict me by: but yer wouldn't catch me pleading to that, neither.'

'Deputy be it always, then. We two are good friends; eh, Deputy?'

'Jolly good.'

'I forgave you the debt you owed me when we first became acquainted, and many of my sixpences have come your way since; eh, Deputy?'

'Ah! And what's more, yer ain't no friend o' Jarsper's. What did he go a-histing me off my legs for?'

'What indeed! But never mind him now. A shilling of mine is going your way to-night, Deputy. You have just taken in a lodger I have been speaking to; an infirm woman with a cough.'

'Puffer,' assents Deputy, with a shrewd leer of recognition, and smoking an imaginary pipe, with his head very much on one side and his eyes very much out of their places: 'Hopeum Puffer.'

'What is her name?'

''Er Royal Highness the Princess Puffer.'

'She has some other name than that; where does she live?'

'Up in London. Among the Jacks.'

'The sailors?'

'I said so; Jacks; and Chayner men: and hother Knifers.'

'I should like to know, through you, exactly where she lives.'

'All right. Give us 'old.'

A shilling passes; and, in that spirit of confidence which should pervade all business transactions between principals of honour, this piece of business is considered done.

'But here's a lark!' cries Deputy. 'Where did yer think 'Er Royal Highness is a-goin' to to-morrow morning? Blest if she ain't a-goin' to the KIN-FREE-DER-EL!' He greatly prolongs the word in his ecstasy, and smites his leg, and doubles himself up in a fit of shrill laughter.

'How do you know that, Deputy?'

'Cos she told me so just now. She said she must be hup and hout o' purpose. She ses, "Deputy, I must 'ave a early wash, and make myself as swell as I can, for I'm a-goin' to take a turn at the KIN-FREE-DER-EL!" He separates the syllables with his former zest, and, not finding his sense of the ludicrous sufficiently relieved by stamping about on the pavement, breaks into a slow and stately dance, perhaps supposed to be performed by the Dean.

Mr. Datchery receives the communication with a well-satisfied though pondering face, and breaks up the conference. Returning to his quaint lodging, and sitting long over the supper of bread-and-cheese and salad and ale which Mrs. Tope has left prepared for him, he still sits when his supper is finished. At length he rises, throws open the door of a corner cupboard, and refers to a few uncouth chalked strokes on its inner side.

'I like,' says Mr. Datchery, 'the old tavern way of keeping scores. Illegible except to the scorer. The scorer not committed, the scored debited with what is against him. Hum; ha! A very small score this; a very poor score!'

He sighs over the contemplation of its poverty, takes a bit of chalk from one of the cupboard shelves, and pauses with it in his hand, uncertain what addition to make to the account.

'I think a moderate stroke,' he concludes, 'is all I am justified in scoring up;' so, suits the action to the word, closes the cupboard, and goes to bed.

A brilliant morning shines on the old city. Its antiquities and ruins are surpassingly beautiful, with a lusty ivy gleaming in the sun, and the rich trees waving in the balmy air. Changes of glorious light from moving boughs, songs of birds, scents from gardens, woods, and fields – or, rather, from the one great garden of the whole cultivated island in its yielding time – penetrate into the Cathedral, subdue its earthy odour, and preach the Resurrection and the Life. The cold stone tombs of centuries ago grow warm; and flecks of brightness dart into the sternest marble corners of the building, fluttering there like wings.

Comes Mr. Tope with his large keys, and yawningly unlocks and sets open. Come Mrs. Tope and attendant sweeping sprites. Come, in due time, organist and bellows-boy, peeping down from the red curtains in the loft, fearlessly flapping dust from books up at that remote elevation, and whisking it from stops and pedals. Come sundry rooks, from various quarters of the sky, back to the great tower; who may be presumed to enjoy vibration, and to know that bell and organ are going to give it them. Come a very small and straggling congregation indeed: chiefly from Minor Canon Corner and the Precincts. Come Mr. Crisparkle, fresh and bright; and his ministering brethren, not quite so fresh and bright. Come the Choir in a hurry (always in a hurry, and struggling into their nightgowns at the last moment, like children shirking bed), and comes John Jasper leading their line. Last of all comes Mr. Datchery into a stall, one of a choice empty collection very much at his service, and glancing about him for Her Royal Highness the Princess Puffer.

The service is pretty well advanced before Mr. Datchery can discern Her Royal Highness. But by that time he has made her out, in the shade. She is behind a pillar, carefully withdrawn from the Choir-Master's view, but regards him with the closest attention. All unconscious of her presence, he chants and sings. She grins when he is most musically fervid, and – yes, Mr. Datchery sees her do it! – shakes her fist at him behind the pillar's friendly shelter.

Mr. Datchery looks again, to convince himself. Yes, again! As ugly and withered as one of the fantastic carvings on the under brackets of the stall seats, as malignant as the Evil One, as hard as the big brass eagle holding the sacred books upon his wings (and, according to the sculptor's representation of his ferocious attributes, not at all converted by them), she hugs herself in her lean arms, and then shakes both fists at the leader of the Choir.

And at that moment, outside the grated door of the Choir, having eluded the vigilance of Mr. Tope by shifty resources in which he is an adept, Deputy peeps, sharp-eyed, through the bars, and stares astounded from the threatener to the threatened.

The service comes to an end, and the servitors disperse to breakfast. Mr. Datchery accosts his last new acquaintance outside, when the Choir (as much in a hurry to get their bedgowns off, as they were but now to get them on) have scuffled away.

'Well, mistress. Good morning. You have seen him?'

'*I've* seen him, deary; *I've* seen him!'

'And you know him?'

'Know him! Better far than all the Reverend Parsons put together know him.'

Mrs. Tope's care has spread a very neat, clean breakfast ready for her lodger. Before sitting down to it, he opens his corner-cupboard door; takes his bit of chalk from its shelf; adds one thick line to the score, extending from the top of the cupboard door to the bottom; and then falls to with an appetite.

* D *

PART II
- David Madden -

CHAPTER XXIV
Rising above the Grit

THE SUN HAS boldly invaded the great smoky, tarnished city of London: illuminating the grand habitations of the rich, which mantle at its touch; unmasking the squalid abodes of the poor, which shyly submit to scrutiny; dispelling the darkness, proclaiming a new dawn; prying into gritty secrets, creeping into hidden corners.

Some of the sun's more adventurous rays, resembling in their shining splendour the tawny hair and whiskers of Lobley, even have the temerity to enter the dwelling of the fell Billickin, picking out its troublesome slates, running along its questionable piping and joists, ascending its vertiginous staircase (the better to view the whole property), luxuriating in the modest comfort of its parlours and bedrooms, and even, like Aesop's beguiling South Wind, persuading Billickin herself to cast aside her shawl of office.

Nowhere is the sun more welcome than in the front parlour of the Billickin establishment, where Miss Twinkleton is seated on a somewhat unforgiving sofa, supplied by the equally unforgiving landlady, and dutifully reading to a semi-attentive Rosa. The warm light plays on the girl's pretty features, as she day-dreams to the accompaniment of Miss Twinkleton's well-practiced reading voice. The modulated tones of the latter are rounded, as a boulder is smoothed by the ceaseless motion of the waves, through the regular practice of nurturing in this manner successive generations of young ladies of good family, gathered together to worship at the shrine of knowledge. In truth, it is an instructional voice which would have drawn the special ire of Billickin, as falling under the rubric that Miss Twinkleton was setting herself to teach *her* something, had that formidably candid contestant been present for the performance. Although in general Miss Twinkleton in the London lodging, and despite the proximity of Billickin, remains in a happy compromise between her two states of being, representing respectively the day and night of her soul, broadly defined as the scholastic and the sprightly, the former demonstrates a tendency to dominate when she is reading, and she reads in what can only be termed a highly Educational Manner, even in the evening.

By mutual agreement, they have together continued to mine the rich seam of novels recounting tales of sea journeys. Odd: why has Rosa in particular become so fascinated by that recondite branch of the art of story-telling? Why does she invariably ensure that a stout volume recounting nautical voyages is ready at Miss Twinkleton's hand, as the hour for reading approaches? Why does she not call for heady romances, for ardent poetry, for light novellas? She knows that Miss Ferdinand, Miss Reynolds and Miss Giggles – especially Miss Giggles – will all be voraciously consuming such fare in their several homes, and will be eager to discuss the content in confidential whispers when they reassemble for the term.

Whatever the reason, Miss Twinkleton heroically reads away about voyages: about sailing and navigating and belaying and reefing; while Rosa pictures brown hands and brown arms performing these various tasks; and likewise pictures a brown face and blue eyes looking far, far across the ocean: looking yearningly back to England. This morning, the sun adds a new lustre to these contented day-dreams.

In the interests of education, and thinking of the time – fast approaching – when her young seminarians will eagerly return to their studies, wherever possible Miss Twinkleton interpolates, in place of vulgar adventure, what she construes as the essential foundations of sea-voyaging: adding a pinch of wholesome detail to flavour the narrative, and leave a rich sediment of knowledge in Rosa's mind. She tells of compasses and lodestones, of astrolabes and sextants, and other miracles of navigation: of trade-winds and capes – whether of good or false hope – and other miracles of sailing; of the stocks and stores carried on board, and other miracles of provisioning; of the great shipping lines, and shipping lanes, and other miracles of trading.

And what are stories without the wonders of geography? The presiding deity of the Nuns' House had brought the two globes, terrestrial and celestial, with her to Billickin's, adding to the cost and confusion of her journey thither – their rotund forms being all too easily miscounted as two additional cabmen, or as a pair of errant trunks, or as considerably more than a brace of Billickins. The terrestrial twin is now put to regular use charting the progress of the intrepid seafarers who have so dramatically entered their lives; Miss Twinkleton often carries the book in her left hand, and continues to read, while with her right indicating the part of the world where the protagonists are involved, or where the prevailing winds will take them, or where they can bunker and reprovision. Meanwhile his celestial brother – for Miss Twinkleton does not tolerate idleness – is employed to demonstrate the subtle arts of steering by the distant stars

Miss Twinkleton is not, however, unjust or unduly demanding of her fair listener. She adjusts the length of her presentations by invariably excluding passages about pirates, or sea-battles, or hand-to-hand combat, or handsome young sailors. It matters little; for Rosa imagines these for herself. Two sunburnt hands and brawny arms feature prominently, and with unvarying success: those same hands and arms which had dragged the youthful Septimus Crisparkle from the treacherous waters, thereby averting a seventh family tragedy: they now regularly wreak havoc among screaming but ineffectual hordes of swarthy pirates, whether of the Barbary or Caribbean persuasion – despite the terrestrial globe, and Miss Twinkleton's dexterous hand, Rosa's sense of geography is not of the strongest.

Miss Twinkleton's improvements to the stories, as she would view the matter, naturally allow her to draw lessons and conclusions, both practical and moral, for Rosa's benefit: indeed these appurtenances attach themselves to the text in a most marvelous manner, and appear to grow out of it like the waving tentacles of some fabled sea-monster encountered in strange seas. The ceaseless search for such instructive appendages is a fundamental part of her system of teaching, developed and practised over the years at the seminary with the resplendent brass plate, and by no means abandoned in exile in Holborn, any more than the wandering tribes of Israel renounced their religion when lead by Moses into the wilderness.

Thus, happily developing the subject of lodestones and longitudes for Rosa's inattentive ear, Miss Twinkleton refers to the intriguingly-named Sir Cloudesley Shovel. Rosa is not sure whether she has fully heard or understood, and indeed in general has become increasingly confused between the odysseys themselves, Miss Twinkleton's amendments, and Miss Twinkleton's illuminating comments, all delivered in the same smooth Educational Voice; not that she minds, or does a great deal to unravel these mysteries, since she has much, of more pleasing matter, to occupy and entertain her. She hears that Sir Cloudesley is portly and florid of countenance (a hint of criticism here, as if Sir Cloudesley does not measure up to Mr Porters, who, although undeniably foolish, was commendably elegant and light of appearance as befitted a man of his accomplishments). The name Shovel appears to Rosa delightfully inappropriate for a man of the sea, and also for one so highly promoted and decorated by a line of grateful sovereigns. But Rosa grasps – or rather it is borne in upon her by Miss Twinkleton's persistence, and through the veil of her languid inattention – that the main weakness of poor Sir Cloudesley is that he is ignorant (head in clouds, muses Rosa); confounded by longitude (showed latitude about longitude); and grounded his fleet upon The Scillies (silly indeed). And is either drowned, or killed for the sake of the gold and silver adorning his fleshy person, as he wades clumsily ashore in his water-logged finery: the unhappy victim of his own failure to set his compass in a systematic and accurate manner. So there is, as always, a pertinent lesson to be drawn by such a practised teacher as Miss Twinkleton from this aberrant episode in the otherwise illustrious history of our Royal Navy.

Suddenly, Rosa is awakened from her long reverie induced by the sun, the soporific sound of Miss Twinkleton's reading voice and her dreams of Tartar. Nautical miscalculation, shipwreck, disaster, drowning, death. Death! This could so easily have been the fate of Tartar, when he also was in the Navy, and perhaps under the command of some red-faced incompetent such as Shovel: ship-wrecked and lost, or dying in battle, or drowning, or catching some incurable tropical disease, or suffering some strange and calamitous amalgam of all these ills.

She feels faint at the thought of what might have befallen him. How lucky she is not to have known him when he was still in the service of his country: she would have known little peace of mind when he was away at sea; and how fortunate it is that he is no longer in the Navy, and that he has given her his word that he would never go to sea again. Curious, that, she reflects: he had quite definitely given her his word in the matter, and at their very first meeting. She silently blesses the deceased uncle for the strength of his prejudice against the Navy, and the experiences and disappointments which engendered this; and, drawing on information derived from the unimpeachable source of Miss Twinkleton, she favourably contrasts Tartar's commendable determination to renounce maritime enterprise, with the rather less fortunate decision of the famous explorer and cartographer Captain Cook not to live in comfortable retirement in Greenwich, but to continue sailing the seven seas, a veritable Flying Dutchman, ultimately meeting his untimely end at the hands of certain inhospitable Hawaiians (the seven seas again being a relic of Miss Twinkleton's teaching, and the occasion at the time of parallel references to the quintessential sevenness of virtues and deadly sins, and wonders of the world, and senses and sages and sleepers, and bibles and bodies and champions and churches). Rosa's pretty eyes open with horror and compassion as she recalls the fate of Captain Cook: deliberately drowned, then cut in to the pieces subsequently returned to his grieving colleagues.

Rosa has been changed by her recent experiences: by the dreadful, horrifying scene by the sun-dial; but also by her solitary journey to London, her warm reception there, the special favour shown her by Mr Grewgious, and the fierce battles between Billickin and Miss Twinkleton, in which no quarter is sought or granted, and in which the dainty shuttlecock receives a regular pounding from the two doughty battledores, and especially from the B. She is become more mature, less saucy, though equally loving. Lumps-of-Delight and a certain stickiness of countenance are things of the past. Were poor Edwin Drood to be present, he would search in vain for the look of pert provocation which had contributed so much to his growing feeling of unease in their relations, to his sense that some vital ingredient was missing in their companionship. Her new existence, and her new acquaintance, have moved new depths in her. The first glimpse of this reformed Rosa was revealed in her skilful yet affectionate handling of her separation from Edwin, in what proved to be their last meeting. In parallel, the childish prettiness is fast growing into womanly beauty.

Chaucer's Prioress, who may well have travelled through dusty Cloisterham in days gone by, when the great Cathedral and the old castle and the hoarse rooks were all younger, rightly proclaimed that Amor Vincit Omnia. She was clearly knowledgeable in affairs of the heart. Had there been space on her brooch, she might with advantage have improved the sentiment by adding a further verb: Amor Vincit et Mutat Omnia. It is so with Rosa. She is changed by love: first by feelings of love for her freshly-minted brother Eddy, then by deep affection for her guardian who came to her rescue like a true – if somewhat shambling – knight errant, and finally by love for Tartar when he entered her life. She feels that she now has an admirer with whom she never quarrels, does not need to quarrel, would not dream of quarrelling. What is there to quarrel about? His affection is unquestionable: ardent and unfeigned: as is hers for him. She looks forward to each new meeting, which was never the case with poor Eddy: never, after the first excitement of their strange betrothal, and their mutual sense of being different and in some way superior to their peers, had worn away, and had slowly and imperceptibly but definitively changed into an unhappy realisation that they had become something of a peep-show, an object of gossip and conjecture, that they were unsuited to each other, and that their dearest wish was to be like others, and make their own choices, by themselves and for themselves.

She has the reassuring feeling that she has found a safe port after a hazardous journey. But, having discovered the port of her liking, of her dreams, she is eager for fulfillment and fruition, rather than uncertainty and delay. She increasingly realises that lodging at Billickin's is but a resting place, and one she has outgrown – if such a little thing could be believed to have outgrown anything. The pre-Christian ancients, such as Dante's omniscient guide himself, who were caught in limbo, must have harboured similar feelings. So, unlike the flightless Dodo, born to be extinct, the old *spoilt* Rosa is not entirely extinguished: just much changed: yet still counting on kindness, and regularly receiving it.

There is a sharp knock at the door, immediately followed by the grand entry of Billickin in gladiatorial mood, her shawl having been loosely draped over her shoulders by her dutiful attendant, in the manner of a military cloak, to acknowledge the warmth of the day, but likewise to be ready at hand in case of a sudden and debilitating attack of personal faintness.

'The day bein' a Monday, Miss, I ham reminded that it is two weeks since the hamiable Mister Grewgious and I signed the agreemient giving right of 'abitation in these rooms to you and the other who is not present and whose name will not pass these lips,' remarks Billickin to Rosa grandly, in accents aspirational with purpose, and pursing, in a meaningful way, the somewhat austere organs to which she refers, as if to underline her resolution that That Name would never again defile them.

'It follows that the agreemient in question 'as but a similar period to run. Rooms as sweet as these is in great demand, and I need to know,' drawing herself up to her full height, twitching at the shawl, and again becoming aspirational 'your hintentions, Miss.'

Rosa opens her mouth to reply, but it is the far from invisible Miss Twinkleton who responds, sensing a rare advantage.

'Rosa, dear, please indicate to that person that we do not act under duress or pressure.'

She speaks to Rosa, apparently ignoring any other presence, alien or otherwise, in the room; her voice is no longer her official reading voice, but the sweet – perhaps slightly over-sweet – tones one might employ, in sorrow not in anger, to correct an errant servant or careless chamber-maid.

'The time for a decision about our future moves is certainly approaching: I require no reminding of that. I shall consult with you, dear, and with the diligent Mr Grewgious, and then we shall communicate that decision in an appropriate manner to the appropriate person.'

She emits a slight sniff as she enunciates this last phrase: someone unacquainted with her background and position in society might even term it a snort.

'I still have some scholarly affairs to detain me in town, and we may wish to extend our lease of these rooms by a week.'

Miss Twinkleton may be speaking to Rosa, but the words are for the ears of Billickin, and the ears of Billickin alone, and launched with sufficient decibels to reach those dainty targets with ease. She launches into the second part of her well-constructed riposte.

'As for alternative tenants, I see no sign of anyone wishing to take these rooms, they gave little indication of recent habitation when we arrived, and there are other rooms available on the top floor, though I cannot believe them to be in great demand, since I understand they have manifold disadvantages.'

A lesser woman, prone to personal faintness, might have wilted; but Billickin is made of sterner stuff, and does not even pause before launching her retort. Her wrath knows no bounds. If before, her lovely lips have looked a shade severe, they are now positively savage.

'I am hamazed at you being asked to return such a reply to a civil request, Miss,' she comments tartly, pulling her shawl further about her, as if both covering her from any further attack, and also keeping the dreaded faintness at bay.

'Were it not for your companion's advanced hage,' savouring the word as she says it, 'I might be tempted to run her out of the 'ouse and into the street the very minute the agreemient ends. Another week, forsooth! I feared the worst when I 'eard that she owned a school. I was at school myself, afore I meets Billickin, and I knows about teachers. They gets ideas of grandiour, and their noses gets stuck in the air. No doubt, I am sure – ' she finishes her point with more conviction than grammar or precise meaning; before re-loading at speed, and firing again upon the hapless enemy.

'Has for scholastic matters, I suggest, Miss, that that is no more than a euphemulism for persuading more parents to part with good money to send their poor unfortunate girls to her seminary.'

In which, it must be admitted that the fair Billickin has landed a telling blow, since Miss Twinkleton has indeed developed a great fondness both for those anonymous-looking envelopes, secreting half-yearly accounts (with their comforting inclusive regulars and heart-warming extras), which accompany her young ladies to their homes at the end of each term: and even more for the discreet but pleasing envelopes in response which return to the Nuns' House with the afore-mentioned young ladies at the start of the following term. But she is not finished, and her speech rises to a peroration at the end, well-aspirated as before.

'As I have remarked before, Miss, I am not accustomed to my word being doubted. But perhaps the old woman has forgotten, hage' she emphasises the word contemptuously 'hage being what it is. If I says that the rooms is interesting to others, that is no inwention, and likewise no deceptin I am sure. And perhaps these others does not wish to climb all those stairs to the top floor. Because, Miss, I would not deceive them, any more than I attempted to deceive you: that is what they would need to do; those rooms being above these. And what if there was a storm? Those damp patches tell a tale, and I am not one to conceal the truth. However much I am accused of telling base untruths by those what don't know, I 'old my 'ead 'igh.'

And her head is indeed singularly high as she delivers herself of these touching sentiments. Rosa, looking at her, is worried lest the Billickin neck might seize up in that over-stretched condition, and leave its owner frozen in the permanent position of someone attempting to peer over a high fence.

'So if you could convey my reply, Miss, I would be under an hobligation. And I await instruction from Mr Grewgious, who can be expected to proceed in these matters without rancour and vulgar habuse.'

On which note the ostrich-like neck miraculously compresses itself like a concertina inward, without apparent damage to its owner, and without a further word she strides impressively from the room, flinging her shawl even further round her, like a performer in some drama at Drury Lane, possibly with a military theme, making a last, dramatic exit.

Once again, Miss Twinkleton has, alas, failed to hold her own. Her opponent is too experienced, too fierce, too rough. Miss Twinkleton does not belong in the same ring, or fight at the same weight; she looks a little flustered, and the breathing is rather more laboured than before.

'The rudeness of that woman is quite unsupportable. I am a little surprised that Mr Grewgious, who seems in other respects so fastidious, recommended her. But the rooms are convenient, and I am inclined to take them for a further week. But that will have to be the termination of our sojourn here, my dear. I shall send a note round to The Staple, and ask Mr Grewgious to negotiate the appropriate arrangement.'

Rosa listens to this exchange, and the conclusion, with growing wistfulness. While increasingly doubting Miss Twinkleton's tactical acumen, she does not like to see her pounded by Billickin, and pasted by Billickin, and generally bested by Billickin. Also, she is abruptly reminded of her own precarious position. Return to Cloisterham has been postponed, yet only for a matter of days. At some point she will need to go back, with two distinct disadvantages. She will be further from the admirable Tartar; and again in the same town as the terrible Jasper, possibly seeing him, feeling his presence, fearing his approach and his possible touch, knowing that he will stare at her, and that his eyes will not leave her lips, so that she will again feel stained. She shudders at the thought, as if the shadow of Jasper had fallen on her, as it fell on the sundial. What is she to do? Where is she to go?

These feelings and anxieties stay with her for the remainder of the day; and she spends much time staring rather mournfully out of the window of her room: which, in truth, does not offer a particularly encouraging prospect, since it looks onto the Mews, where there is a certain prevalence of horse. Imagine her pleasure, then, when Mr Grewgious arrives, and – joy of joys – is accompanied by Lieutenant Tartar. Mr Grewgious rapidly and efficiently disposes of the matter of the extra week's rent with the by now more docile if still candid Billickin, and then they both enter the front parlour.

It is Mr Grewgious who takes the lead.

'Miss Twinkleton, Rosa my dear,' making it quite clear on this occasion that the endearment can grammatically apply only to his ward, and no other, 'I have been remiss. I have been found wanting. But since my fault lies on what might be termed the imaginative side of life, this is, alas, no surprise.' He is bravely chipping these words out of himself in a laborious and angular manner. 'Since I have the highest opinion of Miss Twinkleton and of her qualities', with a slight, and slightly stiff, bow in her direction, 'and since to be with my ward is the greatest pleasure of my long life', with a glance of natural affection and some considerable pride at her, 'I naturally believed that you would both be living in these rooms with pleasure: and, in Rosa's case, with educational advantage. I am aware that Mrs Billickin, relict of the late Billickin, can be somewhat – umps – attritional in manner; but she is both honest and dependable. So I had imagined you to be living here in perfect peace and harmony.

And I am sorry to say that it was my young friend who had to remind me that you might relish some change of occupation, and that we should come up, or rather come round, with an invitation.'

Here he pauses, as if mentally turning a page in his preparatory notes, coughs slightly, and is about to resume when Tartar eagerly joins in.

'Ladies, Mr Grewgious has set the scene most admirably. The fact is, it just came to me, that everyone, however happily settled, may look for new entertainment from time to time. I would like nothing better than to be read to by Miss Twinkleton, and,' taking up a volume and glancing with a little surprise at the title, 'I fancy that this work would appeal to me greatly, though some scenes may be a shade blood-thirsty, for these authors do like to exaggerate so.'

Why does Rosa's pink cheek become slightly pinker: has her choice of reading matter offered too blatant a guide to her affections and secret thoughts? And why does Miss Twinkleton look self-conscious: does she fear that her artful substitutions may now be suspected?

'I am convinced that Rosa must also value her unique good fortune in living here in the company of her dear teacher. But, every now and then, a change can work wonders. A dinner elsewhere: at my quarters, for example. It's all ready. The table is set, the wines are uncorked, it's all ship-shape, and waiting to be honoured with your company,' he ends at a run, his face bright with enthusiasm and expectation.

Rosa is so happy that she almost bursts out with her immediate agreement to this happy proposal, but remembers just in time that it is for Miss Twinkleton to reply to the invitation. Instead, she turns to Miss Twinkleton eagerly, and with those expressive little eyebrows revealing the hopes in her heart. There is a momentary pause while the Wandering Jewess casts a sad glance at the twin globes, as if an evening of improving study in the rotund company of Castor and Pollux will be sorely missed, and looks tenderly at the book which had caught Tartar's attention, as if keen to continue Rosa's education at every possible moment; but in the end she graciously accedes, as Rosa felt sure she would. It is late, and there is more than a hint of the night-time phase of being in Miss Twinkleton's manner.

So they set off for the Staple Inn, Mr Grewgious gallantly accompanying Miss Twinkleton, while his ward is equally gallantly – nay, yet more gallantly – escorted by Tartar. As they go, Miss Twinkleton tells Mr Grewgious of the insupportable rudeness of Billickin, to the latter's considerable consternation; while Tartar regales Rosa with some sea yarns she will not find in books, and certainly not in the somewhat bland ones retold – reinvented – by Miss Twinkleton.

They ascend the stairs to Tartar's chambers, open the door of the sitting room, and the ladies (especially the First Fairy of the Sea) are enchanted by what they find. The Admiral would be amazed to see how his cabin had been rearranged. In the middle stands a sturdy table, on which sits the gleaming little service of plate, all set out and ready for action. Shining forks and spoons stand guard. Glittering knives are braced to assault the enemy. Clean, crisp napkins attend their duty. Sparkling glasses lie in wait, eager to kidnap the wines. Nor are the utensils alone on the field of battle. Their foes are likewise drawn up. There are succulent fish, dressed overall in the most tempting manner; rose-pink shrimps, laid on the plate like so many sharp-eyed ships of the line; exquisite salads designed to attract eye and palette; colourful vegetables, displaying the full range of nature's rich bounty; little rolls, delicately hinting at the fires of Vulcan's forge; and, on a side-table, a panoply of fruits and jellies and creams. Tartar explains apologetically that this is but light refreshment, since the evening is warm and the hour late.

The evening has another welcome surprise to offer. The sun-god himself appears from the garden where he has been busying himself, his red jolly face wreathed with benign smiles, as well as with hair and whiskers; and he proceeds to help Tartar in the task of serving the guests. Not that Tartar appears to require assistance. He displays a feline deftness, surprising in such a powerful man, which could only have resulted from having operated for most of his life in small, crowded working places. He looks as if he could have served a dozen people in half the space; or at least twenty mermaids, scaly tails and all. He is as quick as the flying waiter, though considerably neater and less severely blown – possibly because unencumbered by the immoveable waiter; as nimble as one of the sparrows, though not of the same sooty appearance; and as observant, and as solicitous for the well-being of his guests, as the finest butler in the finest house in England, though in his case it is obvious that the attentive touches come from the heart, and not from anything so dull as training and convention.

Tartar leads the conversation with modesty and ease, his eyes seldom straying far from the fair countenance of Rosa. But – and how this contrasts with those hypnotic eyes of Jasper – she does not appear to resent or fear his attention: far from it. Mr Grewgious continues very gallant to Miss Twinkleton, if a trifle angular of expression. He clearly wishes to convey both kindliness and appreciation for the occasion and their company; and manages to achieve this, as if determined to keep chipping away at the purpose. He greatly improves on his conversational efforts in the forbidding confines of the Nuns' House, largely because he is away from the seminarian atmosphere, and free of the oppressive feeling that he is being examined by an exigent teacher in some abstruse subject, in which he is an unfortunate novice. But, in the main, he is content to sit bolt upright, hands straying towards his knees, benignly contemplating the neat, compact and graceful figure of his ward, who shows to great advantage. For she is blissfully happy. Blushing, delighted and delightful, she forgets the tedium of her days. And alongside her is a singularly sprightly Miss Twinkleton, who is enjoying the occasion marvelously, and has quite forgotten Billickin, and is something reminded of The Wells, and even the attentions of the finished but Foolish Mr Porters.

When the meal is ended, and the cloth drawn, they all repair outside, and find themselves in the magical Hanging Gardens of Holborn. The sun god has set out tables and chairs, and laid out a new platoon of shining glasses and sparkling bottles. The ladies are seated under the rigged awning of the after-deck, and are offered the wines brought up by Mr Grewgious from Aladdin's Cave at the bottom of his stairs, the concoctions spirited into being by Tartar in his neat galley, or rather kitchen, and the waters and minerals graciously supplied by Furnival's for the refreshment of Mr Grewgious's pretty young ward and her chaperone. Tartar ensures that these delights are not unaccompanied with squadrons of biscuits and wafers, skirmishing in the rear of the main body of troops on the dining table, much to the taste and pleasure of the smoky sparrows who chirpily enjoy the garden, and eagerly fall on any loose crumbs.

The grim laws of time seem suspended, such are the pleasures of the evening. But Miss Twinkleton does not forget herself to the extent of staying too late, or appearing indecorous in male company. At some point, therefore, she turns to Rosa, and says that they must not overstay their welcome. There are of course protestations all round, and some pleasing delay; but nevertheless their departure finally becomes imminent. On this occasion, Miss Twinkleton eschews a curtsey, as requiring a little too much yardage in Tartar's compact quarters, and contents herself instead with looking archly at Rosa and Tartar, and knowingly at Mr Grewgious: as if determined to lay aside her reputation as a deliberately pretending old thing, yet possibly gaining one as a potentially gossiping old thing.

Rosa is handed down the stairs by a strong arm – not that it needs all its strength for such a light weight – and they all set off for Billickin's. They walk in the pairs for which their journey hither, and the evening, have provided such ample preparation; and the way seems short indeed to Rosa and Tartar. Poor Eddy. And poor Neville. And lucky Tartar.

CHAPTER XXV
Why so Pale and Wan?

THE SAME SUN which shone on Rosa in Billickin's did its best to shine on Neville in nearby Staple Inn. But if pretty Rosa could easily be discovered and illuminated in her chair in the front parlour, even in the house of the dread Billickin, it was a harder task for the powerful rays of the sun, however omnipotent, to find Neville, ensconced in his attic room directly under the roof, many winding stairs up, and beneath the grimy pane of glass in his garret window. Nevertheless, a few errant rays managed to make the arduous journey, and were rewarded by a glance of genuine pleasure from Neville.

He was seated in his lodgings, doing what he did all day, and much of the evening too: reading, settled in his small, bare room: one might have said study, judging by the number of books, except that it did duty for other rooms as well. There was a cupboard for his clothes, and a hook for his coat, and a rail for his boots, and a bed for his slumber. The heavy, iron-wood, iron-shod walking stick lay in the corner; unused, even on his nightly peregrinations of the city: it carried unhappy memories for its owner.

The books by contrast were his regular companions. His constant study now was the law, consistent with the idea proposed by Mr Crisparkle, and readily agreed by himself, that he should devote himself to reading up that subject. So he was surrounded by great legal tomes, and by lesser volumes of forensic oratory and attested depositions and learned judgements: some the lofty fruit of great wisdom and deep knowledge; some the lesser fruit of deceit and chicanery; some the result of a search for real justice, the betterment of mankind, the protection of the innocent; some the consequence of misused hours, of overweening greed, and of brazen attempts to exonerate and excuse the guilty; some promoting the law as the symbol of the intellectual richness of mankind; some reflecting its role as the assurance of the earthly richness of the lawyers.

Neville worked hard to pick his way through these legal and moral

256

tangles, and was assisted by the eager Mr Crisparkle, when the latter could discover the time to visit the city; although the Minor Canon lacked some knowledge of the wiles of the law, he had an unequalled if seldom trumpeted feel for morality and human decency, and a keen sense that, despite all evidence to the contrary, the law should be used to assist, protect and ennoble mankind. So, between them, they sifted through the weighty material in front of them, and attempted to come out on top of it, rather than being defeated, or falling prey to its toils.

It was weary work, especially for Neville, who, unlike his mentor, had little escape; and he appeared listless, like a caged bird looking enviously through the bars at the lively sparrows of Holborn. Sometimes, as his eyes devoured the books and words in front of him, the image of a certain diminutive and rosy person interposed itself between him and the pages, but he resolutely dismissed it from his mind – or, at least, attempted to. He knew that he owed this to Mr Crisparkle, Helena, Rosa herself, even himself. But the resolution was not always easy to summon: it had to be raised manfully from the depths, like a great leviathan reluctantly dragged to the surface. Life tended to be a perpetual struggle: between his promises and obligations to Helena and Mr Crisparkle, and his own unfulfillable longings. Perhaps this was another reason why he seemed lacklustre. But he knew well enough that they were unfulfillable: and hence what he must do, and what he must avoid. He had given his word, and would hold to it: of that he was quite determined.

There were three people who assisted him greatly in remaining committed to his studies and to his firm resolution.

The first was Mr Crisparkle himself. The Minor Canon not only helped with the legal studies, but visited when he could, tempted Neville out when he could, and provided an encouraging influence when he could. This was at some personal cost, since he lost a little of his own vitality and energy during and after each visit, as if he drew on his own reserves to donate them to Neville, or as if some of the iron of the prison had entered even his well-tempered soul. He tended to depart, saddened by the prisonous look and the prisonous room. This was but temporary, since the brisk waters of Kent washed the cares and worries from him each morning, scrubbing him radiant and clean, and restoring him to his natural state of unbridled optimism.

The second was Lieutenant Tartar, who played his part nobly. In addition to ensuring that Neville had the greenest view in Holborn, and the reddest, for ever throwing out new lines and stays, encouraging compliant beans to run along them, and shoving boxes of opulent flowers along the gutter with his trusty boat-hook, he was a regular visitor. He talked of matters which had nothing to do with the dusty law, or gritty Holborn, or the lurking Jasper (who had occasionally been seen by Neville, as was fully intended by the deeply-grieving and deeply-scheming uncle). He deliberately took Neville out of his immediate surroundings, and gave him a sense of and a feel for something different: seas, oceans, fleets, naval engagements, adventure. He conjured up a vivid picture of life at sea: more exciting than the one in Miss Twinkleton's expurgated readings, though possibly less dramatic than the one in Rosa's fervid imagination. He prevailed upon Neville to tell him about the long journey home from Ceylon: how they had travelled, where they had travelled, what they had seen and experienced. He was greatly amused by Neville's account of Luke Honeythunder, his domination of the evening in Minor Canon Corner, and his premature expulsion from that earthly paradise, and his evident mirth proved infectious. Neville had previously viewed Honeythunder as an object of dislike and resentment, and it was beneficial for him to be shown that the Father of Philanthropy could be laughed at and ridiculed. The happy mood induced in Neville by Tartar's high spirits was briefly tempered by his sudden memories of what had happened subsequently on that same evening in the Precincts, but then as rapidly revived by thoughts of all that Mr Crisparkle had done for him and for Helena, then and subsequently.

The third good fairy was naturally Helena herself, who brought all her powers of pride and persuasion to keep Neville from moping or repining, or bewailing his lot, and to infuse him with something of her own strength and nobility of character.

Very soon after the stray sunbeam, and with the same energy, the same sense of bringing light to a dark place, and the same grateful reception from Neville, Helena entered his room.

'How did you profit from your reading with Mr Crisparkle this morning? I did not wish to disturb you, or interrupt your studies, so I took the occasion to leave our rooms and make some purchases.' She did not add that she had also called on Rosa and Miss Twinkleton, as she often did when Neville was engaged in reading.

'We made much progress. I am so much indebted to the dear, kind man. I do not believe that he likes the study of the law, or feels at ease with it. It would be different if it were canon law; or especially minor canon law, I suppose.'

Helena acknowledged this little sally, and was glad to remark that Neville was at least attempting to appear light-hearted; as ever, the presence of Crisparkle had raised his spirits, and, if there were a touch of Neville in Crisparkle as he left, there was also a little of Crisparkle remaining in Neville.

'I believe that he finds some of the arguments false, and merely disputatious. I have seen his brow wrinkle when he comes across what he regards as a piece of sophistry. His own world is built on selflessness rather than calculation. But, for my sake, he tolerates it, and is very good at both understanding and explaining. He is indeed a saint.'

'My dear, he would not like to hear you say so', she joined in enthusiastically. 'He is so modest and unassuming. He would say that it is but natural to help people: that that is what God would like us to do. It may be natural for him, but it does not seem to come so naturally to all. So I agree with you,' she added. 'We are so lucky to have left our miserable life in Ceylon, and put the dreadful Mr Honeythunder behind us. Whatever our present tribulations, we are better off than before, and than we might be. This is largely due to Mr Crisparkle. He is like a dutiful Saint Christopher, taking you on his shoulder, and bearing you through and above the mighty flood.'

'Or a good Samaritan, turning aside to help one in trouble and distress, rather than passing by on the other side. I wonder whether he really comes from Samaria rather than Cloisterham.'

They were both so pleased with their comparisons, that they sat side by side in companiable contentment for a while. Then Helena, ever fair-minded, had other praise to bestow.

'Tartar has also been most attentive. He has not only proved a solicitous friend to you,' she looked at the garden approvingly, 'he has also baited the trap most effectively. He has made his comings and goings most obvious, rather than springing up through the waterspouts at the back, as he might have preferred, and it cannot be long before whoever Jasper has tasked with watching you in his absence makes his move.'

'I agree, he is an excellent fellow. Yet I cannot but think that he would be better employed in continuing to serve in the Navy rather than in playing nurse-maid to me. His uncle served him a false hand there, I believe. But what would we give or have given for such an uncle, eh Helena? Leaving a fortune, even with onerous terms attached. The only uncle who has come into our lives has blighted them most effectively: like our step-father first, and then our guardian.'

This was said more in rueful self-mockery than self-pity, but it reminded Helena of the need to keep rallying Neville.

'What happiness to have not only Mr Crisparkle helping us, but Lieutenant Tartar as well: throwing you a safety-line, as he throws out lines and stays for the beans. And I do not think that his uncle did him a bad turn. Tartar seems to have plenty to do: with his lodgings, and his plants, and his boats.'

Helena however was not content to leave her point there. Her visit to Rosa had confirmed her in her suspicion that a strong mutual attachment had formed between her friend and Tartar. She wanted to alert Neville to this, in the gentlest way possible, and also discover whether Neville was already aware of this, perhaps from something which Tartar might have inadvertently let slip.

'Besides, he does not spend all his time playing nurse-maid to you, as you put it. I have heard that he has excellent acquaintance in the neighbourhood: Mr Grewgious, Mr Crisparkle, who always sees both of you when he visits from Cloisterham, and others,' she finished a little vaguely. She then paused slightly before continuing. 'I know that it is, or should be, nothing to you, and that her name should not be mentioned between us, but were you aware that Rosa and also Miss Twinkleton were living in the vicinity?'

'I guessed it from something that Tartar let fall accidentally, but which we did not pursue: he, because he is a true gentleman, I because of my firm commitment to Mr Crisparkle,' returned Neville stoutly.

She looked at him gratefully, and with a great deal of sisterly affection and appreciation.

'It is my feeling that by little and little a strong mutual affection is growing between them. I tell you this, not to breach our joint undertaking to Mr Crisparkle, but to ensure that you are aware, and therefore fore-armed.' She left it there, a little uneasily.

Neville laughed, and put his hand on hers: his rather pale and rather lank one on her dark and firm one.

'Don't worry, my dear sister, who looks after me so well, even to the extent of keeping certain matters from me, in case they worry or upset me. My pledge to Mr Crisparkle was given from the heart, and is unbreakable. Tartar is a dear friend and ally. I wish him all possible happiness in life. All happiness.'

He paused slightly, as if weighing his next remark carefully.

'Besides, we have additional reason to be grateful to Tartar, do we not?' He not only does his best for me now, but years ago he saved Mr Crisparkle from drowning. So he is a double benefactor.'

Helena sensed him looking at her curiously, and this added to her feeling that she was being gently teased. She blushed slightly, but was firm in her reply.

'That is indeed a deep blessing for both of us, Neville. Both of us.'

After another short pause, Neville continued.

'But why did you not tell me this before about Rosa? Do you not trust me?'

'Indeed I do, Neville: I trust you fully and absolutely. But I could not tell you that Rosa was in London without explaining the reasons why she had left Cloisterham. I did not wish to add to your worries. I feel that you are now ready for this. In addition, you have already witnessed Jasper haunting around the place, trying to keep reminding you of your presumed guilt, and your exclusion from normal human society, so you already know part of what I am about to say.' She put a comforting arm round him, and looked at him with a steady countenance. 'Let me tell you why Rosa left Cloisterham, as I heard it from Rosa herself.'

So, seated there together in Neville's room, she told him exactly what she had been told that morning in the garden a fortnight previously, when Rosa had suddenly and unexpectedly appeared: of the dreadful scene by the sun-dial, of Jasper's distressing avowal of his love, of the kind of dark power he seemed to exercise over the innocent girl, of his unremitting campaign against Neville whether he were innocent or guilty, of his attempt to blackmail Rosa into silence.

Neville heard her out without a word; but, once she had finished, his anger broke forth. He was livid, tigerish, uncontrollable. Both fists were clenched in a way which would have worried and saddened Mr Crisparkle. He furiously swore vengeance. Not on his own account: he had long known about and attempted to discount Jasper's campaign against him. He loathed and despised the man, and could no longer be hurt by him and his groundless suspicions. No, it was on Rosa's account. How could Jasper behave in that way to that sweet, gentle, unprotected girl? Whom Jasper himself should have guarded as the betrothed of his deeply-loved but lost nephew. How dare Jasper misuse his position in that way?

Helena allowed him to erupt, but then broke in. She was deeply moved within by Rosa's predicament and by Neville' reaction, but outwardly composed. She had to persuade Neville by calm and by the power of reason.

'Neville, my dear, my brother, it is not for you to avenge Rosa. You should not even be thinking or talking of her. She is nothing to you, or you to her. She is far from unprotected. Her guardian, Mr Grewgious, and Mr Crisparkle both know the circumstances, and are ready to help and protect her. I myself am and will remain passionate in her defence. Now,' she trod carefully here, 'Rosa has new friends who are no part of her past, and her dreadful scene with Jasper, but will be equally determined to protect and look after her. Also, think of Mr Crisparkle. What would he think, how would he react, if he heard that you had deliberately set out to hurt and damage Jasper, a man already damaged by the loss of his nephew? Would he not despair? Would he not be accused by others as having misjudged you, been duped by you? What would he have to hear from the Dean, from the Mayor, from his mother? How many times has he defended you, stood by you, stood with his shoulder to yours, stood contra mundum, stood against the petty and small-minded prejudices of the citizens of Cloisterham?' She looked especially noble as she spoke, like Portia defending the properties of justice and its hand-maiden, mercy.

'Besides, as I say, Mr Grewgious and Mr Crisparkle are already aware of all the circumstances, and have their eye on Mr Jasper. They will do what is necessary. Do not ruin their work. And, above all, being falsely suspected of one crime, do not proceed to commit another. We are not alone and abandoned, poor and solitary, as in Ceylon: relying entirely upon ourselves, and our often desperate plans and actions: as when I – unsuccessfully – dressed up as a boy in an attempt to escape. We have good and decent friends around us, to whom we can turn – and have turned – when in need.'

Neville had gradually calmed down as she spoke. When she finished, his eyes filled with tears, and he in turn put his arm round her. The two beautiful, barbarian captives were together again, in full understanding of each other. His mood was now entirely submissive.

'You are right, my dear sister, you are always right. As far above me as the tower. And, once again, you have helped persuade me from error: from vile error. It is as you say. We shall leave the matter to our good friends.'

The brief storm was over. But it had erupted quickly and violently. Helena had entirely overcome the tigers which had been present in her breast, beneath the dark skin. His various tigers, by contrast, while subdued by her acute reasoning, and by his studious manner of life, and by his firm pledge to Mr Crisparkle, still lurked scarcely out of sight.

CHAPTER XXVI
Fair Trading

IN ANOTHER TOWN, Dick Datchery rests on what in effect has become his porch, open to the thoroughfare, appearing to control the passage and monitor its passing traffic. He sits under his lintel, as Mr Grewgious sits under the dry vine and fig tree of PJT, and seems as contented as any buffer in Cloisterham, in the whole of England. Beside him is a table, and some sheets of paper; and occasionally he glances at them, or makes a note as an idea seems to come to him. Being an old buffer, he has probably devised this practice as a way of assisting his faltering memory, and reminding himself of what he may need to do during the day: though for the most part he seems to do very little, but sit there at his ease. His main exercise appears to be to stroll to the Crozier hotel in the afternoon, to pick up his correspondence, of which there seems to be an increasing amount; but, since the Crozier is such an orthodox hotel, and so sleepy, no-one appears to notice this, or take much account of it.

He himself sleeps little these days, possibly because his life is so sedentary. So, this morning, he had risen early, before anyone else was about, and watched the sun rise. First there had been the stirring of the birds, and a beginning of their calls from tree, and roof, and tower, as they sensed what was to come, accompanied by the crowing of the assertive neighbourhood cocks, each determined to make his voice the most dominant; then a lightening of the dark night and an eclipse of the bright stars in the east; then a faint aurora; then some flimsy gleams rapidly becoming sharper; then dawn as the tip of the sun appeared over the earth: or at least, insofar as it concerned the watching Datchery, over Cloisterham. The very fabric of the town had seemed to spring to life with impressive speed and enthusiasm, as if in response to the welcome light of the sun: the lofty battlements of the ruined castle; the brooding square tower of the Cathedral; the roofs of the houses, and the shops of the High Street and the eddying waters of the river; and, finally, the townspeople themselves, as they were summoned from their beds by the whole of nature insistently telling them that the sun was up, that it was another day, and that they had to be about their business.

Having experienced such an inspiring start to a new day, Datchery had modestly retired to his porch: where he still patiently sits and awaits developments.

He has not long to wait. A hideous small boy heaves partly into view. He peers at Datchery from round the main door by which Datchery is seated, while seeming at the same time to twist out of sight of anyone glancing out of the gatehouse windows: anyone with thick, lustrous, well-arranged black hair, say, or equally black and lustrous whiskers.

The resulting contortion of body and features make him if anything even more hideous than usual, and the gap between his front teeth even wider than before. A whistle from him now would indeed be piercing, as coming out under great pressure, like steam from a boiling kettle; but he is unwilling to invite the attention of any mysterious personage in the rooms upstairs. He initially speaks in a harsh, hoarse whisper.

'Is Jasper hup and habout?'

On being informed that he has left for the Cathedral, and that his distinctive singing tones will shortly be audible, Deputy visibly relaxes, and more of him appears. More does not on this occasion betoken better, but the benevolent Datchery does not seem to mind; and he looks at the boy, tolerantly and above all expectantly.

'Yer owes me,' offers Deputy rather truculently. His negotiating style, especially where money is concerned, remains of the stand-and-deliver school, despite the increased trust between him and Datchery.

'Why, Master Deputy?' asks Datchery, reasonably enough.

'I brings yer himportant hinformation. Like the Hangel brings 'Erod', he adds proudly, misremembering some reading he had vaguely heard in the Cathedral one Christmas Eve, when he had abandoned his annual practice of stoning festive decorations and crib figures, in order to turn his tireless attentions to loosely-held purses in the congregation, once again escaping the eye of the less than vigilant Tope as he did so.

'Tell me what it is, heavenly messenger, and I shall determine the reward.'

Deputy seems inclined to argue the point, but then relents. He has proof enough of Datchery's generosity.

'I know where she lives. Her Royal Highness. The Princess Puffer. I know where she lives and puffs her hopium.' He again contorts his face, and in pantomime appears to be sucking greedily at a pipe the size of a large and opulent cigar. 'I 'eard 'er whispering to one of the lodgers at Twopenny's to come and taste 'er mixter. So I knows the way, and am able to give this to my valeeable friend and 'onoured partner, Mr Datchery,' he states graciously. 'At a price, mind yer,' he adds fiercely.

Datchery hears the directions, and decides that the information is worth the shilling already agreed between them. Deputy does not question this judgement, and the money duly changes hands.

So, for once, Datchery forsakes his position in the porch, keeping watch over Cloisterham and its citizens, claps his hat on his head of thick white hair, before absent-mindedly removing it and carrying it under his arm, and takes omnibus and train to London, in order to seek a more detailed audience with her Royal Highness in her commodious palace.

So he follows the route taken by both Rosa and Jasper on their separate journeys, and like them comes into London by train over the house-tops. From the station, his route repeats that of Jasper rather than Rosa. He travels eastward, and then eastward again, further into the grit and the poverty and the misery.

Following the directions provided by her Royal Highness herself, through the less than regal medium of Deputy, he finally reaches a villainous alley, and turns into a miserable court. He cautiously mounts a rickety staircase, a bridge-like structure (indeed, it may once have been a bridge before being purloined and set to its present task) which could well have been the favoured lair of the celebrated troll, except that that predatory beast would probably value his life and bones better than to crouch underneath it. The stairs safely negotiated, and with no appearance of the troll, or anyone else singing "Foll-de-roll", or indeed anyone except the door-keeper lying asleep and unheeding in his bed, he enters a mean and darkened room. It is mid-afternoon, and there is no-one in it apart from the Princess herself. She looks more emaciated, her chin more weazen, and her skin more yellow and stretched than ever.

'What, no ships in, no trade, no customers?' He is tempted to add "Your Majesty", but properly resists the thought.

'It's the price what puts them off. The market price which I has to pay. It don't help knowing the real secret of mixing if they can't afford it and don't visit. Can't pay me. Poor me, poor me. Head, throat, lungs all bad. Lungs dreffle bad. Hands shake so that I can hardly mix. And cough dry, rattling dry.' She coughs alarmingly to illustrate the point, and then relapses into a monotone of mumbling complaint.

Suddenly she looks up sharply and expectantly.

'But what am I doing and saying? Here is a customer. Not from the Docks, but a rich one by the look of it; and one who may return, who will return when he has tasted what I can mix.' Her voice acquires a mendicant whine, and there is a rictus of pleasure across her wizened face. 'One who has more nor three shillings and sixpence in his deep pocket. And a good-hearted one. One who will give that sum and more to a poor old woman. Lie yourself down on the bed, dearie, and I'll prepare the mixter for you. The best you'll get, the true way,' she adds wheedingly.

She fusses round, talking to herself as she does so; and then peers at him with surprise.

'But now I sees yer close up, I knows yer. From Cloisterham, the archway and the Cathedral. But you're a deep one, you are. I never thought, that day in Cloisterham, to see you here. Not the type, I thought. He's not for the trade. He's a proper gentleman. Shows you can get it wrong. As with – .' But she stops herself abruptly, and starts to reach for the thimble, the spoon and the pipe, and those infernal matches which are likely to jump and leap and start, and cause her so much trouble to assemble and light.

For once, however, she does not have to trouble herself with the matches, or the other parts of the grisly ritual.

'No, no,' laughs Datchery, 'you quite mistake my purpose. It is information I seek, not opium. And, like the opium, it's valuable and worth money to you, good money.' He carefully puts his hand into his pocket, jingles it round a little, and takes out certain pieces of silver which he lays out on the table. He puts them in a place where the Princess can see them but not take them: at least, not without his approval and assistance. He watches her carefully, the eyes sharp and the brows dark under the great white mane of hair.

'This is the price for information: about Edwin, and Eddy, and Ned: and about a gentleman in mourning. Surname Jasper, Christian name John. Mr John Jasper. Remember him?'

He silently builds the coins into separate piles, one for Ned and one for Jasper, side by side as befits their close relationship, uncle and nephew, bosom friends, inseparables; and then moves them around on the surface of the table, like draughts on a board. Sideways, and sideways again: full in the Princess's hungry gaze, but never closer to her. Then slightly and temptingly forwards, then provokingly backwards. He has fully secured her attention, and he says softly:

'Tell me.'

She does tell him, her eyes remaining firmly on the silver; and, gradually, the story emerges. Alerted by what Jasper had said about Ned in his drugged sleep, she had followed him to Cloisterham a first time. Followed, but lost him. But she had encountered a young man called Edwin, who had treated her kindly, and for some reason, probably because of the similarity of the names, she had warned him of what was in store for Ned. (Datchery moves one of the piles of draughts in her direction. She cannot take her eyes off them as she continues.)

Then Jasper had revisited, after a long absence. He was in mourning for a relative, and she probed him for information while he was half-asleep, and then followed him: successfully this time. Much of what he had muttered in his sleep was highly suspicious, and gossip in the Travellers' Twopenny had allowed her to identify both Edwin Drood and his uncle. Then, following Datchery's assistance, she had actually seen Jasper in the Cathedral.

Both piles are slightly moved in her direction. Overtly. Temptingly.

'Not so fast. Why did you follow him? It was too late to save Edwin or Ned. You surely knew or guessed that. He was gone six months. Why did you follow Jasper, and seek him out?'

She mumbles incoherently, unintelligibly, her eyes fixed on the piles.

'Was blackmail in your thoughts? Was that why you followed him so meticulously, so cleverly, so successfully? So that he should not escape a second time, and would have to pay you to keep your mouth shut?'

She denies this, strenuously at first, but then as the piles are moved back again a strange look comes into her eyes, and she corrects herself.

'You are right, Sir. I never thought to admit it to another. I heard Jasper say many threatening words about Ned and the fate which awaited him. What he said suggested strangling, though it never came out clear and quite in those words: but his gestures as he muttered about Ned suggested violence and throttling. I heard and saw this a thousand times, a hundred thousand times. The details are burned into my poor mind, I heard it so often, poor me, poor me.'

She pauses, and then goes on.

'Why didn't Ned heed the warning I give him? Ned should avoid anyone who called him Ned: like the plague. I told him, warned him, repeated the danger, the threat, the words about Ned. Dreffle threatening words them were. And then, when Jasper finally returned to me, he was talking about a different thing: a journey, a fellow-traveller, a disappointment, a poor vision, a poor mean miserable thing: no struggle, no entreaty. He says it various ways, laughingly, savagely, cruelly. Yet it seemed to be the same thing. Having heard those threats, heard what Jasper said, before and after, and met the kind young gentleman, who behaved so proper, what could I do but suspect and follow Jasper when he come back, hope to accost him, lay his evil deeds at his feet. And when you thinks about it: him a relation; and Drood but a poor motherless babe.' She is growing passionate and short-winded, and he can hardly keep up, scarcely make out the words as she races through them. To calm her, he pushes the piles slightly closer in her direction. Closer, but not quite there.

She coughs – a horrid, grating, rattling noise, as if death were ever closer – and resumes, more clearly and coherently than before.

'I left Jasper alone on that last occasion. Better to deal with him when he next comes to me, is lying on my bed, smoking my mixter, under my control, in my power. If he don't come, I need to find another was of taking him unawares – but he will come, he will. Can't remain away.' Confident in the power of her mixture, she thinks again of the kindly Drood. 'I'll revenge him. I'll show that Jasper. I'll fleece him, I will. I'll make him suffer.' She coughs again, less dryly this time, and splutters a little; then recovers, looks up with staring eyes, and malignantly shakes those two lean arms and withered fists in the general direction of Cloisterham and the unwitting Choir-Master.

Datchery draws the audience to a close.

'Leave Jasper to me. You will never get a penny out of him. He is too sharp for you. Too sharp, and too ruthless. Do you want to join Drood in the grave?' He looks pityingly at her moribund body, undone by opium.

He finally and definitively gives her the silver. She seizes it.

'Come, that is more than you would ever get from Jasper. Take it, keep it. It is yours. And leave Jasper alone, do you hear: he is mine. He is mine.' His tone is strangely solemn and commanding from an old gentleman of easy manner.

She indistinctly but unquestionably nods her assent, and whispers in a mumbling voice:

'He is yours. But don't let me down, don't let an old woman down.'

He has secured what he wants, and departs, out of the mean room, down the perilous staircase, past the recumbent door-keeper in his dark hutch, through the miserable court, and out into the villainous alley; and from there, still following Jasper on his return journey, through the gritty streets to the railway station, and thence by train and omnibus to

Cloisterham. Where he sinks contentedly into his chair on his porch, thinking to himself, "Another busy day for an old buffer of an easy temper, living idly on his means: and what company I have kept today!", as he resumes his watch on all around him.

But, as he travels, and as he sits, and as he watches, he has a slight sense of unease, a nagging doubt, an unanswered question in his mind about something she had said. What was it? Why was it unanswered? And what was the question?

For this reason, he does not yet chalk a mark on the inside of the corner-cupboard. Time to do that when he has cleared his mind, and determined the way forward. Instead, he takes a blank piece of paper from his table, rests it on his knee, and draws a large, perplexed, demanding question-mark upon it, as if to remind himself of his unfinished business.

CHAPTER XXVII
More Confidences

IT WAS AGAIN time for The Reverend Septimus Crisparkle to leave his comfortable lodging in Minor Canon Corner; leave the china shepherdess, his familiar library (still intact, since the law books which he had lent to Neville had been expressly purchased for that purpose, for they formed no part of Crisparkle's own choice of reading), his boxing gloves, all his lares et penates; and travel up to London. For he felt that Neville would benefit from his presence, friendship and instruction. As indeed proved the case; and Neville felt all the better, and his studies seemed improved, for the visit.

Having finished with his pupil for the day, and seeking the company of a fresh and elevated mind after the cloying embrace of dusty law, the effects of which which lay heavily upon him, Mr Crisparkle enquired whether Miss Landless were at home, and whether she might indulge him in his wish for a companiable walk through the neighbourhood before he was obliged to return to Cloisterham. On hearing that she had gone out and was not yet returned, Mr Crisparkle felt an unaccountable degree of disappointment. His bright, kind, optimistic face fell a little. When might she return? Neville, alas, did not know. It was possible that she had gone to visit her friend Miss Bud, whom he understood to live in the area, in Bloomsbury: he mentioned the name solely to assist Mr Crisparkle, and for no other reason. Mr Crisparkle understood the same; and ventured the thought that he also might call on Miss Bud, to ask how she and Miss Twinkleton were managing in their rented quarters. It was important to ensure that they were encountering no difficulties and suffering no grievances in the unfamiliar city; and, since it was now late in the afternoon, Miss Landless might welcome an escort home through the busy streets between Bloomsbury and Holborn. So, two further pieces of selfless philanthropy on the part of The Reverend Septimus Crisparkle, whose deep well of fellow feeling for others truly knew no bounds.

Of course, he added immediately, if Miss Landless were not at Miss Bud's, it did not signify. He would do what he could for Miss Bud and

Miss Twinkleton; and it could not be supposed that Miss Landless, having coped with the jungles of Ceylon, could not find her way home through a London street. Yes, it did not signify in the least. What was it that made this protestation so signally unconvincing? Was it his woeful countenance as he contemplated the possibility of failing to find Miss Landless at Miss Bud's?

Having enquired in the full generosity of his heart whether there was anything else he could do for Neville on his present mission, and whether the latter might need additional books to be brought soon, and having been assured by Neville that on both counts there was no more he needed, that he was truly grateful for all the many acts of kindness, and that he would now get on with reading by himself to follow up the themes they had identified, tracked down and discussed, Mr Crisparkle departed at a pace a little faster even than his normal, lest by misfortune he might miss catching up with Miss Landless at Billickin's as well as at Staple Inn.

Arriving at Billickin's, Mr Crisparkle admired the lapidary capital letters on the brass door-plate, and their challenging size, and their androgynous quality; and, having determined that this was indeed the place, knocked firmly. He heard the sounds of someone within muttering to themselves, and then taking up and adjusting a shawl, as if preparing for a lengthy and hazardous journey. The door opened to reveal the owner of the impressive capitals, draped in a warming shawl.

'Mrs Billickin?' hazarded Mr Crisparkle.

'Can't you read?' was the somewhat surprising response to a question which, following good Latin precedent, was surely expecting the answer "Yes". 'The plate states Billickin, so all is clear; and that is the only name which you or anyone else require, respectin' the inhabitants.'

Mr Crisparkle apologized for his unintended error, and tried again.

'Do Miss Twinkleton and her young companion Miss Bud lodge here?'

'Sir, I cannot deny that an indiwidual named Miss Bud resides here: a dear girl, I am 'appy to say, despite her educiation and acquaintance; and sadly wanting as she was in healthy wittles, since she had fallen among thieves, or to point the finger of blame more directly, one thief,' (the B's eyes narrowed, and those expressive lips tightened in to a determined horizon as she thought of her plump adversary) 'though much improved now that she has been brought here by Mr Grewgious, and indulged, and given some sense of 'onest 'ousekeeping and 'olesome diet. Sir,' (ending her brief moral peregrination into the virtues of her household arrangements) I freely admit that she lives here. I shall not lie or attempt to cover the fact, or otherwise impose upon you, Sir, though I have to add,' she stiffened as she spoke, 'that I do not know your hidentity.'

Mr Crisparkle smilingly acknowledged her right to this commodity.

'I am The Reverend Septimus Crisparkle, Madam, and a friend of Miss Bud's from Cloisterham. Would it be possible for me to be admitted and see her?'

'Sir, I shall not trifle with you. That is not Billickin's way. I am not 'iding her, you can see her; though I have formed a strangely disfaviourable opinion of Cloisterham and its inhabitants: with good reason, Sir, with good reason. Of the old lady, who is unknown to me, and who is out of my sight and does not exist, of her I say nothink, bar that she is in occupation of one of my sweetest rooms, and that she lives in a style and comfort unknown to her in that Cloisterham. I am given to understand that she lives at what she terms her seminiary, but what to you and me is no more than an 'umble school, when all's said and done.'

With which she opened the door, stepped aside to allow the visitor to enter, and pointed him towards the front parlour. From her introduction, it was unclear whether Miss Twinkleton would or would not be there, but Mr Crisparkle was pleased to discover that she was, and that, despite Billickin's words, and his resulting concerns, looked unchanged, had not somehow departed from her body, and had lost none of that soft plumpness which – it is to be supposed – had once caught the roving eye of the Mr Porters in The Wells.

Even more pleasing to Mr Crisparkle was the fact that Helena was also present in the room, and that she looked contented and pleased to see him and, as ever, grateful that he had journeyed to London to help her brother.

With the condition of Rosa, he was rather less satisfied. True, there was a bloom about her, a depth, almost a maturity, which had been largely lacking up to half a year ago, and he marveled afresh at her prettiness, her young charm. But he deduced from a number of references, and glances, and pauses, that she was worried about the future, and in particular about returning to Cloisterham. He knew all too well why. The shadow of Jasper lay across her, as it had lain across the sundial that day; keeping the warmth and light of the sun from her, as he had kept it from the sundial; setting his black mark on her, as he had set it upon the sundial and the very face of the day. He could sense her spirit fluttering away from the thought of return, and from the dreadful danger it held, as a small bird will flutter and flap away from what assails it, and from what it fears. But what was to be done? Miss Twinkleton had to return to Cloisterham, to the insistent siren-call of her young charges beseeching education, and beseeching it from Miss Twinkleton in person, and from no other; and Rosa could not stay at Billickin's or anywhere else without a chaperone. Mr Grewgious would no doubt be delighted for her to stay near him at Furnival's, but she could not hide there all her life.

'Yes,' mused Septimus Crisparkle to himself, as he surveyed the room and the ladies, one of dark and exceptional beauty, one of beguiling prettiness, but with a slight cloud of uncertainty on her face, and one displaying satisfied self-importance, 'it is time to become more active and involved. To help this young girl, and help steer her feet on to the right paths, into safety.'

He and Helena left together; so he had his wish to walk with her, and to see her safely to Holborn. Surely the sun was shining on Septimus Crisparkle this afternoon; and God in all His infinite wisdom and mercy was fulfilling His covenant with mankind, and was looking after His faithful servant, and rewarding him for all the good he had done, was doing, and would do for others, all the days of his life. Blessed be the ways of the Lord.

As they went together, she told him of her recent conversation with Neville. She told it to him for his ear alone, and in confidence between them. It had been left to her when to tell Neville Rosa's story, and she had chosen her moment. As she had expected, he had reacted with fury, not on his own behalf, but on Rosa's. Whatever he sometimes liked to pretend, her brother was not a selfish or shallow man, but one of generous heart. Crisparkle nodded agreement. She went on to tell him how she had calmed Neville's anger, and persuaded him to put aside thoughts of punishment and revenge. She concluded by saying that she was convinced that Neville kept his word, did his best to put Rosa from his mind, never spoke of her or tried to see her, and appeared to accept, and accept with dignity, the growing understanding between Rosa and Tartar.

Crisparkle listened carefully and attentively, especially to her description of how she had tamed Neville's outburst. When she had finished, he pronounced judgement.

'You remind me of Sandro Botticelli's masterpiece of Minerva calming the centaur: restraining him, teaching him, keeping him from baseness and violent emotion. Without you and your wisdom, I fear that your brother would be lost, despite all his hard work and best endeavours. Those tigers are now seen more rarely, but retain all their ferocity.'

'No,' she returned with passion, 'it is without you and your boundless kindness, support and clear guidance that he would be lost. You are his guardian angel. No, our guardian angel,' she added in a lower tone.

They looked at each other gravely. They had not spoken in this way before, and without Neville present. The kind face of the Minor Canon looked a deeper pink. Helena's beautiful countenance appeared a shade darker, and her black eyes shone.

It was Septimus Crisparkle who broke the silence; and did so, after some internal struggle, by changing the subject.

'By the sundial, during that dreadful scene which still haunts Rosa, Jasper offered his potential sacrifices at Rosa's feet, his tributes which his love was ready to give, his price for her becoming in effect his slave, as he was already hers.' He shuddered as he brought the degraded and degrading picture to mind. 'He listed four sacrifices: his fidelity to Edwin, his overlooking of Neville's "inexpiable offence" against him for daring to love Rosa, his labours in the cause of a just vengeance, and his past and present wasted life. Four different sacrifices were thus said to be offered up; but I note that they are in effect three. Fidelity to Edwin, and his labours in the cause of a just vengeance, are effectively the same. The other two are not the same, but are likewise closely linked: his readiness to stamp his life into the dust, so long as Rosa would take him, however much she hated him; and the punishment or otherwise of Neville's inexpiable offence of daring to love Rosa. So we have three very strong motives and passions at work: hating Neville because he dared to love Rosa, wanting to pin the murder of Edwin Drood on Neville, and his own jealous love for Rosa – his mad love, as he himself expressed it.'

They were talking very earnestly as they walked through the London streets, their heads close, their discourse and concentration intense. Passers-by turned to look as they went their way, the beautiful, dark, exotic girl, and the tall, fresh, amiable Canon, and smiled benevolently at their self-absorption, their sense of sharing a mission, their apparently deep understanding.

He continued, 'So my question is: which was the chief reason for Jasper's pursuit of Neville? Or, to put the matter in another way, how did Neville's supposed sins against Edwin Drood weigh in Jasper's mental balance against the inexpiable sin – and I note in particular the word inexpiable – of loving Rosa?'

Helena was quite equal to the task.

'This is a day for confidences, Mr Crisparkle. I have told you something of Neville, which you as his advocate and defender should know, but which I would prefer others do not learn. Now I can tell you something of Rosa, which you are welcome to use as you wish, and which you may wish to impart to Mr Grewgious as her guardian, if he does not already know it. It happened on the first evening on which we met, the evening which you had kindly intended to welcome us to Cloisterham,' she looked at him with gratitude and affection, 'but which went so wrong, first because of Mr Honeythunder, and then because of Jasper.' No mention of Drood's provocation, or of Neville's temper: these had come later, after Jasper had changed the course of the evening by terrifying Rosa. She proceeded to recount what Rosa had confided that night: of Jasper's undoubted love for her, of his curious powers over her, of his haunting of her, of making a slave of her with his looks, of his obsession with her hands, her lips, of her fear and hatred of him. She had little doubt that mad, unbounded passion for Rosa was the main force which drove Jasper in all things.

Mr Crisparkle was thunderstruck.

'The poor girl! So that explains her behaviour that evening, her increasingly nervous singing, her sudden faint. Poor, poor girl, what emotions she must have experienced, what terror!' He thought of it, and then another, more pleasing aspect of the evening, entered his ever positive mind. 'And what a relief for her to have you to confide in , and provide such a strong and protective influence!' The image leapt into his mind, of Helena comforting Rosa, putting her loving arms around her, protecting her, strengthening her in her hour of need, her hours of need. It was his turn to look at her admiringly and with unstinted affection.

As he did so, thinking of the two of them together, the older one and the younger one, the lustrous dark skin and the pink soft skin, the black hair and the brown hair together, entwined, another, less attractive, image rose unbidden into his mind. He saw himself, on that morning when Jasper seemed so convinced that Drood had disappeared of his own volition, telling Grewgious and Jasper that Neville had confessed himself to being in love with Rosa. He groaned and put his hand to his head; suddenly some of the delight and sunshine seemed to have gone out of the day:

'How could I have told Jasper what had been confided to me? Fool that I was! Not only did I betray a confidence, and cause unhappiness to both Neville and Rosa, but I may unwittingly have provided the motive for Jasper's persecution of Neville. And when I think of the timing: the day before, when Jasper was still believing that Edwin was dead and that Neville had killed him, I would not have dreamed of speaking to Jasper as I did; and later, after my unhappy discovery of the watch and the pin, I would never have unconsciously added to the suspicions so wrongfully directed against your brother. The timing – it was so unfortunate.'

Helena was about to comfort him, say how Jasper could well have discovered Neville's sudden infatuation with Rosa in any case, point out in addition that Jasper seemed instinctively convinced of Neville's guilt from the first, when yet another thought occurred to him, and he suddenly smacked one fist firmly into the other.

'The timing! That's it: the timing! Double fool that I am, as big a fool as any in Holborn, or indeed in Cloisterham, Sapsea always excepted, I was in danger of missing the main point: prattling away about poor Rosa, when she had and has you to look after her; and uselessly chastising myself for something I have always regretted, but can do nothing about. Why, what you have described prefigured the wretched scene by the sundial by a full six months. At one time I might have thought, lightly and foolishly, that it was no crime to fall in love with Rosa; but to pursue her, obsessively and possessively, when her betrothed, his ward, still lived, was entirely different; and – yes – it fully explains and justifies Rosa's subsequent rebuke to Jasper that he was openly and eternally false to Drood.' This comment had puzzled him previously: no more.

He again paused as he fully digested the implications of this new revelation. Yes, it made Jasper both dishonest, by being unfaithful to his nephew, and also untruthful, to himself and to others. But did it do something else? Did it raise a question about his conduct after that evening in Minor Canon Corner: on the night of Christmas Eve, and of his nephew's disappearance, for example? He thought more deeply. He recalled certain images, certain words, certain strange passages, which had been in his head for months, had rested there, had not been acted on, but which had not been erased, because they asked a question which had not been answered, because they seemed to answer a question which had not been asked. A grim suspicion entered his sunny mind for the first time, and dramatically reinforced his earlier resolution to be more active.

Jasper had shown himself a passionate man. Now it was clear that his passion for Rosa was of long standing. This had emerged out of a confidence produced by Helena, who appeared to have no special reason to believe it of particular significance in the case of the absent Drood. Perhaps other such confidences existed. They should be brought together.

Yes, he must become more active. He had been passive too long. He would act: for Rosa, for poor Neville, and for Helena. He would begin by talking to the long-headed Mr Grewgious, who always looked as if he knew or suspected more than he admitted.

He accompanied Helena back to her lofty rooms in the attics of Staple Inn, did not on this occasion interrupt Neville, who remained at his studies, and turned down towards PJT, date 1747, and the more commodious but equally spartan rooms of Mr Grewgious, determined to play a greater role in resolving these mysteries.

* M *

CHAPTER XXVIII
Datchery Revealed

IT WAS A glorious summer's evening at Staple Inn. A slight breeze whispered in the smoky trees which yet adorned Holborn in those distant days, and which took on a richer tinge of green in the soft light which filtered through them and fell on the old brick walls of the Inn. The town sparrows could even play at being country sparrows with some element of conviction. The breeze rippled Tartar's runners which swayed luxuriantly on their lines and stays. His misHisignonette and wallflower flourished in their boxes, in the nooks to which they had been summarily dispatched by the naval boathook. Nature was in her element, even in the midst of dusty London; though the surrounding city, which crowded in on Staple Inn, provided an ever-present reminder of the murky world of men.

Two of the least murky men of our acquaintance were conferring in a set of rooms in Staple Inn. One, an elderly, arid, woody sort of fellow, was seated bolt upright in his favourite window-seat at the open window, with that single hinge in his body, hands firmly on his knees, except when he removed his right hand to take a reflective sip from the wineglass beside him, which he had poured to enjoy while sitting in the evening sunshine; before the second person in the room had arrived to break into his solitary thoughts and reflections. He was generally still and emotionless and imperturbable, though occasionally moved to relieve his feelings by smoothing from back to front what appears to be a mangy fur tippet placed on his head by wilful Mother Nature. Beside him lay his pocket book, and a stump of black-lead pencil, as if recently laid aside after recording something of value

The other, a tall, athletic, benevolent-looking clergyman, was leaning on the chimney-piece above the fireplace. Since it was summer, and there was no fire, his trousers were in no danger from spark or heat. But even if they had been, his mind appeared far away from, and above, such mundane matters. He was concentrating hard, and looked both concerned and determined. In this sober mood, a pair of boxing gloves, primed for action, would not have looked out of place on his powerful hands. And let any potential opponent beware: there was no hint of suet-pudding on his spare frame! He had good-naturedly but firmly regretted any refreshment offered by his host, who was delighted as always to see him, and left the other to taste the glowing wine alone.

They were discussing a certain dark gentleman, whose doings looked more murky by the minute, as their discussion proceeded. Mr Crisparkle, for he it is, had just revealed what he had learned from Helena about her conversation with Rosa on her first evening at the Nuns' House.

'This shows for how long, and with what concentrated passion, Jasper loved Rosa.' He was drawing some conclusions for the benefit of his companion: who might indeed have reached them unassisted, for he is as deep as he is dry. 'He loved her madly, as he freely admitted to her, nay boasted of to her, at the sundial: as if to declare mad love was the way to her heart – it can hardly be considered an unvarnished compliment.'

He was thinking and musing as he went on. 'Self-confessed madness: what does that mean? Had that "one silken thread" to which he also referred at the sundial really been sufficient to protect Drood against his jealous rage? Mad love: it's a powerful image. And in Rosa's cry for help to Helena, there's a strong hint of Jasper's hypnotic powers: used against Rosa, to bring her closer to him, to get him closer to her, against her wishes. Hypnotic powers: that's it! Helena has provided the clue to something else: that one insistent, haunting note played by Jasper that evening, as if bending Rosa to his will. I remarked it at the time, but not its significance.'

His musing now led him in another direction. 'Did he similarly experiment with mesmerism on Drood? There was certainly a curious and very strong bond between them. And, if used on Drood, with what end, and to what effect?'

He mulled over the words he had just used. 'Curious and strong indeed, at least on Jasper's side. For there's also the strange question of the Diary.' Grewgious looked at him enquiringly: Crisparkle enlightened him. 'He told me that his diary was the diary of Ned's life too: it seemed decidedly obsessive to write the diary of another; particularly of a grown man about to marry. And it was written in such an exaggerative style, as he himself once admitted. For whom was it written: Jasper, Drood, or another? He was certainly insistent in showing it to me, more than once.'

Grewgious stirred.

'Let's talk. Your reflections are tending to move in a certain direction. Tell me what is in your mind, Reverend Sir. What do you know or suspect?' As he said this, he took up his pencil and pocket book again, and prepared to apply the one to the other.

'Let's begin with knowledge, or what comes closest to knowledge, and see where it leads us,' returned Crisparkle, still leaning on the chimney-piece. 'I vividly remember one occasion, when I came upon Jasper asleep on his couch. On my approach, he sprang up, deliriously crying out: "What is the matter? Who did it?" His very words, which I remarked at the time because they were so unexpected and so extraordinary. Who had done what, and to whom? Was he sleeping or waking as he said it? And was his mind sleeping or waking as he thought it? The episode is not evidence, but it happened and is a fact: possibly a tell-tale fact: like my next link in a possible chain.' He proceeded to this directly.

'When I proposed to Jasper the idea of a mutual apology between Neville and Edwin, my boy and his, I caught a most perplexed and perplexing expression on his face: an expression which appeared to suggest some close internal calculation, as if weighing advantage and disadvantage, profit and loss. I clearly remember thinking at the time how strange it was. How and why did my straightforward suggestion require such concentrated thought before he replied, before he acquiesced. Again, it is not evidence, but it is indicative of something: yet of what?'

Grewgious seemed to prepare himself for speech, but Crisparkle had something to add. He slightly shifted his stance by the fire-place, and leaned forward in the direction of his companion.

'Forgive me, just one more point. Again, it's not evidence, and I'm not even sure that it is a link, let alone a putative part of a chain. But it is a further piece of puzzling behaviour; and, again, it relates to that curious Diary.' He described how Jasper had again showed him his manuscript pages, this time after Neville had left town, and insistently made Crisparkle aware of his determination both to pursue the murderer of his nephew, and not to discuss the mystery with anyone until he had solved it. 'Why did he do this? Why did he show it to me? And so emphatically? Why did it concern me? He had shown me earlier entries, but why show me of all people his sacred vow to pursue the murderer, who in his view could only be Neville? And why the vow of secrecy? Can you perhaps enlighten me, Mr Grewgious?'

'Not immediately,' replied Grewgious, 'but let's continue to build up our case and our joint understanding of matters methodically, as you began so admirably, before we seek to peer too deeply below the surface.' He again opened his faithful pocket book, consulted it, and cleared his throat mechanically. 'So, it's my turn, Reverend Sir. Let me see if I can add some links to our chain. Some time after Drood's death – or rather I should say disappearance –' he rapidly corrected himself, 'and for reasons which I shall shortly explain, I made a note of what I thought and termed curious incidents involving our local friend.' He once again looked at the small book, and inspected his carefully pencilled notes, to get them off by heart before he started. He then listed various circumstances, going over them as if by rote, as if repeating a lesson, ticking them off on his fingers and nodding his head to emphasise particulars to which he attached especial importance.

'Item the first. The day after Rosa fainted at Minor Canon Corner, and there was the sorry altercation between Landless and Drood, it so happened that I had travelled down to Cloisterham to acquaint my ward with the contents of her father's misguided will. Afterwards, I went to see Jasper, and met him by the Cathedral, at the very jaws of its entrance. He asked immediately "Nothing is the matter? You have not been sent for?" His lips were so white that I noticed that he was moved to bite and moisten them. Why? I cannot believe that he thought I had been sent for because of Landless and Drood. What did it amount to? A few splinters of glass for Mrs Tope to sweep up the next morning, even as Jasper was hurrying round the town to spread word of the affair. What was their foolish quarrel to me: high words between two boys at the end of an evening during which punch was drunk? Why should I of all people have been sent for? I had no responsibility for either of them. I, Hiram Grewgious, had no real role to play.'

A decisive nod of the head, followed by that smoothing action applied to his dessicated locks.

'No, he must have thought that I might have been sent for because of Rosa, because I was her guardian. But why? Because of a slight faint towards the end of a long evening, during which she had entertained the company for some time with her singing, to the accompaniment of her betrothed's uncle on the piano? Hardly a matter for a guardian: especially when the admirable Miss Twinkleton and her new friend Miss Landless were both there to ensure that no harm came to her. So why might Jasper have supposed that I might have been called to Cloisterham? Now you come, clearly revealing the answer to that question, which indeed I already suspected, especially after Rosa told me of the scene by the sun-dial. It could only be because he feared that his role in her faint had been discovered or suspected: that his love, which he had so far managed to keep successfully hidden from everyone except the object of his desire, was now known: that I might be about to confront or expose him, and demand that his unwanted advances end then and there. In short, he inadvertently revealed his guilt by the manner of his greeting.' Another nod of the head, and a light exhalation of breath, as if to say "So much for Jasper. I'll finish with him."

'So far I have only considered Jasper's guilt in the matter of his forbidden love for Rosa,' resumed Grewgious. 'So, on to item the second.' A quick look at the notebook for reference, and he continued. 'At the end of our meeting, and referring to what were still the betrothed pair, I said, for what precise reason I no longer remember, but it seemed the appropriate thing to say at the time "God bless them both!" To which he returned "God save them both!" It sounded falsely, so I emphasised my blessing; and he repeated his formulation, asking whether there was a difference. To me there was: his words suggested that there might be some element of threat to them, and to their proposed union, from which they needed saving. It was a curious word to use towards the nephew he professed to love and to pamper so much. From what did he and she need to be saved? It was equally curious that he did not seem to realise this disparity, as if there was some impediment in his brain, some blockage, some barrier between Jasper and normal human understanding, some lacuna which might lead to – well, to what, I wonder?'

There was no need to refer to the little memorandum book and the pencilled notations again. Grewgious was well-launched, and approaching the most compelling part of his testimony. He remained cool and steady however, speaking with as much passion as if reading an inventory.

'But, Reverend Sir, I believe that I may have gained something of a reputation for dealing with the factual rather than the speculative side of life; and I expect that you came here seeking something rather more material: more solid fare. I rather think that I can provide you with what you are probably seeking.' If nature had provided him with the means to offer a satisfied chuckle, he might have permitted himself one at that moment; but it hadn't, so that is but idle fancy. Instead, he took his bony hands from his bony knees, briefly rubbed them together, as might a cricket, and then restored them to their former resting place.

'Item the third. My ward invited me down to Cloisterham to inform me that she and Drood had broken off their ill-starred union – or semi-union – by mutual consent, and in full friendliness: in fact in better relation than they tended to enjoy when they had been considered as betrothed, when meetings were often fraught, and a certain amount of

— umps — quarrelling and — umps — bickering took place. They had also agreed that it should fall to me to inform Jasper. I think that Drood was a little worried about doing this himself. This was unfortunate for him, I strongly *suspect* — and, Reverend Sir, note carefully the word *suspect*, which I use deliberately — in the light of subsequent developments. And I further strongly *suspect* — the word marginally emphasised in his dry and otherwise flat tones — 'that it was doubly unfortunate that I, in turn, was unable to carry out this important commission until after it had become known that Drood had disappeared, never to be seen again.'

Perhaps it was as well that he had avoided that elusive chuckle: there was tragedy as well as poignant detail in what he had to say.

'So I called on him a couple of days after Drood's disappearance to fulfil the task with which I had been entrusted by my ward, agreed with Drood. I came upon Jasper in his room, when he had just returned from hours of tiring and compulsive searching for the body by the river. He was seated in his easy chair, by the fire, evidently about to fall asleep. I disturbed him,' he added unnecessarily.

'Go on,' urged Crisparkle, 'I believe we are about to unveil a gem of rare price.'

'I certainly think that it may interest you,' admitted Grewgious, modestly. 'I stood in front of the fire, warming my hands, alternately opening and shutting the palms of my hands, looking at him fixedly and sideways the while. I started to tell him about the ending of the betrothal by mutual agreement.' Grewgious described the scene in such detail that Crisparkle could imagine it to himself. 'I deliberately took it slowly, to lessen the shock to him. I knew, or rather believed, how much he loved and cherished his nephew. I was therefore leading into the subject slowly and deliberately, taking my time, so that he would be able to guess what I was about to say before I said it, so that he came to the realisation of what had occurred by himself, before I told him; before I blurted it out, before I laid it before him quite bluntly, because, as you know, Reverend Sir, I am a man of no social graces, no easy manner, no smoothness. All rough, all hard, all dry: like a walnut case.' He again rubbed his hands, which in their texture did indeed resemble a brace of walnut-shells. 'The approach worked. He guessed. But the effect was not what I had expected at all.' Even the dry, matter of fact voice of Grewgious now betrayed some element of excitement as he recalled the scene. 'I suddenly saw a staring white face and two quivering white lips. I continued, looking at him the while, warming my hands, and opening and shutting my palms.' He repeated these gestures as he told his tale. 'I saw a lead-coloured face, and on its surface dreadful starting drops or bubbles, as if of steel. I went on, reaching the point at last. I saw a ghastly figure rise, open-mouthed, and lift its outspread hands towards its head. I said that Drood had intended to go, and he had gone. I saw the ghastly figure throw back its head, clutch its hair with its hands, and turn from me with a writhing action. I finished. I heard a terrible shriek, and saw no ghastly figure, nothing but a heap of torn and miry clothes upon the floor. The image of those torn and miry clothes has remained with me ever since, and I have been quite unable to get it out of my mind'

'And what then?'

'I continued to warm my hands. It was a cold, bleak, hard day, although it was Christmas time; and I am a cold, bleak, hard man, although it was Christmas time.'

Mr Crisparkle was minded to remonstrate at this, for he knew that beneath that arid exterior lurked generous feelings; but he knew that Grewgious would wave away his objections, or seek to smoothe them out of his hair, like so much spare water, and, in any case, he was eager to pursue what the other man had told him.

'And what did you think? And do?'

'I puzzled. I wondered what sort of shock, which aspect of what I had said, could produce such a sudden change in a man? Surely not merely and by itself the news of the breaking of an engagement entered into by the parents of the parties, and in the absence of evidence that the two parties themselves derived much pleasure or profit from it? And why? Above all, why? I continued to look at him, and warm my hands and ponder, until Mrs Tope hurried in and busied herself with bringing Jasper round. Which I also wanted to see, because I wished to hear what he would say, how he would react.

And, while Mrs Tope busied herself, and called Tope, and while together they tended to Jasper, and unable to furnish an answer to the questions which had flooded into my mind, I further thought to myself in a more general way about his appearance and behaviour, and speculated – opium?'

For the second time that day, Crisparkle brought the fist of one hand smack into the palm of the other.

'I must pull myself together.' The idea of that energetic frame being "pulled together" probably gave Grewgious pause for thought, but he remained silent, awaiting the conclusion of Crisparkle's Damascene experience. 'First it takes me time to understand the full import of what Miss Landless is telling me about the conversation between herself and Rosa. Then it takes me years to realise what is absolutely staring me in the face: staring, and waving at me and gesticulating. Except that I do not realise it. It is kindly pointed out to me by a perceptive gentleman, who has seen considerably less of Jasper than I have. Yes, you have it, learned Sir. That glazed look. That occasional film over the eyes. His illness at services.' He mused, and then opened another train of thought. 'But if he were madly in love with Rosa, and therefore desperately jealous of Edwin, what might be the effect of opium on his feelings, on his diseased brain? What might he have thought of, or planned?'

He left the questions hanging in the air. Grewgious did not answer, but started off on his own new line of enquiry, as if the dossier on opium in his overall memorandum could now be considered dealt with: opened, discussed, agreed *nem con*, and closed for the present.

'Item the fourth – or fifth if we make opium the fourth: I was previously a little uncertain where to docket it. There is the evidence of sudden and partly unexpected changes of mood.' Crisparkle looked at him questioningly. 'Let me explain. After hearing of the ending of the engagement, he was suddenly and surprisingly confident that Drood was alive.' Crisparkle nodded responsively, recalling anew his surprise at the time. 'Then, after your discovery of watch and pin, he was immediately and unbendingly convinced that Drood was dead, and that Landless was to blame, even though no body or any other evidence ever appeared.'

'I remember it most vividly.'

'Now it is perfectly logical,' Grewgious uttered the word approvingly, 'yes, logical to conclude that the ending of the bethrothal might – *might* – persuade Drood to slip out of town quietly. But why find that interpretation so suddenly and entirely, so thoroughly and exclusively, convincing? Again, it is perfectly logical,' he liked the word, and rolled it round his mouth appreciatively, 'to reach the conclusion that the finding of the watch and pin suggested murder: but why accept it so definitively, and hold it so unswervingly, in the absence of a body? What was the reason for these sudden swings of mood and opinion? Was this the result of opium working on his mind, and producing curious effects? Or the result of careful reckoning? Of close internal calculation, as you put it?'

A succession of images flashed through Crisparkle's brain: images which had previously been stored separately, but were now brought together: Jasper awakening and asking who had done it: Jasper calculating before accepting the idea of a reconciliation: now Jasper at the door of the dark Cathedral asking whether Grewgious had not been sent for: Jasper asking God to save them both: Jasper collapsing into a heap of torn and miry clothes. At last Crisparkle could answer a question. 'More of the latter, for my money.'

'I am with you, Reverend Sir, I am with you. Indeed, it is possible that I anticipated you.' Grewgious, obviously with something of pressing importance on his mind, unexpectedly rose to his feet and took a few paces round the room at a lively trot. Crisparkle had got used to this mannerism, and assumed that Grewgious was preparing his mind for a bold step – or for admitting to a bold and unexpected step.

He stopped suddenly, in mid-trot, and turned directly to Crisparkle.

'I have a confession: perhaps it is appropriate that I address a priest.' He snuffled to himself in acknowledgement of this little felicity. 'I am an Angular man,' (he was finally prepared to acknowledge this). 'As a result, I act in Angular ways,' (he was sharing a deep confidence). 'This in turn has, or should have, two consequences,' (he has clearly been studying the matter carefully and analytically). 'First, I do not know how a normal man might be expected to proceed: I am for ever feeling my way forward in this world, wondering and groping for,' his hands reflected the word, 'how that normal man, who is so unlike me, might proceed and then acting accordingly: adopting a somewhat indirect approach, resembling that of a crab: and definitely not rushing to conclusions, which might appear obvious to others.

Secondly, not having been blessed with what you might term imagination, I have no right to proceed in a flighty manner. It is clearly so: the case against Grewgious on this count permits no questioning, no opposition.' A decisive nod to underline the point.

'But,' and he proceeded to emphasise the word by repetition, 'but, as I sat in my room, and considered the actions and behaviour of our local friend, I grew suspicious. I turned thoughts and images over in my mind, as I passed my tingling wine over my tongue, and those suspicions grew. I saw that heap of torn and miry clothes again and again and again. So, I took a decision. I am a man of business,' (would this come as a surprise to Crisparkle?), 'and I attempt to follow business-like methods,' (would this catch the Minor Canon amidships, in the solar plexus, in the manner of a punch from a practitioner of the Noble Art?), 'so I decided to have our local friend followed and observed at close quarters, rather as he follows Landless. Indeed, I determined on this course of action about the time when I learned, when we both learned, that Jasper was following your charge and pupil.' Now this admission did catch Crisparkle unexpectedly, and he looked at Grewgious with some astonishment.

'But the purpose was very different,' explained Grewgious. 'He follows Landless to let the latter know that he is under observation, under suspicion. My idea of following Jasper was to investigate him without him being aware of it. Now whether this was the act of a normal or an angular man, I leave you, Sir, to judge. As to whether it was the action of an imaginative and flighty man, I rather fear that it might have been, and therefore out of character, against the grain.' As he sat there, his grain was written all over him, stamped upon him, cut into him, shaping him, defining him. 'Unless, of course, it was so unexpected as to be entirely in character, coming full circle as it were.' He smoothed his hands over his hair, as if these moral and intellectual judgements were quite beyond him.

'So, the idea was formed: now the execution. I briefly thought of undertaking it myself, in disguise, but instantly dismissed the notion. I am too set in my bachelor ways, too chiselled in to my familiar groove, to think of it. Or to get someone like Bazzard to undertake it: it might have appealed to his sense of the dramatic; but he might not have liked it, he might have taken it ill, he might have considered it beneath the dignity of a tragedian. Or perhaps Tartar; but, no, his part was to provide companionship for Landless, and now comfort and hope for dear Rosa. They are both victims of Jasper, to whom that honest sailor is the perfect antidote; he is all brown, outdoor and healthy, as Jasper is dark, brooding and reclusive. In any case, temporary substitution would not have fitted the case. Observing Jasper was not occasional work. I saw it as a full time duty or obligation, if it were to succeed. It required someone on the spot, on his trail, sitting on his very coat-tails, on his doorstep if necessary, ready to respond to the slightest clue, the least indication. So I hired a man to do it: a good man,' (allaying any conceivable suspicion on Crisparkle's part that he might have deliberately chosen a bad man), 'a skilled and professional observer,' (removing any possible assumption by Crisparkle that he had somehow allowed himself to be palmed off with an unobservant amateur), 'a lawyer, and, strange to say, one who believes in justice, in protecting the innocent, in bringing down the oppressor,' (with a snort of "Umps," and a little turn around the room, indicative of support for this phenomenon). 'I have set him to watch Jasper, and to learn all about him and his movements, past and present. Incidentally,' and his bony hands clasped his bony knees in his sudden burst of satisfaction, 'his name is not Dick Datchery.'

'I have heard tell of this man, and seen him. An oldish sort of fellow with a shock of white hair, and something of a military air.'

'That is not how I know him, but I left all details to him. I told him all I knew of Jasper and left it to him. I do not know much about these matters, but that seemed the best way to proceed, and that was how I proceeded.'

At that point, Bazzard entered, looking disgruntled, and running his fingers through his tangled locks, like the reincarnation of Hamlet: except rather doughier of countenance than that haggard Prince, and manifestly less haunted by indecision and self-doubt. These were emotions unknown to the worthy Bazzard.

'Why Bazzard, you are still here. You truly look after me so well, my dear fellow. It must be late, and you have waited long,' enthused Grewgious.

'I'm done now,' responded Bazzard, his big dark eyes remaining dull and unresponsive. 'And I'll be in late tomorrow, to compensate.'

'Why, to be sure, to be sure. Any callers, while I was in conference with the Reverend Mr Crisparkle?'

'None, it was as quiet as the grave,' he observed gloomily, as if to say "What kind of work is this to offer a man of ability and discrimination? Why do I waste my precious hours sitting in your outer office, in Staple Inn, a place which so resolutely keeps my muse at bay?"

'It was all that I could do to keep my eyes open.' Those twin orbs certainly still looked close to sleep.

'Then you must be on your way before you suffer further. Any letters?'

The great tragedian felt in his pockets, and seemed surprised to discover a letter nestling in one of them. He idly glanced at it, and gloomily passed it to Mr Grewgious, whose name was prominently displayed on the envelope, together with a hand-written note in capital letters loudly and unmistakably claiming to all the world that it was urgent.

'There you are,' admitted Bazzard, reluctantly. 'It must have come in during the afternoon.' He still seemed puzzled by its sudden appearance in his pocket, and looked around as if to discover who might have perpetrated this hostile conjuring trick.

'I observe that it is marked as being intended for my early consideration,' commented Grewgious, with the closest he ever came to criticism of his illustrious clerk.

'I follow you, Sir, I follow you,' returned Bazzard obscurely: for the extent to which he followed Grewgious's mildest of rebukes was far from obvious.

'How thoughtful of you not to interrupt Mr Crisparkle and me. It is unlikely to be pertinent to our conversation.' But Bazzard had already gone; and the letter, once opened, immediately proclaimed its relevance. It was in fact a letter from Datchery (as we shall continue to call him as he plays out his role in this tale). Grewgious opened it eagerly, with Crisparkle still there. It provided the gist of what the Princess Puffer had told Datchery (adding substantially to the case building up against a certain dark gentleman), together with an account of the money expended in securing this information.

'This is excellent on all counts. And most business-like to boot. Business is business, and cannot be bettered. I shall reply directly, furnishing him with the new details which you have provided, including your account of what Helena told you, to help build up his picture of Jasper, and of his weaknesses. I have made careful note of your main points. This will greatly assist his efforts.

I shall likewise inform Datchery that you know his identity and purpose, and that you are fully in my confidence on all aspects, as am I in yours.'

Mr Grewgious seemed well-pleased with the turn of events, and made a series of little chopping gestures with his right hand, as if gradually chopping pieces off Jasper, or slicing away at the image of him as a highly-respected man, Choir-Master, and Lay Precentor.

'The case grows apace. As I told you, I had already suspected Jasper's lengthy infatuation with my ward, and its role in causing her fainting that evening: what Helena has just told you confirms this. I could of course have asked Rosa, and would have done so in time, but did not wish to upset her further so soon after her terrible experience by the sun-dial. The sun-dial: that's the point. That wretched scene, which I cannot think of without horror and amazement, did not come out of a clear blue sky. It was part of a pattern of pursuit and pressure,' he triumphantly ended up: unexpectedly and probably unintendedly breaking into alliteration in the excitement of the chase.

He looked momentarily downcast, as his well-organised brain remembered something:

'None of this helps explain why Jasper made a point of showing you his Diary. The reason for that escapes me. I cannot tell you.' Then he suddenly brightened. 'But I expect that Datchery can. I shall bring the matter to his immediate attention.'

A pencil mark in his pocket book ensured that he would do so.

CHAPTER XXIX
A Mayor and Two Deans

ANOTHER MEETING WAS taking place at that very time, in Cloisterham rather than in London. It was not as important as The Field of the Cloth of Gold, for no sovereigns were involved; nor as flamboyant, for there were no jingling retinues of horsemen, though one of the personages was accompanied by his loyal and appreciative henchman, Mr Tope; nor as famous, though the other of the personages was no lesser a figure than the weighty Mayor of the historic town. But, as to the central potentates, it was almost as showy, with one a trim figure, from his shapely hat to his comely gaiters, and the other seeking to emulate him – quite literally – in elegance.

The meeting of Dante and Beatrice by Arno's bridge has entered legend; the arrival of the Queen of Sheba at the court of King Solomon has been celebrated in history and music; the missions of Tristan and Don Carlos on behalf of their kings, and their fabled encounters with Isolde and Elisabetta, proved the very stuff of tragedy; the meeting of Titania and Oberon was "ill-met by moonlight"; and the meeting of the Thane of Cawdor with the weird sisters heralded "double, double toil and trouble"; the confrontation of Elizabeth the First with her great foe Mary Stuart has become a renowned part of our island history, even if it never took place; but the meeting of the Mayor and Dean of Cloisterham stood parallel with these encounters.

For it was only rarely that the two met these days, even though the opportunities were many, and the town small. For the fact was that the Dean felt uneasy in the company of the Mayor. He felt under scrutiny, almost under siege. He felt as if the Mayor was forever disappearing out of his straight line of vision, only to reappear over his shoulder, with the air of a tailor wielding a pin or piece of chalk, or someone holding up a measure. He felt as if his image was somehow being stolen from him, as in a fairy-tale where the wicked magician assumes the mantle of the good to evil intent; or where someone looks into a mirror and hey-presto their soul is spirited away. He can never quite put his finger on any of these feelings, any of these sources of disquiet; he just has a sixth sense that

Cloisterham is fortunate enough, and sufficiently unique in the annals of ecclesiastical governance, to have two Deans to attend its religious needs.

For his part, the Mayor sensed the concern of The Dean, who had a tendency to recoil from him, but was unable to control his wish to copy, to learn, to equal, and then to transcend. He knew that he could not let the Dean wholly out of his sight, else he would miss the opportunity to see his original, and his performances at the auctioneer's desk, his pulpit, would suffer; his appearance would decline into banal laicism, his ecclesiastical manner fade, his aura disappear. If it could be said of so broad a personage, he was in danger of falling between two stools: by attempting to multiply the benefits of each encounter, he ensured that the Dean cunningly kept them to a minimum.

But, on this occasion, there was no escape. Beatrice was well and truly cornered by her wily suitor. Coming down the High Street in the direction of the Cathedral, the Dean and Mr Tope saw the Mayor proceeding in the opposite direction: bearing down like a Spanish galleon in full sail, with the fixed intention of closing with an English privateer. There was no side street or secret yard in which the Dean might seek refuge; and turning and taking to his heels was, he considered, quite out of the question: it would look like retreat, like the religious power giving way in the face of the temporal. In any case the advancing galleon rapidly took the pair hostage by exclaiming as he came:

'Why, it is the Very Reverend the Dean; and his worthy acolyte, Mr Tope.'

The Dean made the best of the matter, and spoke with silky politeness.

'Mr Mayor, this is a rare occurrence, and all the more welcome for that. Our paths cross so seldom. You are busy with the affairs of state, while I work and pray for sinful mankind in my monkish cell.'

Mr Tope was good enough to find the Dean's sally hilarious, not least because he was well aware that the Dean lived in considerable material comfort: together with Mrs Dean and Miss Dean, who were not the usual attributes of a monkish cell.

Mr Sapsea, who is above humour, and largely unaware of it, did not recognise the self-deprecating jest, but placed his thumbs in the armholes of his waistcoat to ensure greater gravitas of appearance and address, and replied portentously that the affairs of state did indeed take their toll, Sir, take their toll, even upon a man as familiar with the world and its ways as himself.

Eager to change the conversation, the Dean pointed ahead, to where the lodging of Dick Datchery lay to the side of that of the Topes, and beneath that of Jasper, and asked:

'What do you make of our latest resident, our settler in Cloisterham?'

'Sir, he is what I term a Character,' returned Mr Sapsea, determining to purchase an umbrella which would be the very fellow to the Dean's. 'A Worthy, who is out of the top drawer, which I call top, because it is at the top. I insist upon it. He possesses the very qualities which allow mankind, as I put it, to rise above the beasts. His manners, his address, his deference to Figures of Authority are all an example to others. I fear that in some ways they put to shame the behaviour of some of the inhabitants of this town towards important civic dignitaries.' He brushed his fingers together with slight distaste, as if feeling the stone-dust of Durdles upon them, and removing it from his person.

'I state this with deep regret, Sir, because this town is a Historic Town,' (as if the Dean had in some way overlooked the historicity of the town), 'a Cathedral town,' (as if the Dean were fervently denying his Cathedral), 'a constitutional town,' (as if the Dean had poured scorn on the very idea of a constitution). 'Datchery's formulation of The Worshipful the Mayor, used, mark this, in direct intercourse with me, has no equal, no superior. You will observe that as you approached I addressed you as the Very Reverend the Dean, as a mark of respect for your status and position. So I take Mr Datchery's form of address most kindly.'

'Yet what, I wonder, has tempted Mr Datchery to Cloisterham?' wondered the Dean, looking at Sapsea quizzically. 'What does he do? It is curious to find a gentleman, who although elderly still seems energetic enough, who does little more than sit in his porch, like the philosopher under his tree, or the seer at the entrance to his tent, however easy his means.'

Mr Sapsea responded to this magisterially, measuring with his eye the exact length and cut of the Dean's whiskers; but if the Dean were expecting enlightenment from this quarter, he was sorely mistaken.

'I fancy that he had heard something of the particular qualities of this town, which I believe to be spread abroad, and with good reason. By this I do not mean merely its physical properties, but its institutions, its gravity, its civic spirit. He likes our ways and our manners,' he went on remorselessly, 'and feels at home. He appears to have developed a particular regard,' he coughed modestly but meaningfully, 'for someone who holds significant office in the secular governance of this town. So do not be surprised that he has chosen to live here, and even see out his remaining days in our congenial company.'

Mr Sapsea is not, it is fair to say, a reflective or self-critical man: except when reflecting on his own genius, or half-tempted to criticise his own modesty in proclaiming it; but, catching sight of Tope's rather sullen face, and indeed glimpsing the tower of the Cathedral rising loftily above them, he wondered whether, in expressing these sentiments, he had rendered just a little much unto Caesar and slightly too little unto God. He moved to repair the damage.

'I for one am certainly not surprised that he has chosen to live in the close vicinity, in the very shadow, of our Cathedral, our famous and historic Cathedral, which has proved such an inspiration to our townspeople over the centuries.'

It was still somewhat proprietorial in manner, and slanted towards lay opinion, but Tope seemed satisfied. The enquiring Dean however continued to probe the riddle of Dick Datchery. His wits were as sprightly as his figure, and he felt that there was a curiosity here which he wished to pursue – albeit in his own rather dilettante fashion.

'With full respect to Mr Tope, and the lovely Mrs Tope, who offers him such admirable support in carrying out his exacting and necessary duties, I wonder that he does not find the lodging a trifle, er, uncomfortable: or perhaps a better word is unusual.'

Mr Sapsea, who was looking enviously at the Dean's comely gaiters, but recognized that he had to draw the line at those, was fully equal to the task.

'Why, Sir, that is the very lodging which makes him feel a part of this town.'

And, for once, the jackass has brayed a truth; for nothing could be more a part of Cloisterham than a lodging which had been sculpted out of its very stone, carved out of its native being, and which was inextricably riveted and bonded to the dwellings of others. Without the presence and support of its close neighbours, Datchery's lodging would not have existed: it was but the space between them: without them, it would have reversed the miracle of Shakespeare's powers of creation, and reverted to airy nothing.

As they conversed, Jasper approached them on the way to his rooms. They exchanged a greeting, but he did not pause. He passed on in silence, apparently on his never-ending quest for the destruction of the murderer of his nephew, like a modern King Pelinore. There was a strange film over his eyes. He looked, to use the word with which Mr Tope had famously triumphed over the grammatical quibbles of The Reverend Septimus Crisparkle, DAZED. He disappeared up the postern stairs.

Sapsea transferred his gaze from the Dean's lapels to the departing figure.

'That young man is a sorry figure, Sir, a sorry figure. I have heard Mrs Tope — and allow me to second your recommendations of that admirable woman,' he looked significantly at Tope, who had now entirely forgiven him for his earlier tendency to dismiss the Cathedral from his enumeration of the virtues of Cloisterham, and in whose mental account book he now stood in credit, 'I have heard dear Mrs Tope, if I may be permitted so to call her,' a further notch to his credit, 'heard her remark that the poor gentleman was very solitary and very sad, and By Heavens she is in the right of it. Even I could not better her description. I hope that you will tell her so, Tope, tell her so.' Tope bowingly indicated that it would be his humble pleasure to do so.

Having got himself back on the rails again, Sapsea's oratory now carried him in a new and different direction, and one not without its dangers.

'It makes my English blood boil,' — boiling his blood would possibly have reduced that flowing outline of stomach by rendering it down, and creating a Sapsea of more modest proportion, albeit not without some pain attached, but fortunately for him that is not Nature's way — 'it makes it boil when I think of the damage done to that poor gentleman by someone who is no more than a young savage, brought out of the jungle and into our community by a Canon,' he ponderously corrected himself, 'a Minor Canon, I should say, with more religion than sense. The resulting damage has broken John Jasper beyond endurance. True Christianity,' he continued indignantly, 'is not about religion or a literal interpretation of the gospels. It is about Englishness and common-sense. It is not, Sir, about Un-Englishness and false charity. I have on occasion been heard to say, to some considerable applause, that charity should begin at home, and not in the tropics.' He waved a majestic hand towards Dover, as if suggesting that the dreaded tropics were to be found the far side of The Channel, and that dusky skins abounded in Calais.

The Dean was understandably annoyed by having the essential tenets of the Anglican Church defined for his benefit by a member of the laity, and one moreover who had the unfortunate tendency to sleep through his sermons (having first taken careful note of what the Dean was wearing), thereby depriving him in the Dean's understandable if partial opinion of any claim to expertise in the matter; but, being an easy-going man with a light manner, he confined himself to commenting that the Thirty Nine Articles were commendably clear on this matter, as on so much else. Knowing that Sapsea had no way of returning this skillfully played ball, since his knowledge of those famous Articles, or any other Articles, was of the flimsiest, the Dean continued his subtle counter-attack.

'I start, as I must, from the proposition that there is no evidence that Neville is a murderer, or indeed that Edwin Drood is dead. Nevertheless, I delicately hinted – no more – to the Reverend Mr Crisparkle several months ago that Neville should leave this town and he saw to it. I also gently intimated – no more – to the Reverend Mr Crisparkle that he should speak out less passionately in Neville's defence. Here I was, perhaps, marginally less successful. The Minor Canon is of determined moral fibre, and unshakeable in his defence of the young man. Provided that they are kept in decent check, for we Churchmen should be neither passionate nor partisan, these are admirable qualities, which I defend – in moderation always. And, Sir, I have to note that it was not the Church which brought Neville to Cloisterham; he was sent here by a noted philanthropist for his education, which was undertaken most zealously by the good Crisparkle.'

There were many arguments here to stop Sapsea in his tracks; but, if that were easy to do, it would have been done many times. He was not used to listening to or being swayed by others; and if the philanthropical Luke Honeythunder had a platform manner, it must be stated that the bourgeois Thomas Sapsea had a pulpit manner. Standing there at his auctioneer's desk, gavel in hand, naming the price, controlling the bidding, taking a nod here, a raised hand there, enjoying the sole right to speak, conducting affairs from start to finish, admonishing here, bestowing patronising praise there, he has not developed the give-and-take of social discourse. Nor did the fair Mrs Sapsea have the temerity to seek to change his ways in their relatively brief sojourn together. Like a ship ploughing its way across the wide ocean, the conversational style of Sapsea was to forge ahead, undaunted by the wind and waves. Occasionally he shifted course, perhaps when feeling the force of an exceptionally heavy billow, the seventh wave feared even by experienced mariners long remembered in ballad such as Sir Patrick Spens, and possibly the incautious and unhappy Shovel: but never for long.

On this occasion, Sapsea took no more than a couple of sentences to dispose of what the Dean had said. Rising slightly on his toes, to get a better look at the top of the Dean's hat, he spoke with the sense of authority which came naturally to him.

'I appreciate what you have done to rid the town of this menace. As a consequence of my office, I can speak for the town in conveying my – our – thanks.' He was thus back to his familiar theme. 'Depend upon it, the young savage, nay barbarian, is Un-English, and capable of any dastardly deeds. Which I dare to call dastardly, which I insist on calling dastardly, because that is a just description of what I term their immoral nature. We are the better for his absence.

Now, Sir, reverting, however briefly, to the most proper address and behaviour of Mr Datchery,' but we can spare the reader the Mayor's further thoughts upon that subject, which was most dear to him. The Dean was less fortunate, but resolved to avoid being caught or taken in this way again. The High Street had some slight turnings, many yards and innumerable close and passages: well, he would in future make better use of them.

The Dean thought only of his home and his dinner, and of how to get there without further ado or delay. He thought of Mrs Dean, and Miss Dean, of warmth and comfort, of table and hearth: and of amiable, companionable silence: above all, of silence. Dominated and drubbed, assailed and assaulted by the flow of words, he listened no more, but instead silently listed to himself the significant points he would include in his Sunday sermon: on tithes, on material support for the Cathedral, on the need for rich endowment in possessions as well as heritage, on moth and rust corrupting the coin in his congregation's pockets and the clothes on their backs, on reward being in Heaven and in Heaven alone.

As a consequence of his mental withdrawal away from Sapsea, and into his own inner and familiar thoughts, the faint inquisitive spark in his mind about the new resident in Cloisterham was rapidly snuffed out. So he thought no more of the riddle of Mr Datchery, or of the unique manner in which he passed his time in the town: for he lacked intellectual rigour and conviction. Life came easily to him, and he took little out of it, or out of himself. He was a pleasant, popular, shrewd, but essentially light man; and therefore missed many of the subtler and deeper aspects of life around him: such as, for example, who and why and what was Datchery.

The Mayor also was not tempted to brood on the mystery of Datchery. Had he been a more thoughtful man, then he might have wondered a little more about who Datchery was, and why he found himself sitting on a porch in Cloisterham. He might have – but he didn't. If only the nose of Cleopatra had been a little longer, or shorter, then – but it wasn't: if Robert the Bruce in his cave had not happened to observe the patient labour of the persevering arachnid, then – but he did: if Don John of Austria had married Mary Queen of Scots, then – : but none of these things happened, and that is how history is. The essence of Sapsea, beneath those folds of cloth and stomach, was to think only of himself, talk only of himself, take interest only in himself. He was the sun around which the planets of Cloisterham orbited and rotated, turning ever to him for their light and illumination, turning away when they could no longer tolerate his burning, corruscating knowledge and intelligence, and the profundity of his insights, and seek rest, ready for his great light to shine on them again on the morrow. The great Sun does not enquire why little Mercury exists, or what its role in the cosmic order might be: surely it exists only to reflect the brilliance and majesty of the Sun in its own small, inadequate way.

Thus it was with Sapsea and the humble Datchery. One day, of course, the latter may be invited into the Mayor's dull, ground-floor sitting-room, and claim his glass, and share the decanter (naturally the smaller share, the donkey's not the lion's), and play back-gammon and learn wisdom at the great man's feet; but not yet; the Mayor is not one to race into the unknown – his build is somewhat against it – and even the highly-regarded Choir-Master had to wait several years for the summons from above.

As they parted, it was obvious that the Dean was eager to be away, for his gaitered ankles, as nimble as elegant, fairly twinkled down the road and around the corner. The Mayor looked after him with some slight surprise; and, although he was usually totally oblivious to the feelings of others, even his insensitive instincts detected a certain readiness, even impatience, to be free of his company. It might have been the frisky flick of his leathered calves as he rounded the corner like a Derby winner which undid the Dean, and gave him away. Sapsea pursed his coarse lips, screwed up his heavy eyes, shook his ponderous jowls, and muttered to himself:

'Well, Mr Dean! Well!' as if this fully clarified the matter in his own understanding.

This was not quite that famous moment in the history of England (which like other famous moments may never have happened, as dull historians tell us), when the Duke of York haughtily plucked the white rose from the overhanging arbour, while his cousin of Lancaster provocatively pulled down the red rose, and challengingly twisted it from its stalk, the while glowering at each other in rage and hatred and contempt; but it was the beginning of something of a schism between Church and State in the fair town of Cloisterham.

Mr Tope was full of the topic when he returned to his house and the welcoming Mrs Tope.

'Fanny, my dear, I sense a scene, I sniff trouble.' He left it there, hoping and expecting that she would press him on the point, and was not disappointed.

'Why, whatever is it? I thought that you were just accompanying the Dean to the centre of town, and then back to the Cathedral. Not much time or place for trouble, I would have thought.'

'The Very Reverend, The Dean, Fanny, The Very Reverend The Dean. Even in the confines of our own house, and between ourselves, we should observe proper form. But that's just it. We were in the very middle of the town, and trouble struck – out of the blue.' He paused again, for effect, but Mrs Tope's eagerness outran his powers of story-telling.

'Why, what on earth happened?'

'Well, it wasn't so much there were *words* between the Very Reverend the Dean and the Mayor, but there seemed to be, well, an *atmosphere*. Not the former's fault, of course; as always he was generous and polite to a fault. The Mayor said some things which could have annoyed him, but didn't appear to: for the Very Reverend,' a shortening introduced here to preserve the niceties, and the proper form of address, but not to risk unduly slowing the pace of Mr Tope's revelations, already held back by the praise which he regularly needed to heap on his patron, 'the Very Reverend is a saint when handling his fellow men. Anyway, I thought that we had survived that hazard, and come out nicely, when at the end the Very Reverend The Dean had to leave and so we did: at something of a canter, because the Very Reverend moves quickly when his stable, no, what am I saying, his home calls to him.

But you should have seen the Mayor's face as we left. Unlike the Very Reverend, who was headed straight for home, I was looking back at him as we turned off the street. He looked thunderous, Fanny, thunderous, and he muttered something under his breath, and he turned on his heel. I didn't like the look of it at all; or of him.'

Fanny looked genuinely worried and concerned. 'Oh dear, I don't like trouble. We don't need it, and the town don't need it, especially after that dreadful murder.'

'Disappearance,' breathed Tope, unfailingly loyal as ever to the Dean.

'Well, disappearance or murder, it makes no difference, and it's left a nasty taste in the town. And now this! Oh dear,' she repeated, 'if only poor Mr Jasper was feeling himself, he could help avoid bad blood between the Dean,' ('The Very Reverend The Dean,' added Tope under his breath,) 'and the Mayor. Because both the Dean,' (Tope rolled his eyes towards the ceiling in anguish, but somehow managed to remain silent), 'and the Mayor think highly of him: though I have seen Mr Jasper yawn sometimes when the Mayor does go on, as it were. He would help resolve the matter, if he could. But he hardly ever seems to go out, now; just stays in his room, and keeps to himself. I don't know what he does. Just tosses and turns on his bed, by the look of it of a morning. I can't see him acting as a peace-maker now; I don't think his poor heart would be in it at all.'

'Blessed are the peace-makers, for they shall inherit the earth,' remarked Tope unctuously. 'Well, I don't suppose that you and I shall solve it my dear. We shall just have to leave it to the Very Reverend, and to God's will,' he ended with some satisfaction, as if the two were one and the same thing.

So having brought tidings of the rift, and being fully satisfied in his own mind that there was nothing he could do about it, Tope comfortably settled in for the evening, leaving his wife worrying rather more than he was about the future, and how Church and State could somehow, unlike that unfortunate ovoid Humpty-Dumpty, be put together again.

CHAPTER XXX
The Terms of the Communication

NICHOLAS MANDER ENDCOMBE is a porter at Staple Inn, and has been for many years. This may, perhaps, hint at a certain lack of ambition and forcefulness in his personality, and that suggestion is not wide of the mark. The slightly grandiose name may convey a touch of dash and swagger, but that is misleading. As is customary, the infant Endcombe did not choose the name for himself, pulling it out of the air with a gurgle of triumph and satisfaction. Endcombe was his birthright, his inheritance from his parents and a long line of Endcombes who had struggled to earn their living in the great city. The Mander was a gift from his fond godparents, in commemoration of his mother's maiden name. The Nicholas was mutually agreed between parents and godparents, who all drew singular satisfaction from it. Alas, it betrayed little imagination, since his paternal grandfather had proudly borne the name for many years, and had passed away only shortly before the young Nicholas was born and inherited it. There was a sense therefore of carrying the flag rather than striking out for himself, which in turn suggested rental rather than full ownership, and more than a mere reminder of mortality.

All the work which had been lovingly put into the naming of Nicholas Mander Endcombe, and thus preparing him for life, is largely wasted. The Mander is generally omitted in his daily line of business. Even Nicholas is rarely used, as he earns his daily bread. Endcombe tends to suffice for the good inhabitants of Staple Inn, when they summon or address him, though the occasional cheery newcomer such as Tartar manages the full mouthful on most mornings.

Endcombe's means are as limited as his ambitions. He is a slight, thin man, with want written all over him: in frame, and deportment and clothing. His hair is lank and ill-cut. He wears trousers which were once blue, and are now shiny with age, a jacket well rubbed at back and elbows, a shirt which shrinks away from public attention, a neckerchief with curiously twisted ends, as if his hands were in the habit of fumbling and pulling at them as he sits at his desk, or looks out of his window, as if prosperity grew somewhere out there, and an old cap which largely defies description. He is the polar opposite of Sapsea, a flute of the thinnest beer compared with a Toby jug overflowing with port wine: where Sapsea's waistcoat bulges outward in a series of soft creases, Endcombe's hangs limply from half-mast; where Sapsea struts, Endcombe edges; where Sapsea preens himself, Endcombe looks abject.

In truth, he is a mean-faced man: with a mean-faced wife and daughter. He has no mean-faced son yet, whose son might in turn proudly carry the name of Nicholas; and to have a son at this stage would be a mixed blessing, as offering the hope of future bread-winning, but also constituting in the short term another mouth to feed. The constant pressure of attempting to make ends meet, when those ends have an innate tendency to part company, and to set off in opposite directions, tempts Endcombe into mean actions: into what is termed *helping himself* when he has occasion and is unobserved; into peering inside envelopes which have been carelessly sealed, just to see what might lie within; into walking the streets with his eyes cast down, just in case small coin may reside there. His eyes are not bright, like those of a jackdaw, but they are as keen.

But Nicholas Mander Endcombe, to restore the dignity of his full title, is not all bad. He does his best to look after the aforementioned wife and daughter, and ensure that any of those additional pickings come in their direction, and in general – and despite those occasional envelopes – he is a loyal servant of Staple Inn: on duty on time on the coldest mornings, and still at his post on the wettest and foggiest evenings; ready to run inconvenient errands; and scrupulous in locking up when he leaves. It is want which keeps him down, and makes him less than he could be. This is part of the all-pervasive grit of the city, which permeates and affects the whole place.

Endcombe has a patron. Not a kind, generous, beneficent patron, like a patron in a fairy-tale; but a dark man, with dark hair and whiskers, and a dark voice, and a decidedly dark and sombre manner; yet, nonetheless, a patron for all that, and a man who has given him money to perform a certain task.

This morning, he has received a communication from this patron. It is not a kind, generous, beneficent communication; it is a dark and sombre communication; three brief sentences, unsigned. Endcombe looks at it again.

'You report that Tartar sees the boy. Warn him off, in the terms I directed. If you succeed, I shall pay you again.'

It is peremptory, it lacks warmth, it spurns the milk of human-kindness, but it has the advantage of clarity. And for Nicholas Mander Endcombe, who is something lacking in letters, it is easy to read, and to understand, and to act upon. The patron knows his man.

Endcombe has a room near the entrance to Staple Inn; not a large room, but sufficient to accommodate the inconsiderable figure of Endcombe and any small pieces of baggage he may have with him. He lurks in this room until he makes out the sound of Tartar's feet rapidly but quietly descending the stairs from his lofty rooms, as if belaying down from the topsail, or flying down the companionway into the mess; as quickly and as noiselessly as a great cat.

Endcombe emerges from his room, or rather his cupboard:

'Good morning, Lieutenant Tartar,' he begins.

'Good morning, Nicholas Mander Endcombe,' he replies cheerily. 'What's on the horizon today?'

'Lieutenant, there's trouble,' responds Endcombe shortly. The fact is that he is not quite sure how to carry out his patron's peremptory instruction and, as a result, is certain to do it badly.

'Trouble? What's that?' asks Tartar in a surprised tone.

'Lieutenant, the trouble is Landless.' He seems to take comfort from regular repetition of the rank, as if it dignifies his replies, and makes them less abrupt; but cannot help feeling that equally the regular repetition exposes the paucity of what he has to say, a molehill of content after the mountain of the grand opening.

'Landless?'

'That's the name. You see him.' He cannot help it sounding grudging.

'Yes.' Tartar looks at him enquiringly, and with dawning suspicion. He did not expect this of the man.

'Well, you shouldn't, Lieutenant.' There, that rank again; it slips out without his being able to control or countermand it.

Tartar tries to make light of it. 'I concede that I have spent much of my time abroad, in the service of my sovereign, but I believe that in this country it is customary to choose one's friends for oneself.'

Endcombe is not sure what to make of this, so ploughs on regardless. He recalls the words originally used by his patron when contracting him, and blurts these out in breathless tones:

'He's dangerous, an animal, he would have cut a man down, there's something of the tiger in him.' He stops suddenly, because he has run out

304

of instruction, and is left twisting idly in the wind, while Tartar regards him thoughtfully.

'That is all very interesting; and revealing. How do you know or suspect this about Landless?'

'From a dark gentleman who knows.'

'Who paid you well?'

Endcombe is uncertain how to respond. He wipes his brow in frustration. He thinks of taking refuge in a subterfuge. It is certainly true that his patron paid him, but not well. Suddenly, however, he has an inspiration.

'Who is a benefactor.'

'Of you?'

This is getting difficult, though there is a way out:

'Of mankind.'

It is not clear for how long Endcombe can keep up the verbal fencing. It is not his forte, whereas Tartar's rapier is keen. Fortunately he is spared by the timely arrival of Mr Crisparkle, who springs down the stairs, more loudly and sportingly than Tartar, and who warmly greets both duelists. Crisparkle looks kindly, as ever, but is much concerned about his pupil, whom he has just been visiting, and who seems more prisonish than ever. Crisparkle's cheeks seem to have acquired an additional shade of health, as if in compensation for the pallor of his pupil; though there is perhaps just a touch less vigour than normal in his manner, as if he had, despite himself, caught something of Neville's listlessness. His annoyance with Jasper, and anyone connected with Jasper, who had played a role in reducing his pupil to this unhappy state, is at its height: which is hard luck for Nicholas Mander Endcombe, who had indeed hitherto been blessed with inadequate luck for most of his life.

'My dear sir,' cries Tartar, 'you are always most welcome at the Inn, and never more than now. Endcombe has just been telling me something most interesting. You should hear it as well. It is much to the purpose. Repeat it, Endcombe. Word for word, now, word for word; just as you told me.'

Endcombe cannot believe his apparent good-fortune. He has been presented with the opportunity to warn two people off Landless: and one of them Landless's principal benefactor. This should earn him a double reward from his dark patron. So he sets off again. Repeating it word for word is not a problem for him: indeed, he can do it no other way. So he does.

As Crisparkle listens, a generous flush rises to his already well-endowed cheeks. But Tartar speaks first.

'What do you say to that? What I say is that this wretch deserves a good thrashing for spying on innocent citizens. Not with the cat o' nine tails, mind you, but with a stout English cane.'

Endcombe cannot believe his ears. Fortunately, Crisparkle again comes to his aid in time of need. He has controlled his wrath.

'Christianity, my dear fellow. Do not harm him. He is obviously acting for another, who has suborned him. We know who did this, and whose words he speaks.'

Endcombe nods approvingly, and mutters under his breath:

'That's it, subordened. That's the very word, Reverend.'

Crisparkle proceeds. 'Remember that God is his judge, as He is of all mankind. We cannot take the role of judgement upon ourselves. Also, remember that you have lodgings here and he is a porter. You need each other. Shake hands upon it and be friends again.'

Endcombe looks even more approving. The Christian gentleman is right, and fortunately he appears to carry influence with the other.

But the Reverend Mr Septimus Crisparkle has not finished. Septimus Crisparkle, Minor Canon, early riser, cheerful, good-natured, sportsman, pugilist, has words to add, for Endcombe's benefit.

'Be warned, my friend. If I learn that you ever again give information to that dark gentleman, or anyone else, about Mr Landless or other lodgers in Staple Inn, you will be in danger of feeling the full weight of my displeasure.' He demonstrates his large fist, and muscular arm, in a way which Endcombe can only find persuasive; and tops this by repeating his regular early morning routine, ending by putting an imaginary foe, probably a spy, in Chancery.

Endcombe looks pitiable. This has not gone well. The ups and downs of his fortunes in a short period confuse him. Now he faces the prospect of no reward on any front. He thinks of his wife and daughter.

Crisparkle immediately relents and repents.

'In my concern for Mr Landless, I may have forgotten myself, and even made threats which are no part of my ministry. The truth is that I am very worried about the boy, and I feel nothing but contempt and anger for his persecutor.' He looks at Endcombe sympathetically. 'Break with the dark gentleman. Do not do his bidding. Be yourself, not his agent. If you leave this city and come to Cloisterham, I shall assist you to find a new position in better circumstance. Here is my card, and my hand upon it.'

Nicholas Mander Endcombe finishes his work for the day, and goes home. The place is poor, but he and his wife have made of it what they can, and have provided for their daughter as well as they can. The main ornaments of the meagre sitting room are a set of fire-irons by the grate, scrupulously polished by Mrs Endcombe over the years; and a sampler diligently sewn by Miss Endcombe, decorated with the alphabet and the numbers up to ten, and also embroidered with the uplifting motto, "Nearer my God, to Thee," perhaps referring to the nearby chimney as a convenient channel of communication, and showing some slight evidence of where a second "e" had been added to "Thee," possibly after parental inspection.

Elsewhere in the room are some small samples of Mauchline ware arrayed on Mrs Endcombe's mantle-piece, the fruits of a visit by her to Carlisle before the birth of their daughter, one of which proclaimed proudly that "My Heart's in the Highlands," though why this should be the case, since none of the Endcombe family had ever visited that majestic but remote part of the kingdom, is more than this history can fathom.

As he arrives back, Endcombe is puzzled and uncertain, and after his supper (a meal which is light by Sapsea's robust culinary standards) he explains his dilemma to his listening wife.

'Here is a gentleman what gives you money for a certain task. It's not much money, but it's easy work.' He thinks of his travails that morning, and corrects himself. 'Well, it's not demanding of the body, more of the brain.' He does his best to be honest with himself, and the formulation is still not quite right. 'Well, the fact is, it's difficult to do well.' Having got it right at last, he proceeds. 'And here is another gentleman, what threatens you, and him a Christian, mind, and a priest at that, but then offers you a job out of London.'

'Why, Nicholas, it's straightforrard. Keep the money you've had, but give it to me for safe-keeping, and for a bit of food and fuel; take no more from that source. As for moving, Staples have been a good employer: well, I can think of worse. You've done long and cold hours. But we've done reasonable here, and there's continuing work. We need to think. Here, we know what we've got; what promises are there for the future? You talk of Mr Crismarkle.'

'Crisparkle, I think,' corrects her husband, lightly, for he depends greatly on his wife.

'Quite so, Crisparkle. What do we have that's dependable from that source? That offers us a reason to leave? But then,' and she looks at him, at this man who works hard and devotedly, with understanding and even compassion, 'you have met The Reverend Mr Crisparkle, and appear to trust him, immediate, and I haven't. So, let's trust to him and to our luck.'

Endcombe is about to shrug his shoulders, as if trusting to his luck was the last thing he would do, or want to do; but then he seems to realise that there might have been a change in that luck, and he holds his peace.

His wife continues:

'So, let's plan; travel down to Cloisterham as soon as you can to seek work; and Beth and I can come as well, or follow you if you've found it.'

The two nod at each other. Do their faces look less mean? Less pinched? Less anxious? Less beset by poverty and grit? Do they experience something called hope? And is it once again Septimus Crisparkle who has provided this precious commodity? Septimus Crisparkle, Minor Canon, early riser, cheerful, good-natured, benefactor, good man, Christian to his very core: Septimus Crisparkle, who has offered hope, and also faith, and charity, and encouragement, and above all a vision of something better, to so many: Septimus Crisparkle, who has replaced Jasper as Endcombe's patron, is in all ways the opposite of Jasper, and constitutes an important witness against him.

* M *

CHAPTER XXXI
The Tower, Revisited

IT IS THE evening. As is his wont, at all times of day, Datchery is sitting in his porch, engaged in his favourite pursuit of observing mankind; and occasionally reading from or jotting on the few papers by his side.

Suddenly a volley of flints hits the side of the gate-house, and part of Deputy appears in Datchery's sight. Only part, but that is hideous enough to suggest the remainder: the extract, to represent the whole. Either he knows that Jasper is out, or he feels fully protected by the benevolent presence of his white-haired patron and paymaster. It is not an exaggeration to suggest that Deputy now has two enlightened and enlightening objects in life: stoning Durdles home, and running errands for Datchery: thus advancing the educational scheme first mooted by Durdles for the benefit of Deputy. The latter is even occasionally dispatched to the Crozier, in a sign of trust and confidence, to collect the growing number of letters addressed to Datchery.

Yet some aura of Jasper may lurk about the place, for the rest of Deputy only gradually appears from around the wall, and the questing eyes and nose, and whistling mouth, remain prominent.

'So, Winks, you are ready to show me the abode of Durdles?'

'I don't know nuffink about 'is habode, but I can show you 'is 'ouse direct. And 'e's in there, asippin' and asuppin'; mainly asippin'.' Deputy pulls the rest of himself round the angle of the wall, and pretends to drink from an enormous imaginary bottle, before wiping a ragged sleeve across his nose and mouth – and indeed most of his face – with what can only be described as relish. Then a familiar look of truculence reasserts itself.

' 'Ere, less of that Winks. I tolds yer. It'd be me death. It's Deputy to you and others. But let's move from 'ere quick. Else that Jasper may return herly from the Kinfreederel.' He is clearly unready to put his new-found status as a protégé of Datchery too boldly to the test, and picks up a handful of stones as a precaution. 'I can feel 'is 'ands throttlin' and chokin' me. But I'll get heven with 'm. I'll dance on 'is grave.' He breaks into a crescendo of heart-felt but ill-choreographed activity.

They proceed to the stony house, collect a stony-coloured Durdles, who had been preparing for the evening in his traditional manner, as described by Deputy, and set off towards the stony Cathedral. On the way, they take leave of Deputy, who departs with a farewell cry of Widdy Warning, and a parting shot with a single stone, as a token of what awaits Durdles when his evening with Datchery is done.

The two proceed, the one bare-headed and with a shock of white hair in the moonlight, the other, beneath his russet-coloured old hat, resembling a moving block of masonry, as if the walls themselves were on the move, like Birnam wood approaching Dunsinane: indeed Durdles himself so simulates the famous Wall in Shakespeare's memorable comedy of the Athenian lovers that it is remarkable that he is not the recipient of a quick volley from Deputy, not because he is out late, but because he merges so architecturally with the dark buildings behind him.

They approach the great black pile of the castle, immense against the night sky, attended by its various fragments of ruin, the remains of fortifications and battlements long gone; they turn to the right, and pass the west front of the Cathedral, where the intricate carvings of the great door and window and pinnacles can only be guessed at, now that the evening light has largely deserted them, and turn right again to discover the door into the crypt.

Datchery is in a sharp mood tonight. As they go, he looks carefully about him, observing everything, taking in everything, from the moment they leave Durdles's gate, until he returns many hours later to his uncomfortable lodging. He is intent, alert and keen: not aggressively and demonically observant like Jasper, but scrupulously and professionally watchful. Unlike Jasper, he is not gazing at Durdles, he is looking carefully at his surroundings as they pass: inspecting, gauging, committing to memory.

Although they follow the identical route, there are other differences from that night with Jasper. There is a bottle which is rapidly appropriated by Durdles; but it is larger, as requested by Durdles, and apparently less potent, since Durdles is less errant in his movements, and less bewildered in his head. Clearly Jasper has a habit of mixing strong potions for others – and on occasion a peculiar-looking pipe for himself – though in the first instance his motives may not always be generous, and may have an element of deep calculation in them.

There are other differences. Datchery helps Durdles to get the bottle right, for he is a companionable soul, though he leaves the lion's share to Durdles, who is indeed only too happy to take it; and he converses with Durdles as they go, for he is a friendly expeditioner, and not as conspiratorially silent as Jasper.

So they descend into the crypt by the small side-door (Durdles produces a key, and Datchery glances at him and it), converse of the old 'uns, look at the tombs, examine the stonework, sound with the hammer as they go, walk up the steps into the Cathedral (the same key again), step through the iron gate which gives access to the staircase leading up to the great tower (a different key, again noted in passing by Datchery), ascend steps and winding stairs to the tower, illuminate with Durdles' lantern gargoyles and angels' heads, disturb jackdaw and rook, admire the view of the sleeping town beneath, descend, and return to the crypt.

And all the time, Datchery talks in a gentle, insistent voice to Durdles, and increasingly but deftly quizzes him on the night with Jasper. As they continue on their way, and as the level of liquid in the bottle miraculously lowers itself, and as it does so leaves rich fragrance in the air, and on the breath of Durdles, the latter becomes more loquacious than he normally is. He has clearly been meditating on his strange time with Jasper, who has evinced no further interest in Durdles's work or knowledge, and, far from learning more from him, or exploring further, has largely ignored him and kept him at arms' length; their day rambles together are a thing of the past, terminated by that single night-time excursion, and Durdles is clearly left with the unavoidable impression that he has been cast aside having fulfilled his mission – whatever that was.

But on their single night excursion together, Jasper managed to leave in Durdles's mind both an unforgettable impression of concentrated malice, and a memorable set of circumstances. 'Durdles, he remembers what happened that night. Depend upon it, Durdles remembers, remembers that night with Mister Jarsper,' is the constant refrain from the stony one.

The patient Datchery learns many things, which he must find of interest, because he perseveres with his light questioning, but which he is careful to avoid appearing to seize on too eagerly. He learns of Jasper's uncontrolled laughter at Neville.

'Mister Jarsper seemed to hear words which Durdles missed, which took his attention or tickled his fancy in some way. What Durdles did note and remember, however, was his sense of menace: of menace and…and what you might call destructive power. Remarkable, that was, quite took Durdles's appetite away.' Durdles is quite disturbed by this remembrance, and eagerly applies himself to his dinner-bundle by way of belated recompense.

Datchery learns of Jasper's abrupt reaction to the tale of the ghostly cry the previous Christmas Eve, as if stung by some comparison, or as if trying to knock the memory of that terrible sound out of Durdles's mind by sharp ridicule and mockery.

'Thinking about it, Durdles believes it was his talking of Christmas Eve which made Mister Jarsper so fierce and abrupt.' But why? What gave special resonance to something which happened on Christmas Eve: surely a time of general joy and celebration; what made it something to be expunged from the mind: surely Christmas Eves, of all three hundred and sixty five evenings of the year, should be remembered and treasured?

He learns of Jasper's alarm and fury at the possibility that he might have been followed by Deputy, and the violence he offered him. Which was doubly curious, since his night-time excursion with Durdles had been openly discussed, and Durdles had been with him all the time, from start to finish, hadn't he? So what secret was he so concerned to protect? What had he done which he would not wish another to see? What might Deputy have nosed out and voiced abroad? And why did he move so softly that night?

'Durdles noticed him moving silently along, and Durdles thought: Why, this is a curious sort of expedition, an unaccountable sort of expedition.'

And he learns of Jasper's apparent fascination with keys that evening at Sapsea's.

'He held them, examined them, weighed them, clinked them. Durdles had to say to him: take care of them wards, Mister Jarsper; don't make a pitch-pipe of them, Mister Jarsper.'

By the time that they have returned to the crypt, Durdles is in a drunken state – although the liquor produced by Datchery is unadulterated, the quantity consumed by Durdles is prodigious – and, as a result, reaches that state in which he is able to recall with clarity his dream on his night with Jasper: recall, and in beery reminiscence tell Datchery, who has been the recipient of so many confidences that evening.

'Durdles dreamed of lying there, asleep, and yet counting Mister Jarsper's footsteps as he walked to and fro, to and fro. Durdles dreamed that the footsteps died away, and that something touched Durdles, and that something fell from his hand. That something clinked and groped about. Then that Durdles was alone; and that when he came to, there was Mister Jarsper walking among the lanes of moonlight, beating his hands and feet. Then Durdles recalled his dream, looked down, and there was the key of the crypt door.'

'This is a most interesting dream,' says Datchery, most politely; and he is polite, indeed over-complimentary, because some might consider the dream a little thin in content. But that is the way with Datchery; he is always polite, and as a result learns what he wishes to learn, is told what he wishes to be told: a polite old fellow who gets his way, and beguilingly hears what he wants and needs to hear.

'A most interesting dream,' he repeats, 'and is that the same key which you have in your hand now?'

Durdles looks down blearily.

'Yes, that's it. That's the key to the small side-door into the crypt. Also opens the door at the top of the staircase from the crypt into the Cathedral. Durdles knows all these things, he does. Remembers them, he does.'

He struggles unsuccessfully with a recalcitrant outer pocket in his coat, breathing heavily the while, and swaying silently from side to side; tries the pocket of his trousers instead, and comes out with his two foot rule, which he abruptly rejects with a curse; and returns to his obstinate coat pocket, from which he finally and triumphantly brings out the cherished prize: another key.

'And this is the key for the door leading to the Tower steps: Durdles knows them all, better even than Mr Tope; and knows things that Tope don't know, that Tope isn't even aware of.' He attempts to tap the side of his stony nose with his stony index finger, but fails to make contact: which is better than managing to put it up his nostril or into his eye.

So Datchery is steadily building up his knowledge, both of the Cathedral and its secrets, and also of the night of that unaccountable expedition; and is doing so in the manner of a trained investigator, proceeding slowly and carefully, and advancing on a solid platform of knowledge and goodwill. Building on the goodwill, he thanks Durdles most warmly for a most interesting evening, intimates that he is ready to conclude their tour, and go to his bed, but only when Durdles has rested sufficiently, and is ready to make the journey home. How different from the terse impatience and the grudging tones of Jasper.

As if without thinking, he lifts Durdles's dinner bundle to a more convenient place on a piece of stone beside him; and, as he does so, comments on the weight. Surely this contains more than the remains of dinner? Another bottle, perhaps?

Durdles chuckles in the same beery manner, and proceeds to open the bundle in question. He does so carelessly, for his hands are shaking a little; and out pour, to his evident regret, some nameless substances which were the crumbled remains of his meal, and which will make a veritable feast for the mice of the place when the men have retired to their beds (or wherever Durdles chooses to take his rest that evening). Firmly at the bottom of the bundle, each in a separate fold, sit a number of keys, one considerably greater than its fellows. Durdles pulls it out in triumph.

'There it is: the Sapsea key. Of great size and weight. Like the Mayor himself.' He laughs loudly and inordinately at this witticism, for rather longer than is merited by the jest; and, having put himself in such good humour, hands the key to Datchery. 'There, feel the weight of that. Durdles keeps the keys by him, because he likes to admire his work,' he adds obscurely.

Thus honoured, Datchery takes the key and feels it softly. Softly, because Durdles likes to see keys well used and handled with care. Not picked up and played with, and idly examined and then ignored, and carelessly clinked and possibly damaged: but held in gentle and appreciative hands.

'That is as you suggest a mighty key. Would it be possible to feel the other two Cathedral keys: as a comparison, so that I can better judge the Sapsea key?' Always polite, always seeking permission, taking nothing for granted, or making Durdles feel uneasy.

Durdles takes the two keys, peers closely at them, and solemnly hands them over. 'That's for the crypt and upper door; and this one is for the tower. Durdles don't forget.'

Datchery takes them, still handling all the keys with the care and even reverence which Durdles clearly expects and appreciates. Satisfied that his charges are in safe and reverential hands, Durdles laboriously readies pockets and bundle to receive them back – for his movements are slow and sluggish tonight, as on all nights, and he has many pockets from which to choose – Datchery steals a close look at the keys in the light of the lantern. Yes, his sensitive fingers have not misled him, there is a trace of wax on the least-used of the three keys, the Sapsea key. He also looks with particular interest at the crypt key, as if trying to impress the details of its design on his memory. When Durdles is all prepared to take the keys back, he readily surrenders them, sees them stored safely back in their appropriate resting places, and they proceed out of the crypt together, locking the door behind them as they go.

There is no Deputy to greet them as they emerge into the open air: how Jasper would have preferred that to have been the case on his night with Durdles. Perhaps Deputy is unavoidably detained by his duties at the Travellers' Twopenny, though the precise nature of these remains a little hazy, to himself and others. Or perhaps he is away, out of the building, for his health, or busy stoning late travellers on the road, though most of mankind is long abed by now. Or perchance he is even taking a little rest himself, now that he is a busy person with two important jobs to perform: but, even were that the case, it is unlikely to extend to forty winks.

Whatever the reason for the absence of Deputy, Datchery bids goodnight to Durdles, who without the assistance of Deputy seems more inclined to attach himself to a convenient buttress of the Cathedral, and to take his rest there on his hind legs, rather than to make his way home, past the Monks' Vineyard, and the pile of quick-lime, and the stony lumber and the saws.

Datchery returns to his porch, looking back towards the Cathedral and castle as he does so. Night having long fallen, he cannot make out the buildings, but knows exactly where they are, and how they look. The stranger is now totally at home in Cloisterham, and fully at ease. It is no surprise that he has decided to see out the remains of his days in the town, in these familiar surroundings he know knows so well: as well as he knows all his near neighbours and their habits. And now he has an exact knowledge of the inside workings of the Cathedral, and of its sepulchral crypt and singular tower, and of its doors and keys and secret passages; and of much else besides.

He goes his way under the gatehouse and into his uncomfortable lodging beside the postern stair, and readies himself for sleep, for it is late, and he has much to do and think about the next day.

CHAPTER XXXII
Minor Discord in Minor Canon Corner

IT WAS A wet day in Cloisterham. The rain poured down in a steady stream, soaking the town and its streets and yards, soaking the castle on its eminence overlooking the river, soaking the Cathedral and its surrounding buildings and ruins. It poured down on the schools, including the seminary of Miss Twinkleton, which lay abandoned by its proud proprietress, who was still in London with Rosa; it tumbled down on the auctioneer's house, and dripped down the nose and whiskers of the effigy of Mr Sapsea's father; it gushed over the gate-house, though Jasper was so taken with his own thoughts that he scarcely noticed; it so insistently pelted down on the Travellers' Twopenny that even the urchins of that hospitable hostelry were forced to remain within; it spared nothing that existed on the face of Cloisterham's rich earth; and, ultimately, it found its sinuous way through subterranean streams and passages and channels down into the tombs and graves lying beneath the town.

Fields and gardens were sodden, and the rich Summer vegetation flattened, by this early harbinger of Autumn. At the best of times, the town tended towards an earthy and somewhat damp flavour, which came seeping out of the crypt, out of the ruined walls, out of the old 'uns, out of Durdles; an ancient, mouldy, chilly kind of flavour; and this was accentuated on wet days such as this. The resulting miasma lay heavily on the town, its buildings and its inhabitants; and few possessed the necessary spirit or valour to rise above the diluvian conditions, challenge the weather, and, in effect, say, 'Do your worst, I shall go about my business, and will not be dissuaded from making the best of matters.'

Even Mr Sapsea was for once not raised up by the thought of his own remarkable profundity, but sat slumped in his dull ground-floor sitting-room, looking gloomily at his portrait, his eight-day clock and his weather-glass. It is a rare day indeed that these household gods fail to remind him of his superiority to the rest of mankind, but on this day they did not succeed. The weather-glass appeared to be in especial disfavour, perhaps because it had proved deficient in warning him of this

316

day of rain and flood; from time to time he glared at it, and occasionally shook his finger at it, as if to remind it of its scientific and informative duties, tutting magisterially as he did so. He might have been tempted to tap it sharply in punishment, but for his suspicion that the mercury might sink to new depths in retaliation. The eight-day clock, which served to remind him how slowly time was passing on such a dismal morning, was largely ignored for that reason. Instead, Mr Sapsea had put his trust in the decanter of port; and while no challenger to the drinking powers of Durdles, and generally more sociable than the stony one in his drinking habits, regarding the ceremony of drawing forth the glasses as another occasion to hold forth, had already taken off a glass or more.

Mr Sapsea also cast the occasional glance towards a book lying in his ample lap, which seemed to revive his spirits. Now it was unusual for Mr Sapsea to be seen with a book in his possession, for he was not of the reading tendency, and preferred to pluck his knowledge straight out of the ambient air, or dredge it from the deep recesses of his four-square head, rather than look to an author to deliver it into his keeping. He even had a marked liking for drawing attention to this feature of his character, and make it part of his regular presentations on Sapseaship, which he was ready to give to anyone who had time and inclination, and to some who had neither: 'Authors, Sir! Books, Sir! I don't need 'em, and I don't trust 'em. If I want a fact, I think about it, and there, it comes into my mind. If I need an argument, it's the same: I think about it, and it springs conveniently into my mouth. As to judgement: that, Sir, is already resting in my brain, ready to burst forth.'

But this book was different. It consisted, not of dull print, the work of impenetrable authors, but of instructive pictures, the fruit of esteemed portraitists: copies of the likenesses of politicians, statesmen, and Ministers, even Prime Ministers: for Mr Sapsea had quite given up copying the Dean (no Very Reverends in the Mayor's thoughts now), or thinking him a proper object for study. As leader of the State party in the town, he now sought his models in the lay hierarchy; and who better than a Prime Minister to lead the way in dress as in politics? In his person, and in his attire, Mr Sapsea was now at the forefront of the anti-religious establishment; and even in the auction-house, wielding his gavel, the pulpit manner had become the dispatch box manner, and he eyed his potential purchasers as a Minister stares at his back-benchers, rather than as an Archbishop regards his congregation: though heckling was still considered quite beyond the pale.

Mr Sapsea's eye fell on his own portrait, and despite himself he winced.

He could not conceal the fact that there was something undeniably – well – ecclesiastical about it: the hand half-raised as if in benediction, the collar which hinted at priestly garb, the look of a man bowing slightly before his maker. It dated from the days when he had worshipped at the shrine of the Dean, and reflected this: the days of his servitude, his slavery, his Babylonian captivity, before his deliverance and glorious exodus. Well, his mind was finally made up: he would have another portrait painted: no, two, one for his sitting-room, and one for his office: portraits of Sapsea as Mayor, Sapsea as English bulldog, Sapsea in full temporal regalia. Despite the day, he swelled with pride and self-aggrandisement. Finally he bestirred himself, rose to his feet, raised both arms, and bodily lifted the picture down from the wall: before reseating himself, breathing heavily with the effort.

Elsewhere in the town the spirits of the townspeople fell as steadily as the rain and their barometers. The single pawnbroker looked wearily and morosely at his unredeemed stock, and seemed ready to wring the neck of the stuffed parrot which had stood on its perch in the back of his shop for many years. The jeweller despaired of custom, and fell to day-dreaming about a world in which the Elephant and Castle carried a stream of eager purchasers to his door, perhaps even including the diminutive Rosa, all coming to hear and follow his advice on what personal items of jewellery they should wear – for in his view Cloisterham did not boast many salesman such as he. The Topes sat silently in their rooms, she darning an item for Jasper, he appearing to be lost in deep study, but in fact turning over in his mind not very much of little moment. Even Datchery had drawn his chair back by a few paces, to avoid the downpour, but otherwise remained on his watch: not that there was much to watch that rainsodden morning.

Normally, when there is gloom or dullness or nothingness (or nothing more than Sapseaship) in Cloisterham, there is an exception in Minor Canon Corner. The healthy countenance of Septimus Crisparkle generally exudes liveliness and kindness, while the face of the china shepherdess is bright, cheerful and calm. But, for once, on this day, even Minor Canon Corner had not escaped a touch of the prevailing gloom. The two had just finished their breakfast, and should have been enjoying their usual degree of tranquility; but, despite the loving and mutually affectionate glances, there was the slightest whiff of discord, of grapeshot, in the air, and Mrs Crisparkle was addressing her crochet work in a particularly determined manner.

This was all the more curious since all the ingredients for their usual harmony were present. The brisk early morning walk and refreshing swim (for Septimus Crisparkle is not a man to be deterred by a few drops of rain from taking exercise) had been followed by a bout of fisticuffs, all of which left him in excellent fettle, and ready to do justice to an ample breakfast; grace had been said by Mrs Crisparkle; ham, eggs and toast had been consumed in a generous quantity, at least by the Minor Canon; Mrs Crisparkle had presided over the tea-urn, and served the Superior Family Souchong to both of them. So what could have gone wrong, what could have come between this contented pair?

The serpent had entered the Garden of Eden; a small serpent, it has to be admitted, and notably lacking in venom; but still a serpent – at least in the critical gaze of Mrs Crisparkle. Septimus Crisparkle had made the mistake of mentioning Helena Landless, and compounded his error by praising her qualities: her character, her nobility, even her beauty.

Mrs Crisparkle stiffened, and her lips tightened; her cap unmistakably vibrated. She looked less like a china shepherdess, than a flesh-and-blood shepherdess whose sheep had been caught misbehaving in Arcadia and were about to feel the full effect of her disapproval.

'But, Sept dear, she is the accomplice of that murderous wretch who has brought so much sadness to poor Mr Jasper – Mr Jasper who has always taken infinite pains for me, and cared so much for my feelings. Why, I remember him telling me about the drunken – the drunken brawl, for I can call it nothing else, that night when you would have said nothing to me. She stands by her brother, and zealously defends his innocence, against all the evidence assembled by dear Mr Jasper.'

'But Ma dear,' said Septimus lightly, 'there is no evidence against Neville.'

'He came home in a drunken state that first evening, bringing dishonour upon himself and this house, and that's enough for me. And it should be enough for you, but that you are foolishly fond of the boy, Sept dear.' She tossed her head, and the cap vibrated again, more vigorously this time. This boded ill for her ensuing comments, which were not long in coming.

'As for beauty, her complexion is close to that of a female Ethiope.' There could be no doubting to whom the *her* referred, and the train of thought, though no name was mentioned. It was highly unlikely that Mrs Crisparkle, in the secluded recesses of Minor Canon Corner, had ever seen an Ethiope, male or female; but she knew her Shakespeare, and this also gave her her next line of attack: for she was determined to defend her Sept against the wiles of the dusky enchantress, and would do what she could to arm him against her seductive charms.

'And the leopardess cannot and does not change her spots. She has completely thrown in her lot with her brother, leaving the comfortable quarters offered by Miss Twinkleton at the Nuns' House – which we took the trouble to arrange, Sept, which we managed for her – in order to join her brutish brother in London. Shame on her!' She took the hooked needle firmly in her right hand, and pulled the yarn in a determined and meaningful manner, as if dealing with a recalcitrant Landless, or indeed a pair of them.

Septimus Crisparkle, whose cheeks were always of healthy hue, and who had become yet ruddier as his mother offered her thoughts on Helena, rubbed his ear vigorously, and then gently attempted to guide the conversation, which was in danger of spiralling out of control.

'But, Ma dear, that shows the nobility of which I spoke. She has gone to help her brother. Neville is suffering, he is weak, he is in declining health. She has gone to minister to him, to breathe new life into him, to strengthen him.'

'Sept, dear, I cannot believe my ears.' She obviously felt the need to clear those decorative pieces of chinawork, since she again tossed her head so strongly that the cap shook like the crest on an affronted peahen. 'Why should anyone wish to strengthen Landless? Bless me, Sept, everyone knows of his diabolical strength. Poor Mr Jasper has testified to this many times, and to the difficulty he had in prising the knife from his grasp before it was repeatedly thrust into poor Edwin Drood.' Clearly the tale of that ominous night has gained in the telling; how many times has the cook, now almost an eye-witness, gone over and improved and embellished the details? 'I must add that that poor gentleman, despite all his torments and sufferings, remains the soul of politeness to me, and is ever most obliging. It is a matter of great regret to me, Sept, that you have become so distant from Mr Jasper. It is quite as if that black temptress and her brother have established some kind of hold over you,' she saw him stir impatiently, and added: 'it is because of your kindness and charity, dear Sept. Sometimes I think that you are too good for this wicked world. You spread bounty wherever you go, but you are too indiscriminate, too indiscriminate.' She took his hand and squeezed it affectionately. But this did not deter her from her headlong pursuit of supposed sins to attribute to the Landlesses.

'I had almost forgotten, now it appears that she has dragged Rosa after her to London. The cook at the Nuns' House, who is an admirable woman, and remarkably well-informed for someone who spends most of her life in a kitchen, told me this last week.' Septimus strongly suspected that cook was a lady of remarkable imaginative powers, and, not to put too fine a point on it, was guilty of "making up" many of her revelations; but did not wish to further strain matters in Minor Canon Corner, so wisely kept such heresies to himself. 'Cook said that Rosa had upped and gone: those were her very words. With poor Rosa in London, and close to Landless who has openly boasted of his so-called love for her, who knows what influences and iniquities and infamies she is exposed to.' A vigorous nod accompanied each of these nouns, listed in ascending order of dishonour, to press home the points of the indictment.

Despite himself, and the tenor of the exchange, Septimus Crisparkle could not but be amused as Mrs Crisparkle piled Pelion on Ossa in this heroic manner.

'Ma, dear, I know the reason for Rosa's sudden departure for London. It has no connection with the Landlesses, and casts no shadow on them: rather the reverse, since Miss Landless has been most kind and solicitous to Rosa there. Landless is, I believe, aware of her presence in London, but certainly has not seen her, or even attempted to do so. Additionally, and perhaps the cook, who is sometimes – er – absent-minded, in story-telling if not in cooking, forgot to tell you of this, Miss Twinkleton has herself moved to London, to act as Rosa's companion, mentor and chaperone.'

If he thought that reasoned argument would make headway, he has quite misjudged the matter.

'Well, *I*,' she accentuated the personal pronoun, '*I* don't know the reason for Rosa's removal to London, and fear the worst. And, look, you've made me pull the needle too hard.'

After a brief pause, Septimus Crisparkle, a doughty fighter for truth, as well as a lover of peace and concord, tried again. 'Ma, I remember you telling me that she,' again, there was no doubt who the *she* was, 'had an influence over her brother, implying that this was for the good, and that I should praise her for this. This is what I am doing now, yet still appear to be in the wrong in your eyes.'

'Bless me, Sept, bless me, you don't understand the matter. As I said, you are simply too generous-hearted for this world. It is all a matter of degree. Even if she is better than him, it does not follow that she is good. If this plate,' she pointed to hers, 'is cleaner than its fellow,' she pointed to his, 'it does not mean that we should put it out unwashed when the Very Reverend the Dean comes to dinner. Also, it may be the case that he has some evil counter-influence over her.'

Sensing difficulties, and acknowledging that Septimus was probably her superior in analogy and logic, she did not attempt to repeat her parallel with the plates, and left her argument hanging there: or almost there.

'That is often the case with these natives. Cook says that their ways can be imponderable. At least, I think that was what she said. That is why it is better to keep them abroad, in Ceylon. I can't think what Mr Honeythunder was up to in bringing them to Cloisterham; and quite spoiling our supper party,' she added illogically.

The discussion was at an end. Septimus Crisparkle pondered the matter; he foresaw difficult times ahead; and he had not even responded to his mother's animadversions on the subject of complexion.

To help leave the subject behind them, Septimus Crisparkle reached for the morning newspaper; not in any attempt to exclude his mother, or avoid her gaze, but precisely to include her in a new and different activity. He also reached therefore for his large, ridiculous, and above all ineffective spectacles; and indulged in a little play-acting. He peered at the paper, and attempted to read out a brief paragraph: but, abandoning the effort, and blaming the font, or type, or the size of the print, he passed the article to his mother for further elucidation. She remained troubled by their conversation, and could not so readily put it behind her. She was very settled in her views, and not easily persuaded, or persuadable at all; and could sense that, in this instance, the same was true of Septimus, however easy and amiable his manner.

She did not therefore immediately accept the proferred olive-branch, but gave it as her opinion that she detected some hint of malaise or even fever in her son, probably as a result of swimming on a day when so much water abounded everywhere. She was deaf to Septimus's jest that, precisely because the day was as it was, swimming made no difference, and certainly made him no wetter. She remained of the opinion that he was slightly fevered, and therefore prepared him an infusion from the egregious medicinal herb-closet on the upper staircase-landing. He could not tell what mixture of nauseous ingredients it comprised from that herbal penitentiary, but saw it mixed before his eyes with the equanimity of an early Christian facing a lion, drank it down manfully and good-naturedly, felt that he had paid his penance for disagreeing with the china shepherdess, and set out resolutely through the teeming rain to the Cathedral.

She watched him go, walking at his usual rapid pace, paying no heed to the weather, but again as usual ready to show every consideration to anyone he passed on his way, essaying a few lines of his favourite choral music as he went. She watched him until he passed out of sight, at which point she felt the force of his absence, and even regretted the strength of some of her assertions in their exchange: while, of course, remaining of the view that she was totally in the right. Nevertheless she determined to go to the Nuns' House, and learn more of the departure of Rosa and then Miss Twinkleton: from Mrs Tisher, mind, Mrs Tisher – she would not demean herself by gossiping with the cook. But, of course, if she happened to see the cook, or pass her on the stairs, on the way in or out, it would be highly impolite not to speak to her, or pass the time of day, or ask after Miss Twinkleton: highly impolite, and not to be thought of. Not that she felt for a minute that she might be in the wrong about Miss Landless, mind you. Certainly not in the wrong; but it would be well to confirm her assessment from other sources. The cap vibrated slightly as she nodded her agreement to this prudent course of action.

For his part, as he went, Septimus knew that a vigorous walk would clear his head, and allow him to think his thoughts; and think of – well, no matter, let him think, let The Reverend Septimus Crisparkle, Minor Canon, devoted Christian, genuine philanthropist, guide and mentor, good man, good son – and, who knows, good husband and good father – let him think what and as he wishes.

CHAPTER XXXIII
The Riddle of the Keys

DICK DATCHERY, ELDERLY gentleman, retired from public life, benign old buffer by temperament and disposition, settler in Cloisterham, was seated in his porch, doing as he always did: seeing, looking, observing; and, on this occasion, also ruminating. Ruminating about the keys: the keys which interested Jasper: and which therefore also interested him: ruminating and deducing.

The starting point for his deductions was that Jasper had taken three keys from Durdles that night in the crypt, while Durdles was lying in drunken stupor: the key to the crypt door from his incapable hand, the key to the tower from his unguarded pocket, and the Sapsea key out of his unattended dinner bundle; that he had taken the keys away and made wax impressions of them, while Durdles slept; that he had then returned two of the keys to their resting places, and left the crypt key on the ground by Durdles, as if it had fallen from his hand; and then patiently waited for Durdles to regain consciousness naturally, wakened by the shift in the light of the moon: patiently waited, walking among the lanes of moonlight, beating his hands and feet to keep out the bitter cold.

Where had he made the wax impressions? The most likely theory was that he had slipped back to the gate-house, still moving silently and slyly through the night, and made them there: hence his later acute fear that he might have been seen by Deputy when on his way there or back, or even engaged in this work: he had not reckoned on anyone being awake and at large at that hour. Once he had the wax impressions, he could have had copies made in London, on one of his journeys there, or in Maidstone; far too risky to use one of the locksmiths in Cloisterham itself.

So the question which Datchery now posed himself was: where were those copies now? He drew a professional distinction between these. Jasper had absolutely no right to the Sapsea key, which Datchery sensed was somehow central to the mystery. If the two Cathedral keys were found in his possession, this would occasion less surprise and comment; Jasper could claim that they had been handed him by his predecessor some five years previously, since it was considered useful for the Choirmaster to have duplicate copies in case of necessity. Jasper could even claim that he had not seen the reason for this, but had not questioned it at the time, and had not used the keys subsequently.

Datchery developed these two lines of speculation. Jasper's deliberate theft of the unmistakable Sapsea key, which if found on him would immediately have given away whatever game he was playing, and led to enquiries and investigations, suggested that he had a specific reason for taking it, and further that, once used, it would surely be jettisoned. There was probably no need to keep it, and every reason not to. There being no such requirement to dispose of the Cathedral keys, they were probably hidden somewhere to which Jasper had regular access. Who knows, he might have considered that they could even prove to be of further use to him.

Datchery again checked his deductions, and discovered a further point. If it was correct that the Sapsea key was to be used once, and then disposed of, then it followed that Jasper had utilised it to dispose of something for which he had no further use, to exploit the tomb for something he wished to be rid of.

So where were the copies now? First, where might Jasper have disposed of the Sapsea key, hoping that it would never be recovered? Someone, probably Jasper, had tried to rid themselves and the world of Drood's watch, chain and pin by throwing them into the river, in Cloisterham Mill; and would have succeeded, but for the sharp eye, swimming prowess and super-human perseverance of the Minor Canon. The great Sapsea key was far heavier than a shirt-pin, and would have sunk deeper into the thick mud at the bottom of the pool. It could well have escaped the despairing clutches of Septimus Crisparkle, however supple his long fingers, as he repeatedly dived into the murky waters. In any case, the Minor Canon had been looking for a body, not a key: the pin had been but a chance discovery.

As for the Cathedral keys, Jasper was unlikely to have hidden these in his rooms. Mrs Tope was an enthusiastic cleaner and tidier; and, given her husband's employment, she might even have recognised the keys. Moreover, why take unnecessary risks. Jasper did not need to keep the keys close to him, in a place where his ownership was obvious. There were many places to which he had ready access, but where his involvement would be easily deniable, if necessary.

Datchery put his imagination to work: possibly in the Cathedral itself, for example; somewhere in the chancel, perhaps; possibly in the very choir stalls, where Jasper often resorted for practice, chanting out the choir music in a low and beautiful tone, rolling out the notes in his deep, dark, velvety voice; the sounds of a man in a state of grace, with perfect pitch and balance, with nothing on his conscience; just feeling the unutterable sadness of the loss of his nephew; and where, as he sang, he could lean down, without a break in the harmony, to feel where he has hidden the valuable keys, just in case he needed them again, and to check that they were still safely there.

Early the next day, Datchery forsook his place in his porch, and set off on a fishing expedition. He was not, however, carrying rod, line and hook, but what looked like a large powerful magnet, and a length of twine – concealed under his coat. He set off from town down the long High Street; but then, observing that he was not being attended or followed, and was on his own, he veered off towards Cloisterham Mill. He was hatless, and his white locks were flowing in the breeze, and he was enjoying himself; he strode along, rather more briskly than his normal pace around the town, and he sang to himself as he went. The singer may have been confused: "A-hunting we will go" is not normally sung to the familiar tune of Widdicombe Fair, and down-alongs and out-alongs tended to intrude; but he did not care. Knowing that he was unobserved, and off duty, he was determined to make the most of the late summer's day, and his release from his porch of duty. He was glad to be active, and to be on the trail of something specific, after the long days of looking and watching and observing and thinking: fruitful though these had proved.

Out of town, as he went, there were fields and meadows, and herds and flocks, and hens and horses, and paths and rides, and birds and insects. Nature was singing and buzzing and humming and lowing and neighing and clucking. Alongside him, as he made his way towards the Mill, he occasionally caught sight of the river, itself abundant with life and movement. Above was the blue sky, and the unthreatening clouds, and above all the sun. He thought to himself with amusement: what a joy on such a day to be alive, and to be a buffer was very Heaven.

He reached the Mill, and looked down into the deep, glistening waters: wondering at the abilities of the Minor Canon, who had repeatedly dived into those waters at the coldest time of the year, and come up with his trophies; but not tempted to emulate him, even on a benign Summer's morning. Instead, he took his place on the bank, at the far side, so that he could see if anyone approached, tied his magnet on his twine, and started to pull the magnet over the bottom of the water.

It proved a lengthy search. The sun beat down upon him, and those insects began to annoy. He grew hot, and cursed his long white hair: surely a barber should have been requested to reduce those flowing locks, in honour of the Summer months. Suddenly, the thought of his cool and shaded porch became more attractive; but he toiled on.

Repeatedly he felt his magnet attract something from the depths, and pulled it in, but always in vain. How many generations had thrown away, or lost, or overlooked some trifle which then somehow found its way to the bottom of the Mill pond. Everyone who had passed through or stopped in Cloisterham seemed to have carelessly disposed of or abandoned something with metal in it. Soldiers had parted company with daggers, stonemasons with chisels, abbesses with trinkets, monks with rosaries, adventurers with compasses (like Sir Cloudesley's): here was the detritus of centuries, the testament to Cloisterham's long and often dramatic history: here was the treasury of the past, the relics of the old 'uns methodically divined by Durdles, and whose dust formed such a prominent part of the topography and the atmosphere of the place; and all was lying in the depths of Cloisterham Mill, deep down in the thick mud, to be discovered and liberated by Datchery.

The pile of odds and ends beside Datchery grew, and he grew weary. Then, finally, his magnet seized another prize, and he drew it up; and it proved to be a key, a great key. It was a key which asserted itself, a key which made a statement about its owner, which proclaimed his importance and prestige, which called the world to take note. It was the identical twin of the great Sapsea key; by rights, Datchery should have seen this, and with a blush retired; but he didn't. He landed it, pulled it off his magnet, and his search was ended.

Without ceremony or regret, he pushed the remainder of his haul back into the Mill – Alberich or the Rhine Maidens could dispute over ownership of this treasure trove for as long as they wished, for all he minded – and picked up the jewel he wanted, the key. Not having his dinner bundle handy, nor indeed, possessing one at all, he put the key in his right-hand pocket, and with considerable satisfaction – for the old buffer with the white mop of hair had had a long, tiring, but eventually successful day – he set off back to town and his beloved porch.

But, having regained his lodging, and safely hidden the key, he did not immediately resume his station upon the porch. Instead, he headed for the Cathedral: enjoying himself, taking his ease, not hurrying: an elderly gentleman luxuriating in the beauties of his surroundings, his chosen place of retreat, the town where he had retired and was planning to see out his days. He greeted his good friend Mr Tope, and asked whether the latter might be able to assist him. The fact was that there was a minor patch of damp in his inner room. He knew little of these matters. Could Mr Tope, whose views he greatly respected, and whose knowledge of these affairs was well-attested in the town, possibly advise and give his valued opinion.

Tope bustled off in a self-important manner. Datchery observed him depart, then hastened into the Cathedral, strolled down the nave and ascended the steps into the choir. Here, shielded from view by the handsome stone screen, he immediately turned to the side, and made for the choir-stalls, knowing from his previous visit the very place where the Choir-Master would sit, remembering seeing Jasper chanting and singing, musically fervid, and all unconscious of the Princess shaking her skinny fist at him from behind the shelter of a pillar.

Safe from scrutiny, Datchery looked around, fingered some promising-looking pieces of paneling, discovered nothing, then felt instead with his foot, found a loose board, cautiously pulled it up and to the side, and saw a couple of keys resting in their hiding place. He examined them closely, was convinced by detailed scrutiny that one was the key to the side-door of the crypt, and replaced them carefully for safe-keeping (the crypt key deliberately placed to the left, for ease of recognition and recovery), in case Jasper regularly checked the contents of his make-shift safe. He then slipped the board back into position with his nimble (and surprisingly young-looking) fingers.

He returned to the day light, outside the Cathedral, just as Tope also returned, loudly opining that the damp was a minor affair, and not worth bothering about, and would not inconvenience Mr Datchery in the least. He said this in a slightly pitying tone, as if addressing an ignorant and unworldly incompetent. Who knew little of life or damp or water.

Datchery, ever polite and considerate, made a point of thanking Tope profusely, and in particular remarking on his helpfulness, and highlighting his gratitude and the debt he owed. Tope had an uneasy sense that he was being overpaid, and that he had possibly appeared a little dismissive of Datchery's concerns.

Safely back in his inconvenient room, Dick Datchery opened his corner-cupboard in a satisfied kind of way. He took the chalk from the shelf, and painstakingly added another thick line to his growing score.

Another thick line, which extended from top to bottom of the board, and which added to the pattern which was starting to take shape: it was starting to resemble a set of iron bars, such as are placed on the windows of prisoners: or, with cross-markings added, a portcullis, such as prevents an escape from jail: or a whole series of gallows, placed side by side, as if for a multitude of executions. A multitude: or just one?

CHAPTER XXXIV
The Secrets of the Ring

THE NEXT DAY, Datchery attends evening service in the Cathedral. He sits in the stall from which he had viewed both Jasper and the Princess, and from that vantage point observes the paucity of the congregation. Despite the general emptiness of the place, and the feeling that many exciting events must be taking place elsewhere in Cloisterham, which have drawn the crowds away, the choir, led by the illustrious Choir-Master, are outstanding in harmony and diction. They tell the world that The Lord hath put down the mighty from their seat; and hath exalted the humble and meek; that He hath filled the hungry with good things; and that the rich He hath sent empty away. The words ring out through the Cathedral, around the close, across the town: and the insistent, deep, dark voice of Jasper is ever-present: perhaps just a shade too insistent and dark and deep and ever-present.

After the service is ended, Datchery comes across to congratulate the Choir-Master. The latter is a little hasty in his acknowledgement, but the whole town knows that the poor gentleman is not himself, because of the disappearance of his nephew several months ago, and the suspicions which attach to a foreigner, a dark stranger from Ceylon, who spent a little time in the town, but who is now gone.

Mr Datchery certainly must know it, because he does not seem to mind Jasper's rather less than fulsome reaction to his words of praise, does not turn on his heel and walk away from the place, but nods after the Choir Master as the latter leaves first. He then lingers in the choir, the very picture of a man with time on his hands, taking in his surroundings, admiring the high altar, the carved choir-stalls, the wall decorations of leopards and fleur-de-lys, and the fine floor: hands clasped behind his back, whistling very gently and tunelessly to himself as he goes, with just a hint of Uncle Tom Cobley and all, occasionally peering forward.

He even takes a pace or two up the steps of the stalls, and seems to look very closely at something which has caught his attention: another piece of carving, perhaps, a veneer, or even something let into the floor. Whatever it is, his hands unclasp and reach forward, as if possibly removing something – perhaps a layer of dust – to view it better; then they clasp again behind his back, but not before the left hand has dropped something into his left pocket; then he quickly stands up and looks around, looking for someone perhaps; no, he continues to look round him at the wonders of wood and stone-work, then slowly and deliberately heads for the Great West Door, like an elderly sort of fellow (with something of a military air about him) taking his time and enjoying himself. He again unclasps his hands, the better to greet Mr Tope as he finally goes out, and feels for something in his right pocket; probably a handkerchief, no it is coins for the poor-box from the kind old gentleman; finally bids farewell to Tope, and hopes he has not kept him; and leaves for his lodging, the key to the side-door of the crypt safely on his person.

Why only the key to the crypt? Why not the key allowing access to the mighty tower? Because his work tonight is not up in the skies, in the heavens, looking down on the sleeping town, and the townspeople; his work is down on earth, beneath the earth, down in the musty recesses of the town, among the dust and the dirt, among the old 'uns and the odour of death and decay.

He sits on his porch, and observes and watches and listens and waits: above all, he listens and he waits. He listens as the cawing of the rooks gradually dies away as they settle for the night in the elms and in the roof and tower of the Cathedral. He listens as the Cathedral clock regularly strikes the quarter-hours. He waits as he watches the moon rise, and begin to spread the softness of its gentle beams across the town. He waits as the lights of the houses gradually go out as the good people – yes, and the bad, too – retire to their beds. He waits as he senses that Jasper has turned in for the night, prepared to be visited by who knows what dreams and visions and images; he believes that he hears his feet stumble slightly as he goes up his stairs, possibly carrying a curious looking pipe, to assist his slumbers, and perhaps bring a feeling of release from the cares of the world; he sees that Jasper has left that red light burning, as it has burned for so many nights, including on the night of the great storm and of the disappearance of Drood, burning steadily all night in the lighthouse.

He waits as he hears the Topes heading for the matrimonial couch, and before too long he hears the somnolent snoring of Tope; no visions or interrupted slumber for him, just deep contentment as he unconsciously contemplates his comfortable existence, his easy relations with the

Dean (even in his dreams he remembers to add The Very Reverend the Dean), his superiority to bumbling incompetents such as Datchery (no Mr appended), who know not the first thing about damp, or water, or gutters or drains.

He waits as the stars become brighter, and as the moon rises loftily in the sky. The whole firmament looks down upon little Cloisterham, insignificant in its nook by the river, scarce big enough to support its mighty Cathedral. The powerful moonlight creates a pattern of light and shade, an outline of black and white; it is a monochrome of a town, a chiaroscuro mosaic of a town.

He still waits. He waits until he hears the sounds of Deputy stoning Durdles home; first he catches a snatch of 'Widdy, widdy, wen! I ketches 'im out arter ten,' which then fades away into the darkness, and hears the receding noise of smartly-thrown stones hitting their prescribed target with a dull thud as the pair go their way, providing Deputy with an enlightened object in his life as prescribed by the philanthropic Durdles: it being a curious fact how little philanthropy emanates from The Haven, despite the proliferation of beetle-browed Professors, and how much from other unlikely sources.

Then he moves. Now is his chance for observant and unobserved investigation. The night is quiet, with the moon providing sufficient light to assist him find his way, though he carries a lantern to help him through any darker passages. Tonight, it is his turn to tread softly and silently. Why does he do this? And why does he head for the crypt, which should surely be left for the undisturbed slumber of the old 'uns at this time of night? What if they wake, and resent the intruder? What if those bodies, or their spirits, summon their long-hushed voices, hoarse from the dust and the damp, and call on him to stop, to be gone from their presence, and not return? What if they wake the dogs, or the town, or Jasper?

On Datchery glides. He moves nimbly for someone blessed with such a shock of white hair. He produces the key from his left pocket, opens the door of the crypt, and descends the stairs into the darkness. At the bottom he carefully lights his lantern, for his way is partly obscured. He moves forward past the little underground chapel; his path lies among the dead ones; no longer meeting promiscuous with crook and mitre; but just lying in their tombs, ready to crumble at the sight of Durdles in their midst: or of Datchery, if he has designs upon their tombs. But he has only one tomb in his mind, and it is not the tomb of an old 'un. It is of someone recently interred, who through the munificence of her husband has a fine tomb, and an even finer inscription. The lucky woman is greatly blessed, in death as in life.

Datchery looks around him, and listens carefully; then opens the Sapsea tomb with the great key, and peers within. The odour of death and decay, ever-present in the dank air of the crypt, is infinitely more oppressive in this confined space, but Datchery does not permit himself to be deterred from his task.

At the back of the tomb is the place of the coffin which contains the mortal remains of the fortunate Ethelinda Sapsea nee Brobity; her mouth possibly still shaped to breathe the reverential words "O Thou", as if in permanent appreciation of the fact that Mr Sapsea's eye had lighted upon this humble handmaiden; or possibly ready to rebuke a retiring and blushing stranger.

Towards the front of the tomb, at the side, is a bundle of something: possibly some rubbish left by Durdles, or more probably Durdles's men, since Durdles seldom dirties his hands with manual labour: it remaining a mystery to one and all how he has acquired that stony look and colour and texture when he spends so little time sawing or chipping or chiselling the raw product.

Datchery puts his lantern inside the tomb and takes a closer look at the strange and obtrusive bundle. He is saddened, but not surprised. He sees a lipless mouth gaping at him; a pair of empty sockets staring at him, nothing but a slit where a nose should be. He sees a tumble of bones. He sees a body, or rather what remains of a body. It looks as if some agent, possibly lime, has removed flesh and clothes, apart from a few scraps of loosely-hanging flesh. But it has left – what? Something previously hidden, well protected from human eyes by clothing: clothing now pitilessly eaten away and consumed by the voracious lime. It glints brightly at him from among the decay and destruction all around. It is a ring; a lady's ring; a rose of diamonds and rubies delicately set in gold – how brightly those cruel stones shine; a ring, but not on a finger, set on a skeletal hand; it is just lying among the bones; perhaps it had fallen from a finger as the flesh was eaten away; or possibly it had been in a pocket, an inside pocket for protection, for safe keeping, before the owner could protect it no longer, could no longer keep it safe, because the owner was dead, disposed of and eaten by lime.

Datchery puts his handkerchief over the palm of his hand, leans forward, takes the ring, wraps it, and puts it carefully into his inside pocket: a methodical man, Datchery, and well-suited for the task he had been given.

He turns his attention to the bones. They themselves are as yet unaffected by the lime. Whoever had poured it on had not the trick of stirring it. So they survive to tell their tale, whatever that tale may be, assisted by the ring as a material witness. But what is this? Maybe they have more to tell than had immediately struck Datchery; for now he looks more closely he notices that there is a further mystery in this terrible tomb, this tomb of two corpses, of double death. For the bones are sadly broken and disarranged. This is not the work of quick-lime. It looks as if the owner of the bones has been attacked by a mad assailant, with manic strength: attacked, and beaten, and crushed.

A crazed attack: these things cannot be done quietly, especially in a small, peaceful, sleepy old town like Cloisterham; surely the victim would have shouted out, screamed for help, alerted the neighbours, tried to raise the town; surely there would have been noise, and confusion and struggle; surely this would have been audible, even if done on the night of the great storm.

Here is a new and unexpected puzzle. In discovering the body, and finding a clue, he has unearthed an even larger mystery. He may have moved two paces forward; but this is a decisive step backward. Yet he has resources to call upon; the time has come for a meeting with Hiram Grewgious; a meeting with Grewgious and Septimus Crisparkle, since Grewgious had brought the latter into the picture, and clearly trusted and valued him.

Satisfied with this plan, if not with the entirety of his night's work, Datchery locks the tomb, retraces his steps, emerges cautiously into the night air, looks around for any sign of Deputy but finds none, locks the crypt door, and makes his silent way back to his lodging. He takes up his chalk, and marks a slightly wavering line, of no great length or conviction, on the wall: he has made the progress he expected, and also found that gleaming ring, which he did not expect; but, above all, he is puzzled and worried by the condition of the body. He did not expect that: what did it mean?

He takes out the ring, and inspects it: as if it will bring enlightenment. Perhaps it does, now he has time and opportunity to think about it in a cool manner, away from the crypt and the old 'uns and the terrible tomb; for he nods his head once or twice, and looks more satisfied. But then he is once more oppressed by thinking of those bones, those broken and disfigured bones.

The following morning he strolls to the Cathedral, easily escapes the attention of Tope, who is grandly supervising the cleaning of the Lady Chapel, and returns the crypt key to its hiding place, nestling again beside its fellow, to the left.

The Sapsea key is hidden away behind Datchery's corner cupboard, safe from discovery, and ready to be put to further use when required.

For Datchery is now ready to act on what he has discovered, and equally on what he has not yet discovered: primed for action, and prepared to share with others the results of his findings, including the mystery of those shattered bones. Perhaps they will help him find the answer – or possibly the answers.

* M *

CHAPTER XXXV
The Gospel Makers

EARLY THE NEXT day, well before the town was stirring, Datchery walked down to Minor Canon Corner. He knew that it was Crisparkle's custom, before the rest of mankind was awake, to stride down to some part of the neighbourhood by the river, and submit his rosy forehead, rapidly followed by the remainder of his healthy body, to the waters of Kent; and he planned to fall in with him on his return. He was not misinformed; and, like a prescient highwayman, his planning was amply rewarded; he saw the Minor Canon coming up from the river, aglow with health, with still some signs of the dampness which he had failed to towel off in his haste not to disappoint his mother by appearing late for their daily ritual of breakfast.

As he came, the Harmonious Canon sang melodiously to himself:

'Like kidlings blithe and merry, like ki-i-dlings bli-ithe and me-e-erry, O ruddier than the cherry – ' but paused politely when he saw the waiting figure.

Seeing that Crisparkle was in something of a hurry, Datchery came straight to the point.

'Sir, we have not met, but I know who you are, and your reputation. I believe that you know of my role, and purpose; and who I work for, and why.'

Crisparkle halted politely, extended his hand in greeting, and was careful to betray no hint that he might be in haste.

'Why, Mr Datchery,' he returned, 'we are most expeditiously acquainted. This is extremely welcome. I did not seek you out before, because I did not wish to intrude or in any way compromise your work. What can I do to assist you now?'

'I have important information for you and Mr Grewgious; a clue, but also a puzzle,' answered Datchery with a slight frown: not directed at Crisparkle, but at himself, for being unable to present a final and conclusive picture of Jasper's villainy. 'It is important that we meet urgently, later today. Let us travel separately to Staple Inn, to avoid observation, and possible suspicion on the part of Jasper; and then follow the precedent described to me by Mr Grewgious by meeting at Tartar's, if that is convenient to him, in order to escape any prying eyes.'

'An admirable plan, which I shall follow to the letter,' returned Crisparkle, clapping his two hands together, for no better reason than that he had taken no vigorous exercise for more than a minute.' I shall miss the "Alternate Musical Wednesdays", but that must not stand in our way. I have had as much pleasure singing George Frederick's music by myself outside as I would in a room indoors with fellow singers: nay, more, since the open air is more tolerant of musical error than the chamber.'

He beamed happily: but then, acknowledging the need for haste, continued, speaking rapidly and enthusiastically,

'You go straight to Tartar's: his rooms lie on the top floor of the stairs on the far right of the building. I shall meet you there, having collected Mr Grewgious from his chambers: for we can I believe be confident that I shall find him there. Whoever gets to Staple Inn the sooner can bring the excellent Tartar into the picture. I have every certainty that he will put himself out for us; he is a most selfless gentleman. I am most happy to learn that there has at last been some progress in this dismal affair. Farewell, Sir, and may God help our efforts, and lead us to the truth.'

Datchery certainly felt that some divine assistance would not be out of place, and was about to say so, when he saw that the energetic Minor Canon was already bounding on his way, to the Corner, to boxing, to breakfast (and keeping well clear of the contentious subject of Helena), to London and to Tartar's: and even, if time permitted, to a few minutes spent with Neville to go over some legal texts which he had been perusing in his spare moments. He was a man of great vitality and endeavour, the Minor Canon, and most of it was devoted to serving God's purpose, and helping his fellow men.

Inevitably, given his speed of motion, and despite the number of duties he had to perform before leaving, Crisparkle was on the train first and at Staple Inn first. There was insufficient time for the intended call on Neville, so he made his way straight to PJT, date 1747, to collect Mr Grewgious. As expected, he found the latter in his rooms, seated under his dry vine and fig tree, writing a memorandum of incorruptible integrity in his crabbed hand. When he heard what was afoot, he immediately laid aside his task, and the two proceeded together: a Priest of Just Temper; and a Professional Janitor of Trusts. Together they sought out

Tartar, who was at work in his garden, and explained what they sought. He immediately assented, as his guests fully expected; but Grewgious was reminded that Tartar, although knowing other parts of the story, knew nothing of Datchery, who was yet to arrive. Grewgious rapidly enlightened him, speaking as if from a prepared text, still and upright, voice dry, hands occasionally employed to produce a chopping gesture for greater effect.

Tartar grasped it all, asked a few pertinent questions, and ended by congratulating Mr Grewgious on his perspicacity, and Septimus Crisparkle on his support for the noble project to clear Neville's name, find the real murderer of Drood, and help protect Rosa. (He mentioned the third last, but his listeners gained the impression that in reality he listed it somewhat higher, and his voice shook just a little as he named her and the mission of supreme importance to protect her). He did not of course know Datchery, but expressed himself as satisfied that Mr Grewgious would have chosen just the right man and no other for the job: more than satisfied, fully convinced.

Tartar had but one suggestion to propose; if they sat for the meeting in his main room, there was just a chance that they might be seen from outside, either from another room or from the far side of the street, and their presence together, and the length and intensity of their conference, might be marked and remarked upon. What did these four men have in common, and what did they have to discuss in such depth? To avoid such speculations, they should meet in the garden, which was covered with trellises and a nautical awning, and where their deliberations would continue quite unobserved. Grewgious immediately saw the good sense of this, and Tartar hurried away to prepare a table and seating. He sang happily to himself under his breath as he went, and created seating arrangements which would have fully satisfied the courteous King Arthur and his Knights of high renown. A Practical and Jolly Tar.

In the midst of this, Datchery arrived: A Patient and Judicious Traveller: Perhaps Jasper should be Troubled.

At his appearance, Grewgious laughed; or, rather, emitted an odd, dry, wheezing sort of sound, as if his throat could do with a good oiling: which in truth, it could, for he did not often laugh outright. But it was clear that the intention behind the laugh was benign and cheerful, so no-one minded the unusual method of delivery. Perhaps the next time that Grewgious laughed, it would sound better.

'Why, Will, I did not recognise you.'

Datchery also laughed, and made an altogether more convincing job of it. As he did so, he removed the wig of flowing, white locks, and emerged many years younger and looking surprisingly sharp. His notable black eyebrows gave him a keen and penetrating gaze, no longer obscured by the elderly locks. The blue surtout remained however, still giving him that ineffably military air.

'I made myself an old buffer for the part,' he explained, dangling the hanging wig from his index finger as he spoke, and swinging it slightly and dismissively. 'It disarms suspicion: no-one cares about an old fellow, or questions what he is doing or why. Even though I sit on Jasper's very door-step, no-one, not even Jasper, seems to suspect me or my motives. I caught the Dean looking at me in a strange and questioning way once or twice, but that soon passed: not a gentleman of great intellectual rigour I suspect.' He was about to add that he could see why the Dean had entered the Church not the Law, but fortuitously his eye alighted on Crisparkle just in time and stopped: he had no wish to offend his new friend, whom he could immediately recognize as a generous and sensitive soul. Instead he continued with an explanation of his tactics. 'So I could sit on Jasper's door-step all day, with no questions being asked.'

'So, that's what you did do, no doubt,' interposed Grewgious, admiring the cunning of the scheme.

'Exactly: sitting, looking, observing, noting. No-one asks themselves 'Now, what is that old buffer doing?' because I am doing just what old buffers do. Now, if I stood forth, or rather sat forth, as a young man, I would invite attention: attention and everything that follows: questions and suspicions and surmises: all of which are bad for the noble art of detection. Even His Worship the Mayor might smell a rat, as he would no doubt phrase it in his original way, with ponderous pauses for heavy emphasis, and winks to a waiting audience, expected to hang on his every word.' He stopped himself, and smiled.

Crisparkle recognised a fellow doubter at the court of King Thomas. 'So, Mr Sapsea is not one of your favourite characters?'

'No, but for purposes of cover and concealment I am forced to seek out his company more often than I wish; he is the essential bell-wether (if I am permitted to use that expression of the Mayor without lese-majesty), the ultimate seal of approval for a stranger come to settle in the town.'

His hand passed over his bared head, and he looked a liberated man. 'It is wearing, though, to bear that great pile of hair. How good life seems without it. I feel as if I am wearing a hat all the time, even inside; making it two when I remember to put the real thing on my head.' He lightly tossed the offending wig onto a chair in the entry hall, in a place convenient for being replaced on his head before he went out into the street, so that he would not be seen without his disguise: a cautious man, Will, and one unlikely to be caught out by events, even unexpected ones.

Tartar ushered them through to the garden: the garden which Rosa had brightened by her presence that magical evening when she had dined with Tartar and Grewgious: and which was now set out as if for a conference: which indeed it was. He then poured them sherry into twinkling glasses from a gleaming decanter.

'To refine our senses and our wits,' he remarked as he did so; and then, with feline deftness, produced dainty biscuits from a neat cupboard in his kitchen; as if he had been an illusionist, though the biscuits proved real enough. And so they settled in the garden, well away from prying eyes, and Datchery began.

He started, not with explanation of why he had sought an urgent meeting, but with a sudden surprise. He put his hand into his inside pocket, and with a flourish produced an object wrapped in a silk handkerchief. He unwrapped it and produced a ring: a rose of diamonds and rubies set in gold. Grewgious started, but being a man of great control and reserve, said nothing; he just stared at it with double sorrow in his eyes, looking more angular and arid than ever, and contemplating the tragic association of that elegant circle of elements, of metals and jewels, with death and departure and deep loss. Datchery told the company how he had come into possession of the ring, with full details of his finding of the body.

Then Grewgious sadly took up the melancholy story, with a heavy air, as if he like Datchery had looked upon death in all its misery and horror. He recounted how and when and why he had given the ring to Edwin Drood, and how only he knew that Drood had it on his person. Drood had not mentioned the fact even to Rosa in their last interview – he knew this from Rosa; and Jasper knew nothing of the ring – he did not even know that the engagement had been broken, or that it had been spoken of between Rosa and Drood in their last meeting.

Datchery resumed his narrative.

'So the ring confirms the body I discovered as that of Drood. That solves the mystery, or rather the first part of the mystery: why did Drood disappear? So, on to the next stage: who killed him? I suspect that I have no surprises here: certainly nothing to equal the finding of the ring.

But let's review the evidence we have, recognising it to be in the main circumstantial. Clearly my working hypothesis was that Jasper had killed his nephew: that was where the suspicions of Mr Grewgious pointed, and the basis on which I was invited to investigate. Nothing I have discovered threw any doubt on this theory, or suggested that anyone else was guilty or complicit.

Now we have the evidence of the keys, the discovery of the ring, and confirmation that the killer knew of the watch and pin but was unaware of the existence of the ring. We also know that Jasper was passionately in love with Drood's betrothed, but again unaware that the betrothal was a thing of the past. Who else had the combination of motive to kill Drood, together with access to copies of the all-important keys and such intimate knowledge of Drood's personal habits that he knew that Drood would be wearing only two tell-tale pieces of personal jewellery, without the need to check?'

He added in parenthesis: 'He should of course have searched the body, instead of assuming that it carried only the watch and the pin. It was careless, and I should add typical; for most clever criminals are detected through some small but in retrospect obvious defect in their calculations. That is what provides employment for detectives – and for criminal lawyers. Yes, this was the fatal flaw for Jasper, the final link of the chain.'

'An invisible chain, riveted to heaven and earth,' uttered Mr Grewgious, surprising even himself by this apparent flight of fancy. 'Yes, the error of errors,' he added more prosaically.

Datchery further underlined the point by laying his hand firmly on the table, palm down, as if pushing something beneath the surface: was it any remaining doubt about Jasper's guilt? Grewgious in turn ticked the point off, with his right thumb on his left, no doubt feeling that his somewhat reluctant decision to entrust the ring to Drood had been vindicated, albeit in the saddest of circumstances.

Datchery glanced round, and politely enquired – for he remained polite even without his wig – whether anyone wished to challenge anything he had said: was he running ahead of the evidence?

'I have no doubt of his guilt: no vestige whatever,' said Grewgious, solemnly: 'I have called him a brigand and a wild beast, and I repeat that.'

'Nor I,' added Crisparkle gravely, aware that in saying this he was condemning one of God's creatures, unheard, but being morally certain in the matter.

'I know little of the circumstances, or of the man; but, knowing what he did to Rosa, and in a different way to Neville, and, yes, to Endcombe, I believe we are justified in assuming him guilty also of murdering his nephew,' concluded Tartar, grimly; before his innate sense of natural justice compelled him to add, a little grudgingly for such an open-hearted and generous man, 'or at the very least, for we have not yet heard the further evidence, of being fully capable of it.' That scene by the sun-dial was clearly at the forefront of his mind: and, had he been a judge, he would have had little scruple in reaching for the black cap once Datchery had completed his presentation of the case.

'Nevertheless,' added Grewgious, ever the man of business, and taking and extending Tartar's slight reservation, 'although the evidence is compelling, it remains, as you remind us, circumstantial. How can we add to it, especially now that we have the body? Could you reconstruct the crime for us, and tell us what else you have discovered?'

Datchery responded.

'I think I can tell you what happened, in most essentials. Let me rehearse the probable sequence of events. Edwin Drood returns from his visit to the river, and goes straight to his uncle's house, leaving Landless to walk home to Minor Canon Corner, as the latter has told us. Since it was already after midnight (the timing was confirmed by Jasper), and Landless was due to make an early start in the morning, which in the event he did, it certainly seems likely that he went directly home, and immediately took himself to bed.

And what of Drood? He has been depressed all evening. He is tired from all the emotions of the last few days: the break with Rosa and with so much of his past life and expectations; his imminent departure from Cloisterham and then from England; the meeting with the old woman and her strange words of warning, brought home to him every time that Jack calls him Ned that evening – and it is many times; the evening itself and his need to be on best behaviour with Landless, in whose company he still feels a strange uneasiness; the walk to the river and back through the violent, stormy night, with branches wrenched by the wind from trees and tiles from roofs; and the river itself, in spate before the storm, its energy and power truly fearful – just standing by it would have sapped and daunted a man even in the best of spirits.'

'I remember the night well, and the extraordinary power of the wind. It was as if God spoke, as he did with the great flood,' agreed Crisparkle. 'Even a fit young man like Drood would have felt the effect.'

'There may have been another disturbing emotion in his mind,' continued Datchery, with just a hint of uncertain enquiry in his voice. 'Possibly there are thoughts of Miss Landless in his over-wrought brain as he returns to his uncle's.'

Mr Grewgious glanced at the speaker apprizingly, but Mr Crisparkle looked surprised and a little worried: 'What is that?' he asked, with a hint of abruptness unusual for the gentle-mannered Canon.

'Oh, just a little idle speculation of my own,' returned Datchery, mildly. 'I wondered whether it had been an additional element in the famous quarrel, to which it would have added some neat symmetry, and whether the break with Rosa opened new possibilities for the young man. Miss Landless herself would have remained oblivious of any such feelings on Drood's part.' He glanced at Crisparkle beneath his dark black eyebrows. 'But no matter,' he added lightly.

His voice resumed its more confident tones.

'So, overall, it is not surprising that on his return Drood is tired and wishes to go straight to his bed. Perhaps he does, and is murdered in his bed, while he sleeps; it is possible, but not I believe likely. I think that Jack wants a few more minutes with him, to add piquancy to what he is about to do, to savour his impending triumph, to indulge himself, before he murders the youth who, he still believes, intends to marry the girl he loves; the girl whom he adores with a mad and dark passion, which holds him in a vice-like grip which will never be broken. So Jack detains him. Clever old Jack finds a way of keeping him there when he is desperate for rest: and Edwin indulges him; as he ever indulges and seeks to please his uncle, no his friend Jack, whom he believes dotes on him. How does Jack do this? I believe he mixes him one of those stirrup-cups, which he is so adept at stirring, and which he creates with such immediate results, in order to mark Edwin's departure the next morning. So they toast each other, Jasper in pure wine, Edwin in evil and adulterated punch; and then, when he is feeling just a little fuddled, on top of his tiredness, Jasper strikes. He kills him.'

'How?' asked Grewgious quickly and unexpectedly.

Equally unexpectedly, Datchery smiled slightly: 'I shall come to that shortly.'

With which Grewgious had to be content.

'What does Jasper do next?' resumed Datchery. 'He rapidly removes watch and pin, which would identify the body. He lifts the body – for Drood is still but a youth, and Jasper a strong man, and the distance is

343

not far – and carries it to Mrs Sapsea's tomb, to which he possesses the key, and lays it in there. He then collects and pours on quick-lime: there is a mound of lime by the yard-gate out of Durdles's hovel; I have observed it there, as no doubt did Jasper. Jasper knows that Durdles will be lying in his bed dead drunk, having been stoned to his house by Deputy the previous evening: dead to the world, unaware that his precious lime is being stolen, largely oblivious of the great storm, until he is roused in the morning to come and repair the tower and roof: no sooner gathering his men and starting this work before word races round the town, as word invariably manages to when there are evil tidings to relate, that Drood has vanished and has probably been murdered by Landless, who has likewise disappeared.

Let's return to Jasper: having finished with the body and the lime, he hurries to Cloisterham Mill, and disposes of all the incriminating material: watch and chain, shirt pin, Sapsea key: all safely consigned to the waters. Safely? That is what he believes. He has failed to notice, unlike our eagle-eyed friend some days later, that the watch has caught in the weir.'

'Only Septimus would have had that suspicion of something glittering in the water, and then been able to act on it,' wonderingly remarked Grewgious, who was altogether too dry and nutty to contemplate swimming.

The ever practical Tartar was stirring slightly.

'Could I ask something? I recognise that all this is silent work for Jasper that night; but how can he do all this without being observed or disturbed, or above all without the fear of being observed or disturbed?'

'A very acute question,' returned Datchery. 'But remember that it's the night of the great storm. It's not only Durdles who is already long inside his hut. Many of the lights in the Precincts have been blown out by the blasts of wind, it is dangerous to be outside, there is flying debris everywhere, the streets are empty, and the inhabitants of Cloisterham are lying in their beds, their bed-clothes over their heads, praying that their chimneys will not topple and crash down through their roofs. In the morning all is different: the wind has fallen, and they creep out to inspect the damage and begin the repair work, starting with the Cathedral tower and clock.

By this time, Jasper is long finished, and is on his way to Minor Canon Corner to raise the alarm. He is white from all his nocturnal efforts, and only half-dressed; he has abandoned his outer clothing, partly for effect and to suggest that he has only just jumped from his bed in a panic; but also because his clothes are sodden: sodden, and also torn and mired with telltale traces of mud, lime and, perhaps, blood.'

Grewgious looked up with appreciative interest. Crisparkle was also in a position to recognise the significance of the point, and nodded once or twice, reflectively. Datchery paused for a moment to gather his thoughts before proceeding.

'At this point, Jasper is engaged in an artful piece of calculation, which he has to get right: artful because there are several conflicting ingredients in it, and he has to get the balance correct. What elements go into this? First, there is the danger of the body being found and recognised as Drood's, before the lime has time to do its disfiguring work, for example by Durdles on one of his evening prowls: he has the key and endless opportunity. If it is discovered, there is a danger of Jasper being a suspect. So he must find a way of immediately throwing suspicion on Neville, and ensuring maximum publicity for his suspicions; in this the timing and circumstance of his raising the alarm is impeccable, and he is helped by the lucky chance that Landless had already set off that morning on his journeying: this looks like guilt and flight. Landless had no doubt confided to Jasper and Drood the previous evening that such was his intention; who knows, Jasper may even have got wind of this already, perhaps overheard Landless telling someone else,' (Datchery's eyes fleetingly brightened, in sudden recognition, but he did not interrupt his narrative) 'and worked to strengthen Landless's intention to make a really early start, despite the weather; this is something that I can ask Landless when I have the chance to interview him. I have not previously left Cloisterham in pursuing the case: except to call on the old woman, as I reported.'

He was about to add something, but evidently decided against it and continued, from where he had briefly paused.

'Second, he well knows that there is no real evidence against Neville, and therefore a danger that as this gradually becomes clearer, the finger of suspicion may start to point elsewhere. So he wants the hue and cry, and the excitement, to die down as quickly as possible: the case rapidly to grow as dead and cold as the body safely hidden away in the Sapsea tomb. The best way to ensure diminishing interest is to have no body; or, even better, to find a way of proving as clearly as possible that no body exists. No body, no crime, and therefore no guilt.'

'Ah, the search which Jasper so easily persuaded our Mayor that that worthy himself had suggested,' noted Crisparkle.

'The unsuccessful search,' commented Grewgious drily, emphasising the adjective.

Datchery leant forward, resting his arms on the table, his palms open.

'Quite so. Jasper stimulates a painstaking search for the body, undertaken in an area as far as possible from Cloisterham Mill where he has concealed the tell-tale personal jewellery. Days of searching produce no result, and – naturally – no body. Yet they allow Jasper to advertise in the clearest possible manner his devotion to his nephew, and thus help avert any seeds of doubt or suspicion. They also keep the idea of the guilt of Neville in the public eye, discouraging any tendency to look elsewhere for the criminal, but without exciting any fresh interest. Better still, they allow him to solve the problem of those dirty outer clothes, which have to be kept from suspicious eyes, and above all the keen gaze of his cleaning woman Mrs Tope as she goes about her work in his rooms. What is the best disguise? Why, days of searching for the body in mud, in shingle, in reeds, in brambles, among the stakes and jagged stones, all of which produce those torn and miry clothes in which he returns from his unavailing search.'

His audience, realising the importance of those torn and miry clothes, could readily imagine them, though only Grewgious had seen them.

Datchery went on with his description.

'Thus he appears before Mr Grewgious in those theatrically mired clothes, well pleased with himself and his performance to that point. All is going smoothly and according to plan. But Mr Grewgious, God bless him,' he glanced fondly at the upright figure sitting to his right, his hands firmly on his knees, and looking unblinkingly straight ahead of him. 'Mr Grewgious tells him something which changes everything. He tells him that Rosa and Edwin had broken their engagement. Jasper feels the ground opening beneath his feet, and himself falling into the chasm, at the sudden ghastly realisation that the murder which he had just committed, the murder of his own nephew, his sister's child, his closest relation, his ward, had been unnecessary, had not advanced his cause one iota. No wonder he falls into a dead faint.'

There is silence all round at Jasper's evident predicament.

'When Jasper comes to, he is being tended by the Topes, who are satisfyingly solicitous and attentive: but what is this? Mr Grewgious is still there: still awkwardly and determinedly there, looking stolidly at him, watching his recovery, saying nothing, offering nothing, just making his life more difficult. What does Grewgious know or suspect? What indeed? Jasper simply does not know, cannot work it out. Grewgious's face shows nothing, betrays nothing: an empty dial on which Jasper cannot read the time. Mr Grewgious, Sir, we are indeed fortunate to have you on our side in this miserable affair.' Datchery again looked fondly at the dry and angular figure to his right. Grewgious smiled at him in a kindly way, and made that curious gesture of appearing to dry his already sere hair with both his hands: as if he and not Crisparkle had leapt straight out of the river that morning before meeting Datchery and hastening to the meeting.

'So, as he regains consciousness, Jasper has to think fast. He does so while he eats and drinks frantically; he has little appetite, but he desperately needs the time to collect and order his thoughts. Once again, he passes the test with some success: we are not dealing with a fool, despite his elementary mistake in overlooking the ring. He immediately grasps that his behaviour on hearing the news will tend to invite suspicion; not just in Mr Grewgious, but in the minds of less acute observers. So he forces himself to think calmly; after all, there is no evidence against him – yet. He cannot change what has just happened, but he can seek to alter the surrounding circumstances: or, at least, try and find a way of making both facts and circumstances look different, by altering perceptions, by changing impressions, including those which he himself has been sedulous in creating. Jasper allows Mrs Tope to assume and spread the word that the faint has been induced by weariness and hunger. Meanwhile, he devises and puts about the theory that this new revelation about the ending of the engagement makes it more likely, almost certain, that Drood has simply absented himself from Cloisterham, has abandoned his old life. This may not convince the sage Mr Grewgious, but it appears to do the trick elsewhere, or at least provides a new and different talking-point, and takes the pressure off Jasper, for a time, and serves his wish to allow excitement to abate, and the trail to grow cold.'

'It shows tactical dexterity; but, speaking as a plain sailor, and as someone to whom this is terra nova, or incognita, I find it a little obvious,' observed Tartar thoughtfully: 'but that is probably only because we have such an expert to guide us through these mysteries,' he quickly and generously added.

'I did not believe it, because Drood would have waited to see me, as he had agreed with Rosa, before leaving Cloisterham. But Jasper knew nothing of that conversation, of our agreement, and therefore misjudged the matter. He sometimes acted like a man on a treadwheel,' offered Grewgious, 'with problems approaching him, and him having to deal with them piecemeal.' He chopped a few approaching problems with his right hand.

'Yes: or on a helter-skelter,' suggested Datchery more imaginatively. 'The problems come at him thick and fast, and he does not always deal with them successfully, especially in the period after the murder. I often wonder whether murderers realise that the real problems come later, after the planned deed has been done, and when they believe – and had hoped – their troubles to be at an end.

In Jasper's case, he was already making unnecessary mistakes even before the murder. You recall the jeweller who testified about Drood's watch after its discovery. I subsequently wrote to him, via a colleague in my chambers, with a number of questions, without revealing who I was or that I was already in Cloisterham: simply indicating a technical interest in the case, and in the unusual aspect of the evidence provided by the recovered watch.

He was flattered, as I had planned, and his reply was fuller than it need have been. It included two nuggets of information. One was that he was already aware, before Drood appeared in his shop to have his watch wound and set, that Drood's sole jewellery was watch and pin: thus unintentionally establishing himself as a possible suspect for the murder, but one whom I could instantly dismiss.' He permitted himself a brief smile, before continuing.

'The other was quite extraordinary. His source for this piece of information was none other than Jasper himself. Now, why was Jasper going around Cloisterham, before the murder, providing to outsiders intimate details of Drood's jewellery: details which he knew were of vital importance to himself and to his crime? It could surely only be because of nervousness, because those details were preying on his mind. He was so preoccupied with the thought that he had to find those items on the body of his dead nephew, recover them from the corpse, and then find a way of disposing of them, and disposing of them finally and irretrievably, that the words came tumbling out when he was talking to the jeweller. He must have been horrified by what he suddenly found himself saying. Because those possessions were of crucial importance to Jasper: if found with the remains of the body, they would provide certain identification, even if the remainder were eaten away; and, if discovered in their place of concealment, they would instantly suggest foul play, which was not Jasper's purpose in his carefully-planned murder.'

Despite the horror of recounting a murder, the cold-blooded murder of a nephew by his uncle, Datchery could not help deriving some enjoyment from telling the tale, and revealing his skill in reconstructing it, and this showed in his manner and his words. He also had more than a sense that Grewgious had already worked out at least the greater part of the story. He once again looked appraisingly at the figure beside him, who appeared to be checking the various points being made by Datchery against some mental memorandum of his own.

'For fate has not finished with Mr Jasper: by no means. The discovery of the jewellery by our athletic friend Septimus Crisparkle,' he smiled warmly in the latter's direction, 'that discovery again changes everything. It suggests, as intimated just now, death rather than disappearance. So, yet again, he has to change tack, and throw all suspicion on Landless: assisted by widespread public malice and the boundless stupidity of Mr Sapsea. Once again, though, Mr Crisparkle plays a notable role: this time in defending Landless, and ensuring that the so-called case against him does not succeed by default. So Jasper has to work yet harder at convincing everyone of Landless's guilt, and in keeping the case in the public eye. Jasper can rejoice that the enterprising swimmer did not find the Sapsea key: it would have complicated the case against Landless, perhaps even prompted Durdles to say something about his nocturnal excursion with Jasper, and certainly led to the discovery of a body which is still largely uncorrupted. So Jasper's luck holds, and every minute which passes make it less likely, he believes, that the body is identifiable as Drood's. He does not, of course, know about the hidden clue, the ring.'

'Yes, so all that explains those greatly exaggerated changes of mood which puzzled us earlier,' commented Crisparkle to Grewgious.

'We were right, though: it wasn't the opium, it was artfulness,' responded Grewgious.

'In order to keep up the pretence that Landless is guilty of Drood's death, even in the absence of a body, Jasper fixes upon the idea of unceasing pursuit and hounding of the boy, haunting his life, torturing him by perpetually reviving suspicion. This has a dual purpose: ensuring that, in the public mind, there is only one possible suspect for Drood's murder; and also, if possible, driving Landless into making some foolish and apparently suspicious error, such as running away, or changing his name. Luckily,' and he looked at Crisparkle as he said this, 'Landless had a steadfast and wise friend who persuaded him against such damaging behaviour; a friend who would indeed have been ready to keep Neville in his own house in Cloisterham, as proof of a total belief in his innocence, for all the world to see, if the Church – I was about to say militant, but I suspect that supine is closer to the mark – had not taken a hand.'

Datchery was still looking benignly at Crisparkle, both in continuing admiration for the role which the Minor Canon had played throughout, but also because he was approaching a difficult point in his narrative, a narrows which he would have preferred to avoid, or circumnavigate, but which for the sake of completeness he had to confront. He went on.

'And it was absolutely vital that that friend gave Neville such sound advice, which the latter might not have accepted so readily from another source. For, as Jasper later boasted to Rosa, there are ways of piling up a case even against an innocent man. Jasper was more than ready to pile up that case with the utmost diligence. I have already provided ample reasons for this: and there is another, equally compelling.' The others felt Crisparkle stiffen: he well knew what was coming.

'For entirely honourable reasons, which do him nothing but credit, and as Mr Grewgious is already aware, Mr Crisparkle had confessed to Jasper Landless's feelings for Rosa.' Septimus shuffled uneasily, but both of Datchery's points were correct; he had passed this confidence to Jasper, and he had done so for the purest of motives; but how he wished he had not done so. How he wished that it was possible to wind back the clock, and undo what he had done. But he was a stoical man, as well as an honest and conscientious one, and he knew that it was not possible. If clocks could be rewound in this way, Drood would still be alive, Mrs Sapsea and Mr Tisher would still be with us, and even all the deans and vergers from Cloisterham past would be present in our midst, causing the utmost confusion, not least for their current successors. So he did not attempt to interrupt Datchery, who was continuing his argument.

'Landless's ardent passion was, as Jasper put it to Rosa, an inexpiable offence in his eyes; it was another motive for him to hate, hurt and pursue Landless, and do all he could to pin the crime of Drood's murder on him.'

'You are absolutely right, of course. Mea culpa,' acknowledged Crisparkle sadly.

'My dear friend, if I may call you so, I did not say this to suggest any guilt on your part. It was rather in an attempt to lay all possible facts and motives on the table; and also to contribute to the picture of the various pressures on Jasper's mind, to which I shall now come.' Grewgious looked up with sharp attention, as if this was an aspect of the affair which particularly interested him as well.

'Just consider what was going on in Jasper's mind the while. He knows that, realistically, he will find no determining clue against Landless; can find none, because none exists. Landless, well-advised as ever by Mr Crisparkle, refuses to play into his hands by making a false move. So Jasper is left playing for time until the mystery is all but forgotten, and in essence left unsolved. I believe that Jasper must have realised, almost from the first, that this was going to be the likeliest outcome, and that Mr Crisparkle's stalwart support for Landless was likely to stymie him: not by throwing suspicion back on himself, but by setting the bar of what constituted evidence against Neville at its proper height.' He was doing his best to compensate for having to follow the thread of the narrative through the awkward narrows of Crisparkle's confession to Jasper. 'But remember that, in the end, producing proof positive of Landless's guilt does not matter to Jasper; the main object is for his own guilt in the matter to remain well concealed.' Again, that gesture by Datchery of pressing his hand on the table, palm down, this time appearing to reflect Jasper's concern to conceal his guilt and suppress any possible suspicion.

'You are right,' Grewgious could not stop himself from eagerly joining in. 'Covering his own tracks: that is what matters most to Jasper.'

'What about that curious Diary entry? Where does that come in?' asked Crisparkle suddenly, recalling Jasper's dramatic gesture and impressive look in showing it to him.

'Yes, that's an interesting move: interesting and, I think, revealing. Apart from recording his conviction that Drood was dead, which was already well known, and his own determination to pursue the murderer, which again was already clear, it also states his intention nevermore to discuss the mystery with any human creature, until a clue was in hand – or words to that effect. This was the only new element. Now, the reason for it seems obscure, until one recognises that it is nothing but a self-defensive mechanism. The self-evident purpose is to avoid a succession of difficult enquiries about the success of his quest: for he knows that he can never make progress, will never have clues in hand. So, it is better to avoid the necessity of constantly having to admit this, and he finds a way of achieving this; yet one which, carefully analysed, actually throws some suspicion back on Jasper.'

'Like that time when he incautiously asked whether I had been sent for, after Rosa's faint,' added Mr Grewgious, ever ready to spot a parallel. 'Or like your interpretation of his curious conversation with the jeweller,' he added, equally quick to assimilate new information.

'Yes, they were all flaws, but not fatal ones: mis-steps on the treadwheel, or the helter-skelter: not easy to spot at the time, and therefore in the short term innocuous; but easier to pick up later, when they start to form part of a pattern. That is the advantage of the excellent idea of sharing information, which Septimus Crisparkle initiated.' He had more than made amends for following the thread of the story through those awkward narrows.

'I should have started the process earlier,' bemoaned Grewgious, 'but thought that anyone in Cloisterham would have considered me even odder than I am – which is surely odd enough for most tastes – if I presumed to suspect Jasper. As a result, I felt great satisfaction, and – yes, excitement,' he looked surprised at himself, 'when Septimus came to me with his suspicions.'

'Yes, but you had already brought in our good friend and colleague Dick Datchery to help us, and that was obviously our first and biggest advance,' pointed out Crisparkle, ever ready to praise another. 'But one aspect of that journal entry still puzzles me,' he persisted. 'Why did Jasper show it to me? By that time we were scarcely on speaking terms.'

'Two reasons, I think. First, he had showed you the earlier entries, initially throwing all blame on Neville, and then retreating; he wanted to bring the story up to date, as it were, to demonstrate that all doubts were gone. Secondly, because of the high regard in which you are held in Cloisterham, and because of your readiness to take Neville's part, he wanted you in a sense to be privy to what he claimed were his thoughts. He may have suspected that there would be comment or criticism about his decision to retreat into secrecy, and he wanted you to be able to say that you had seen the Diary entry explaining his vow. In this curious sense, he wanted you in a way as his witness, even his advocate. Who better from his point of view? Do you follow my, or rather Jasper's, line of reasoning?'

'Yes, and you are absolutely right. I recall an earlier occasion on which he referred to me as a witness to his state of mind,' Crisparkle readily agreed; and then added reflectively. 'Were there no under-hand villainies to which he would not stoop in his plotting?'

'None,' responded Datchery laconically: 'but all proved equally fruitless. So, to return to the main story, Jasper has made his position marginally more comfortable, and warded off enquiries and possible suspicions – but at a cost. And what is that cost? By making himself yet more solitary and separate and unapproachable.'

'And unhappy?' ventured Tartar.

'And unhappy. The pressures on him, on his mind, must be enormous: and yet greater once he knows that he has lost Rosa, that she has run away from him, that he has no more power over her. For two reasons: first, what does Jasper have in his life to look forward to? If he appeared close to madness in the extraordinary scene by the sun-dial, in making his declaration of love for Rosa, in exposing his tactics quite so clearly (yet at the same time in hiding his violent passions under a largely calm exterior, in revealing his deeper emotions principally in the workings of his face, and the exaggerated gestures of his hands) what must his feelings be now, now that Rosa has fled? Secondly, he does not know who she is with, and, above all, what she has reported, and to whom; and he must realise that the scene by the sun-dial, if taken together with the other mistakes he knows he has made, finally raises the finger of suspicion against him.

Which brings us to the present; and at this point I must pause, and take a sideways step.'

He did not do so literally, but lifted his glass of sherry to his lips and took a slight sip, and likewise took a rather more relaxed and meditative stance in his chair. His listeners also unconsciously shifted a little, and prepared themselves for a change of tack.

'How did Jasper become Jasper; how did he become a mad, murderous, treacherous wretch, evil beyond belief, the very essence of dangerous, selfish and heartless criminality? I have naturally been making discreet enquiries. He was not the product of an unhappy union, of cruel or unloving parents; he came of a contented family. When young, he was particularly affectionate towards his sister, who was considerably older than him, and who married Edwin Drood's father before they both died young. It was therefore considered quite natural for him to become in due course the guardian of Edwin, and appear to love and cherish him so much: to become so wrapped up in him, as Mrs Tope puts it. So far, then, no explanation of the horrible wonder which Jasper became.

Then I discovered an interesting fact. Drood's father is buried in Cloisterham, near the unfortunate Mrs Sapsea; Durdles cut the tomb and the inscription and showed it to me with some pride. It was natural for him to be buried there, since the family had its roots in the neighbourhood. Now, and this is the striking aspect: his wife is not buried there, in the same tomb, nor even in Cloisterham, even though her family also had close local connections.'

'How curious that I never noticed!' exclaimed Crisparkle. 'And, above all, how strange!'

'Strange: and suggestive: so I probed the point. Two rumours reached my attentive ears: not painted full of tongues, but faint whispers of distant times and half-forgotten events. There was some talk of an unhappy marriage, and even perhaps of a separation: dark talk of a suicide, which meant that any wish for burial in the grounds of a Cathedral might have produced complications and undesirable publicity: better therefore for the interment to take place away from Cloisterham, somewhere suitably remote.

There were still many gaps in the story, many uncertainties in what was beginning to take shape. What was however starting to become clear, from my various researches, pursued by a mixture of discreet local enquiry and correspondence with some outside Cloisterham whom I could approach in total confidence, and from whom I could hear through Crozier's without exciting attention, and above all without leaving my sentry-post on Jasper's doorstep for too long, was that the death of a beloved elder sister wrought a complete change in him. He grew solitary and lonely, moody and gloomy: as dark and saturnine as his countenance; his only real contact with people was through the music which he loved and sang so beautifully – or appeared to love, for I doubt whether a man who could stoop to murder, and such murder, and surround and protect his evil deed with such a a tissue of deceits and subterfuges, could genuinely have a soul to appreciate the beauty and purity of ecclesiastical music. But that is no more than another conjecture or fancy which came to me as I sat watch on my porch,' he added quietly, and without expanding the reference to a parallel thought, since he felt that his earlier theory that Drood had developed an interest in Miss Landless had caused some pain and concern in Crisparkle.

'Then something which had been gnawing at the back of my mind suddenly leapt to the front, and emerged as an inspiration: an inspiration which I fear had been overlong in coming: perhaps those white hairs had started to take control of my once sharp brain.' He was clearly thinking with some distaste of his wig.

'It was a phrase used by the old woman whom, borrowing Deputy's words, which I cannot better, I shall call the Princess Puffer. In her confused mumblings and whisperings she had called Edwin Drood a motherless baby. Why? Had she known him as a baby; and, through her opium haze, confused this with their later meeting? And why motherless? Had she known him both as a baby; and later, when his mother was newly dead? Was this the explanation of her hatred, of her desire for revenge? It certainly furnished a more convincing motive for her pursuit of Jasper than thoughts of blackmail, which she had earlier suggested (or which I, in my foolishness and naivete, had put into her mind): which a confused old woman, trembling like a leaf and dying of opium poisoning, was in little position to execute against a man of considerable local standing, a man fully supported and backed by the Mayor himself.' He bowed slightly, eyes lowered, as if Mr Sapsea himself was present at their deliberations.

'I sought her out again: yes, a second visit to her den. I shall spare you the details of our meeting, of her prevarications, of her falsehoods, of her mutterings, of her wheedlings, of her complaints, of her repetitions, of the many things I had heard the previous time, with certain additions. But at last we got there. My – belated – intuition was proved correct. She had been at one time, long before the opium habit took hold of her life and being, the servant in the house of Edwin Drood's parents. The full, sad story emerged: sad for her as well, and it may indeed have started her on the downward road towards the opium den. After the birth of Edwin, his mother Jenny grew melancholy and distraught, never recovered her health and spirits, and gradually lost her reason. There was nothing that anyone could do to help her overcome this, or revive her interest in her life and her child.

During this period, the family moved away from the Cloisterham area, as Drood became a partner in an engineering firm and decided to live nearer London, so the town remained largely unaware of the full story. Drood did what he could for his wife, but there was a further complication; as her illness took control of her, she falsely suspected her husband of infidelity, of infidelities, and shunned his company. One day, she was found drowned. It was unclear whether this was accident or suicide, but it was considered better to bury her away from Cloisterham. It was the drowning which drew the two grieving husbands, Bud and Drood, together, and thus led to the next twist in the tale; the unofficial betrothal of their two infants, and to the consequences which are familiar to us.'

'How terrible,' exclaimed Tartar, probably thinking also of the drowning of Rosa's mother.

'What a sad and tragic story; and how awful for all concerned;

including Jasper,' said Crisparkle, compassionately.

'You are perhaps going to say more of Jasper, and the effect on him,' hazarded Grewgious.

Datchery again tasted his sherry, reflectively, and helped himself to a very small piece of biscuit; but, conscious of his work as story-teller, and unwilling to follow Durdles's example of leaving it unmunched at the side of his mouth, left it instead untasted on the plate in front of him.

'Indeed I am. Just let me complete the tale of my discoveries from the Princess She had known Jasper from the time when she worked for the Drood family; but by the time he frequented her den, her powers of sight, observation and comprehension were much impaired, and she did not immediately recognise someone she had known only as a boy or youth in the dim light entering the dark room from the dank and miserable court. After all, she scarcely recognised me again in that room, although we had met but a fortnight or so before.' He shivered as he remembered his visits to that noisome place. 'It was only later that she realised who he might be and determined to follow him and find out more about him and about who the Ned might be and if possible warn him: that was on the first occasion, when she lost Jasper but met Drood, but again did not immediately comprehend who the latter was. She had last seen him as an infant. Nor, at that stage, had she conflated the names Edwin and Ned. Whether Drood had a presentiment of who she might be we shall never know.'

Tartar recharged the small glasses from the sherry decanter, again moving most deftly and inconspicuously for a large, strong man: he certainly had the sailor's trick of negotiating with ease in a confined space, a tight harbour.

'So much for the Princess's testimony. My main interest in all this, as Mr Grewgious correctly deduced, was how it related to Jasper. He of course would have believed his sister's delusions about her husband; and so he blamed Edwin Drood for his sister's mental distress, and the father for causing her death. This would have helped explain his growing alienation from the rest of mankind, his lack of trust, his distance, his tendency to go his own way, his lack of interchange with his fellows. I then learned more details about him, and the full story continued to fall into place. He was away, first at school, and then studying the music which became the centre of his life, if not his inspiration; but then moved back to Cloisterham when he was appointed both Choir-Master and official guardian to his nephew, Edwin. I believe that at this point his mood grew yet darker; the return to Cloisterham would have brought back vivid memories of his sister, and he was now very closely connected with someone he deeply resented.'

'Opium?' asked Grewgious concisely.

'Yes. It was also probably at about this time – I have to be a little vague, since I am unable to ask Jasper, and the Princess is understandably uncertain on dates – that he began to take refuge in opium: the effect on a dark, brooding and potentially violent man can be imagined. Then, he fell hopelessly – and I use the word advisedly – in love with Rosa.' It was Tartar's turn to stir slightly: slightly but determinedly. 'Edwin was now an impediment, and gradually Jasper seized on the idea of murdering him to get him out of the way. This would have been at first only a slight whisper in his mind, indignantly dismissed; then a more insistent component of his dark thoughts; then entertained as an idea, as a possible way forward out of his frustrations and difficulties; then, finally, enthusiastically embraced and endorsed as a convenient but fully justified way to get rid of the egregious Drood, and take Rosa for himself. That is how the criminal mind works: ordinary people can generally find justifications for their minor peccadillos; criminals can convince themselves that they have a right to murder.

No doubt in parallel the scheme or schemes for committing the crime were developing in his mind. This was no unexpected crime of passion, no sudden rush of blood bringing about an unforeseen and unplanned murder. The Princess's testimony about Jasper is crystal clear on that point: it was long in his mind, revealed to her by his sub-conscious mutterings under the influence of opium. As his determination grew and planning advanced, he used and manipulated extraneous events to further his purpose, most obviously the arrival of Landless and the ill-fated quarrel with Drood; again, I have no direct evidence for this, not having spoken to Neville, and denied the chance for differing reasons to speak to Drood and Jasper, but I strongly suspect that Jasper deliberately fomented the quarrel between the two hot-headed young men, and cleverly brought it to a head. Occasionally events seemed to conspire against him. One such occasion was Mr Crisparkle's admirable scheme for a reconciliation; but he always managed to find an effective way through the new difficulties – after close internal calculation – and this time made the hated reconciliation itself the cover for the murder.'

'Ah, the murder,' exclaimed Mr Grewgious, 'we come to that.'

'Yes, the murder: and the question of how.' For the first time in his telling of the story, Datchery was looking a little fatigued. The ever-observant Tartar offered him a small glass of water, which he gratefully accepted; but he did little more than just moisten his lips: those shattered bones, and his inability to explain them, were preying on his mind. 'The murder. The Princess is adamant that Jasper intended to strangle Drood. She was convinced that she had heard, and even observed, Jasper strangling someone in his dreams a thousand times: without at that stage realising who the someone was. Throttling or choking would have been relatively easy to do; and, above all, would leave no tell-tale blood in Jasper's rooms. And there is another aspect: you will recall Jasper describing the ties between him and Edwin as silken threads: was this perhaps a careless association of ideas, an inadvertent reference to the silk scarf with which he intended to do the deed?'

Crisparkle started at the mention of a scarf, and his hand flew to the side of his head in a gesture of silent horror. Datchery glanced at him, quickly and enquiringly.

'He was wearing a large black scarf of strong close-woven silk, slung loosely round his neck, on the evening of the reconciliation, the dinner,' said Crisparkle unhappily, in a low voice. 'I thought that his throat might have been tender, and therefore took especial trouble to congratulate him on the service, and on the exceptional quality of his singing. And we talked for several minutes in high good humour, and he readily accepted all my warm words and compliments. And – and, to think that he had murder in his heart all the time we were speaking, a wicked, deliberate murder long planned in the coldness of his heart, in the evil of his mind – and that I was looking at the murder weapon, which he was coolly sporting in front of me.' He shook his head unhappily, possibly wondering how and why his God, his kind God, his omnipotent and omniscient God, could allow such things to happen in His world.

Datchery naturally sympathised, and was even able to offer a scrap of comfort.

'I agree that it is awful to contemplate what Jasper hid within himself as he dispassionately went about his business of planning the killing of Drood. But I am not convinced that you looked on the murder weapon on that fateful evening. Consider the evidence.

First, the killing of Drood had not gone quite according to plan, judging by what the Princess understood of Jasper's mumblings and ramblings. The death had been too easy, too rapid, and was unsatisfying in some unexplained way.

Secondly, why the broken bones which I discovered when I found the body? Had Jasper struck him rather than strangled him, and as a result, killed him too easily? Had he missed the feeling of strangling, the close contact with the victim, the satisfying feeling of the noose tightening round the neck, the initial half-cry of surprise by the victim, the appealing look, the anguish, the frenzied struggling, the quivering of the body, the feeling of possessing the power of life and death, the remorseless choice of death: slow, painful, lingering death? Or had he strangled him, and then, his passions inflamed, still thinking of Rosa and all his frustrations in that quarter, proceeded to attack the body? His own nephew? On Christmas Eve? And with what? The iron-shod stick, purloined from Landless? No, the latter had it with him the next morning. His own poker, seized from the fireplace beneath the fateful portrait of Rosa? But then that and the carpet and so forth would have required careful cleansing before being discovered by the diligent Mrs Tope. Jasper had planned this murder long and carefully: would he really have done something at the last minute which complicated his task, which made discovery more likely? Surely any last-minute change would have been in the other direction, to make his crime safer, undiscoverable. Those broken bones remain, for the present, a mystery.

There is a third point I should bring to your attention: a question, rather than a problem as such: but I cannot find the answer: why did Jasper copy the Tower key? What was his projected purpose in the Tower that evening, or on another evening?

In short, my friends, I know that Jasper killed Edwin Drood, and why, but I cannot tell you how.'

He sat back in his chair, and at last the waiting morsel of biscuit received the attention it fully deserved: as did, again, Tartar's excellent sherry.

His listeners had in large part sat enthralled and unstirringly through this long explanation. Now, as Datchery finished, they all relaxed, and expressed their feelings in their own ways. Tartar gave a short, incisive whistle and gazed approvingly at his beans, no doubt giving silent thanks that Rosa had escaped the clutches of this evil monster. Septimus Crisparkle, still disturbed by the reference to the black scarf, was also experiencing difficulties in containing his own emotions, now that he had learnt how coldly and calculatingly Jasper had abused and traduced his pupil Neville in order to cover his own guilt; and was still recalling with unabated dismay how he had inadvertently stoked Jasper's hatred directed against his protégé. Neville would have been amused to see Septimus's great right fist clenched in anger. There was a sudden "Umps" from Mr Grewgious, before he relieved his feelings by plunging round the room with an ungainly jig or two, and some lines of doggerel:

> 'I'll sing you four, ho! Green grow the rushes, ho! What is your four, ho!'

But he rapidly recovered both poise and judgement.

'Nevertheless, my dear fellow, there is much that is clear. We have the body – habeamus corpus. We have the ring and therefore the identification. We have the evidence of the various keys. Tomorrow morning we shall call on His Worship the Jackass, and lay our case before him. Mr Jasper will have much explaining to do.'

So the four dispersed and went their several ways. Septimus Crisparkle did not go to call on Neville: his emotions were still stirred, the meeting had been a long one, and he needed to return to Cloisterham. Alas that he did not: it could have prevented much grief and unhappiness. Was it written in the stars that he would fail to see Neville as planned? Or was it the working out of God's purpose?

CHAPTER XXXVI
Other Listeners

THE MEETING, AS carefully managed, took place well away from prying eyes. In fact, there were no eyes to pry: the former agent of the local friend, the enemy, had been identified, as envisaged by Mr Grewgious and, separately, by Helena, and had then been effectively neutralised – even turned – by Tartar and Crisparkle, especially the latter; the local friend himself no longer visited London, and was far away in Cloisterham, unaware of the net closing on him, and still fondly believing that his agent was at work, isolating Neville from friends and acquaintances, hunting and haunting him, ensuring the misery of his existence; and there were no other allies of the local friend in the vicinity. He was not a man who encouraged friendships or alliances. The four were therefore unobserved and undisturbed in their hanging garden high above the city, their oasis of calm and greenery in the gritty desert of London, accompanied only by the unnaturally black sparrows seeking the crumbs of Tartar's magical biscuits.

They may have been well away from prying eyes in their lofty eyrie, but not from prying ears. For Helena and Neville were in their sitting room, with the window ajar, and they heard every word, every grim detail. They were listening at the beginning of the lengthy narrative, and they were listening at the end, they did not utter a word, and they did not stir, unmoving though by no means unmoved. They listened intently as Datchery explained the mystery, reported the finding of the body of Drood, described the likely course of the murder, set out the intricacies of what happened thereafter, and tackled the puzzle of Jasper's character and infamy. They listened with particular attention and indignation to Datchery's account of the various stages of Jasper's campaign to ensure that the guilt for Drood's sudden disappearance was ascribed to Neville and no other.

Not until the four had left Tartar's rooms did the two stir. They had heard Datchery out together, in close harmony, but their reaction now was very different. Neville was understandably incensed with rage and frustration at what he had heard of Jasper's behaviour.

'I shall seek him out, confront him, beat him, kill him. I was ready to do that to my step-father to save you, Helena, and I am ready to do it to him now, for my own revenge. The man is evil and dangerous, and does not deserve to live, must not live.'

Helena was calm, powerful and imperious.

'Neville, I understand your feelings, but you must not use these words, think these thoughts. We are not still in Ceylon, at the mercy of that dreadful man. We are in England, where there are laws and justice. You are yourself studying for the law, and should know this better than I. Also, we are not the savages we were when we first appeared on these shores, and were even prepared to hate dear Mr Crisparkle, who has done so much for us.' Her voice softened as she spoke of him. 'We have been educated, and know the ways of civilisation. Others, who know these ways better than we, for they have all lived longer in this country, also know of Jasper's infamy, indeed discovered it by bringing all their knowledge together, and carefully working it out, are determined to deal with him. They are level-headed, they are knowledgable, they have a plan. Leave the pursuit and punishment of Jasper to them.'

Neville was unconvinced.

'You are wiser than me, my dear sister, but you miss the point. I have been greatly wronged. I have been falsely accused. I have been deliberately and maliciously singled out for suspicion, ignominy and abuse. As a result, I have a role to play, which I must play, for my own sake, to assuage my feelings. Yet you are right, I won't kill him. I promise not to kill him, but I shall confront him and demand revenge, demand justice.' His voice rose as he spoke, and drove himself into yet greater anger. 'When I think of how he heard of my plan to leave Cloisterham early on Christmas Day, encouraged me in my purpose to leave as early and as silently as possible, warned that any delay would make it harder to leave the warmth and comfort of Minor Canon Corner on the day of the great festival, argued that the only way to forget about those comforts, and overcome thoughts of the loneliness and fatigue which would be my lot, was to get quickly on the road and out into the open; and all the while planning how to make my decision to leave Cloisterham for a while look like escape and flight after committing a cowardly and dastardly crime; why, my blood is so roused at the thought that I can hardly think straight. Perhaps I can't for the pain, and the rage and the injustice. But I do know that I have to do something and cannot just leave it to others.'

'But, Neville, my brother, I pray you, please do not put yourself in the wrong: I was about to say again, which would be unfair, since you and Drood – and, above all, Jasper – shared the guilt on that first occasion: but the word serves to remind us how others would see the matter. If you were to resort to an act of violence now, then the labours of Septimus Crisparkle in attempting to clear your name, and of Datchery and others in exposing Jasper, would be wasted. Cloisterham would continue to regard you as violent and untrustworthy, and – yes – even capable of murder when your blood was up: a savage beast, incapable of taming; as I have heard you yourself admit. And you know what people will be likely to think, when their suspicions about you are once again aroused. Even in the matter of Drood you will be found wanting, and even complicit; they will be all too ready to point out that the bad blood between you and Drood facilitated Jasper's plan of murdering his nephew.

There is a lesser matter, but still of importance: I, as your sister, would continue to attract some of the renewed criticisms directed at you, just when I can at last see some prospect of emerging from under the dark cloud of public disapproval. Think of me, think of Septimus Crisparkle, and yes – as he would remind us at this point – think of God, who holds us all in his hands. You have no rights of judgement, of punishment, of retribution.'

'Yes, sister, but Jasper had no right to, as it were, steal my soul and use it for his own purpose, and my disgrace. You must admit this. He created a different Neville, a creature capable of murdering Drood in cold blood, and foisted this on Cloisterham, when it was he who struck down his nephew. He stole my identity and used it for his purpose. Surely this justifies punishment – by me?'

Helena thought before answering. She was loth to bring Rosa into the argument. Crisparkle had forbidden the two of them to discuss her, in her view correctly, and she had no wish to rekindle Neville's interest and passion. But she still thought both lovingly and protectively of Rosa, and for her sake, and to warn Neville of the pitfalls, determined to mention the unmentionable.

'Neville, my dear, you will be surprised to hear me speak of Rosa. But it is for one purpose and one purpose alone: to help dissuade you from following the wrong course of action. Think of the effect on Rosa if you attack Jasper. Think of the wagging tongues and the malicious gossip. Thanks to the machinations of Jasper, your infatuation for Rosa became widely known. It is now likely to come out that Jasper also loved Rosa, and that that was the cause of her precipitate flight from Cloisterham.

363

If you were to attack him, it would all too easily be interpreted as an act of jealousy, of fighting over the poor girl. Alternatively, you might be considered to believe yourself her champion, punishing Jasper for killing her youthful companion Drood. For her sake, Neville, do not do it. She would be hurt and damaged all over again, just when she has found greater security and happiness in her life.'

She paused, but then steeled herself to continue, to play the last card in her hand, in the set, and finish her argument. She spoke gently.

'Do not forget, Neville, the growing understanding between her and Tartar. He is a good friend to her, as to us; he is helping her to overcome the horror of the scene by the sundial. Do not spoil this and raise old spectres which she is putting behind her.'

It was a tribute to the force and honesty of her personality, and also to the essential nobility and selflessness of Neville's character, that this appeal worked. He rapidly relented.

'Helena, dear, how do you always manage to see things so much more clearly, and so much more correctly, than I do. You are entirely right that, whatever my justified grievances, I must do nothing to hurt Rosa, who has already suffered so much in this matter, or bring a new blush, or fresh sorrow, to her cheek.' She looked at him appreciatively, but warningly, and he had the grace to smile self-deprecatingly.

'You are again right, sister, I must avoid thinking of her, or picturing her, least of all that pink little cheek, and I am now determined to keep off the subject Above all you are correct in reminding a budding lawyer,' she again glanced at him, but saw that the slip was both unintentional and unremarked on his part, 'that someone studying for the bar, at however an early and untrained stage, should be the last person to try to take the law into his own hands. How can lawyers earn an honest living, as I hope for both of our sakes I am able to do, if might were to usurp the prerogative of right?' He laughed happily: a rare enough sound in those pinched lodgings.

The rest of the day passed sociably and amicably. It was a warm and pleasant evening, and for once they strolled out together to enjoy it, he proud of her beauty and carriage, and glad to have her on his protective arm. It was as if the disasters and troubles of the past few months had passed, and they were fully back to the unity and closeness of understanding and purpose with which they had arrived off Joe's transport in Cloisterham. They were equal in spirit and grace, though she remained the stronger, the leader.

After walking, they sat and talked over the texts which Neville had read during the day, and which he had not yet had the chance to discuss with his tutor. So, as in the old days, the two young minds worked at them together, puzzling, parsing, examining, the two heads together in their labours. Then they parted for their beds, though Neville determined to read further that night. He expected Septimus Crisparkle in the near future, had even had unrealized hopes of seeing him that day.

Despite the harmony and ease of the evening, however, Helena was troubled and did not attempt sleep. She knew that Neville had been badly damaged, first by the wretched quarrel with Drood, and its outcome, and then by the six months of suspicion and the consequent misery he had endured. He had increasingly kept to himself, and stayed indoors, and his health and spirits had suffered. Their own mutual love and self-reliance had not abated, but she sensed that she was able to do less for him than she hoped, than she believed she might, and than she both could have done and had done in the past. The strange and unexpected events of the day had been cathartic, and certainly helped him overcome that listlessness and dejection which had been pervading his character of late; but the shock had been great, especially to someone in a weak state of health, and in previously low spirits. She had been worried, though not surprised, by the fury and violence of his reaction, and realised that his tigers still lurked very near the surface. Above all, she feared some further reaction on his part to what he had learned that day.

Helena knew Neville and his mind, probably even better than he did himself. She knew that his character had its weaknesses, and that he could give way to those traits of which he himself was the sternest critic: that he could be secret and revengeful and mean. She realised that, when he had said that she was in the right and that he deferred to her judgement, he genuinely meant this in all honesty. She fully understood that he wanted an evening of study followed by an unbroken and reviving sleep, hoped to wake fully rested, feeling that a heavy cloud had been lifted from him, and planned to remain quietly in Holborn, while awaiting the results of the morning's meeting with the Mayor of Cloisterham: for even that worthy could hardly believe Neville guilty having heard the testimony from Datchery and the others. She knew well what Neville wanted, hoped for and planned, at least in the course of a companiable evening; but she equally understood that this happy turn of events was, alas, a chimera.

For she knew that those tigers within Neville which had been awoken were now unlikely to rest or allow him to rest. She knew that he would be awake for part of the night: might indeed never go to sleep: and that during the night, in the dull, dark hours, he would brood, and think of the wrongs which he had suffered. She further and instinctively knew that his resentment would grow; that his determination to pursue and punish Jasper would re-emerge, more slowly but more powerfully this time, until it became unendurable; and that he would throw himself from his bed, which offered no sleep, and burst out of the house, and that she would be unable to stop him. Yes, she understood this quite well: even if she were able to stop him a first time, she could not mount guard over him, hour after hour: initially thwarted, he would find opportunity to escape, and would do so, feeling in his rage that even his sister had turned against him, and that he was being denied what he saw as his right. His previous listlessness would be turned into a negative cast of mind, into sullenness, into pessimism, into acting thoughtlessly and selfishly because any other route seemed unpromising.

So, resourceful as ever, she determined on a different stratagem. She would precede Neville, and reach Jasper before him. She had little fear of Neville actually harming Jasper, even in a furious assault: his power and endurance were much diminished by his long sojourn indoors; while Jasper was a tormented soul of considerable strength, who, like Joe, could probably deal with Neville single-handed. No, she was not worried about actual physical harm, though she had warned Neville of the damage which even an attempted assault would do his already low reputation in Cloisterham. Rather, she was concerned that Neville would inadvertently warn Jasper of the noose tightening round his neck, and would allow him to escape justice by some means. She was determined to prevent this, and to get to Jasper first. She was well aware that she would be able to act with greater care than Neville, with superior subtlety, and get from Jasper what she wanted, without alerting him, or giving the game away.

And what was it that she decided upon as she sat there, turning over in her mind the events of the day, and planning the future? What was it that her fierce if bridled spirit was determined to seek from Jasper, to get from him? Nothing less than the final clue to the mystery, the missing piece of the puzzle, the remaining secret: the revelation of how Jasper killed his nephew: to get this from Jasper, from his own lips, and then take it to Datchery and Grewgious – yes, and Septimus Crisparkle as well – and lay it at their feet, as her gift to them, her tribute. How she would achieve this, she did not yet know; she would determine her approach by judging Jasper's state and demeanour when she caught up with him; but she was supremely confident in her ability to confront or beguile Jasper, whom she did not fear in the least, to extract this information from him, to deliver it to her allies, and to achieve this before Jasper had any inkling of what she was about, before he had any opportunity to escape his fate.

Helena had worked all this out while Neville was yet reading. When she heard him cease, blow out his light, and get into that bed which alas offered so little prospect of calming sleep, she noiselessly left her room, equally noiselessly opened and closed the front door and descended the stair, took a cab to the station, and caught the first available train to Maidstone. All this was achieved while Neville was still tossing in his bed, vainly seeking sleep, and before his troubled mind started to review and revise his agreement with Helena that he should leave the pursuit of Jasper to Datchery and the law.

It was very early morning in Maidstone when she arrived. The breeze was beginning to stir the trees, betokening a change in the weather, after the untroubled warmth of the previous day. The town was asleep, and there was no Joe, and no Elephant and Castle, to convey her to Cloisterham. But although the citizens slept, there were one or two carts in from the country on their way with produce for shops and markets. She saw one of these which appeared to be heading north, for Cloisterham, and asked the driver whether this was the case, and, if so, whether he could give her a ride.

He looked surprised, but answered civilly enough: 'I am, and I can, Miss.'

She got up onto the box beside him, with such grace that again a look of surprise and even wonder appeared on his face.

They moved off.

'This is an odd time to travel, Miss. Lucky for you that there were carts such as mine. Better to be safe in one's own house at such an hour.'

She answered the implied question.

'There are occasions when it is not possible to choose the time for one's travel. But I can assure you that, when I finish with this mission, I shall return to my own lodging in London, and at a more Christian hour.'

'You are not running away then, Miss. You certainly don't look the type,' he glanced sideways at the handsome and dignified figure beside him, 'but I did wonder.'

She smiled.

'No, I am not running away, if anything I am running towards – ' She deliberately left the sentence unfinished. 'You will note that I carry no luggage, so am unlikely to be fleeing the ancestral home.'

'I had remarked that, but wondered whether you might have left in haste: that likewise explaining the hour.'

'In no haste, but under the necessity of helping my friends.'

He had to accept it, because it was clear that he was going to get no other explanation. And he did accept it, because it had the ring of truth. She spoke with such composure and certainty that he was convinced that here indeed was someone who would help her friends, and do it expeditiously and above all successfully.

Their talk turned to other, less personal matters; and never had the journey between Maidstone and Cloisterham sped by as it did for him that night. It was not that his horse suddenly acquired the hoofs of Bucephalus, or the wings of Pegasus; it maintained the same steady pace which had taken cart and driver along this road so many times, neither hastening nor delaying, and requiring neither reins nor whip. No, the time appeared to speed by as a result not of physical condition, but of circumstance, and the presence on the box beside him of a girl of singular beauty and resolution. He was charmed, despite his initial suspicion about her nocturnal adventure, and considered it a great honour to drive her wheresoever she pleased. If a fairy-godmother had appeared and sprinkled his old cart and his old horse – and even himself – with gold-dust, he could not have been more surprised or delighted with the events of that night. He remembered for a very long time the fine, dark lady whom he drove that morning. He remembered it even more clearly, and with yet greater pleasure, than Joe recalled the day when he had extended his protection to Rosa, and to her very little bag, and had been entrusted with the precious burden of Rosa's love – intended for Miss Twinkleton.

They arrived at Cloisterham before anyone or anything was stirring. The rooks were still in their nests, in the trees, in the Tower. Cathedral and castle were invisible in the darkness, though one could sense their lurking presence. The moon and the hanging stars were shrouded with cloud. Nothing moved.

Even Deputy seemed to be asleep, though no doubt with one eye open in case of trouble – or opportunity. Helena gratefully – and gracefully – thanked her horse-drawn benefactor, and made her way through the town, unobserved, as far as the Gatehouse. And so she, for the first and last time in her life, went up the postern stair.

* M *

CHAPTER XXXVII
Delirium

JASPER LIES ASLEEP: or half-asleep: or a quarter-asleep. He lies across the foot of the bed, with his clothes still on, merely his cravat loosened, his shoes off, his head resting on his left arm. Why does he lie like that? As if dead to the world, but far from unconscious, his brain working and spinning out of control, permitting him no mercy, no satisfied slumbering, no refuge from the thoughts and images which assail him.

He is drugged; or half-drugged; or part-drugged. He is dreaming, and delirious, and thinking and talking; thinking and talking to himself, thinking and talking of himself.

All nights are bad now: like this one. However often he takes the drug which he hopes will offer sweet oblivion, his midnight spectres stay with him until grey dawn. Perhaps he has allowed himself to get too used to it, too addicted; perhaps he has lost the art of mixing – but, if that is the case, how does he learn it again? He shudders at the mere thought of revisiting the old woman; his contentment in her room, in her company is ended. Never again would he sing himself into drugged sleep on that miserable bed, in that miserable room. He thinks of her hands on him, stroking him, feeling him, and he shudders uncontrollably.

The drug is losing its effect, giving him some longer periods of clarity and semi-consciousness. There are many things he wants to get straightened in his bewildered brain, to explain, to himself, and who knows, in certain circumstances, possibly to others. His mind is moving into and out of consciousness, into and out of comprehension, into and out of sense; and, at the same time, he is flickering seamlessly between incessant thought, and occasional speech: the latter, when it comes, expressing itself in a low, intense, careless muttering. He is thinking about many things: about his childhood, about his youth, about his sister, about Edwin Drood himself, but it is not always intelligible, even to himself. The words are pouring into his mind in profusion, in confusion.

'Tried to care, do my duty, look after him, for sister's sake.'

Yes, he had tried to do his duty in caring for Drood. He had done it for his sister, his dear sister, his dear dead sister, who had been like a mother to him. For her sake, he had even tried to like Drood. To like him? He had been obsessed with him: obsessed with his ease of manner, his supercilious way of treating others, his self-confidence. He had admired it: admired him. Thought, as he saw him with others: here was his nephew, his ward, whom he had brought up to be a fine fellow, engaging and sociable, superior and condescending. Lounging, the world all before him, a life of change and excitement. Journeying: ha! – journeying.

Yes, he loathed Drood's manner, and he loathed him. Don't moddley-coddley, there's a good fellow: like anything better than being moddley-coddleyed.

'Yes, Ned, like being kissed by Pussy, or kissing Pussy, there, that's better isn't it, Ned: the two of you kissed under the elm trees by the Cathedral that evening: I saw you, kissing each other fervently, her raising her face to you, kissing as if you would never stop, until you saw me and parted. Kissing, kissing.' He had followed them still. To see what they did next.

He groans as he lies there, thinking of that kiss, those kisses. He had never kissed her, done no more than touched her with his outstretched hand: outstretched because she was far from him, pulling away from him, recoiling from him. Never kissed her: though he had watched her face, watched her lips, watched her lips until they were engrained on his sight, on his brain, on his heart.

Then his mind is off down another track, but still thinking of Drood, still fascinated with Drood.

'Loathed it: loathed him.'

He enunciates the words with emphasis:

'I loathed him.' He remembers the words: 'Any dinner, Jack?'

'What a jolly old Jack it is: please to carve, Jack, for I can't. Of course he couldn't: never troubled to learn: why should he? There was always someone else for the carving, and the thinking, and the planning and the hard work. There was his uncle, no friend, no near contemporary, Jasper: Mr John Jasper, Lay Precentor and Choir-Master: no Lay Precentor and Choir-Master and fraud' (he laughs drowsily, as this addition takes his fancy). 'For Edwin Drood there was engineering, dreams of Egypt, shaking the place up, gaining reputation, taking Pussy.' *Taking Pussy*: he stops laughing abruptly.

Taking Pussy. Taking her from him, from his sight, from his dreams, from his – bed? Pussy, Pussy, twisting the knife in the wound, in his heart. Taking and shaking: shaking. Shaking his – Jasper's – nutcrackers at her. Calling her names: Miss Scornful Pert: Little Miss Impertinence. Intolerable: she had the right to show scorn and indifference to him: she showed it to everyone else – including to him, Jasper. Traducing that beautiful and enchanting – that cold and indifferent – that frightened and wilting – that cowed girl.

'I can, will possess her.'

He ought to have hit Drood: struck him there and then. But that would have given the game away, shown his hand. Given himself away!

'Take it as a warning, Ned,' why had he said that, laid his inner self bare? He just had to control himself, somehow, all the time. Had to control not strike.

'Control not strike. Control not – '

The juxtaposition of the words control and strike appears to worry him. He relapses into silence for a few minutes. But then he becomes restless, he stirs, twitches spasmodically and twists his body. The Princess Puffer would have understood the signs, would have expected some new revelation; she would have rolled the body slightly with a wizened hand, and put her ear close to the mouth: the cat gently stroking the stomach of the trapped and half-slain mouse. But she is not there to hear what he says.

He is on a new track; but it is a track which is evidently familiar to him. He is back in the place and time where he spends so many of his half-sleeping, half-waking hours; he is in his rooms, this same room, but not in the present, rather on that fateful Christmas Eve, going through the events again and again, repeating the actions which ended Drood's life, and changed his own life, yes and Neville's life too; just as he had done so many times before, planning, savouring, triumphing; but yet –

Suddenly he is dimly aware of another presence in the room, a silent arrival, an apparition. It is not the Princess Puffer, it is not someone pressing against him, feeling him, probing him. It is a girl of extraordinary beauty, who in the gloomy, sickly-smelling room, slightly coloured by the red light burning beneath, emanates youth and radiance; and it is standing at some distance from him, not seeking his secrets, but seeking to influence and even control him in some curious way. For a second, his confused brain believes it may be Rosa, come to visit him, to seek forgiveness for having fled from him, to repent for her behaviour, to offer amends. His dark, misty eyes, betraying their familiar film, look in her direction, gloatingly, possessively. But, even in his confusion and longing, he can see that it is not Rosa who is there and looking at him commandingly. The figure is dark, tall and dignified. He thrusts at it and tries to clutch it, but it easily eludes him, floats away; and, as he falls back, gasping, once again looms over him as he lies there.

'I do not fear you, Mr Jasper, as I told you once before, on that evening, when my immediate suspicions about you, and your feelings towards my dear friend Rosa, rapidly became certainties,' says Helena, with unwavering firmness and poise. She had heard about the opium from the mouths of Grewgious and Datchery, when she and Neville had overheard the conference in the garden; and she was immediately convinced that the man lying in front of her was under the influence of the drug (for there were Lascar seamen in Ceylon as well, and opium had a certain reputation), that she therefore had him at a disadvantage, and that his future recollection of the scene about to be played out would be scanty at best. She also suspected that, undisturbed, he was likely to spend many hours in hazy slumber after she planned to leave, which would allow a comfortable amount of time for the case against him to be made to the Mayor long before he could make a move. So she was determined to be bold.

'I have come to avenge Edwin Drood, to help my brother, and above all protect and defend Rosa from your further unwelcome advances. You will rapidly come to regret the ways in which you overbore, terrified, and sought to defile her.' She stares at him unblinkingly as she speaks, fixing him with her firm, intense, fiery dark eyes, looking straight at him, into him, peering into his very soul.

Yet even worse is the firm voice, which carries absolute authority and absolute determination.

'You stand accused of the murder of a man, of your nephew, of Edwin Drood. Do you plead guilty or not guilty?'

He is confused. Is he in a court of law? The firm voice suggests so. Charged with murdering a man? Again, the firm voice suggests this. How can this be? The crime was perfect, undetectable: so perfect and undetectable that it was no crime, no crime at all. When there's no crime about the house, there's –

He stirs again, uneasily, but when he recovers his wandering wits, he is still in the courtroom: so is she. He begins to explain, to make the case for the defence. It will all be easy enough, but he needs to start at the beginning, to build his explanation. Then the judge, or whoever this proud girl has turned into, will understand.

'Edwin Drood was not a man, he was a boy, an arrogant, spoilt, provocative boy. His attitude towards Rosa, towards me, yes towards Neville, who saw all his vanity and conceit,' – perhaps this would help placate her – 'was insupportable. He behaved as if life and rewards came without effort, without any attempt to earn or deserve them. He only needed to call his Pussies by the dozen to make them come,' – was he speaking from painful memory? – 'People cannot behave in that way and escape just censure and due punishment. He acted as if it were beneath him to take the effort to pluck the golden fruit that hung ripe on the tree. But,' his voice becomes more frantic, and rises above a mumble, 'I saw them kissing that evening. Kissing passionately, fervently, kissing like lovers, kissing as if they were saying good-bye, goodbye for ever. Forever,' a manic laugh, 'yes, that's right, they were.'

Some sense in his tortured, tired brain is telling him that this will not do as the case for the defence. It sounds too much like jealousy, like a confession, a confession which will mean the scaffold. The scaffold! More feelings of agitation, more contortions of the body, more wriggling by the mouse.

He is still in court, so he still has the chance to make amends for his initial, blundering attempt to explain. He can hear the judge, who still seems to be the tall and imposing girl, saying in the same firm voice: 'Just tell the truth, Mr Jasper, the truth.'

And somehow, hearing her voice, he wants to tell her the truth, the whole truth. He finds himself wishing to help her; knowing that in doing so he will help himself, exculpate himself; and then she will help him; it is all so clear; it shines out like a light in his dazed world.

'I did not murder Drood. I did not raise a finger. Yes, I had thought of it, planned it, longed for it, committed it in my thoughts, in my dreams, a thousand times, hundreds of thousands of times, millions and billions of times. I determined to do it at the time of the reconciliation proposed by Crisparkle – who ever stood in my way, but this time offered a priceless opportunity. At first I was horrified by his idea. I would lose the cover, the suspicions about Neville I had so carefully built up. Then I saw how I could do it. Suggest a meeting to confirm the reconciliation: bring the three of us together again, and thus provide the chance I could use. Better still, in his reply, Drood proposed a dinner. It was perfect. After the dinner, rid of Landless and relaxing with Drood and discussing the evening, I would find occasion to strangle him with my scarf: with my large black scarf of strong close-woven silk: and then dispose of the body in the Sapsea tomb. With all suspicions thrown upon Landless.' An ugly chuckle, and his hands clench and grasp, clench and grasp again.

A thought appears to strike him. After all, he is not a monster, he is not bereft of humanity, of human feelings and emotions. The Sapsea tomb: Mrs Sapsea's tomb: hasn't that poor woman suffered enough? Can't she be permitted a little peace at the end, in her death, requiescat in pace? Too bad, why did she marry that canting, prating jackass? Her tomb was the perfect place, just as Landless was the perfect suspect, the perfect dupe; and the key was already in his possession.

He mutters on.

'How many times have I strangled Drood with that scarf? In my imagination, always in my imagination. Always, at some point, I found myself strangling him, with the scarf; we were together, I was pulling the scarf tight; and we reached the end, his end, together; and then I was free, and Rosa was mine, in my power, at last. Free for plucking, for wooing, for winning, for – '

Once again, he pauses. This is again getting out of hand, it does not sound like the case for the defence, he must do better. He checks his chain of confused and heated thought, and starts anew, resumes his mutterings. As he tells the story, remembers and rehearses the events of the past, the voice gradually grows stronger and more coherent.

'But, Judge, My Lord, no My Lady, members of the jury, it was not like that. It was the storm which gave me the idea, the new and wonderful and exciting idea, the inspiration, the final touch. I had already had opportunity to influence – mesmerise – both Drood and Rosa; just dabbled to test my powers; showed I could make a slave of her, draw her to me against her will; direct his mind when I wished to; so I knew that I could do it. Could do it and would do it; and do it now for a purpose, my purpose, my punishment of Drood, my pursuit of Rosa.

I had already realised that the storm would be the perfect cover for my plan: it would blanket any noise, and no-one would be abroad to observe what I did. But I could do better than that: I could make the storm itself the killer: the storm and the great tower, together, in unison, fulfilling my purpose.

So, when he returned from visiting the river with Landless, I mixed him one final glass of punch. He protested, of course, said he was ready to turn in for the night. But I persuaded him, as I always did; played on our friendship, our nearness in age, our closeness. I said that we needed to celebrate both the success of the evening, and the welcome reconciliation with Landless, which had been the success of my dear boy, not of me, the humble host; and also drink to his departure, a stirrup-cup to say farewell before he left in the morning. Yes, another stirrup-cup, another departure, why did the young fool not suspect, why didn't he leave then and there, rush out into the night, back into the storm, better that than face me. But he didn't.' Jasper is gasping and panting with the effort of talking, of explaining, of remembering, of attempting to explain, to convince.

'So I mixed, and he drank, and very soon he felt the effects: it made him drowsy this time, and easy to influence. I played with him, enjoying the experience for one last time; I told him how he was going on a journey, the famous journey, the journey I knew so well, a very long journey, leaving in the morning, perhaps even sooner than that.

As I talked, I fixed him with my black gaze, with the look of intensity and intentness which I often summoned when talking to him, to prevail over him, to bind him to me, to break the colt, to take the young puppy in hand. He was tired, and offered no resistance, and easily fell in with my wishes. The tremendous noise and commotion of the storm provided the perfect background; he was still I think slightly drunk from feeling the full effect of the storm outside, beating directly on him on his way to and from the river, the punch added to the effect, and the sound of the elements still battered his senses. I suggested that he ascend the tower to view the storm from there; it would be better and more impressive than by the river, and he would see much more of its effects. It was so simple: I had in my pocket the key to the gate giving access to the tower.'

He checks himself; this is a point which he feels he needs to explain to the judge, otherwise he fears that she will not believe his testimony. But he has to think, and do it carefully to carry conviction. He stares at the wall for inspiration, and then continues, speaking now slowly and carefully.

'You must not think that I am claiming to carry all the keys of Cloisterham in my pocket. Even Durdles cannot manage that.' He essays a light laugh, supposing how many separate pockets Durdles would require, but it goes horribly wrong, and comes out as an evil cackle, so he reverts to the spoken word without adornment.

'No, I just had the crypt and tower keys on my person: and the big key of course, the great key,' inadvertently, he winks knowingly, before recovering himself, 'had them copied, that night with Durdles; just in case. As I planned the murder, I was determined to leave nothing to chance. So I had and kept the key to the tower, in case it came in useful, which it did; and he was in no state to question why I had it or its fellow.'

As he returns to his tale of that night, his voice again picks up speed, and starts to race ahead, as if experiencing the events all over again.

'I went with him, opened the way through the crypt to the tower, and then pointed him on his way. I said that I would not accompany him, having no head for heights. "Poor old Jack; what a feeble old Jack it is," he said as he went up the circular stair unsteadily: his last words. Up he went, up and up, round and round, and disappeared from my view. The strength and noise of the wind was frightful and terrifying, but he was under my spell and hardly seemed to notice. Up he went on his difficult and dangerous journey, his hazardous and perilous journey. A slip would be destruction. He went the journey, and never saw the road, or where it was leading. Up and up he went, obedient and docile. I could make out his footfalls for a short way, and then lost them in the thunder of the storm.

I turned on my heel, and retreated back the way we had come together, locking the doors behind me as I went: there was no way he would be returning that way, could survive up there in the howling wind and the driving rain. Lead from the roof, stones from the summit of the tower, even the hands of the clock, were all ripped away and cast to the ground. The debris was falling all around me, but I didn't mind: I felt elated, immortal, as I walked along the north side of the Cathedral, awaiting him. Soon, he followed the lead and the stones and the rubble. He fell, he crashed to the ground, without a word or a cry. His body lay beside the old Norman Tower, just at the point where he had fallen from the roof. It looked crushed and beaten, as if by a heavy iron-wood stick.' The manic laugh again, then silence and muttering.

'But it shouldn't be found, mustn't be found, won't be found.'

Then, in a clearer voice.

'So I set him on his way inside, and welcomed him and bade farewell outside. He lay there, dead.'

A slight pause before he continues.

'Dead, but not by my hand. All I did was to get rid of the body, give it decent burial in a tomb, alongside a worthy woman, with a husband of great substance.' He giggles inanely at the jest, but then grows more serious.

'Hardly a hanging offence, ladies and gentlemen: especially,' and here he grasps his hair as he shouts in rage and grief and pain, 'especially as I did not profit from his death.'

In his agony, he does not hear, or sense, the fair judge leaving; but suddenly he feels that she is no longer in the room.

Fully awake now, he staggers to his feet, but then sits heavily on his bed, shaking uncontrollably, head in hands, bemoaning his woes. The death of Drood had brought him nothing. Rosa had fled: where? Landless was out of sight, and there was no word from the man charged to watch and harrass him: why? Worse, his own relentless pursuit of Landless was doomed from the start. He had proudly boasted to Rosa that it was possible to pursue both the innocent and the guilty; how circumstances could accumulate against the innocent, and one wanting link condemn the guilty; but he was unable to produce or concoct or fabricate or direct evidence against Landless. There was no body. It was lying and disintegrating in the tomb, without identification. How could he prove murder against Landless? Instead, he was left, slinking about, hiding, keeping an eye in every direction, sneaking to and fro, dodging up and down, looking for – nothing!

He had miscalculated. When he had overheard Landless telling Crisparkle of his plan to leave Cloisterham the morning after the evening reconciliation, he had thought that the gods were smiling on him, that events were playing into his hands. He had immediately grasped the opportunity he would have for throwing indelible suspicions upon Landless, and had laughed and laughed at his good fortune. He had been almost unable to control himself. But he had been wrong. He had celebrated too soon and too thoughtlessly.

Starting to lose full consciousness again, he gives up sitting and falls back on the bed, in the same posture as before: it seems to come naturally to him. His hand reaches out for something, but fails to find it: another cause for misery and the utmost dejection.

As he lies, as he feels his room seeming to move around him, he thinks and broods. Killing Drood had been too short and easy. There had been no satisfaction, no excitement, no triumph. There was no struggle, no physical dominance, no feeling of mastery, no consciousness of peril. It was a poor, mean, miserable thing. It was the poorest of all his visions. It was not worth the doing, it was done so soon. It was not like the dreams of strangling Drood; of squeezing the life out of his body; of punishing him for being Drood and betrothed to Rosa, of seeing his soundless mouth begging for mercy; of overcoming his febrile but impotent attempts to free himself; of hearing him gasping for breath which would not come – could not come; perhaps of sensing the neck crack, like a nut in the jaws of a nut-cracker; of feeling him suddenly go limp; of seeing him fall to the floor, mouth gaping, body lifeless.

Lifeless; that was his own existence now. Wasted and empty; cramped monotony; the Cathedral, the choir, the town, all the things he hated; ahead bleak nothingness; desolation of heart and spirit; a man living his very life apart; opium no longer the cure as he brooded on his miseries, but too often the cause.

Half-consciousness claims him again. He is back in the courtroom: why? Why has he not been acquitted? Acquitted without a stain on his character? Hadn't the judge been listening, was the jury asleep, hadn't they realised that he had not killed Drood, that he was innocent, innocent? Had the judge really left? Why had she left?

But here was a new mystery to unravel. There still appeared to be a judge in the room. He could not see this person, yet seemed to hear a voice. And that voice was undoubtedly male. A nasal, legal whine, quite unlike the steady voice of the female judge: the judge who had listened to him. This new judge had not even been present for his explanation, for his defence. What kind of trial was this: when the judge had not heard the words of the defendant?

As a consequence, this new judge, this false judge, this ignorant lying judge, is leaping to the wrong conclusions. Listen! The sentence of death is being pronounced. To be taken to the place of execution, to hang by the neck until dead. This is a travesty. He tries to cry out, to appeal, to stop the case; but no sound comes. He is powerless.

CHAPTER XXXVIII

I come, Graymalkin

NEVILLE RISES EARLY, though he is a long way after Helena. He leaves their lodging, believing her to be still there and asleep. He does not check, because he does not wish to disturb her. This is now a difference between them. She retains that perfect knowledge of him, that natural understanding of all his thoughts and actions. But he does not know and predict her with the same certainty, with the same automatic unity of spirit and feeling. It has been lost to him, squeezed out of him by worry, and by hiding indoors away from the sun. It represents another, and very fundamental, loss for his life and well-being, as a result of Jasper's cruel persecution.

It had been just as Helena foresaw, as she knew and understood in her whole being. During the long, black night, Neville's fury, his anger directed against Jasper for his infamy, his baseness, finally boiled over again, fuelled by the newly-acquired knowledge as to why Jasper had been so intent on persecuting him. Helena's wise words were all swept aside in Neville's rush of self-pity; it was not her honour, or even that of Rosa, which had been deliberately and systematically impugned; it was not their lives which had been deliberately poisoned; it was his quarrel, and his alone; he had to fight his own cause. And, in the dark of the night, Helena was not there to control his headstrong and selfish urgings; to argue that the evil deeds of Jasper had affected her and more especially her dear friend Rosa as well, that they also had suffered at the hands of that cruel and unnatural monster, that Neville had no unique right of vengeance; to remind him that Datchery, well advised by Grewgious and Crisparkle, had the matter in hand. There were no contrary voices and calming arguments.

Neville descends the stairs, and hastens towards the station. He is now the hunted turned hunter; but there is still something of the hunted in him, as he hurries through the streets, feeling them somehow hostile to himself and his mission. He looks haggard and careworn, and blinks in the bright light of morning.

The weather has changed. There is a powerful wind from the West, and it is bringing with it rain and storm. The trees are bending before it, surrendering leaves and dead twigs; dust and rubbish blow around the streets. Neville can feel the rain in the wind as he goes, and soon the first squall drives across Holborn and assaults his hastening figure.

He scarcely notices, for he is fulminating angrily as he hurries along: the name Landless had been given him at his birth, and was all too appropriate: Landless he was, and Landless he remained, without status, relying on the kindness and generosity of Septimus Crisparkle, because Jasper had stolen his good name and reputation.

As he crosses the River Thames, a sudden blast of wind and rain sends a black shudder across the surface of its waters, raises little waves, and even crowns them with crests. There is another squall as he reaches the station, and takes the train. The rain follows him from London, overtakes him, and anticipates him in Maidstone. The squat bus is waiting. Neville takes a place inside, rather than on the box by the muffled figure of Joe; the storm provides a good excuse for keeping apart. He and Joe see each other, and eye each other, but say nothing. Neville is back to a world where people recognise him, and connect him with certain past events. He does not relish it, and it adds to his sense of injustice and resentment against Jasper. He will show these people who was really responsible for the disappearance, nay murder, of Drood; make them eat their words; force them to choke over their suspicions and their baseless allegations; and wring an apology from them.

The bus arrives at Cloisterham, and Neville alights, still doing his best to ignore Joe. The wind continues blustery, though it now seems to be blowing the rain away, driving the clouds before it, rather than bringing the storm. Neville remains largely oblivious to such things. His mood remains fiery as he starts to walk down the High Street, keeping mainly to the side of the road, and avoiding the gaze of passers-by. This is the place where he had felt the first stirrings of happiness in his life, where he had been welcomed by Septimus Crisparkle; and not only welcomed, but listened to and believed in. The figure of the Minor Canon, pink and polished, and benevolent and Christian, rises up before him and he can scarcely suppress a sob. This could have been the turning point in his life, his fresh start; instead, from the very first evening, he became enmeshed and entrapped in Jasper's web of selfish villainy and deceit. From that first evening, he could not walk outside without being looked on and whispered about as a dangerous savage; even inside his own lodging in Minor Canon Corner, it had been clear that Mrs Crisparkle also regarded him in this unflattering light. She had a tendency to glance about her, and seek possible places of sanctuary with her eyes, when in his company; and he had heard her remonstrating with her dear Sept, and counselling him to take care. Yet, without Jasper's machinations, the high words between him and Drood would have gone unremarked, their quarrel would not have been inflamed, he would have returned quietly to his room that night, and would not have met Drood again before Christmas: by which time the latter would no longer be betrothed to Rosa, leaving a possible opening for others.

Even in his mood of resentment and self-pity, he immediately ceases this train of thought, and forces himself to stop thinking of Rosa in this way. The kindly figure of Septimus Crisparkle is still in his mind, this time in mood of stern remonstrance: he vividly remembers the ban imposed by that conscientious teacher, and his own pledge to erase Rosa from his mind. He also glimpses the image of his sister, imploring him wordlessly and compassionately to listen to Crisparkle and do what is right. In any case, Tartar is now on the scene; he knows full well that he has lost Rosa for ever, and even in his rage he would not contemplate doing anything to offend or hurt his latest friend and guide and comforter.

His anger directed against Jasper is however unabated: perhaps even heightened by these conflicting emotions and recollections. Neville strides along, his heavy walking stick firmly clasped in his clenched right fist. He is in control of himself and his emotions; but is both confrontational and determined: determined to seek revenge for his lost opportunity of happiness, his lost hours. Jasper's evil plotting, his haunting and tormenting, his maligning and impugning, had deprived Neville of life and youth, driven him inside, kept him indoors, banished him from human intercourse, made him seek darkness and refuge, and worn out his daily life, grain by grain. And, now he is out and about, back in Cloisterham, and again the butt of anxious asides and contemptuous glances.

Even though he is deliberately not looking around him, he senses this reaction as he passes through the streets, where the citizens are making use of the break in the clouds to go about their morning business. He glimpses people and faces he half-remembers. There is Mrs Tisher, the sole numen of the Nuns' house, in Miss Twinkleton's absence, and greatly missing the latter's improving conversation during the long evenings, albeit now accompanied by the cook who is accounted a doughty conversationalist herself, and eager to convey the gossip of the day: they are out together doing some morning shopping, no doubt for the seminary. Pretty Mrs Tope is also abroad, still worrying about Mr Jasper, whom one scarcely sees these days, poor man, he is still so took up with that sad business of his nephew, and who knows how he spends his days and nights, he looks so dazed, and his clothes and bed so crumpled, and that curious smell in his room of a morning.

Neville feels them stiffen and stare, and heads turn. He hears some of the sentences and half-sentences: "thought he had gone for good"; "for good! For bad, you mean"; "What's he about now, sloping along?"; "up to something: look at his mean, weasely face"; and, definitively, in the cook's rich and resonating contralto, "Why, that's the boy wot upped and threw the decanter and the cutlery at that poor young Master Drood like a tiger, before going for him with a sabre," – was cook in danger of confusing her tigers? – "and then done him to death by all accounts."

So, he is back, and still the subject of gossip and speculation and malice: all Jasper's work. Yet he has no plan. He is uncertain what to do. He just wants to find Jasper, to confront him, to pour forth his angry passion.

Perhaps because he remains uncertain about his future actions and plans, but also because he feels light-headed as a result of having been outside in the open air since first dawn, after his months of seclusion away from the daylight, and possibly also because he sub-consciously wishes to avoid the prying and hostile eyes, his feet do not succeed in taking him directly to the Gatehouse. They take him on a curious circuitous route through the town. He does not escape the dull yards and quiet alleys, which nevertheless do have the advantage of removing him from the growing throng in the High Street.

What he does escape, however, are the attentions of Helena, who is awaiting his likely arrival by train and Joe's omnibus, but is uncertain where best to do this. She does not wish to wait too near Jasper's Gatehouse; she has finished with him, extracted from him what she wanted, and does not wish to see him again, or to attract or inspire any suspicions. Equally, she does not wish to wait too near the place where Joe's vehicle disgorges its customers, lest she be seen to await someone – Rosa, after her sudden disappearance, or Miss Twinkleton, after her departure for London with the seventeen, or was it eighteen, trunks and packages, or even her unhappy brother, after his long absence from the town – and thus draw unwanted attention to his return. So she resolves to wait further up the High Street, between the entry to the Gatehouse, and Joe's terminus, and, as a result, entirely misses Neville as he unwittingly evades her.

He passes the two mechanical figures, the demonic representatives of Time and Death, facing each other, and sawing the raw stone in Durdles's yard, lively and remorseless at their joint labour, like devils armed with pitch-forks relentlessly shoveling the bodies of the damned into the flames of Hell. How many monuments are they preparing? One? Two?

Finally, and after his indirect approach, he arrives at the Gatehouse from the rear, from the Cathedral side. Helena is still on duty, further up the street the other side of the Gate, unaware of what had happened, but starting to feel uneasy. Where is he? She cannot be wrong in what her whole soul tells her about Neville's intentions and state of mind. She knows that he is near her, somewhere in Cloisterham: but where?

Neville reaches the postern stair. He knows his way up: all too well, alas! The stair, and Jasper's rooms at the top, are always connected with unhappiness, with tragedy in his life: first the dreadful quarrel with Drood on that first evening: then Christmas Eve, an awkward occasion which he had tolerated but found it difficult to enjoy because he and Drood were so obviously uneasy and on edge, while Jasper was so very lively and even ebullient in manner, and which led to murder, suspicion and impeachment: and now he is there again, mounting the same steps, heading for the same rooms. He should therefore have stayed away, not mounted the stair, repudiated his mission, returned to London, gone out of his way to avoid his nemesis Jasper, kept away from him at all costs. A voice in his head tells him all this: is it Helena's, is it Septimus's, is it his dead mother's?

But he does not listen, or heed; instead, he goes boldly up the postern stair, just as the rain-clouds release a sudden, final but momentary shower of heavy raindrops.

CHAPTER XXXIX
The Condemned Cell

JASPER IS STILL dreaming. Dreaming? He is delirious, hallucinating in his ravaged and confused mind.

He now finds himself in the condemned cell. There are the dank grey walls, the cold rough blocks of stone, the bars which look old and rusty but which can resist the most frenzied attempt to break through them, the miserable small window designed to keep the light out and reveal no view and no sight of anything of the outside world, the remains of the untasted meal and glass of brackish water on the rickety table, the total absence of anything which could be used for escape or resistance or suicide. A bare, empty, depressing, miserable place, with a bare, empty, depressing, miserable purpose.

He can hear the rustle of the solitary warder keeping careful watch outside: and occasionally hear him move and take a pace, and see his basilisk eye at the peep-hole. There is no way out, no way back: Drood is dead, and cannot return: Jasper is guilty and cannot escape.

He starts to mutter again, more disjointedly this time, unsteadily, as if feeling the slight weight of a skinny arm lying across his chest and stomach.

'Two women. Made me. Unmade me.' Wasn't there a verse of Dante he had learned at school? Dante: Purgatory and Hell. Forget Heaven. Journey too far. *Cammin di nostra via*. Divine Comedy. What was there of divinity or comedy about life?

He pauses, as if for thought, but it is not thought but spurts of confused memory and association which are murmured through his dry and caked lips.

'Jenny. Sister. Sister, a mother. Happiness. Gone; gone, destroyed by Droods. Destroyed by dreaded Droods. Dreadful, dreaded Droods. Dre – ' He falls silent, but his mind and face work.

Rosa. A ray of hope, of loveliness. He pictures her, and groans and writhes. She had filled his life, consumed him. Nothing else mattered to him, nothing else existed. Only she could save him, guide him through the abyss. Give him what he wanted, when everything else failed him – even the pipe. Failed him and enraged him and ground him down. Dreaded Drood, hateful Cathedral, terrible town. Dreaded, hateful, terrible. Dreadful, hateful, terrible. Dreffle. Yes, the old woman was right. 'Dreffle, dreffle, dreffle.' Another thought comes to him, and he stops his chant excoriating town and Cathedral and Drood.

'Killed for her, make her mine. But she has gone, gone – '

Silence, and then a longer sentence, a memory from the Cathedral, a text which he knew and must have pondered, looked upon as a lifeline as he confronted what he had done.

· 'When a man turneth away from his wickedness which he has committed, and doeth that that is lawful and right, he shall save his soul alive.' He even manages a few notes of plainsong in his deep voice: the Princess would have recognised the sweet tones.

He stops, and again there is silence. The silence reflects a pause for anguished thought, and then the muttering begins again.

'Too late. No redemption.' The word redemption seems to trigger something in his brain, and he becomes more alert, more awake.

'How can I save my soul when I have committed murder? How can I turn from that? Turn? From murder? How can murder be undone? Even if the soul can be saved, how can I, my body, be saved when I lie in the condemned cell?'

He rapidly rejects the notion as absurd. Who could possibly have proposed it? He cannot think.

Instead, and as so often, he finds himself delving back into memory: not of murder this time, but of his past life, of the women who had played a role.

'Two women? Three.'

The old woman, the ghastly, dying old woman, the complaining old woman. But she had the trick, she knew how to mix, provided brief comfort, enjoyment, release. No, not comfort, alleviation. He likes the word alleviation, which suddenly comes to him, and smiles as he lies there. And repeats it. And says it:

'Alleviation.'

Alleviation from pain and grief. He thinks of another word, and smiles the same smile: temporary.

'Temporary alleviation: that's it. Talking like a doctor now. Hate doctors and doctors' phrases.'

Their argot. Their patina of words artfully contrived to enhance their standing and confound their patients. The words again form on his lips, as he renews his muttering.

'Same doctors who failed to save Jenny.' The smile turns to a snarl, which looks more natural on his face. Canting hypocrites. Incapable, canting hypocrites. Incapable, canting, cretinous hypocrites. He starts to chant again: 'Canting, cretinous – ' He is quite enjoying this, and the snarl relaxes. He thinks further. Enjoyment. Release. The door to glorious dreams of murder, throttling Drood. Throttling dreffle Drood. Dreffle-Drood. The door? Closed. All doors closed. 'Ladies and Gentlemen, this door is pronounced closed.'

And what was wrong with the mixture now. It grew weaker, slower, less potent, but more poisonous and debilitating. Like the murder itself, less satisfying. He lacked the secret, the trick. She would not tell me.

'Why lose my custom, deary? Why give away trade, when times is bad, chuckey? As they are; as bad as my poor lungs,' So, it simply led to complaint. Tirades and complaints. Used to be worth it for the mixture. But no more.

He appears to recoil, to shy away from something: something or someone who is rolling him gently, insistently. Surely he had decided never return to her, never. Yet he seems to feel the thing again, stirring him, soothing him, asking him about the journey, the murder, the murdered, the murderer.

The murdered: the murderer. He sees the grim outline of the gallows, feels the harsh rope round his neck, senses the sudden chasm opening beneath his feet, experiences the desperate fear, the sharp pain, the finality, the nothingness. But what is this? His past life already seems to have passed in front of his eyes, so there is nothing more to see, but what is happening now? It is as if he, Jasper, is suddenly divorced, separated from his body. He is a spectator at his own death. He sees his mortal remains brutally cut from the gallows, cast aside, and tossed into a sack. The body of Mr John Jasper, Lay Precentor and Choir-Master at Cloisterham Cathedral, highly respected member of the town and society, intimate of His Worship the Mayor: just tossed into a common sack. And then taken for burial; thrown into the ground and buried: buried, but not before a spadeful of quick-lime is unceremoniously poured over the sack; just like the quick-lime he had inexpertly poured over the body of Edwin Drood, spilling some on his outer clothing. Still divorced from his own body, the spirit of Jasper is horrified and appalled by the dreadful justice and infernal symmetry, but understands the aptness of it all.

The figure on the bed shrieks aloud, and wakes. Awakes as a sudden cold clutches at him. The door opens, and Neville Landless strides into his room.

CHAPTER XL
Blood will have Blood

JASPER SEES THE figure in front of him, talking, shouting, gesticulating, waving a heavy stick in its clenched right fist; demanding an apology, restitution, satisfaction, the magistrate, the police. But, however furious and desperate, the figure does not attack his inert victim. Some sense of decency and decorum, some memories of the moral counsel and Christian earnestness of Septimus Crisparkle and the sweet but powerful pleadings of Helena, seem to stay his hand. Also, Neville has not thrown off the fatigue of his long journeying, which weighs him down.

This gives Jasper his chance. He gathers all his strength, and makes for the door. He is a powerful man, and tends to violence when he is returning from his visions and fantasies to the world inhabited by other human beings. He seldom seems to remember or mind that other smokers do not like being pounced upon, and seized, and turned, and dragged to the floor; but it is part of the pleasure and satisfaction which Jasper used to derive from his visits to the den. The domination over other men, silencing them if they dare to be "intelligible", the physical gratification of seizing and bullying them: that is what was sadly wanting in his murder of Drood, the cause of much subsequent regret and despair. He savagely shoulders the youth aside, using more force than he needs, and rushes for the door and the stair.

As with Neville, he does not have a plan, but he has instincts to assist him. Finding himself out in the bright morning light, he shies away, and has only one object; like any fugitive animal he makes for the dark. Directly in front of him, he sees the gaping mouth, the Great West door, of the Cathedral, surmounted by the monumental window. Inside, he sees the welcoming, cavernous darkness, smells the musty air, the compound of wood and leather and candle-wax and vault and damp and dust, senses the deep shadows and the gloomy corners; and rushes in through the folding door earlier opened by Tope. He sees that venerable figure, Chief Verger and Showman, self-importantly gesturing an excursion party out of the chancel, and in dumb but authoritarian show pointing to a sign with a single minatory word "Private" written upon it in Tope's fair hand. All this takes a little time, and means that Tope sees nothing of what ensues, and is quite unable to keep the patrons of the public bar of the Crozier Hotel, or even the solitary waiter, regaled over the years to come with a definitive account of the events about to unfold. The role of Neville in particular was absent from any of the myriad fictions produced by Tope in this period.

The dank air helps clear Jasper's mind as he draws breath. He briefly thinks of seeking asylum by the high altar; but how will that help save him from the savage hard on his heels, who probably knows nothing of such niceties as sanctuary, and carries an equally savage stick, and will probably prove less reluctant to use it a second time? He glances round, and, avoiding the centre of the Cathedral, makes for the passage to the left of the choir. This leads through to the oratory, but he is thinking of escape not prayer. Then, to his left, he sees another door: smaller than the western entrance, but equally friendly to a fugitive. More friendly. It is the door to the lofty tower; it also lies open; the good Tope has not been idle that morning, and has prepared everything for the arrival of the bell-ringers. Jasper races through it, and up the tower. Up, up, up; away from his pursuer.

But his pursuer waits behind. Uncertain of purpose, and infirm of body, he does not follow Jasper far into the church, let alone up the tower. After a few uncertain paces into the sudden darkness, he halts and then retreats, retracing his steps back into the clear air and the open space between Cathedral and castle.

There, he forces himself to stop, to think, to decide what to do. Jasper has no escape; he is up the tower and there is no way out for him without being seen from where Neville now stands. So he does not need to follow him. This determination, and the pause for further thought which it allows, permits further reconsideration, deeper questioning of himself. What would he do if he did follow Jasper? Confrontation in Jasper's room had signally failed: why would a further meeting up the tower, or on the ground in front of the Cathedral, achieve any more? What indeed is he attempting to achieve?

As he broods, he suddenly realises what he should do. He should do what he should have done in the first place, what Helena had begged him to do, what the clear light of day was steadily persuading him to do, overcoming the black hours of night which had engendered his madness and his whole sorry – and ineffectual – expedition. He should withdraw from the role he had foolishly assigned himself, and leave the pursuit of

Jasper to others more capable than himself; and, as a first step, he should seek out Septimus Crisparkle, confess all, and tell him where Jasper now was. As ever, Crisparkle would be his saviour. He turns away, and once again, after a gap of several months, finds himself following the familiar path to Minor Canon Corner.

But Jasper knows nothing of Neville's change of heart and plan. He urges himself forward, his one thought to get away, as far and fast as possible. He is incapable of thinking beyond this. Having mounted the first winding set of steps, he sets off towards the great tower rising majestically above him: forward and upward. Across the roof, and through the rafters under the next, higher roof, and up into the bell-ringing chamber under the weighty, silent bells. The hoarse rooks cease their croaking and cawing, and flee at his approach.

In the ringing room, he hesitates. The dark and warmth are comforting. But the shakes are returning. He wants to sit down, sit in a chair, hold it tight, hold himself tight, steady himself. But he can't: he has to move forward. He glances at the ladder up to the tower, and the shaking grows stronger. He looks round frantically. There is a small door to his right. He makes for it, and thrusts it open.

He rushes out into the confusingly bright light again. He is over the North Transept, on the other side of the edifice to Minor Canon Corner. He sees the town lying beneath him: the spreading ruins of the old abbey, the streets and alleys, the castle and river, the lofty trees, the river with its barges. He sees the clouds rolling across and away, the dark grey to the East, and the bright light to the West. But, above all, he sees the habitations: the red-brick houses and the red-tiled roofs; and the inhabitants moving around like small insects.

He peers down at the scene below him with new interest. Why, there's his escape; the way to avoid his pursuer; he can simply walk out onto it, into it, and hide himself again. Escape his isolation, hide among those clustered houses, among those anonymous people. Away from the savage and his stick, away from suspicion, hidden safely in the hospitable and unquestioning town. In his excitement, he runs rather than walks across the wet and treacherous flag-stones: towards the parapet, towards the edge, towards safety.

His body topples from the tall tower, falling outwards as it descends, and plummets to the ground. But he does not hit the ground. He is instead caught; but he is not held up by magic, or by angelic hands. He is impaled on the tip of one of the iron railings which lie beside the grave-yard to the West of the North Porch, the grave-yard where Mrs Sapsea and – yes, Edwin's unhappy father – are buried and commemmorated. He hangs there, like a great black rook awkwardly fallen from its nest in the belfry, motionless, lifeless. Perhaps that is why the rooks of the neighbourhood start to collect and gather round, as if one of their number is missing. But it is the body of a man which is hanging lifeless from a murderous spike.

The tower has avenged Drood, and punished Jasper. He has indeed fastened the crime of Drood's murder on the murderer, as promised in the Diary entry shown to Crisparkle so many months previously. He has devoted himself to his own destruction, and has most effectively succeeded.

CHAPTER XLI
The Aftermath

GREWGIOUS, DATCHERY AND Crisparkle have not been idle. They have made their separate ways to Cloisterham, foregathered in Minor Canon Corner, and now called or rather waited upon the Mayor. They attended him in his office, which he has redesigned after the manner in which he considered a ministerial office might be furnished; and, to complete the similarity, the Mayor, as was his present wont, was attired in what could only be termed ministerial dress: nothing of the clergy about him at all. The very thought of spats would revolt him.

Datchery, again fully equipped with snowy white locks, has done most of the talking. He wished to put aside the wig for good, as well as that peculiar third-person way of addressing the Mayor, but Grewgious did not allow him to do either. He was worried about confusing, and perhaps annoying the Mayor, by admitting to subterfuge. Grewgious well knew that this would be no easy meeting: presenting the Mayor with new and different facts, and ones which ran counter to all his previous views and prejudices, was no light task.

For similar reason, he had entreated Datchery to keep his presentation as brief and to the point as was possible: nothing to confuse or challenge Sapsea; no theoretical disquisitions on the youth and character of Jasper; no reflective strolls down memory lane; no thoughtful evocation, however pertinent, of the memories of the Princess Puffer. Such were his stern admonitions, delivered as if read out from a previously prepared memorandum: just the bare facts: the finding of the body, and the ring, and the keys: and the resulting, if circumstantial, case against John Jasper. Grewgious agreed to fill in the details about the ring; and did so in his usual dry manner, bolt upright in his chair, occasionally underlining a point of particular significance with a short jab of his right hand.

Sapsea heard them out with rapidly increasing surprise, disbelief and anger. If Datchery had not shortened his presentation, as artfully advised by Grewgious, his patience would have burst long before the close of what he was clearly determined to consider a tale of cock and bull. His motives for treating their tale with contempt were many and various: as Grewgious had correctly surmised, he did not readily take to new information which caught him at a disadvantage; he did not like to hear criticism directed against someone he had taken under his lordly wing and befriended in such a patronal manner; he suspected that Crisparkle, whom he already loathed as an example of Un-English Christian charity and as an opponent of Jasper, had found some underhand way of exonerating Landless, whom he also loathed; he felt that his eight-day clock and his weatherglass, both re-established in his affections unlike the disgraced portrait, and both emblems of the England he knew and honoured (and to which he felt he rendered honour by his existence and high office in Cloisterham), were in some way under attack from the enemy, led by the hordes from Ceylon; and, not least, with the schism in mind, he believed that, by taking aim at Crisparkle, he would also discountenance the Dean and the Church party – and even, if he could find a way of manipulating a difference between Crisparkle and the Dean, whom he knew was already concerned by Crisparkle's advocacy of Landless, split his opponents.

Faced with this complexity of emotions and motives, the Mayor's brain – never the most nimble of mechanisms – demonstrated a distinct tendency to seize up. He could not immediately marshall his arguments, but simply blurted out the first thing which entered his head. Inevitably, it was the personal aspects of the revelations which entered the lists as the first champions.

'In my wife's tomb,' he spluttered, 'you were there, Sir. In Mrs Sapsea's very company. Forget the ring and your preposterous story of a body. It was an act of impertinence, Sir. Of immorality, Sir, of immorality,' he blustered, as if expecting them with a blush to retire.

Datchery was equal to the task.

'My presentation was clearly at fault, and I must apologise to the present company, and in particular to His Worship The Mayor. Otherwise His Worship would immediately have grasped the point that I did not of course open the coffin of Mrs Sapsea, so her uncorrupted body will have remained inviolate and undisturbed in its handsome stone coffin provided by the munificence of His Worship, guarded by the inscription painstakingly indited by none other than His Worship, sleeping peacefully in the town she loved, and loved more especially because of her blessed if alas brief union with His Worship; and also that it was not your humble servant who desecrated the tomb, but Mr Jasper. I merely followed the clues which presented themselves, in order to help solve a crime which has benighted the reputation of this fair town, and even by extension its civic officials: which is both unjust in itself, and a compelling argument for bringing the sad case to a speedy resolution.'

But, despite Datchery's efforts and silver tongue, Sapsea was not to be mollified, or so easily brought on board. The former's emollient words had merely allowed the Mayor time to attempt to order his thoughts, and turn to the next page of his denunciation. He was at that moment in the act of pinning his next thesis to the door of Wittenburg Cathedral.

'What do you mean by impugning the honour of my good friend and colleague, Mr John J-Jasper?' he thundered, stuttering slightly in his astonishment and indignation. 'He is a man of integrity, of sensibility: when I listen to him singing in the choir,' – which, in truth, Mr Sapsea has not listened to for many years, for, just as he sleeps through the Dean's sermons, his main thought during the choral music is how appropriate it would be to have an anthem which would hymn the wisdom and knowledge of Mr Sapsea, perhaps setting to music a few lines laboriously but elegantly penned by himself – 'why, I think to myself, here is a man of taste, as I put it. Furthermore, although he is a young man and greatly my junior, he is my friend, and that in itself should protect him from – from Detractors.'

He frowned at them.

'Mr Grewgious, I am truly sorry to find you of all people in this company, in what I call this atrocious plot.' Mr Sapsea's less than benign opinion of Septimus Crisparkle – "A very Nazarene, Sir, a Nazarene!" – was well known, after the unfortunate differences over the character of Neville Landless; but the stock of Mr Datchery has indeed fallen fast: there were few buyers on the look-out for Datchery shares in the Mayor's office that morning.

Mr Sapsea had not completed his eulogy of Jasper.

'I like to call him a pillar of the community;' a phrase which had suddenly occurred to Mr Sapsea, and presented itself in its full profundity; 'as I say, sound to the core, and at the core. What you have dared lay before me are no more than suspicions: unfounded and baseless suspicions.'

Datchery did his best:

'If his Worship the Mayor would like me to rehearse the details again, not because his understanding is in any way inadequate; but solely because of the paucity of my presentation – '

But he has shot his bolt. Like a mediaeval monarch, Sapsea no longer listened to his former favourite, who had committed the ultimate sin of censuring another favourite in the presence of the king. Datchery would be fortunate to escape with his head intact and still firmly secured to his neck. A proven tragedian such as Bazzard would have performed wonders with the scene of the sudden downfall of the white-haired courtier.

The Mayor was left with only one person in the room whom he was prepared to speak to.

'Grewgious, let me address myself to you, sir. If indeed a body has been discovered at long last, and despite the inadequacy of the police and other, self-appointed, detectives,' he looked malignantly in the direction of Datchery, who was however, unconcernedly engaged in shaking out his hoary locks, 'then I shall issue a warrant for the arrest of Landless, and we can finally make progress in proceeding with that long-suspended case: suspended, I must underline, through no fault of the magistrate.'

This time he glared at Crisparkle; but the latter's thoughts were elsewhere. He had been stimulated by Sapsea's minatory words into reminding himself that he must send word via Grewgious that Neville should on all counts remain in London until this case was finally dealt with, and must avoid Cloisterham until the Mayor had somehow been persuaded that there was no case against him: which was clearly likely to prove a lengthy task. The Mayor's audience had therefore reduced itself rapidly to one, as is often the case with such leaden orators, and also reflecting his decision to address himself to only one of the company; but since that one was Grewgious, the case for Neville's defence lay in capable hands.

'But, Mr Sapsea, there is no shred of evidence against young Landless.' Grewgious spoke with precision and authority. 'By contrast, Jasper had the key to the crypt hidden in the choir, in the Cathedral; and, by such evidence as we have, and the testimony of Durdles relating to that strange nocturnal expedition, had access to the key of your wife's tomb.'

Sapsea swept this aside.

'Mr Grewgious, this is but unfounded fancy. I do not know what tales Datchery has been telling,' – the latter's relegation is complete – 'but, luckily, I know the world. I know it, and feel it through my finger and thumb, through my gavel. That is why my fellow citizens have chosen me as their Mayor. I am not a Receiver and Agent, nor yet a Minor,' (he emphasised the word) 'Canon, nor yet a – a – a Churl;' this said with growing disparagement rising to indignation; 'I am the elected Mayor.

As such, mankind is what I often term an open book to me. Durdles is a Character, as I have likewise said; but he is also a drunken sot, and no weight should be put upon his testimony. Also, I can scent a miscreant, Sir; and that miscreant is Neville Landless.'

As he pronounced these last words, with sufficient volume to give full effect to them, there was a gentle rap upon the door. It was a light knock, as made by a female hand, but, despite being a knock at the Mayoral door, was not as timid as it might have been, or as the Mayor might have wished. The door opened, and Neville Landless's sister entered. There was little doubt that she must have heard the mayor's concluding peroration. Indeed, given the undoubted power of the stentorian Sapsea lungs, half the town could have heard those damning words.

Having missed Neville, and now uncertain where he could be (she remained certain that her intuition was correct, and that he was in Cloisterham, not in Holborn), and totally unaware that he had already confronted Jasper, and that the latter was now dead, she had determined to visit Minor Canon Corner to pursue enquiries – and perhaps even find Neville – there; and, more especially, to seek the assistance of The Reverend Mr Crisparkle. In making her way there she had deliberately avoided Jasper's Gatehouse, and added some minutes to her journey by taking a longer way around. Arriving at the house, she was told that Neville had indeed been there but a few minutes before, but finding the Minor Canon not at home, had gone his way: this naturally had increased her concern, without providing any clue about his then whereabouts. Further informed by the helpful maid that Septimus Crisparkle was closetted with the Mayor, together wth Mr Datchery, and a curious dry-looking man, and realising that she possessed important evidence which would greatly assist their presentation to the Mayor, Helena had immediately realised the need to abandon for the time her quest for Neville, and had hurried to the meeting, and arrived just as Mr Sapsea was – again – loudly pinning his noble colours to the mast of her brother's guilt. Was it this which brought the slight blush to her dark cheek? Or was it something else about the room and the company? Could it be Crisparkle's welcoming glance in her direction as she entered, for example?

Sapsea continued to hold the floor, as he had done for most of his life.

'Dear Madam, it is always a pleasure to admit a young and personable lady into one's presence, even if one of – ahem! – somewhat rich and – and native mien. But please understand that we are engaged in a discussion of serious matters, which may, indeed do, concern you, but which you will little comprehend. I suggest therefore – nay, propose – nay, insist – that you withdraw; and perhaps take up a little embroidery, or whatever else Mrs Tisher may find for your edification, until we have concluded: for I understand that Miss Twinkleton is still unfortunately away, for unexplained reasons. We miss her in our society and in our counsels.' Sapsea, as ever, talked as if speaking for the whole town; but, as he did so, rather more private thoughts of that plump and attractive person, with just a hint of a cottage loaf about it, rose unbidden in to his mind: he sternly repelled them.

Helena looked at him haughtily, and, he regretted to note, without respect.

'But, Sir, I have found the missing part of the mystery. I know exactly how John Jasper killed Edwin Drood, which he has personally confessed to me.'

Surprise, approbation and congratulation were clearly written on the faces of three of those present in the room after this stunning statement by the handsome, lithe girl, who spoke with such simple authority, but not on Mr Sapsea's. He flushed crimson with annoyance and impatience, rose angrily to his feet, and fairly shouted:

'Enough of this mummery. I will be heard!'

But, alas for his dignity, this was not to be the case. There was a sudden uproar outside, as of somebody attempting to catch a wild animal, and conspicuously failing. This was followed by the sharp sound of a stone being thrown in anger, and hitting flesh, accompanied by a cry of 'Gerroff, and let me be!' The door was flung open, and Deputy entered, coolly blowing a whistle of triumph through the gap in his front teeth.

Sapsea, already incensed, was beside himself, his air of authority blown to the four winds. He incautiously grabbed at the intruder, but his movements were lumbering, and he failed to make any contact at all. Deputy ran round him, shouting, 'Ya-a-ah! Stoopid,' as he went, and then took refuge behind his favourite, Datchery. Safely ensconced there, he issued a pronouncement. 'Now, will yer all stop seizin' and 'inderin'. I got news fer yer all.'

The Mayor still seemed reluctant to listen, and was shouting to his staff to come and evict the intruder, though they still appeared to be licking their wounds in the outer office. Again, it was Mr Grewgious who took control, pasting down the hair on his head with his hands as he did so.

'Mr Sapsea, it seems to me that this young – er – boy,' and he looked at Deputy's hideousness with new surprise as he took it all in, 'it seems to me that this young – umps – man has something to tell us. And, since this is a morning for surprises,' he glanced appreciatively in the direction of Miss Landless, 'perhaps it would be sensible and prudent and – ha! – businesslike to listen to what he has to say.'

The Mayor said nothing, so Mr Grewgious courteously gestured to Deputy to take the floor, a new experience for that doughty spirit. But he proved equal to the task.

'Just now, I was walking round the Kinfeederal, for my 'elth,' he added, looking provocatively at the Mayor, as if challenging that luminary to contradict him by suggesting that he had been up to some mischief, but the pillar of civic society had fallen silent; so Deputy, now the master of the field of battle, continued. 'And at the side of the Kinfeederal, at the back of the grave-yard, I come across that Mister Jasper,' he spat out the words contemptuously, then paused for effect, before adding dramatically, 'or rather 'is body, hanging from the railins.' The effect was instantaneous and deeply gratifying. There were sharp intakes of breath, and then silence, as the various people present in the Mayor's office digested this piece of information. Deputy definitely had his audience; and, although unversed in the black arts of oratory and rhetoric, understood instinctively that this was the occasion to embellish his account a little.

'Ye', spike right through 'is 'eart, 'is black 'eart, and out the back. Pokin' out, it was. I looked, special.' Since he still held his listeners in the palm of his hand, he felt it appropriate to draw a moral from the tale, in case this was overlooked by omission. 'That's wot come of histin' a boy off of 'is legs, and chokin' 'im and bustin' 'is braces. 'E'll be sorry now. Worse nor a sharp flint to the back of 'is jolly old 'ead. But it's too late. 'E'll be in 'Ell by now, 'e will.'

At this, Deputy performed a morbid little dance of triumph and revenge, possibly representative of a man vainly seeking to avoid the eternal flames lapping at his feet: accompanied by another, piercing whistle, indubitably directed at the shocked figure of the Mayor.

But the fight had entirely left Sapsea, at least for the present. He sat down heavily, and silently allowed the others to file out of his presence. It was only later that he heard, or wished to hear, Helena's testimony. But she made it her business to give a full account to Grewgious, Datchery, and – of course – the third of the three musketeers, Septimus Crisparkle, as soon as she could. But, having once again amazed them, as much by her character, ingenuity and perseverance, as by the strange and terrible tale she had to relate, she then left them to seek out Neville, wheresoever he might be.

Chapter XLII
Cloisterham Weir

THERE IS A solitary figure by the Weir: not Septimus Crisparkle, about to plunge in, or alternatively drying himself after invigorating exercise; someone who knows the place less well; someone who lacks the Minor Canon's crystal-clear complexion and ruddy skin (for that renowned singer with his prolonged outdoor exertions has also grown ruddier than the cherry); someone who likewise lacks Crisparkle's clear conscience; someone who appears to be drawn to the Weir, to the water, but to contemplation, rather than exercise.

Neville sits by the Weir, staring into the waters. The wind and rain have passed, leaving peaceful skies: the ground is wet, but Neville is untouched by such material discomforts. Since he had failed to find Septimus Crisparkle after having left the Cathedral that morning, he has not had the benefit of his wise and just, but above all calming, judgments. So he is left to himself and to his own far from soothing reflections. As he looks into the watery deeps, he is not seeking a watch, or a pin, or any other clue; he is just sitting, staring, thinking, regretting. His part in Jasper's death is unknown. No-one saw him or suspected him. But this does not absolve him in his own eyes – he knows his role all too well; his conscience rebukes him, and he is fully conscious of his shortcomings. He had failed to heed Helena's advice, and thus has let her down; he had ignored what he knew Crisparkle would have counselled, and thus has let him down; he had dismissed from his mind the warning, from both Helena and Crisparkle, that he should avoid appearing in any guise as the champion or suitor of Rosa, and thus risked letting her down as well. He has let them all down, and done so cravenly, disappearing during the night, into the night.

He had seen Jasper's body caught on the railings as he walked disconsolately back past the Cathedral after his failed mission in Minor Canon Corner. Some interested bystanders were starting to gather, including a young boy of hideous aspect, who was taking a particularly close and intrusive interest. Neville carefully kept his distance. Briefly, he had rejoiced, felt delight, seen the hand of fate, even – so help him!

– the hand of God. But then he had realised how he has helped Jasper to escape trial and punishment, assisted him to discover an easy way out; how he had acted selfishly and foolishly, without forethought or plan; how he was out of control, a tigerish savage, as he had been all his life.

He had no idea where he was walking, no plan, either before or after seeing the body of the dead Jasper. But somehow, as in the case of his friend and mentor Septimus Crisparkle on that mysterious and momentous starry night many months before, he suddenly and without any clear intention found himself walking in the direction of Cloisterham Weir.

Now he is by the Weir, and all these thoughts are still running through his head. He looks back to the town, and can see the Norman keep and the tower: the tower from which a man had fallen to his death, pursued by another, by a craven assassin. He runs his fingers through the cool waters, and looks round at the open fields around him. These scenes and sensations, so different from those of Holborn, should have brought solace and balm, but fail to do so. He is still enumerating his faults: he was secret and revengeful, false and mean. Furthermore, he can hear Mr Crisparkle's steady voice describing him as sullen, angry and wild. The steady drum-beat of self-reproach, of self-accusation, repeats itself again and again. Mr Crisparkle, good man that he was, had attempted to take him in hand and reform him. He had failed because of Neville himself, because of his inescapable weaknesses. Helena had tried to help him, using the powers of love and persuasion; but she had failed because he was headstrong and self-willed. Rosa had – indirectly, since they had no direct communication – tried to help him: she had never rebuked him, though he had played an ignoble role in the events leading up to Drood's death: according to Helena, she had always appeared gentle and understanding: at one point she had sent him her remembrance and sympathy, and asked him not to hate her – hate her! But she had not succeeded, could not have succeded, because Neville had ultimately been selfishly determined to punish the wrong done to himself, regardless of the potential or real damage to others, instead of sensibly leaving it to those more knowledgeable and better-equipped than himself. He had failed everyone. By a hideous irony, the only person he had assisted was his persecutor, his tormentor, his enemy, and the real murderer of Edwin Drood: Jasper himself.

How could Rosa love, or have loved, or ever love, such a man as himself? Tartar was far better than him: and far better for her. Rosa. He had lost her, forever and finally. There was no hope. What remained for him? He looks again into the mill-pool, into the waters, which bubble and beckon in front of him. There are no pool-maidens, or nymphs, or naiads: just the promise of certainty, of finality, of eternity.

He looks away, and falls once again into lamenting. He should have let the law take its course, instead of interfering: interfering and blundering. Now he has blood on his hands; he has driven Jasper to his death. That it was ignoble blood, which would have been spilt in any case by decision of the law courts of England, was of no account: neither in his view, nor, he believed, in the sight of God. The question was: what right did he have to spill it? And the clear answer was: none! Septimus Crisparkle was, as always, right; God was the searcher of all hearts; and he knew in his heart that, again, he was in the wrong. Again? Surely it was an article of faith between brother and sister that that word was unfair. No, he must be clear with himself. In that ridiculous quarrel with Drood, between two young turkey cocks, preening and running at each other, he was in the wrong: however much he and the loyal Helena had argued at the time that he had been provoked beyond endurance: he had been the first to resort to violence, to allow himself to be foolishly enraged: and it was his endurance and patience which had been found lacking. Now, again, he was wrong; but this time he would not hide behind words, take refuge behind Helena' loyalty, he would freely admit it: he was totally in the wrong.

But what was the consequence of this admission, this piece of candour? He was tainted, he was dangerous, his passions were too strong and unbridled, he was incapable of doing right, he must die: he must die.

He must die? He checks himself. What is he saying, where is his train of thought leading him? To perdition, to sin, to Hell. To take his own life would appear to confirm his guilt in the whole matter from the very first words with Drood through to Drood's murder and then to the death of Jasper. What would Septimus Crisparkle think when he heard that Neville appeared to have taken his own life, and without knowing more of the details and reasons? The very thought appalled him: Mr Crisparkle, good man and Christian that he was, would inevitably blame himself: fault himself for not calling to see Neville, and enquire about his reading, after that meeting in the garden; believe that somehow he had failed Neville, and left him short of support and advice at a crucial time. He could not allow this, he could not do this to dear Mr Crisparkle.

Then, darker thoughts return. What of the future? He unhappily realises that it would be his fate to let down and disappoint Crisparkle again and again, repeatedly, just as he has in the past. So now was the time to end this pattern of behaviour. He had killed Jasper without right, albeit not meaning to. His own life was forfeit. Better to end it all now.

He returns to gazing at the waters: the deep, welcoming waters. He sinks deeper into reverie: deeper and deeper. And gradually, imperceptibly, silently, he allows his body to slide down into the glistening and unresisting waters of the Weir. How welcoming they feel, how cleansing. Into, down and under. He feels his manifold sins wash away: his dirt, his grubbiness, his imperfections. He makes no attempt to struggle, to float, to live.

Suddenly, a strong hand seizes him from above, gets hold of him, drags him to the surface, and hauls him up onto the bank. Neville finds himself looking into the fond and benevolent but troubled eyes of Septimus Crisparkle. Once again, some unknown force had brought Septimus to this place, and given him a task to perform; last time a task which caused many difficulties and tribulations for Neville, this time one which saves him. Once again, Septimus does not know how he finds himself there, but he arrives in the nick of time, just as Neville is sliding under.

'Neville, my dear boy, what happened? You must have fallen asleep: and, sleeping, fallen in. Luckily, I came just as you slid under. Come, you are soaking and trembling: let me carry you back to town.'

Mr Crisparkle lifts the body. It is desperately light and unresisting: the months of pursuit and hiding indoors, as an outcast, a moral leper, have taken their toll. It clings to Mr Crisparkle, and they continue in this wise on their way back to town and the sanctuary of the Nuns' House.

Their conversation is not extensive: both have plenty to think over as they go. Neville says nothing about the scene at the Weir; but, as they get nearer town, confesses in broken sentences to his role in Jasper's death.

Septimus does not look surprised; he had suspected something of the kind.

'Neville, I am very glad that you told me, and congratulate you for it. You must of course tell your sister as well; it is better for you to have no secrets from her. It is not the only confidence that the three of us have agreed to share between us,' he adds softly and regretfully, wishing for the millionth time that he had not fallen into the mistake of sharing this secret with Jasper, and thence with the whole of Cloisterham. If Neville also thinks this, he gives no sign of it, but readily agrees to what Septimus has proposed, and feels all the better and stronger for it. He had always assumed that he would confess everything to Helena, with whom he shares everything, and who would almost certainly guess it in any case, but was unwilling to divulge his infamy in the affair to a wider circle, and was relieved to have Mr Crisparkle's sanction for this.

As they approach town, Septimus lowers Neville to the ground, and sets him on his feet. He does not wish to attract idle gossip, or risk encouraging speculation, by being seen to carry the young man. Certainly, Neville cuts a bedraggled, damp, and initially woebegone figure as they walk together, arm in arm; his late baptism in the Weir has only served to draw attention to his forlorn air and pallid features, and mark the change wrought in him by months of suffering; but gradually there begins to be a touch more confidence in his demeanour, and a new spring in his stride, as he recognises that he is alive, that his tormenter Jasper is dead, and that he has Crisparkle for his saviour, benefactor and friend. He looks up shyly at the purposeful Canon walking beside him, as ever the picture of health, but at much less than his usual, vigorous pace (since on this occasion he is determined not to leave Neville nowhere), and is rewarded by an encouraging smile, a squeeze of the strong hand, and a whispered 'Courage, mon ami.'

At the Nuns' House, they ask for Helena, who very soon comes out to them. She is naturally delighted to see her brother, for whom she has been searching ever since the meeting with the discomforted Sapsea, but surprised and concerned by his appearance.

Crisparkle hurries to explain:

'Neville was asleep by the Weir, exhausted by the events of the morning, which he will tell you about shortly, and accidently slipped into the water. Such drowning can happen so easily, and out of the blue – just think of Rosa's poor mother.' He is careful not to envoke the unhappy spirit of Edwin's mother. 'By great good fortune, I arrived on the scene just in time to save him, and pulled him out; just as our friend and ally Tartar saved me so many years ago. Like Tartar, I may even have made use of poor Neville's hair for the purpose,' he finishes gamely, determined to apply a light touch.

Despite the levity of his final comment, and the parallels, deliberately introduced by the Minor Canon to throw Helena off the scent, by demonstrating that accidental drownings were not uncommon, she immediately grasps what really happened. She looks at Crisparkle, with gratitude and understanding – yes, and love – in her face, and then at Neville; and, for once, she is unable to conceal a look of pity.

But the first thing is to remove all traces of his unhappy experience in Cloisterham Mill. With the kind permission of Mrs Tisher, and in the absence of the young ladies of the academy of learning, Neville is able to avail himself of the ablutionary facilities to dry his clothes, and improve his appearance; though not before he has fully confessed to his sister his part in the death of Jasper, emphasising that this is known only to the three of them, and should remain in that tight circle. Since he is able to assure her that this has Mr Crisparkle's agreement, Helena readily and gratefully assents.

The question then arises where brother and sister will spend the night. Return to London is quite out of the question after the events and excitements of the long day. Helena can of course stay in her room in the Nuns' House, forsaken only to comfort and succour her brother in Staple Inn. But Neville? Yet again that well-known good fairy, Septimus Crisparkle, has the answer. Neville will naturally return to his old quarters in Minor Canon Corner. The story of Drood's disappearance now being clear, there is no need any longer to observe the banishment so indirectly and implicitly imposed by the cunning Dean. The Canon will himself explain the circumstances to the china shepherdess, and ensure no objections from that precious piece of porcelain. The various activities of the morning appear to have imparted a new confidence and sense of authority to Mr Crisparkle.

This new mood rapidly and patently shows itself later that afternoon. Neville has retired to rest after his exertions, and Helena seeks out Mr Crisparkle to thank him from her heart for all he has done for her and her brother that day, and on so many previous days.

'Mr Crisparkle, I believe that God Himself has sent you into our lives to look after us and save us from ill.' He repeats that little gesture of putting his finger to his lips, and replies quietly: 'And I believe that God Himself put you into my life.'

She looks up at him with sudden surprise, mixed with overwhelming pleasure, as he continues.

'Miss Landless, Helena, I can keep silent no longer. Had you a guardian, I should probably be speaking to him at this moment; but the eloquent Mr Honeythunder has in effect abandoned that role; and if anyone might now be considered your guardian, it is probably myself; thus putting me in an invidious position, except that I know from my heart that, as guardian, I fully accept and concur with what I am about to say as suitor.'

What has happened to The Reverend Mr Septimus Crisparkle, Minor

Canon, athlete, benefactor, teacher, committed Christian? Only a day previously he would have looked uncertain and embarrassed in saying what he is about to say; would have been tempted to beat about the bush, and proceed indirectly, and falter; and now here he is, taking charge of the conversation, and even managing a slight joke at his own expence. What indeed has happened? Love can do strange things.

'From my heart, I wish to say that I love and admire you greatly, and that I wish you to be my wife. I wish you to be an inseparable part of my life, and in my life for ever. I too believe that God brought us together, through the perhaps surprising intervention of Luke Honeythunder, and meant us to love each other and to be man and wife.'

What could be more different than Jasper's tormented and brutal wooing of Rosa by the sundial? What could be more noble and honest that Mr Crisparkle's straight-forward declaration of love for Helena, and his offer of his hand in marriage? Helena's response could not be other than to accept on the spot, and then burst into a flood of happy tears as she sees her own wishes fulfilled, and a new security and stability entering her life.

There is only one, small matter to be resolved.

'Helena, my dear, as I am now at last permitted to say, could we at first keep this a secret, even from your brother? I need a little time, and a way, to accustom my mother to our union. The fact is that she has lost six children, and come to rely inordinately on me. It will be a huge change for her to have me married, and therefore with another woman in my life: in the very forefront of my life. I need to accustom her to this change gradually, and need a little time to do this. No suspicion of our engagement should reach her ears before I have prepared her, and ensured that she will give a warm welcome to her new daughter in law.'

He is careful to say no word, give no hint, of his recent conversation with his mother, and her evident distrust of Helena, which he knows it will be difficult to remove. But he does not need to mention or allude to this; the alert and perceptive Helena already knows it full well. She immediately agrees to what he proposes; and fondly muses that there is no man alive more ready to sympathise with the feelings of others, and no man less able to practice deceit, even in a noble cause. It is the second time that day that she has looked beyond his words to find an inconvenient truth which he has done his best, and quite unsuccessfully, to conceal from her. She smiles at him with pleasure and love in her heart, and tenderly prays for a miracle which will help to sway Mrs Crisparkle's mind and affections.

For a miracle it will need.

* M *

CHAPTER XLIII
Departures

THE VERY NEXT day, Mr Grewgious called upon Rosa and Miss Twinkleton at Billickin's. For some reason, Tartar attached himself to Grewgious for this purpose, and both seemed to consider this a good idea.

Once past the fair Cerberus of the apartments, Grewgious and Tartar rapidly apprised the two of the fate of Jasper, with the attendant details of his horrible crime; they said nothing about Neville, because neither they nor anyone else except the three knew either about his part in Jasper's death, or about his mishap in Cloisterham Mill – or ever would.

Rosa's immediate reaction was one of relief. Various pictures and memories flashed through her mind: the scene round the piano on the night of Helena's arrival in Cloisterham, and her consequent confession to Helena of her fear of Jasper; her parting from Edwin Drood, with the fearsome figure of Jasper lurking in the background, totally unsuspected by the innocent Drood; worst of all, the grotesque and horrible encounter by the sun-dial. All these were given sharpened significance by the knowledge of Jasper's purpose and intent: his wish to murder Drood to gain her; she had been right to fear and loathe Jasper, and to seek escape in flight, and poor Drood had been naïve and guileless to trust him. Escape in flight: yes, for who knows what Jasper might have done to her in his wrath and despair when she rejected his impassioned advances. She once again recalled the scene by the sun-dial: the working features, the convulsive hands, the wicked and menacing face, the hypnotic eyes, and yet the frighteningly easy attitude: what was the man capable of? But she had escaped; and now she was free of him, free to walk the earth and return to Cloisterham, without Jasper setting his black mark upon her. She exulted at the thought, and at her deliverance.

Yet, even as she exulted, two unrelated thoughts came to her mind. One was a realisation of her great good fortune, and the way in which luck had smiled on her. She had escaped the dreadful man, and found sanctuary among friends (glancing rapidly and gratefully at Grewgious and Tartar in turn: no, it would be truer to say Tartar and Grewgious).

Whereas, for poor Eddy, murdered for her sake, there had been no escape, no possibility of succour. Poor, poor Eddy, killed in cold blood by his uncle, just like those little princes in the Tower, just when he and she had finally learned to love each other as brother and sister, and his life and prospects beckoned. The tears leapt unbidden to her eyes.

The other thought was more surprising. She found it difficult to put the shadow on the sun-dial out of her mind. She had been physically touched by a man who had six months previously dispatched his nephew to his death in order to win her in his stead: killing him, not in a sudden fit of crazed passion, but after months of planning and keen anticipation. She was surprised that her hand was not marked for life by his touch: she looked down at the hand in question, and was relieved to see it lying in her lap, pink and a little plump and very pretty, and above all untouched by the horror of the sun-dial: Tartar followed her glance, and looked with similar pleasure at the little hand, imagining it in his own brown fist. She vividly remembered the frightful vehemence of Jasper, combined with the absolute powers of self-repression; she still felt that his declaration of love had soiled her, and still shuddered at the stain of its impurity; but yet, suddenly and amazingly, she felt sorry for him. Why, the man had been mad, a monster, totally deranged. What must have been going through his head by the sun-dial, what was in his dazed mind as he smoked opium, with what visions must he have been tortured, what torments must have lurked behind the respectable face he showed to the world. Above all, what and how he must have suffered; and what a horrible way to die!

These two contrasting thoughts, and particularly the more surprising sudden feeling of sorrow for Jasper, completed the transformation of Rosa from being a sweet and adorable but spoilt and whimsical girl into a mature and thoughtful – but still captivatingly beautiful – woman. Poor, poor Drood; poor, poor Neville; and lucky, lucky, Tartar.

There being no reason to remain in London, and every reason for Miss Twinkleton to return to Cloisterham, they resolved to leave the next day. Announcing the early departure to the fell Billickin was no light matter, though eased by the fact that the rent was already paid, and was not returnable – or returned. This did not prevent that formidable lady holding forth to Rosa at some length about old ladies who kept changing their minds and seemed unable to keep to a plan: acceptable, no doubt, in their own school, or seminiary as they would insist on calling it, since the girls were no more than slaves to the whim of the owner, or slave-driver, but totally unsatisfactory when it involved others with their own plans and bread to earn. She finished this salvo by declaring candidly that she would not deceive Rosa, but add that the elderly lady brought to her welcoming arms by Mr Grewgious had proved a most particular disapintmink to her.

Although understanding and acknowledging the warm desire of the presiding deity to return to the Nuns' House, and the attractions of Mrs Tisher's company, as soon as possible, Rosa was in something of a flutter. As she had discovered on her flight to London on that fateful day, Cloisterham was some way removed from Staple Inn, and that magical land up the bean-stalk. She naturally assumed that Tartar was capable of taking the railway, for he seemed capable of everything and anything; or alternatively, setting sail with the admirable Lobley down the Thames and up the Medway to Cloisterham: but the question was, would he, and how often?

She need not have concerned herself. It was not for nothing that Tartar had commanded a ship of Her Majesty's fleet – albeit a modest one, with challengingly low ceilings and tight corners; and his old masters, the Lords of the Admiralty, would not have been surprised to learn that the young Lieutenant's own plans were laid: newly and freshly laid, and already in the process of being implemented, for he had already taken the precaution of speaking to his good friend and ally, Rosa's guardian, on their way hither. So Rosa was already surrounded by two ships of the line even before the boarding-party arrived: not that she wished to escape, let alone fire upon those fine vessels.

It was naturally to be expected that any proposal from Tartar would be delivered ship-shape and Bristol-fashion, and so it proved. It was not romantic: romance could await a more propitious occasion, without the close attendance of the angular Mr Grewgious and the proprietorial Miss Twinkleton, and with the fiery Billickin breathing at the door; but it was clear and to the point. Tartar hung his proposal on the ready acceptance of his suit by Rosa's guardian, as he would hang lines and stays for his runners; put forward his good fortune in being left his uncle's property and hence able to support a wife, as he would shove a box of wallflower with a boat-hook; and ended by stating right out that he wished to take Rosa for that wife, as if planting out mignonette with a flourish. The result of this bold engagement was never in doubt, and a blushing Rosa was soon being embraced by a motherly Miss Twinkleton, and by an indubitably delighted Mr Grewgious.

The scene of departure the next day was just as confused as the day of Miss Twinkleton's arrival. It was indeed further complicated by two factors: the inability of Rosa to concentrate on anything so mundane as packing and departure, and the determination of the B to get in the way on every possible occasion, interposing herself and her trusty shawl among the trunks and packages, loudly referring to the mental confusion of the old lady as she did so, while significantly adding to it by her presence, and complaining all the while that all this upheaval was making her feel faint.

'Well, Miss, I do understand that the *haged*,' emphasised as before 'the *haged* tend to put their own comfort above all other consideration, most particularly the comfort and well-being of others, including those unfortunate enough to suffer from swoons,' she exclaimed, drawing her shawl protectively closer round her as she did. Poor Miss Twinkleton, who was feeling anything but comfortable as she juggled suitcases, hat-boxes and a tip to the young gentleman who was seeking to place them in a brace of hansom cabs, despite the series of countermanding orders he was receiving, fortunately failed to hear this sally; but would no doubt have heard the next, already forming on the lips of the redoubtable Billickin, and intended to take what she regarded as her honesty of expression to new heights of candour, when fate in the form of Tartar took a hand. Like Blucher at Waterloo, that capable officer appeared out of nowhere in the nick of time, silenced Billickin with his presence, gathered, counted and stowed the pieces of luggage, gave directions to the cabbies, paid off the young gentleman, and accompanied the two ladies on their journey to the railway station, promising to visit them at their house in Cloisterham the very next day.

Tartar was accompanied on his mission of mercy by Mr Grewgious, who drily and efficiently removed the B from the scene, in case she should find her tongue again – that organ was never long silent – and cause further mischief. He accompanied her to her own prized parlour, courteously helped her off with her shawl, and sat down in his abrupt and upright manner, with a flick of his coat-tails to either side of his chair, to listen to a recital of Billickin's woes, starting with a lament for the absent Mr Billickin, but rapidly developing into a ferociously candid attack on the selfishness of Miss Twinkleton, ending only when the cab conveying that lady was heard to roll away from Billickin's door.

'And good ridderance,' she concluded triumphantly.

Mr Grewgious looked at her, with a puzzled expression chiselled on his long, bony face, beneath that mop of mangy, yellow hair.

'Mrs Billickin,' he started.

'Just Billickin,' she retorted.

'Ma'am,' he began again, unwilling to fall into what appeared a discourteous form of address, despite being so invited, 'you speak most disapprovingly of Miss Twinkleton. She, in turn, appears to be somewhat – umps – critical of you.' He was choosing his words with care: he did not wish to detonate further explosions. 'I must confess to being at a loss to explain or understand this.' He left it there, with the question unspoken.

'Mr Grewgious, you are a gen'leman and an 'onest soul. I shall therefore take you into my confiderance.' She drew herself up to her full height, in a state of overpowering candour. 'The fact is that I knew that indiwidual,' – the name would still not sully nor cross those adamantine lips – 'before she lodged 'ere.' Mr Grewgious looked up in surprise. 'Before she moved to Cloisterham, she owned a school – or seminiary as even then she called it – in Bloomsbury. I 'ad the unhappy duty of being a parliour-maid at 'er,' she paused, 'hestablishment, when I was still a young girl livin' at 'ome 'ere in the city. She was a shrew, a wirago, a termagerant!' She had clearly been storing up these terms of abuse over the years, ready for just such an occasion. 'Forever complaining that I were moving 'er books and 'er papers and 'er bloomin' globes, she was. Those same globes she 'ad 'ere: I recognised 'em, immediate. That, that – persencution in Bloomsbury were the start of me feelin' faint, and needin' to wrap up close; just as her scanty feeding 'armed my blood. Well, I left, walked straight out, I did, left her and joined another 'ouse, very commodious it were, most unlike 'er's, but not afore there was words betwin us. I stood my ground then, Mr Grewgious, and I stand my ground now.'

She was still standing it firmly and implacably, in her hall, as Mr Grewgious took his polite departure. The sense of puzzlement had not left his face or his mind, however; for he distinctly remembered Rosa telling him that she had understood the B to say that she herself had been a pupil at a boarding-school like Miss Twinkleton's, and that Rosa had therefore assumed that this might somehow be the reason for Billickin's instant dislike of Miss Twinkleton, as representing a deeply-resented authority. He shook his head sadly as he realised that he had in no way succeeded in getting to the bottom of the mystery.

Rosa and Miss Twinkleton were not the only people leaving London that day. A family of three was also making its way out of the town on what was for them a journey of discovery. Nicholas Mander Endcombe had given notice at Staple Inn, and was engaged in taking his wife and daughter towards Cloisterham. They had no furniture, despite his long years of service, so all their worldly belongings including the pewter, the sampler, and the Mauchline, could easily be fitted into the trunk, which Endcombe was now entrusting to the baggage department of the train. At Maidstone, it would be transferred to the Elephant and Castle, and Joe would carry it and the passengers to Cloisterham. And what would await them there? They did not know. But Endcombe had Mr Crisparkle's card in his wallet, and that seemed to be a talisman to him, and to Mrs Endcombe. At various times, Miss Endcombe had addressed her parents on the subject of what they would do in Cloisterham, and where they would live, always to meet with the calming reply:

'The Reverend Mr Crisparkle will look after us.'

A curious response: for what had the various Reverends and Right Reverends and Very Reverends in the city of London managed to do for Endcombe, or anyone in his situation; but the benevolent Septimus definitely radiated an aura, and a willingness to help, which had convinced her parents, or rather her father: and this was sufficient for Mrs Endcombe and Miss Endcombe. So they departed in hope, and all at the same time, rather than with Endcombe travelling first to seek work; for their trust was in Crisparkle, and the name of Crisparkle was often on their lips. Joe heard it, and was able to direct them towards the good, if still Minor, Canon, on their arrival at their destination.

A few minutes later, they found themselves knocking hopefully at the door in Minor Canon Corner, and asking whether it was possible to speak to the Reverend Mr Septimus Crisparkle. It was, and they were ushered into that gentleman's study. Septimus rose welcomingly to his feet, immediately recognised Endcombe (though the latter was looking less pinched and down-trodden than he did in London), and invited them to be seated.

'I expect that you have come about a job,' he said in a matter of fact way, as if jobs grew on trees in Cloisterham, and it was perfectly normal for a family to leave London and come down in a speculative way and pluck one from a low-hanging branch.

'Well, you did suggest it, Sir, and I sort of thought – ' It was not immediately clear what Endcombe sort of thought, so his wife helpfully explained.

'The fact is, Sir, that London is no place to live and bring up a daughter, if you don't have what you might call money. So we are in the way of falling on your generosity, as you did suggest it to my husband.'

Septimus smiled on the family.

'You did well,' he responded. 'As for lodging, I shall put you in Crozier Hotel while we look for other accommodation; as for work, I shall have a word with the Dean later this morning. I already have an idea in mind, which I shall want to discuss with him. The maid will show you the way to the hotel, since the geography of Cloisterham is somewhat complicated. Just remember to keep looking out for the tower: that's the way to find your way around. As for company for your daughter, there are many young girls in the town, including the servant girls at Miss Twinkleton's seminary, but that can wait until you are more settled.'

So, there it was, and it seemed as if it were a simple task to pick up job and lodging in the town, so long as you were in the energetic and capable hands of The Reverend Mr Septimus Crisparkle. Only Septimus himself knew what a difficulty he would have in persuading the Dean to employ an additional member on his staff, since the Dean was a man who preferred income to expenditure; indeed, preferred income to many commandments and aspects of religious doctrine, and was wont to consider expenditure as the eighth deadly sin.

Septimus therefore needed a plan, and after a brisk and refreshing walk through town, he had one ready. He fell in with the sprightly Dean as the latter was making his way from comfortable deanery to commanding Cathedral, and after some initial words of greeting, turned the conversation the way he wanted.

'Mr Dean, I am getting a little worried about Tope.'

'Tope? Why? Surely you need have no worries about a man who has the fair Mrs Tope to look after him,' quoth the Dean, with more than a hint of archness.

'It's a combination of two things: first, his arthritis, which I believe is troubling him increasingly; secondly, he seems to have so much to do. His tasks as Chief Verger keep him for long hours in the Cathedral, but he also, I believe, likes to accompany you around the town, as a kind of companion and acolyte. He derives great pleasure and no little honour and benefit from being in your company, and hearing your conversation. In turn, I believe that it adds to your status to be seen to be accompanied wherever you go; not of course that you need this, but it shows the regard in which the Bishop and Diocese hold you.'

The bolt so shrewdly shot by the cunning Minor Canon struck home;

but, in truth, the shot was not a difficult one to bring off. Numerous little asides by the Dean had of late indicated that beneath that comely exterior lurked ecclesiastical ambition, and that thoughts of a Bishopric for himself were not absent from his mind. He was therefore eager for signs that he was not overlooked, and that his seniors recognised his worth and his aptitude for promotion.

'What is your suggestion, then, Septimus?'

'I thought that perhaps we could employ someone as a kind of Under-Verger, to undertake some of the more arduous tasks about the Cathedral, freeing Tope for more time to act as your *fidus Achates*,' (for he knew that the Dean prided himself on his knowledge of classical literature and the liberal humanities, like so many of the senior priesthood): adding insinuatingly 'for as long of course as he is able to keep pace with your nimble and youthful stride around your Precincts.' The Reverend Mr Septimus Crisparkle was increasing in cunning with each passing sentence, as he moved to snare his man.

The Dean saw the prospect of another sub-rook added to the staff of the Cathedral, and liked what he saw: another attendant to stand around in the Cathedral, looking important and busy; another lackey to keep those importunate visitors under control, and ensure that the poor-box was regularly brought to their attention; another foot-soldier in the war of the roses against the Mayor, whose retinue was by comparison scanty. Then, suddenly, a slight shiver of disappointment ran through the Dean's elegant frame.

'A new appointment! Surely that means, er, expense.'

'I think that I can find someone who would not cost too much, who is used to running errands, and who would want the work. I dare say he could make himself useful by taking round the plate at the midday service, when we normally do not take a collection. And, after all his years of devoted work on behalf of the Cathedral, we should think of Tope: he would rush at the chance to be your, be your, well, liveried attendant.'

The dean looked smug, but did not wish to be seen as immediately agreeing to something which would cost good money, contrary to his normal practice: it might set a poor example to others.

'It's an unusual suggestion, Septimus, but worth consideration. It is very good of you to worry about Tope, and this may prove just the answer, but let me think it over. I promise you a reply soon.'

And Septimus Crisparkle, who well knew what the answer would prove to be, was well satisfied with his work as he returned to Minor Canon Corner, striding along even faster and more enthusiastically than ever.

In Cloisterham itself, another departure was taking place. The single old buffer was taking leave of Mrs Tope and his inconvenient – but undoubtedly well-placed – lodgings. He did not appear inconsolable at his departure, and was rapidly shaking the dust of Cloisterham off his footwear, as well as flinging his ostentatiously white wig over a neighbouring hedge in what can only be described as an ebullient manner. He determined never again to wear a wig: except when appearing in court. He had also evidently abandoned his intention of settling in Cloisterham, and even seeing out his days there: possibly because those days have suddenly lengthened by several decades: and indeed was never seen there again. As His Worship the Mayor put it in his inimitable way,

'I always said that the fellow was a bounder, and an imposter; a bounder, Sir, and an imposter; and I am never wrong.' Then, with his forefinger raised magisterially in the air, as if accepting a bid from a grateful supplicant: 'I know mankind, Sir, I know mankind.'

For Neville and Helena, there was no departure. Both remained in Cloisterham, and their few effects were sent to them from Staple Inn. Neville was now most welcome back in Minor Canon Corner, and not only by the Minor Canon himself. Even in the sharp, bird-like eyes of Mrs Crisparkle – perhaps we should now say Mrs Crisparkle senior, since another may soon be elevated to that coveted title – Neville was now a reformed character. The tigers had been driven out of him, washed out of him. He was pale, weak, listless, grateful for everything and anything, profuse with his thanks to the Crisparkles and anyone else who did him a kindness, and, above all, totally devoted to Septimus. Mrs Crisparkle saw all this, recognized the change, sensed the suffering, and warmed in a maternal way to Neville. Thus was one of the possible causes of anxiety to Septimus removed.

But another still remained. His mother remained distinctly and ostentatiously reserved towards Helena, towards his beautiful and wise bride to be. Helena was again living in the Nuns' House, able to share in Rosa's happiness and her excited talk of her forthcoming marriage; but able to say nothing of her own, and uncertain whether her marriage could or would take place. Mrs Crisparkle, after the promised talk with Mrs Tisher, had probably withdrawn, at least to herself, though not to Septimus, her more extreme allegations against Helena; and her improved feelings for Neville had also undermined some of her harsher arguments against his sister; but she still professed to consider Helena proud and haughty and even self-willed; and, such is the enigma of human feelings and emotions, that the warmer she seemed to feel to Neville, the colder she appeared to grow towards his sister. Septimus had need of many invigorating walks up to his favourite fragment of ruin, much soothing contemplation of the grand view over river and pasture and hills and dales, in the promising light of dawn, and in the romantic gloom of dusk, in order to calm his feelings, and work off the frustrations of his position: and generally to convince himself that Dr Pangloss was correct, despite the appearances, and that all was for the best in all possible worlds, and that all would indeed come out right in the end.

Yet, Dr Pangloss had a trick or two up his capacious sleeve, and demonstrated this in the most extraordinary way. For the deus ex machina proved to be none other than that remarkable philanthropist, that spirited humanist, that vigorous benefactor, that outspoken orator, that pugilists' pugilist, Luke Honeythunder.

For, a few days later, Mr Honeythunder visited Cloisterham for the second and last time. It was his purpose to spread the gospel of Philanthropy to the deserving: yes, and to the undeserving too: he would force it upon them, thrust it down their throats, whether they liked it or no. He would philanthropise them until they begged for mercy, until they prostrated themselves before him, until they hugged his knees in penitence, in brief until they submitted. For the town had fallen upon sorrowful times; it had lost its honoured Choir-Master in a terrible accident: and who better than Luke Honeythunder to console them, to convince them that they should all be brothers, to force them to become brothers, to bind them together with tight fraternal twine of his own devising, to weld them in eternal brotherhood, to turn them violently away from their past ways and to find a new life: beginning with a pledge to contribute substantial monies to The Haven, in order to demonstrate their zeal for brotherhood and the new philanthropical horizons opening before them. They should put down their names as Members of the Haven, and thereafter speak as Honeythunder spoke – or rather bellowed.

A secondary purpose was equally dear to the heart of Luke Honeythunder, if indeed he possessed such an organ: to demonstrate to all and sundry that there was no connection between him and the savage miscreant Neville, that his guardianship of the latter had long ceased, that he had washed his hands of the boy, and that the egregious Minor Canon was solely to blame for any catastrophe which had befallen as a result of Neville's presence in the town, which was befalling on his regrettable return, or which might befall in future if he remained: for the Philanthropist was determined to avoid all moral and economical liability in the matter.

As was his wont, he travelled down by the train, and then made straight for the omnibus, shouldering others aside in his haste and determination. Joe, seeing his burly figure advancing, hastily put a brace of slender school-boys on the box beside him, and courteously gestured Honeythunder to the inside of his conveyance: where he shared the inadequate space with some generously proportioned matrons of Cloisterham, who were travelling with equally generous allowances of luggage. That self-promoting gentleman, who had been looking forward to a spell in the open air, and to adding further colour to his already choleric countenance, was therefore in a thunderous mood when he arrived in town. It was clear to all who saw him alight from the vehicle that Honeythunder, in full philanthropical fervour, was determined to strike about him, and to strike hard.

He headed directly from the High Street to Minor Canon Corner. It had been his purpose to begin elsewhere, and in particular to pay his respects to the Mayor, and engage his support in calling upon all the citizens of Cloisterham to become brethren, and contribute their respective mites to the cause. But the spirit was upon him, and he determined to start with those who he felt might stand in the way of his philanthropical purpose, and epecially the denizens of Minor Canon Corner: in rising order of importance and miscreancy, Mrs Crisparkle, Helena Landless, Neville Landless and The Reverend Mr Crisparkle. As a result of his uncomfortable and constrained journey in the jolting wooden omnibus, his blood was – as the pugilistic profession might have put it – up, and the platform manner was full upon him. The very timbers of the platform had entered his soul, and he was ready to pull a mote out of his neighbour's eye, aye and tug out the beam too if necessary and if opportunity offered; he felt exalted, and both physically and morally above mankind and therefore, like a great snake, poised and ready to strike.

On arrival at the Corner, he found Septimus and his mother at home, together with Helena, but Neville out. Honeythunder regretted the absence of one of his principal targets, but was nothing deterred. He was courteously invited to sit, Septimus carefully selecting a sturdy chair which would not splinter under the weight and vehemence of his philanthropy, and he directly held forth

'Mrs Crisparkle, Ma'am, I rejoice to see you. I have not forgotten that evening when you were so kind as to invite the stranger, the lone wanderer, to your home, and make him welcome: even though I recall that the seating was a little tight, and the service somewhat tardy, if the coffee was a trifle speedy; and allow him the chance to lay his discourse before the other, less worthy, spirits. An evening when Mr Jasper, whom I mourn, Madam, I mourn, was present, and contributed to our philanthropical deliberations.' Jasper, on that occasion, had been as silent as the grave, looking obliquely at Rosa, and would have offered little, even if the platform bombardment of Honeythunder had faltered for a second: which it hadn't.

'An evening which, I remember, Ma'am, led to most unpropitious developments, which might have been checked if I had been able to remain here rather than being impelled to hurry back to London.'

How false and selective is human memory: for Honeythunder was by now convinced that he had had urgent need to return early to the capital, to fulfill a task which he had to undertake, and which only he could undertake: and that he had done so only to the evident distress of his hosts, and with the insistent cries to remain and enlighten them further ringing in his ears; that Mr Tope had temporarily abandoned his duties as assistant to the parlour-maid and had personally gone on his knee to beg him to stay; that Mrs Crisparkle had shed a bitter tear at his departure; and that, as he went, he had heard on all sides tributes, not only to his eloquence (which he had heard so often), but also to his surpassing benevolence (which, in truth, were rarer coin).

Encouraged by these memories of things past, Honeythunder touched new heights in his rhetorical flight, addressing himself to Septimus, but also, indirectly, to Helena.

'Unpropitious developments. Sir, I have taken refuge in a platitudinous circumlocution, which is not my way. By George, Sir, it is not the way of Luke Honeythunder. I speak straight, Sir, unlike a Christian – or so-called Christian – gentleman in my presence. Straight, and directly to the point. Hear me then, and do not attempt to steer me from my task by feeble and simple-minded objections.'

'Such as facts, you mean,' suggested Crisparkle mildly, not quite knowing where Honeythunder's eloquence was leading, but strongly suspecting that it was to the detriment of himself and Neville.

'Facts, Sir,' boomed Honeythunder, sitting all-square, with his fists planted on his knees, and his brows knitted, 'I shall give you facts, however much you seek to conceal them. There has been murder in this town, Sir. Murder, and then a strange fall from a tower. Now you tell me that these are unconnected, and that the fall was in no way strange.'

'I said no such thing, nor have had the chance to,' protested Crisparkle, but was again swept aside by the tidal wave of words.

'These events have brought death and dishonour to this town. They have also brought me, in a double capacity. First, as representing the Haven of Philanthropy. These deaths would not have occurred, had the townspeople attended the lessons of the philanthropists and loved their neighbours as their brethren. Will you, Sir, dare to dispute this? Because, if you do, you will be defeated by my superior weight of argument. They should love their neighbours, and should be chastised until they do so; whipped with scorpions, until they love their neighbours and form the new brotherhood of Cloisterham. Any contrary voices should be cast forth from the town.'

As he said this, he squared his shoulders, with hands still on knees, and seemed to sway a little as he sat, as if seated on the box seat of a conveyance: leading Crisparkle to believe that he was thinking of Joe, and the differences he had had with the town charioteer.

'So that is the first part of what I regard as my mission to this unhappy town, which appears to have been misled by such an inadequate representative of the established religion as yourself, who knows not the meaning of brotherhood among men.' It was Mrs Crisparkle's turn to attempt to intervene, in defence of her son, but she also was left bobbing and jerking in the wake of the Honeythunder dreadnought as he ploughed on, regardless. 'Permit me, Ma'am. You shall all be made to love each other, with heavy penalties for those unprepared to see the error of their ways, and repent. For this unequalled opportunity to follow the path of brotherhood and amity – at least amity for the deserving, and obloquy for the remainder – I shall ask no more than a contribution to the Haven, which is offering the town the chance of redemption and a new start.

My second purpose is more specific. I have told you, Sir, that I have broken all communication with that youth and his sister, to whom I was once the unhappy guardian.' He glanced gloatingly at Helena, but she was looking away from him.

'I come here to repeat this decision formally and publicly. I shall demand a meeting with the Mayor to make my position clear. For it is obvious that these tribulations have been brought upon this town by that untamed savage. He should be cast out as a scapegoat, thrown forth into the desert. But such is the base immorality of the youth, that, who knows, he may be tempted to take his own life, as final, inexpungeable proof of his own guilt and culpability.'

As he said this, he glared challengingly at Crisparkle: at the Haven there would have been thunderous applause at this bold speaking, and hats might have been thrown into the air, as Honeythunder, having bored his man, and gouged his man, and mauled his man, and stamped on his man, was encouraged to knock his man to the canvas. So Honeythunder lunged in again, arms pumping and fists swinging:

'And, if that were his intention, if matters come to that, it were better that no interfering busybody would intervene – '

It was at this point in Honeythunder's gunpowderish ministrations that the miracle, which had been long prayed for by Helena, occurred. Honeythunder had over-reached himself. Even the mild Crisparkle reacted:

'What are you daring to say?'

Helena, well aware that her brother, in his afflictions, had indeed attempted to take his own life, and being determined to protect that knowledge for ever, was stung by the coarse brutality of the philanthropist's manner and arguments, and burst into those tears which neither the cruelty of her step-father, nor the travails of her brother, nor her own distress, had yet drawn from her. The china shepherdess, remembering how Honeythunder had harangued and criticised her dear Sept at that dreadful supper party that awful night, and furious that the attacks were continuing, was horrified by what she heard, partisan for her new favourite Neville, and deeply affected by Helena's obvious misery. Tears also sprang to her bright eyes.

Crisparkle did the only thing he could do with honour; he opened the door and indicated that, since the eminent philanthropist had reduced both of the ladies in the house to tears, it were better that he should leave; reminding his unwanted guest that he had upbraided him before on the subject of his platform manner; adding that perhaps he should seek out the Mayor, since they appeared to have much in common in the way of philanthropy, if by that they meant believing and devising and circulating uncorroborated rumour, and calumniating the innocent.

Honeythunder unabashedly departed in platform manner, thrusting his hands deep into his pockets, his shoulders squared for thrusting townspeople out of his way, loudly proclaiming that he had completed his mission, that he had never previously been expelled from a house in such a summary manner (if true, a tribute to the patience, not to say the feebleness of his fellow men), that he would never see the gullible Crisparkles and any heathen Landlesses again, and that he was delighted to erase them completely from his mind, to wipe them from his memory. And, in this high temper, he departed from Minor Canon Corner with such haste and ferocity and determination, that he quite forgot to call on the Mayor; and so he left Cloisterham, and was never seen there again, which was a matter of regret neither for the town nor for the philanthropist; and, as he went his platform way, he left Mr Crisparkle in a state of indignation unusual for that mild soul, and a solicitous Mrs Crisparkle trying to comfort the still weeping Helena, her white hair pressed against the raven black locks.

The elder woman looked down sympathetically at the distressed figure half-lying in her lap, evidently wondering why and how she had thought this unhappy girl proud and haughty. Why, she was no more than a girl, who had suffered much for her poor brother, but had tried to do her best for him. Septimus saw these changed emotions in his mother's face, and decided to risk all.

'Ma, dear, it does my heart good to see you comforting Miss Landless in that manner.' His opening was both true and uncontentious, but he could not long continue in that manner, and soon had to proceed onto more demanding terrain, like a pioneer venturing across territory strewn with petards, which an incautious step could detonate: he had no choice. 'I hope that you will both be sources of great comfort and support to each other in the future.' He could not keep a slight quaver out of his voice as he said this: a quaver both of deep love, and of pleasure that this moment, long-awaited, long-dreaded, had come at last.

Mrs Crisparkle looked up quickly, her cap vibrating, and her sharp face puzzled and questioning.

'Why, what do you mean, Sept? You sound so serious.'

'I am serious, Ma, dear: never more serious in my whole life: for the girl you are comforting is the girl whom I love, and whom I intend to marry.' Helena turned, rose and looked at him with her shining black eyes in her tear-stained face, proud and stately and handsome beyond words; but with a slightly worried expression, as if uncertain whether Septimus had chosen the right time for this revelation. Mrs Crisparkle also rose to her feet, and looked with astonishment and surprise, first at Septimus, then at Helena.

'But, Sept, what – I – I don't understand – '

It was Helena who saved the day. She flung her arms around the china shepherdess, and hugged her closely to her. The shepherdess seemed initially to take against this sign of affection, and there was a slight struggle as the cap vibrated; but then she felt the warmth and ardour of the embrace, and gently returned it. Septimus put a comforting arm about both, and looked and felt like a victorious general who was at last able to send reassuring dispatches back to his capital, written on a flitch of parchment steadied on the taut canvass of a convenient drum.

Thus it was that Honeythunder achieved, quite by accident, and without intention, a unique piece of real and genuine philanthropy. He never knew it; and, had he known it, he would have ground his teeth with annoyance and vexation. The Haven never knew it; and, had it known it, there would have been calls for Honeythunder to be expelled for conduct unbecoming, for adding to the sum of human happiness without causing an equal and opposite amount of human unhappiness, for achieving a result without denunciation or elimination or inflammation or concatenation. But Septimus knew it, and ever after remembered Luke Honeythunder in his prayers at the close of day: probably the only man in the kingdom, or the world, or the universe, or the cosmos, who did so. Blessed be the name of Luke Honeythunder, who has wrought these deeds: and of God, Who knoweth and planneth all things.

Back in London, in his rear room in Staple Inn, Hiram Grewgious locked away the recovered ring in the escritoire. Earlier he had cogitated, in his dry and angular manner, whether he should present the ring to Tartar to give to Rosa. He had debated the question with himself, weighing the arguments, chopping them into little shreds and then reassembling them, fashioning them and refashioning them; but, however he shaped and reshaped the arguments, they always came out firmly against the proposition.

First, and at the most prosaic level, it was very likely that the methodical Tartar had already procured a ring of his own to plight his troth to Rosa; it was almost certainly already stowed away in a neat drawer in a neat cupboard in his neat quarters, probably wrapped in a fragment of silk to keep it clean and shining and safe and free from harm.

Secondly, that was not the purpose for which he had been handed the ring; the ring was intended to bring to fruition the long engagement between Rosa and Drood; it was not designated to cement the union between Rosa and anyone else.

Thirdly, he felt that the proper place for the ring, denied its proposed usage, was in the drawer which had been its home for so many years, and from where he had only reluctantly drawn it forth to entrust to Drood. In a way, the ring had played its part, had carried out some clear purpose; for it had helped to bring home to Drood the thought that was already in Rosa's mind, that their engagement was a sham, destructive of friendship between them, and should be ended: and that was a further reason for Rosa not wearing it, and for no-one else giving it to her in token of betrothal.

Grewgious smoothed his hair forward as he realised that there was a further aspect to this argument about the ring having played out its purpose, and made its own unique contribution to the drama which had unfolded. It had clearly and unambiguously identified Drood's body; and, just as clearly and unambiguously, pointed to his murderer. Its role was acknowledged, its office completed, and its place was in the cupboard.

There was a further, separate reason, for replacing the ring in its former place of concealment, which Grewgious did not like to admit, even to himself, especially to himself: he liked to have the ring in the escritoire, he liked to think of it there, where it had been so long. For it was Rosa's mother's ring, and his last and only direct link with her. As he placed the ring in its resting place, he looked at it mournfully, if those wooden features bequeathed him by careless Mother Nature could be said to show as uncertain and shrinking a quality as mournfulness. He put it in and locked the cupboard, returning the key to his fob.

There the ring would remain until the end of his days. He could not bear to lose it or to give it away. Only after his death would it be retrieved, and sold into circulation, the proper usage for a twist of metal and precious stone created by a craftsman for the pleasure and admiration of mankind.

Grewgious returned to his table, and poured himself a glass of ruby-red wine. He sipped it appreciatively, thinking of Rosa, of her growing beauty and maturity, looking forward to her wedding, reflecting approvingly on Tartar, realising that his guardianship was coming to an end, speculating on a generation of new Tartars perhaps; but, being Grewgious, not congratulating himself on the success and loving care with which he had helped Rosa through the crisis in her affairs. After all, he would have told himself firmly, he had done it for Rosa herself, and for her mother, and therefore, at the last, for himself.

Chapter XLIV
New Beginnings

DESPITE THE COLD of the late autumn, and the deep-red leaves from the Virginia creeper ominously blowing around the streets and yards by the Cathedral, providing a reminder that the long Summer was well and truly over, and that Winter was already knocking at the gate, the old town and especially the Cathedral close was in festive mood. For the venerable building was to be the site not just of a wedding, but of a double wedding. Two close friends had decided to pay this homage to the links between them, forged in difficult and often testing circumstances, while one of the intended husbands was a Minor Canon of the Cathedral, and the Dean in person was to officiate.

Let us take a look at some of the congregation as they assembled, when the great day had finally arrived. Pride of place, in the circumstances, went to Mrs Dean and Miss Dean; but other persons of note, and familiar to the reader from these pages, were also present. One was Miss Twinkleton, owner and head of the seminary where the two brides had studied, and kind mother in her own way to both girls – for they had no other – accompanied as ever by her close confidante Mrs Tisher, who needless to say had heard a great deal about that foolish but worldly Mr Porters the previous evening. Also there, and ornamenting the front pew, was the mother of one of the bridegrooms, Mrs Crisparkle, together with her sister, that other piece of Dresden china, contentedly enjoying another chance to reunite in addition to the annual re-matching, and her brother-in-law who was sitting proudly between them, his dog collar proclaiming his profession, or rather vocation. In the same pew sat Neville, an especial favourite with Mrs Crisparkle on account of his meek bearing and excellent manners.

Also there were the Topes, and Mr Tope's new assistant Endcombe together with his wife and daughter. The Endcombe family had now moved into the rooms vacated by Dick Datchery (who had received but regretted an invitation to the occasion, perhaps feeling that his youthful appearance might cause some surprise and even indignation in the town); and such was Mrs Tope's pleasure at their arrival, and what she saw as the resulting promotion for her husband, and therefore for herself in the eyes of the citizens, that she had graciously made an additional room available for the daughter: a room that Dick Datchery had not wanted or needed, since he spent most of his time sitting in his porch, and had no interest in retiring deeper into the building away from his former quarry.

Not that the porch was now untenanted; for Endcombe, having been much enclosed in Staple Inn, followed Datchery in keeping the front door open for much of the time on warmer days, and often sat there, taking the air, though he was less diligent than his predecessor in taking careful stock of the passers-by. Endcombe had also taken to watching the rooks, seeking them out, looking at them as they circled and wove and poised and lingered, and from time to time landed in the trees and on the roofs and on the ground. As he explained it to Mrs Endcombe: 'I like to watch them and their ways and their patterns. They seem to act like people: all collecting and cawing together. You couldn't watch them like that in London: only starlings and sparrers there.'

Lobley took his allotted place towards the back of the Cathedral. The previous day, he had brought Tartar's yacht down from Greenhithe to Cloisterham, just in case his master had the opportunity to use it during one of the remaining days of good weather in the Thames estuary. He was lodging at the Crozier, and finding it assuredly orthodox and sleepy; but, unlike the false Datchery, was not tempted to claim that he would take up permanent residence in the town.

Also among the congregation for the occasion was Durdles, who had indirectly played his own role in the discovery of Jasper's terrible crime; though he sat a little apart from the others, surrounded by what looked like a dusting of mortar and lime and stone-grit on the wooden pew; and occasionally falling to munching what resided in his dinner-bundle; while those who sat closest were from time to time regaled with a powerful scent of spirits, as of a bottle being surreptitiously opened, and a pull of its contents swallowed, no doubt in celebration of the double ceremony taking place, and also to make the bottle right.

As he sat, and as so often when he was in the old Cathedral, he recalled to mind that unaccountable sort of expedition with Jasper; and also, puzzlingly, that curious ghost of a cry, the ghost of one terrific shriek, and the ghost of the long dismal woeful howl of a dog, which he had heard the previous year, almost twelve months before. Was it imagination, reality, a portent, a warning, something from this world, or another, what? He could not say. As always a discreet and comforting pull at the bottle seemed to calm his nerves, and preserve his beery composure. A philosophical mood descended on him, and he confided to himself under his breath,

'Durdles says, it wasn't the cry which was important, it was the sharp reaction of that Jarsper, which showed his base criminal intent.'

Deputy was not on the invitation list; but that young man had managed to slip into the side of the church to enjoy the spectacle; and, on this occasion, was not tempted to pick the pockets of any of the guests: which led to him ruefully remonstrating with himself afterwards, as the loss of a potentially valuable source of rich pickings.

Also uninvited, for good reasons, were Luke Honeythunder, who had renounced Landlesses and Cloisterham in so very final a manner; and the Mayor, who had still not come to terms with the facts that Neville was blameless in the death of Drood, and that Septimus Crisparkle was proved both sagacious and fully vindicated. The absence of an invitation widened the rift in the town, between what might be termed the Church faction and the Town faction, because the Dean was delighted to brandish his resplendent white rose, to take the part of the Crisparkles, and see even less of Mr Sapsea, whereas the wise men of the Town Council felt that the ruddy red rose, and the ruddy red face, of Mr Sapsea, had been sorely slighted on this occasion.

Needless to say, Rosa and Helena had invited all their fellow seminarians to their weddings, to avoid any further disappointments on the part of those fair nymphs. The excitement and chatter in the Nuns' House the previous evening, when the girls were having their supper, and preparing their clothing for the morrow, had been tremendous. Particular zest and hilarity had been imparted to the occasion by the knowledge that Rosa was marrying a sailor. Miss Ferdinand had adorned her healthy features with a full imperial and ferocious whiskers of burned cork, it being assumed that the majority of sailors were bearded like pards, as a result of a communal failure to carry their shaving tackle on board with them; Miss Reynolds sported one earring rather than the more customary two, and was seen swinging a paper cutlass; Miss Giggles performed a lively little horn-pipe, accompanied by the bearded Miss Ferdinand on comb-and-curlpaper.

The next day, however, their behaviour was most decorous, and a credit to Miss Twinkleton. In truth they were silenced by how very handsome, and how very brown, Rosa's sailor proved to be, and by the contrasting beauty of the two young brides.

Rosa was pink, and blushing, and soft, and dimpled, and utterly charming, as after the ceremony she walked down the aisle with her bronzed husband; the pink and the brown together: perfect and harmonious on this special occasion, though any rowing or soccer or jockey clubs would do well to avoid the over-rich combination of extravagant tones in their proud colours.

Helena, by contrast, was handsome and lithe, quick of movement and limb, black of hair and eye, beautiful though no longer barbaric; one look at her suggested that the tall, gentle looking man, who loped beside in slightly ungainly manner, in a desperate attempt to slow his normal energetic pace as they walked together down the nave, had once again been overpaid, though this time it was his turn to kiss her hand after they had been made man and wife.

Everyone remarked on the excellence of the service, and especially the quite extraordinary quality of the music, which touched all hearts. It was as if a great weight had been lifted from the choir by the death of Jasper. Although his own voice had been, strange to say, a thing of beauty, his increasingly glowering presence, his nervous temperament which caused him at times to rush some of his musical fences, and his distance from his fellow men, all had tended to suffocate the talents of others, who were largely reduced to the role of an audience, or of part-time singers. Relieved of his presence, spirits and voices were raised to the heavens; and the town itself seemed to rejoice that a dark shadow had been removed from the face of the day.

As she listened, Rosa remembered that evening when she fancied that she could distinguish the voice of Jasper in the resounding evening chord of the service. But, now, she did not shudder; she knew that the poor, unhappy, wicked, sinful man was dead, and far from her; and she was convinced that, though now finally reduced to the rank of a spirit, and an unhappy one at that, he was unable to continue his ghostly following of her through the massive walls of the Cathedral; though, once or twice in the course of the day, she may have grasped the comfortably solid forearm of Tartar just a little more firmly, as if just to confirm that all was well and that he was still there, beside her, and that her present happiness was not just an idle dream.

After the service, the company repaired to the Nuns' House for the traditional glasses of white wine and slices of pound-cake, handed round by the hand-maidens of that august establishment, for Miss Twinkleton was determined to emphasise her own role in the happy outcome to the sad story of Edwin Drood, and give herself new content for her evening discourses, since the tales of the Wells and Mr Porters, however foolish and finished, were growing a little, a little, well, long in the tooth, if not yet tall.

Mr Grewgious found himself talking to Miss Twinkleton at some length, or rather being talked at for some length, and suddenly realised that here was his chance to solve the problem which had been puzzling him. He seized his moment as Miss Twinkleton paused to draw breath, just momentarily smoothed his head nervously with his two hands, as if seeking courage, and boldly dived in.

'I understand, from a remark of Mrs Billickin,' there being no-one of a candid nature present to rebuke him for using the longer and more usual form of address, 'that you were already acquainted with her.'

She looked at him quickly.

'Yes, She was a parlour-maid. A most unsatisfactory and rebellious child. She was called Trott in those days. Naturally, I dismissed her.' Her voice was sharp at the memory. 'She has not aged well,' she added, and left it at that.

They were about to move on to another topic, but at this point were joined by Mrs Crisparkle the elder. After a few minutes, Mr Grewgious moved away. So, it was true: the two had known each other previously. But why had neither acknowledged the other when they met? Was the hurt really so deep from those events years ago? In that case, why had they not referred to them, disputed them anew, fought their old battles, rehearsed familiar phrases (he smiled involuntarily as he thought of the B's emphasis on shrew, virago and termagant, words bottled up over all those years), rather than forever seeking new fields of warfare, novel bones of contention, fresh affronts? What was it in the female mind which produced these puzzles?

He strolled towards the garden, with his great length of throat matching his long ankles and heels sheathed in white stockings, pondering these questions; and, like an angler patiently playing a fish, secured the answer he had been seeking. It was really quite obvious. Both the B and Miss Twinkleton had wished to keep their earlier differences to themselves: Billickin, because she wished to preserve the fiction that she had been at boarding school as a pupil not as a maid, Miss Twinkleton because she did not wish to admit that she had totally failed in training a young girl committed to her care. At loggerheads on all else, they were united on this.

As he looked around in a satisfied way, Mr Grewgious espied Neville looking a shade forlorn and lonely on such a happy occasion.

'Why, of course,' thought that benevolent gentleman to himself, again smoothing his hair, and then stretching his long, dry fingers, 'that young man will greatly miss his sister, who has been so close to him in all ways. I am sure that he will always be welcome in Minor Canon Corner, and knows that, but it is a different thing when a beloved sister is married. Though how should I know, since I have no sister, close or distant, and was born middle-aged?'

Despite these glaring deficiencies in his circumstances and upbringing, and because tireless in seeking out and doing right, he approached the young man, and asked him how he was, and what he planned to do now.

'Why, Sir, to continue my study of the law, even though my kind benefactor Mr Crisparkle will probably have less time to help me, now that he has married my sister, and is also likely to play a larger role in the life and work of the Cathedral, with the Dean more involved in assisting the deliberations of the House of Bishops, I understand.' Neville might have said dancing attendance on the House, a phrase particularly appropriate to those sprightly gaiters, but was insufficiently versed in the ways of mankind to put that interpretation upon it.

Mr Grewgious again stroked his head, thoughtfully and carefully.

'I have an idea, though I am not sure whether it is a good one, and look to you to be the judge.' He took a sideways pace, and then another pace back to where he had started. 'Yes, you to judge, you to judge.'

'I would consider you a far better judge than me, Sir, since you know more of the world.'

'Do I? The world? I'm not sure. But since this idea concerns you and your future, it seems to me to follow naturally that you are the proper judge.' He paused again, to make sure that he had the elements of his proposal firmly in his mind, and then started, occasionally emphasizing a point with his little chopping gesture.

'I understand that you wish to continue with your study of the law, and I agree that it offers excellent prospects for a young man such as yourself.' Chop. 'I know that you have worked and read with my esteemed friend Mr Crisparkle, who is an admirable person in all respects: virtuous and selfless.' Chop. Chop. 'But the law is a specialised subject in many ways, and though I have no doubt that he is a most assiduous teacher, with sound knowledge of canon law, he cannot be expected to be a complete guide on all aspects.' Chop. 'It could therefore be that, having provided essential encouragement and a firm grounding, he may be ready to step aside while we seek more professional assistance. As you say, his other duties are increasing, and, in his modest way, he would be the last person to stand in the way of new arrangements, always provided that they indeed offered an improvement.' Chop. Chop.

'I have a friend, Mr Will Watson, who is a lawyer, but not just a lawyer.' The thought of Will wearing a snowy white wig rose unbidden to his mind, but he resolutely kept it at bay. 'He is naturally drawn to cases where there appear to be strong elements of misuse, whether legal or otherwise, and evidence of human suffering as a result. Now, it seems to me that you would be likely to have an interest in such aspects of the law; and I am sure that, if you are interested, and if you authorise me to speak to Will on your behalf, we could get you articled.' Chop.

'Mr Grewgious, Sir, I am quite overcome with your kindness. With you and Mr Crisparkle, I now seem to have in this country nothing but benefactors who repeatedly go out of their way to help and look after me, It is just as my wise sister, Helena, always said.'

'You realise, of course, that working with Mr Watson in his law firm would mean living in London; and away from your sister, though I have no doubt that you would always be a welcome guest in Minor Canon Corner.'

'Yes, I realise that, Sir, and in a way welcome it. I do not wish to be a burden on my sister, let alone on my dear benefactor Mr Crisparkle, and feel it better that, as a rule, we live apart.'

'Then we need to retain those lodgings in Staple Inn, at least for the present. And since I suspect that Mr Tartar, having so far accustomed himself to life on shore and away from confined spaces and solitary nights on board ship as to have got married, will soon move out of his rooms into something more spacious, we may perhaps think in terms of you taking those in due course.'

'Mr Grewgious, you are a very magician: though an unusually kind and thoughtful one.'

But Mr Grewgious had not completed his acts of genuine philanthropy for that week. On his return to London, he set about disarranging and rearranging his room, to the amazement of any visitor who happened to look in. The main purpose seemed to be to make more space for others, for a veritable company. The new arrangements gave every appearance of being temporary rather than permanent, since one could still make out the distinctive and soothing shape of the old room hiding behind the new.

The next day he completed these changes to his habitual surroundings, and succeeded in making himself look very dismal and out of place. There was no sign of Bazzard to assist him, nor did Mr Grewgious seem in any way surprised by his absence. In the afternoon, food was brought from Furnival's, by the special intervention and assistance of the flying waiter and the immoveable waiter, though more by the former. The flying waiter also brought several cases of Furnival's wine with him, though the immoveable waiter naturally called for more. These preparations complete, the pair of them withdrew, and Mr Grewgious descended to his cellar at the bottom of the stairs, and brought up various bottles which sparkled and twinkled in the unaccustomed light of day. Then the two waiters returned, the flying waiter being assigned the duty of serving from a variety of dishes set upon too small a table, while the immoveable waiter presided over the wine-bottles, as if he were the very host, ready to dispense the contents into the waiting glasses scrupulously cleaned by the flying waiter.

Soon the guests, who had clearly been long and warmly awaited, began to appear. They did not seem to know Mr Grewgious, nor he them, and in truth made little attempt to make his acquaintance, preferring to attack his food and drink as if they had long been starving in assorted ill-provisioned garrets; which, indeed was the case, since these guests were all authors of Bazzard's acquaintance, his intimate circle of acolytes and devotees. But the host did not seem to mind, or consider such behaviour discourteous; he believed it to be a natural part of the artistic temperament, and an intrinsic element of unrecognised genius, to behave in this way; and so he stood there in a quiet and angular manner, smiling benevolently on the company.

Then Bazzard finally appeared. A great cheer went up from his peers.

'He's here at last, well done, Bazzard, well done, the English Racine.' They clapped him on the back, and gathered round, drinking to his success. For "The Thorn of Anxiety" had finally been brought out before the expectant public in printed form. Now it was true that Mr Grewgious had paid all the production costs in full; that the initial print-run was small; that indifference to the publication had been near universal; that for some reason Bazzard had not dedicated The Thorn to his kind patron, who might have been tempted to buy copies of his own to give to friends or relations, but instead to a singularly misguided genius who had not even felt moved to depart from his habitual routine in order to attend the celebration; that the rest of the company felt envy rather than genuine pleasure; that each wondered why the book had not been dedicated to him in recognition of his special qualities and the inspiration he had proved for Bazzard; that all were tormenting themselves with the question why Bazzard's book had been published while their masterpieces languished in oblivion; and, finally, that the food and wine was finite and all but finished: nevertheless, publication was publication, and should be celebrated.

Then Grewgious produced his special touch. He requested the immoveable waiter to wield the corkscrew and open the special bottles of wine from the cellar, which the latter did with an air of surly resentment, and the flying waiter to take it round in new glasses, which he did with alacrity and good grace. When all were served, and just before some led by the puffy-faced Bazzard had finished their freshly served glasses, he consulted his memorandum book, looked round, cleared his throat, cleared it again more noisily to attract attention, and embarked upon a short speech.

'Gentlemen, it is my pleasant duty to offer you all a celebration on the occasion of the publication of Mr Bazzard's book. Now I am not an author, and could not be an author, and would not be an author; and, even were I an author, I know that I would be quite incapable of writing a play, still less a tragedy. But I understand that everyone else in this room is an author: and authors, moreover, who fully measure up to the task of writing tragedies: who are, in short, tragedians. So you all understand the great achievement of fathering a book which is then brought into the world in the form of a printed copy.'

Renewed cries of "Good old Bazzard", accompanied with calls for more wine to drink his health: for these are thirsty tragedians.

'But there is only one author whom we are thinking of tonight, and that is Bazzard. This is his evening, his celebration, his achievement; so it is not the occasion to think of the work and struggles of others,' besides, he wouldn't like it, and might take it ill, thought Grewgious to himself wryly, 'so my toast is Mr Bazzard, and "The Thorn of Anxiety".'

Another cheer, and a flourishing of glasses in the air, and the sound of wine disappearing down a host of gullets, and a further round of replenishment. The room looked expectantly at Bazzard, but the great tragedian was in no mood to make a speech, or give effusive thanks to Mr Grewgious. He therefore contented himself with saying, 'Mr Grewgious, Sir, I follow you, and I drink to you,' which he did copiously before looking around for the flying waiter to recharge his glass.

The wine being soon finished, the company did not linger, and Mr Grewgious was left contemplating the disorder of his room, determining to put it to rights first thing the next morning, and musing, this time not on the minds of the fair sex, but upon the enigma and curious ways of genius.

CHAPTER XLV
The Seeds of Time

AFTER THE EXCITEMENTS of first the deaths and then the weddings, the fictitious old town of Cloisterham resumed its normal ways. But in a world of change, there is no such thing as normality, however much citizens of towns like Cloisterham fail to see this, however much they deny it and resent the suggestion as an insult, and regard change as something which has already – and ineluctably and unrepeatably – happened. Many things in Cloisterham indeed remained unchanged, but there was also much that was new.

The new was the more obvious and notable, which makes it all the more curious that it was so rapidly swallowed or ingested by the town and treated as a natural part of the old order, as if it had always been.

The first change – but, then, perhaps Cloisterham was right, and it was no great change: suggesting that a dogmatic insistence on eternal verities is the correct approach – was that Mr Sapsea as Mayor, and as presciently foreseen, in due course came up with an address (which proved to be a linguistic insult to the long-suffering English Grammar), and was knighted: was made a knight: the word made knight: the blood made knight: the flesh made knight. This was and is the ultimate honour for any jackass – for all jackasses. Arise, Sir Jackass! Flaunt your finery. Brandish your new gewgaws, bellow your old heehaws. Arise, Sir Jackass, arise and bray!

Sapsea was minded to present this accolade, or deserved accolade as he preferred to think of it, or even well-deserved accolade, as a significant victory over the forces of the Church, and to declare victory on that basis; but since his Council were more cautious than he, since Mr Crisparkle of all people found it impossible to hold a grudge, and made it plain that he wished an accommodation, since the Dean felt that he was very soon on his way to advancement, and therefore disinclined to pursue a local rift, and since even the Mayor seemed to be regretting his separation from half his fellow-citzens – and voters – the elders of the town declared a draw, with honours even on the two sides, and the great

435

schism of Cloisterham rapidly collapsed, and was soon replaced by the normal processes of gossip and intrigue: which marked, once again, a return to normality.

There was another change affecting Sir Thomas, as we now should call him. A new effigy, almost life-size, appeared on the auctioneer's house, overlooking the Nuns' House, next to that of the father in the very act of announcing a sale; it showed Sir Thomas himself, "going up" with a air of undeniable smugness, and carrying his address firmly in both hands, lest a playful zephyr steal it from his nervous grasp, and he be left – for only the second time in his life – speechless.

At about the same time, Sir Thomas looked again at the old sitting-room portrait of himself, and relented. Perhaps it was rather good of him after all: the benediction appropriate to a knight; the collar a delicate touch; the humble look a thing of wonder in such a distinguished and successful man. He decided to have it rehung in his sitting-room, the only modest additions being a mayoral chain of office painted majestically round his neck by the skillful artist, and the insignia of knighthood shown pinned to his swelling breast. There were, after all, plenty of places for the new brace of portraits to hang, and much demand for pictures of such an important local figure.

Winter was now beginning to relax its grip on the town, and the first signs of Spring were starting to appear. The castle looked less grim on its hill, as small flowers began to adorn the grassy sward around it. The tower of the Cathedral appeared less forbidding as the evenings lengthened, and the light grew stronger. The river took on more inviting tones, and lost something of that muddy appearance which betokened winter floods.

A touch of spring was also in the mien and step of Sir Thomas. For, realising that the former Miss Brobity was now more than two years in her handsome tomb, surmounted by the equally fine inscription, that it was not good for a man to be alone, that he still felt in what he was wont to describe as his prime, and that he had a new prize to bestow in his generosity of heart on a future wife – nothing less than the resounding title of Lady Sapsea – he determined to seek a new helpmate.

In truth, he did not have far to look. Right across the High Street from his house lay the seminary owned by the pleasing and sprightly Miss Twinkleton. He took to casting his gaze upon her. To this end, he abandoned his dull ground-floor sitting room, giving on his paved back yard, and instead transferred himself – and shortly after, his portrait – to his upper parlour giving on the street, from where he could overlook the school and its inhabitants; and he habitually walked abroad at times when he knew that he was likely to meet the fair school-mistress. He greeted her, and raised his hat to her, and looked on her most kindlily.

He finally called upon her; and after a certain amount of wordy preparation, largely devoted to himself, and his manifest merits as man and public servant, he formally asked for her hand in marriage. She was rather less awe-struck, and rather more articulate than Miss Brobity on a previous occasion, but equally less definitive in accepting the great honour being offered her. Her response was to prevaricate, to express her gratitude, but to ask for time – possibly a month or so – to consider the proposal and return a proper reply. For, on the one hand, it was so sudden, and she had never considered marriage, least of all to the portly Mayor; but on the other hand, she could see advantage in the match, and was on the threshold of being beguiled by her cumbersome suitor. So, after ponderous leave-taking, the torpid serpent returned to his house, and shapely Eve remained in the Nuns' House to think the matter over.

There were already two major changes, of which we are already aware, affecting the Nuns' House, since the two young ladies, as we must now call them, had left to be with their fortunate husbands. In the case of Rosa, as Mr Grewgious, that arid but acute commentator on the human condition, had predicted, Tartar had left his modest abode in Staple Inn for the command of a more commodious mansion in the country. He obviously felt ready for the succeeding phase of his odyssey onto dry land, but being a judicious tar he compromised: he bought the house not only in the general vicinity of Cloisterham, so that he and his wife could visit their friends in the Cathedral town, and especially the Crisparkles, but also close to the sea, so that he could keep his yacht on the water there. He had many plans to take his wife out to sea, and then, in due course, his family; for it seemed inevitable that pretty, pink little Rosa would soon have a pretty, pink little child – and then more. This would not, in Tartar's opinion, constitute "going to sea", in terms of the self-denying ordinance which he had so freely and willingly given to Rosa so early in their acquaintance: it would constitute a mere and most pleasurable excursion, like going up the river from Temple Stairs.

So, the Nuns' House had inevitably lost its rosebud: there was no-one to be looked after, and petted, and spoilt, and made much of, and above all loved. Nor was there Helena to be admired, and honoured, and envied for her looks, and generally looked up to. There were no ready substitutes; though Miss Giggles could give a passable impersonation of

Rosa, when the girls had feasts or balls, and there was no shortage of volunteers to play the part of Tartar.

In entering their new kingdom, the Tartars were intrigued to discover in due course that one of their near neighbours was a Mr Porters. In truth he seemed a little elderly and distinctly unworldly and not especially foolish; his legs showed some tendency to twine in an unfinished way when he walked without a stick; but his mind was keen, his bearing good, and his manners still gallant. At one point Rosa plucked up the courage to ask him whether he knew and remembered Miss Twinkleton. He displayed the utmost pleasure at hearing her name, and regetted the fact that he had lost contact with her for so many years. Rosa communicated all this to Miss Twinkleton, with the suggestion that the latter come down to visit them, and resume acquaintance with her former admirer. Miss Twinkleton immediately fell in with this suggestion, and it was not long before a happy reunion took place. There was much talk of The Wells, and dances and suppers and theatres: and these lively memories seemed to have such a reviving effect on Mr Porters's frame and legs, that it was very soon decided that there was everything to be said, and no disadvantages, in making the reunion a more permanent affair. Mr Porters and Lieutenant Tartar took themselves to Maidstone on a secret mission; after which a more formal proposal was made, was immediately accepted, and a ring changed hands.

And, so, Miss Twinkleton returned to Cloisterham with the ring upon her finger, for all to see: to the consternation of Sir Thomas Sapsea, who would now need to look elsewhere if he wished a lady to his name, but who thanked himself that, in his considerable wisdom (which never ceased to amaze him), he had not communicated the fact of his proposal to anyone else, and was therefore in a position to deny it utterly if it were bruited abroad; and to the rage of Billickin when she heard the news, as Miss Twinkleton (soon to be Mrs Porters) made sure she did, very soon.

The Nuns' House itself was then changed in yet another way (but still the citizens of Cloisterham persisted in pretending that nothing was changed, and all went on as before). The presiding deity decided that she would depart to live with her new husband in his house near to the Tartars, consoling herself at her prospect of abandoning the charges with the thought that she would be on hand to teach the young Tartars as and when they appeared, taking charge of those youthful minds as soon as their fond parents wished it. It was therefore agreed that Mrs Tisher, as having long imbibed Education at the fount of wisdom, would remain in charge of the seminary, though teaching only the younger girls, and deputing the teaching of their elders to another brought in specially for the purpose: a promotion from the wardrobe, and a return to the better days, which would have greatly surprised the departed Mr Tisher, hairdresser or not.

In Minor Canon Corner, meanwhile, the breakfast ritual continued, but with Helena Crisparkle present: Helena Crisparkle: how Helena and Septimus and, yes, even Mrs Crisparkle herself, liked the sound and implications of those two names in conjunction; and all three of them looked forward to the day when the house would be blessed with the appearance of little Crisparkles, to make up for Septimus's six lost siblings, and to bring pleasure to the heart of their fond grandmother.

For all was harmony in the breakfast room in Minor Canon Corner; with only the occasional slight vibration of the cap to indicate momentary displeasure: but usually directed against dear Sept for some marginal shortcoming on his part, especially when his character showed signs of being too generous, too magnanimous, too forgiving. There was one other change to the morning routine. Septimus had been persuaded, by the joint entreaties of Helena and his mother, of the Mrs Crisparkles senior and junior, to forsake his habit of an early morning swim. Both argued that, without the intervention of Tartar so many years ago, he would not still be with them. Helena's beautiful eyes also reminded him of Neville's recent near calamity: Cloisterham Mill in particular was a place of ill-omen.

Of course, Septimus had powerful counter-arguments, had he wished to deploy them: the Tartar incident was many years ago, since when his head had broken the surface of the still waters of Kent on many thousands of occasions; he knew those waters like the back of his hand; and he was now a powerful and skillful swimmer. But he held back, and accepted the discipline of no more solitary swims, however calm and inviting the waters. He laughed chidingly at them, but would not have dreamed of ignoring their joint appeal: their new unity and companionship was too precious to him. He knew that the absence of an early morning swim followed by a hearty breakfast might allow the development of a certain amount of unhealthy suet-pudding round his waist, but was confident that he could keep any excesses at bay with an even more vigorous early-morning walk followed by the ritual of pugilistic exercise. He knew that his mother would not be sufficiently cruel or unfeeling to attempt to place a ban on boxing as well, despite her concerns about pier-glass and blood-vessels. And inwardly, and yet again, Septimus gave silent thanks to Luke Honeythunder for the miracle he had brought about by a severe overdose of platform manner and untutored verbal fisticuffs.

A new Choir-Master had been appointed by Dean and Chapter. Vividly recalling what had happened to Jasper, the Dean was determined to keep a close eye on his health and general demeanour: or, rather, determined that someone else should keep a close eye; for, as he reasoned to himself, it was of little use for a man who would so soon move or be elevated to another appointment to undertake this role, and better if it be deputed to someone who would be remaining at the Cathedral for some time: for the Dean showed increased zest for early preferment as the prospect receded.

'Septimus, you will, I am sure, take a close look at the well-being of our new lay precentor. We all know what happened to his – ahem – his predecessor, and we would not wish to suffer another such – er – calamity. It would be bad for our reputation, and bad for revenue. There is no profit in such goings-on. So would you be so good as to keep an eye, dear boy. Just look out for any signs, any – well – dazes. You know well what I mean.'

'I shall do so, Mr Dean, and tell him that, in the circumstances, you take a special interest in his health and welfare.'

'That's the spirit. Health, yes, yes. And welfare, quite so, quite so. And you also, Endcombe,' he added, as the latter, who had been hanging back, was encouraged by the ever-observant and kindly Crisparkle to join them, 'could you help to welcome and look after our new song-bird, and ensure that he does not go off his feed?' Mr Tope was highly but respectfully entertained by this.

'I am sure that the diligent Mrs Tope will make him feel at home, but the good Tope, while an excellent and sharp fellow, has other – er – important duties, and you will be on hand to keep old Nick away from the Gatehouse.' Tope was deferentially sharp enough to find this highly diverting.

Endcombe, eager as ever to assist his patron, Septimus Crisparkle, and to prove him correct in bringing the Endcombe family to Cloisterham, and offer him employment in the Cathedral, hurried to volunteer his services in ensuring that the new choirmaster did not descend to the devil.

But perhaps the greatest change was in Deputy. It appeared that even the hard heart of that young gentleman had been touched by the double wedding, and by the quality of the music and the singing. He seemed to hear it for the first time, and it spoke to him. Perhaps that was because he heard it properly for the first time, without the insistent sound of Jasper's sinister and hated voice. So, to the astonishment of all, he joined the Cathedral choir; and, although his voice had a slightly sibilant edge to it, on account of the gap which nature had left at the front of his mouth, and although it took him time to sort out aspirates and non-aspirates, since he had not studied that question previously, and although his knowledge of the sacred texts was at first a little faulty, since he could not read, and his tone uncertain, since music was another closed book to him, he rapidly accustomed himself to his new role, and started to have words and music by heart; and to help himself in these new achievements, determined both to devote time to practice rather than to the throwing of stones, and to take to his bed earlier. So the sound of a husky young voice singing religious music was often to be heard around the Cathedral Precincts, replacing the noise of volleys of stones landing full on their various targets, and the accompanying shouts of pagan triumph.

Durdles was inordinately proud of the new career being followed by his young charge.

'Durdles knows what you can achieve by giving a young fellow an enlightened object in life. Puts his feet on the right path, it does. Shows him what can be achieved, if you show application and consistency. Durdles and his methods helped him there. It wouldn't do for everyone, mind: everyone has to be found his own objects.'

How in future Durdles managed to get home before dawn broke, without the active assistance of Deputy, this history knoweth not.

Only two real traces of the old Deputy remained. He always kept a supply of stones ready in his pocket, just in case of attack by the gangs of urchins who still infested the town; and he was, by common consent, quite the most hideous choirboy in England.

So, apart from the urchins, what has not changed in the historic old town? Much remained as it was at the beginning of this tale: the dust, the damp and the gloom of the place: the dead ever-present in their tombs, in their headstones and epitaphs and memorials, in the dirt and grit of the place, in the gardens, in the radishes and lettuces; the musty air of the Cathedral and the dank, heavy atmosphere of the crypt; the rooks who circled round the tower, and landed in the trees, and cawed their hoarse comments on the change of the seasons, and on the weather, and on the black-coated clergymen as they flock in and out of the Cathedral; the echoing silences of lunchtime at Crozier Hotel, where the single buffer had showed his name to an interested crowd of one, and where he had received a heavy post without exciting attention; Joe, forever driving his heavily-loaded Elephant and Castle, from Cloisterham to Maidstone to Cloisterham to Maidstone, and still remembering the pretty young girl, with the excessively small bag, whom he had carried that evening, and whose love he had faithfully – if respectfully – given to Miss Twinkleton; the carrier who had brought a fine, dark lady, with some indefinable majesty about her, to Cloisterham early one morning; the single pawnbroker with his unredeemed stock, still unchanged and still unredeemed; the sun-browned tramps in the summer, the travel-stained pilgrims; the busy High Street and the quiet closes; and the Strangers, with a blush, retiring.

And the real Cloisterham also lived on. Unlike its fictional counterpart, its oppressive respectability was untroubled by the heavy burden of two linked deaths. It was likewise innocent of nurturing or harbouring a man such as Jasper; and possibly innocent of choosing a man such as Sapsea to be its Mayor – though many towns seem capable of this particular piece of foolishness, and then compound their error by reelecting their Sapseas, and further drive the nail into their own urban coffins by allowing their Sapseas to go up with an address, and getting their Sapseas knighted, and spurred and booted, for Heaven's sake.

The real Cloisterham lived on, with its historic buildings: the Norman Cathedral built by Bishop Gundulf, together with the vestiges of the former abbey lying around them, and also the later Romanesque additions to Gundulf's work; the fine castle, once alive with the clatter of mailed feet, and the jingling of bridles and armour, but now silent and abandoned, and the sturdy Norman keep surrounded by fragments of ruin: both proof of change and transience in human affairs, for all to see, or such as choose to. The real Cloisterham lived on, with its wide river, flapping gulls, brown-sailed barges, and heavy crop of seaweed at low tide; and with its visitors and tramps and pilgrims, treading the path trodden many years before by the ill-fated William of Perth, and drinking at the public houses, including the Bull Inn.

All lived on, well away from the bustle of the restless world outside: all lived on, telling their tale of change and changelessness: unchanged and unchanging, changed and changing.

Chapter XLVI
Another Dawn

IT IS COLD, grey dawn: again. Dawn, when some men, from various backgrounds, from various professions, for various motives, to satisy various desires, greet the morning by rising unsteadily, shaking from head to foot, and supporting their trembling frames upon their arms, before sitting suddenly and holding themselves tight in a chair.

London. Think not of the centre of the city, and its monarch and Parliament and peers, its shops and arcades and parks, and its smart lawyers and clubs and men about town. Forget even Holborn, and Staple Inn and those black sparrows dreaming of the countryside and recreating it in this urban waste, and Billickin and her slates and her joists and her shawl to keep out the cold, and the river where Tartar used to moor his boat, and the streets which poor Neville used to tramp every night. Forget all this, and go eastward and eastward again. Follow the road taken by Jasper many times and Datchery but twice: make the journey made by Jasper many times and Datchery but twice. Go eastward along the river, which at this point is acting less as a major thoroughfare and important artery of the city's trade, and more as a cess-pit or sump for what the city wishes to get rid of: an area for the disposal of material and human waste. Upstream, as the stage directions for Calisto tell us, the River Thames is attended by two nymphs, representing Peace and Plenty; here it is attended by two waifs, representing Poverty and Filth.

The scum and ooze and rank odour of the river have their parallel in the thick mud of the streets, the engrained dirt of the courts and alleys, the joyless squalor of the tenements. In the middle of this scene of neglect and putrefaction is a miserable, mean court; in the middle of this court a miserable, mean dwelling; in the middle of this dwelling a miserable, mean room, and in the middle of this room a miserable, mean bedstead, with its post hanging awry and topped by a rusty spike: on which tumbled bedstead lie respectively, in varying states of undress, unconsciousness and decrepitude, the Princess Puffer herself and her visitors: lascars, sailors and Chinese, (or, as the old Deputy would have it, jacks and chaynermen and hother Knifers).

Although time has passed, the Princess is much as she was when Jasper still lived. She keeps up her mumbled litany of chronic complaint about her aches and pains, about her cough and her lungs, about lack of custom, about the high price of opium, about what life offers her and where it has brought her: though it is unclear whether anyone in that room is attending her, or capable of attending her. But the skin of her face is more stretched and parchment-like, her hand shakes more, the walls of her lungs are thinner and more than ever like cabbage nets, her voice is more distant and her cough has a more pronounced rattle. Were Jasper still alive, it is unlikely that she would be capable of shaking her yet more skinny arms at him.

But he remains in her thoughts. Where is the missing one? He was ever an honest payer. Why doesn't he come, why doesn't he come again, having returned after the long delay? Had he seen her shaking her fists at him in the Cathedral, and resolved to come no more? Had he started to suspect her for some other reason, and decided to avoid her? Had he felt her feeling him, trying to seek out his secrets? Any or all of this is possible, probable even, but she rather doubts it: she has such faith in her powers of mixing that she knows that, if alive, he will come again.

Has he followed the nephew he murdered and died, sinking under the weight of his own misdeeds? Is he dead and in heaven: this last can at least be ruled out? Is he dead and suffering the torments of hell? Or – once again, this possibility raises its head – has the hell-hound cut the traces, cheated her, and taken his custom elsewhere? No, again she consoles herself, she doubts this: he well knows that no-one has the trick of mixing like her, the poor old soul with the real receipt. No-one. So it is probably death after all.

Apparently reassured by this morbid thought, she turns over and drifts off into sleep. What visions does she have? Does she dream of butchers' shops and public houses and much credit? Of an increase in hideous customers, and the horrible bedstead set upright again, and the horrible court swept clean? No. Somehow, perhaps because she was thinking of Jasper, brooding about Jasper, speculating about Jasper, she dreams Jasper's dream, though Jasper is dead, and has no further need of it, no claim to it.

She dreams of a glorious procession past an ancient English Cathedral, and its massive grey square tower: a great pageant taking place right in front of her eyes; or is it even closer, and in her very mind? The drug gives her imagination greater powers: the colours are almost too bright, the music too flamboyant, the tableaux too vivid. The men and animals and weapons are close to her; she can feel the tread of feet and hooves, sense the movement, smell the odours as they pass by. Then come the dancers and the musicians: closer and closer, with the blasts of music, and whirl of dresses; closer; too close, they are overwhelming her, trampling her, smothering her, suffocating her..

She stirs and wakes suddenly, pulling the sheet away from her face where it had rested. The visions have disappeared; the vivid and frightening figures are no more. They are all gone. All she can now see is the sharp spike of the broken bedstead. There is no Cathedral, no tower, no great landscape and no glittering procession. The proud Sultan, his retinue of attendants, the clashing cymbals, the flashing scimitars, the caparisoned elephants, even the dancing girls strewing flowers as they go, have all passed by. The bright lights are dowsed, the colours have departed, the music has stopped. All have gone, and left not a wrack behind.

Only the keen and murderous spike of rusty iron remains, thrusting upwards: grim, pitiless and destructive.

* U *

www.ingramcontent.com/pod-product-compliance
Lightning Source LLC
Chambersburg PA
CBHW022348020726
47500CB00002B/169